LION & LAMB

A list of titles by James Patterson appears
at the back of this book

JAMES PATTERSON

& DUANE SWIERCZYNSKI

LION & LAMB

C

CENTURY

1 3 5 7 9 10 8 6 4 2

Century
20 Vauxhall Bridge Road
London SW1V 2SA

Century is part of the Penguin Random House group of companies whose addresses can be found at global.penguinrandomhouse.com.

First published in the UK by Century in 2023

www.penguin.co.uk

A CIP catalogue record for this book is available from the British Library.

ISBN: 978–1–529–13655–5 (hardback)
ISBN: 978–1–529–13656–2 (trade paperback)

Printed and bound in Great Britain by Clays Ltd, Elcograf S.p.A.

The authorised representative in the EEA is Penguin Random House Ireland, Morrison Chambers, 32 Nassau Street, Dublin D02 YH68

www.greenpenguin.co.uk

For Parker and Evie

— D.S.

PROLOGUE
SUNDAY, JANUARY 23

ONE

12:20 a.m.

THE NIGHT Philadelphia lost its mind, police officer Deborah Parks was patrolling the Ninth with her rookie, Rob Sheplavy.

He was a nice enough kid, maybe a little overeager. They'd been together since just after New Year's Day, when the red-and-gold holiday decorations were quickly replaced by Eagles-green banners to celebrate the team clawing its way to the NFC playoffs.

Now it was just after midnight on a freezing Sunday in late January, when Philly was at its darkest and coldest. The Birds were facing off against the Giants, and aside from a few rowdy drunks with their faces painted green, the residents of the city had apparently decided to take a collective breather before tonight's kickoff.

As they went around the Museum of Art toward Eakins Oval, Sheplavy's face lit up. "Check out that sweet Maserati."

Parks followed his sight line to the sports car, which had been detailed with a laser-blue holographic wrap. The thing literally glowed in the street, where it appeared to have paused at a stoplight at the far end of the traffic circle. Only problem: The traffic circle had no light. But still, the Maserati had come to a dead stop, nose slightly out of its lane.

"What is up with this guy?" Parks said. "Look, we're going to pull up a little closer and I'll check it out. You stay here."

"Wait—can't I come with you?"

"I need you to hang back. And don't touch the radio!"

Parks hated being rough with the new kid. But he had a tendency to go rogue, and she knew something was off about this even before she climbed out of the car.

As Parks moved closer, she could see someone slumped behind the wheel of the glowing vehicle. Was the driver passed out drunk?

No. The body language was all wrong—his head was tilted at an unnatural angle, his shoulders were completely still, and there was no sign of breathing.

Parks glanced back to make sure the rookie was where he should be. "Stay in the car, Sheplavy!"

If the rookie heard, he didn't respond.

Steeling herself, Parks moved to the driver's side, hand near her service weapon just in case this guy turned out to be (a) alive and (b) drunk and pissed. But she knew that would be the best-case scenario.

Parks called out to him, trying to wake him up. The driver didn't stir. She reached in and touched the side of his neck with two fingers. The man's skin was ice cold, and there was no pulse.

Parks had forgotten to put on gloves, and when she lifted her fingers away from the driver's neck, she was surprised to find them tacky. She looked down at her hands and realized that the city's new LED streetlights had made the body look as if it were covered in shadows.

But it was blood. *So much blood…*

TWO

Audio transcript of police officer Deborah Parks's body-cam footage

OFFICER DEBORAH PARKS: What are you doing with that radio in your hand?

OFFICER ROB SHEPLAVY: I called in the plate number. Figured I'd save us some time.

PARKS: Damn it, Shep, what'd I tell you about shutting up and staying off the radio?

SHEPLAVY: Why are you freaking out? We're supposed to call this in, right?

PARKS: I told you to wait, and that's all you needed to know. Now get out of the car and get the crime scene tape out of the trunk.

SHEPLAVY: What happened over there? Is that guy all right?

PARKS: No, he's pretty much the *opposite* of all right. Which is why I need you to go in the trunk and dig out some flares and crime scene tape.

SHEPLAVY: (*Grumbles*) Jesus . . .

PARKS: You got a problem, rookie?

SHEPLAVY: Whatever's in that car, I can handle it. I'm not a toddler.

PARKS: Look, I'm sorry for snapping. But you just put out the license plate of a potential murder victim's car over the radio. You know who listens to the police band? TV reporters. Not to mention people bored or twisted enough to come check out a crime scene.

SHEPLAVY: I'm sorry, I didn't—

PARKS: Everybody's excited about the first dead body until they actually see it.

SHEPLAVY: Oh, Christ. Look, I said I'm sorry...

PARKS: It's fine. Just remember rule number one: Do not touch *anything*. You got me?

SHEPLAVY: I know. I promise, Parks, I'm good.

(*The officers approach the Maserati. The vic is partially obscured by the wheel and the door of the Maserati. Sheplavy crouches down for a better look.*)

SHEPLAVY: You've gotta be kidding me.

PARKS: What is it?

SHEPLAVY: It couldn't be... I mean, tonight of all nights?

PARKS: Sheplavy, *what*? Hey, you okay? Take a deep breath. We need to secure the scene. I'm thinking this is a carjacking gone wrong, that's all.

SHEPLAVY: I can't believe...

PARKS: Look, we're going to see this kind of thing from time to time. Are you... Sheplavy, are you *crying*?

SHEPLAVY: I can't believe it's actually *him*.

PARKS: Can't believe it's who?

SHEPLAVY: Look at his face!

THREE

AS THE rookie was sobbing, a tall man in a dirty gray hoodie cut across Eakins Oval.

When he spied the two cops, he stopped in his tracks. He pulled his phone from his pocket and snapped a photo. Then he inched closer, a stunned expression on his face.

"Hey, back off!" Parks shouted. "Crime scene!"

Too late. The hoodie guy snapped another photo and ran away, thumbing something into his phone as he went.

"Hey! Stop!"

A photo of the vic was going to be online in a matter of seconds. Shit! But what was she supposed to do, chase after him and—what? Confiscate his phone? While leaving a rookie alone at his first murder scene?

It turned out that Parks had been right to worry; when the two images of the blood-covered man in the Maserati hit social media, it was over. The news traveled worldwide at breakneck speed. People enlarged the grainy photos until the victim's face was pixelated but identifiable. The reaction everywhere: utter astonishment.

Some claimed the photos were photoshopped or deep-faked. But most who saw the images believed they were real. The powder-blue Maserati alone was confirmation of the victim's identity.

Online there was collective grief and an instantaneous outpouring of tributes. There were also macabre jokes, as always. And even though it was well after midnight, locals began to gather at the scene, arriving from Center City and Spring Garden and Fairmount and West Philly. As the crowds got bigger, more images from the crime scene spread online. Some people took awkward selfies in an attempt to place themselves in this historic moment. Some simply stared in shock. Some wept inconsolably, held by their friends.

Fortunately Parks and Sheplavy had been joined by half a dozen other officers from the Ninth, and they'd established a wide perimeter around the car, so between that and the wall of bodies, the victim's face was largely blocked from view.

Unless you were in a helicopter.

Parks had been right about local TV news always keeping an ear on police radio. An overnight staffer chained to the assignment desk at the local NBC affiliate heard the word *Maserati* and had a cop friend run the license plate on a whim—maybe some local CEO or sports figure had been involved in an embarrassing traffic accident.

But when the Maserati's owner's name popped up, the staffer knocked over his Diet Coke in his scramble to get to the assignment editor.

That station's news chopper was kept at Penn's Landing, which was thirty minutes from any location in the city. The art museum was so close, however, that the chopper was circling overhead within five minutes. A minute after it arrived, the station was interrupting the local broadcast to go live with footage from the air.

Until they had official word from the Philly police brass—that meant a captain or higher—the station couldn't confirm exactly who was in the powder-blue Maserati.

But the word was already out, and distraught fans on the street knew the truth.

Philadelphia would never be the same.

FOUR

1:02 a.m.

HOMICIDE DETECTIVE Mickey Bernstein, forty-three, was the son of a Philly PD homicide legend, Arnold "Arnie" Bernstein.

Dad was famous for working the city's most violent cases and resolving them with lightning speed, usually thanks to his hunches and gut feelings. He nailed gangsters (the guys who blew up Leo "Chicken Man" Caranchi) and serial killers (coed slayer Herman "the Guru" Bludhorn). Every administration since the early 1960s loved Arnie—he got results. Nobody questioned him. Ever.

Arnie's only son operated in much the same way—except Mickey had a degree from UPenn under his belt and extensive forensic training to back up his hunches, so he got even more respect than his famous father.

What was not to love? He was a street-smart cop with an Ivy League degree who knew how to talk to TV and print journalists. *Philadelphia* magazine had run a fawning profile on him a few years back, and the cover still hung in his parents' retirement home in Margate, Florida.

If you were doing a true-crime doc about something that happened in Philly and you *didn't* check in with Mickey Bernstein, you were just not doing your job.

So when Mickey climbed out of his glossy black Audi A3,

murmurs rippled through the crowd, and TV reporters started fighting their way to him. Mickey pushed past them and made a beeline for the crime scene.

The detective was easily identifiable—six foot three with the kind of handsome, chiseled face that you see on coins. The looks, people assumed, came from his mother, a statuesque Atlantic City showgirl back in the day. (Arnie was many things, but attractive wasn't one of them.) In a city starved for celebrities, Mickey Bernstein would probably have been a star even if he weren't police royalty.

Parks saw the detective approaching and hurried over to meet him. The sooner she could put this scene in Bernstein's hands, the better.

"Well, this isn't how I imagined spending my Sunday morning," Bernstein said with a sly smile. "Are you the one who caught this?"

"Yeah, me and Sheplavy. He's my partner."

Bernstein assessed him in about two seconds. "Rookie?"

"Uh-huh."

"You made the ID?"

"My partner recognized him right away."

Bernstein raised an eyebrow. "And you didn't?"

"Not really a sports fan."

"Heresy, Officer Parks!" Bernstein exclaimed with fake outrage, clutching his chest. "How can you call yourself a Philadelphian?"

Ordinarily this kind of comment out of a detective's mouth would have rubbed Parks the wrong way. And throughout the brief conversation, most of his attention was on the scene. But something about Bernstein's delivery—that boyish smile and deadpan sarcasm—made it okay.

The detective crouched down by the corpse as if he were about to have a little chat with him. *So what happened here, buddy? Looks like somebody punched your ticket real good.* "Something's missing, Parks."

"What's that, Detective?"

"Anyone else come near this crime scene after you arrived?" Only now did Mickey Bernstein give Parks his full attention. He studied her face for tells. His eyes were ice blue and didn't miss a thing.

Parks felt guilty even though she'd done everything by the book. Damn, this guy was good. "No, Detective," she assured him. "We kept everyone away."

"How about the rookie?"

"No, he's fine."

Bernstein went back to examining the scene, a sour look on his face.

"What's missing, Detective?" said Parks. "If you don't mind me asking."

"A certain piece of jewelry."

"All due respect, how could you possibly know that?"

"Do me a favor, Parks. Can you push those crowds back a bit more? I want to take a look in relative peace and quiet."

"Of course."

"And, oh—the missing piece of jewelry? It's a Super Bowl ring."

FIVE

FOR DECADES, the City of Philadelphia had been promising its hardworking police officers two things: sparkly new headquarters and a state-of-the-art computer system.

Neither had appeared yet. Mickey Bernstein was sitting in the same building, the concrete Roundhouse on Race Street, that his father had worked in years ago. Dad had used an electric typewriter to hunt-and-peck his murder reports, but Mickey didn't have it much better. He was forced to use a nearly comatose PC with an operating system twenty years out of date.

Eh, screw the things you can't change, Mickey thought. That was one of many twisted pieces of wisdom from Dad. Mickey cracked his knuckles and got to work.

Philadelphia Police Department / Homicide Division

Case No. 22-9-3275

Investigating Detective: Michael Bernstein

2445 Captain called with a report of a Black male found dead inside sports car in front of art museum.

2450 Notified my partner, Detective T. Mason, #4977, of the murder. She was at least thirty minutes out so I headed to the scene alone. I was already in Center City, just a few minutes away.

0100 Arrived at scene. Briefed by Officer Parks, #6332, who was first at scene. Partner: Officer Sheplavy, #8841. Parks reported a man in a gray hoodie in area at the time of her arrival. Witness took photos with a phone and fled scene. Parks did not pursue. See statement, attached.

0130 Coroner investigator V. Waters arrived at scene. Rolled prints of victim identified as Archie Hughes, DOB 12/27/89. Crime lab tech Wolfinger completed photographs. Victim suffered GSW. No shell casings found at scene.

0200 Requested all surveillance video in immediate vicinity.

0241 Coroner took possession of body. Cleared scene.

0437 Made death notification to Hughes's wife, Francine Hughes, 10███ Country Club Drive, Radnor, PA.

Which brought Bernstein up to the present, 5:00 in the morning. This was going to be a crazy day, with zero chance of sleep in the foreseeable future. He hit the PRINT key and prayed it worked; Bernstein didn't want to have to wait for some guy in IT to show up so he could begin the murder book that would define his career.

Small miracle—the pages printed without a hitch.

Bernstein saved the file and got up to find a gallon of coffee. Then he stopped. Sat back down. Cracked his knuckles again.

Better to pave the road now and save himself some grief later.

SIX

HIGHLY CONFIDENTAL
EYES OF THE POLICE COMMISSIONER ONLY

Madam Commissioner:

The Archie Hughes case is a guaranteed clusterf██, even if everything goes right. However, I have some thoughts on how we might minimize the damage.

The Eagles quarterback is arguably the most talented pair of hands ever to touch the pigskin. If he's not the greatest of all time, he's a serious contender for the title. Archie Hughes's family, friends, and fans all over the world will demand swift justice. We must give it to them.

I was next up on the wheel for this case, as the captain will confirm. But I understand that this may not sit well with the rank and file, who might assume it was handed to me on a silver platter. Also, full disclosure: I am on friendly terms with Eagles ownership, though I did not know Mr. Hughes personally. Nonetheless, I know I am the best detective for this case, despite the optics.

My suggestion, Madam Commissioner, is that we create a task force. Let the city know we have all hands on deck.

Not only will we have the eyes of the entire city on us, but there will be massive national and international media attention. It's vital that we have a unified voice giving simple, direct updates on the status of the investigation. I volunteer my services for this role.

As you know, I have excellent relations with the local news outlets and have appeared on national news multiple times over the past ten years.

The truth is, this case will most likely be solved with surveillance cameras, which is how we solve ninety percent of homicides. I'll be working closely with my colleagues in the Special Investigations Unit to review the footage and we will have answers soon. As my dad liked to say, "We don't sleep until the killer is tucked neatly into bed."

Thank you in advance, Madam Commissioner. I hope we can bring this case to a rapid and satisfactory conclusion.

Yours,
Det. Michael Bernstein

SEVEN

11:50 a.m.

WINTER LANDSCAPING on Philadelphia's Main Line was mostly about preventive care. Which was why Mauricio Lopez, fifty-three, had winterized the sprinkler system way back in October and wrapped the young trees to protect them from frost. He'd also fertilized in advance of the first hard freeze. And he made sure to replenish the mulch as needed.

Mauricio insisted on using the leaves he raked up in the fall as mulch in the dead of winter, despite his employer's wife telling him not to bother, that they could afford to buy a fresh supply. Mauricio told her it was not about the money; it was about the health of the roots beneath the freezing soil. The mulch acted as an insulating blanket. Nature supplied it for free. Why not use it?

Much of that work had been done, so Mauricio had little to do aside from occasionally pruning dead branches and brushing road salt away from the front-facing bushes. Otherwise, daily maintenance of the vast grounds was simply a matter of looking around for anything out of place.

And Mauricio saw something *very* out of place late Sunday morning.

Any foreign object on the ground almost always turned out to be an errant golf ball from the nearby country club. Sometimes the children in the neighborhood left a baseball or toy. Once Mauricio even found a hobbyist's drone that had crash-landed near a birdbath. And occasionally, there were dead animals—birds, mostly. When Mauricio found them, he quickly disposed of the corpses. If the kids were around, they'd want to hold a funeral. Which was sweet, but it ate up a lot of his workday.

This morning, he noticed a foreign object that was mostly buried in a flower bed. The only reason Mauricio saw it was that the low winter sun glimmered off its surface.

A car, Mauricio thought. The older child had had an obsession with Matchbox sports cars last summer; this had to be one of them.

Mauricio knelt down, hearing his knee joints pop, and brushed away some of the frost and mulch covering the toy. But it wasn't a little sports car buried in the flower bed.

Mauricio Lopez lived his life largely unplugged. He had a landline so Mrs. Hughes could reach him as needed, but he avoided "smart" devices. He did not own a computer, TV, or radio. He enjoyed reading books about ancient history. He liked to garden.

So when Mauricio arrived for work that morning, he had not heard the news about his employer. For all Mauricio knew, Mr. Hughes was preparing for this evening's game. In fact, despite his closeness to the family, Mauricio Lopez might very well have been the only person in the tristate area who didn't know Archie Hughes had been shot and killed in front of the art museum the night before.

But still, the sight of a gun caused him to tremble violently.

MONDAY, JANUARY 24

CHAPTER 1

7:32 a.m.

AFTER EXECUTING the most perfect display of parallel parking ever seen in the city of Philadelphia, Cooper Lamb realized not a single soul had witnessed it.

Not his ex. Not his children. Not a random passerby. Not even a meter maid, who normally would be on him like a heat-seeking missile. If no one saw this private eye's incredible display of automotive prowess, did it actually happen? It was another bummer in a long string of them.

Lamb fished his phone out of his jacket pocket, hit the memo app his assistant, Victor, had loaded for him, and began to speak. He always felt better when he was talking out loud.

COOPER LAMB / VOICE MEMO #0124-735

Victor, I regret to inform you this is the end of the world.

Maybe not your world. But my world, for sure. I am currently sitting in my car trying to process it all. Trying to figure out what I'm going to tell my kids. Damn... what *am* I going to tell my kids?

Don't transcribe that last part, Victor. Yes, I know you're not personally transcribing these words, that the computer program you designed is doing all of this automatically. But humor me. I can't stand the idea of talking to a machine.

So let's review the facts at hand while I await the arrival of my lovely and brilliant offspring, whom I adore completely.

Fact number one: Eagles starting quarterback and national treasure Archie Hughes was shot to death last night. The entire city is in a state of shock and mourning. We woke up to a different world today, Victor.

Fact number two: The NFC championship game has been postponed for some unknown amount of time. Which means nobody will know what to do with themselves until it's rescheduled.

Fact number three: I was not in possession of tickets to the game, but maybe this is an opportunity. Victor, can you see if there are tickets available? Possibly something in a box? Maybe some fans won't be able to make it, they'll be so heartbroken over the loss of the amazing Mr. Hughes. A guy can dream, right?

Fact number four: On Saturday I placed a fairly sizable bet—on the Eagles, of course—with my army buddy Red Doyle down in Atlantic City. I was already sick to my stomach knowing I'd have to wait twenty-four hours to see how it turned out, and, more important, if I'd be ducking my landlord for the next two months or not. Now I get to enjoy a full week of anguish and torment. Victor, next time I mention making a bet, talk me out of it.

Fact number five: Speaking of disappointed, at this very moment my kids are running out of their mother's house and...oh, it doesn't look good. Seems as if the awful news has reached my children's impressionable ears. To be continued.

CHAPTER 2

THE REAR passenger doors of Cooper Lamb's car were wrenched open and his children climbed into the back of his vehicle with the force of a small hurricane.

"Dad!" his son exclaimed. "Did you hear what happened to Archie Hughes?"

His daughter was already annoyed. "*Of course* Dad heard. But what I want to know is, who would do something like this the night before the game?"

"Are you going to find Archie's killer?"

"Are they going to cancel the Super Bowl?"

"Do you already know who killed Archie, Dad?"

Lamb clutched the steering wheel tight to avoid being sucked under and drowning in all that raw emotion.

His wonderful, amazing, and, at times, exasperating children—Ariel, ten, and Cooper Jr., eight—lived with their mother in a three-bedroom townhome in trendy Queen Village. Funny how you blink and things become "trendy." This used to be a solid immigrant neighborhood; Lamb's own ancestors had toiled at the factory that received sugarcane from the Caribbean and processed it to satisfy America's never-ending sweet tooth. For years Lamb's great-grandfather wouldn't even *look* at sugar, let alone eat dessert.

Happily, that particular family trait went to the grave with the old man. Lamb was starving, and he was sure his kids were too.

"How about a quick before-school breakfast at the Down Home Diner? I could practically inhale a stack of buckwheat pancakes right now."

"Dad!" Ariel cried. "Are you even listening to us?"

"Just don't let me drink from the maple syrup container again. Last time I did that, I was up all night."

"Dad!"

"I was up all night peeing. Very, *very* slowly..."

"Ewww!" Cooper Jr. said.

"Jesus, Dad."

Lame dad humor? Guilty as charged. But had Cooper also managed to change the conversation and stanch the flow of tears from his children's weary eyeballs? Yes, Your Honor. No further questions.

"I will explain all that I know over breakfast at Reading Terminal Market. I don't care to discuss homicide while driving through Center City. It makes me... twitchy. Until then, strap in and start contemplating the menu. I know you two have it memorized by now."

"Father," Ariel said solemnly. "You're trying to distract us with food, but we're serious. We want to know what's going on."

"Daughter, I hear your question, but right now your mother is approaching and she doesn't look entirely pleased."

Sure enough, Lamb's ex, the former—and possibly future?—love of his life, was approaching the passenger side. Ariel helpfully pushed the button to lower the window.

She had never been Lori Lamb; Lori Avallone thought she wouldn't be taken seriously at the museum with an alliterative name. Lamb had considered offering to take *her* name, but Cooper Avallone sounded like a country-and-western lounge singer, so that was out.

"Don't worry, I'm taking the kids to breakfast," Lamb said.

"They already ate," Lori replied. "It's almost eight, and they have to be at Friends Select in twenty minutes. For future reference, the school frowns on the kids cutting first period to eat waffles."

"We do it all the time!" Cooper Jr. said.

"When we're with Daddy, we do," Ariel confirmed.

"You were supposed to be here an hour ago," Lori said.

"I was . . . wrapping up a case."

"Does this 'case' have a name?"

"*The People versus Cooper Lamb.* Because people are *always* getting on my case."

Cooper Jr. knew he shouldn't laugh at that, but a giggle escaped his lips anyway.

"Thank you, son," his father said, turning and lifting his hand for a high five. The look on his ex's face, however, revealed exactly zero amusement. Both Cooper Sr. and Cooper Jr. put their hands down.

"I'm sorry, Lori. I'll do better." Lamb searched her eyes for a reaction but failed to find the one he'd hoped for. "I *mean* it."

Thing was, Lamb actually *did* mean it. If this was the end of the world, and it was sure looking that way, he'd better start getting his act together.

But first, pancakes thick and fluffy enough to choke a horse. Book learning could wait.

CHAPTER 3

11:02 a.m.

"JUST SIT back and relax."

"I am perfectly relaxed."

"Oh, and you can take your sunglasses off."

"I know I can. I prefer not to."

"Um, is it too early for a nice glass of wine? We have red and white."

"Red *and* white, huh. Tempting, but I don't like to drink while I'm working."

The girl in the disposable face mask and nitrile gloves smiled. Or at least, her eyes smiled. "But are you working right now?"

"I don't know. Are *you*?"

Veena Lion knew that was probably too much, but the young nail tech had lost all credibility with the wine thing. *Red or white?* Then again, maybe she was expecting too much from a random Korean nail joint on this end of Chestnut Street.

Veena liked to change things up, rarely visiting the same salon twice in a season. Mostly because she resisted the idea of having a regular place where people could easily find her. That ruined the indulgence of having her nails done in the middle of the morning.

Said indulgence lasted for another seventy-five seconds before Veena Lion's phone alerted her to an incoming call. She lifted a hand from the manicurist's table and tapped the bud in her ear twice.

A haughty voice spoke. "This is the district attorney's office. Is this Veena Lion?"

"What is this concerning?"

"You'll have to speak with the district attorney about that."

Veena sighed. "Why don't you spare me the suspense."

"As I said," the voice continued, barely containing the speaker's annoyance, "you'll have to talk to the dis—"

Veena tapped the earbud, ending the call. She exhaled slowly, letting the tension leave her body. The girl in the mask raised her eyebrows. Veena held up her index finger: *Wait for it.* Her phone buzzed again.

"Apologies, Ms. Lion—please don't hang up!"

"Who is this?"

"It's the district attorney's office! This is about Archie Hughes. Might you have a moment or two to speak with Mr. Mostel?"

"Let Mr. Mostel know that I'll stop by his office at my earliest convenience."

"Couldn't you spare a moment now?"

"Right now," Veena said, "is not convenient."

Veena ended the call. Waited. The phone did not buzz a third time. The girl in the mask raised her eyebrows again. Veena shrugged. The girl in the mask resumed her work. "You know what? I believe I will have some wine."

"Red or white?"

"Consider what you know about me, then follow your instincts."

The nail girl's mask twisted up, barely hiding the wry smile beneath. "I thought you didn't drink while you were working."

"Sometimes it's absolutely necessary. And *sometimes* happens to be right now."

While Veena waited for her beverage, she tapped her earbud three times.

CHAPTER 4

Transcript of encrypted message exchange between private investigator Veena Lion and her executive assistant, Janie Hall

VEENA LION: Looks like we're getting the Archie Hughes case from that dirtbag Mostel. I hate the creep, but how can we resist something like this?

JANIE HALL: Hang on. You sure about this, boss? Do you remember the document you signed swearing you'd never, ever work for the DA again?

LION: This is different.

HALL: You had me notarize that document.

LION: Ha, that's right. I did, didn't I?

HALL: Not only that, but you had me become a notary just so I could notarize that document. There was a course, a written exam, a background check, not to mention the fees—

LION: Thereby giving you a lucrative side hustle. You're welcome.

HALL: My point is, you were pretty sure about never working with DA Mostel again.

LION: Point taken, but this is the Archie Hughes case. There is no other case right now. This is the Beale and Adderall of murder cases.

HALL: Are you speaking your texts again? Did you mean the *be-all and end-all*?

LION: My fingers are occupied at the moment.

HALL: Ah, nice. Which color did you pick?

LION: You'll see in about twenty minutes when I'm back at the office. In the meantime—

HALL: In the meantime you would like me to compile every possible scrap of coverage and footage from the past thirty-six hours as well as the usual deep-background dossier on Mr. Hughes and all of his known business associates.

LION: And everything the police have. Did you get that last part, Janie?

HALL: Oh, I see Detective Mickey Bernstein is on the case.

LION: Easy there, lady.

HALL: Yum.

LION: Archie Hughes files first, flirt with the handsome detective later.

HALL: Yes, boss. Anything else?

LION: A triple draft latte from La Colombe, please.

HALL: Cold espresso? You know it's like two degrees outside, right?

LION: I have to swallow an ingestible recorder capsule and it goes down easier with something cold.

HALL: Is that a good idea, Veena?

LION: The latte or the hidden recording device?

HALL: Either. But especially the device.

LION: It will dissolve in a few hours, you know that. Just make sure the file has uploaded to the server and have a transcription prepared.

HALL: What I mean is, if Mostel finds out—

LION: I'm after the truth, no matter what state privacy laws say. Also, that pompous windbag won't suspect a thing.

CHAPTER 5

Transcript of conversation between Veena Lion and Philadelphia district attorney Eliott K. Mostel

ELIOTT K. MOSTEL: So, to be clear, you're prepared to swear on a Holy Bible that you don't have a tape recorder on you? Like, anywhere?

VEENA LION: Do you see a recording device anywhere, Eliott?

MOSTEL: I'm not falling for that again, Veena. You tape *everything*. I found out the hard way, if you recall. I'm thinking of the Gillespie case specifically.

LION: I recall the Gillespie case. Specifically. And I never used the tape in court.

MOSTEL: I just want to make it clear that if you *do* have such a device and this conversation is being recorded right now, it's a felony. Pennsylvania takes privacy law seriously.

LION: Do you want to send me to jail or do you have a job for me?

MOSTEL: At times I find you needlessly infuriating, Veena. Do you know that?

LION: How about we skip the flattery and get down to it.

MOSTEL: Can you at least take off the sunglasses? I'd like to see your eyes as you insult me.

LION: No.

MOSTEL: You drive me [unintelligible].

LION: That makes two of us, Mr. District Attorney. Please continue.

MOSTEL: As you know, we're going to have to eventually prosecute the son of a bitch who killed Archie Hughes. I want an airtight case, and I'd like your help.

LION: I'll do it on one condition. Just a simple question, but I want the truth.

MOSTEL: Ask away.

LION: Was I your first call or was Cooper Lamb?

MOSTEL: Veena, how long have we worked together? You know you are my first and only choice when it comes to these kinds of cases.

LION: Eliott, there's never been a case like this. And I want to know where your head is at. If Lamb turned you down and I'm merely your backup—

MOSTEL: I swear to Jesus, you were my first call.

LION: You're Jewish.

MOSTEL: Can we please focus on the murder of one of our most beloved and high-profile citizens?

LION: Fine. I'll take the assignment. I'm going to need a direct line to your office, someone on call twenty-four/seven, preferably one of your top ADAs. Real-time updates, with my executive assistant blind-copied on every piece of correspondence.

MOSTEL: Done, done, and done. And naturally you'll have access to everything the police know in real time.

LION: I'm more interested in what the police *don't* know.

MOSTEL: What a coincidence. That's what interests me the most too.

LION: Afraid I'm not following you, Eliott.

MOSTEL: (*Pause*) I'm going to be frank with you. Mickey Bernstein pushed his way onto this case and I don't like that. Frankly, I don't like him.

LION: Sounds a little personal.

MOSTEL: No, what I mean is, I don't trust him. He's dirty, just like his old man. Everything he touches is tainted. He and his family are symbols of how corrupt this city used to be. We don't live in that city anymore.

LION: So prosecute him.

MOSTEL: Yeah, *you* try getting past the big blue wall. Especially when it's led by Her Majesty the commissioner, who is too focused on her path to the mayor's office to care about the carnage on the streets.

LION: You don't think the commissioner is keeping her eye on the ball?

MOSTEL: Look, forget I said anything—and see, this is why I'm paranoid about you taping every single conversation. Let's keep this about Archie Hughes.

LION: Agreed. (*Pause*) Oh, and Janie, you can stop the transcription here.

MOSTEL: What? Who are you talking to? You said you weren't recording this!

LION: Just a little joke, Eliott. Tell me what you have.

CHAPTER 6

12:05 p.m.

ELIOTT K. MOSTEL kept an incredibly close eye on the mayor's office.

Veena knew this to be quite literal. The district attorney's office occupied several floors in a high-rise that sat catty-corner from the mammoth pile of Philadelphia City Hall. If you ran a rope from one building to the other, you could zip-line from Mostel's private office down to the mayor's reception room.

If only it were that easy. Mostel desperately wanted that job for himself and considered the police commissioner his fiercest rival.

None of this political maneuvering mattered to Veena. But whatever came out of Mostel's mouth had to be viewed through this filter.

"Archie's wallet, watch, and Super Bowl ring are missing," Mostel said. "So it's theft on top of murder."

"Not unexpected."

"Well, how about this for unexpected—they've already found the murder weapon."

Veena adjusted her sunglasses. "Where?"

"In a flower bed behind the Hughes mansion, out on the Main Line."

This was a bombshell. Veena tried hard not to show any reaction. "Ballistics are solid?"

"I have no reason to doubt the technicians or the report. But wait until you hear whose prints they found on the barrel."

"The prints of his wife, Francine Pearl Hughes."

"How did you know?"

"About a third of all homicides are perpetrated by someone close to the victim."

Mostel nodded solemnly and let the fact hang in the air for a moment. "This is completely confidential, by the way. Nobody else knows except at the highest levels. And it's going to stay that way until further notice."

"Understandable." Veena maintained her poker face, but her mind was whirling with possibilities. Either Francine Pearl Hughes—who'd been Philly's sweetheart since she was just a kid—had murdered her superstar athlete husband in cold blood or she was innocent but certain forces were determined to have the world think otherwise.

Francine Pearl Hughes was arguably more famous than her husband. She'd rocketed to fame as the lead singer of a preteen R and B trio from West Philly. Multiple Grammy Awards later, she embarked on a solo career, and each album she released broke new ground and shattered sales records. And only last year, her film debut in a wildly popular indie feature (*The Guilty,* Veena noted with no small amount of irony) resulted in an Academy Award nomination for best supporting actress.

Now imagine telling the world that this same brilliant woman had pumped a bullet into her superstar husband's chest the night before one of the biggest games of his career.

No wonder Mostel was bringing in the big guns (namely, Veena). Screw this up in public and you might as well point a gun at your own career.

"I want you to put together your own murder book," Mostel said. "Do your thing, work your magic, but keep it a completely clandestine and independent investigation."

"No matter what I find," Veena said.

"No matter what you find."

"And you'll give me everything I've asked for—I have your word on that?"

"Yes, you do. And you can record me saying that if you'd like."

"No need, Mr. District Attorney," Veena replied.

CHAPTER 7

12:07 p.m.

"YOU GUYS must be losing your minds."

"We are very concerned for our client."

"I'd be concerned too," Cooper Lamb said, easing his tall, lean body back into the lawyer's two-thousand-dollar leather sofa. "Because it's obvious she did it."

"I'm sorry... what did you just say?"

"Can you hold that thought for a sec, Lisa?"

Cooper fished inside his jacket, retrieved a small fabric pouch, and pulled out a tiny morsel of dried salmon. His associate Lupe, a year-old Rhodesian ridgeback, snapped to full attention. Cooper said, "Gentle," then held out his hand, treat nestled in his palm. The noble Lupe quickly and carefully made it disappear.

The defense attorney, Lisa Marchese, was momentarily distracted by this utterly adorable display. Then her brain patiently reminded her of the last thing Cooper had said.

"Lamb, did you say my client is guilty?"

"I said *she did it,*" Cooper repeated, and he hated repeating himself. "No idea how she feels about it."

"Let me get this straight. Francine Pearl Hughes, the bereaved wife—you honestly believe she killed her husband?"

Cooper looked around the spacious office for an imaginary judge. "Your Honor, Counsel is badgering her guest."

"For Christ's sake, Lamb. How can you possibly say such a thing about Francine?"

Cooper rubbed Lupe's head and murmured something about not paying attention to the mean lawyer lady and her profanities.

Both private investigator and pooch were sitting in the posh 1818 Market Street offices of Kaplan, DePaulo, and Marchese LLP, the city's top criminal-defense firm. Senior partner Lisa Marchese had asked to meet with Cooper at nine a.m., but he told her he had other plans. (He did; morning walks with Lupe were sacred.) He ignored calls from the DA's office—Cooper hated that guy—and finally agreed to a noon meeting with Marchese. "I'm bringing my associate," Cooper had warned her, not letting her know that the associate happened to be canine. But everybody loved Lupe. He instantly improved the vibe of any room.

"I'll tell you exactly how," Cooper told Lisa. He gave Lupe another dried salmon treat for being a good boy, then continued. "You just told me that her prints were found on the murder weapon, which ballistics has definitively matched to Archie's murder. The weapon was hastily buried in a frozen flower bed on the Hughes estate. My guess is, sooner or later there will be surveillance footage connecting her to the crime. There are dozens of cameras on the parkway; I'm sure there will be multiple angles of your client pumping a few slugs into her husband's heavily muscled torso, then hurrying away from the scene of the crime."

Lisa Marchese stared at him in horror. "You don't really believe that, do you?"

"No, but I'll bet you're terrified that a jury might believe it. That or whatever compelling version the DA's office is putting together as we speak."

Marchese exhaled. "You scared me there for a moment. I was

afraid the legendary Cooper Lamb, ex–army intelligence and the best PI in the city, had lost his mind."

"Flatterer."

"We'd like you to clear Francine's name. And, if possible, find out who really killed Archie."

"Of course."

"The police will have their own ideas, but we want the truth."

"Who doesn't?"

"So, can we count on you to join the team?"

"Hell no."

CHAPTER 8

Transcript of private conversation between Cooper Lamb and Lisa Marchese, senior partner at Kaplan, DePaulo, and Marchese, captured using an ambient recording app on Lamb's smartwatch

LISA MARCHESE: You're seriously going to walk away from the biggest murder case in Philadelphia history?

COOPER LAMB: Why don't you try Veena Lion? She's the best. Well, second best, if I may be so immodest.

MARCHESE: Maybe we already called Veena.

LAMB: Nah, she'd never work for you guys. She hates big law firms even more than she hates authority figures.

MARCHESE: You've had no problem cashing our checks in the past.

LAMB: And in the past, the checks have been generous. But when it comes to... what did you say? "The biggest murder case in Philadelphia history"?

MARCHESE: Ah. I see. You're negotiating.

LAMB: Of course I am. I wouldn't want you to lowball me simply because I'd kill for this job. I loved Archie and I pretty much bleed Eagles green. I bet on them every week, even during their not-so-stellar seasons. And I've had a massive crush on

Francine Pearl ever since that music video where she's wearing that . . . ah, never mind. But yeah. I'm all in. Wait, what are you writing there?

MARCHESE: How's this for a retainer?

LAMB: That is . . . impressive. Lupe, my faithful friend, I think that will keep you in dried salmon treats for months to come.

MARCHESE: So we have an agreement?

LAMB: Just one thing. Two things, actually.

MARCHESE: Go on.

LAMB: I'll need full access to the team. And the owners.

MARCHESE: You don't honestly believe one of Archie's own teammates murdered him, do you? Or the Sables?

LAMB: Maybe I'm a huge fan *and* milking this situation for all it's worth.

MARCHESE: I'm sorry, what?

LAMB: Maybe I promised my kids some autographs.

MARCHESE: But—

LAMB: Or maybe I'm really good at my job, and you should trust my instincts.

MARCHESE: (*Sighs*) Fine. What's the other thing?

LAMB: If you hire me, I'm not going to stop until I find the truth.

MARCHESE: That's what we want.

LAMB: Even if the truth is very bad for your client?

MARCHESE: (*Slight hesitation*) That's what we want, Lamb.

LAMB: You've got yourself a private eye, Marchese.

CHAPTER 9

1:12 p.m.

COOPER LAMB fork-and-knifed his way into a hot pork sandwich at the DiNic's counter at Reading Terminal. Sitting one stool away was Victor Suarez, his unflappable assistant, nursing a mug of black coffee.

"So what do you want?" Victor asked.

Cooper shook his head, then pointed a forkful of broccoli rabe and pork at his assistant. "No, my friend. Question is, what do *you* want?"

Victor sighed. Or perhaps it was just him exhaling—the differences were subtle, and even a trained ear like Cooper's had a difficult time telling them apart.

"I mean," Cooper continued, "you can't just sit at this counter and torture yourself with that sad, lukewarm cup of alleged coffee. The roast pork here is the best in the world."

"I assume you've got a list for me, boss?" Victor asked.

"Of course I have a list." And with that, Cooper began to reel off the items. He was confident Victor could find him the information he wanted because Victor Suarez could find out *anything*. Seriously. No matter the organization—the local police, the Feds, freakin' Facebook—Victor knew how to slip through the digital back door. He'd take a discreet look at the most highly protected files and go—no one ever knew he had been there, and it wasn't as if Victor himself went around bragging about it. Sometimes Cooper wondered if his longtime inside guy had seen so much brain-melting top secret intel that he no longer reacted to any news, no matter how shocking.

"I need everything on Archie Hughes—"

"Already compiled and on this flash drive." Victor slid a slender metal fob across the counter toward his boss.

"No so fast. I'm also gonna need everything Mickey Bernstein has."

"On this same flash drive."

"Yeah? Well, how about everything Mickey Bernstein is thinking now and will be thinking soon, including what he'll order for breakfast tomorrow? And while you're busy hacking into the detective's brain, also get me a full background on the lovely Mrs. Hughes—one Francine, née Pearl."

"It's on the same—"

"Flash drive, got it." Cooper slid the flash drive off the counter with his finger, palmed it, and made it disappear with a flourish. If Victor was impressed by this semiprofessional demonstration of close-up sleight of hand, he didn't let on.

Hiring someone with the hacking prowess of Victor Suarez might have given other investigators pause. But the way Cooper saw it, Victor must have dug deeply into Cooper's past, and since he'd still agreed to work with him, Cooper couldn't be in better hands.

"That it?"

"No," Cooper said. "Have some pork, put it on the company tab."

"I'm good."

"Yes, you are. But this isn't a cold case. Things are going to evolve very rapidly."

"As things happen, I'll have them for you."

"You sound pretty sure of yourself there, Victor."

"That's because I *am* sure of myself."

Cooper tried to see beyond his assistant's stony expression, catch a glimpse of the man's inner life. But such a thing was impossible. Cooper shrugged. "All right, go do your nerd thing. I have two very important phone calls to make, and the sound of your furious illegal hacking distracts me."

"Whatever, man."

CHAPTER 10

Transcript of Cooper Lamb's phone call to Red's Bar and Grill, Atlantic City

COOPER LAMB: Lemme talk to Red.

BARTENDER: Red's busy.

LAMB: Yeah, yeah, he's not too busy for me. Put the old buzzard on.

BARTENDER: Telling you, he's not here.

LAMB: Which is it, he's busy or he's not there? Tell him it's Cooper Lamb.

BARTENDER: Who am I going to tell? The thin air? It's the middle of the day, there isn't nobody in this place, it's freakin' dead.

LAMB: That's *Cooper Lamb*. Go on. Say my name out loud.

BARTENDER: What kinda name is that?

LAMB: Just say it.

BARTENDER: I ain't sayin' nothing.

LAMB: Sayyy it . . .

BARTENDER: You're a goddamn pain in the ass, you know that, Lamb? Here you go.

RED DOYLE: Hey, kid, what's up?

LAMB: Nice employee you got there.

DOYLE: Trained him well, didn't I? He's better than a German shepherd in the front yard.

LAMB: I'll bring Lupe in sometime to meet him. They can talk dog to dog.

DOYLE: Okay, enough chitchat. You're calling about Archie Hughes, right?

LAMB: You sit at the dark nexus of the criminal underworld, Red. Tell me what you know.

DOYLE: Next of what? I don't know anything. Not this time, Lamb.

LAMB: Red, don't do me like that.

DOYLE: No, I'm serious. I'm not playing around here. You know how many people are calling me about their bets? This is costing me boo-coo bucks.

LAMB: Speaking of…

DOYLE: Oh no, don't you freaking start with me too!

LAMB: It's just that, without Archie on the team, I'm not feeling as bullish about the Birds, if you know what I mean.

DOYLE: If I hear anything about the murder, I'll let you know. But in the meantime, your bet stays the same, capisce?

LAMB: You are an international man of mystery, Red. I'm counting on you.

DOYLE: Yeah, yeah, I'll keep my ear to the ground.

LAMB: Right next to your mind in the gutter.

CHAPTER 11

Transcript of phone call placed by Cooper Lamb to a private number

COOPER LAMB: This is the Federal Bureau of Homework Management. May I speak to Ariel Lamb, please?

ARIEL LAMB: *Dad*, I know it's you.

LAMB: I'm sorry, I think you have mistaken me for some other odious authority figure. I am calling to let you know that... well, hold on a moment. Can you put your brother on the line as well? I do not care to repeat myself.

ARIEL: This isn't 1995, Dad. There are no other *lines*.

LAMB: This is super-serious and of deadly importance, Ms. Lamb. And your brother needs to hear this as well.

ARIEL: Don't you have work to do or something?

LAMB: That's exactly why you need to put your brother on the phone. He's going to lose his tiny little mind.

ARIEL: (*Shouting*) Coop! Dad's on the phone! (*Pause*) He said he's coming.

LAMB: How's Mom doing, by the way?

ARIEL: I'm not a double agent. Instead of this sneaky way of checking on Mom, why don't you just ask her?

LAMB: I am *not* being sneaky.

ARIEL: Are *too*.

LAMB: Am *not* to infinity!

ARIEL: (*Sighs*) Coop's here.

LAMB: Goody. Can you both hear me? Am I on speaker? Excellent. Tomorrow I am headed into the mouth of madness that is the locker room of the Philadelphia Eagles. Yes, your father, the man who provided quite a bit of your DNA, will be interviewing the possible NFC champions tomorrow. I'd like you to give me your autograph requests in order of preference.

COOPER LAMB JR.: Cool!

ARIEL: Isn't that highly unethical? To use your privileged access for personal gain?

COOPER JR.: Will you shut up, Airy?

LAMB: No, Coop, my boy, your sister makes an excellent point. And you know what? I'm scared straight. See this leaf? It's turning over. Thanks for setting me straight, daughter.

ARIEL: Uh-huh.

LAMB: (*Whispering*) Coop, text me who you want. Don't tell the killjoy.

CHAPTER 12

FOR IMMEDIATE RELEASE
MONDAY, JANUARY 24
STATEMENT FROM COMMISSIONER MAHONEY REGARDING THE INVESTIGATION INTO THE DEATH OF ARCHIE HUGHES

As the city of Philadelphia—and, indeed, the world—continues to mourn the loss of "Greatest of All Time" Eagles quarterback and beloved father and husband Archibald "Archie" Hughes, I want to assure my fellow citizens that justice will be sure and swift.

We have created a special task force composed of dozens of highly trained detectives, forensic analysts, and scientists.

Detective Michael Bernstein is leading the task force investigating this brutal crime, and he assures me they have made tremendous progress in the past thirty-six hours. There are already several persons of interest.

Our hearts and prayers are with Archie's friends and family, especially Francine Pearl Hughes and their wonderful children, Maddie and Archie Jr., in this extremely difficult time. I urge the citizens of this city to treat the family with the greatest respect and understanding and refrain from any ugly public displays. Such behavior will not be tolerated.

If you have any information regarding the case, you may contact the department safely and anonymously on our tip line.

CHAPTER 13

9:50 p.m.

"HENDRICK'S MARTINI, up, with Noilly Prat vermouth, just a splash, and three blue-cheese-stuffed olives."

Veena Lion gave her order without looking up from the menu. The bar was dim, but her eyes remained hidden behind her sunglasses.

"And I'll have the Citywide Special," Cooper Lamb said. "Thanks, sweetie."

Veena raised an eyebrow. "You know we're not at Dirty Frank's, right?"

"The Citywide Special, as the name implies, is honored all over the city," Cooper said. He looked up at the server. "Is this not true?"

The server smiled shyly. "I'll see what I can do." Cooper watched her leave, then turned to see that Veena had been watching him watching the server leave. "What?"

Veena shrugged. "She's going to bring you the Rittenhouse Hotel version of the Citywide, you know."

"A thimble's worth of WhistlePig and a jewel-encrusted goblet of Duvel?"

"My point is, it's going to be more than five bucks."

"Good thing you're picking up the tab."

"Oh, am I?"

"Of course you are—you've got that big DA paycheck coming."

Only now did Veena remove her sunglasses. She placed them on the table between them. Cooper knew her secret. She didn't wear shades to be mysterious. It was the intensity of her jade-green eyes. When Veena Lion looked at you, you felt as if she were gazing into the secret chambers of your soul. This made most people supremely uncomfortable.

But it worked the other way around too. Veena's eyes often betrayed what she was really thinking. "You're working for Francine Hughes," she said, pure delight in her eyes.

"Technically, her *lawyers* hired me."

"No need to get technical with me, Cooper."

"Oh, I know. I just didn't want you getting all jealous, imagining a scene that never happened."

"You mean the scene where the hot grieving superstar heaves her bosom in your direction and plies you with alcohol until you swear to her that you'll find her husband's killer?"

"Eh, something like that."

"Speaking of..."

Their drinks arrived. Veena coldly noted the presence of *four* blue-cheese-stuffed olives. While she no doubt preferred overkill to the alternative, Veena liked her directions to be followed to the letter. The server was trying too hard, and the slight hint of disapproval in Veena's eyes made Cooper smile.

"And for you, handsome, a Citywide Special," the server told Cooper as she set an oversize tumbler and a pint glass in front of him.

"Which here at the Rittenhouse is defined as..."

"If you can guess what's in that glass," the server said, "the drink's on me."

"You know," Veena said, "it's not technically a double entendre if your meaning is painfully obvious."

"I'm sorry? I—"

Cooper interrupted. "Challenge accepted! But if I get it right, I'm still paying five bucks. Otherwise, it's just not a Citywide Special."

"You've got a deal."

Veena rolled her eyes.

Cooper sipped at the shot like a hummingbird sampling the nectar of a daylily, paused to consider, then unceremoniously knocked the rest of the shot back.

"The fluid in that glass," Cooper said, "was definitely alcohol."

The server laughed, maybe a little too much, and left Cooper and Veena to their libations. Cooper raised his pint glass and turned to Veena. "Shall we toast?"

"To what?"

"To working another case together."

"We're not working this case together," Veena said. "In fact, we're working for opposing sides. You remember, don't you? Prosecution on one side, defense on the other?"

"Ah, but we're still on the same side."

"And what side is that?"

"The side of truth, no matter what."

CHAPTER 14

10:01 p.m.

"TRUTH IS, this case is a flaming garbage fire," Veena said, then downed half the martini. It was cold and bracing and exactly what she needed.

"Please," Cooper said. "Not with us working together as a team."

"Cooper, the only thing worse than being on a team *with* you is being on a team opposite you. Which is why I wanted to meet."

"And here I thought you just wanted to tie one on. Speaking of..." Cooper looked around for their server, who had departed only a few moments ago.

"We're friends and all, but I want to establish some ground rules," Veena said.

"Perfect. This calls for a drink."

"Rules first, drinks after."

"Okay, fine," Cooper said with a slight pout in his voice.

"We share everything. I mean every last shred of intelligence."

"Done."

Veena blinked. "Really? That was too easy."

"Not at all. It's the smart move. I mean, my man Victor can grab anything he likes from your files—"

"Just like my number two, Janie, can from yours."

"See? So we're saving valuable snooping time. Anything else?"

"Yes. We need to agree that we won't trust anything that comes from Mickey Bernstein."

"Done," Cooper said. "I hate that tall handsome prick. He's nothing but a haircut, a Penn degree, and a last name. What else?"

"No bullshit, now—who do you think killed Archie Hughes?"

"My gut take right now, based on the available facts?" Cooper asked. "Some of which came from Bernstein's initial report?"

Veena made a sweeping *The floor is yours* gesture with her freshly manicured hands.

Cooper nodded. "It was a random carjacker. He saw the fancy Maserati, not the guy behind the wheel. Once he realized who he'd killed, he took the Super Bowl ring to pawn it for some getaway money, but then figured out it would be like tattooing *Guilty* on his forehead."

"Interesting theory. So this random carjacker is also a master criminal who can evade dozens of surveillance cameras in the area and knows how to elude the cops in a citywide manhunt?"

"Eh, beginner's luck," Cooper said. "This is probably the guy's first time, which is why Mickey B. and his goons are having so much trouble finding him. And until they do, the entire city will continue to lose its collective mind. So that's my take. Who do you like for this?"

"Oh, the wife killed him," Veena said. "Absolutely."

"Really."

"No doubt about it."

Cooper made a *Give it to me* motion with four fingers.

"Let's put aside for the moment *why* Francine Pearl Hughes definitely murdered her husband," Veena said. "Instead, let's discuss why they'll never arrest her."

"I don't know. Could it be because . . . she absolutely didn't do it?"

"No. It's because this city loved her long before any of us had even heard of Archie Hughes."

"True. Francine is Philadelphia's sweetheart. What was that cringey soul trio she used to front?"

"You're pretending like you don't remember the Puritones, but I know you do."

Cooper smiled like a boy caught in a fib. He was completely unaware that their server was approaching as he broke into a horribly off-key rendition of the Puritones' hit "Cross My Broken Heart." Veena considered Cooper a highly talented investigator who had many skills across a variety of disciplines. Singing wasn't one of them.

"I'll swear it to the ennnnnnd," Cooper crooned, *"cross my broken heaaaaaaarrt!"*

"So glad Lupe isn't here to see this," Veena said.

"Can I, uh, get you anything else?" the server asked.

"Only my dignity," Cooper said, his cheeks slightly red. "As well as another round."

"Not for me," Veena said. She downed the second half of her martini.

"Come on, one more," Cooper pleaded. "Cross my broken heart?"

"Nope." Veena left cash, including an incredibly generous tip for the server. "By the way," Veena told her, "don't go home with him. He's a gifted orator and can probably talk you into it, but do yourself a favor and pass."

"I'm mortally wounded," Cooper said, clutching his chest.

"What business is it of yours?" the server asked. "Are you his ex or something?"

"Maybe someday," Veena said.

TUESDAY, JANUARY 25

CHAPTER 15

6:45 a.m.

THE WINTER gust skimming across the surface of the icy Delaware River was cold enough to cut through cloth, skin, and bone. Cooper Lamb and Lupe were standing at Penn's Landing looking across the river toward Camden, New Jersey.

They'd been partners for almost a year now. Lupe—Cooper Jr. called him "Loopy"—had entered Cooper's life just one week after his wife had left it. Friends joked that poor Lupe would soon grow tired of Cooper's bullshit and file for emancipation. Cooper didn't doubt it. Sooner or later, everyone had enough of him.

Cooper didn't have to turn around to know that Victor Suarez was approaching. He could hear Lupe's happy little yelps. The dog adored Victor.

"Damn, it's cold—who decided to meet out here?" Cooper demanded, shivering.

"That would be you, boss. To make it easy for you to head down I-95 straight to the Linc, remember?"

"Poor Lupe here peed icicles a few minutes ago."

"So here's what I've got. This won't be announced officially for another hour, but the Eagles-Giants game has been rescheduled for this Sunday."

"They're not going to try to push back the Super Bowl?"

"Turns out, you can't move a thing like the Super Bowl."

"Only a week between games. That's rough."

"Just keep it in mind as you talk to everybody this morning. The tensions are running a little high at the Linc, from what I hear."

"What else you been hearing?"

"I picked up some interesting details from the players' chatter on their various private social media accounts."

"Private accounts?"

"Separate from their public accounts, which are run by their management teams. This is what they use to hit on women and generally act stupid. Anyway, if the chatter is to be believed, you're going to have a long suspect list. Not many people on the team—or on the staff, for that matter—liked Archie Hughes very much."

"Reallllly."

"Quite a few players seriously *hated* the guy, as a matter of fact."

"Professional jealousy or something else?"

"Yeah, there was a bit of *something else*. Some of them are convinced that Archie was cheating on Francine."

"How could any mere mortal step out on a woman like Francine Pearl?"

"Don't know yet. But from reading their messages, I got the idea that some of the players would be more than happy to comfort Francine in her time of need."

"Those dirty dogs," Cooper muttered. "Sorry, Lupe. It's just an expression. Anyway, good work, Victor. Do you have a list of the players who seemed the most hostile or angry?"

"Texted it to you a few minutes ago."

"How about the ones who have taken a fancy to the Widow Hughes?"

"That would be the entire team," Victor said. "But I also texted you a list of the players who were especially vocal about it."

"Among themselves." Cooper pondered this for a moment.

"Think two of them teamed up to take out their quarterback and move in on his hot wife?"

"You don't pay me to make those kinds of guesses."

"I don't, but I'm asking you anyway. You're the one listening to this chatter."

"Pretty sure two people plotting to kill a coworker wouldn't do it on social media. Not even in direct messages. These guys sounded like they were just venting to each other, maybe even joking around a little. Or just being horndogs."

"Thanks, Victor. Lupe here speaks their language. I'll see if he can get one of them to confess."

"One more thing, boss. I'm coming along for the ride."

CHAPTER 16

Transcript of phone call placed by Cooper Lamb to a private number

COOPER LAMB: Good news, not-yet-fully-grown humans. I've decided to ignore professional ethics and totally hook you up with some Eagles autographs. Don't worry, I'll get those first, because I've got some tough questions to ask, and I'm probably going to have to be put in traction when I leave this stadium. If you don't know what *traction* means, look it up. Preferably using Google Images, because it will freak you out.

ARIEL LAMB: Sir, this is a Wendy's.

LAMB: Nice one, daughter! Now quit blabbering so I can get to work.

ARIEL: Do you have Lupe with you?

LAMB: Please. Would I *ever* leave home without my secret weapon?

Excerpt from Cooper Lamb's interview with Eagles receiver Lee McCoy

LEE McCOY: Cute dog, man. They just let you bring him back here? What the heck is he, anyway?

COOPER LAMB: Lupe here is a Rhodesian ridgeback. But never mind him for the moment. I'm here to talk about Archie.

McCOY: My brother!

LAMB: So you two were close?

McCOY: Dude. C'mon. Are you serious? Were we *close*? How can you ask me that? I would die for that man.

LAMB: Looks like he beat you to it.

McCOY: I'm sorry?

LAMB: Nothing. Did Archie ever talk about threats against him or his family? You know, overeager fans stalking him, anything like that?

McCOY: We get that all the time. I mean, when you're a public figure, it comes with the job. I don't expect you to understand, but it's a real pain in the ass.

LAMB: I'm sure. Have *you* received threats?

McCOY: Well . . . no. I don't think anybody is crazy enough to come at me, you know what I mean?

LAMB: Yeah, I know what you mean.

McCOY: Can I, uh, give your dog a treat?

LAMB: Depends. Can I have an autograph for my kid?

[Cooper Lamb's handwritten annotation: *McCoy—a lot of bluster, but not much to back it up. All bark, no bite.*]

Excerpt from Cooper Lamb's interview with Eagles center Bobby Devaux

COOPER LAMB: You played center at Notre Dame, right? I was a huge fan.

BOBBY DEVAUX: Wait up. Who do you work for again?

LAMB: I'm just doing a little routine background work for Francine's lawyers.

DEVAUX: Yeah, you can drop all that *routine* stuff with me. Not a damn thing routine about this case and you know it. This city is losing its damn mind.

LAMB: Then help me out here. Who should I be talking to? Did Archie have any stalkers, any enemies? What are the police missing?

DEVAUX: I'd be curious to hear what you've found so far. You're working for Frannie's lawyers, so I guess you want to take some of the attention away from her.

LAMB: You think she deserves the attention?

DEVAUX: Of course not. I love Frannie. I just don't know what you want from me.

LAMB: Look, I'm just starting out here, and I was hoping you could help.

DEVAUX: Don't detectives always try to figure out who'd benefit the most from someone's death? Also, people might take you more seriously if you didn't bring your [expletive] dog.

LAMB: I suppose an autograph is out of the question.

[Cooper Lamb's handwritten annotation: *Devaux—guarded. Probably a cat lover. Also kind of a dick.*]

Excerpt from Cooper Lamb's interview with backup quarterback Terry Mortelite

COOPER LAMB: I'll bet you wish this was all happening under different circumstances.

TERRY MORTELITE: Well, sure, but don't worry. We're gonna win this thing for Archie!

LAMB: I mean, you must have dreamed about this day—being the starting quarterback! That has to be a career high, right?

MORTELITE: Look, I'm just gonna give everything I have for Archie and Frannie.

LAMB: Were you two close?

MORTELITE: No, but I'd like to be. I mean, especially now. She must be lonely. I haven't reached out to her yet, but it's a weird time and—

LAMB: I meant you and Archie, but sure, let's keep going down this road. If Francine were here right now, what would you tell her?

MORTELITE: I just want to make her proud. If you talk to her, will you tell her that for me?

[Cooper Lamb's handwritten annotation: *Mortelite—had the most to gain, clearly has the hots for Francine. Too obvious.*]

Excerpt from Cooper Lamb's interview with tight end Jimmy Tua

COOPER LAMB: I'm really sorry for your loss. Everybody is telling me how close you were to Archie. To the entire Hughes family, for that matter.

JIMMY TUA: Yeah, thanks. I still can't believe it's real. Feel like I'm walking around in a dream these days. The world's worst dream.

LAMB: Since you were all so tight, I wanted to talk to you about the gossip flying around about Francine.

TUA: (*Angry*) What gossip?

LAMB: Everyone always points a finger at the spouse.

TUA: Someone points a finger at that beautiful woman and I'll snap it off and make 'im *eat it,* you feel me?

LAMB: Easy, my friend. I'm on her side!

[Cooper Lamb's handwritten annotation: *Tua—big guy. Built like a side of beef. AVOID BEING PUNCHED BY THIS MAN. Unlike the other players, Tua seems truly close with the Hughes family. Especially Francine.*]

CHAPTER 17

1:14 p.m.

"HOW'D IT go with the team?"

"It was just like a football game," Cooper said. "Lots of waiting, and I feel like I've taken a series of blows to the head. Did you get what you need from the front office?"

Victor was scrubbing his hands with a disinfectant wipe. His motions were thorough and meticulous, as if he were prepping for surgery. Cooper's assistant was borderline OCD when it came to leaving zero physical traces behind.

"Yeah, I had plenty of time before the Sables came back. Speaking of—that's them over there."

Across the broad green field, a lean, tall man was huddled with two obese men who looked like unmade beds. The latter were Harold and Glenn Sable, the father-and-son owners of the Philadelphia Eagles. They carried themselves like a pair of feudal lords watching over their knights, vassals, and peasants as they made furious preparations for war.

The tall man approached. Cooper knew him by sight, the handsome bastard. Enter homicide royalty, Detective Mickey Bernstein.

"The Sables seem awful chummy with the homicide dick," Cooper said to Victor.

"What do you mean?"

"Look at them all," Cooper said with disgust. "Laughing and backslapping. Does Detective Mickey look like a man hell-bent on finding the killer of the greatest quarterback ever?"

"I don't know, Cooper. You're the one who's good at reading people. All I know is, whatever their deal, we'll know a lot more by the end of the day."

Cooper turned to face Victor and clutched at nonexistent pearls in mock horror. "My God, Victor! Please tell me you didn't do something . . . *illegal*?"

"I've got their offices and reception areas fully wired for sound. Oh, I wired up their matching convertible Rolls-Royce Dawns, too. Even if these guys had someone doing routine security sweeps—and by the way, I checked their financial records, and they don't—"

"Nobody will be able to spot your bugs," Cooper finished. "Excellent work, as always."

Victor shrugged, which was about as close as the man came to accepting a compliment.

"Now, let's see if I can rattle these big boys a little," Cooper said.

"I'll let you know."

CHAPTER 18

Transcript of Cooper Lamb's interview with longtime Philadelphia Eagles owners Harold Sable (age seventy-one) and Glenn Sable (age forty-eight)

COOPER LAMB: First of all, let me tell you both how sorry I am for your loss.

GLENN SABLE: (*Muttering under breath*) *Loss*—yeah, that's the word for it.

HAROLD SABLE: (*Annoyed*) Glenn...

GLENN: What?

HAROLD: How can we help, Mr. Lamb?

LAMB: You two knew Archie better than almost anybody. Can you tell me if anything seemed, you know, *off* in the weeks leading up to the playoffs?

HAROLD: See, here's the thing. It's interesting you're asking *us* this question. Your client could tell you a lot more than we ever could.

LAMB: My client?

HAROLD: You're working for Kaplan, DePaulo, which means you're working for Francine. I mean, why else would you be here?

LAMB: Look, I want the same thing you guys do—to find Archie's killer. Which is why I'm asking you, again, if anything seemed strange in the past week or so. Maybe somebody you didn't recognize hanging around? Any of the players have a beef with him?

HAROLD: You gotta be crazy if you think one of my boys did something like this to a fellow player!

LAMB: Of course not. But sometimes tempers flare, somebody speaks out of turn, and the next thing you know...

GLENN: You're not going to find anything like that in this franchise. It's been one hundred percent hustle. I mean, it's the freakin' Super Bowl on the line! Going all the way would mean everything to us.

HAROLD: And the city of Philadelphia. You have to admit, Mr. Lamb, this city could desperately use a win. On so many levels.

GLENN: And every single member of this franchise is focused like a laser on that goal. There's no time for beefs or rivalries or whatever the hell you said. Who you should be looking at is the family.

LAMB: I'm pretty sure his children didn't leave him for dead in front of the art museum.

HAROLD: (*Shocked*) Mr. Lamb, my son didn't mean—

GLENN: Pop, don't do that. I'm perfectly capable of saying what I mean. But seriously, I don't know why you're wasting your time here when you should be grilling the nanny.

LAMB: The nanny... (*Checks notes*) You're talking about Maya Rain?

GLENN: Just giving you a friendly heads-up. You should seriously talk to her. If there's trouble in that household, look no further. She's pretty hot. For a hillbilly from West Virginia.

LAMB: Trucker's tan, blond from a bottle, couple of missing teeth... does that kind of thing float your boat, Glenn?

GLENN: What did you just say to me?

HAROLD: Glenn, I'm sure Mr. Lamb is just teasing.

LAMB: No, Mr. Lamb is just trying to do his job. Francine Hughes deserves better than cheap cracks and innuendo.

HAROLD: We have nothing but love and compassion for Mrs. Hughes. She is truly a legend. But so was her husband, and he meant the world to us. I'm talking personally—I'll forever be in his debt. So please do us a favor and find out who did this. No idea what kind of retainer you've got from Kaplan, DePaulo, but I promise you, the Philadelphia Eagles will handsomely reward you.

LAMB: I'm not in this for the money.

GLENN: Not in it for the money? What kind of bull■ is that?

CHAPTER 19

COOPER LAMB drove north on I-95 toward Center City with Victor slumped comfortably in the passenger seat, right knee propped up on the dash.

As a rule, Victor refused to drive. When he was barely a teen, Victor had hacked his way into an insurance company's servers, read a bunch of mortality tables, and vowed never to sit behind the wheel of a motor vehicle. When told that he was taking the same risk by being a passenger, Victor merely shrugged and said that it was up to God.

This would seem like a complication, but Victor was very skilled at using public transportation—without paying—to reach every corner of the city. Victor almost always beat Lamb to any given destination.

"I presume you were listening to my chat with the Sables. Did I rattle them?"

Victor shrugged. "The hillbilly crack was kind of cheap."

"I was dealing with vulgar men."

Again, Victor shrugged. It was his favorite form of personal communication, which drove Cooper a little nuts. He liked to joke that if Victor ever wrote a tell-all memoir, it would be about three pages long.

"Anyway, you promised me a surprise," Cooper said.

Victor reached between them and handed his boss a thick black binder bursting with pages. "Here's my report."

Cooper grabbed it, weighed its heft. "How did you find time to do all of this?"

"The business office has a good laser printer. And, yeah, I might have raided their supply closet a little."

"Nobody questioned you?"

"I'm a Latino dude in khakis and an off-white polo shirt futzing around with office equipment. No one batted an eye."

"God bless the bigots." Cooper placed the binder in his lap and used his right hand to awkwardly thumb through. It contained a dizzying array of invoices, e-mails, and tax documents.

"Keep your eyes on the road," Victor warned.

"It's going to take me all day to read this."

"The first five pages are a summary."

Cooper thumbed backward. "So they are."

"But let me just tell you what's in there. Basically, the team is a mess from the top down."

"Tell me about the top."

"Business operations are a joke. There's, like, no oversight. The Sables are tax evaders, gamblers, extortionists, and con artists. They try to screw anything that moves, and I mean that literally. It's amazing the business side of this team hasn't already imploded."

"Yeah, they don't seem to be guys who bother with the little things," Cooper said. "Business ethics, sound accounting practices, personal hygiene…"

"Boss, you don't know the half of it. You'll find the rest in the report."

"What about the players?"

"There are summaries of dozens of quashed lawsuits and NDAs in the files. But to sum it up: These guys are spoiled brats. Most of them, anyway. Nobody's telling them no, and when they get into trouble, the team's lawyers keep everything quiet. They employ *very good* lawyers. And lots of them."

Lamb continued to flip through the binder until he reached a short transcript at the very end. "What's this part?"

"I'd seriously appreciate it if you focused on the wheel, boss."

"This looks like a transcript of—"

"Your interview with the Sables, yeah."

"Transcribed in real time and printed a minute later? You're incredible, Victor."

"If I'm so incredible, maybe keep your eyes on the road so I don't die."

"For you, my friend, anything."

CHAPTER 20

12:23 p.m.

VEENA LION was sitting on a Paoli/Thorndale train headed to Ardmore holding a legal pad on which she wrote names, drew arrows, crossed names off, and added them again, ranking all the people who had a reason to kill Archie Hughes.

A dull gong from her phone interrupted her brainstorming. The gong meant a text from Janie, but when Veena flicked open the message, there was no text, only a camera icon. *Okay, it's story time.* Veena tapped the image and listened over her earbuds.

On-screen was Janie, who had positioned her own smartphone to capture her desk with the computer's display cocked at a precise angle to avoid glare or distortion. Always thoughtful, that Janie. "Apologies for all of the . . . awkward," Janie said, waving her hands around as if to illustrate *the awkward*. "I received a small tsunami of files and footage from the DA's office. I was going to cc you on all of it, but since it required a bit of explanation, I thought it would be easier to walk you through it. I mean, I can show you the whole thing when you get back to the office, but . . . okay, I'll stop talking and just show you."

Veena couldn't help but note that right next to Janie's keyboard was a half-demolished hoagie from Cosmi's in South Philly. Specifically, the Godfather: prosciutto, soppressata, and enough roasted peppers and sun-dried tomatoes to stock a salad bar.

On the monitor, black-and-white surveillance footage from a section of the Ben Franklin Parkway.

"Okay, here's the Museum of Art on the night of the Archie Hughes shooting. The interesting thing is that Archie's car is parked just out of view." Janie paused to take a bite of her hoagie, then continued to narrate through the prosciutto. "Sorry. I'm starving. Anyway, you can sort of make out a bumper."

Janie tapped a few keys. The image zoomed into that bumper, then back out again.

"The weird thing is, Archie managed to stop his Maserati inside a perfect dead zone between two surveillance cameras."

That can't be a coincidence, Veena thought.

"I know what you're thinking," Janie said. "That can't be a coincidence, right? I went back and checked on where those cameras *should* have been aimed. Looks like both of them were angled approximately twenty-three degrees away from where they were supposed to be pointed, creating that dead zone."

This was a setup, then. Either Archie Hughes was lured to that exact spot or someone had dumped him and his car there, which implied he had been shot and killed elsewhere. *Please tell me you went back and checked when those cameras were moved,* Veena thought.

"Before you ask," Janie said, "I went back and checked both feeds. The cameras were moved six minutes and twenty-three seconds before the police discovered Archie Hughes's body."

There we go, Veena thought.

"But that's not the best part," Janie continued. "Watch this."

She tapped a few keys and took a bite of her Godfather as the computer jumped to another stream of surveillance footage. It took Veena a couple of seconds to identify the location: Spring Garden

Street, between Twenty-Third and Twenty-Fourth Streets, just a few blocks from the art museum. "Check out *this* guy."

On-screen, a white male hurried up the street, using his T-shirt as a mask to cover his nose and mouth; a gray hood covered most of his head.

"This was captured just minutes after a couple of patrol officers discovered Archie's body. Definitely looks like he's running for his life, doesn't it?"

"There was a reference to him in the police report," Veena said.

"Yes, but this is the first time he's popped up on surveillance. We now have a better physical description."

Could be an athlete, Veena thought. *Maybe even a football player.*

Transcript of encrypted message exchange between Veena Lion and Janie Hall

VEENA LION: Stellar work, Janie. Enjoy the rest of your Godfather.

JANIE HALL: Sorry about that, V., but a girl's gotta eat. You headed to the Linc to figure out which member of the team had it in for Archie? Need me to prep some background files on the team?

LION: That would be fine, but no, I'm not headed to the stadium. I was just sitting here realizing that I need a window into the Hughes household.

HALL: Please don't tell me you're going to break into their mansion.

LION: Who am I, Cooper Lamb? I'm just going to follow your lead.

HALL: ???

LION: Can you send me the home address of their personal chef? The one the file said they'd just fired?

CHAPTER 21

1:07 p.m.

VEENA LION was horrified the moment she stepped into Chef Roy Nguyen's cramped kitchen.

Not by the kitchen itself, which was compact, clean, and tidy. So tidy, in fact, it looked as if Chef Nguyen rarely cooked a meal at home. No, Veena was horrified by the lunch Chef Nguyen was currently preparing: leftover spaghetti. At some point, the sauce-heavy pasta had been a take-out meal, and now the chef was frying it up in a high-end skillet over a medium flame. Sauce smoked and splattered as the chef pushed a wooden spoon around the edge now and again.

"Hungry?" Chef asked.

"I had a late breakfast," Veena lied. "So, I understand Ms. Hughes let you go fairly recently?"

"Let me go?" Chef asked. He made an annoyed huffing sound. "Let's get it straight. That snooty bitch *fired* me. Over, like, nothing."

"Have you found employment somewhere else?"

Chef Nguyen stared at the tangled strands of spaghetti as if they could tell his fortune. "It's not exactly easy to line up another gig like that one. You have no idea how hard I busted my balls trying to get her attention in the first... hey, you're not even listening to me!"

Chef had looked up in time to catch Veena furiously thumbing her phone.

"I am listening to every word. But I'm also texting a headhunter friend of mine, who will be contacting you within the hour. She specializes in matching executive-level chefs with discerning families."

Chef's grimace disappeared. "Are you... are you serious?"

"Just pay attention to your phone over the next hour. Her name is April White."

"Why would you do this? You don't even know me."

"You're actually doing *me* a favor. April's clients will be falling all over themselves to retain your services. But help me understand something."

Chef turned his attention back to his sizzling pasta, which was on the verge of burning. "Sure. Yeah. Anything."

"Tell me about your time in the Hughes residence. Sounds like they were a very tight-knit family."

"Ha. Only three members of that family were truly tight."

"Mom and the kids?"

"Please. Parents are *supposed* to be tight with their kids. I'm talking about the threesome."

"You're going to have to tell me more."

"First I want you to try some of this."

"No, really, I'm fine. If my assistant, Janie, were here, she'd be all over your, uh, leftovers."

"I really just insist. I can see you give me those *Ew, gross* stares. You think I'm just heating up leftovers, but don't judge it until you put a forkful in your mouth."

With a flourish that finally revealed the man's skill, Nguyen spooned a small sample of the fried pasta into a glass bowl. He stabbed the pile with a tasting fork, then slid the bowl across the counter toward Veena.

"Go on," Chef said.

Veena knew the point wasn't negotiable. She twisted the fork around until she had a few thick strands of pasta in a tight little ball and put it in her mouth. She had to admit, the fried spaghetti was insanely flavorful, with a perfect blend of crispy bits and soft noodle bits. It was an entirely different approach to the household staple.

"You seriously need to make this for April," Veena said. "She'll lose her mind."

"Oh, this? This is nothing. Just lunch, you know?"

Veena made a series of mental notes (which she would commit to a yellow legal pad during the train ride home): *Chef Nguyen more than what he shows on the surface. He hides his massive ego behind a faux everyman exterior. He is the savory bite behind the fried pasta. What is he hiding?*

"So tell me about Archie, Francine, and Maya."

Chef Nguyen smiled and swirled himself a bite of spaghetti. "See, you figured it out for yourself. The threesome."

"But only *you* saw how they behaved."

"Oh, believe me, everybody saw. They were shameless. Everybody on the Main Line talked about them. And I should have known better. The moment I crossed that Maya Rain chick, my days were numbered."

"What did you do, ask her out?"

"Of course I asked her out. Have you *seen* her?"

Veena said nothing as she twirled more pasta around her fork. She hated herself for wishing there were more in her bowl.

"It's the whole nanny thing too. Sweet and shy on the outside, but once the kids are tucked away in bed . . ."

"You can stop painting the picture, Chef."

"What if I don't want to, Ms. Lion?" he said, chuckling.

CHAPTER 22

Transcript of phone call placed by Cooper Lamb to a private number

COOPER LAMB: Hey, it's your old man. Guess who I'm going to be meeting in two minutes.

ARIEL LAMB: Francine Pearl Hughes.

LAMB: Whoa! Nailed it on the first try.

ARIEL: C'mon on, Dad. You're working for her law firm, so one can only assume you'll be meeting with Francine at some point.

LAMB: You're good, kid. Unlike your dopey brother.

COOPER LAMB JR.: Hey! I'm standing right here.

LAMB: Relax, sparky. I knew you both were on speaker this whole time. I could hear your snuffles. By the way, are you taking your allergy medicine? And shouldn't you be getting back to basket-weaving class or whatever they teach at that expensive Quaker school?

ARIEL: Ignoring you. Say hello to Ms. Hughes for us! Tell her we're huge fans.

LAMB: I'll bet I'm a bigger fan than you guys.

ARIEL: Oh, really. Name one Francine Pearl song.

COOPER JR.: I hate that allergy medicine. It tastes like puke.

LAMB: If you could learn how to swallow a pill, you wouldn't have to drink the puke. As for your question, my dear doubting daughter: "The Star-Spangled Banner."
ARIEL: That's not a Francine Pearl song.
LAMB: I heard her sing it once. At a Super Bowl, in fact!

Cooper Lamb had been in more impressive homes than this. But those homes were Monticello, the Hearst Castle, and 1600 Pennsylvania Avenue. And none of those homes had had Francine Pearl Hughes living in them.

"Sit anywhere you like, Cooper," Francine said. "I'll be right with you after I get the kids their snacks. Care for something to drink?"

"Just some tap water for me and my dog, Lupe, if you don't mind."

"I think we can do a little better than that," she said, smiling.

Most people would be pondering the correct drink request. Not Cooper. He was too busy strategizing the proper place to sit. Sure, this was a friendly interview at his client's home. But make no mistake, Francine's kitchen was also her battlefield. Especially now that she had fired her general (Chef Roy Nguyen) and assumed command of all the family meals. She might be dressed in the casual manner of a Main Line mom, but she was still a superstar.

"I have some updates for you," Cooper said, opting for a spot directly across the kitchen island from Francine as she sliced vegetables to accompany kid-size trays of pita and hummus.

"Really?"

Not really. This was one of Cooper's favorite techniques, especially with an interview subject who was theoretically on your side. You didn't show up with a tape recorder and a list of questions. No, you acted like a proper houseguest and came bearing a gift—information. This made you collaborators, not detective and witness.

"The team is a mess," Cooper said. "The Sables are up to their ears in corrupt schemes, and the players are more or less kindergartners with millions in disposable income."

"That's not really an update, Cooper," Francine said. "That's been my reality for the past five seasons."

"Why didn't you encourage your husband to take his considerable talents elsewhere?"

"I presume you never had the chance to meet Archie in person. Nobody could ever *encourage* him to do anything he didn't want to. I'd better get these snacks to the kids—"

"One second, Francine. I really think there's something rotten with the team, and it may have something to do with your husband's death. I'm hoping you can point me in the right direction."

Francine's smile—her armor—faded a little. Only now did she look like a woman trying desperately to keep the oceans of grief at bay.

"Archie liked to say that he was *in* this world, but he was not *of* this world."

Cooper stared at her across the kitchen island. "You just tied a knot in my brain."

"What he meant was, he knew what he was getting into with the Sables. But he kept his nose clean and his head above the filth. The team had nothing to do with Archie's death. At some point, when the media calms down and cooler heads prevail, the police will find the truth."

"And what is that?"

"That Philadelphia is a violent city, and sometimes it takes even the best of us. Can I feed my kids now?"

"I'm sorry . . . just one more thing. Please."

Francine stared at him.

"Look, I *have* to ask this question," Cooper continued, "because it's going to come up sooner rather than later."

"Go ahead."

"Why were your prints on the gun found in the garden? The gun you said you didn't recognize?"

Francine nodded and smiled, as if she had been expecting this question. "I've just told you that Philly can be a violent place. If you grow up here, you're taught to protect yourself. All of this"—she waved a hand around her designer kitchen—"doesn't mean a thing if you can't take care of yourself."

"So you and your husband kept guns in the house, and you've handled them all at some point?"

"When I told the police I didn't recognize the gun, it was like saying I didn't recognize a particular hammer in a toolbox. Why would I? I never gave it much thought."

The explanation was delivered casually. But Francine locked eyes with Cooper with such intensity, she was clearly issuing an unspoken challenge: *Go ahead. Tell me I'm lying.*

Cooper stared right back. *Hey, it's not me you have to convince.*

Finally, Francine broke the tension. "I'd better get the kids fed, Mr. Lamb."

"I have a feeling they may have already feasted on my dog."

"Lupe? Are you kidding? They love him!"

"Everybody does," Cooper said. "He's the worst private-eye sidekick ever."

CHAPTER 23

2:21 p.m.

"OH, AND this is Maya," Francine told Cooper.

Maya Rain—the "hillbilly from West Virginia," as Glenn Sable had called her—was sitting cross-legged on the floor with the Hughes children as they played with Lupe, who was relishing all of the attention.

"Traitor," Cooper told his pup.

"Quiet, kids. Mr. Lamb is a private eye," Maya said in mock fear. "His job is to listen to everything we say."

"I think Mr. Lamb is a sheep!" announced five-year-old Maddie Hughes, who was utterly adorable. *"Baaaaa,"* she said. This was followed by a giggle fit.

"I've been called worse," Cooper said. "And don't worry, Ms. Rain, I'm just here to retrieve my partner, Lupe, who is clearly falling down on the job. Unless he's managed to take statements from all of you between treats?"

Three people in the room—Francine, Maya Rain, and Maddie—smiled at the joke, but not twelve-year-old Archie Hughes Jr.

The boy sat on the floor too, legs crossed, but his attention was miles away. Cooper had seen that look before. Back when he was in the army, Cooper had spent countless days in Fallujah and Baghdad staring into the eyes of children who'd lost a parent and couldn't understand why everyone was acting like nothing was wrong. Cooper felt his heart implode.

Maya Rain caught Cooper looking at Archie Jr. and quickly stood up. "Let me show Mr. Lamb out while you kids have your snack."

"Thank you so much, Maya," said Francine.

"Children, I'll be right *baaaaaack,*" Maya said, which made Maddie giggle all over again. Maya looped her arm through Cooper's and gently guided him toward the servants' entrance.

The touch wasn't flirtatious—it was as if she knew he needed to touch another human being in that moment, which was even more startling.

Transcript of recorded conversation between Cooper Lamb and Maya Rain

COOPER LAMB: I'd love to speak with you too, if you have a minute.

MAYA RAIN: Not here. Not right now.

LAMB: Where and when?

RAIN: Hmm. That eager to see me again?

LAMB: I'm just doing my job, and your name has come up a lot.

RAIN: I'm sure it has. I'll be in touch.

LAMB: Where and when?

RAIN: I don't know. The kids keep me pretty busy most days. Cleaning up messes, that's what I do.

LAMB: Funny—looks like we're in the same business. But name the time and place. Seriously.

RAIN: I'll let Lupe know. And be careful on your way out, Cooper. Mr. Lopez is picky about the grounds.

* * *

Transcript of recorded conversation between Cooper Lamb and Mauricio Lopez

COOPER LAMB: Hey, you're Mr. Lopez, right? My name is Cooper, and I'm working for Ms. Hughes's lawyers. Do you have a moment?

MAURICIO LOPEZ: That stupid dog is going to dig up my garden!

LAMB: That dog's name is Lupe and he will do no such thing. I wanted to ask you about the g—

LOPEZ: I can't speak right now. I'm sorry.

LAMB: It's just a simple question and nothing you haven't already told the police.

LOPEZ: What is that in your hand? No tape-recording!

LAMB: I promise I'm not recording. I have a nervous habit of holding my phone.

LOPEZ: Please, I'm very busy today.

LAMB: I promise this will just take a second. It's a matter of life and death.

LOPEZ: Fine. What is it?

LAMB: I can't seem to keep my hydrangeas alive from season to season. What am I doing wrong? You can be honest with me.

LOPEZ: (*Confused*) What?

LAMB: The winter months in Philly, they're brutal. Obviously you do a ton of work maintaining these grounds. I mean, that's how you saw the gun, right?

LOPEZ: I have to go now—

LAMB: But Ms. Hughes said it would be okay if we spoke.

LOPEZ: I believe she would be very angry if we spoke.

LAMB: No, she said it would be okay. Well, she *implied* it would be okay. I mean, we're all on the same team here! What have you got to lose?

LOPEZ: (*Sighs*) Everything, Mr. Lamb. I have *everything* to lose. My job. My status in this country. My freedom.

LAMB: Has someone threatened you, Mr. Lopez? Because if that's the case, we can protect you.

LOPEZ: Nobody has threatened me, Mr. Lamb. I live always under this threat. Now, please, take your dog and leave the grounds. I have much to do to repair the mess he's made.

(*After a gap in the dialogue of approximately one minute, a car door slams.*)

LAMB: You heard that, right, Victor? Mr. Lopez has a problem with Lupe, which clearly means he's evil. Kidding. But seriously, he may know something. I need to find out what. And Maya Rain . . . okay, I need to know *everything* about her.

CHAPTER 24

REPORT TO C. LAMB BY V. SUAREZ
TUESDAY, JANUARY 25

Finished my latest analysis of audio surveillance at the Hughes home and there is nothing unusual to note after you left.

You asked me to keep an ear out for the nanny, but she spends most of her time with the kids. She's good at keeping them distracted. Very inventive, lots of creative brain games. Stuff like having them look outside and tell her the makes, models, years, and colors of all the cars they see. (I found myself distracted by this too, to be honest.) The Hughes kids are quick. Who knows how they'll eventually turn out, but they might make great private investigators someday. Maya Rain is quite the teacher.

Francine Pearl Hughes spends a lot of time shopping online. I'm tracking all internet activity and I have a list of the high-end clothing and jewelry stores she's been visiting. The clothing appears to be purchased for herself, though I do not know the nanny's measurements. (Yes, I'm working on it. Ms. Rain's digital trail is either thin or carefully obscured.) The jewelry appears to be for a woman, presumably Ms. Hughes.

One other thing, boss—and this may be nothing, but I wanted to mention it anyway: Francine Pearl Hughes does a lot of singing around the house. Her own hits, but also older show tunes and stuff from the Great American Songbook. This is not surprising, of course, because Ms. Hughes is a singer, and I'm sure she's keeping her vocal cords in shape. Could be just habit. But is this the behavior of a woman in mourning for her husband?

More updates as I learn them. As I type these words, however, I hear there's a visitor to the Hughes home—your old friend Veena Lion is there to talk to the nanny.

CHAPTER 25

4:37 p.m.

"THANKS FOR agreeing to speak with me, Ms. Rain."

"Of course. Ms. Hughes thought I could help. I just have one request, and this is on the advice of the family lawyer. Please don't record this interview."

Veena Lion pretended to give it some thought. "Okay, I won't."

While Veena paused, she took a quick mental snapshot of Maya Rain, who did not appear to be your stereotypical home-wrecker. Her lithe body was clad in a tailored Banana Republic top and pants—rugged enough for someone who chased after children all day, classy enough for a member of the Hughes household's staff.

"Can you say that out loud?" Rain said, smiling.

"You want me to say that I'm not recording our conversation?"

"Thank you."

As a rule, Veena recorded all of her conversations. This was a matter of habit as well as personal protection. She was forever in pursuit of the truth, and while the truth could be twisted, tape never lied. But something told Veena it was best to relax that rule for the moment.

Veena matched Maya's warm smile with one of her own. "How did you come to work for the Hughes family?"

"Everybody in town has a salacious story about that," Maya said, blushing a little. “You know, rumors that Archie picked me up while I was waiting tables at Gullifty’s or stripping at Delilah’s or something along those lines.”

“Is that where you were working before you came to take care of the kids?”

“Which one, the family restaurant or the high-end strip club?”

Veena could tell Maya was teasing her. “You tell me.”

“The truth is much more boring than that, I’m afraid. I’m working toward my master’s in psychology at Villanova, and my adviser recommended me for the job. There was a lot of competition from people in the department because, you know, the Eagles and all that. But I’m not even a football fan.”

“Don’t let anyone hear you say that in this town,” Veena said.

“Tell me about it! It’s better to admit you’re a mass murderer or something.”

“Did you grow up on the Main Line?”

“No. Pretty much the opposite of the Main Line—Buckhannon, West Virginia. Ever hear of it?”

“I’m afraid not,” Veena lied. She recalled the 2006 mining disaster near Buckhannon that took a dozen lives, and she’d seen a documentary focusing on the town’s opioid epidemic. And she could hear echoes of Appalachia in Maya’s voice, which Maya took great pains to hide. She probably hadn’t become “Maya Rain” until she’d crossed the state line into Pennsylvania.

“Then you’re just like everyone else,” Maya said, examining the tops of her shoes. “I’ll admit, Buckhannon doesn’t have a lot going for it. I spent years saving up my babysitting money so I could escape. And strangely enough, all of that work landed me here, taking care of the sweetest children in the world.”

“Here’s what bothers me,” Veena said.

Maya’s eyes narrowed. “What’s that?”

“You’re too good to be true.”

"I've been told that," Maya said. She laughed. "But all I do is clean up messes. It's pretty simple, really."

"Seriously, though, do you enjoy your work with the Hughes family?"

"Are you kidding? Archie and Maddie are amazing. Even now—especially now, going through the shock and grief of losing Archie . . ." She seemed to search for words. "I hope that someday I'll be as strong as Mrs. Hughes and those kids. Want to meet them?"

CHAPTER 26

VEENA KNEW the kids were a deflection, but she went along with it; she'd wanted to meet them anyway. The boy was in sixth grade, and the girl—who was a miniature version of her famous mother—was a kindergartner. Both were absorbed in their handheld devices and barely noticed Veena's entrance.

"This is Miss Veena Lion," Maya said. "She's a private investigator who is working with the district attorney."

"Rowrr," Maddie said, then collapsed into giggles.

The son, Archie Jr., looked up. "You're helping the DA find out who did this."

"I'm trying my best, Archie," Veena replied. "What are you watching on your phone?"

"Just some stuff on YouTube."

"The hour before dinner is device time," Maya explained. "I don't want you thinking the worst of me."

"No judgments here. I live on my phone."

"The police asked us lots of questions already," Archie Jr. said. As he lowered his phone Veena stole a glance at the screen. Based on the graphics and framing, the boy was watching some sort of true-crime show.

"Yeah? What kinds of things did they ask you?"

Maya rubbed Archie Jr.'s shoulders. "You should probably wash up before dinner."

"Lions go *rowrr,*" Maddie said, then giggled again.

"That's right, they do."

"Do all private eyes have animal names?" Archie Jr. asked.

Responding to Veena's puzzled expression, Maya said, "A colleague of yours was by earlier today."

"Ah, Mr. Cooper Lamb," Veena said, nodding.

"Lambs go *baaaaa* and lions go *rowrr,*" Maddie announced. "Do you know his dog, Loopy? He's so cute!"

"I know Lupe, and he is indeed adorable," Veena said. "But watch out for Mr. Lamb. Sometimes big bad wolves like to hide in sheep's clothing."

This caught Maya's attention, just as Veena had intended it to.

CHAPTER 27

HIGHLY CONFIDENTAL
EYES OF THE POLICE COMMISSIONER ONLY

Dear Madam Commissioner:

A quick update on the Roy Nguyen situation.

I know speculation has run wild in the media. It's understandable—first, someone murders Archie Hughes, then, barely two days later, his former personal chef is badly beaten and shot. (I'm keeping in constant touch with the hospital, by the way, and will let you know the moment his condition improves . . . or worsens.)

This is why I immediately drove to Ardmore to learn what I could from the Lower Merion PD. Cutting to the chase, this appears to have nothing whatsoever to do with the Archie Hughes murder.

From what I hear, Nguyen is big into sports gambling. And while it's true that he had a lot of money riding on the Birds this year, I understand he owes quite a bit all over town. It's messy, but it could explain why a well-known chef would have taken a high-paying gig in the Hughes home.

I spoke to the Lower Merion detectives and forensics team. They're still working on their report, but it's clear that the attack was about intimidation, and things rapidly escalated. There were signs of a pretty brutal struggle inside Nguyen's apartment (broken furniture, doors) that spilled over into the hallway, where the chef was shot in the chest twice, at close range.

If this were a professional hit, Nguyen wouldn't have heard him/them coming, much less had the opportunity to fight him/them off. (It's possible there were multiple attackers, but all signs point to a single perp.)

My unofficial take: A leg-breaker showed up to scare some money out of Nguyen. The chef fought back, which caught the leg-breaker by surprise. Things spiraled out of control. The leg-breaker pulled a gun, at which point Nguyen probably tried to take it away. Two shots to the chef's chest later, the leg-breaker hightailed it out of there. (Again, had this leg-breaker been a pro, he would have made sure Nguyen was dead.)

I want to assure you that I will follow every detail of this case as it develops to see if there are any solid connections with the Hughes murder. But at this point, my gut is telling me no.

And like my dad used to say: "When your gut is talking, listen to it. Then go eat something."

Yours,
Det. Michael Bernstein

CHAPTER 28

Transcript of conversation between Detective Michael Bernstein and Glenn Sable, co-owner of the Philadelphia Eagles

GLENN SABLE: Mickey, my man. What's up?
MICHAEL BERNSTEIN: I don't know yet. I'm calling you from Ardmore. Maybe that will tell you something.
SABLE: What the hell's in Ardmore?
BERNSTEIN: A personal chef who may have baked his last soufflé.
SABLE: Shit, the Asian guy? Is he gonna make it?
BERNSTEIN: It's kind of touch and go. He's young, though, and I've seen people pull through worse than this.
SABLE: How could it be worse? I heard he took two in the heart.
BERNSTEIN: Two in the chest. Bullets are funny things. They can follow all kinds of paths in a human body.
SABLE: You have the chance to, uh, talk to the chef?
BERNSTEIN: Glenn, the dude's unconscious.
SABLE: No, no, I mean before. Like, about the other thing.
BERNSTEIN: It wasn't on my to-do list. Listen, my friend, I have to ask, just to make sure...
SABLE: Ask what?
BERNSTEIN: How much was the chef into you for?

SABLE: Hold on a sec. You think *we* had someone do this?

BERNSTEIN: Look, I'm not judging, I'm just asking. I told you before, I need to know everything, no matter how minor.

SABLE: Far as I know, the chef was current. I didn't even know he was part of our thing until my dad told me.

BERNSTEIN: So you had nothing to do with...

SABLE: Screw you, of course we had nothing to do with this!

BERNSTEIN: Glenn, calm the hell down, okay? And don't get me wrong, this was not anything professional. But it does look an awful lot like someone paid the chef a visit to smack him around a little, and things went haywire. I just want to be sure I know all of the details before I, you know, massage things.

SABLE: You want a massage, *Mickey,* go to a rub-and-tug. Don't call me up and accuse me of this bullshit. What, did I offend your tender sensibilities?

BERNSTEIN: No, man, I'm just sitting here enjoying my afternoon.

SABLE: Look, I'm sorry. I know how hard you're working. Things are just tense around here. I've got private eyes up my ass—

BERNSTEIN: Who?

SABLE: You know. The sheep guy.

BERNSTEIN: (*Chuckling*) You mean Cooper Lamb?

SABLE: Yeah, him. He's working for Francine, so I gotta play nice, but there's a guy I'd like to put through a wall.

BERNSTEIN: A lot of people feel the same way.

SABLE: Then maybe somebody should do something about it.

BERNSTEIN: I'll look into it.

SABLE: Yeah, you do that.

CHAPTER 29

Transcript of encrypted message exchange between private Veena Lion and Janie Hall

JANIE HALL: Hey, V., you know that chef you interviewed earlier today?

VEENA LION: Oh, did April find him a job already?

HALL: What job? No. Veena, this is important: He's over at Lankenau. Someone beat the hell out of him and then shot him twice. You there? You've been typing a long time…

LION: Is Roy alive?

HALL: I'm waiting for a call back from one of the nurses. She's a friend from high school, a straight shooter, so she'll give me the real deal.

LION: Okay, I'm headed there now. Give me any updates as soon you hear.

HALL: Of course. But V., be careful out there.

LION: I appreciate that, but I'm not the person who was attacked.

HALL: Sure, but the person who did the attacking is still out there. And he might have been watching Chef Nguyen. More to the point, he might have watched you meeting with Chef Nguyen just a few hours ago.

CHAPTER 30

Transcript of Detective Michael Bernstein's recorded interview with Justin Sugarman, aka Shuggie, currently residing in a homeless camp on Lemon Hill

MICHAEL BERNSTEIN: Justin? Hey, man, you around? I'm looking for Justin Sugarman!

JUSTIN "SHUGGIE" SUGERMAN: Quiet down, yo, I'm tryin' to sleep.

BERNSTEIN: That you, Justin? It's your old pal Mickey Bernstein!

SHUGGIE: Man, stop that Justin shit. You know everyone calls me Shuggie.

BERNSTEIN: Ah, there you are. Come on out, let me see that pretty face. How's it going, Shuggie?

SHUGGIE: Living my best life, man. You know me. The usual ups and downs. Mostly downs, if I'm being honest. But I don't let that keep me down, if you know what mean.

BERNSTEIN: I don't understand half the shit you say, if *I'm* being honest. But I think you can help me out with something.

SHUGGIE: No way, man. I don't help the police. Y'all hear that? (*Shouts*) I don't help law enforcement, like, ever!

BERNSTEIN: Save the outrage, Shuggie. No one else is around right now. Who could handle all the raccoons and garbage?

SHUGGIE: No, that's cool, man. You always insult people whose help you desperately need?

BERNSTEIN: Often as I can. Did you happen to see Archie Hughes's Maserati a few nights ago?

SHUGGIE: Come on, man. Get out of my camp.

BERNSTEIN: This so-called camp belongs to the city. I could tell *you* to leave.

SHUGGIE: Yeah, that's just perfect. Price hardworkin' people out of every affordable living space so we're all forced to live in a dump like rats. And then you want to take away our dump! So what are the rats supposed to do, huh, Mr. Detective?

BERNSTEIN: I don't know, Shug. Maybe the rat should just answer my questions. Did you see the Maserati or not?

SHUGGIE: Screw you.

BERNSTEIN: You'll have to talk to the missus about that, but I don't think she's flexible.

SHUGGIE: I'm serious, man. I don't need this grief.

BERNSTEIN: In that case, Mr. Working-Class Rat, start packing your things because I'm gonna have a sanitation crew up here in twenty minutes, and you'll be spending the next few days fishing your crap out of the Schuylkill.

SHUGGIE: [unintelligible]

BERNSTEIN: What's that, Shuggie? Couldn't quite make that out.

SHUGGIE: I didn't see no Maserati.

BERNSTEIN: But...

SHUGGIE: But... I heard about a guy who's trying to fence a Super Bowl ring. That might be of some interest to your current investigation.

BERNSTEIN: See that, Shug? I knew you were the right man to talk to. Who's selling the ring?

SHUGGIE: You must be high if you think I'm giving you a name.

BERNSTEIN: Dude, you're as high as giraffe balls right now. And I *know* you're going to give me a name because you don't want me throwing your skinny little ass into the river with the rest of your junk.

SHUGGIE: Damn, man.

BERNSTEIN: Come on. Nobody's around—it's just you and me, brother. Tell me a name. I probably know the guy already.

SHUGGIE: Brother, my ass. You know the guy. It's Percy.

BERNSTEIN: Crazy Percy Marshall? From Kensington?

SHUGGIE: Told you.

BERNSTEIN: What's Crazy Percy doin' with a Super Bowl ring?

SHUGGIE: I'm just telling you what I heard.

BERNSTEIN: Okay, Shug.

SHUGGIE: He's killed people, you know.

BERNSTEIN: Is that a fact.

SHUGGIE: I'm serious. You'd better be careful out there.

BERNSTEIN: Always am.

SHUGGIE: No, man, don't you get it? The line? You know, from *Hill Street Blues*? Probably before your time...

BERNSTEIN: Try that joke on my dad sometime. I'm sure he'd appreciate it.

SHUGGIE: Your daddy was a psycho fascist and everybody in the city knew it.

BERNSTEIN: Want to know a secret?

SHUGGIE: What's that?

BERNSTEIN: I'm worse.

CHAPTER 31

8:37 p.m.

TWO SURPRISES awaited Veena Lion at Lankenau Medical Center.

One was the armada of TV reporters blocking the entrance to the emergency department. She'd known word would travel fast, and the media was starving for any crumbs they could link to the Archie Hughes murder. But it was rare for TV reporters to beat Janie Hall on a breaking development. This case was going to test all of them.

The second surprise was waiting just behind the security checkpoint, which Veena got past by telling the officer she was Roy Nguyen's personal attorney. "How many lawyers does this guy have?" asked the beleaguered Lower Merion cop. "Your colleague is over there, by the vending machines."

Cooper Lamb, who was no lawyer, was busy ripping open a plastic bag of turkey jerky. *"Rowrr."*

"Baaaaa," Veena replied.

"I didn't know you were close with the chef."

"Yeah. He makes incredible fried spaghetti."

"If that's an in-joke, I'm missing the gag."

"Life doesn't revolve entirely around you, Cooper. What's the latest?"

The latest was that Roy Nguyen was still in surgery, and the hospital was clearly not prepared for all of the attention or the constant inquiries from private investigators.

"So we might as well go for a cocktail," Cooper said. "Unless you want to get in on this jerky with me. We can even split a root beer."

"I need to talk to Roy the minute he wakes up."

"Get in line. The police are downplaying this, but did you know that Chef Roy was fired by the Hughes family just *two days* before the murder?"

"Yeah, I did."

"Do you know why?"

"Of course."

"See, I don't think you do. He probably told you that Francine Pearl was just a bitch or something. But no, the dude flat-out *stole stuff* from the house. Watches, jewelry, sports memorabilia. And he was caught on a *nanny cam*."

Veena frowned. "That doesn't sound right. Who's your source?"

"Nobody you'd know."

"Is it Red from Atlantic City? Your old army buddy?"

"Damn it. I wish I'd never told you about him. Look, Red knows his stuff. Including the fact that your boy Roy owed a lot of people in Atlantic City a lot of cheddar. Which would explain the not-so-petty larceny from the Hughes home."

Veena considered this and replayed some of their lunchtime conversation. She thought about her legal-pad list of suspects. She thought about Maya Rain. But mostly, she considered that the day had been a very long one.

"Throw that crap away," she said, "and let's have that cocktail."

CHAPTER 32

9:08 p.m.

EARLY IN his career, Mickey Bernstein had spent a few years undercover. He'd told his superior he just wanted more street experience. But his real motivations were more complex.

A lot of it was wanting to be out from under his dad's thumb. But it was also the secret thrill of letting himself disappear into the rougher sections of the city and enjoying some of the pleasures associated with those places. Being the son of Philly's most famous cop meant he'd grown up under constant scrutiny, both inside his home and out. It was nice to slip into another man's skin.

And he could still do that from time to time.

Like now, walking toward a dive bar near the infamous intersection of Kensington and Allegheny. They said this area was slowly gentrifying, just like nearby Fishtown, but Mickey knew better. Woe to the hipster moron who stepped off the El looking for avocado toast and a craft IPA. Mickey didn't want to look like that. Or, even worse, like a cop. So he'd pulled on workman's clothes, skipped his evening shave, and got into character.

Bernstein opened the door to Dmitri's and found an empty barstool. People gave him the usual once-over, but nobody seemed to make him. He ordered a shot of Jack, a Bud back, and a fifty-cent bag of greasy potato chips. In the corner was a long-defunct

Donkey Kong console that now doubled as an ashtray and a place to hang Christmas lights, which were apparently up all year.

Mickey's dad loved places like this. Real salt-of-the-earth joints in the old working-class nabes. For all he knew, his dad had dragged him and his mom here at some point. Young Mickey had probably pumped some quarters into that very Donkey Kong machine.

When Mickey was two rounds in, Crazy Percy walked through the front door. Nobody bothered to look up. According to Mickey's regular snitches, Crazy Percy was always in here this time of night. Mickey didn't even have to come up with a tactic for the approach; Crazy Percy slid his large frame into the empty stool to Mickey's left.

"Hey, Crazy. Want a beer?"

"Oh, shit, man." Percy's frame deflated a little. "Gimme a Jack instead. A double."

Mickey nodded his permission to the bartender, who didn't exactly measure as he poured the whiskey into a tumbler.

"You look like garbage," Percy told Mickey, which was quite a statement coming from a man nicknamed "Crazy." This was not a nickname Percy embraced, but for years he'd been the guy who was willing to do pretty much anything (steal cars, break legs, maybe even murder) for low, low prices, so the moniker was hard to shake. Percy was forever looking for a way to turn a fast buck, but he always undervalued himself. With a little ambition, Mickey thought, he could be a proper criminal.

"I couldn't be better," Mickey said. "In fact, I'm getting married."

"Thought you *were* married."

"I'm in the market for a ring, and here's the thing—my sweetheart is a huge Birds fan. I mean, she, like, lives for it. So I'm looking for something like . . . a Super Bowl ring."

Percy groaned, then downed his whiskey as if it might be taken away from him.

"Heard you had a line on one," Mickey continued. "Something really special that just came on the market."

"I wouldn't even know what a Super Bowl ring looks like. What, does it have little footballs or buffalo wings on it or something? I don't know what you're talking about."

"Percy, you're breaking my heart here."

"Look, okay, I know where you're going with this. I didn't have anything to do with Archie Hughes."

"But you saw his car."

Crazy Percy stared at his drink, knowing that this conversation could go one of two ways. He decided on the easy way. "Yeah, I did. There was another fancy car parked nearby too."

Mickey tried to hide his excitement. "You remember the make and model?"

"A Bentley. Red or maroon, something like that. The thing was gorgeous. Couldn't believe somebody had left it out there that time of night." The thought of boosting it had clearly crossed Percy's mind. But maybe he wasn't *that* crazy.

"Did you see anyone behind the wheel? A woman, maybe?"

"Nah, there was nobody in the car. Unless they were hiding in the back seat."

"You sure?"

"I didn't see a soul. Not until you cops rolled up, and then I got the hell out of there."

The car, though. That was enough.

Francine Hughes drove a red Bentley.

CHAPTER 33

9:32 p.m.

"WHAT'S THAT? Hang on, kiddos, let me find out. Excuse me, miss?"

The waitress at the Rittenhouse Hotel bar was the same one from the night before, but gone was any hint of flirtation. In its place was an icy veneer. Veena must have *really* rubbed her the wrong way. That's what Veena did for a living, but Cooper needed to make it right. He liked it here.

"Yes?" she said quietly.

"I'm on the phone with some old war buddies...okay, that's a lie." Cooper showed her his best smile. "My *kids* are on the phone, and they have a very important mixology query. What's the real difference between a Rob Roy and a Shirley Temple? I mean, is it the same thing only sexist?"

"Order your kid a Rob Roy," the waitress said, "and I could have you arrested."

"Come again?"

"You're thinking of a Roy Rogers, which has Coke in it. A Shirley Temple uses Sprite. That's the difference."

"You hear that, kiddos? This impossibly beautiful woman just saved me from prison." Cooper looked up at her and mouthed, *Thank you.*

But it was something else—probably the words *impossibly beautiful*—that melted the ice, and suddenly all was calm and good in the lounge at the Rittenhouse Hotel once again.

That is, until Veena Lion arrived, pulled out her chair with a teeth-shredding scrape, and barked out an order for a double martini with three blue-cheese-stuffed olives, easy on the vermouth. Cooper said good night to his kids, told them he loved them, and placed his phone on the table.

"Okay, what the hell is going on with this case?" Veena said.

"So are we finally past the whole ethics thing? Can we talk straight?"

"We shouldn't be talking at all, but I need to know the truth."

"Amen to that. And here come our libations."

They drank in silence for a while, recalibrating their nervous systems. Then Veena said, "Speaking of the nanny cam..."

"Ah," Cooper said. "So you've met the lovely Ms. Rain too."

"Eh. She's too good to be true."

"I like her."

"Based on?"

"Gut feeling. I know, I know, I'm keeping an open mind. But I'm going to be terribly disappointed if she had any part in Archie's murder."

Veena watched him carefully with her green eyes, analyzing every word, every micro-expression. "My God. How did you do it?" she asked.

"Do what?"

"Fall in love so quickly."

"It was easy. Happened the minute she slipped her arm through mine and escorted me into the garden."

Cooper's intention was to playfully jab back at Veena for that falling-in-love wisecrack. But she surprised him by leaning across the table and kissing him on the cheek.

"That almost hurt," Cooper whispered.

"Rowrr," Veena whispered back.

"Does this mean you want to come for a sleepover tonight?"

"No, it does not."

"Well, that hurt even more." Cooper was confused about where all of this was going. Was it the usual flirtatious banter? Or were they about to cross *all* the lines in their professional relationship?

He had just resolved to hang in there and find out when a harsh *buzz* on the table broke the spell, followed by a second *buzz* a moment later.

Both of their phones.

Lion and Lamb scooped up their devices quickly to read the incoming flurry of texts from Janie and Victor, respectively. The TV newscast droning in a corner of the lounge had the same breaking news one minute after that.

"Holy God, Chef Nguyen—" Cooper muttered.

"Didn't make it," Veena said.

WEDNESDAY, JANUARY 26

CHAPTER 34

3:13 a.m.

THE CELL phone on Cooper's nightstand vibrated. Lupe gave a short, muffled bark—more of a *woof*—to alert his master. But his master was already on full alert. "Shhh," he whispered. The pup immediately fell silent.

Cooper reached down and grabbed the shotgun he kept clipped to the underside of his bed. Cooper knew the easiest way to disorient a target in his home at night was to call him. While your target fumbles for the phone in the dark, you take your shot; it's over before he's even fully awake. Cooper refused to make that mistake.

Only with the Winchester SXP Defender pump-action shotgun in his hand did Cooper answer his cell.

"Honey," he said calmly, "I told you *never* to call me at work."

The person on the other end of the line hesitated. Cooper heard a confused muttering before the caller finally snarled: "Walk away. That's what Chef Boyardee should've done."

Cooper said, "Red—is this you?"

Click.

CHAPTER 35

EARLY MORNING was the best time to do a home search, in Detective Mickey Bernstein's professional opinion.

Surprise 'em while they're not fully awake and still in their pajamas. When you have a choice, serve that search warrant before the coffee machine drops its first drip.

In this case, however, Mickey *didn't* have a choice.

He'd left Dmitri's around ten o'clock and pulled an all-nighter that involved the commissioner (already on board), his homicide captain (a pushover), a federal judge (an elderly political hack), and his counterpart at the Radnor Police Department (a nobody). Even with the dice loaded, for a while there Mickey wondered if it would actually work. Testimony from a lowlife named Crazy Percy wasn't exactly the strongest piece of evidence. However, that piece was needed for all of the others—most important, the murder weapon in the Hugheses' flower bed—to click into place.

It helped that the judge was a longtime pal of his father's and was used to wild Bernstein hunches. The moment His Honor signed off on the search, Mickey mobilized his team but pretended that the Radnor PD was taking the lead.

They knocked at exactly 6:03 a.m.

Francine was up and looked almost as if she'd been expecting company. *Nobody rolls out of bed this put together,* Mickey thought, *not even a multiple Grammy winner.* She was breathtakingly gorgeous. She even smiled at him.

"Good morning, Detective."

"Sincere apologies for the early-morning call, Ms. Hughes. I hope you understand that an investigation like this follows its own timeline."

Mickey had rehearsed what he would say to Francine on the ride over; this was the best he could do on zero sleep and in his wrinkled clothes. She seemed to take it in stride.

"You've got quite a crew with you," Francine said, looking over his shoulder at the small army of uniformed officers waiting for the signal to proceed. "I'd better put on more coffee."

But even a super-gracious host like Francine couldn't keep up with the sheer number of investigators examining every inch of her house. Little Maddie Hughes tried to pitch in, bringing the uniformed officers homemade chocolate chip cookies ("Our friend Maya helped us bake them last night"), organic lemonade, and helpful pieces of advice such as "Remember to check the bottom of the hall closet!" and "Don't forget the safe room!"

Mickey floated around the house checking in with various teams who'd been assigned different parts of the sprawling mansion. "I'm sure the Oval Office is tucked away somewhere here," grumbled one of the uniforms, who probably lived with a wife and three kids in a cramped Northeast Philly twin. Mickey shot him a look that told him he agreed but *stow it right now*.

Whenever he could, Mickey put eyes on Francine Pearl Hughes. She was eerily calm for a woman watching more than a dozen strangers examine every detail of her home. Calm for a woman suspected of murdering her husband.

Two developments threatened to break that calm. First, Archie's $400,000 Patek Philippe watch, which was reported missing from his body the night of the crime, was found mixed in with Francine's jewelry. How do you misplace nearly half a million bucks?

And second, ammo for a Glock was found in the garage, tucked behind gardening supplies. Not exactly hidden, but a weird place for live rounds.

"Keep searching," Mickey told his men.

"Hey, Detective?" said a tech named DeNardo. Mickey couldn't remember his first name for the life of him. Something like Dan or Drew? Whatever. He was the computer forensics guy working for the Radnor PD.

"Yeah, whaddya got?" Mickey said.

"I found a text to Archie Hughes. Something you probably haven't seen before."

"I doubt that, DeNardo. We seized all of his devices, remember? We've had techs all over his cell phone, his laptop, his tablet—"

"True, but I guarantee you haven't seen this."

This turned out to be a PlayStation 5 hooked up to a flat-screen TV that took up half the wall. This was Archie's toy; the kids weren't allowed to play video games—Mom's rules, no ifs, ands, or buts. Right now, a game was on-screen. Looked like elves with machine guns... or something. Mickey wasn't a gamer.

"What's this, DeNardo? You think one of the pistol-packin' little people did it?"

"Ha-ha, no. This is Worlds of Wrath—the shared-world FPS game?"

"You're speaking Latin, only dorkier," Mickey said.

"I won't get into it, but you fight monsters throughout history while you chat with other players. What makes this game unique is the social media component. You can send screenshots and short clips as messages out into the real world, and vice versa."

Mickey's blank expression encouraged DeNardo to hurry it up.

"Anyway," the computer guy said, "at some point, Archie must have sent Francine a clip of an awesome move or something, because she responded via text. He kept that up, and at first it was all playful, but things devolved over the past few weeks. And then, just a few days before the murder . . ."

DeNardo thumbed the game controller and a series of text messages from Francine to Archie appeared in giant letters on the flat-screen, as if it were evidence presented in court:

I'm tired of this. So, so tired

And:

You can't hide forever. We have to deal with this

And, most damning of all:

Maybe someone will teach you a lesson someday

CHAPTER 36

8:17 a.m.

"WE'RE TOO late," Lisa Marchese said.

"No such thing as too late," Cooper Lamb replied.

"What are you talking about? This is the textbook definition of *too late*!"

To be fair, this did seem to be the case. The Hughes home was crawling with law enforcement as well as local news teams hoping to capture the perp walk of the century. News vans up and down the street, two—no, now *three* helicopters circling, live feeds picked up internationally. At this moment, there was no other breaking story in the world.

Word had spread with lightning speed: Francine Pearl Hughes was about to be arrested for the murder of her legendary husband.

Thanks to Victor—who was alerted the minute a Mickey Bernstein–friendly judge signed off on the arrest warrant—Cooper had had a half-hour head start, time enough to pick up Francine's attorney and start racing to the Main Line.

But reporters still beat them to the house, most likely tipped off by their secret sources inside the Philly or Radnor PD. They were *not* going to miss this shot.

"Why didn't she call you the moment Bernstein showed up?" Cooper asked Lisa Marchese as they climbed out of his car.

"I don't know, Lamb. My client said she had her kids to worry about."

"Well, you find her and make sure she doesn't say a word to anybody," Cooper said. "I know she's Philly's sweetheart, and she's going to want to reassure her fans, but—"

"Come on," Lisa interrupted. "This isn't my first murder case."

"Yeah, but this is your first Francine Pearl Hughes case. Besides, that's not the point. I want you to stall until I can figure out a way to keep your client from being paraded in front of the cameras. Once that happens, she's as good as guilty."

"Hold on," Lisa said. "You work for *us*, remember? I need you to chase something down."

"Whatever you're about to tell me," Cooper said, gently leading Lisa by the arm toward the house, "I can guarantee it's not as important as the next five minutes."

"Just let me say this! The rumors about the chef are true."

Cooper Lamb stopped dead in his tracks. "Tell me quick."

"Roy Nguyen was up to his puffy white chef's hat in debt. The man was a serious gambler."

"We've all had bad nights at the poker table," Cooper said, pretending like he was hearing this for the first time.

"You don't understand. I'm talking *epic* losses in Atlantic City. To the point that he started stealing from the Hughes household."

"Damn," Cooper said, wondering how long he should feign shock before urging the lawyer inside the house.

The tendons in Lisa's neck were standing out; she was clearly exasperated. "Don't you get it? This is the whole case right here. It was an inside job, engineered by Roy Nguyen. What's more valuable than a Super Bowl ring? Forget that—what's more valuable than *Archie Hughes's* Super Bowl ring?"

"You really think Chef Roy would kill a legend for a hunk of gold?"

"No. I think it was a heist that went horribly wrong, and for some reason, the Philly cops are super-eager to pin it on my client."

"Speaking of..."

Letting the lawyer delay things had obviously been a mistake, because here was Francine, perfectly coiffed and handcuffed, being led by Detective Mickey Bernstein down her own neatly manicured garden path, lush even in January.

CHAPTER 37

REPORT TO C. LAMB BY V. SUAREZ
WEDNESDAY, JANUARY 26
(SENT WITH ENCRYPTION AND RED-FLAGGED, WITH DELIVERY CONFIRMATION)

You're going to want to read these two documents right away, boss—but let me walk you through them. I yanked them from the police servers just a few minutes ago.

The first document is the full report on the gun the police found at the Hughes home. Ballistics has positively linked the weapon to the bullet in Archie's body. Nothing shocking there. I scanned it for obvious mistakes or technical missteps, but it looks solid; I'm confident this is the murder weapon.

The second document, however...now, this one took a little more digging because someone tried to erase it earlier today. But I saved the doc, and I've authenticated it. Hang on to your hat, but the murder weapon? It's been in police evidence before.

That's right. The gun that was used to murder Archie Hughes

spent the past six years in police-evidence lockup. I don't know when it was removed from the evidence room or who checked it out. Give me some time. But the attached should be enough to make it clear that someone who had access to the evidence room was involved in this murder.

CHAPTER 38

Transcript of encrypted message exchange between Veena Lion and Janie Hall

JANIE HALL: OMG.

VEENA LION: You know I hate that, Janie. Skip the drama and just tell me what you found.

HALL: Sorry, V. Mistook you for a human being for a moment there. Human beings, as you may recall, enjoy a dramatic buildup to earth-shattering developments in an ongoing case.

LION: Hate sarcasm even more than dramatic buildups.

HALL: You're no fun. Anyway, guess who lives in a penthouse apartment she can't possibly afford on the salary she earns as a high-profile yet humble nanny?

LION: Maya Rain.

HALL: Like I said, you're no fun. Anyway, I'm kind of shocked here. Based on your notes, she seemed so nice. So normal. And now she's a murder suspect!

LION: Nice and normal on the surface. But it's a carefully constructed surface, although it would probably fool the casual investigator. I need to break through all of that.

HALL: What do you need? Deep backgrounding? Dark-web stuff?

LION: The layout of that fancy penthouse.

CHAPTER 39

9:16 a.m.

"CAN I help you, miss?"

"I'm sorry, could you please just hold this?"

Veena Lion was awkwardly juggling her phone, a legal pad, a fine-tipped black marker, a large cup of coffee from La Colombe, and a mixed bunch of gerbera daisies she'd picked up at a stand on Eighteenth Street.

The overload was intentional. She had just stepped inside the swank lobby of 10 Rittenhouse, and the doorman was trained to help. This would make them instant collaborators. Possibly even allies.

The doorman carefully stabilized the coffee, then held the bouquet of flowers as Veena organized the rest of her supplies. The nervous energy radiating from her movements made the doorman all the more eager to put her at ease.

"It's okay, miss," he purred. "Take your time."

"Thank you so much... Curt," she said, reading his name tag.

"No worries at all, we've all had those days," Curt replied. "Who are you here to see?"

"My friend Yvette Rivera," Veena half lied. "I thought I'd surprise her with flowers and a Fishtown medium roast."

Veena *did* have a friend—well, a former client—who lived at

10 Rittenhouse, an ex-lawyer who was a coffee junkie and loved houseplants, even though none of them lasted long in her care.

"Oh, gosh, Ms. Yvette is out of the country at the moment! Though I know she'd appreciate those gifts."

"Oh," Veena said, pretending to be completely flustered by this information. In fact, she knew Yvette Rivera was in the Caribbean for the month; Janie Hall had double-checked. "Do you, by any chance, like Fishtown medium roast?"

"Never had it, but a hot cup sounds really good right now."

"With my compliments," she said, gesturing to the cup already in his hand. "The flowers too. I'm actually allergic."

"Wow, really? Thanks, Miss . . ."

"Veena Lion, and it's my pleasure. My father worked in a building like this many years ago." Veena's father had done no such thing. "The people you must see . . ."

Curt the doorman was sipping the hot coffee and nodding along. Within two minutes, a friendship had been cemented. Now they were just two friends chatting.

"You'd better believe it," Curt said. "Fanciest address in town."

"Yvette told me she'd seen everybody—Patti LaBelle, M. Night, even Kobe now and again."

Curt made an awkward sign of the cross, coffee cup in hand. "God rest his soul." But then he got an impish gleam in his eye. "And speaking of, you know who else I saw a lot of not too long ago?"

Veena leaned forward as if ready to receive nuclear secrets. "Who?"

"Archie Hughes."

"Really," Veena said, feigning astonishment. "Oh my God. That's incredible."

"I know! Look, I'm not supposed to talk about the comings and goings of residents or their guests, but he's pretty hard to forget.

Especially with what's going on right now. You been following the news?"

"Such a shame. That family's already been through a lot."

Some sources required a team of horses to drag even basic information from their mouths. Curt was not that kind of source. He was positively gushing, and it was clear he had been dying to tell someone, anyone, about his personal connection to the murdered football legend. This segued into a story about the last time he'd seen Archie Hughes play at the Linc and what they'd cooked at the tailgate party outside the stadium, but Veena was here only for confirmation that Archie Hughes had regularly visited 10 Rittenhouse—a luxury residence well out of the financial reach of most nannies.

As Curt held forth on how to cook beer brats on a portable grill without drying them out, Veena scanned the control desk of the lobby. She finally found what she'd been looking for.

"I hate to ask you this, Curt, but would it be okay if I used the ladies'?"

Of course it was not a problem. They were friends, weren't they?

CHAPTER 40

THE HALL to the restrooms also led to the elevator bank. Veena knew this from a glance at the floor plan behind Curt's desk. She rode a car down to the subterranean garage and hoped that Curt would be too entranced by the gerbera daisies to notice her in the security camera's feed.

At least not until she confirmed something important.

The garage floor was so immaculate, you could picnic on it. Bentleys and BMWs and Audis filled about half the spaces, and carpeted walkways guided residents from their vehicles to the elevator banks. But only the rare few had access to what Veena had spotted at the lobby control desk: a private elevator leading to the penthouse.

"She can come and go as she pleases," Veena mumbled to herself. "Any visitor she wants can go up without being seen."

Awfully nice setup for a nanny from West Virginia, recruited straight out of Villanova. Definitely not everyone's grad-school experience in the City of Brotherly Love. *So who's paying your bills, Ms. Rain? And what are you giving them in return?* Surely it was something more than helpful parenting tips.

Physical spaces always helped Veena put herself in the minds of her quarries. She saw what they saw, felt the same ground under her shoes, took in the same smells. Janie liked to poke fun at Veena's slightly mystical approach, but it worked. As long as you had uninterrupted time to—

"Excuse me," an irritated voice said, breaking the spell. "What are you doing? You can't be down here!"

"Of course I can," Veena replied even before she turned around to see a tall security guard moving quickly toward her. He was trying to use his size to appear menacing. His hand even hovered near his belt, within reach of a pepper-spray canister. Veena knew she could easily outrun him if it came to that. The man's bulk would slow him down.

Not that she would give him the pleasure of a pursuit.

"How did you even get down here? You can't reach this level without an ID. Let me see yours."

Veena evaluated the man (according to his name tag, his name was Vincent—of course it was) and instantly clocked him as an extreme law-and-order type. The usual avenues of the law were most likely closed to this clod, so he had channeled all that misplaced ambition into this job. And ooh, was he itching to use that pepper spray.

"Vincent," she said, "let me stop you right there. I have an important message from the DA for you."

The man blinked. "For me? Seriously?"

Veena nodded, reached slowly into her pocket, and took out a business card embossed in blue and gold—official city colors—with the name of her sometime employer. The security guard took the business card and examined it with the same reverence a woman would give her best friend's engagement ring.

"What's the message from DA Mostel?" Vincent asked, astonished at this turn of events.

"He said to tell you to go away."

To Vincent's credit, he did as he was told.

CHAPTER 41

11:00 a.m.

IF HIS job didn't depend on his being online, Victor Suarez would never go online.

As it was, Victor left zero traces of himself on the internet. As far as the web was concerned, he had never been born.

He could not understand people who left pieces of their lives all over the place (on Facebook, in Google searches, in countless smartphone apps) for practically anyone to pick up. Did they also leave their doors unlocked and their windows wide open? It was the same thing to Victor.

But most people went through life assuming that whatever personal information they released to their banks (or their favorite online retailers or even their local pizza shops) would be guarded by the employees of those institutions with their lives. The truth was, most organizations' internet security wasn't worth a damn. And the few companies that actually bothered...well, they didn't bother to stay current. State-of-the-art cybersecurity ate into profits, after all.

Lunacy.

Victor poured himself another extra-large mug of strong black coffee—he was trying to graduate from Diet Coke—and spent an hour doing a deep dive into all things Hughes family.

He skipped the online troll stuff. That was basically useless. Anyone with an internet connection could have an opinion about anything; opinions were as common as hydrogen atoms.

No, what Victor loved were the document trails, the paperwork backdrop of the universe: Legal agreements nobody bothered to read. Direct messages that senders assumed were private. Interoffice memos that meant nothing to most people in the outside world...except Victor, who would put them aside until he found the place where each one fit.

All the information on everyone was out there. Sometimes it was in bits and pieces, like a shredded document. You just needed the mental tape and stamina to put it back together again.

Like the Google Maps search Francine had run on her phone a month ago, directions to a modest building in Center City, Philadelphia.

The address felt random until Victor realized it was *the office of the city's top divorce lawyer,* Charles "Chuck" Castrina. From there, it took only a few minutes to figure out the full story. Francine Pearl Hughes had officially retained Castrina's services that very day. Victor's boss, Cooper Lamb, was going to turn cartwheels.

Victor took another slug of coffee, thinking, *Not the same as Diet Coke, not even close,* and kept digging.

Now here was something interesting—the people trashing Francine were not the usual online trolls. These were high-end trolls. Online gamblers, mostly high rollers and whales, all of whom were none too pleased about the postponed NFC championship game. They felt like the rules had been changed; this was not the same bet it had been just a few days ago.

Conspiracy theories were abundant. Many centered on the excesses of the Eagles' father-and-son owners. And quite a lot of them linked Archie Hughes's murder to someone trying to influence the outcome of the game and, possibly, the Super Bowl. Victor believed some of the theories in these private posts; these were people with real money on the line.

Still, there was no smoking gun—nothing concrete to share with Cooper yet.

But Victor continued to dig. He put on another pot of coffee but made a mental note to restock his minifridge with Diet Coke. He could handle only so much coffee.

CHAPTER 42

12:13 p.m.

"I CAN be there by four," Cooper told the annoying jerk on the other end of the line.

"As I told you, there are no appointments available today," said the annoying jerk, who was somehow employed by the top divorce lawyer in the City of Brotherly Love despite being an annoying jerk. "Or for the remainder of the week."

"And as *I* told you, this is a professional matter, not a personal one," Cooper said. "I don't need a divorce lawyer. I'm already happily divorced."

"Doesn't change the fact that there are no appointments available."

"Tell him it's Cooper Lamb. Chuck knows me!"

"Chuck knows a lot of people."

"Do you realize how disrespectful you're being?"

"I think I'm being *extremely* respectful of my boss's time."

Ordinarily, Cooper Lamb would opt for the dripping-with-honey approach. Kindness and flattery—maybe even a harmless bribe—worked most of the time. But ten seconds into the phone conversation, Cooper had known he was up against a different type of gatekeeper. One who'd been hired because he was a sadist who took great delight in swatting away all potential distractions.

"Let me guess," Cooper said. "You're a UPenn grad. You've got that Ivy League arrogance about you."

"Insulting me won't magically open a time slot."

"No, but it might make you realize how much you don't want me showing up uninvited at your office at four p.m."

"Is that a threat?"

"You catch on quick! You *are* a UPenn grad!"

"No, but I am a former Temple running back, and I will happily escort you to the sidewalk if you even dream of showing up here without an appointment. In fact, I hope you do. Then I could skip my evening workout."

Cooper liked this guy. Of course, the dude was still an annoying jerk. But the ex-jock's passion for quick, insulting responses was admirable. Few people took such joy in their work. Even fewer threatened physical violence so eagerly.

"Listen, Mr. Temple Owl, I've gotta go pick my kids up from school. And they get cranky if I don't take them for a snack right away. But you'll be seeing me at four p.m."

"Looking forward to it, Mr. Lamb. I suspect it's been a while since anyone kicked your ass."

"You'd be surprised," Cooper replied. "Do you want me to get you anything from Reading Terminal while I'm there? Maybe a cannoli?"

"I don't want a cannoli."

"Who the hell would turn down a free Termini Brothers cannoli? There's something seriously wrong with you. See you at four."

The annoyance spiked in the assistant's voice: "Don't you d—"

CHAPTER 43

COOPER LAMB gave his best bloodcurdling Bela Lugosi impression: "Hello, children of the *night*."

"It's three o'clock, Dad," said Cooper Jr., hurling his overloaded schoolbag into the back of the car.

"Excellent point. Who's hungry for a midafternoon snack?"

"I'm guessing *you* are," Ariel Lamb said.

"Okay, you talked me into it. Though let's make it Italian pastries at Reading Terminal, since I don't have much time and I have to take you home to your mother and then slingshot back to see a divorce lawyer over at Eighteenth and Market."

"Why do you need to see a divorce lawyer? You and Mom are already divorced."

Cooper exhaled and leaned back in the driver's seat. "So *that's* why she's been so distant lately."

"Dad!" Cooper Jr. exclaimed.

"I kid, and you children know that. Your mother is so amazing, we practically didn't need a lawyer when we parted ways."

"Is that why she owns the house now?"

This was the problem with raising smart, independent-minded children: They knew *exactly* where to slide the shiv between your ribs.

"Like I said, the woman is amazing."

* * *

Transcript of conversation between Cooper Lamb and Prentiss Walsh, executive assistant to divorce attorney Charles Castrina

PRENTISS WALSH: You brought your dog with you?

COOPER LAMB: His name is Lupe. He's here to make sure you fight fair, Mr. . . . Prentiss Walsh? Seriously? Your parents named you Prentiss? What, did they lose a bet with God or something?

WALSH: Gotta be honest, Lamb, I didn't think you'd actually show up. But look, Chuck's not in, and I honestly don't expect him back the rest of the day. (*Lengthy pause*) Is there really a cannoli in that bag?

LAMB: Sorry. Cannoli is for closers.

WALSH: Huh?

LAMB: If you want to be a *closer,* tell Mr. Castrina I'm here, and this flaky, crunchy tube of Italian sweetness will be yours.

WALSH: And I told you, he's not—

LAMB: Here. (*There is the sound of a paper bag landing on a desk.*)

WALSH: Wait. I can just have this?

LAMB: Enjoy. In the meantime, Lupe! Make sure Prentiss here doesn't come out from behind his desk. (*Lupe growls.*)

WALSH: Come on. You can't do this. This dog shouldn't even be here!

LAMB: Just enjoy your snack. I'll be right out. (*A chair creaks. Lupe growls again. The chair creaks again.*)

WALSH: (*Shouting*) Chuck! That asshole private eye is here!

LAMB: Thank you for announcing me.

* * *

Transcript of conversation between Cooper Lamb and Charles Castrina, Esq.

CHARLES CASTRINA: What, no cannoli for me? I gotta say, Lamb, you bribed the wrong guy. I don't even know that guy's name.

COOPER LAMB: Lucky you. Listen, Chuck, I'll bring you a whole box of goodies from Termini Brothers if you'll be straight with me.

CASTRINA: You know I can't do that, but hey, thanks for stopping in.

LAMB: Fine. I'll show you all my cards. I'm working for Francine. So are you, apparently.

CASTRINA: See, let me stop and correct you right there. I am *not* working for Ms. Pearl.

LAMB: Interesting omission of her married name. Anyway, I hear you, Counselor. There's no need for a divorce lawyer when your spouse is dead. Thing is, Chuck, this is *exactly* why Francine needs our help.

CASTRINA: Oh, it's *our* help now? Are we teaming up? Do continue.

LAMB: They're trying to railroad Francine and I need to know why.

CASTRINA: I'd love to know too. She's a goddamn national treasure and I can't believe anyone would have the nerve to mess with her.

LAMB: So help me out.

CASTRINA: Can't do it, partner. You call it helping Francine; I call it betraying a client's sacred trust, and if she wanted me to break that trust, I'm sure she or one of the overpriced attorneys at Kaplan, DePaulo would let me know. As of right now, they haven't, so I think we're through here.

LAMB: I'm going to give you round one, Counselor. But that just makes me hungrier. I'm going to find out *everything* you know. And some things you wish you knew.

CASTRINA: How are you going to do that? Looks like you're out of cannoli.

CHAPTER 44

4:32 p.m.

FRANCINE PEARL Hughes's arrest early that morning had been met with shock all over Philadelphia; her release from jail after arranging for bail felt like a party.

There were a smattering of protesters, of course, obsessed Birds fans bundled up in Eagles sweatshirts waving posters of outrage. These were the rare Philadelphians who embraced Archie Hughes as the greatest player of all time and yet hated his wife because they blamed her for every time the Eagles stumbled. *Ah, he's distracted by his pop-star trophy wife*. Or: *She should mind her own business and not distract him so much.*

And now the latest variation: *Oh yeah, she was jealous of the team's success so she totally had him killed.*

But those "fans" were in the clear minority. Most of the people gathered outside were there to cheer on Francine. And maybe to be part of a historic moment in the city.

The only person neither protesting nor cheering was Cooper Lamb.

Somehow Francine sensed his presence in the crowd. Maybe it was because he was the only human being standing perfectly still. Once they locked eyes, Cooper began to clap. Slowly. Theatrically.

As if to say: *If you had told me the truth, and all of the truth, you might not be in this position right now.*

He watched Francine carefully, and her reaction sort of stunned him.

Francine Pearl had spent most of her life in the public eye. She knew how to smile even when she felt like dying inside. And to be sure, she smiled at Cooper.

But it was only a half smile. A weary admission that it was hard to keep a positive outlook when your entire world was burning down.

Was it possible she'd loved her husband despite it all?

CHAPTER 45

Transcript of encrypted message exchange between Veena Lion and Janie Hall

JANIE HALL: You busy, V.?

HALL: Okay, no response... I've got a lot to share here, so try to keep up.

HALL: Kidding!

HALL: You know how I'm always saying there are some things you're never going to find on a computer? Well, I hit the streets and did some old-school journalism, just like in the old days (three years ago, when you hired me away from the Dying Tabloid That Shall Not Be Named). You're not going to believe what I found.

HALL: I keep teasing and rambling in the hope that you'll respond, but you must be busy, so here goes...

HALL: Archie Hughes wasn't paying nightly visits to Maya Rain only. He had another gal pal (sorry; I cringed just typing those words) at another swank penthouse, this one in a condo in Old City. I interviewed the community relations manager. I also interviewed the guy who owns the comic-book shop across the street, and boy, was he happy to talk to me.

HALL: Comic Book Guy said he used to see Archie Hughes duck into the building from an entrance off an alley. He had a perfect view from the front window of his nerd emporium. He says he may even have a pic or two on his phone, because he bragged to his buddies. I'll forward it as soon as he sends it to me. I think he's trying to get me to go out for a drink with him in exchange for the photo; I'll have to break his heart gently.

HALL: Suzanne, the CR manager for the building, was a bit more reticent at first. But she opened up a little once I dropped the strong hint that I worked for the DA. (Not a lie, right? I mean, I work for you, you're currently working for Mostel...)

HALL: Anyway, I kept at her and she finally admitted Archie Hughes had been a frequent visitor to the penthouse. The current occupant of which is Rosalind "Roz" Cline. Somebody you might want to speak to. I'm thinking, *Kept woman*. But Suzanne didn't want to speculate on that. Didn't want to go anywhere near that, in fact.

VEENA LION: Good work, Janie.

HALL: There you are! Were you just letting me ramble on?

LION: You shouldn't ever imply you work for the DA, because that's not true. Find another way next time.

HALL: Sorry, V.

CHAPTER 46

Transcript of conversation between Veena Lion and Suzanne Hingston, community relations manager of the Villas at Elfreth's Alley

VEENA LION: Let me make myself clear. I work for District Attorney Eliott K. Mostel. So unless you and your management company want me to come back with a subpoena and a small army of investigators...

SUZANNE HINGSTON: We take our residents' privacy seriously. And shouldn't a police detective be interviewing potential witnesses?

LION: The district attorney's office routine employs its own investigators.

HINGSTON: Well, you don't even have a warrant. I know that much. I checked.

LION: Okay, fine.

HINGSTON: What are you doing? Oh, wait—*do* you have a warrant in there? Listen, I'm not trying to start something with the DA or anything—

LION: Calm down. This is not a warrant. This is five hundred dollars cash. I'll wait if you want to count it.

HINGSTON: I don't need to count it.

LION: But you're not taking it either.

HINGSTON: I'm seeing only *half* a warrant there.

LION: Ah. (*Pause*) You know, used to be I could buy some cooperation with only a quarter of a warrant.

HINGSTON: The times they are a-changing.

LION: Just make sure it's a full warrant's worth of information, Ms. Hingston.

HINGSTON: Thank you. (*Pause*) Her name is Rosalind Cline. She used to work as a hostess in one of those big casinos in Atlantic City. Don't ask me which one, because I don't know. All I know is she's still back and forth to AC all the time. I think she's there more than she's here.

LION: Wouldn't her employment history be in her rental application?

HINGSTON: If she were the one paying the bills, sure. But a private company takes care of it.

LION: Go on.

HINGSTON: What do you mean, go on? What else is there? I hardly know her, and you'd have to pay me a hell of a lot more than a grand if you want me opening up her personal files.

LION: I don't need her files.

HINGSTON: What, then?

LION: Just tell me about her.

HINGSTON: I don't know what you mean. Who cares what I think about her?

LION: When you see her walk through the lobby, what goes through your mind? Pretend I paid you a thousand dollars to tell me the truth.

HINGSTON: (*Pause*) Honestly? I think, *Who does that bitch think she is?*

LION: Well, that was candid.

HINGSTON: It's not just me. Everybody here hates her. She's a lousy tipper. And I don't care how good-looking you are, that doesn't give you permission to treat people like dirt. Swear to Christ, some of the people in this place are horrible human beings.

CHAPTER 47

REPORT TO C. LAMB BY V. SUAREZ
WEDNESDAY, JANUARY 26
(SENT WITH ENCRYPTION AND RED-FLAGGED, WITH DELIVERY CONFIRMATION)

Take a look at the attached video clip and isolated frames, then come back to this document.

Yes, that is Francine Pearl Hughes in that video. (Rest assured, I used a facial-recognition program to confirm the match.)

I didn't start out looking for Ms. Hughes in this particular location. I had been attempting to place her near the art museum on the night of the murder. I was not successful, so I expanded my search geographically and chronologically. Within minutes, I had a match elsewhere in the city, three days before the murder.

Details on the video:

Ms. Hughes and her male companion are on the 100 block of Chestnut Street, closer to Second Street, in front of a Belgian restaurant/brewpub. This was at 9:47, according to the time stamp from the surveillance camera.

I don't know if Francine and her companion dined at the restaurant before the images were captured; a standard check on all of their credit cards came up with no record of either of them dining anywhere that evening. It's possible that they paid cash. I have a call in to the restaurant's owner; I'll update you when I know more.

While it is difficult to make out specific details from the video, I took the best single frames, enlarged them, and used image-enhancement software to bring things into focus. As you can see, Ms. Hughes and her companion are holding hands, hugging, and embracing.

Even without image enhancement, you can probably recognize the identity of her companion. He's a hard man to miss: Eagles tight end Jimmy Tua.

CHAPTER 48

COOPER LAMB / VOICE MEMO #0126-735

To whom it may concern: This evening I'm headed back down to the Linc, the very place where Eagles dare, on Sunday, to clinch the NFC championship. By my side is my faithful companion Lupe, who is expert at working the crowds. Even a crowd as hostile as the one I'm about to face.

Yeah, it's safe to say the Birds ain't gonna be happy to see me. I am definitely a distraction they don't need.

But you know what? I don't give a shit. I've got questions that demand answers. Questions for Mr. James "Jimmy" Tua. Specifically, this: Why were you fooling around with your best friend's wife just three days before he was murdered? As the kids say, it's not a good look.

What do we know about Jimmy Tua? For one, he's kind of a genius. Scratch that—he's a *certified* genius. Victor found the test results and everything. And that high-powered mind is encased in two hundred and seventy pounds of sheer muscle.

So you'd think a big guy with a big brain would know better than to step out with his bestie's best girl. Especially in public.

Yeah, I know. Chestnut Street was dark, and it was sort of late…for the Quaker City, anyway. But still, you're two of the most recognizable figures in Philly, and you're out canoodling in public?

Francine and Jimmy *had* to know what they were doing. Which tells me that they'd reached a point in their affair when they really didn't care if anyone saw them or not. You don't go waving matches and a can of gasoline around unless you're ready to burn the house down.

There are more pieces on the board than anyone is willing to acknowledge. We've got Francine and Jimmy and, possibly, Archie and Maya. Though Francine and Maya don't act as if they're opponents on the battlefield of love. They're downright chummy, in fact.

So maybe Archie and Francine were going to separate amicably, and their new lovers were waiting in the wings? That's right, ladies and germs, an Eagles pun. But if that's the case, who killed Archie? And did it have anything to do with Francine and Jimmy Tua?

There are at least two people who know the truth about them. One of them just made bail and has clammed up on the advice of her attorney—i.e., my employer. The other is currently practicing for one of the most important games of his career. And I'm about to ruin his day.

CHAPTER 49

5:57 p.m.

THE FIELD was buzzing with nervous energy. Practice squads were running through passes and rushes with the active players, trying their best to imitate the Giants and impress the higher-ups. Everybody's gotta serve somebody.

Cooper Lamb found Jimmy Tua hydrating along with a handful of his teammates. His skin was slick with sweat, even in this bitter afternoon cold.

"Hey, Jimmy," Cooper said.

"Hey, it's the private eye with the cute dog," Jimmy said. "What's up?"

"Can we take this conversation to the sidelines?"

"That's where we happen to be standing, my man. Besides, I have no secrets from my teammates."

"This might be an exception. It's about Francine."

There was an instant electric-shock jolt from the burly players gathered around Jimmy Tua. It was as if Cooper had set off a firecracker at their cleats. But Jimmy himself didn't flinch. He gave Cooper a murder stare, as if daring him to go on. Naturally, Cooper dared to go on.

"More specifically, about the two of you," he said. "Being together."

Yep, check, please—that was the unspoken attitude of the surrounding players, who began to drift away from Jimmy, Cooper, and Lupe. They didn't stray too far. They didn't want to be directly involved in the ugly conversation that was about to happen, but they stayed within earshot just in case Jimmy Tua tried to rip the private eye's head off. The last thing they needed before the NFC championship game was *another* murder.

"What are you saying?" Jimmy said quietly.

"Do I have to spell it out for you? I thought you were a smart Bird."

"Yeah, you'd better spell it out, big man."

"Fine. I'm saying you've been having an affair with your best friend's wife. The same woman who was just arrested for the murder of your best friend. But I guess that's not as important as the big game this Sunday—"

By the time Cooper spoke the words *this Sunday,* Jimmy was already charging forward. But Cooper was fully aware the attack was coming. He'd watched the tension and anger building in the huge man's body from the beginning. It was as if Jimmy had been braced for this line of questioning, but Cooper was the only guy who'd been stupid enough to ask.

To the untrained eye, it probably looked as if the players were running a small drill by the sidelines. There was Jimmy Tua rushing forward like a missile and six other players scrambling toward him as if to intercept that missile.

And standing directly between Jimmy and the players: Cooper Lamb.

Cooper knew that only one thing would prevent Jimmy Tua from plowing him into the freshly cut Bermuda grass at their feet. And that one thing was Jimmy's IQ.

Jimmy Tua was a powerhouse full of rage, but he was also a

thinking man. And a thinking man wouldn't throw away his career over an insult from a PI.

(*Would he?* Cooper prayed he wouldn't.)

Right up to the last second, Cooper thought he might have made a grave miscalculation. This is how his life would end. And in front of his beloved pooch, no less.

Jimmy Tua's nose came to a sudden halt a few millimeters away from Cooper's. Only then did Cooper understand that he'd been spared. Fortunately, he'd held his ground the entire time. If he was about to be snapped in half over a tight end's knee, he'd do it on his terms—no flinching.

"You don't know what the hell you're talking about," Jimmy said.

"Didn't know you were a big fan of Belgian beer," Cooper said. "Especially right before a championship game."

There was the instant spark of recognition. Jimmy knew that Cooper knew. How Cooper knew didn't matter.

Cooper had saved this piece of information for this specific moment—it was meant to push Tua completely over the edge and get him to say something stupid. Victor had talked to the brewpub's owner as well as the bartender who'd been on duty that night.

Oh yeah, Francine Pearl Hughes and Jimmy Tua were there. Oh yeah, they were making out. But a huge cash tip was incentive enough for the bartender to keep his mouth shut.

That is, until Victor made it sound like he was affiliated with the Federal Bureau of Investigation. No cash tip can cover that kind of tab.

The rage inside Tua built to the point where Cooper thought the tight end might actually pummel him. Cooper could smell the fury on the man's breath before three linemen grabbed Tua and pulled him away. It was a struggle.

"I know exactly who you are, asshole! Where you live and what you do."

"Hey, I know who you are too," Cooper said, bright smile on his face. "You're Jimmy Tua! All-Pro, right?"

Phone call between Cooper Lamb and his children

COOPER LAMB: Kids! You're never going to believe this!
ARIEL LAMB: What's that, Dad?
LAMB: Guess who I just met—Jimmy Tua! What a great guy.

CHAPTER 50

Transcript of private conversation between Cooper Lamb and Lisa Marchese, senior partner at Kaplan, DePaulo, and Marchese

LISA MARCHESE: What the hell is that?

COOPER LAMB: This is a digital recording device. As per Pennsylvania law, I am notifying you that I am taping this conversation.

MARCHESE: I'm sitting at a bar having a late supper. Do we have to make this so formal?

LAMB: Clearly, Counselor, you're also working so that you may expense your small plates and double martinis.

MARCHESE: Are you going to update me on what you've dug up on the chef or do I have to buy you dinner first?

LAMB: No, I'll wait until you're done.

MARCHESE: What's the matter with you? I'm girding myself for a long night. People at the firm are losing their minds . . . not that I have to explain myself to you.

LAMB: Yeah, you kind of do. Because if you want me to help you save Francine, you're going to have to come clean with me.

MARCHESE: We're going to save Francine because she's innocent.

LAMB: Well, that's not what it looks like to the police. Unless there's something you're not telling me.

MARCHESE: Like what?

LAMB: Like *everything*. Whatever you know, I need to know it too. Which is why I brought this recording device.

MARCHESE: I truly have no idea what you're talking about.

LAMB: That's the problem we keep running into, isn't it? Everybody's tiptoeing around the truth like it's an infectious disease or something. For instance, why didn't you tell me Francine hired Chuck Castrina?

MARCHESE: Keep your voice down!

LAMB: Ooh, that got your attention. I guess I should be grateful you weren't taking a sip of your drink, otherwise I would have been treated to a shower of Grey Goose.

MARCHESE: Who told you about Chuck?

LAMB: No, Counselor. You first.

MARCHESE: Turn that thing off.

LAMB: Do you promise to tell me the whole truth and nothing but?

MARCHESE: (*To bartender*) Danny, can we move to the booth in the corner? Thanks, hon.

LAMB: I'm taking that as a yes.

CHAPTER 51

THE RESTAURANT was an old-school steak house on the first floor of the Market Street building that housed the offices of Kaplan, DePaulo, and Marchese. It had charming waitstaff in vests, portraits of local notables hung on the walls, excellent cheesy bread in a basket offered gratis. So many of the attorneys dined here regularly, it was the firm's de facto cafeteria, the place to be seen. If you wanted privacy, you headed to the fringes of downtown. Or possibly to New Jersey. For now, however, Lisa Marchese would have to settle for the quiet zone of the corner booth near the kitchen.

"Is that thing off?"

"Here you go. Powered down completely. If you want, I can dunk it into your double martini. Now, tell me what you've got."

Marchese frowned. "I'm not going to tell you, but I can show you. If you promise—and I can't stress this enough, Cooper Lamb—if you promise this information will stay inside your skull. No cute leaks to the press, none of your usual bullshit."

"If it helps Francine, then yes."

Lisa dug into her briefcase. Cooper thought she was about to bring out a file folder marked CONFIDENTIAL or something absurd like that, but instead it was an iPad. She quickly entered a password, then another one to open a vault file, and then looked into the camera to activate the facial-recognition software.

All of which was a huge relief to Cooper, because if it existed digitally, his man Victor would have no problem snagging a copy. He could pluck information from an Apple device as skillfully as a Dickensian pickpocket lifted a wallet.

She rotated the iPad toward him. "You want to know about the real Archie Hughes? Read these."

CHAPTER 52

Transcript of phone call between Cooper Lamb and his children

ARIEL LAMB: How was your meeting with the divorce lawyer?
COOPER LAMB: The dude dodged my questions like a total pro. He didn't even respond to my cannoli bribe!
ARIEL: Not everyone is a sugar monster, old man.
LAMB: Speaking of monsters, look who just showed up—it's my best frenemy, Veena Lion! Say hello to Ms. Lion, children.
COOPER JR. and ARIEL: (*In singsongy unison*) "Hello to Ms. Lion, children."
VEENA LION: (*Laughs*) They're definitely *your* kids. Hello, Coop and Ariel! My sincere apologies for taking your father away for a business meeting.
COOPER JR.: It's okay. We have homework anyway.
ARIEL: Do you always conduct your business meetings in a bar?
LION: I would like to tell you otherwise, but yeah, pretty much.
LAMB: Wait, wait—how do you know we're in a bar, young lady?
ARIEL: Only, like, about a *million* clues. Glasses clinking, murmuring voices, the sound of a cable sports channel in the background. Also, it's nine p.m. Where else would you be this time of day?

LAMB: Well, I hate to break it to you, Ms. Junior Detective, but you are one hundred percent wrong.

LION: (*To server*) Miss? I'd like a Hendrick's martini up with three blue-cheese-stuffed olives.

ARIEL: You were saying, Father?

LAMB: I was saying—ahem—you are one hundred percent wrong about the cannoli. Nobody turns down a Termini Brothers cannoli. The lawyer is clearly hiding something, and that's why I'm here in this church basement discussing my most recent case with Ms. Lion.

LION: Wow. The ease with which you lie to your poor children.

ARIEL: Uh-huh. Just make sure you take a cab home from the church basement. You shouldn't be driving.

LAMB: I will take all appropriate measures, children. Don't you worry about your old man.

COOPER JR.: See you tomorrow morning, Dad!

"I have something very important to show you."

Veena smiled and beckoned with her fingers. "Oh yeah. Gimme."

"Hang on now," Cooper said, smiling. "This stays between us. I mean, like, in *the vault*, okay?"

"Of course. *The vault*. Why would this be any different?"

The vault was their mutually agreed-upon term for a discussion that would remain completely off the record, no matter what. A free zone for private eyes. Even if those private eyes were threatened with prison by a federal judge.

"This lies deep, deep, deep in the vault."

"Fine. I'll keep it in the deepest, darkest chamber of the vault."

Cooper nodded, then slid a manila folder across the table, which was beaded with moisture from their drinks. Veena placed her fingertips on top of the folder and began to pull, but Cooper kept an iron grip on it.

"What is it?" Veena asked.

"This is ugly stuff."

"I've probably seen worse."

"Sure, but not from a national hero."

Cooper meant it. Hell, it had been painful for *him* to read. He almost wished he could bleach the memory of this file out of his brain cells. What was that old saying, about how you should never meet your heroes? It was too late for Cooper to meet Archie Hughes but not too late for him to learn what kind of man he'd been.

"It's fine," she replied. "Don't tell anyone, but I'm not much of a sports fan."

Cooper nodded and released his grip on the folder. Veena removed her sunglasses and flipped open the file.

Usually, Veena Lion gave very little away. Her frustrated opponents called her "the Sphinx." But as Veena read the series of printouts in the file, her eyes widened and her jaw dropped just a little. She might have been a stone-cold professional, but she was also a human being.

The file contained a series of screenshots of texts, each on its own page.

Where are you

Your appointment can't be taking that long

Hey, baby, let me know where you are, I'm worried about you, that's all

Come on, text me back

Baby, where are you

You there?

Baby, come on

Where are you, anyway? I called the salon and they said you'd left hours ago. This is NOT cool

Don't you dare ignore me, bitch

You had better call me back now, I swear to God

I can have your phone tracked, you know. You want me to do that?

F███ me

I see where you are

Really love to know what your fans would think of you right now, you f█████ whore

There's not enough fancy makeup in the world to cover up a broken nose, you hear me? CALL ME NOW

And the texts raged on and on and on. "Well, this is completely awful," Veena said, closing the file.

"Warned you," Cooper replied.

"Here's what I don't get."

"What more could you want? Archie Hughes was an abusive son of a bitch and no one knew it except Francine."

"That part is perfectly clear. What I don't get is, why would you share these with me? Do I need to tell you how much Mostel would love to get his hands on this file?"

"Because we want the same thing," Cooper said. "The truth, no matter what. Remember?"

"But I'm working for the DA, and you're trying to keep Francine Pearl Hughes out of prison. Sharing this with me doesn't help you one bit."

Cooper took a large swallow of his drink. "Normally, I'd agree with you. But in this case, the texts came directly from Francine's lawyer. Which I think is very interesting, don't you?"

"I do," Veena said, drumming her fingers on the bar. "Why would Francine's own lawyer willingly hand over a big fat motive that pretty much damns her client?"

"Lisa Marchese is one thousand percent certain that Francine didn't kill her husband."

"So what? Easy enough for her to hire someone to do it for her. A pro who turned out to be a little careless or forgot to make it look like a proper carjacking."

"No. I also believe Francine had nothing to do with it."

"You're being paid to believe her," Veena said.

"I'm working for her," Cooper replied, "but I believe her anyway. Our killer is still out there."

CHAPTER 53

11:02 p.m.

"SO WHO do you like?"

"Nobody on this planet at the moment," Veena said, stirring the dregs of her second martini with a single blue-cheese-stuffed olive speared on a wooden toothpick.

"I'm sorry," she continued. "I can't stop thinking about those texts. How can two human beings be so awful to each other? You start out with the best intentions, maybe you even think you're in love. You promise to take care of each other, be there for each other no matter what. But time passes, as it always does, and there comes the inevitable day when all of those promises are forgotten. You can't remember why you're even together. How did you end up trapped like this with a person you can barely stand? Do all relationships come with an expiration date?"

"No, no," Cooper said. "I meant who do you like for the game on Sunday? I'm waiting for a call from Red. You want in on some of the action?"

Veena didn't know if she should laugh or dump the remnants of her martini over Lamb's head. Instead, she slipped on her sunglasses and tried to force herself to sober up. They poured them strong here.

"Sure, I'll play along," Veena said. "Put me down for a thousand bucks on, um, whatever team is *not* the Eagles."

Cooper grinned. "You have no idea who's playing, do you?"

"Does it ultimately matter? Overpaid gladiators in heavy padding dancing back and forth on a lawn. I mean, what is created? What possible benefit is there to mankind? Is there a point other than distracting beer-guzzling, nacho-eating Americans for an evening of capitalism and brutality?"

"I don't know, V. Maybe it's a good thing that we channel our collective aggressions into something frivolous rather than killing each other on the streets."

"Plenty of people get killed anyway."

Cooper held up a hand as if calling for a time-out. "Hang on," he said, sputtering a little. "Rewind a sec. How can you *not* bet on the home team? How are you even a Philadelphian?"

"No idea," Veena said. "But it will be worth losing every penny of that thousand bucks for the reaction you just gave me."

Cooper smiled and leaned back. "Nicely done, Ms. Lion."

"Rowrr."

"Baaaaa."

They locked eyes. There were no more elements of the case to discuss. They'd run out of jokey banter. It was just the two of them, practically alone in this bar, with the server washing martini glasses and generally minding his own damn business.

The phone on the bar top buzzed, breaking the spell. Cooper scooped up his cell. "Hey! Red! Glad I caught you, man."

Veena watched Cooper as he placed their bets. He really did put her down for a grand! She had been kidding, but oh, well. The words coming out of his mouth were all nonsense to her. But his mouth curled occasionally into a boyish, playful smile, even though Red on the other end of the line couldn't see it. Was that meant for her? Veena didn't care. She wanted it anyway.

Without notice or preamble, Veena leaned forward and pressed her lips against his. She delighted in the surprised murmur that escaped his mouth—"Mmm, lemme get back to you, Red"—before pressing her case further. She heard his phone hit the bar top, and not gently. He cupped one side of her face with his hand and settled in for a long, searching kiss, totally unafraid of being seen.

Veena was relieved. Cooper Lamb was just as drunk as she was.

During a break in the action she whispered into his ear, "I like us like this."

"So do I. Let's go to your place."

"No," she said softly. "I mean I like us like this, at this moment in time. No expectations, just us. Nothing to complicate things. I don't ever want to hate you."

"Just keep my mouth busy so I won't say anything stupid."

Ah, but it was too late. The moment was over. Veena leaned back on her stool. The bartender busied himself with washing pint glasses and trying very hard not to notice their impromptu make-out session.

"Danny, can we get the check?"

Cooper blinked. "So that's a no to your place?"

"Right away, Danny."

She had to give Cooper credit. He tried to play it cool and gently nudge her back into the zone she'd just left: Touching her hand. Asking her to take off her sunglasses again. Suggesting they split a rideshare, you know, so they could discuss the next steps of the case. Veena gently rebuffed all these advances and gathered her things. "Give Lupe a kiss for me."

"Hang on. The *dog* gets a kiss too?"

"Just be glad you didn't bring Lupe to the bar. You would have been completely out of luck."

CHAPTER 54

REPORT TO C. LAMB BY V. SUAREZ
WEDNESDAY, JANUARY 26
(SENT WITH ENCRYPTION AND TRIPLE RED-FLAGGED, WITH DELIVERY CONFIRMATION)

Boss—this is important. Please read this before you talk to anyone else. I have solid confirmation on the Archie Hughes abuse allegations.

This comes right from a private server in the Radnor PD. As I've mentioned before, almost every police department's intranet is a joke. They might as well pin every confidential file to the nearest utility pole. But the one in the Radnor superintendent's office is different; they spent a bit of money keeping this one locked down tight, with no connection to the internet.

Of course this is no big deal for me. I have a source inside the Radnor PD who has a way to access this server. You've told me time and again that you don't want to know how the sausage is made. Fair enough. But just know that the full cost of this particular sausage will be included in my next invoice.

On that confidential server were two reports of calls to the Hughes house, one in October, another in late December. The circumstances were vague initially but were later reported as a dispute between the gardener and the pool-maintenance man (October) and teenage kids goofing around in the neighborhood (December).

However, these calls were downgraded after the fact. The initial reports were clearly domestic violence calls, and both reports ended up on the superintendent's private server.

There is no record of who placed the reports on the confidential server, but it's fair to assume that this was the decision of the superintendent, as he is the only one with access.

I've attached the compete files, which include photos of Francine Pearl Hughes. Needless to say, they are graphic.

My contact knows what is in these reports. Don't worry; this person is rock solid and trustworthy. There will be no leaks. But my contact did pass along a warning to me to watch my back.

So I'm passing the same along to you. Keep your eyes open, boss.

THURSDAY, JANUARY 27

CHAPTER 55

COOPER LAMB / VOICE MEMO #0127-735

Once more I sit in an ice-cold car on a freezing street in downtown Philadelphia. I think I've been doing this job too long. When I die and my life flashes before my eyes, about eighty percent of it will be me sitting in an ice-cold car on a freezing street in downtown Philadelphia.

Except this time is different, because this city is on the verge of exploding and I'm watching a bunch of volatile chemicals swirl around, ready to combust at any moment.

Speaking of volatile...

Hi, Maya Rain. Your lights are on. You awake up there? Cleaning up messes? Did you fall asleep studying? Or are you entertaining someone special at this late hour? Perhaps the same someone who is paying for that condo, since I know even a top-drawer nanny couldn't afford a place like that.

Yes, I know this is sort of stalkerish behavior. Scratch that—this is *straight-up* stalker behavior. But Maya is the one piece that doesn't quite fit. Doesn't make sense that someone this special would be involved in this case by accident.

Okay, yeah, I heard what I just said about Maya being special. Victor, you can stop rolling your eyes.

Let's talk about the other volatile chemicals at play. Starting with the chemicals in my own lab.

Francine is potentially the most volatile chemical of all. In a weird way, it'd be so much easier if I knew she did it, because then I could take steps to minimize the blowback. Hell, those psycho texts from Archie would acquit her in the eyes of most Philadelphians. The bastard essentially threatened to break her beautiful face. Not a good look, Mr. Greatest of All Time.

But I know she didn't kill Archie, even if she's not telling me everything. But why is that? Is it because she's protecting her children? If so, from what? Let's say Archie and the Sables were up to some shady Super Bowl stuff. Any kind of shame associated with fraud the children might feel is nothing compared to seeing their mother sent to prison for life. Must be something else.

Who can tell me about that something?

Maybe Lisa Marchese. Wait—*of course* she knows, otherwise she wouldn't have handed me those text messages, right? Victor, redouble your efforts on her law firm's servers. I know you've already searched them, but there must be something in a file somewhere. Maybe there's a hidden server inside Marchese's office, one that requires the talents of one of your secret sausage men.

Okay, I can't believe I said that last part out loud.

Who else, who else... well, who else is obvious. I'm parked outside of her condo right now.

Maya Rain had a front-row seat to the Hughes Family

Drama for the past few months. She's in a unique position to know most, if not all, of what Francine is so desperate to hide.

Maybe I should just climb out of this cold car, walk up to Maya's condo, and ask her in person.

CHAPTER 56

1:04 a.m.

"WHAT'S THIS?"

"One hundred American dollars, my friend. And this is the part where you nod your head, pocket the cash, sit back, and return to whatever show you're watching on your cell phone."

Curt the doorman sighed, leaning back in his chair. "I really can't do this again."

"Again?" Cooper Lamb asked. "What, do you have total strangers handing you a hundred bucks all the time?"

Lupe, waiting patiently, let out a tiny yelp as if to underscore his master's question.

"You'd be surprised what people offer me to let them sneak into this building. Look, brother, I need my job more than I need a hundred bucks."

"So now we're negotiating. Cool. Tell you what—I'm going to leave three hundred dollars with you for safekeeping. Who knows how dangerous it is up there? One of your residents might try to mug me and my dog."

"Uh-huh."

"And if I don't come back down to reclaim my money, just pocket it until you see me again."

"I've got an awful memory for faces."

"Even dog faces?"

Curt the doorman tucked the money into his breast pocket without so much as another glance at Cooper, as if to prove how bad he was with faces. Cooper walked to the elevator and rode it up to the penthouse level. Thanks to Victor, he knew exactly where to go and which doorbell to ring. And hey, the lights were on.

"Come on, Lupe, let's see if your favorite nanny is awake."

Lupe matched Cooper's pace the entire length of the hallway, though he did give him a side-eye glance: *We really doing this? Bothering this poor lady at one o'clock in the morning?*

She answered almost instantly, which both relieved and worried Cooper. Had she been expecting him? Did she catch a glimpse of him down on Eighteenth Street; was she reverse-stalking him?

"Hey, Maya," Cooper said. "Is this a bad time?"

CHAPTER 57

Transcript of private conversation between Cooper Lamb and Maya Rain, captured using an ambient recording app on Lamb's smartwatch

MAYA RAIN: Hello, Mr. Lamb. And hello, Lupe! So great to see you again.

COOPER LAMB: Great to see me or great to see the pooch? And please, call me Cooper.

RAIN: Actually I was talking to Lupe. I know you make house calls, Cooper. I just wasn't expecting you at *my* house.

LAMB: And this is a very nice house, in one of the most desirable areas of the city. Do you have, like, seventeen roommates or something?

RAIN: No. I live alone. And right now you're about to say, "Gee, the Hughes family must pay really well if you can afford a place like this."

LAMB: That would be rude, and I am nothing if not professional. I was about to insinuate that you had a sugar daddy.

RAIN: I don't have one of those either. I'm just a simple girl from West—

LAMB: Virginia, yeah, you've mentioned that. Can I come inside to talk for a minute?

RAIN: Sure, but not with your recording device running.

LAMB: I don't have any recording devices running. (*Extended silence*) Okay, fine. How did you know?

RAIN: Because you are a professional... or something like that.

LAMB: Fair enough, Ms. Rain. Here, I am officially turning off my top secret recording device, which no one ever notices.

RAIN: Oh, I noticed—

CHAPTER 58

"I FIGURED it was a smartwatch," Maya Rain continued. "Men don't wear wristwatches anymore, not since the smartphone came along. Come on inside. Can I get you something to drink? Some water for Lupe?"

"Actually, would you mind if I used your restroom for a moment? I spent a long time down in my car in the freezing cold working up the courage to knock on your door."

Cooper used a casual tone of voice meant to put her at ease. He was also taking a mental snapshot of her condo. Spare, high-end furniture (possibly rented), generic framed art, not much in the way of screens or electronics. If his daughter, Ariel, were here, she would tag this place a "grown-up apartment," a jab at his own cluttered digs.

"The guest bathroom is to your left," Maya said. "And before you waste too much of your time, because it's awfully late and I suspect we've both had a long day, you're not going to find anything personal in the medicine cabinet."

"I'm sorry?"

"You know—no telltale prescription bottles, no bag of heroin taped to the inside of the toilet tank, nothing like that. Isn't that what detectives do, pretend to use the bathroom and then engage in a little impromptu profiling?"

"Uh, I really just have to relieve my bladder. But thanks for the heads-up."

She's good, Cooper thought as he closed the door behind him. *Too good to be true.* Of course he intended to scour her bathroom for any revealing details. Just because she'd told him not to bother didn't mean he wouldn't try.

But as Maya had warned, there was literally nothing to reveal, except that she had a taste for expensive grooming products and furnishings. The vanity was white Carrara marble on top, solid wood below, with soft-close drawer glides and brushed-chrome fixtures. This guest bathroom was pristine enough to perform brain surgery in. Cooper felt like a heathen using the facilities.

Back in the living room, Maya was waiting for him with an ice-filled tumbler garnished with a wedge of lemon.

"I probably shouldn't," Cooper said. "I still have to drive Lupe home."

"It's mineral water, to help replace your fluids."

"I didn't have to go *that* badly."

"What did you want to talk about?" she asked, guiding him to her midcentury-modern couch, made of an impossibly soft woven fabric and supported by stubby walnut legs.

"Can I be totally straight with you?" Cooper asked as they sat down. "I'm trying to save your boss, and for whatever reason, she's reluctant to tell me the truth. I know she didn't do it. I'm just looking for evidence so I can prove it to the rest of the world. You're in a unique position to help me do that."

"You want me to betray my employer's confidence?"

"No. I just want to know what you saw."

"Which is also betraying her trust."

"Maya, I'm just going to come out and ask you: Did you see Archie hit Francine?"

For the first time, the nanny seemed speechless. This was good. Cooper pressed his advantage by pulling out prints of the photos that Victor had found. He fanned them out on her walnut coffee table. It was difficult to look at them, even though he'd seen them before.

"Oh," Maya said.

"Look, I know Francine didn't kill Archie. But after seeing these, I wouldn't blame her if she had." Instead of looking at the photos, Cooper studied Maya's face. She was taking it all in, but there was a hardness there, as if she were unwilling to *let* it all in. He saw a professional detachment in her eyes. Cooper doubted they taught that in grad school.

"Yes," Maya said after a while. "There were incidents."

"You saw Archie hit Francine."

Maya nodded. "I asked her if she needed my help finding someone to talk to. She swore me to secrecy but also assured me that this was nothing new, and she knew how to handle her husband. I knew better than to press."

"Even as a crime happened right before your eyes?"

"This is just between you and me, Cooper," she said quietly. "But Francine gave as good as she got."

"Does that include murder?"

Maya smiled and shook her head. "I should know better than to talk to a private eye at one in the morning."

"Come on, you know how this looks. And it's going to look even worse when it all comes out. I'm trying to help Francine."

"When all you've got is a hammer," Maya said, "everything looks like a nail."

"And that means?"

"You think I was Archie's side piece, that he bought me this penthouse apartment and filled it with beautiful things—a taste of the good life I'd always craved back in West Virginia. Is that right?"

"If Archie wasn't paying for it, who is?"

"That's none of your business." Maya reached out and touched the side of Cooper's face. "Don't get me wrong. I like you."

"I like you too," Cooper said, then gently took her wrist and guided her hand back to her lap. "Which is why I hope you're not hiding something. Or worse. Because I'm not going to stop until I find out what really happened."

"I know," she said. "Which is why you should be careful out there."

"Why is everyone always telling me that? Do I have a bull's-eye pinned to the back of my jacket or something? And if so, does it at least match my socks?"

Maya stood up, indicating their late-night meeting was over. Lupe took the cue and popped up from the floor expectantly.

"If multiple people tell you the same thing," she said, "it just might be the truth."

CHAPTER 59

"I NEED to see you. Right now."

"Cooper, it's two in the morning. I've got a long drive ahead of me. Don't you remember? We did this dance already."

"It's not about that. I'm talking about our case."

"I have to leave for Atlantic City in . . . ugh, like four hours."

"It will just take a minute. You and Janie hitting the craps tables?"

Veena Lion paused. She was wide awake and wouldn't be going to sleep anytime soon. She'd been at her kitchen table poring over stacks of documents and was feverishly mapping out their case and all of its possible tangents on a legal pad. She'd tried to shake off the effects of the martinis (and her bar-side make-out session with Cooper) with work and endless cups of black coffee. None of it helped. Veena felt jittery. Maybe she should just power through the rest of the night and try to catch a nap tomorrow. Even though she never, ever took naps. "How soon can you get here?"

"I'm parked in front of your building."

"Of course you are."

Cooper was at the door before Veena could decide what to cover with a blanket or push into a closet. Whatever. They'd known each other a long time. If a messy apartment was a deal breaker, then so be it.

"You know, it's been forever since I've been here," Cooper said. "I like what you've not done with the place."

"I wasn't expecting company at two a.m."

"Anyway, I just spent some time with the elusive Maya Rain."

"At her invitation?"

Cooper raised his eyebrows. "Are we jealous, Counselor?"

"No. I'm just trying to figure out her game."

"Me too," Cooper admitted. "But I think she's one of the good guys."

"Do you think that because you want to justify sleeping with her?"

"That's absurd." Cooper made a show of looking around the messy apartment. "Speaking of, do you still keep your bed in the adjoining room?"

"Cooper..."

"I just don't see a place for us to sit down and discuss the case. We're both tired, and I know I think better when I'm lying flat on my back."

Veena didn't respond. She knew Cooper's argument style; they'd dance around it and he'd try to slip something past her on a technicality. And she was honestly too exhausted to go through the steps to reach that point, so she reached out, took his hand, and led him toward her bedroom.

"Wait—is this a yes?"

"This is us lying in bed and discussing our case."

"Pants on or off?"

"Pants," Veena said, "are absolutely on."

CHAPTER 60

COOPER LAMB stared up at something he'd never thought he'd see: the ceiling of Veena Lion's bedroom.

He'd certainly hoped to gaze at it at some point. But Veena was mercurial. There was no way to confidently predict what she'd do at any given moment. For example, this: Veena leading him down the narrow hallway to her dark bedroom. Taking him by the shoulders. Leveling her gaze at him, her eyes almost glowing in the dark, so close he could feel her warm breath on his neck.

And then Veena shoving him backward until he bounced onto the surface of her bed, which was covered in stacks of clean laundry.

Veena spun around and dropped backward too, bouncing him—and the tumbled stacks of laundry—a second time.

"Was it good for you?" Cooper asked, deadpan, as they lay next to each other.

"The case," Veena reminded him.

"We should move in together," Cooper said.

"We've had this conversation on a number of occasions, remember? We determined there was no way we could be with each other all the time."

"Right, right. Because one of us would end up trying to hide the other's corpse and attempt to get away with the perfect, untraceable murder—"

"Even though we both know there is no such thing as the perfect murder."

"Well, that's only when we are investigating them," Cooper countered. "If one of us is dead, and the other is determined not to get caught, then I think that person would have a strong chance of getting away with it."

Veena sighed. "See, this conversation right now is why we could never live together. I'm literally dizzy."

"Good, because now that you're weak and swooning, it's my turn to ask a question."

Lupe naturally chose this moment to jump onto Veena's bed. He selected a location near her head and curled himself into a ball. It had been a long, cold night for him, much of it spent outside in a cold car or inside a stranger's apartment. Veena's home, however, was one of Lupe's favorite places. He adored her and everything associated with her.

"Hi, loopy Lupe," Veena whispered, giving him scritches behind his ears. "Such a good boy."

"So, um, back to my question. It's serious. A matter of life and death."

Veena rolled over and gave Cooper affectionate scritches behind his ears too. "Aw, is someone jealous?"

"Not in the least. But my belly could use some rubbing."

"You said something about a serious question?"

Cooper hesitated. He never let his guard down completely with anyone. Not with his ex, certainly, not even when she was his wife, which might have been the root of their problems. And not with his children, because they deserved a steady, stable presence and he was a grown-ass man; they didn't need to know when he was worried or stressed.

With Veena, however, it was different. Sure, they joked and sparred and flirted. He drove her more than a little nuts. But a rock-solid trust had developed between them over the years, probably because they were variations of the same animal. He loved that she took off her sunglasses for him. So what the hell, right?

"There's a strong chance that someone will try to kill us if we keep going with this investigation," Cooper said.

Veena narrowed her eyes. "What makes you think that?"

"People keep warning me away. Even Victor is telling me to watch my step, which is an astounding display of emotion for him."

"Since when does Cooper Lamb listen to warnings?"

"Since the warnings are coming from witnesses and suspects involved in this case. Even Maya the nanny told me to watch my back. And when a childcare provider is telling you to be careful..."

"So do you want to stop?" Veena traced a thumb along Cooper's jawline.

"Hell no. I just wanted to let you know that I would still respect you if *you* decided to stop."

"Well, I'm not stopping until we find the truth."

"Even if it kills us?"

Veena removed her hand from Cooper's face. She extended her pinkie and waited until Cooper got the hint and wrapped his pinkie finger around hers.

"Pinkie-swear that if one of us gets killed," Veena said, "the other won't rest until the killer is brought to justice."

"Pinkie-swear," Cooper said, gently shaking her pinkie twice. "But what if they get both of us?"

CHAPTER 61

Transcript of encrypted message exchange between Victor Suarez and Cooper Lamb

VICTOR SUAREZ: Sorry for the early wake-up text but I've got three important items for you, boss.

COOPER LAMB: New phone, who dis?

SUAREZ: [No response]

LAMB: You're no fun, Victor. Go ahead, what do you have for me?

SUAREZ: Item one: Just received confirmation Detective Mickey Bernstein was already en route to Eakins Oval *before* Archie Hughes's body was discovered by the P/Os who called it in.

LAMB: WHAT? That means... you have this absolutely nailed down?

SUAREZ: [No response]

LAMB: Okay, okay, dumb question. But how do you know? I need to be sure this is rock solid before I go gunning for Dick Mickey. If I'm going to have the entire homicide department wedged sideways up my ass, it has to be for a good reason.

SUAREZ: I traced Bernstein's complete movements starting twelve hours before the crime. Confirmed by his personal phone's own GPS, backed up by traffic cams both here and in New Jersey.

LAMB: Tell me about Jersey.

SUAREZ: That's item two. Bernstein was in AC earlier in the evening.

LAMB: Blackjack? Baccarat?

SUAREZ: Poker. High rollers' table. I've got house footage detailing how much he lost and exactly how he lost it. He only left because of a phone call, at approximately 7:18 p.m.

LAMB: Who?

SUAREZ: That would be item three. The call came from the Eagles' business office.

LAMB: From Papa Sable or Younger, Fatter Sable?

SUAREZ: Still running down a record for that call...if it hasn't been scrubbed.

LAMB: You have to find that call, Victor. That could be the key to everything.

SUAREZ: Which leads me to believe it's already been wiped. But I'll try. Also, your suspicion about Bernstein working for the Sables turned out to be accurate.

LAMB: He's their fixer, right?

SUAREZ: They're making sizable deposits to a secret account of Bernstein's. No one, not even his wife, has access to this account.

LAMB: Damn it, I hate being right. There's no way Bernstein should be allowed anywhere near this case, yet somehow, he's the guy calling all the shots.

SUAREZ: I'm working on that too. A source tells me there's a memo somewhere in which Bernstein spells out exactly why he's the man for the job.

LAMB: Stellar work, as usual.

SUAREZ: Rain has a very faint digital trail. She's either a true nobody or a ghost.

LAMB: I'm not sure which disturbs me more. Anyway, time to turn up the heat under Tricky Mickey.

SUAREZ: You're going to have to settle on a nickname for him, boss. I can't keep up.

LAMB: Ha-ha-ha. Get back to work.

CHAPTER 62

Transcript of call from Cooper Lamb's phone to Detective Michael Bernstein

ARIEL LAMB: Hello, I would like to speak with Detective Bernstein, please.
MICHAEL BERNSTEIN: Uh, yeah, this is... wait, who is this?
ARIEL: (*Muffled*) Dad, he's on the line.
BERNSTEIN: Hello? Hello?
COOPER LAMB: (*Muffled*) Oops, thanks, honey. (*Pause*) Hey, Detective! Glad I caught you. This is Cooper Lamb. Got a minute? I have something very important you should know.
BERNSTEIN: Hang on—was that one of your kids just now?
LAMB: Yeah, that was my daughter, Ariel. I'm driving her and her brother to school, but I thought it was super-important to reach out to you right away. Don't worry, they understand. Kind of goes with the territory.
BERNSTEIN: What do you want, Lamb?
LAMB: I mean, I imagine you share a little shop talk with your youngsters now and again. "Boy, you kids should have seen the floater we pulled out of the Delaware this afternoon, talk about fleshy bloat—"

BERNSTEIN: I don't have time for this.

LAMB: Kids, the detective says he's too busy to speak to someone involved in the case he's investigating. Does that sound right to you?

BERNSTEIN: Lamb, I swear to God...

ARIEL: I think he should at least talk to you.

LAMB: Do you hear that, Detective? Out of the mouths of babes.

BERNSTEIN: Make it quick.

LAMB: This is too serious for the phone. Let's meet up in one hour. You pick the place.

BERNSTEIN: Can't do it.

LAMB: Are you serious? What, do you have to drive down to Atlantic City this morning? Or are the Sables expecting you to report in?

BERNSTEIN: The f███ did you just say to me?

LAMB: Whoa, whoa, whoa! Detective! I've got you on speakerphone. Do you really want to curse like that in front of my kids?

BERNSTEIN: Kids, I sincerely apologize for the profanity. But your dad is a scumbag who shouldn't have you on speakerphone during a work call, so I'm hanging up now.

LAMB: Come on, Mickey! Be a mensch, meet with me! I can help.

BERNSTEIN: You know how you can help? Do better by your children, ass███.

"I believe the homicide detective just hung up on me," Cooper said as he negotiated the busy traffic circle around Philadelphia's City Hall.

"Admit it," Ariel said, "you wanted him to hang up on you, didn't you?"

"I wanted to see what he would do when I said key words such as *Atlantic City* and *Sable*."

Cooper Jr., who was sprawled out in the back seat, had been listening to everything with a bemused smile on his face. But now he couldn't resist. "Is that cop working for the owners of the Eagles?"

"Yeah," Ariel said, "is he like their bagman or something?"

"Where did you learn about bagmen?"

"We are your children," she replied. "We pick up everything."

"I'm so proud I could weep."

CHAPTER 63

Transcript of recorded interview with Rosalind "Roz" Cline conducted by Veena Lion and Janie Hall

ROZ CLINE: Jeez, do you always wear those things inside? You look like you're with the Secret Service or something. All I see is myself talking to myself.

JANIE HALL: I assure you it's nothing personal, Ms. Cline. Veena is light-sensitive.

CLINE: What do you mean, light-sensitive? You're inside a casino. It's practically midnight in here all the time.

VEENA LION: Let's not talk about my boring sunglasses. I want to hear all about you. I'm fascinated how you keep one foot in Philly and one foot here. Kind of the best of both worlds?

CLINE: Nobody uses the word *best* in connection to either Philly or Jersey. I'm guessing you two didn't grow up here.

LION: Where did you grow up?

CLINE: Blackwood, New Jersey. Pretty much right at the beginning of the expressway.

HALL: Did you attend college nearby too?

CLINE: College? I didn't even finish high school. That's the big lie they push—work your ass off so you can graduate from high school, and don't you dare miss a day or you won't get the perfect-attendance award! And God forbid you're not accepted to the right Ivy League school—you're doomed to a lifetime of failure. Never mind that if you go to college, you're chained to a lifetime of debt. No, I knew it was all a racket from a young age.

LION: How young, exactly?

CLINE: Finished ninth grade and that was all I could stand. Can I get another coffee? Maybe with a little Irish in it this time?

HALL: I'll take care of that for you right away.

LION: Thanks, Janie. While we're waiting, I wanted to ask you about Archie Hughes. How long did you know him?

CLINE: Who said I knew Archie Hughes?

LION: Of course you knew him. He was paying for your apartment.

CLINE: I don't believe . . . that is utter bull■! Who told you that? I'm serious. I want to know a name.

LION: It's not important. Especially if it's not true.

CLINE: Is that why you're here? To drag me into this whole murder mess? No, thank you. And you can keep your coffee. I have things to do.

LION: Please, Ms. Cline, wait. You have to understand something. I'm buried in bull■ from everyone around Archie. I'm talking his wife, the cops, the lawyers. I need someone to tell me the truth about the man. Someone who has nothing to gain.

CLINE: Is that what you really want? The truth?

LION: Absolutely.

CLINE: You're one of the few. (*Sighs*) I can't tell you how tired I am of this city. Everybody's always making assumptions about everybody else. *Ooh, how can that dirtbag possibly afford that Lexus? Ooh, look at that stuck-up b■ in her Old City condo, she must have a sugar daddy somewhere.* They never think, *Huh, maybe that lady did it all for herself.*

LION: Tell me how you did it, then. I'm one of those suckers who has a perfect-attendance certificate in a drawer somewhere, and I'm still paying off my law school tab. What do you know that I don't?

CLINE: I know plenty. (*To Janie Hall*) Oh, thanks, hon. (*Sips*) Wow. You did Irish this up.

HALL: I told them to give me an Atlantic City pour.

LION: You were saying, Ms. Cline?

CLINE: The trick is to figure out what people want and come up with a way to give it to them. No guilt, no shame, no fuss, none of that nonsense.

HALL: And you've figured this out?

CLINE: Oh, sweetie. A long time ago. And if you can give people want they secretly want and make sure they never, ever feel bad about wanting it . . . well, they will reward you.

LION: I'll bet poor Archie needed that kind of escape now and again.

CLINE: Oh yeah. I don't think people appreciate what it's like to be in the spotlight all the time. Sure, there are perks. But the stress and pressure and constant scrutiny can be awful. And that wife of his . . .

HALL: Francine?

CLINE: I can't hear one of her old songs on the radio without feeling homicidal. Nobody knows what Philadelphia's so-called sweetheart put that poor man through. She's a real pill.

LION: And you'd make Archie feel better.

CLINE: I know what you're thinking, and no, he didn't pay for my condo. I can afford it all on my own. Money is not one of my worries.

HALL: So your thing with Archie was for real.

CLINE: I'm gonna pretend you didn't just imply that I'm a whore.

HALL: No, it's sweet! Sorry, that came out all wrong.

CLINE: Everybody knew the NFL superstar, but very few people knew the real Archie, the sweet kid from Detroit. I don't even think Princess Francine saw that part of him. When something struck Archie as funny, he laughed with his whole heart, you know? God, I loved spending time with him. Wasn't nearly enough, but it was enough. It had to be.

LION: Do you think his wife knew about your relationship?

CLINE: He only stayed over a few times...she watched him like a goddamn hawk during the off-season.

LION: How have you been coping with your loss?

CLINE: I'm drinking Irish coffee first thing in the morning, what does that tell you? Speaking of, if I could trouble you for another...

CHAPTER 64

10:18 a.m.

JANIE STEERED their rented Honda Civic down the Atlantic City Expressway toward Philly as Veena, in the passenger seat, furiously scribbled notes—underlining phrases, drawing arrows to related ideas, circling key words.

Janie loved watching her boss work. It was like Veena was spilling the contents of her brain onto a series of yellow legal pads. Janie ordered them in bulk and sometimes had a hard time keeping up with the demand.

"What did you think of Ms. Cline?" Veena asked.

"I wish I could down a shot of her confidence," Janie replied. "She seems to have life pretty much figured out."

"She's a mess, and her so-called confidence is yet another mask she wears. She's still that same frightened ninth-grader who turned people-pleasing into a way of life."

"Whoa, V. Kind of harsh, don't you think?"

Veena shrugged and continued making notes.

"But yeah, I guess I can see that," Janie said. "What tipped you off? Was it the Irish coffee?"

"No—the constant need to impress us. Only people who feel inferior do that."

"Well, one thing was clear," Janie said. "Roz was totally into

Archie Hughes. She spoke of him like he was the love of her life, not a casual fling."

Veena nodded. "She also knows a lot more than she's saying. She probably thinks she's protecting his memory, but I'm sure she's also treading carefully. Above all else, Roz Cline is a survivor, and she doesn't want to get sucked into the whirlpool."

"So what's the plan?"

"We stay on her until we learn what she knows. Roz was wary of me, but maybe she'll cozy up to you, my underling and her potential enabler."

"Me?"

"You're the trusted underling. She'll want an inside track on what I'm looking for, and you're in a unique position to give it to her. Drop her a text. Tell her you loved what she said about living without shame, and gee, you really wish you could do that too. Maybe offer to buy her a drink, see where it goes."

"I'm still hung up on the word *underling,* V. Is that how you see me?"

"Good—you can use that!"

Janie frowned. "Not exactly what I meant, but point taken."

"Meanwhile, Cooper Lamb will be watching Archie's other romantic entanglement, Maya Rain."

"Cooper? I didn't realize we'd partnered up with the opposing team."

"We're both trying to figure out the truth. That puts us on the same team."

CHAPTER 65

COOPER LAMB / VOICE MEMO #20127-735

The kids have been safely deposited at school and I'm back in front of Maya Rain's condo like a real creep. It's been only a few hours since I saw her, but it feels like a lifetime.

Victor, if you're listening . . . ah, who am I kidding, you're the only person who listens to these things. But please ignore all of this stuff about me pining away for someone who's a possible witness in the biggest murder case in Philadelphia history. Because that would be wrong, and I would never, ever act on it.

Anyway . . .

Maya isn't scheduled to be at the Hughes house until noon, which means she'll probably be headed downstairs to her car around eleven fifteen. I slipped the garage security guy a crisp hundred-dollar bill to let me know the moment she calls down for her ride.

At first he was weird about it, but then I casually mentioned that I was trying to stop this annoying lawyer chick working for the DA from hassling Maya. Garage Dude was all too happy to help after that. I probably didn't even need to slip him the hundred. Thank you for being you, Veena.

My plan is to follow her until we reach the Hughes home, then come up with some pretext to knock on the door...some detail I forgot to follow up on. I don't know. Maybe you can help me with that, Victor.

Speaking of, I'm finding it hard to believe that you're coming up with zilch on Maya Rain. I mean, this is *you* we're talking about here, Victor. Keep trying. I need to know everything about her.

Okay, *need* is a strong word. I *want* to know everything about her.

For the case!

I think Archie was paying for Maya's apartment despite what she says. I think she and Archie had some kind of relationship that was extramarital but also somehow had the blessing of Francine. Hey, it's the twenty-first century, people are gender-fluid and relationship-fluid these days. Maybe Archie and Francine allowed each other to have little dalliances...just as long as they cleared them with each other first.

For all I know, Francine hired Maya as a nanny and trusted her, liked her, and then Archie expressed an interest, and Francine thought, *Sure, why not? I trust her, I like her, and I could literally destroy her if she moves in on my husband for real.*

I'll need to watch the Francine-Maya dynamic a little more to know for sure. But Victor, if you can find any kind of document trail regarding Maya's employment at the Hughes house, that would be huge. A high-profile gig like that would definitely require a state background check. You have any sources in Harrisburg who could help us out?

I just can't believe someone as amazing as Maya popped out of the West Virginia woods and into a multimillionaire's Main Line mansion without leaving some traces.

CHAPTER 66

COOPER LAMB / VOICE MEMO #20127-735 (continued)

Okay, now that I've been thinking about it some more...

Here's the lame and obvious version: Francine was tired of being abused by her ultra-famous, ultra-wealthy husband and used some of that wealth to hire a hit man to take him out and make it look like an accident.

The problem with this take? It ignores all of the shady characters and circumstances surrounding Archie's murder. There are too many moving parts that don't fit into this neat, tidy narrative.

For example, there's the NFL factor and another obvious version. A hack private eye would say, *Duh, somebody wants to throw the Super Bowl. What better way than killing the Birds' star player? It takes him off the field, shakes the confidence of the team.*

The problem with this theory is that Archie's death seems to have had the opposite effect on the team. They've been galvanized into winning this one for Archie, and the city is more Eagles-crazy than ever. And it also ignores the other shady circumstances and characters.

Mickey Bernstein, for one. Unless he's moonlighting as a hit man, what's his role in all this? Why was he speeding to the crime scene before anyone knew it was a crime scene? What do we know about Mickey?

We know that Mickey Bernstein is a bagman for the Sables. We know he was headed to Archie's body before anyone officially reported it. We know that he lobbied the commissioner and possibly even the mayor to run this investigation. All of this speaks to someone who (a) knew about the crime in advance, and (b) wants to completely control the investigation of said crime.

But why?

Now I'm starting to think this does have everything to do with the Super Bowl. Sometimes the obvious and lame theory is correct, because crooks and killers are often obvious and lame.

I need to see if this theory has legs...

Transcript of Cooper Lamb's phone call to Red's Bar and Grill, Atlantic City

COOPER LAMB: Let me speak to Red, please.
BARTENDER: I don't know anybody named Red.
LAMB: Let's not do this again, sparky. Put him on.
BARTENDER: Fine, whatever.
LAMB: Don't stop being you.
RED DOYLE: Yeah, what's the good word, Cooper?
LAMB: I was hoping you could tell me.
DOYLE: It's a s■show here, if I'm being perfectly honest. All of

the heavy guys are jittery. I feel like I'm talking all of them down off the ledge. It's like I'm a friggin' therapist instead of your friendly neighborhood bookie.

LAMB: And that's exactly why I'm calling. Who has the most to gain from the championship game being delayed?

DOYLE: Nobody. This whole thing sucks and it's freaking everybody out.

LAMB: Come on. You telling me there's no angle to be played with the delay?

DOYLE: This isn't like throwing a fight or something, Lamb. It's too public. Everybody knows what happened.

LAMB: Yeah, but once you place a bet, there's no changing it. I mean, that's the first thing you told me once we started doing . . . uh, business together.

DOYLE: That's right. Except in this case, the game was pushed back a week, and whenever you go past seventy-two hours, all bets are literally off. So people can adjust their wagers accordingly. Look, I know you're working some private-eye angle here, but I just don't see it. If there were a way to make some bank from this whole mess, believe me, I'd be doing it.

CHAPTER 67

Transcript of phone call between Maya Rain and Glenn Sable

MAYA RAIN: Hello, Glenn.

GLENN SABLE: Hey, yeah, just checking in . . . er, Maya. Seeing how you're doing and all. It's been a crazy f████ week, hasn't it? What are you up to?

RAIN: Just getting ready for work. And you?

SABLE: Did I catch you heading into the shower? Or maybe out of it? In which case, maybe we can FaceTime or something.

RAIN: About to step out the door in a minute, actually. Francine and the kids need me at noon today. Something I can help you with?

SABLE: Ah, no, nothing like that. I was just worried about you, kid. And it's been a while.

RAIN: The Hughes family have been through a lot, and I'm doing my best to keep the kids happy and distracted.

SABLE: What? Oh, yeah. Right. But that's not exactly what I meant, Vanessa.

RAIN: I'm sorry?

SABLE: I mean Maya. Apologies. I've got so many names running through my head.

RAIN: That's okay, but I really have to go. My ride's here.

SABLE: I understand. Hey, if you get the chance, maybe you could stop by after work. It would be great to catch up. Maybe have a drink or three.

RAIN: I'm going to be with Francine and the kids fairly late.

SABLE: Well, maybe I'll stop by there. I haven't been down to Rittenhouse Square in a while.

RAIN: That might not be the best idea, with all of the media attention lately.

SABLE: You're not giving me a lot to work with here. (*Laughs*)

RAIN: I really have to get going, Glenn.

SABLE: No, sure thing. But listen to me, and I'm deadly serious here. Be careful out there. You see anybody following you or acting weird, I'm your first phone call, you hear me?

RAIN: I appreciate that, Glenn, I really do. Talk to you soon, okay?

SABLE: Especially if it's one of the private investigators on the case. There are two of them—one working for your boss, the other for the DA.

RAIN: I'm not worried about them at all.

CHAPTER 68

11:29 a.m.

COOPER ALMOST didn't see her.

He had been expecting a tip-off call from Garage Dude. He'd also kept an eye on the front entrance. If Maya Rain darted out for a prework latte, he wanted to know about it. But that commanded only a small part of his attention. The rest of his brain was busy running through the scenarios and possibilities of the Archie Hughes murder—mostly to distract himself from the scenarios and possibilities with Maya Rain.

And then Cooper glimpsed something in his peripheral vision that forced him to sit up behind the wheel and take a closer look.

There—in the alley. A side entrance to the building meant for employees, deliveries, and trash pickup. There stood Maya Rain, carefully dressed for a day in the nanny trenches and still managing to look obscenely beautiful.

Cooper rubbed his eyes. He'd slept so little that he felt like hammered garbage. Yet Maya, who'd also been up late, appeared perfectly refreshed, ready for anything. He'd have to ask her for her beauty secrets one of these days.

But first, he wanted to ask Maya what she was doing standing in the alley next to her condo.

"You should be down in the garage, climbing into your sensible

Subaru like a good nanny," Cooper muttered to himself. "What—or who—are you waiting for?"

Cooper realized that this was a perfect opportunity to look at her, *really* look at her, in an unguarded moment. What did her face reveal when she thought no one was paying attention?

But from his vantage point parked on the east side of Eighteenth Street, he couldn't make out her features. Not in much detail.

He reached under his seat for the hard case resting there. Years ago, in a completely different universe, his then-wife had made a then-outrageous purchase for him: high-end Canon binoculars. "Doesn't every private snoop need a quality set of snooping goggles?" she'd said at the time, a little woozy with vodka martinis and still very much in love. Cooper couldn't believe it; he'd promised to treasure them always. A bittersweet memory. Like so many from back then.

Cooper flipped open the case and saw the shape of the high-end binoculars in dark gray padding, but no binoculars. *What?* A thief would have smashed the window and then stolen the case too, for maximum resale value. So what had happened to them?

If Cooper had to guess, he'd say they were at the bottom of Cooper Jr.'s underwear drawer. The boy did love to "borrow" his dad's PI gadgets. "Memo to self," Cooper muttered, even though he wasn't actively recording. "Discuss with son how 'borrowing' works."

Cooper squinted. Didn't help. Then inspiration struck. He pulled out his phone, hit the camera app, pointed the lens out his window, then used his fingers to zoom in on his target. Not perfect, by any means. But better than squinting.

He tapped the RECORD button, telling himself this was just him being a professional investigator, not a creep.

Maya's face was as placid as the top of a cool lake. If she had troubled thoughts, she wasn't allowing the tension to bubble to the surface.

And then Cooper's view was obscured by something large, pale, and blurry.

He lowered the phone, rubbed his eyes, and took a better look. A late-model white Ford Bronco was slowly making its way down the alley. Something pricked at his brain—he *knew* this car. But from where?

There was something on the rear panel, a sticker of some sort. Cooper pointed his phone camera at the Bronco and used his thumb and finger to enlarge the image.

It was an FOP sticker—Fraternal Order of Police. And the black license plate frame had a discreet motto running across the top and bottom:

OUR DAY BEGINS

WHEN YOUR DAY ENDS

Cooper couldn't believe it. This was Mickey Bernstein's car.

CHAPTER 69

COOPER'S MIND was reeling with the possibilities even as Maya slid into the Bronco's passenger seat, pulled the belt over her shoulder, and clicked it in place. All without paying much mind to what she was doing, as if she'd done it dozens of times before.

Maya and Mickey the detective? Now, that was a pairing he never would have predicted.

Sure, he could imagine Bernstein making a few clumsy moves on the hot nanny, figuring she was anonymous enough not to matter. But this was something different. And it was not the usual business of a cop picking up a witness either. For one thing, that would never involve just one detective. No, this was friendly, familiar. Which meant they were allies . . . right? Or maybe Maya knew something, and Tricky Mickey was coaxing it out of her with false promises of police protection—all of it off the books, because Bernstein was working his own angle.

Cooper hurriedly opened the city streets app on his phone to see where this alley led so he could pick up their trail. He couldn't pursue Bernstein directly down the alley; the veteran cop would spot him in a microsecond.

The app offered some good news: The alley ended at a side street that would take you north to Sansom Street or south to Walnut.

But the bad news: He didn't know which direction Bernstein might be headed. That depended on where he was taking her.

A left turn onto Walnut could mean he was headed to the Roundhouse at Eighth and Arch for something official—or something meant to *seem* official.

A right turn could mean Bernstein was giving her a lift to the Main Line for work...or perhaps taking her to the Sables' head office at the Linc.

And if Cooper chose wrong, he would lose them.

Cooper put his hand on the gear shift, ready to spring into action whenever Bernstein hit the gas. But he lingered. Bernstein and Maya were talking about *something,* their faces only inches apart.

He wished he could go back in time and have Victor wire Bernstein's car for sound. "Memo to self," Cooper mumbled. "Have Victor invent time machine, then travel back and bug Mickey's ride."

For a fleeting second, Cooper considered the direct approach—running up to the car, pounding on the windshield, smiling, and making a *Roll down your window* gesture—just to see where the conversation took them.

But Bernstein would most likely give him the finger and peel off down the alley. Besides, Cooper's sole advantage was that neither Mickey nor Maya knew Cooper was there. So he would flip a coin at the end of the alley and try to follow them. Maybe their destination would tell him everything he needed to know.

But there was one thing Cooper Lamb wasn't prepared for.

Maya moving closer to Bernstein and giving him a long, slow, deep kiss.

A nuke went off in Cooper's skull, and his senses fuzzed out for a moment. Was he actually seeing this? Son of a bitch!

Okay, there was no way Detective Mickey was Maya's sugar daddy. Not unless he had a small fortune tucked away in a metal box under some floorboards somewhere. Cooper knew what homicide detectives took home, and he could not float Maya's apartment on top of his own house.

But forget all of that for now.

Why the hell was Mickey Bernstein heading up this investigation?

Before Cooper had a chance to consider that question, the white Bronco rocketed down the alley.

This was it.

Time to toss that coin.

CHAPTER 70

COOPER LAMB / VOICE MEMO #20127-735 (continued)

I am currently in hot pursuit of Mickey Bernstein, big-deal homicide detective.

I'm recording all of this just in case something...well, weird happens. This is Philadelphia, after all. And everybody's been telling me to watch my back. So maybe a recording of these next few minutes will come in handy for the person investigating my murder.

Please, don't let me be murdered.

Victor, if I am murdered, avenge me.

I guessed correctly, by the way. Mickey turned right, heading toward Sansom Street, which means he's going to the Linc or the Main Line.

Victor, I don't know if you're listening to this in real time or not, but in case you are, work your magic. Tell me where Bernstein is headed.

Okay, you must be busy. No magic for now. I have to do this the old-fashioned way.

Bernstein is continuing down Sansom Street. At some

point he has to turn, otherwise he's headed into the river. I am following close behind. But not too close. Bernstein is police, and he knows when he's being followed.

Okay, he's taking a right on Twenty-Second Street, which makes sense. This will take him to the on-ramps for the interstate and then to everybody's least favorite highway, the Schuylkill Expressway. Ah, Mickey, but are you taking the freeway west, out of your jurisdiction and into the chilly embrace of the Main Line? Or are you taking it east, down to the Linc?

The next few minutes will tell us everything...

Oh, s■.

I think he spotted me.

S■, s■, s■.

This is *not* good, Victor.

If Bernstein saw me, all he has to do is call it in, and within a minute I'll be pulled over, and who knows how that might go? At best, I'll be slapped with a dozen tickets for fictional violations. At worst, I'll end up...

Okay, he definitely sees me. I'm turning around now.

CHAPTER 71

AS COOPER Lamb drove home, he expected that any minute he'd be pulled over, arrested, and possibly shot. His name would be added to the hundreds of murder victims in Philadelphia every year, because when it came down to it, what was one more?

None of those things happened.

Cooper obsessively checked his rear- and side-view mirrors, looking for any hint of a police vehicle, marked or otherwise. No such hint appeared, which worried him even more. What if Bernstein had someone *else* coming for him? Some shadowy player from the underworld—someone who Cooper wouldn't hear coming until it was far too late?

But he made the short drive back to his brownstone at Twentieth and Green without incident. He even successfully parallel-parked. (Again, without anyone around to appreciate it.)

Cooper went upstairs to take a shower. This was where he did his best thinking, and he had a lot to think over. He undressed, stuffed his clothes in the hamper, knelt down, and pulled out the Browning Black Label 1911-380 clipped to the underside of his bed. He carried the weapon into the bathroom, twisted on the shower water, and adjusted the temperature to just shy of scalding. Cooper needed to shake the chill from his bones and the adrenaline from his muscles. The Browning was just in case someone broke in and tried to kill him while he relaxed.

Only twice before had he felt compelled to bring a firearm into the bathroom, and both times he'd debated the best place for the weapon. Top of the toilet tank? No, because then it became a race between himself and an intruder. Resting on the water pipe? Too precarious, and Cooper couldn't stand the idea of the inevitable *Philadelphia Daily News* headline: "Private Eye Shoots Self in Shower." (*Does it hurt, getting shot right in yer shower? Ha-ha-ha-ha.*)

Cooper tucked his Browning into his mesh shower caddy, which he'd purchased mainly as a place to keep his gun. The fact that it also held soap and shampoo was a bonus.

But now it was time to sort out the facts. Maya and Mickey. Rain and Bernstein. How did that happen? And what did it mean? Bernstein worked for the Sables. Had Bernstein and Maya met at some Eagles event where all the members of the Hughes family (and, of course, the nanny) were present? That would be the innocent answer. But there was nothing innocent about this situation.

So most likely the murder had brought them together...but the murder had just happened on Sunday. Bernstein and Maya looked like they'd known each other a lot longer than a few days.

Cooper lowered his head, allowing the scalding water to pummel his neck and shoulders. He needed sleep. But the Maya Rain situation felt like a thorn in his brain; he couldn't properly relax until he plucked it out of his gray matter.

Fortunately, Cooper didn't have to leave his brownstone to pick up the kids; they had a half day at school, and his ex was picking them up early to catch an afternoon matinee. "You're not the only fun parent," his ex had said. Cooper wanted to tell her not to worry about that. He was the opposite of fun right now.

The detective spent the rest of the day brooding. Lupe followed his master's lead and seemed extra-contemplative as well. Cooper set up camp on the sofa, which gave him views of both his front door and the window overlooking Green Street. Lupe perched next to him, head on Cooper's lap.

At some point Cooper must have fallen asleep, because Lupe's sharp series of barks jolted him awake. His hand grabbed the Browning tucked between two cushions, and his brain tried to fix on a target—the door or the window?

But nothing was happening inside or out of the brownstone. The sun had set a while ago, and the neighborhood was dark…

Except for the flashing lights that danced across the window.

Cooper crouched down low, listened, then peered outside. A white Bronco was crawling down Green, flashing its headlights, followed by the piercing, repeating electronic chirp of a portable siren. The driver gunned it down the block.

"Hello, Detective Bernstein," Cooper mumbled. "What brings you out this evening?"

Clearly Bernstein wanted to send a message. But was it just a warning or a prelude to something else? Maybe it was a distraction to keep Cooper's eyes on the street while someone came through his front door.

"Lupe," he whispered. "Eyes sharp."

Lupe gave a quiet, low growl in response. He was on the case.

The second drive-by happened a few minutes later, and Cooper tensed up all over again. But the third, a minute later, with a constant flutter of electronic chirps, just annoyed him. If Bernstein was going to do something, he should just do it already.

On the fourth drive-by, which was a full half hour later, Cooper realized this was the point. To keep him on edge, to let him know he'd crossed a line.

FRIDAY, JANUARY 28

CHAPTER 72

2:11 a.m.

"VICTOR? GOOD, you're up."

"What's up, boss?"

Cooper wasn't surprised Victor Suarez was awake in the middle of the night. A true surprise would have been finding Victor asleep or—even more shocking—out somewhere enjoying himself.

"Can you shake down an address for me?"

"Sure," Victor replied. "Just as soon as you stop talking like a 1950s private eye."

"Be kind to your favorite employer. I've had a rough day."

"Mickey Bernstein, right?"

"How did you know?"

"How did I know what? Mickey's been the puzzle piece that hasn't fit this whole time. I figured you'd eventually want to go knocking on his door. Okay, got a pen?"

"Hang on. You found it that easily? What, do you have access to the home addresses of all Philly cops?" Cooper knew quite a few guys on the force, and they were super-cautious about any scraps of personal information leaking out on the internet. They often came to him looking for the name of a good web cleaner, a high-tech private eye (of sorts) who would scrub all traces of them off the web. Not that this helped them when dealing with a specialist like Victor Suarez.

There was a strange sound on the other end of the line, like an elephant clearing its throat. Cooper quickly realized this was the sound of Victor Suarez *laughing*.

"Good one, boss."

"Whatever. Let me have the address."

"You want the rundown on his wife and kids too?"

Cooper knew Victor was kidding. At least, he *hoped* he was kidding.

CHAPTER 73

FOR DECADES, Northeast Philadelphia had felt almost like a suburb, a place somehow *apart* from the city, even though it rested firmly within the city limits. The lawns were wider, the houses slightly bigger. For years, it had been a haven for middle-class families fleeing the blue-collar neighborhoods of the inner city. But recently it had become a glorious melting pot, much like the rest of Philly.

Except for this part of it.

Mickey Bernstein's slice of Northeast Philly held on to that 1950s white-flight feeling—outsiders most certainly *not* welcome. This neighborhood was so far to the northeast, it was practically Bucks County.

Cooper pulled up in front of the homicide detective's house. A massive lawn crawled up to the main entrance of the Colonial-style home and its three-car garage, from which hung a tasteful Eagles flag, the new white Bronco parked outside. Whatever job Bernstein was doing on the side clearly had its perks.

What was Cooper thinking, taking the fight to Bernstein? He knew this was a total grade-school move: *You showed up at my place, I'm gonna show up at yours. Only I'm not going to hide in a white Bronco.*

No, it wasn't that. Cooper wanted to talk to Bernstein face-to-face. He was tired of being brushed off and chased away. He wanted straight answers.

Cooper pounded on Bernstein's door with the side of his fist. Inside, a dog yip-yip-yip-yipped like it had lost its fool mind. Cooper pounded again. *That's right, pooch, wake up your owner. And the owner's wife and kids while you're at it. Let's get the whole family down here to talk about Daddy Detective's afternoon with Maya Rain.*

Slowly the house creaked to life. An upstairs light switched on. Blinds were parted with fingers, then shut again. The dog continued to express its very strong feelings about the visitor at the front door. Slippered feet slapped their way down a hardwood staircase. A vestibule light flickered to life. The door opened. A blinking murder cop looked at him.

"You gotta be kidding me," Bernstein said.

"Clearly you had an urgent need to see me," Cooper said. "Figured I'd save you the trouble of coming to my place again."

"It's two in the goddamn morning. Who gave you my address?"

"Tell me, Mickey, back in the academy, didn't they teach you that dating the nanny of a murder victim's family might not be the *best* look?"

"Get the hell out of here."

Bernstein was wearing a robe, but Cooper could tell that was for show. The homicide detective had none of the telltale signs of sleep, and his breath carried the sweet-sharp odor of whiskey.

The yipping dog—some indeterminate breed that reminded Cooper of a dust mop—appeared between Bernstein's legs to complain a bit more. Cooper forced a smile as he locked eyes with the noisy little bastard and reached into his jacket pocket.

"Hey!" Bernstein said. "Keep your hands where I can see them!"

"Easy," Cooper replied. He pulled a small plastic baggie of dog treats out of his pocket. “Lupe loves these things. I think your pooch will go crazy for them.”

Before Bernstein had a chance to protest, Cooper was taking a knee and grabbing one of the nuggets (“Paw-Lickin’ Chicken”). The Yipping Dust Mop was suspicious but also intrigued by the scent.

“Don’t you give my dog anyth—”

The protest was cut short because Cooper made two moves in rapid succession. He dropped the treat for the Dust Mop, then he clenched his right fist and sent it rocketing skyward on a collision course with Bernstein’s face.

The homicide detective was caught completely off guard. Usually, a person taking a knee in front of you doesn’t have the advantage in a close-quarters fight. But Cooper didn’t intend this to be a fight. He was betting that his strength, speed, and weight would knock Bernstein for a loop.

Which it did. Blood gushed out of the detective’s nose and mouth, and the blow had the bonus effect of rendering Bernstein unconscious. Cooper had heard people say this was difficult to do in real life. He supposed that was true, but the army had taught him many ways to do exactly that.

“Good dogs deserve treats,” Cooper said.

Cooper pushed Bernstein’s body all the way into the vestibule and dropped a few more treats for the Dust Mop before he pulled the door shut. Cooper wasn’t a total monster.

CHAPTER 74

7:41 a.m.

"WOW, DAD."

"'Wow, Dad' what?"

"You look like you slept rough in the street," Ariel said.

"You're not too far off the mark, daughter. And who taught you about sleeping rough?"

Truth was, Cooper hadn't slept at all since assaulting the city's most famous homicide detective. He was pretty sure that single uppercut had placed a target firmly on his back. Bernstein hadn't been goaded into a fevered response, but Cooper knew for sure there would be a response. Maybe Bernstein would slip up, and it would be something he could use to help Francine.

"What's on the agenda today, old man?"

"Glad you asked," Cooper said. "Today's goal is convincing my own client to help me save her life."

"You're seeing Francine Hughes again?" Ariel asked.

"Why, yes, I am. Private eye to the stars, that's your dear old father."

Cooper Jr. leaned in from the back seat. "Do you think Francine could get us tickets to the game on Sunday?"

"You mean you want me to ask the grieving widow for tickets

to a game her late husband should have been playing? That might not be the smartest move, my boy."

Ariel shook her head. "That would be unethical."

"Yeah, but this is *Dad* we're talking about," Cooper Jr. said.

"Hey, Dad is sitting right here! And by the way, private eyes have a very strict ethical code."

Cooper Jr. frowned. "But you told me you became a private detective because you didn't want anyone telling you what to do."

"Plus you can set your own hours," Ariel added.

"Don't you two have schoolwork to finish or something?"

Transcript of conversation between Cooper Lamb and Francine Hughes

COOPER LAMB: Thanks for taking the time to see me, Francine. I wanted to ask you about Maya.

FRANCINE HUGHES: You're too old for her.

LAMB: Um, that's not what I'm asking.

HUGHES: Sure, sure. I see the way you look at her.

LAMB: If I'm looking at her in a particular way, it's because I'm trying to figure out how she fits into this case.

HUGHES: What do you mean? Maya looks after the kids. I have no earthly idea why you're trying to drag her into this.

LAMB: I'm not dragging her anywhere. She seems to live at the center of this thing, Francine. Did you know she's dating Mickey Bernstein?

HUGHES: (*Pause*) What she does in her time off is none of my business.

LAMB: You have no problem with your nanny being in a relationship with the man investigating your husband's murder?

HUGHES: I think we're through here, Cooper. You should probably go.

LAMB: If you want me to help your defense team save you, you're going to have to tell me everything you know about Maya and Bernstein.

HUGHES: I said we're through. I need you to leave.

LAMB: Hey, I'm on your side here!

HUGHES: Well, it doesn't feel that way. Sometimes you're no better than those reporters who call and text and e-mail all damn day. What does my nanny's personal life have to do with anything? It's all just gossip.

LAMB: Francine, it's clear we have one tiny problem between us.

HUGHES: And what's that?

LAMB: You're constantly lying to me.

HUGHES: (*Sharply*) Excuse me?

LAMB: Hey, it's okay. Sure, it makes my job a bit more challenging, but it ultimately doesn't matter, because I'm going to find the truth, no matter what. It's what I do.

HUGHES: Well, here's some truth for you. I didn't murder my husband. Maybe the prick deserved it, but I didn't kill him.

LAMB: Now we're finally getting to the truth.

HUGHES: I should fire you.

LAMB: *Please*. Put me out of my misery.

CHAPTER 75

"NICE ARM!" Cooper shouted with real delight, cradling the football to his chest.

And it was true, there had been surprising power behind the toss. But Cooper had to stop himself before continuing the thought: *An arm just like your father's.*

Cooper had found the twelve-year-old Archie Hughes Jr. outside alone, lost in his thoughts, toeing a Wilson Duke NFL football around the frosty lawn. The sight broke Cooper's heart. Cooper knew he should be down at the Linc, squeezing the Eagles' owners for answers. But he had never been a guy who could turn his back on a kid. He'd asked Archie Jr. how far he could throw that ball. And damn, did Junior show him.

"Let's do that again!" the boy shouted.

"Give me your worst," Cooper said, tossing him the pigskin. The kid caught it effortlessly and with a grace that belied his age. Cooper hoped that was because Archie had spent time out here practicing with his kid. Those memories would mean everything down the line.

Cooper knew this from personal experience. He clung to the few memories he had of his own father like faded wallet photos.

After Cooper and Archie Jr. had tossed the ball around a few times, with Lupe serving as their cheerleader, Maddie Hughes and Maya Rain emerged from the house. Maddie roared with delight when she saw Lupe.

"I love the Lamb's doggy!"

Lupe, the little glory hound, bounded over to Maddie for some chin scratches.

Cooper's attention was all on Maya, so much so that he failed to notice that Archie Jr. had hurled the football. Cooper caught it at the last possible second, and the blow took his breath away.

"Nobody taught you to keep your eye on the ball, Cooper?" Maya asked.

Cooper coughed, then tossed the ball back to the kid. "I thought I was."

"He's pretty amazing, isn't he?"

"It's good to see you again, Maya."

"I don't seem to be able to shake you," she said.

"Exactly how hard are you trying?"

Was that shyness on her face right now? Or flirtation? Whatever it was, Cooper didn't want to ruin the mood just yet by mentioning her boyfriend the homicide detective. "Is there somewhere we could talk?"

Maya glanced over at the Hughes kids playing with Lupe. "Not here. Let's talk in the pool house."

"Because sure, talking inside the pool house in the middle of a freezing January day isn't suspicious at all."

"Or we could do this another time."

"Pool house it is."

Cooper told the kids to look after Lupe, and he let Maya lead the way.

CHAPTER 76

Transcript of private conversation between Cooper Lamb and Maya Rain, captured using an ambient recording app on Lamb's smartwatch

COOPER LAMB: This place is huge! You could fit my entire brownstone inside here. Twice.

MAYA RAIN: Interesting you mention that. Why were you outside my apartment yesterday morning?

LAMB: You saw me down on Eighteenth Street, huh?

RAIN: I was waiting for you to come upstairs and tell me whatever was on your mind, but you never did.

LAMB: Maybe I was working up the courage until your boyfriend showed up in his white Bronco.

RAIN: Ahh, so you saw Detective Bernstein pick me up. Is that what this is about?

LAMB: Detective, huh? So formal. Especially considering you two started kissing after you climbed into the passenger seat.

RAIN: You know, Cooper, I didn't think you were one of those sleazy private eyes who goes around taking photos of married men with their younger lovers. Guess I was wrong about you.

LAMB: Is Bernstein your sugar daddy? Because I have no idea how he swings your Rittenhouse Square condo on his police salary.

RAIN: Bernstein has nothing to do with where I live. I'm not dating him. You have the wrong idea about so many things.

LAMB: Maya, this is f[illegible] hopeless. I already know who's paying for that place of yours. In fact, I'm going to pay him a visit this afternoon. I just wanted you to tell me the truth. Just one time.

RAIN: You're free to speculate however you want.

LAMB: By the way, who's Vanessa?

RAIN: Are you just throwing random names at me to see if I'll react?

LAMB: It's either your real name or another identity you use. I'm leaning toward the former.

RAIN: I don't have an alias or a pseudonym or an alternate identity. Just being me is enough.

LAMB: If only I knew who you really were.

RAIN: You're looking at her.

LAMB: (*Pause*) I'd better go before Maddie and Archie Jr. decide to formally adopt my dog.

CHAPTER 77

Transcript of private conversation between Cooper Lamb and Eagles co-owner Harold Sable in his office at Lincoln Financial Field

COOPER LAMB: Honestly, Harold, I don't know how you keep all of these plates spinning on all of these poles.

HAROLD SABLE: What're you talking about, plates and poles?

LAMB: I mean you must be crazy-busy right now, but you seem perfectly calm in the center of the storm.

SABLE: Is this why you had to see me right away? You want free lessons in time management?

LAMB: Just the expenses alone. I mean, how do you keep track of it all? Cars here, travel there, all of those luxury suites…

SABLE: Oh, I get it. You're delivering some kind of private-eye monologue. Well, go ahead, don't let me stop you.

LAMB: Not to mention all of the condos and apartments around town. I've seen Maya Rain's pad. That place can't be cheap.

SABLE: And now we come to the point. Only there's one problem—who the f■ is Maya Rain?

LAMB: You know exactly who she is.

SABLE: Maya, Maya…oh, right, the nanny. You think *I'm* paying for Archie's nanny's apartment? Isn't she living at Villanova or something? I still don't see how this is any of my business or why you're wasting my f████ time with this nonsense.

LAMB: Nonsense? You were covering for Archie by taking care of his mistress's penthouse. Anything to keep your star quarterback happy, right?

SABLE: If Archie had anything on the side—and I'm not saying he did—he could certainly have afforded to pay her living expenses on his own.

LAMB: Not if he wanted to keep it supersecret from Francine.

SABLE: You actually think Archie and this Maya were a thing?

LAMB: I *know* Archie and Maya were a thing.

SABLE: (*Laughs*) No, a████. Maya and the *detective* are a thing.

LAMB: (*Pause*) Really.

SABLE: You just don't get it. I know you're zipping around town trying to connect the dots and all. But you can't make it fit, can you? That's because there are no dots to connect. People are gonna do what they wanna do whether or not it's convenient for you. So he's banging the nanny. Who gives a s██? People do all kinds of crazy things.

LAMB: Crazy things like work for you?

SABLE: What's this, now?

LAMB: I know Bernstein's on your payroll.

SABLE: Unbelievable. Where'd you get that?

LAMB: You denying it?

SABLE: Yes, I'm denying it. Bernstein wishes he were on my payroll—he'd do a lot better than what the city gives him. No, I like Mickey because I was pals with his old man, and yeah, I might throw him some tickets now and again, but I throw a lot of tickets around. See, there you go again. Connecting dots that aren't even on the same page.

LAMB: (*Pause*) I really have this all twisted around, don't I?

SABLE: That's the first smart thing you've said today.

LAMB: Well, thanks for setting me straight, Harold. You're actually saving me a lot of time.

SABLE: Tell you what, Lamb. Just to show you what an outstanding guy I am, I want you to be my guest this Sunday at the game.

LAMB: You think I can be bought with a ticket to the game everybody in the world wants to see?

SABLE: I'm not trying to buy anything. I'm just a generous guy by nature.

LAMB: In that case, can you spare three tickets so I can bring the kids?

SABLE: Like I said before, you're unbelievable.

CHAPTER 78

12:25 p.m.

THE TRAFFIC on Third Street just above Market was slower than usual up to Arch Street. Something was off; Veena had an uneasy feeling. She looked up at the skyline for black smoke or news choppers or both but saw nothing out of place. That made her worry all the more.

"Driver, please pull over," Veena said. "We'll get out here."

Their rideshare driver seemed stunned by the very suggestion. "But I'm supposed to take you to Second and Arch."

"Charge us for the whole trip, and I'll add an obscene tip," Veena said. "Come on, Janie. We're walking the rest of the way."

"You got it, V."

They hurried east on Market. The brutal winter winds chilled by the nearby Delaware River blasted their bodies as if trying to push them away.

"Why did we get out here? What's going on?"

"Hopefully nothing, but..."

"But what?"

"Traffic is never this slow. To me, that means police activity."

"And Roz Cline lives nearby..."

They hurried down Market Street, fighting the cold wind. At the far end of the block, near the ramp leading to Penn's Landing, there were two police vans blocking traffic, and street cops were steering pedestrians away. As they closed the distance, even more police cars arrived, lights flashing, along with an EMT truck that squawked and squeezed through the blockade, forcing its way up Second Street in the wrong direction.

"This is such a huge response," Janie said. "What the hell is going on?"

"There are no fire engines," said Veena. "Just police and EMTs."

"I don't like this."

"You still have your old press pass, right?"

"Five years out of date."

"They probably won't pay too much attention. We should head up the walk to Church Street. Maybe we can sneak past the police along Christ Church."

Veena was right; nobody paid them much mind as they wound their way through the police vehicles toward Roz's condo. A crowd had gathered outside. Veena could hear snippets of conversation that chilled her blood even more than the January cold:

"Can you see anything from here?"

"Trust you me, you don't want to look."

"I need to get back to my apartment. This totally sucks."

"Anybody actually see her jump?"

CHAPTER 79

Transcript of conversation between Janie Hall and Stephanie Weddle, captured using an ambient recording app on Hall's personal phone

JANIE HALL: Oh my God. I can't believe this. We were just with her yesterday...

VEENA LION: Before we let our imaginations run wild, let's find out for sure.

HALL: Hang on. Oh, I know that cop over by the condo entrance. Let me see if she can tell us what's going on. (*Pause*) Hey, Steph! It's me, Janie Hall.

OFFICER STEPHANIE WEDDLE: Huh? Oh, hey, Janie. I didn't know you were still on the beat. Thought you'd retired a few years ago when that rag of yours folded.

HALL: Wasn't *my* rag, thankfully. I just gave them words in exchange for money. And yeah, I'm still at it. Hey, what happened here? I was trying to make my way up Third when everything just ground to a halt.

WEDDLE: You don't wanna know.

HALL: Come on, Steph. Of course I want to know.

WEDDLE: Heh-heh. Off the record?

HALL: As always.

WEDDLE: What about your friend over there, the elegant-looking lady you walked up with?

HALL: That's Veena. She's a lawyer, so we have that confidentiality thing going.

WEDDLE: Is that right?

HALL: That's right.

WEDDLE: Okay, well . . . we don't know if this is a suicide or something else. A resident on the top floor tumbled off the balcony and landed in the alley.

HALL: Oh God.

WEDDLE: Yeah, it's a mess. And I mean that literally. The poor man who found her is having a real hard time of it.

HALL: Who is it?

WEDDLE: The man who found her?

HALL: No, the victim.

WEDDLE: I don't know if I should tell you that. Even off the record—you understand.

HALL: Of course, Steph, I totally get it. But the thing is, we were headed over here, to this building, to visit a friend of Veena's. She wasn't feeling too good, and we were worried about her.

WEDDLE: I don't know, Janie. I'd better ask someone . . .

HALL: Just give me a first name so my heart stops racing. Please?

WEDDLE: Damn it, Janie. (*Lengthy pause*) Okay, her first name is Rosalind. But the building super says everyone calls her Roz. Please tell me that's not your friend's friend.

HALL: Thank you, Steph. I really appreciate it. You've just put my mind at ease.

CHAPTER 80

"IT'S HER."

"Uh-huh," Veena said, staring off into the distance.

Janie Hall blinked. "Did you hear me, V.? It's *her*. Roz Cline. I just got confirmation from my cop friend. They found her body on the sidewalk. I pretended I didn't know her to get information from Steph, but it's looking like—"

"I already knew it was Roz."

"—she either jumped or was...wait, how did you know it was Roz?"

Veena wasn't looking at Janie. She was focused on the alley next to the building. Janie followed her gaze and saw burly guys in suits stepping out of the side entrance. She recognized most of them from her police-beat days. They were homicide.

Veena said, "I knew because of him."

Among the murder cops: Mickey Bernstein. He seemed to be running the show, instructing his colleagues on the next moves.

"This freakin' guy is everywhere," Janie murmured.

"And he shouldn't be anywhere near this."

"Why's that?"

"Because he's currently my number one suspect in the murder

of Archie Hughes. And who was our most promising lead? The woman who was just shoved from her balcony."

"We don't know for sure that's what happened, V."

"She sounded like she was in love, not suicidal. Either way, Bernstein is the last person who should be investigating Roz Cline's murder, because he's probably the one who did it."

"Come on, V. I know he's a scumbag, but that's a huge line to cross."

The two of them took in the bustling crime scene together. Janie tried to absorb the details like a newspaper reporter. That meant looking for the *telling* details—the small things that would bring this scene to life for a reader later. The body language of the police (upset, blasé, confused). The behavior of the lookie-loos gathered on the sidewalk (rowdy, sad, suspicious).

And, of course, anything striking about the murder victim herself—anything to bring her to life for a few more seconds. Janie was no longer a reporter, but she still found the technique useful, especially when Veena asked for her take. And her boss *always* asked.

Veena Lion, however, took in crime scenes in a different way. Instead of using her eyes and ears like recording devices, she analyzed the scene like it was a life-size board game. Who were the key players? What did this recent move mean strategically? Who had been in the best position to make that move?

And sometimes, Veena just stepped right onto the game board and started playing along.

CHAPTER 81

Transcript of conversation between Veena Lion and Detective Michael Bernstein, captured using an ambient recording app on her phone

VEENA LION: Detective Bernstein! You got a minute?
MICHAEL BERNSTEIN: Not really, Veena.
LION: Fine. You don't want to talk to me, I'll find people who will.
BERNSTEIN: Hey! Wait up and listen to me for a sec. You're gonna want to stay away from this one. I'm not saying that as a threat. I'm saying it as your friend. Just be patient. You and the DA are going to get the outcome you want.
LION: All I want is the truth, Bernstein.
BERNSTEIN: Oh, you'll get the whole story. Don't worry.
LION: I'm not so sure. Are you going to tell your superior officers about the connection between this murder and the Archie Hughes murder?
BERNSTEIN: Who said this was a murder? And what does one have to do with the other?
LION: Thought as much. See you soon, Detective.
BERNSTEIN: What do you mean, soon?

* * *

Transcript of interview with James Papaleo, doorman at the Villas at Elfreth's Alley, conducted by Veena Lion and Janie Hall

VEENA LION: Excuse me, are you the employee who found the body?

JAMES PAPALEO: God, I wish I hadn't. You have no idea. There are some things you can never erase from your brain.

JANIE HALL: I'm so sorry, Mr. Papaleo. I know how hard this is. But we're just trying to figure out what happened here.

PAPALEO: Like I told the other cops, I just heard it. I didn't know what I was hearing, but it sounded like a ton of produce fell off the back of a truck, you know? A loud, wet . . . *cracking* sound.

LION: Did you know Roz Cline pretty well?

PAPALEO: Yeah, I did. Everybody did. She was the life of this place. Really nice girl, very popular. I don't understand this, I really don't.

HALL: When you say *popular,* what do you mean exactly? Did she entertain a lot of friends?

PAPALEO: Nah, not a lot. She wasn't a partyer like that. Really classy lady, real discreet. And the people she—what did you say, *entertained*? Well, they were classy people too.

LION: People like Archie Hughes?

PAPALEO: No offense, Detectives, but I think I should be discreet too. I mean, Archie obviously had nothing to do with what happened to poor Roz here.

LION: But Archie *did* visit often, right? Never mind, you don't have to answer that. I have all the sign-in logs from the management company.

PAPALEO: Don't know what good that'll do you.

HALL: What do you mean?

PAPALEO: People like Archie Hughes pay a visit, their names don't go into the sign-in logs. Too many crazy Eagles fans out there.

Somebody sees his name on the log one day, and before you know it, you've got a crowd camped outside. The poor guy didn't want to be bothered.

LION: Or caught.

PAPALEO: What was that?

LION: Never mind. I'm guessing their friend Maya Rain wouldn't be on the visitor logs either.

PAPALEO: I don't know any Maya Rain. Who's that?

HALL: What about Roz's other friend . . . ah, sorry, I'm blanking here. What's her name . . . (*Snaps fingers*) Super-pretty, in her twenties . . .

PAPALEO: You probably mean Vanessa. Yeah, she and Roz were really close. Really sweet ladies . . . oh no. You're asking because you have to break the bad news to Vanessa, right?

LION: I have a feeling she already knows.

CHAPTER 82

Transcript of encrypted message exchange between Cooper Lamb and Veena Lion

VEENA LION: What's the latest?

COOPER LAMB: Oh, nothing, just a leisurely day avoiding the police, sparring with a nanny, and trying to wrestle information out of an obese multimillionaire. Right now I'm waiting for the young ones to finish their pricey Quaker education for the day so I can feed them sugar and regale them with tales of violence before dropping them off at their mother's place.

LION: Roz Cline is dead.

LAMB: You've gotta be s████ me! Okay, you have me beat. What happened . . . oh, wait. Was Roz the Old City jumper? It's all over KYW.

LION: I'm down here right now. Guess who else is here?

LAMB: Bernstein.

LION: Yep.

LAMB: Thank God.

LION: ?

LAMB: If he's there, that means he's not stalking me and looking for an opportunity to have me arrested or shot.

LION: ??????

LAMB: Long story. But wait, why is he there?

LION: We have a dead NFL superstar, a dead celebrity chef, and a dead Atlantic City hostess. The first two are murders, and I'm pretty sure the third is one too.

LAMB: And Mickey Bernstein just happens to be there in record time for every killing. You should ask him why that is.

LION: Tried that already. He told me I should steer clear of this for my own good. He said he was telling me because we're old friends.

LAMB: I didn't know you two were close.

LION: I didn't either. I'd be tempted to ask him out if it weren't for that triple-homicide thing.

LAMB: Seriously? You think Bernstein killed all three of them? I mean, Mickey had a head start on Archie's murder, but I don't think he pulled the trigger himself. Victor tracked his movements.

LION: Even detectives have partners.

LAMB: So now it's a conspiracy?

LION: It already was, by definition.

LAMB: Touché. But we have nothing solid tying Mickey to any of these killings. If anyone has a reason to show up at a murder scene, it's a freakin' murder cop.

LION: So you think Bernstein is innocent?

LAMB: Hell no. He practically has a neon GUILTY sign over his head. But we need to prove it.

LION: Two potential witnesses have been killed. Who else is left to squeeze?

LAMB: We make the rounds again. And this time, we squeeze harder.

SATURDAY, JANUARY 29

CHAPTER 83

CONFIDENTIAL DOCUMENT FROM JANIE HALL TO VEENA LION, FOUND ON AN ENCRYPTED SERVER

Okay, V., consider this file extremely private and incredibly confidential. This is why I'm not texting you this information. If you have a place where you keep supersecret information—stuff so secret you don't even tell me about it—put the contents of this entire folder in there. RIGHT NOW.

This is because I'm about to admit to a crime.

First, my justification for the crime, then the crime itself.

I went home yesterday thinking a lot about Roz Cline. The woman who was about to become my new best friend. Her sudden death . . . her murder . . . hit home in a way I wasn't expecting. I didn't want it to be for nothing. She deserves better than that.

But the truth is, she's just a bit player in the murder of the century. And the people on the other side—whoever they may be—aren't playing fair. So why should we? This, then, is the motive for my crime. (Crimes, actually.)

Now to the means and opportunity for said crime(s).

I know you like to tease me about my tortured dating life. And it is tortured. But it used to be tortured with a purpose. Since I'm in a confessing mood, and since this document will never see the light of day (right, V.?), I'll admit that when I was a tabloid reporter, I preferred to date useful individuals.

"Useful" meaning in a lowly position yet connected to the halls of power. (It didn't hurt if they were a little hot too.)

A few years ago, before I came to work for you, one of my useful dates was a guy named Prentiss Walsh. A bit of a smacked ass, to be honest, but ambitious. He'll probably be mayor someday. And he just so happens to be the executive assistant of Charles Castrina, divorce attorney to the Philadelphia stars.

Well, last night I called Prentiss. He was very happy to hear from me. He suggested I go to his place. I told him I was a little tipsy and happened to be at a bar right around the corner from his office. He told me he'd be right over. I told him I'd have another drink while I waited. He told me to have two. I had nothing stronger than a club soda with lime.

Well, hellos led to flirtations, which led to more drinks (whiskey for him; club soda masquerading as gin and tonic for me), which led to my bold suggestion that we raid his boss's high-end liquor cabinet. I mean, it was just around the corner, and I knew Prentiss had the pass card and keys...

I know what you're going to say, and believe me, I already said those things to myself. But remember what I told you about the other side not playing fair?

Anyway, this wasn't a long shot; I know a few things about Prentiss. For one, he has a larcenous streak, so the idea of getting hammered on Chuck Castrina's expensive scotch while possibly making out with a former reporter on Castrina's ten-thousand-dollar Chesterfield leather sofa...well, this would be too great a temptation to resist. And the other thing about Prentiss? He's pretty much a lightweight. We made it to the sofa . . . and that was it before he passed out.

I helped myself to the file cabinet. The keys were on Prentiss's ring.

I found Francine Hughes's file.

And V., let me tell you, I wish I'd had a few drinks before opening that folder of horrors.

I scanned everything and dropped it into this folder. Take a look for yourself. Just be warned—it is entirely awful.

CHAPTER 84

REPORT TO C. LAMB BY V. SUAREZ

SATURDAY, JANUARY 29

(SENT WITH ENCRYPTION AND RED-FLAGGED, WITH DELIVERY CONFIRMATION)

Some quick but extremely vital updates. Please read carefully, boss. I'm going to call you after I end this to follow up.

And I know you're going to ask me about sources, and I'll share what I can with you at a later date if you really need to know. But in the past, you've expressed strong disinterest in all of my "dark-web geek stuff," as you call it. So it's up to you. Just know that this information comes with the usual caveats.

I have a very solid lead on Roz Cline's killer. Yes, killer. Her death was no accident; this was a one-hundred-percent professional hit.

What's interesting is who they hired. The job didn't go to local muscle—and that upset the local muscle a great deal. Instead, the job went to an upper-echelon gunman who works out of both Vegas and Atlantic City. Expensive as they come, and absolutely bold and brazen. My sense is that he's the guy you bring in when you have champagne problems. The local muscle grumbled about it, but it's clear they're afraid of him, so they didn't grumble too loud.

Why bring in a hitter this expensive for a casino hostess like Roz Cline? It stands to reason she must have had some expensive information about Archie Hughes in her head.

I'm still working on identifying this hit man. Even an alias will help me track him, although I doubt he's still on the East Coast.

I'm also searching for who hired him, though the clients in these situations are always very well shielded (as you can imagine). But even if I can't find the client's identity, knowing what channels he or she used will be helpful. There are only so many ways you can find a killer for hire, and the method of communication will tell me a great deal about the client.

More updates as I learn them.

But I can't stress this enough: Watch your back out there. You know me, boss. Very little frightens me. Well, I am very frightened by the types of people who are involved in this investigation.

Keep your head low. You know your tendency to take a wild leap, maybe piss off the wrong person? Yeah, don't do that. At least not until you hear from me again.

CHAPTER 85

6:03 p.m.

VEENA LION found herself sitting across from Cooper Lamb in his backyard (although *backyard* was a stretch for the concrete slab behind his brownstone), both of them on rickety beach chairs, knees touching, passing a cold bottle of Yuengling Lager back and forth. There were four more holstered in the cardboard carrier at their feet. The beer would stay perfectly cold. The sun had set, and outside felt like the inside of an industrial freezer.

"Can't we take these to your kitchen table?" Veena asked.

"I don't spend nearly enough time in my backyard," Cooper said. "I thought it was one of the selling points of this place."

"This is a glorified alley, my friend."

"Yeah, but it's *my* alley; no one else has access but me. I was thinking this spring I could put a grill out here, maybe hang a few twinkle lights. You think the kids would like that?"

"I think this alley is so narrow, the kids will have to watch from inside as you flip burgers."

"The other selling point?" Cooper continued as if Veena hadn't spoken. "No one would think to plant a bug out here."

Veena's eyes narrowed. "You think somebody wired your place?"

"I have to assume so, yes. Yours too."

"It doesn't matter," Veena said. "I won't need words to explain what I've found." She removed the folder from her briefcase and handed it to Cooper, who in turn handed her the Yuengling. Veena finished the bottle, slid the empty into a slot, and removed another beer from the cardboard carrier.

Cooper quickly read Janie's memo, then flipped to the next page. It was a printout of a photograph, just like every other item in this folder.

Cooper was puzzled. He flipped to the next. And the next. And the next, and soon, the images fell together into a complete picture. Just as they had for Veena.

Cooper looked up and locked eyes with her. His eyes were wet. Veena passed the beer over to Cooper. He nodded his thanks, drained half of it, passed the bottle back, and continued flipping pages.

Veena pulled out her phone and did a quick search for *Francine Pearl Hughes* and *Kennedy Center*. The video was the first to appear in the search. It was a concert from last summer, with the president and his wife in the audience. Critics ranked her iconic performance as right up there with greats like Aretha Franklin, Beyoncé, Patti LaBelle, and Pink.

Veena pointed at Francine's arms on the screen.

"Yeah, it's a nice dress," Cooper said.

"But look at the style. That dress? On a hot summer evening?"

Cooper squinted, then slowly understood. "He hit her only where clothes would hide the bruises." He said it softly, not because he was afraid of being overheard, but because he was still reeling from what he'd seen in the folder.

The abusive texts were bad enough. But the violence inflicted on Francine's body earned her abuser a special place in hell.

The bruises somehow looked raw and tender, even though he was seeing them in two-dimensional, black-and-white images. He felt as if touching the photo would make the subject flinch.

Big powerful hands inflicted that damage. You could make out the dark purple finger marks from where he'd grabbed her and decided to make her suffer.

The folder was stuffed with similar images from all over Francine's body—where no one else would see.

No one except Archie.

"Keep flipping," Veena said.

"I don't know if I can."

"You have to."

"What am I going to see?"

"Just keep flipping."

Cooper continued flipping, and soon the images changed. Were these bruises shot at a different angle? It looked like Francine Pearl Hughes had somehow shrunk, as if the savage beatings had diminished her, made her a frail shadow of herself.

But the photos weren't of Francine. Once Cooper understood, he felt an atom bomb explode in his chest.

"He hit the kids too."

SUNDAY, JANUARY 30

CHAPTER 86

2:57 p.m.

"I CAN'T believe we're actually doing this!" said Cooper Lamb Jr.

"Me too," replied his father, although without quite the same level of enthusiasm.

That they were attending the NFC championship game wasn't the surprise. Harold Sable had honored his promise; a cream-colored envelope with the team logo had been waiting for *Mr. Cooper Lamb and Family* at the will-call window. But there were no tickets inside.

Instead, Cooper had pulled out a handwritten note instructing him to take the enclosed green plastic card to a particular luxury box and swipe it through the reader. Cooper led his children to the elevators per the instructions.

Cooper was reasonably sure that Harold Sable wasn't the one who'd written *XOXO* at the bottom of the note.

"Isn't this just a wee bit unethical?" asked Ariel Lamb as the elevator doors closed. "I mean, taking championship-game seats from someone who might be implicated in a murder?"

"Accepting seats may be a little unethical," Cooper replied. "But it's not as if we're hanging out with the owners in their luxury box or anything."

"Dad," Cooper Jr. said. "These are the elevators to the luxury boxes."

Cooper turned to his children and winked.

One swipe of the card led them into Glenn Sable's lair, which was directly next to his father's (bigger) box. The reactions from those gathered inside told Cooper everything he needed to know. A look of shock—perhaps even fear—flickered on Glenn Sable's face before he covered it up with a scowl.

The Hughes children were there, and they squealed with delight the moment they saw Cooper, thinking he had Lupe with him. Alas, he had left his constant companion with his ex-wife; a stadium full of screaming fans wasn't the ideal place for the pup. After hearing that, the Hughes kids waved shy hellos and turned their attention back to the pregame festivities taking place on the field.

But Maya Rain was there, and she wore a warm, knowing smile as she locked eyes with Cooper. Of course she was the one who had arranged this.

"Thank you," Cooper told her.

"For what?" she replied.

"X-O-X-O?"

"Mea culpa," she said, smiling. "I like you, Cooper. I couldn't have you and your family sitting out there in the cold. What good is a personal connection to the team if you can't exploit it every once in a while?"

"Well, I appreciate it. So do my children."

"They are very welcome. Your wife couldn't join us?"

Cooper smirked. "I'm divorced. But I think you knew that."

"How would I know that?"

Cooper had a half dozen responses to that question: *Because you're super-observant, and I'm not wearing a ring. Because we've been walking a flirtatious line for days and never once did you bring up other partners. Although you don't seem to have a problem with married men.* But he let it go. "Speaking of personal connections, where's Francine?"

"She wasn't feeling up to this today," Maya said. "And I don't think anyone could blame her. But the kids wanted to see the game, so I agreed to take them."

"Another tough day at the office, huh?"

Maya leaned in close, as if she were about to reveal something dark and personal. She touched the top of Cooper's hand; her fingertips were cold. "I'm not exactly a sports fan," she whispered.

Cooper, pretending to be scandalized by this confession, held his hand to his mouth. He saw Glenn Sable throwing eye-daggers his way. Apparently this particular private eye was most unwelcome in Glenn's luxury box.

Not that his children noticed. They were too busy joining the Hughes children in a raid on Glenn's Eagles-themed dessert bar. There was plenty of Stock's pound cake with green frosting, Termini Brothers cookies in the shape of the team logo, and ice-filled coolers holding tubs of Breyers mint chocolate chip.

"I don't think the little big man likes that we're speaking," Cooper said.

"Little big man doesn't like a lot of things."

"Such as?"

"Let's just say that Francine isn't here right now with her children because she's not exactly welcome."

"Glenn has a problem with Philadelphia's sweetheart?"

Cooper was suddenly aware of the lack of space between them. Good thing his children were laser-focused on the overflowing buffet of sugar.

"The Sables thought Francine was bad for Archie's career. That she distracted him from his commitment to the team. Pulled him closer to show business instead of the game."

"God forbid Archie make someone *else* money," Cooper muttered.

"I guess they wanted to squeeze every dime out of their investment before he retired."

"It's not just that," Maya said. "The Sables even tried to block Francine's halftime performance at this year's Super Bowl."

Cooper couldn't help himself—he threw Glenn Sable some eye-daggers of his own.

CHAPTER 87

TAKE AWAY the shocking murder. Take away the unprecedented weeklong delay. Take away all of the naysayers who said the Eagles wouldn't go any further without Archie Hughes's almost supernatural touchdown passes.

If you had been dropped down into a stadium seat and told absolutely *nothing* about this game, you'd still quickly realize you were watching the greatest nail-biter of all time. Despite everyone believing that the Giants would humiliate the Birds, the Eagles stood firm. New quarterback Terry Mortelite held his own, working well with receiver Lee McCoy. By halftime, the Eagles were down by only three points.

Ordinarily, Cooper Lamb would have enjoyed such an exciting nail-biter. But his focus stayed on the occupants of the luxury box, most of whom were cheering and shouting and absolutely giddy with the thrill of possible victory. Even those who weren't jacked up on sweets had delighted expressions on their faces; they all looked like they'd been handed a surprise gift from the football gods.

All except one person—the man who should have been the happiest. Instead of celebrating along with the rest of the box, Glenn Sable looked like someone had urinated all over his fancy dessert table.

Cooper decided to wander over to Glenn for a mood check. And maybe get some long-overdue answers.

"Jimmy Tua is an absolute madman on the field," Cooper told the younger Sable. "I can't believe what I'm seeing. You must be turning cartwheels."

"Game's not over yet," Glenn grumbled. He refused to look Cooper in the eye.

"Ah. You're being cautious. I can respect that."

"That ain't it, Lamb. Archie should be down there right now. None of this feels right without him."

"Your players are honoring him the best way they can. They're clawing their way back."

"Yeah, yeah."

"Though I'm not sure Archie deserves it."

That got Glenn's attention. He didn't seem able to process what he'd just heard. Was it a joke or an insult or something else? Cooper let the little big man sort through his very big feelings for a moment before leaning in close.

"I saw what that monster did to his wife and children," Cooper snarled. "And you're a monster for protecting him."

"You think you can go around saying whatever you want," Glenn said quietly. "But that's not the way the world works."

"I want no part of a world where cruelty to children is not only accepted but rewarded."

"Speaking of, why don't you take your kids and leave."

"What, did they finish your favorite ice cream?"

Glenn could no longer keep his voice quiet or calm. "You want me to call security? Let Cooper Junior see Daddy get his ass royally kicked?"

Maya Rain appeared between them with the stealth of a boxing referee. "I'll take the kids down to your car, Cooper."

"Ha, look at that!" cried Glenn with fake delight. "You need a nanny to bail you out. Yeah, real tough guy. You're as soft as your last name!"

"I am soft, you're right," Cooper said with a smile. "Ordinarily if someone said that, I'd threaten to break his bones, but I'm too lazy to wade through all that fat."

Maya slowly closed her eyes. "Oh, boy." She opened her eyes and placed a hand on Cooper's chest. "We should go."

"What did you say to me?" Glenn said, as if he were preparing to fight Cooper.

"You can't bury the truth forever," Cooper said. "That's not the way the world works."

CHAPTER 88

Transcript of conversation between Cooper Lamb and Maya Rain, captured using a recording app on Lamb's smartwatch

COOPER LAMB: Thanks for being the cooler head up there.
MAYA RAIN: All part of the job. Cleaning up messes—
LAMB: Is what you do, right?
RAIN: Something like that.
COOPER LAMB JR.: Dad, can we turn on the radio so we can at least *hear* the second half of the game?
LAMB: What? Oh, right. Hand these keys to your sister and turn on the power. Do *not* turn on the engine, you got it?
COOPER JR.: Got it.
RAIN: Smart idea. Because we need to talk.
LAMB: Well, there isn't a pool house handy, so I had to improvise.
(*Ambient sounds of power windows being raised, and a muffled sports broadcast behind the recorded voices.*)
RAIN: I can't believe what you said to Glenn.
LAMB: I'm tired of everyone lying. Did you know what that monster did to Francine and the kids?
RAIN: I didn't know . . . everything. Not until after, when it was too late to do anything about it.

LAMB: Sounds like Archie deserved some cosmic payback. Part of me is glad he's dead.

RAIN: Don't say that.

LAMB: That's not going to stop me from finding out who killed him. The Sables know a lot more than they're saying.

RAIN: Sure, but I thought you would have been a *little* more professional. Especially considering you were a guest.

LAMB: To steal your favorite line: It's all part of the job. It's what *I* do.

RAIN: What *are* you trying to do, Cooper?

LAMB: Some people don't tell the truth until you push them out of their comfort zone, make them a little miserable. But I'm sure you knew that, otherwise you wouldn't have invited me into Sable's luxury box.

RAIN: No good deed goes unpunished.

LAMB: Is that why you were surveilling Roz Cline? You were trying to do a good deed?

RAIN: Who told you about . . . never mind, it doesn't matter.

LAMB: We'd save each other a lot of time if we were honest. I don't know how you fit into all of this, and I can't tell if you're trying to help me or throw me hopelessly off track.

RAIN: You think way too much of me.

LAMB: Here's some honesty: I think about you a lot.

RAIN: (*Pause*) Cooper . . . we can't do this.

LAMB: Because you're with Mickey Bernstein? How did you even meet him?

RAIN: I should get back to the kids.

LAMB: Give me one more minute. Tell me why you were watching Roz Cline. You know she's dead, right? Pushed right off her penthouse balcony in the middle of the afternoon.

RAIN: I know, Cooper.

LAMB: Of course you know. Bernstein is investigating that murder too, even though he should be a million f███ miles from all of these cases.

RAIN: I don't ask Mickey about his business, and he doesn't ask about mine. How we met doesn't matter, but it has nothing to do with Archie's murder.

LAMB: So why keep tabs on Roz Cline?

RAIN: I did it for Francine. I know this may not make sense to you, but she's become my dearest friend. I was hired to care for her children, but I came to care for her too. That's the way it happens sometimes. And the thought of anyone hurting her... I just couldn't let that happen.

LAMB: How could Roz hurt Francine?

RAIN: Cooper, my friend, I think you know exactly how.

LAMB: None of this makes sense. You know that, right? Help me out here.

RAIN: That's what I've been doing, whether you believe me or not. Kids' messes aren't the only messes I clean up.

LAMB: Who's looking out for you?

RAIN: That's sweet. And I truly mean it. So few people look out for each other these days. Especially in this city.

LAMB: So let me protect you.

RAIN: Go listen to the rest of the game with your kids. I think the Birds are going to give people a big surprise.

LAMB: Says the non–sports fan.

RAIN: Call me an optimist.

CHAPTER 89

"WOW, DAD, game of the century and we're sitting in your car," Ariel said. "Can't wait to tell my grandkids someday about the epic championship game I *almost* saw."

"Ingrate. Up until an hour ago, you were feasting on sugary sweets in one of the owners' boxes! Tell your grandkids about *that*."

"This is so lame."

"Shhh, quiet for a second."

Cooper didn't want to care about the Eagles or the game or anything else that wasn't related to the three murders he was investigating. But he couldn't help it; the game *was* one for the record books. It was a nail-biter right up to the very end, when the new quarterback managed some kind of insane Hail Mary pass (and oh, did Cooper regret not being able to see it) and, with just *seconds* to go... clinched the Eagles' victory.

"Dad."

"Wow, wow, wow," Cooper said, stunned.

"Dad," Ariel said. "I can't believe we missed that!"

His daughter was right. He should have waited to squeeze Glenn Sable until after the game was over. Maybe that would have revealed another piece of the puzzle, because one thing was clear: Glenn Sable had not been happy about the prospect of an Eagles victory.

Did he have Archie murdered to ensure the team's loss? And if so, why? A winning team was far more profitable than a runner-up. None of this made sense.

"Well," Cooper said, "at least there's the Super Bowl to look forward to."

"Where are we going to watch that?" Cooper Jr. asked. "In a dumpster behind the stadium?"

"Keep joking, kid," Cooper replied. "Wiseasses don't go to Chickie's and Pete's for a celebratory dinner."

"We'll never get a table there. Not on a day like this."

"You're lucky to have a father who knows a guy who knows a guy. There's a table waiting for us."

"Don't drink too much beer when we're there," Ariel said. "Mom doesn't like it when you drink too much beer, then drive us home."

"I promise I will drink an entirely appropriate amount of beer," Cooper assured his daughter. "Now, let's beat the crowd and feast on some Crabfries."

CHAPTER 90

REPORT TO C. LAMB BY V. SUAREZ

SUNDAY, JANUARY 30

(SENT WITH ENCRYPTION AND RED-FLAGGED, WITH DELIVERY CONFIRMATION)

Here's what I've been able to learn about this hired killer.

He has no real name (or aliases) that I can pin to a driver's license or passport. But he has two nicknames: "the Quiet One" and "Tesla." The names are a nod to this hit man's silence and speed. If you want a hit done fast and clean with zero traces, you pay extra for the Quiet One.

No law enforcement agency, domestic or foreign, has been able to gather more than scraps about the Quiet One. (I know; I looked.) The FBI won't even acknowledge he exists, attributing his work to various other people. As if it would be bad form to admit total defeat.

But for the Archie Hughes and Roz Cline killings, the Quiet One seems to fit. There was zero forensic evidence left behind; no cameras caught the murder; and the killer eluded the authorities despite police officers being on the scene almost immediately.

The missing Super Bowl ring is the only part of this that feels off. The Quiet One would not bother with such a souvenir—unless his client had insisted on it. That said, it still feels out of character.

Under my own alias, I tried to reach out to arrange some kind of meeting with the Quiet One or one of his associates. I was pretty much laughed out of the dark web. The kind of people who can afford to hire the Quiet One are way above my pay grade...or even one that I can reasonably fake. Every overture I made was quickly shut down.

And I'll be honest: I'm worried about trying again, because I'd rather not catch the Quiet One's attention. You treat me fair, boss, but I don't want to die for this job.

This should tell you a lot about who might have hired the Quiet One to kill Archie Hughes. These are not ordinary wealthy people. They look down on new-money types like the Sables. We're talking about the highest echelon of the wealthy, individuals who reshape the world as they like. You have to ask yourself, why would these people want Archie dead?

Hope you and the kids had fun at the game. I'll admit to being incredibly jealous that you were able to witness firsthand the Hail Mary pass they'll be talking about for decades to come.

I'll send more as I learn it.

Oh, one more thing—this just came in. It's about Maya Rain. See the document attached to this message.

CHAPTER 91

9:48 p.m.

COOPER DRANK more than an appropriate amount of beer.

Not with the children, of course. He had his two standard bottles of Yuengling Lager and enough crab fries to soak up every last ounce of that beer. The mood at Chickie's and Pete's was festive, and of course Cooper loved celebrating with his kids. But he was very distracted.

One distraction was Victor's most recent report, which was even more alarming than the first. The Quiet One, huh? Why were they working so hard to find a killer who could disappear without a trace, eluding the FBI, Interpol, you name it? How could two private eyes from Philly possibly hope to find him?

But that was academic for now. The second, and bigger, distraction was Maya Rain. Cooper couldn't help but think he'd missed an opportunity back at the Linc. Maybe there was something he could have said to unlock her mental vault. Cooper liked her a lot but didn't trust her; maybe she felt the same way about him. Behind the flirtation, they were both cautious, professional people.

Maybe he should try again, convince her that he was worth her trust.

While settling the tab at Chickie's, Cooper bought a six-pack of Yuengling and stashed it in the trunk of his car. After dropping off his children—and once again hearing the story of how Dad had ruined the championship game for them—Cooper drove across Center City to Eighteenth Street. As it was Sunday, there were parking spots available. He parked in essentially the same spot he had a few days ago and nursed his beer while waiting for Maya to return home. Although maybe she had plans with Mickey Bernstein.

At the tail end of Cooper's fourth lager, Bernstein dropped Maya off. They kissed goodbye. Maya went upstairs.

Cooper was nowhere numb enough. It still hurt.

He thought about drinking the fifth and sixth beers. Instead, he went into Maya's building. The two lagers were enough of a bribe for Curt the doorman—hell, the entire city was in a celebratory mood. Besides, Curt recognized Cooper. "Go on up. I'll let her know you're on the way."

While consuming beers one through four in the driver's seat of his car, Cooper had planned his speech—this was how he'd earn her trust and work his way into her heart. But when Maya opened the door, his brain refused to cooperate, so he said the first thing that came to mind, an item he'd just come across in Vincent's latest file: "You own a Glock forty-four."

"Good to see you again too, Cooper. Do you want to come in?"

So much for trust. Well, in for a dime, in for a dollar. "That's the same model that killed Archie Hughes."

Maya closed the door behind him. "You think I killed my own employer?"

"No," Cooper said. "I'm just following the evidence. Did anyone have access to your gun besides you?"

"Before I start talking about my personal firearms—which, by the way, are perfectly normal in West Virginia—can I offer you something to drink?"

"I've had enough to drink," Cooper said. "Schuylkill punch will be fine."

"I don't know how to make that cocktail."

"Just turn on the tap."

Where was he going with this? Cooper didn't know, but the document that Victor had sent while Cooper and the kids were at Chickie's and Pete's clearly showed a Glock .44 registered to Maya Rain at this address. Recent permit too; Victor said it had been pushed through the system in record time. Why would a nanny suddenly need to pack heat?

When Maya returned from the kitchen, she was holding a gun.

CHAPTER 92

"I'M NO expert," Cooper said, "but I'm fairly sure that's not a glass of water."

"I'll get that in a minute," Maya said.

"Would that be *after* you kill me?"

There was one of those horrible, elongated moments—a second or two in actual time that feels like an eternity when you experience it. Both of their lives could hinge on what happened next.

"You really do think the worst of me," she replied, breaking the tension. "No, I brought this out to show you my high-school graduation present from my father. Very ladylike, isn't it?"

Maya snapped open the wheel of the small pearl-handled revolver and showed him the empty chambers. She moved with the grace of a person who had grown up with guns. Cooper was simply relieved he wouldn't be forced to pull his own piece and engage in a gun battle with the most beautiful woman he'd ever met.

"Adorable," Cooper said. "But that's not the gun I was talking about."

"But this is my point," Maya said. "I don't know how you learned about the Glock, but that was a gift from Detective Bernstein. I guess he thinks I'm just some rube from West Virginia, so I need to have some personal protection."

"Where is the Glock?"

"That's the weird thing—I don't know. Maybe he took it back when he realized I had my own gun and a permit to carry? I honestly hadn't thought about it until you mentioned it."

Cooper's mind spun with possible explanations, all of them sinister. Among the worst was the idea that Bernstein was trying to frame Maya, taking advantage of her kindness and her proximity to the murder victim. Could be that he wasn't dating Maya; he was merely getting close enough to tighten the noose around her slender neck.

"I know where the gun is," Cooper said. "It's booked into evidence."

Maya's face twisted with revulsion. "Are you saying *that* gun was used to kill Archie?"

"Possibly," Cooper said. "If we knew for sure, we'd be that much closer to finding his killer."

"I'll get that water now. And a drink for myself."

Cooper followed her into the kitchenette. She opened the tap to fill a tumbler, then turned around to find Cooper very close.

"There's no one else here," Cooper said. "It's just the two of us now. If you tell me what you know, I'll do everything in my power to protect you."

"I'm not the one who needs protecting."

"What do you mean by that?"

Maya sighed. "Archie had enemies on and off the field. You don't want to provoke them."

"What, you don't think I can handle myself?"

"Clearly that's what you think about me."

Cooper had to admit she had a point.

"Listen," he said. "All I'm saying is, if you let people like Bernstein and the Sables into your life, they're going to want something in return. They always do. Maybe it's something as simple as sex. But sometimes it's more. A lot more. I don't want you getting hurt."

Maya smiled. "Look, I have my eyes open. Mickey is just... we're having fun. We both know what this is. And the Sables, yeah, they're sleazebags, but they're mostly full of bluster. They're harmless. I've had to deal with guys like them all my life. I know how to handle them."

"The same words have been spoken by every victim," Cooper said, "right before she realizes she *can't* handle them."

"Do I look like a victim to you?"

Maya Rain filled the tumbler with water and gave it to him. And in that instant, Cooper saw her mask slip a little. He saw a fierceness in her eyes, and it caught him by surprise. Maybe it was anger, maybe it was lust, maybe it was something else. Cooper could have responded with another question. Or a kiss...

But his instincts told him to go in the opposite direction. So he dumped the water into the sink, walked out of the apartment, took the elevator down, and left the building.

CHAPTER 93

THE WALL exploded just to the left of Cooper Lamb's face. Hot fragments stung his cheeks as he dived to the sidewalk. Without even thinking, he pulled his Browning from his underarm holster and returned fire.

The shots came from the service driveway next to Maya's building. The same driveway where Bernstein had picked her up the other day.

That you, Mickey? You jealous bastard.

Cooper kept firing at the shadows as he ran, hoping his would-be killer would seek cover and allow Cooper to reach his car on Eighteenth Street. And Cooper almost did. But the assassin was quick and clearly unafraid. Return fire chewed up the asphalt under Cooper's feet. He was already moving fast, but he dug deep and found the fuel to move faster. Cooper's wartime responses kicked in—he made it to the other side of his car without being hit. Bullets shattered the window over his head. Beads of glass rained down into his hair. This assassin meant it.

Yeah, but so did Cooper.

He reloaded quickly and returned fire over the hood of his car. Six shots, all aimed at the killer's center of gravity—based on his best guess of where that was, of course. The killer was still hidden in the shadows. But Cooper had had plenty of experience in the army firing into the shadows at people who wanted him to die.

Cooper crouched down and listened closely. Total silence except for the far-off wail of a siren. Gunfire in this part of Philadelphia was rare; someone had called it in.

Either he'd hit the gunman or the gunman had fled the scene.

That meant that with every second, the shooter—and potential witness—was either slipping farther into the afterlife or putting more distance between himself and Cooper.

Do you think you hit him, Cooper? There was a third possibility: the shooter was waiting for him to stick his head up so he could blow it away.

Nobody lives forever, Cooper told himself. He darted out from behind the car and ran toward the service driveway. At the other end, he spied a vague form running away, pumping his arms and legs and moving with preternatural speed.

Damn it.

CHAPTER 94

COOPER REMEMBERED exactly where the service driveway led: to a side street that took you to either Sansom Street or Walnut Street, depending on which way you turned. As he approached the driveway's end, he flipped a mental coin, then hung a right toward Sansom.

It was the correct move. Cooper caught sight of the shooter as he raced to the left, headed west down Sansom.

Whoever this guy was, he had the speed of an Olympic sprinter. Cooper was surprisingly fast too, especially given his height. But he had to ignore the pounding of his heart and the screaming of his muscles to keep pace with the shooter.

Cooper hoped this guy would hop into a car at some point so he'd have a legitimate reason to give up the pursuit. But no. The shooter continued to run. So, what, had he taken public transportation to the hit?

By the time the shooter reached Twenty-Second and Market, Cooper realized that he might have done just that. The guy was headed down a set of concrete stairs to the underground trolley line.

Cooper skidded to a halt just before the stairs. Could be a trap. Shooter could be waiting at the bottom for Cooper's silhouette to appear, and then *blam-blam-blam*—slaughtered Lamb.

He waited. The seconds piled up again. Cooper hated this. The shooter was probably catching a trolley right now.

Except...wasn't it too late for that? These lines ground to a halt around eleven p.m. Most likely, the shooter was down there waiting for him.

Screw it.

Cooper crouched and peered down the stairs, Browning in his hands. Fluorescent lights flickered on the grime and litter. There was no shooter.

He bounded down the stairs, ready for an ambush. *Where are you?* He listened carefully.

The tiled walls of the station echoed with a peculiar sound. Something slapping. It was faint, but it was fast and consistent in its rhythm. Cooper turned the corner and saw that he was right, the station was closed. But there was enough room above a security gate for someone very determined to scale it and jump down to the other side.

Down to the tracks. And that's when Cooper understood the slapping sound. They were footsteps.

The shooter was escaping through the trolley tunnel.

CHAPTER 95

THIS WAS probably one of the worst ideas in the long, troubled history of bad ideas. Cooper knew this. But he scaled the gate anyway.

The army had prepared him for these kinds of insane activities. Climbing tall barriers. Hunting prey in the dark. Running until you thought your heart and lungs would burst in your rib cage.

But none of those activities usually took place in a cold urban environment like this one: a freezing, grimy commuter tunnel that plowed under the Schuylkill River.

Yep. A seriously bad idea, for sure.

But Cooper knew he couldn't turn around and make the loser's march back to his car on Eighteenth Street. When someone tries to blow your brains out, you don't just turn the other cheek so he can take another shot. Cooper needed to find this bastard and make him explain.

So into the tunnel he went, pumping his legs as fast as he could.

The terrain was dark and treacherous. He had to avoid the rails and trash and vermin (yeah, he could hear them complain and squeak) while still matching the speed of the shooter, who was barely visible at the far end of the tunnel. Why did he have to be so fast? Why couldn't they have dispatched a weight-challenged hit man, some dude named Mel or Irv who could be caught easily?

Cooper couldn't help thinking about what Victor had told him about the Atlantic City hit man, aka Tesla or the Quiet One. The assassin notorious for speed (check) and stealth (check). Is that who Cooper was chasing through this damn tunnel?

On top of all that, Cooper idly wondered (as he ran, ran, ran) how wide the Schuylkill River was, how long this tunnel went on. Did the Quiet One have an end point in mind? Or did he think there was no way Cooper would be stupid enough to pursue him down here?

Sorry, Tesla, Cooper thought. *I am that stupid.*

The tunnel seemed to go on forever. Cooper wouldn't have been surprised to see signs for Pittsburgh. But he turned a bend, and the dim glow of the next station appeared in the distance. Thirty-Third Street, right in the heart of the University of Pennsylvania's campus. Maybe the Quiet One was returning to his dorm in the quad.

The sharp crack of a push bar on a metal gate told Cooper that his quarry was headed to the surface.

Ignore your pounding heart. Ignore your burning lungs. Get up there, Cooper. Go bag yourself a hit man.

When he reached the street, he saw a surprising number of students around. Probably coming home after a long night of post-Eagles-win revelry. Cooper scanned the slowly moving bodies for the one body who looked out of place. *Come on, Quiet One, show yourself…*

"It's a cop!" someone cried.

Cooper spun around to find the tipsy student was talking about *him*.

"You don't belong here!" the doughy-faced kid in John Lennon glasses shouted. "Get off our campus, pig!"

"Did you see a slender man with a gun run through here?"

Cooper asked him and his friends. But they either didn't hear him or didn't care to answer. They closed ranks around Cooper, feeling emboldened by the lager or cider or shots in their systems.

"Defund the police!"

"'I can't breathe!'"

"Blue lives suck!"

Cooper tried to ignore them as he looked around for any trace of the Quiet One. If the shooter was smart—and clearly he was—he would have slowed down and blended into the crowd. But Cooper would recognize him. Not that he had a description, but he'd spent the past twenty minutes watching the shooter *move*. He was pretty sure he could identify him by body language.

The students, however, were determined to give him as much grief as possible. They blocked his attempts to look around them and continued shouting slogans at him.

"All cops are bastards!"

"Defund the po-po!"

"I don't believe this," Cooper said. "You've got a problem with me, but you guys are cool with a professional killer roaming the campus?"

The Quiet One—if indeed that's who Cooper had been chasing—was nowhere in sight. Cooper had lost him. He holstered his Browning and willed himself to take slow, steady breaths.

A young woman with blue hair practically spat in his face. "When's the last time you murdered someone, *pig*?"

"Ask me again in a couple of days," Cooper replied.

CHAPTER 96

COOPER LAMB took the long way home.

Not because he wanted to. He would have loved nothing more than to crash for a few hours and allow his stressed body to recharge. But that might be a fatal mistake. The shooter had known exactly where to find Cooper tonight, so he most certainly knew where Cooper lived. Cooper could be stumbling right into an ambush.

Okay, part of him didn't care—an early death would let him catch up on his sleep. But Cooper needed to see this case through to the end. And, if nothing else, get a little payback after that guy had tried to remodel Cooper's face with a bullet.

The long way home meant a meandering route up Thirty-Fourth Street to the Philadelphia Zoo (*Hello, lions, I'll say hi to Veena for you*), then across the Girard Avenue Bridge and past Girard College, the nearly two-hundred-year-old boarding school originally opened for fatherless boys. This reminded him of Archie Hughes Jr. Strange to think that in another era, he might have ended up here.

From there, he took Corinthian Street down to his own neighborhood, skirting along the east side of the Eastern State Penitentiary. Its guests had included Al Capone and Willie Sutton; today, the former prison catered to history buffs and haunted-building freaks.

Cooper liked the place because the Dead Milkmen shot the video for "Punk Rock Girl" inside its walls.

On Green Street, he saw no obvious signs that anyone was watching his brownstone. Still, Cooper hopped a fence and made his way to his backyard—what Veena had dismissed as a glorified alley. Okay, maybe this *was* an alley. The place felt extra-claustrophobic now that he was steeling himself for a possible attack.

Cooper checked all possible entry points in the back of his brownstone, looking for anything out of place. Everything seemed fine except for one detail.

No excited Lupe noises.

Lupe always greeted him eagerly when he arrived home. In fact, whenever Cooper entered through the back, he always saw Lupe's excited face looking down at him from the bedroom windows.

He wasn't there now.

Cooper doubled back and made his way around to the front of his building. He slid his key into the lock with surgical-level care and precision to avoid making any noise. He kept his front door well oiled with WD-40 specifically for moments like these. Stealth was everything; some old army habits died hard.

The front door opened into a foyer and long hallway. His Browning was empty, but his possible attackers didn't know that. If it came to it, he could use it as a distraction while planning his next move.

But if they'd hurt Lupe, there would be no planning needed. Cooper would punish them. Punish them *permanently*.

Cooper moved down the length of his hallway, taking care not to step on the floorboards that creaked.

Gun in hand, he slowly opened his bedroom door to find...

Lupe staring back at him from the bed. *Oh, you're home.*

Next to him was a slender form wrapped up in his comforter. The form stirred, then rolled over into a new position.

Cooper felt all the tension in his body dissolve at once. He undressed and slipped into bed next to Veena. The world was a dangerous, screwed-up place, but somehow this made it okay. For tonight, anyway. Veena stirred, pushing her body back into Cooper's.

"Love you," she whispered, then went back to sleep.

MONDAY, JANUARY 31

CHAPTER 97

7:13 a.m.

ON A few occasions, Cooper Lamb had felt the need to shower with a gun close by. But walking his dog with a gun? This was a first.

One hand he kept on the leash, the other in his jacket pocket, fingers wrapped around the grip of his fully loaded Browning. His would-be killer was still out there, and Cooper would be foolish to venture outside without protection.

Lupe knew something was up. Cooper was sure the pup could feel the tension because he kept an extra-vigilant eye on Green Street, scanning for possible threats. Of course, to Lupe, a threat usually meant a squirrel. With the energy Cooper was radiating, the poor dog must have thought a fifty-foot squirrel was rampaging up the Ben Franklin Parkway.

No squirrels attacked. No gunmen either.

When Cooper returned home, Veena was already in the shower. Cooper unhooked Lupe's leash and walked into the kitchen to start breakfast. This Monday demanded something huge and greasy to soak up all that anxiety. Lupe kept a close eye on Cooper's movements in case a spare treat might be thrown his way.

In one oversize pan, a pile of sliced potatoes and bell peppers for Cooper's world-famous epic hash browns. In another pan, four thick slabs of scrapple, a Philly favorite. It was misunderstood by the world at large but incredibly delicious when grilled to perfection. Who cared that scrapple was essentially a gray block of all the parts of the pig that couldn't be sold separately and that most people put it in the same category as haggis? With the right amount of Pennsylvania Dutch seasoning (which Cooper suspected was largely pepper), it became a delicacy right up there with caviar.

"Oooh, scrapple," Veena said with honest delight as she sat down at the table. She was freshly scrubbed, and you would never know her clothes had been draped over Cooper's desk chair all night. Cooper, however, looked as if he'd rolled down a hill and slept in a gully. A shower was definitely in order.

"So what's next?" Veena asked as they were finishing breakfast.

"What, this artery-clogging feast wasn't enough for you? Should I put some baby backs on the grill?"

"With the Archie Hughes case," Veena clarified.

"Oh, what's next with *that*," Cooper said, then added with a note of solemnity, "Well, considering I was almost killed last night in pursuit of the truth—"

"Whatever," Veena replied. "What's next?"

"I'm actually being serious here, V. Someone took a few shots at me outside Maya Rain's building. I trailed him all the way to Penn, but I lost him in the crowd."

"Maya Rain's place. Huh."

"Yeah. She said something that's been knocking around in my skull all morning."

"I'm sure she did."

"No, not like that. About Archie having more enemies than just the ones on the field."

"You're thinking Archie himself was in some kind of trouble. This is interesting. Maybe our focus is too narrow. Let's think outside the NFL."

"Sure, but the NFL was Archie's entire life. To the point that the Sables were jealous when Archie spent time with his family."

"That's not entirely true," Veena said. "Janie found some financial breakdowns that...well, never mind that for now. But Archie's credit cards say that he spent a lot of lazy afternoons at the Merion Golf Club."

"You think his golfing buddies got mad and ordered a hit? What, did he play multiple balls on the same hole?"

"I doubt that's punishable by death." Veena polished off the last of her hash browns, then walked her plate into the kitchenette. "I'm just saying it's something we should look into."

Cooper pondered this. "Fair enough. I'll do it."

"But you made this lovely breakfast."

"And almost took a bullet to the brain! I don't know why you're not making a bigger deal out of that."

"Well, he missed, right? I'm going to bring the leftovers to Janie." Veena was already scooping eggs and hash browns into a plastic container.

"Anyway, I know the club a little," Cooper said. "It'll be easier for me to slip inside and ask some questions."

"Hmm. I don't think she's much of a scrapple fan. That's all you and Lupe."

"Generous of you! I'll let you know what I find."

"Bye, Lupe, sweetheart!" Veena called.

Bye, sweetheart, Cooper thought. He groaned as he dragged himself to the shower; he hated having to dress up and look semirespectable.

CHAPTER 98

Partial transcript of Cooper Lamb's conversation with Richard Gard and Loren Feldman, longtime members of the Merion Golf Club

COOPER LAMB: They really pour these bottomless Bloody Marys stiff here, gentlemen. (*Palm slaps a tabletop*) Hoo-ah!

RICHARD GARD: That's one of the best perks of the club, if you ask me. And thanks for this round, Cooper. Mighty kind of you.

LOREN FELDMAN: Jeez, stop pushing the kid. If he wants to join, he'll join.

LAMB: You know, I think you guys are talking me into it. And that's not just the rail vodka talking. (*Pause*) Tell me one thing, though. Archie Hughes was a member, right?

GARD: Boy, was he.

FELDMAN: Hey, enough of that. You want to get us kicked out?

GARD: What? It's not like it's a state secret or anything.

LAMB: What's a state secret? Ah, come on, guys! I'm, like, the world's biggest Birds fan. You gotta tell me!

GARD: Archie liked to gamble. Like, on everything. You could be standing on a street corner flipping a quarter, and he'd show up and want to make a wager.

FELDMAN: Yeah, but that wasn't the problem.

LAMB: What was the problem?

FELDMAN: The problem was, he was the worst gambler I ever met. He lost all the damn time! Whatever winning Archie Hughes had in him, he saved it for the football field. Which is good, because that's how he could afford to do all that losing.

GARD: Aw, Archie wasn't that bad.

FELDMAN: Wasn't that bad? How do you lose *half a million bucks* during so-called friendly rounds of golf?

LAMB: Whoa. He lost *how* much?

GARD: Look at who's spilling state secrets now.

FELDMAN: You started this! But yeah, he lost that much. Easy. I know a guy who pretty much financed his Margate summer home with what he took off Archie Hughes. Guy called his place the Eagles Nest. Which I think is pretty hilarious.

GARD: If you want some good Archie Hughes stories, you need to talk to Ben E.

FELDMAN: Oh yeah, Ben E. has all the great stories. Not only from here but down in AC too.

LAMB: Who's this Benny?

GARD: Come on, you're not that young! I'm sure you've seen Ben E. Franco. Legendary seashore comic. For a while there, he had a couple of men's clothing shops down on South Street. Maybe that was before your time.

FELDMAN: The old prick did have the best commercials! Remember the one where the models in bikinis came out and whipped him because he was selling his suits for too low a price?

LAMB: Sounds like my kind of guy. How can I get hold of Benny?

FELDMAN: No, it's not *Benny*. It's *Ben E.* E., like a middle initial.

LAMB: How can I get hold of Ben E.?

GARD: I don't know. Can you walk straight?

LAMB: If it makes you gentlemen feel better, I'll call a cab before heading over to him.

GARD: No, no. That's not why I'm asking.

LAMB: Then what does it matter if I can walk straight or not?

GARD: Because he's sitting right across the room.

CHAPTER 99

Transcript of conversation between Cooper Lamb and Ben E. Franco, semiretired Atlantic City entertainer

COOPER LAMB: Mr. Franco?

BEN E. FRANCO: If Mr. Franco owes you money, he said he'll be right back after he visits the cash machine.

LAMB: Ha-ha, nothing like that, Mr. Franco.

FRANCO: So formal! Call me Ben E. As long as we're so close, why don't you pull up a chair and buy me another mimosa.

LAMB: You got it. (*To waiter*) Excuse me, could you bring Mr. Franco another?

FRANCO: So what can I do for you, young man? You want an autograph for your sweetheart? Because, you know, she can have the real thing for next to nothing. Hell, at my age, I might even pay *her*.

LAMB: Heh. Your friends Rich and Loren over there said you had some good Archie Hughes stories.

FRANCO: Rich and who? Oh, the *alte kaker* over there with the lady's first name? Ah, they ain't my friends. They're hangers-on. Rich made a lot of money gouging people one billable hour at a time. I should know. He was my entertainment lawyer for years! And as for Loren Bacall, Christ on a cracker. The man can't handle his liquor. One time he was hauled in front of a judge. The judge says, "You've been brought here for drinking." Loren says, "Okay, let's get started."

LAMB: Ha-ha-ha, that's good, Ben E. But I'd really love to hear about Archie.

FRANCO: God rest his soul.

LAMB: You two were close, I gather.

FRANCO: You gather? What are you, a migrant field worker? No, we weren't close. That big bastard owed me a lot of money.

LAMB: Archie owed you money?

FRANCO: Are you kidding? Archie Hughes owed *everybody* money.

LAMB: How much money are we talking? Loren said it was something like half a million.

FRANCO: Ha! Don't listen to that souse, he has no idea what he's talking about. Archie owed a lot more than that. (*Whispering*) I'm talking *millions*.

LAMB: Come on.

FRANCO: Kid, you know I'm a kidder, but I ain't kidding about this. I've been around this town for way too many years and never saw anyone throw money away like Archie Hughes. He did it here, and I heard he owes millions out in that desert town too.

LAMB: Vegas?

FRANCO: No, the Gobi Desert. Yeah, Vegas! Where else do people go to hand over their hard-earned cash in exchange for the cheap flash of a leg and a piece of rubber chicken at a lousy buffet? Come to think of it, his buddy was in just as deep. And look where it got them.

LAMB: Which buddy?

FRANCO: You know, that ass█ chef who got himself killed last week.

LAMB: So you think their gambling debts had something to do with their deaths?

FRANCO: (*Long pause*) We've been joking around, kid, but listen to me. And listen to me carefully. This is serious business. Always has been. This is the way of the Mob. They want you to have a good time, drink their wines, feel up their girls, watch their ponies run. Whatever. But when the bill comes, you'd better be ready to open your wallet and pay. The entire organization runs on this principle. If people don't pay, the Mob goes away. And let me tell you, they're not going anywhere.

LAMB: Makes sense. But how do you get someone like Archie Hughes to pay?

FRANCO: If someone serious decides to welsh on a bet, you send someone serious to speak with him.

LAMB: What kind of serious are we talking about?

FRANCO: I think you know exactly the kind of *serious* I'm talking about. Look how Mr. Greatest of All Time ended up. Nobody's untouchable, Mr. Lamb.

LAMB: (*Slight pause*) You know who I am?

FRANCO: You've been asking a lot of questions around town. People have noticed. *Serious* people.

LAMB: I'd be happy to speak with these people. Maybe they can help me straighten all this out.

FRANCO: You don't understand. I am trying to help. I know this Mob guy. Capo. Friend of mine. Keeps a collection of other guys' balls in his man cave. He'd be happy to add yours to the collection. You're pissing off people. You're pissing off the *wrong* people. (*Pause*) Now, if you'll excuse me, I have to go shake the dew off my lily. Watch your back, kid. And your front.

CHAPTER 100

2:01 p.m.

VEENA COULD drive . . . technically. She just wasn't comfortable driving. But even though Cooper had tried to pace himself at the country club, he was in no condition to rocket down the Atlantic City Expressway. The mix of vodka and subtle death threats had clouded his mind. Which meant he handed his keys to a very reluctant Veena.

Cooper tried to keep her calm as she weaved in and out of traffic. "Look, it's a sleepy Monday in January. We'll have the whole city to ourselves."

"Yes. Just us and the gangsters you count as friends."

"Hey, Red is *not* a gangster," Cooper said. "At least, I don't *think* he is. Though if you're in business with a bunch of gangsters, I suppose that, strictly speaking—"

"And what about the associates of this Ben E. Franco guy?"

"He didn't name names. He didn't have to. But don't worry. I know the usual suspects—the next generation of the old Philly Mob. I'm not going to approach them until I vet them with Red."

"You couldn't have just called Red?"

"Some conversations need to happen face to face. Besides, I thought we deserved a little break. We'll talk to Red, then rent a penthouse for pennies and knock back some complimentary glasses of wine."

"Don't you have to be back in time to pick up the kids from school? And Lupe from your ex?"

"The Eagles just won the championship. Do you think anybody—let alone teachers—is in school today? Hey, keep your eyes on the road."

"You know what? Before we drive home tomorrow, I'm getting hammered, so you'll have to drive."

"Fair enough."

CHAPTER 101

CASINOS WATCH YOU.

There are no blind spots, no hidden corners—nothing is left to chance. If you ever want to record a few minutes of your life in complete detail (and from multiple angles), simply walk onto the main floor of a casino.

But Cooper and Veena weren't feeling *that* kind of watching.

When casinos watch you, it's like a mama bird making sure you aren't trying to run off with one of her chicks. This was a different kind of watching. More like a bird of prey sizing them up for the kill.

"Am I crazy," Cooper said, "or do you feel all kinds of eyes on us?"

"Oh, good. I thought it was just me."

"Well, Ben E. did say the Mob was well aware of our activities. I'm sure they're all wondering why we just checked into Caesars on Monday afternoon."

"Maybe we just can't say no to the slots," Veena said.

"Ben E. would have a crude double entendre to share off that one."

"And you don't?"

"I think I'm hungover. Let's get settled, then go have an early cocktail with Red Doyle."

"Didn't you just say you were hungover?"

"No better way to avoid crashing to the ground than by pulling back on the stick."

"Your best friend Ben E. would have a crude joke about that one too."

"I think he's my new hero." As Cooper spoke, the phone in his jacket pocket vibrated. "Hold on. Got a message from Victor."

REPORT TO C. LAMB BY V. SUAREZ
MONDAY, JANUARY 31
(SENT WITH ENCRYPTION AND RED-FLAGGED, WITH DELIVERY CONFIRMATION)

A quick heads-up, boss. I know you're in AC with Ms. Lion. Just keep your eyes open. I confirmed this with three different sources (including the New Jersey Turnpike Authority): Mickey Bernstein's in AC too.

CHAPTER 102

"RED, MEET Veena. We're working the Archie Hughes case together."

"Yeah, yeah. Before I say a word, if the two of ya are secretly recording me right now, that would be a violation of New Jersey law."

"Come on, Red," Cooper said, "I wouldn't do you dirty like that. Besides, Jersey has a one-party consent law. We wouldn't need your permission."

"You for sure would do me dirty," Red replied. "I'm giving the lady the benefit of the doubt."

"We are not recording this conversation, Mr. Doyle," Veena said.

They were sitting in the cocktail bar of a hotel originally known as the Boardwalk Regency; it was one of the area's oldest hotel-casinos, opening in 1979, just after gambling became legal in Atlantic City. There had been a dizzying series of owners over the years and flirtations with a dozen different themes and styles, each one trying to find the secret mix of ingredients that would lure Philadelphians to AC instead of Vegas. None of them quite worked, so now the place was capitalizing on its old-school status—1979 was all the rage again, apparently.

Red Doyle had grown up in Atlantic City, and it showed. His

prematurely aged face seemed chiseled from granite and cured with years of alcohol and tobacco. He was off the cigarettes now, though; he contented himself with his whiskey sour. Veena had already polished off a glass of chardonnay and ordered another. Cooper stuck to a mug of Yuengling Lager.

"I need your confirmation on something," Cooper said.

"Unofficially," Red said. It was a demand, not a question.

"As always," Cooper said. "We know Archie owed quite a bit of money around town. We're trying to figure a ballpark estimate."

"Heh. A *bit* of money, huh? Whatever your guess might be, I guarantee the actual amount is way higher."

"Half a million," Veena suggested.

"Honey, please." Red waved his hand like he was trying to swat away the very notion. "Archie *wished* he owed me only half a million bucks. He was into me for about a million three."

"Wait, wait," Cooper said. "One point three million just to you alone?"

"Easily that much," Red said. "Word was that he owed something like seven million between here and Vegas. Mostly here."

Cooper whistled in horror or surprise—or maybe both.

"Why didn't he just pay?" Veena asked. "The man's contract with the Eagles earned him at least fifty million a year."

"That's the funny thing about high rollers like Archie," Red replied. "They really, really don't like to pay."

"And what happens when someone like Archie doesn't pay?" Veena asked.

"That's the thing. Nobody would be stupid enough to put out a hit on the GOAT. I mean, that's just bad for business."

"Ben E. Franco seemed to think that's what happened."

"Ah, Ben E. Franco is full of shit. That guy has been recycling jokes since the days of JFK, and half of those were lifted from Joey Bishop."

"Okay," Cooper said. "But let's take your case, Red—how do *you* make your displeasure known?"

"Well, for one thing, I stop taking their bets."

"Let's say you do that. What's next? I mean, no offense, Red, but you're up my ass sideways when I'm, like, a day late."

"I can't believe I'm listening to this," Veena said. "What are you two, thirteen?"

"Small-timers like you, Lamb—no offense—always pay up quick. They know that word travels fast, and if they screw up a few times, they're done."

"And with Archie?" Veena asked. "Plenty of people were still taking his bets."

"Yeah, how could they refuse, right? I mean, they were counting on him paying up eventually."

"Except he died before he paid up," Cooper said. "Can't imagine you're too happy about being down a million and a half bucks."

"Eh, it'll sort itself out. Always does."

"I don't think the Mob was so philosophical about being owed millions of dollars by Archie when he was alive."

"No, they weren't."

"So what did they do?"

Red shook his head. "Look, they wouldn't send a shooter. No way, no how. But they would send someone serious. Someone who specialized in reluctant clients, let's put it that way."

Veena leaned forward. "You're talking about the Quiet One."

CHAPTER 103

RED TURNED pale. "How do you know about that?" he whispered.

"You think you're my only source?" Cooper said, taking the baton from Veena. He kind of relished these moments when he had a leg up on know-it-all (and seen-it-all) Red Doyle.

"You two—you really like sticking your pricks in the hornet's nest, don't you."

"That's what I'm known for," Veena said, deadpan. "Sticking my prick wherever I want."

"I'm sorry, Ms. Lion. But seriously, you have no idea what you're doing."

"Oh, I don't know," Cooper said. "We've met the opposition. I'm pretty sure this Quiet One tried to silence me last night."

"Nope," Red said. "If someone sent... *that one* after you, we wouldn't be talking right now. I would be trying to decide whether or not it was worth driving to Philly for your goddamn funeral."

"You don't think the Quiet One killed Archie?" asked Veena.

Red frowned, then signaled the bartender for another whiskey sour. "Is it possible? Sure. But it wouldn't make no sense. The professional you're talking about would cost too much, even for a debt as sizable as Archie's. Just wouldn't make sense."

"What about Roz Cline?" Veena asked.

"What about her?"

"Why did she have to die?"

"I have no earthly idea, but she kind of put herself in that position. Once she sank her hooks into Archie, she was sure to parade her fatted calf all around town. You ask me, she got what she deserved."

"She deserved to be thrown off her balcony?"

"Buy the ticket, take the ride."

Cooper watched Veena struggle to contain the rage simmering inside her. Not that anyone else could tell, especially Red. But Cooper knew she was using all of her willpower to keep from knocking Red on his ass. "Speaking of tickets, what's our favorite policeman Mickey Bernstein doing in town?" Cooper asked.

"How would I know?"

"He works for you, right?"

"Nice try, Lamb. No, Mickey is not currently in my employ. He's down here all the time. Maybe he's a big fan of the Knife and Fork, I don't know."

"You've been a big help, Red."

"I'm not sure what you want from me. But hey, one more thing, just between the three of us—"

Cooper interrupted. "I know, I know, we should watch our backs."

"Oh, no, you two are way past that point. I'll do what I can, but you keep screwing around with hornet's nests, you're gonna get stung."

"You're a big fan of that metaphor, Red."

"I don't know why you came here showing your faces around town. You could have picked up the phone, you know."

Cooper wasn't facing Veena, but he could practically feel the heat from her eyes. There would be an *I told you so* later on.

"In fact, if you two were smart, you'd drive back to Philly right now. Don't worry about the room, I'll take care of it."

"Trying to scare us off, Red? You nervous about where this investigation is headed?"

Red smiled. "Please. I'm just trying to keep one of my small-timers from getting killed."

CHAPTER 104

4:04 p.m.

"LET'S HIT the boardwalk and think," Cooper said.

Veena nodded and led the way out of the hotel and onto the nearly empty boardwalk outside. The sky was slate gray, and the winter Atlantic Ocean was restless, pummeling the khaki sand like it had a grudge against it. This was not a place you wanted to be in the off-season. But Cooper liked the salty air, always had, going back to the days when his parents would bring him to AC. The scent brought back happy memories because even the most troubled families could call a truce on vacation.

But something felt off. And not just because they were in Atlantic City in late January. They reached the steel railing on the far side of the boardwalk and looked out over the sand.

"Red knows more than he's telling," Veena said.

"To be fair, though, we've always had a strange dynamic. He enjoys holding things over me. He's like a creepy uncle or something."

"And yet you place bets—large amounts of money—with this man."

"Hey, you heard him. I'm just a small-timer."

The boardwalk wasn't entirely empty. There was a man in a clear rain poncho and a fedora lingering by their hotel's entrance. Taking a break between shifts at the slot machines, most likely.

"Do we take his advice and leave?" Veena asked.

"Hell no," Cooper said.

"That's what I was hoping you'd say. So how do we find these mobsters you claim to know?"

Out of the corner of his eye, Cooper saw the man in the clear rain poncho start walking toward them.

"Cooper?"

Something off about his face. Distorted features, like he was a burn victim and had endured months of skin grafts. Or maybe it was the winter sun playing tricks on Cooper's eyes.

But then Cooper saw the stranger in the clear rain poncho take aim.

There was no time to cry out. He slammed into Veena with his left shoulder as he pulled the Browning out of his jacket pocket. His intention was to push Veena out of harm's way—push her all the way to friggin' Ventnor, if he had to—and return fire on this bastard.

The bad news was that Cooper moved too suddenly and powerfully to stop his own momentum. He fell on top of Veena, and his gun went skittering across the boardwalk.

The good news was that this probably saved their lives, because the man in the clear poncho wasn't anticipating this and fired above their heads. Bullets sparked against the steel railing.

"Shit!" Cooper yelled. They were defenseless and completely out in the open. The only play he had left was to scramble to his feet and charge at the man. Sure, Cooper might take a bullet. He might take multiple bullets. But if that gave Veena time to find cover, it would be worth it.

Cooper tensed, preparing to sprint. But something grabbed the collar of his jacket and jerked *hard*. Immediately he was reminded of a seashore attraction: the Hell Hole, a ride where you're spinning so fast, you almost don't feel the floor fall away from your feet.

For two seconds, Cooper had no idea how or why he was falling.

When sand exploded in his face, and he saw Veena still clutching the collar of his jacket, he understood.

She had pulled him off the edge of the boardwalk—and out of the line of fire.

Maybe Cooper had saved her life a few moments ago, but she had absolutely just saved his life.

"Thank you," he said, struggling to catch his breath.

"Thank me later," Veena said quickly. "Crawl under the boardwalk *now*."

They scuttled like crabs under the wooden walkway as bullets chopped into the sand. The killer in the poncho was intent on seeing this job through.

Veena dragged Cooper across the sand, back toward the casino.

"Wait!" Cooper whispered.

He looked up at the underside of the boardwalk. Hazy light poured through the gaps in the planks. Creaks in the wood revealed the gunman's path. The man knew they were hiding down there, so he was following them, keeping pace with them, lining up his next shot.

There was a peculiar melody cutting through the silence, not far away. The man was whistling a tune. Familiar, yet out of place, given the circumstances. What the hell was it? Cooper wondered.

"Under the Boardwalk"—the Drifters' hit from 1964. That's what it was. This scarred-up hit man had a peculiar sense of humor. Cooper Lamb did not want to die under the Atlantic City boardwalk listening to that goddamn song.

He reached for Veena's arm, but a bullet punched through the boards and cut through the patch of sand between them. The shooter knew exactly where they were hiding!

Veena was digging in her purse, most likely for her phone. He wanted to tell her not to bother—even if the AC police responded, they'd arrive just in time to load his and Veena's shot-up bodies onto a meat wagon. But he didn't dare make a sound.

"Cover your ears," Veena said. She pulled a COP .357 derringer from her purse and started firing toward the boards above them. *Blam-blam-blam-blam!* She blasted four shots through the weather-beaten wood. A moment later, they heard a heavy thud, like a sack of potatoes hitting the boards.

When enough time had passed, Cooper and Veena climbed back onto the boardwalk and walked up to their assailant. All four bullets had blasted into the man's chest. Now that Cooper was closer, he could see the man's face wasn't scarred. It had been hidden behind a clear plastic Halloween mask.

Veena crouched down and pulled away the mask. Cooper expected to see Mickey Bernstein, but for the umpteenth time today, he realized he'd made the wrong assumption. The man's face wasn't familiar to either of them.

"Is this the Quiet One?"

"No idea."

"Is he the one who tried to shoot you last night?"

"Roll him over so I can see the back of his head; maybe I'll recognize him," Cooper said. "Are you okay?"

"I'm okay."

"I didn't know you had a gun."

"I live in the city, what do you expect?"

"You used to be famously anti-gun."

"I used to be someone who wasn't on the Mob's hit list."

CHAPTER 105

THE SURPRISE punch knocked Red Doyle out of his chair and set off a noisy chain reaction in the nearly empty lounge. Red's cocktail tipped over and flooded the tabletop; his chair flipped over in the opposite direction and bashed into a chair at another table.

Cooper didn't care. He kicked all of the furniture out of the way so that Red couldn't hide from the ass-beating he was about to receive.

"The hell's the matter with you!" Red cried out, half worried and half furious.

"You sent a killer after us," Cooper snarled.

"I didn't send anybody after you!"

That earned Red a literal kick in the backside, which flipped the man over onto his belly. Cooper planted a knee in Red's spine and twisted his right arm behind his back.

"Agh!" Red screamed. "You lost your damn mind?"

"I want you to think about spending the rest of this year without the use of your arms," Cooper said. "And that's just the beginning unless you start telling me the truth."

"I'm not saying another word to you, asshole. I'm going to let the police do all of the talking. You forget—this is *my* town."

Cooper was so focused on deciding which of Red Doyle's joints he was going to dislocate first that he didn't notice Veena crouch down in front of the bookie and place the barrel of her petite handgun against his bony forehead. She lowered her sunglasses.

"I was just forced to kill someone," Veena said calmly. "This is something I'm going to have to carry with me forever. But let me tell you this: I have zero problem doing it again."

Cooper could feel the fight leave Red's body. Whatever he saw in Veena's eyes, he believed it.

"I'm telling you the truth," Red said softly. "Whatever just happened to you, I had nothing to do with it. I was trying to *warn* you. You two have big fat targets painted on your backs."

"Why?" Veena asked. "Because someone shot a football player in downtown Philadelphia and we're trying to find out who pulled the trigger?"

"No. Because you're poking around at one little corner of a very dangerous situation."

"Detail it for us."

"Take that gun off my head."

Veena took the gun off his head, and Red exhaled before continuing.

"The Sables bet huge on the NFC game yesterday."

"Illegal, but not surprising."

"No, you don't understand. They bet against the Birds."

"What?"

"You're finally getting it, aren't you? This has the makings of the biggest gambling disaster in ages, and the Mob wants no part of it. They want to shut this down completely and bury anyone who knows about it. What happened to Archie is sad, but they don't want any loose ends."

"So they *did* send the Quiet One after him."

"No! I'm telling you, that would be the opposite of what they'd do. It only brings more attention to this whole thing. I mean, look at you two. You wouldn't be sticking a gun in my face if Archie were still alive."

"There's more, isn't there?"

"If I tell you more, we're all dead."

CHAPTER 106

"IT'S ALREADY over, Red. Everything's going to come out sooner or later. You might as well tell me now."

"Goddamn you, Cooper. Get me a drink first."

"Tell me, then I'll buy you a bottle."

"You're going to owe me more than that. Too bad I'll never have the chance to collect, because my body will be rotting in the Pine Barrens." Red ordered a drink anyway. Another whiskey sour. The bartender made a half-hearted attempt to intervene, maybe show those two the door. But Red waved him off, grumbling about the bartender not stepping in a few minutes ago when Cooper Lamb was kicking his ass. Neither Cooper nor Veena cared for another drink. Bad idea to pour alcohol on top of all that adrenaline.

"In a way, you two were right. This *was* about Archie Hughes."

"How?" Veena asked.

"Archie was supposed to throw the NFC game, and—*poof!*—his debts would vanish. Complete reset."

"The Sables agreed to this deal?" Cooper asked.

"The Sables came up with this deal! The way they tell it, it was the only solution to an impossible situation. Yeah, the team loses, boo-hoo. Philadelphia is used to losing. Nothing new there. But Archie has the boot taken off his neck, the Mob gets its money, and the Sables recoup their losses and then some, so it all should have worked out fine."

"But it didn't," Veena said. "Because someone killed Archie before he could throw the game."

"Do you finally see what I mean? Why would the Mob kill the man at the center of the plan? No, this was something else. A fluke, dumb freakin' luck, punishment from God, who the hell knows. The rest of us have to deal with the aftermath. Including you two."

"What do you mean? Why us two?" Cooper asked.

"You two are loose ends. And now maybe I'm a loose end too."

Cooper realized Red Doyle wasn't being a prick—he was terrified. In his own way, he had been trying to steer them away from this situation before it was too late. But now, with a dead (alleged) Mob triggerman rapidly cooling outside on the boardwalk, there was no turning back. They would have to see this through to the end.

Cooper put a hand on Red Doyle's shoulder. "Hey, we still good?"

Red turned to Cooper and opened his eyes wide in genuine surprise; he looked as if Cooper had just told him that he'd won the Pennsylvania Lottery and then that he had terminal cancer.

"You're unbelievable, Lamb. You know that?"

TUESDAY, FEBRUARY 1

CHAPTER 107

5:02 a.m.

THE TROLLEY Car, out on the fringes of Northeast Philly, was open twenty-four hours a day, seven days a week, cash only. Cooper Lamb had always thought this was the perfect setup for armed robbery. Hit 'em right after Sunday brunch and walk away with a mint. Well, maybe not a mint. The prices were so reasonable, that stolen dough would get you as far as Allentown. Maybe.

Cooper chose the place and extended the invitation; Mickey Bernstein accepted it.

Yeah, Cooper was still stunned by that. He'd assumed he'd have to go knocking on the homicide cop's front door once again, and it was very likely such an encounter would end with a fistfight and handcuffs. A diner was a neutral spot and a clue that maybe Bernstein was willing to share some information.

Either that or Bernstein wanted to lure Cooper to an isolated parking lot at crazy o'clock in the morning so he could finish what he'd started a few nights ago outside Maya's apartment building.

After all, it wouldn't be the first time Mickey Bernstein showed up early to a homicide.

Cooper was pretending to study the menu when Bernstein arrived a few minutes before the appointed time. He slid into the booth across from Cooper, who had arrived even earlier to choose this table: right in the middle of the dining room, in full view of pretty much everybody, next to the battered upright piano and microphone.

Yes, the Trolley Car featured live entertainment, although Cooper had never witnessed it himself.

"Need a minute to look over the menu?" Cooper asked.

"Pretty sure I have it memorized by now," Bernstein said, then gestured to a waitress, who changed course immediately to take care of the celebrity cop's order. "Black coffee, sweetie, and a toasted bagel with cream cheese. Thanks."

Cooper hadn't been planning on ordering anything, since he wasn't hungry, and this meeting would most likely not be a pleasant one. But he mirrored Bernstein's order, substituting a Diet Coke for the coffee.

"I'll level with you," the homicide cop said. "On everything."

"That's very kind of you."

"Just one rule," Bernstein said. "No tapes."

"I promise, I'm not taping anything."

"Yeah, I hear you saying the words, but I'm dead serious about this. I know all the tricks. Don't make me dunk your watch in your Diet Coke."

"Bernstein, I'm not even wearing a watch. I could give a crap about recording you. I just want to know the truth."

"Fine. And I'll give you the truth. But I don't think you're going to be very happy when you hear it."

"Why's that?"

"Because you're going to realize what a freakin' idiot you've been."

CHAPTER 108

THERE WERE three reasons Cooper Lamb had chosen the Trolley Car for his meeting with Mickey Bernstein.

One: The physical location. Close enough to I-95 for Cooper to make a quick getaway if he had to, but the diner was also in Bernstein's neck of the woods (the so-called Great Northeast), so it was in his comfort zone.

Two: The crowd. Plenty of potential witnesses in case things went sideways.

Three: The piano.

And this was key. Cooper remembered it from a long-ago trip here with the kids; they were mortified when he waved a lighter and shouted, "'Free Bird'!" even though no musicians were around. ("Dad, you seriously need a therapist," Ariel told him.) But the piano and microphone were perfect hiding places for secret recording gear.

Which was why he'd brought Victor here three hours earlier and promised him a heart-stopping omelet if he'd wire the piano and mic for sound.

As Cooper had said, Bernstein wouldn't find any trace of a recording device... unless he decided to lift the lid of that upright and start poking around.

* * *

Transcript of conversation between Cooper Lamb and homicide detective Michael Bernstein

MICHAEL BERNSTEIN: Yeah, I gave Maya Rain a gun. And yes, that gun turned out to be the murder weapon.

COOPER LAMB: Why would you give Archie Hughes's nanny a gun?

BERNSTEIN: Because of Archie Hughes! Come on, you know what kind of company he kept. Take away the gambling lowlifes and rappers and street gangs and God knows who else, and there were still plenty of criminals who would've loved to pick Archie's bones clean. I wanted her to be able to protect herself, just in case.

LAMB: Are you in love with her?

BERNSTEIN: Who, Maya? Yeah, maybe I am. But who the hell isn't?

LAMB: Bernstein, come on. Why the hell are you still on this case? You should have recused yourself a week ago.

BERNSTEIN: What, because I'm having a little fling? Grow up, man. Do you know how small this town is? If I had to recuse myself every time I knew someone on the fringes of a homicide investigation, I wouldn't investigate any murders. Don't be like those idiot reporters who look for gossip when at the end of the day, it doesn't matter.

LAMB: You just told me you gave your secret girlfriend the murder weapon used in the highest-profile murder in the city's history. Would we call that the *fringes*?

BERNSTEIN: Clearly, someone lifted it from her bag at some point, hoping to do exactly this—confuse the issue.

LAMB: And what is this issue?

BERNSTEIN: Archie traveled in some rough company, and it caught up with him. I'm trying to find out who was behind it.

LAMB: Is that why you took on the Roz Cline case?

BERNSTEIN: Cline definitely set Archie up with some of this rough company. I think they wanted to silence her so nobody would be able to trace it back to them. So, yeah, it's a related case.

LAMB: You any closer to finding out who "they" might be?

BERNSTEIN: The investigation is ongoing.

LAMB: Please. You're telling me you have no idea at all?

BERNSTEIN: In my experience, you either know who did it right away or it's a long slog to figure it out. This is one of those long-slog cases.

LAMB: Huh. I thought you'd have a hunch or something. Like your old man.

BERNSTEIN: (*Through a mouthful of bagel*) What can I tell you.

LAMB: Well, I've got something to share with you too.

BERNSTEIN: Yeah?

LAMB: Veena Lion probably killed the Quiet One yesterday. I helped out a little, but she did the heavy lifting.

BERNSTEIN: The quiet who? What the hell is that supposed to mean?

LAMB: For a little while, I thought *you* might be the Quiet One. But now I see that I'm completely wrong about that.

BERNSTEIN: I don't know what you're talking about, but look, I gotta go. Hope this clears things up.

LAMB: You didn't finish your bagel.

BERNSTEIN: Hey, I've gotta work on that case you want me to solve so bad.

(*Long pause; there are diners murmuring and the clatter of silverware on plates in the background.*)

LAMB: Please tell me you got all that, Victor. (*Pause*) Also, I need you to hit an ATM for me. Mickey stuck me with the tab, and I didn't bring any cash.

CHAPTER 109

"ANYWAY, SO, yeah, I was listening in the whole time. Bernstein is full of crap."

They were driving south on I-95, headed toward Center City. Cooper dodged rush-hour traffic as Victor crouched in the passenger seat with a laptop on his knees. He was still hacking as he maintained his end of the conversation.

"What specifically was crap?" Cooper asked.

"Pretty much everything that wasn't self-serving," Victor replied. "But what was most interesting were the things he left out."

"Such as?"

"His other two jobs, aside from the Philly PD."

"Two jobs, huh? Well, we already know one of them. He works for the Sables."

"Yep. And I found a digital trail leading from the Eagles' head office to Bernstein's secret bank accounts. He's been working for them for three years now."

"Doing what, though?"

"It's not like there's a memo line on the checks that says *Fixer* or anything. But the amounts vary, so I'm guessing that's what he is. If the Sables have any problems, then Bernstein is there to take care of them."

"Who's the other employer?"

"This was a little trickier, because the amounts deposited were more infrequent, and I had a hard time tracing them. At first."

"And..."

Victor was silent except for the clacking his fingers made on the laptop keys. Cooper didn't push him. The man was doing his research in real time.

"Okay, this isn't locked down as tight. But as I'm reading through some older clips about Bernstein's father, I'm starting to figure out the connections."

"Victor, what are you talking about?"

"The Mob."

"Philly or Atlantic City?"

"Boil it down and it's all the same Mob, has been since the 1920s. One big screwed-up family, and the Bernsteins have been their silent fixers going back decades. Mickey is just following in his father's footsteps. And his grandfather's, for that matter. Mickey's grandfather used to run errands for Joe Ida and Angelo Bruno."

Cooper watched the skyscrapers of Center City slide into view. Old knockaround guys like Ida and Bruno wouldn't recognize Philly anymore. Their sons and grandsons had transformed it—with the help of the police and the politicians they kept in their pocket. It wasn't new corruption; it was the same corruption with a twenty-first-century sheen.

"Hold on," Victor said suddenly. "Pull over."

"What—right here on I-95? Are you crazy?"

"Boss, pull over! Now!"

CHAPTER 110

SOMEHOW, COOPER LAMB defied space and time (and the morning rush hour) to force his way onto the highway's shoulder. Which wasn't much of a shoulder. Officials had been rebuilding I-95 almost since they'd first slammed it through the river wards back in the 1970s, and now they were expanding it by another two lanes. Construction gear and debris littered the side of the road. It was a miracle Cooper hadn't crashed into an asphalt spreader.

"I hope this is worth almost dying for," Cooper said.

"Oh, it's worth it," Victor told him.

"What is it?"

"A page of high-end escorts."

"If you're lonely, Victor, I recommend a Dungeons and Dragons club or some other nerd-friendly gathering."

"Yeah, funny, boss," Victor said in a way that made it plain he did not find Cooper's joke even remotely funny. "No, these pages were heavily protected in the first place, top-notch encryption, then scrubbed from the internet."

"How did you find them?"

"Avid fans collect this stuff in the hopes of catching someone famous on their way down," Victor said, "or on their way up."

"There's always a screenshot."

"Funny you say that. This is why I had you pull over." Victor turned his laptop so that Cooper could see the screen. If Cooper had been watching himself, he would have seen a classic Hollywood double take.

"Is that Maya Rain in a slutty Halloween costume?"

"No," Victor said. "This is Vanessa Harlowe in her work clothes."

"A long way from West Virginia," Cooper mumbled, staring at the image and trying to square it with the flesh-and-blood woman he'd come to know. She was gorgeous in real life. On-screen, she looked like a CGI character, like someone had attempted to capture her natural beauty but produced a cheap caricature instead.

"What does that mean?" Victor asked.

"Nothing. So she was a hooker."

"Five years ago, in AC. Based on what I'm seeing, Vanessa Harlowe was at the top of her game. Fifteen hundred an hour, ten grand for the night. She worked with someone else you know—Rosalind Cline."

"Let me guess. Her madam."

"They don't call it that anymore, boss."

"Well, she's not a madam anymore either."

CHAPTER 111

12:27 p.m.

FOR MAKING a discovery this huge, Janie Hall thought she deserved lunch at the Sansom Street Oyster House.

While waiting for her boss, Janie sat at the raw bar and ordered a dozen assorted oysters from up and down the East Coast. Wellfleets from Cape Cod; Glidden Points from Maine; stormy bays and sugar shacks from Jersey. *And* a double shrimp cocktail.

This was just for starters.

The food was its own reward, but Janie also enjoyed knowing that her reporter's instincts were still strong. When something nagged at her, it was the reporter inside her brain urging her to follow up, ask another question, keep pushing.

The ring. Like a Tolkien fantasy novel, it all came down to the ring. In this case, the missing Super Bowl ring.

It bothered Janie and fit none of the narratives Veena had been entertaining (professional hit man, personal grudges). A stolen ring made no sense with any of those. Why would a hit man take a Super Bowl ring when that would serve as a blinking red arrow pointed right at him? Maybe someone with a grudge would take the ring as a trophy, but again, to what end? The moment someone discovered it, the killer was as good as exposed.

No. A stolen ring meant a robbery.

As her boss and Cooper Lamb took a trip down to the shore, Janie called up one of the useful individuals in her life, this one from about five years ago.

The name he'd given Janie was Travis, but she knew it was fake. Travis was a kind of dark alternative-universe version of Cooper Lamb—a fellow shamus, but completely amoral and perfectly at home in the underworld. (Janie *did* enjoy the occasional bad boy.)

She had been writing a piece on high-profile art heists on the Main Line, and her reporting led her to Travis, a private eye who specialized in recovering stolen goods (for a steep fee), as long as the police were kept out of it. Only one of his quotes—on background—made it into the piece, but Janie and Travis had ended up downing more than a few martinis at the Continental over the years.

Which was where they'd met up the night before.

"Tell me who would try to fence a stolen Super Bowl ring," Janie said.

"Somebody really stupid," Travis replied.

And she would have left it at that if Travis had not followed it up with "You know, it's funny you say that. Last week I had some idiot reach out through one of my associates trying to sell Archie Hughes's ring. Even if it was real, the ring is radioactive. I can't imagine who would buy it. If someone is selling it, it'll be on the street, for crackhead prices."

A noise next to Janie snapped her out of her reverie—the legs of the next stool over scraping against the tile floor.

"Did you start with a dozen oysters or did you order only three?" Veena asked.

"When you hear what I've got, you're going to buy me another dozen," said Janie. "And a chilled lobster tail."

CHAPTER 112

JANIE SLID the slip of notebook paper to her employer. Veena lifted it from the counter, unfolded it, read the name and address Janie had scribbled on it.

"Who's this?"

"Quite possibly the guy who killed Archie Hughes."

"Some random guy from Kensington is now our lead suspect?"

Janie walked Veena through her conversation with Travis, the recovery specialist from the previous night. It had taken another two martinis, but Travis finally agreed to give Janie the name and address of the moron who claimed he had Archie Hughes's Super Bowl ring and wallet.

Travis was convinced this was a dead lead; a man smart enough to evade every surveillance camera in the Museum of Art area wouldn't go shooting his mouth off about having the missing ring.

"But the guy might not know there *is* footage," Veena said.

"Exactly," Janie replied. "Which made me think, what if this *was* just a carjacking gone wrong?"

Veena started riffing. "This guy thinks he's just boosting a fancy car but then sees who he's robbing, freaks out, and shoots him."

"He doesn't want to go away empty-handed, so he takes what he can carry."

"Archie's wallet. And his Super Bowl ring."

"It's possible, right?"

"Only one way to find out."

Veena pushed her stool back and prepared to leave. Janie grabbed her arm. "Wait."

"Don't worry, just put the tab on the company card," Veena said. "Good work."

"No, it's not that. I don't think you want to be going up to this guy's apartment alone. That neighborhood is rough—I covered crime up there for two years. And with your painted nails, fancy shades, and expensive shoes, you're kind of a target."

Veena smiled. "Yesterday I shot and killed a professional hit man. I also threatened to put a bullet in an elderly man's face. I don't think I'll have a problem."

Janie started to laugh, but the sound died in her throat as she clocked Veena's expression and realized she wasn't joking. Before she could form a follow-up question—she had several—Veena was adjusting her shades and heading out the door.

CHAPTER 113

WHEN CRAZY Percy Marshall had woken up this morning, he hadn't thought he'd open his front door and find a gun pointed at his heart that afternoon. For one thing, he didn't know that anyone knew (or cared) where he lived. Big difference from a week ago, when he thought his luck had changed. But now, as Crazy Percy looked at the pretty lady holding the tiny gun, he realized it was worse than ever. He sighed.

Transcript of conversation between Veena Lion and Percy Marshall

VEENA LION: May I come inside, Mr. Marshall?
PERCY MARSHALL: Can I just say no?
LION: No.
MARSHALL: Then, sure, make yourself at home. Want a beer?
LION: No, thank you. I'd like you to give me the Super Bowl ring and the wallet.
MARSHALL: Yeah, yeah. Figured that's why you were here. Why didn't Bernstein come down here himself? Hey, wait—you didn't show me your badge. I don't think that's legal. You're supposed to show me your badge.
LION: The ring?

MARSHALL: Okay, okay.

(*Long pause as Marshall leaves, pulls open a kitchen drawer, returns.*)

LION: Tell me how you got these.

MARSHALL: You know how I got these.

LION: Tell me anyway.

MARSHALL: I was walking, minding my own business, when I saw this crazy-ass car just sitting in front of the art museum. I got closer and realized who was inside it. I figured he was passed out or something, in which case I would have called for help. But no—he was shot, man. Someone killed him! I didn't want any part of that.

LION: But before you ran away, you helped yourself to his Super Bowl ring and wallet.

MARSHALL: But I just gave them back to you! So it's kind of like I borrowed them, right? Or held on to them for safekeeping?

LION: And you have no idea who killed Archie.

MARSHALL: Oh, I didn't say that.

LION: Excuse me?

MARSHALL: Yeah, I know who killed the quarterback. And for the right price, I'll tell ya.

LION: For a price, huh? Okay. How much is your life worth to you?

MARSHALL: What do you m—? Hey, come on, now, you don't have to point that friggin' thing at me!

LION: Let me repeat: How much. Is your life. Worth to you? Because to me, it's worth absolutely nothing.

MARSHALL: You're no cop.

LION: Never said I was.

MARSHALL: I want that ring and wallet back, missy.

LION: Never going to happen. Now tell me who killed Archie Hughes.

MARSHALL: F███ you.

LION: I'm not a cop, but I am working for the district attorney. And I have zero problem explaining to them that I found a shot-up corpse in possession of a dead man's ring and wallet. Who do you think they're going to believe? Oh, that's right, they'll have to believe me, because you won't be able to say a ███████ word.

MARSHALL: Man. This week keeps circling the drain.

LION: Tell me who killed Archie.

MARSHALL: I can't.

LION: What did I just say?

MARSHALL: No, no, no! I can't tell you because I don't know their names. But I can show you. It's right here on my phone.

CHAPTER 114

Transcript of encrypted phone conversation between Veena Lion and Cooper Lamb

VEENA LION: Where are you? What are you doing?
COOPER LAMB: I'm looking at vintage screenshots of high-priced Atlantic City call girls. How about you?
LION: I'm about to catch the Frankford El. Can you meet me at Thirtieth Street Station in twenty-five minutes?
LAMB: You know, I'm pretty wrapped up in this research at the moment.
LION: I'm sure you are.
LAMB: Our friend Maya Rain? She used to be one of Atlantic City's finest escorts. And, even better, she used to work for Roz Cline.
LION: Incredible.
LAMB: Also, I discovered that Mickey Bernstein moonlights for the Atlantic City Mob, which runs all of the escorts in town. So it's not a huge leap to assume that Mickey and Maya go way back.
LION: Nice work, Cooper. But I can do you one better.
LAMB: Ha! No, you can't.
LION: Yes, I can.

LAMB: Impossible. There's no way you can top this. I'm like one baby step away from figuring out this whole sordid story. I just have to sort out why the Mob wanted Archie dead a week before the championship game. I'm thinking it was some kind of—

LION: Cooper.

LAMB: What.

LION: I have a video clip on my phone showing Archie's killers leaving the scene of the crime.

LAMB: I'm sorry, you have what, now?

LION: I'm also wearing his Super Bowl ring on my middle finger.

LAMB: No, you're not.

LION: Yes, I am.

LAMB: No, what I mean is, you should absolutely *not* ride the Frankford El wearing Archie Hughes's Super Bowl ring. Someone will knife you for it. Hell, *I'd* knife you for it.

LION: So you can sell it for crackhead prices?

LAMB: What?

LION: Never mind. Okay, okay, it's in my pocket now. Are you going to say it?

LAMB: Say what?

LION: Are you going to say, "Veena, how on earth did you manage to solve this case all by yourself?"

LAMB: No. I figure you'll tell me all about it when I pick you up from Thirtieth Street Station in twenty-four minutes.

LION: Perfect. Oh, and bring your gun. And leave Lupe at home.

CHAPTER 115

AN HOUR later, Cooper Lamb and Veena Lion knocked on the front door of the Hughes estate and were met by a monster.

"You two need to leave right now," Jimmy Tua said, practically growling the words. "Francine doesn't want to see you."

"She's my client," Cooper protested.

"Well, consider yourself fired. Goodbye."

Tua slammed the front door in their faces. Tried to, anyway. Cooper threw out his palm and stopped the door a few inches from closing. Tua pushed. Cooper held firm, but he knew he couldn't do this forever. Maybe not even for another few seconds.

Tua let up for a moment, but only to ask a couple of questions. "Are you insane? Or do you want to leave here with a broken arm?"

"Look, man, I know you mean well and you have the family's best interests at heart. But the future of this family depends on us speaking with Francine right now."

"Get the hell out of here."

"We're not leaving."

"Now."

Cooper turned to Veena. *You want to give me a hand here?* is what he started to say, but all he got out was "You want to" before Jimmy Tua launched an atomic bomb against the side of Cooper's skull.

Actually, it was Jimmy's fist. But the effect was the same.

Cooper's conscious self lagged a few seconds behind his physical body, which was doing a clumsy tap dance down the Hugheses' walkway. He couldn't blame his legs. They were trying their best. But ultimately, their best wasn't good enough.

CHAPTER 116

EVENTS USUALLY happened in threes.

Veena firmly believed that. And since she had pointed her derringer at three different people in a twenty-hour period, she assumed she was done with gun incidents.

But Jimmy Tua had disproven that axiom when he knocked Cooper Lamb on his ass, forcing Veena to draw her weapon and point it at a living human being a fourth time.

Tua was not impressed with the gun. Not in the least. Where he'd grown up, people were always sticking guns in each other's faces. "You're not gonna shoot me."

A chunk of the wooden doorframe directly above Tua exploded. Splinters showered down on his head. The tight end flinched, then locked eyes with Veena. She knew she looked like a madwoman capable of pretty much anything. He hadn't seen that often where he'd grown up, especially not in a woman's eyes.

"That was me missing," Veena said. "Next time I won't."

Jimmy Tua seemed undecided about what to do next. Backing down wasn't in his DNA, but this crazy lady with the derringer seemed serious. He was saved by a voice calling out from inside the house, "Jimmy, it's okay."

Francine Pearl Hughes appeared behind the massive athlete. She reached up and touched his shoulders, encouraging him to look at her. Tua seemed reluctant to take his eyes off Veena—what if this lady opened fire on *both* of them? Francine was gently insistent. Tua turned to face her.

Cooper Lamb, meanwhile, had gotten to his feet, but he looked confused. Veena wondered if he knew what year it was. "You alive over there?" Veena asked.

"I'm just quietly applauding myself," Cooper said, "for not pursuing a career in the NFL."

Okay, Cooper was fine. Jimmy Tua, however, looked like he was on the verge of tears. This was a little boy in a big man's body, a boy who had tried his best but let down his friend. Francine stood on her tiptoes and wrapped her arms around him. Tua settled into the hug, relieved. Maybe he hadn't failed her and the children after all.

"I love you," she whispered. "So, so much." Her voice was barely audible, but Veena heard her.

Then, slightly louder, she said, "Let me talk to these good people now. I'll call you later, sweetheart."

Jimmy Tua nodded in agreement and left without another word and without looking either Veena or Cooper in the eye. Which was okay. If the rule of threes held up, they'd see Jimmy again soon.

CHAPTER 117

"IT'S NOT what you think," Francine said.

"Okay," said Cooper, following Francine up the hallway. "Tell me what you think I think."

"That Jimmy and me are a thing. I mean, I know how you private eyes like to collect salacious gossip."

Francine was slurring her words a little, possibly due to alcohol or a couple of Xanax or just plain exhaustion. Cooper watched her walk, preparing to catch her if he had to. Hopefully it wouldn't come to that. Cooper was sure he was wobbling a bit after that hurricane-force punch from the Eagles' star tight end.

"Well, that's not the case. We're not. For one thing, Jimmy is gay."

"Yes, we know," Veena said.

"We know pretty much everything," Cooper said.

If she had been slightly drunk, Francine Pearl Hughes sobered up instantly. "Come into the parlor."

CHAPTER 118

MAYA RAIN was sitting there, although the children weren't around. Maybe they were busy elsewhere in the house or out with friends. But Veena was pretty sure that Francine and Maya had sent them to their rooms the moment she and Cooper knocked on the door.

"I have something for you," Veena said. She reached into her pocket, pulled out Archie's Super Bowl ring, and held it out to Francine, who stared at it unbelievingly. She hesitated to take it, as if Veena were trying to hand her a cursed talisman.

"How on earth did you find— "

"That's what we're here to discuss," Veena said.

"Francine, we don't have to do this now," Maya said, rising from her chair. "In fact, I'm going to insist that we don't do this now. Let me call your attorney and have her arrange a proper meeting."

"Have a seat, Vanessa," Cooper said.

"I'm sorry, what did you say?" There was no anger in her voice. On the contrary, Maya seemed amused.

"I saw a bunch of your old escort ads, Vanessa. You were beautiful then, but I like your current look a lot more. What I'm wondering is, which name is real, Vanessa or Maya? Or is it something else entirely? Am I talking to a Wanda June?"

Maya smiled. “I still like you, Cooper. Even though you say the cruelest things sometimes.”

Francine’s confusion seemed genuine. “Will someone explain to me what’s going on?”

“Happily,” Veena said, giving Cooper a look that said *Please stop taunting the potential murder suspect.*

CHAPTER 119

"WE HAVE proof that both of you were at the scene of the murder," Veena explained. "I have a video clip on my phone that shows your car, Francine, and the figures of two women who look like you and Maya. It won't take much digital forensic work to positively match both of you to those women."

Maya smiled. "It was the guy in the hoodie, right? I thought he was snapping a photo of Archie's car."

Veena was puzzled. "So you admit you were there?"

Maya shrugged. "Go on."

"Obviously, one of you drove Archie there in his own car with the other following in Francine's burgundy Bentley, the only other car you had available on such short notice. Which means that Archie was shot and killed elsewhere, and his body was left in his car at Eakins Oval so that it would look like a carjacking gone wrong."

"No," Francine said quietly. "It was a message."

Cooper's jaw dropped. "I'm sorry—what did you say?"

"Archie and I met at the Museum of Art. I was performing on the Fourth of July, and he was one of the parade guests. We met backstage. He told me he'd been in love with me since he was a kid. I figured I ought to say goodbye to him in the same place I'd said hello."

Cooper couldn't believe what he was hearing. "Francine, you do realize you're admitting to killing your husband, right?"

"No, she's not," Maya said. "Also, at best, you have evidence of us leaving the scene of a crime. And I don't think you even have that. You two like to bluff."

"The murder weapon was buried right here! In the flower bed in back of your house!" Cooper said.

Francine shot Cooper and Maya cold, hard looks. "Keep your voices down. Please."

"Could have been a home invasion gone wrong," Maya continued. "Archie resists and is killed. The killers force us to drive with them to the art museum to dump his body. And then they get frightened and let us go."

Cooper shook his head. "So these alleged home invaders forgot to bring a gun and had to borrow yours, Vanessa? The very one you received from Mickey Bernstein? Who, by the way, should be a thousand miles away from this murder investigation."

"Stop it, I'm begging you!" Francine shout-whispered.

"The details don't matter," Veena said. "We just want the truth. That's *all* we've wanted since the beginning of this thing."

Francine lowered her head and shook it gently as if to the beat of the saddest, slowest ballad she knew. She was beyond weary. This entire conversation seemed to drain the life from her body. "I don't know what you want me to say," she said.

"Easy," Veena replied. "Just tell me which one of you shot and killed Archie."

CHAPTER 120

"*BAAAAA,* SAID the little lamb."

The noise was so out of place, it startled all four adults in the parlor. Cooper was the first to realize who it was and responded to the comment.

"*Baaaaa,* little one," he said. "Come on out from your hiding place."

Five-year-old Maddie crawled out from behind a sofa, and a moment later her older brother stepped into the room with a solemn look on his face. Cooper expected him to say something along the lines of *Sorry, Mom, I accidentally threw a football into the windshield of the Bentley.*

For the first time since Cooper had met Maya, she appeared horrified. "I told both of you to stay in your rooms," she said with a coldness in her voice that was as far away from Mary Poppins as you could get.

Francine, trembling with uncontrollable anger or fear or maybe both, said, "Both of you. Upstairs. *Now.*"

"No, Mom," said Archie Jr. "I have something to say." He looked at his sister. "Maddie, go upstairs. I have to talk to these people about something important."

Maddie saw the seriousness in her brother's eyes. Her lower

lip trembled. She didn't understand what was going on. Maddie looked over at Cooper for reassurance. Cooper felt himself slip into dad mode. He smiled, nodded. "It's okay, sweetie," he said softly. "Your mom will be up in just a moment."

Maddie wanted to do a lot of things in that moment. She wanted to *baaaaa* at the man with the funny name (and the cute dog). She wanted to run to her mother and jump into her arms. She wanted to understand why everyone was so angry and sad all the time.

But in the end she turned around and went up to her room. She had a stuffed lamb on her bed, a gift from Nanny Maya just a week ago—though the timing meant little to Maddie. She just loved the stuffed animal and hugged it tight.

CHAPTER 121

"I KILLED Dad," Archie Jr. said, his voice barely a whisper.

"Archie..." His mother began to protest, but she trailed off when she realized that all hope had evaporated. There was no way for him to take back what he'd said. No way to rewind any of this, although she would have given almost anything to do so.

"It's okay, Archie," Veena said. "You're in a safe place right now, and we're all here to help you. You don't have to be afraid."

The kid unconsciously balled his hands into fists as he worked up the nerve to continue. "My mom and Maya didn't want you two to know that, but I didn't want to lie and get them in any more trouble."

"We understand, buddy," Cooper said. "And by the way, what you're doing right now is incredibly brave."

"I don't feel brave."

"I know that's not how you feel," Veena said, "but your mother couldn't be prouder of you. Isn't that right, Mom?"

Archie Jr. looked over at his mother. Francine could only beam love at her child as she slowly nodded. "You can tell them the truth."

"I'm sorry, Mom."

"It's okay, baby," Francine said. "And they're right. You're the bravest person I've ever met."

"Can you tell us what happened?" Veena asked.

Archie Jr. relaxed his hands as if he'd just realized he'd been clenching them. "I shot Dad," he said. "I knew it was wrong, but . . . I had to do something. When Mom found out, she asked where I'd gotten a gun, and I'd found it in Ms. Maya's bag but I didn't want to get her in trouble, so I lied and said I found it near school."

"And then you buried it in the garden," Cooper said.

"Yeah. But the police found it anyway. Or Mr. Mauricio did, and he told the police. I swear I didn't mean to get Ms. Maya in trouble."

"You didn't, Archie," Maya said, forcing a smile as if that would hold back her tears. It failed.

"Why did you do that, honey?" Veena asked. "Why did you shoot your dad?"

Archie Jr. swallowed. "I *had* to."

Cooper nodded. "Tell us what your dad said."

"It's not what he said. It's what he did."

"What did he do?"

Archie Jr. didn't reply, but the way he looked at his mother confirmed it for Cooper. The boy had known *exactly* what was going on. Archie Jr. hadn't cared if his father hit him. But his father hitting his mother was too much. What kind of young man could let his mother be beat up, even if it was his own father doing the hitting?

"Dad always said blood is thicker than water," Archie Jr. continued. "Nothing was more important than Mom and me and Maddie. I think he forgot that. I was just trying to remind him."

"How?" Veena asked.

"I didn't mean it. I just wanted him to stop and listen to me. So I pointed Maya's gun at him so he would stop. I didn't want to . . ."

"It's okay," Cooper said. "It's not your fault."

"But it *is* my fault!" Archie Jr. yelled. "I should have known Dad wouldn't stop! He tried to take the gun, and I just wanted to pull it away from him, and I must have pulled too hard and..." The boy trailed off and stared off into space as if it were happening all over again.

Cooper fought hard to control the tightening in his chest. It felt like the onset of a heart attack, but he knew he was just trying to avoid crying in front of everyone. He glanced around the room and realized he didn't need to bother. All of them were sobbing.

CHAPTER 122

THE SUN had set by the time Cooper and Veena got on I-76 and headed back to Philly. It was rush hour but everyone was leaving the city, so they hit very little traffic. It seemed like someone had turned down the volume of the world. Philadelphia was cold and quiet.

"You going to tell that prick DA about this?"

"No," Veena said. "Not about little Archie, anyway. You telling Francine's lawyer?"

"Pretty sure she knows. Starting to think she hired me for window dressing. 'We got the best, Your Honor,' and so on."

"So we finally know the truth."

"Yeah, we do."

"We should be happy about this."

"We should."

"So why does the truth feel so horrible?"

Cooper drove in silence, mostly because he knew the answer to that question. A lot of people thought that life was a struggle between virtue and temptation, angels and devils, good and bad. But that wasn't the case. The truth was, life was often a choice between bad and worse. Neither of those options felt good, but human beings were compelled to choose, hoping everything would turn out okay despite all evidence to the contrary.

CHAPTER 123

9:09 p.m.

"ARE WE doing the right thing?"

"That's a loaded question," Cooper said. "So the only answer is to get loaded."

They were back at the bar in the Rittenhouse Hotel. Same low-key bartender, same flirtatious server. But they felt like they were sipping martinis in an alternative universe. Nothing about this world felt right, so they took comfort in each other's company. Which in itself felt strange. Could Cooper Lamb have imagined doing this with Veena, his former nemesis, two weeks ago?

"Seriously," she said. "There's no way Francine would ever be convicted. No jury in the world would punish a woman for protecting her own child."

"I don't think there would be a trial," Cooper said. "I imagine that even a hard-ass like Mostel would cut a deal to keep this family out of the courtroom."

"Even if I believed that, it's nothing but a waking nightmare for Francine and those kids."

"And the monster who beat them gets off the easiest. Death is too good for him."

"The greatest of all time."

"And, somehow, the worst."

They finished their initial round and considered ordering food but opted for another round instead. By the end of the third round, they were ready to hide away from this twisted world. For a little while, anyway.

"How about we go to your place this time?" Cooper asked with what he hoped was a knowing gleam in his eye.

"We can't."

"Why not?"

"We're already here."

"What do you mean?"

"I currently live here," Veena said. "At the Rittenhouse Hotel."

"What, is your apartment being remodeled or something?"

"No. I've decided to sell the place and forgo apartments altogether. Hang on, hear me out. I crunched the numbers and realized I was wasting a ton of money on a physical space I almost never occupy. Factor in the upkeep of that space, even if I hired help—which I would never do—and it's even more wasted time and money. So my plan is to hop from hotel to hotel. I'll stay until a place bores me, then move on. If I like a place enough, I'll go back to it."

Cooper looked as if he'd taken another punch from tight end Jimmy Tua. "Wow. So all this time, we could have been enjoying our drinks in the comfort of your room, which is just a short elevator ride away?"

Veena shook her head. "Nope, not in my sanctuary. Nobody goes inside except me. Oh, and housekeeping. That's another thing I decided."

"That is the most Veena Lion thing I've ever heard."

"Besides, I prefer your place."

"You mean you prefer Lupe."

"Mayyyybe . . ."

"And the kick-ass breakfast I make when I'm a little hungover or have escaped the clutches of death."

"Also very possible. So shall we head to your place?"

"Wait. Exactly when did you make this decision about your apartment? And did it have anything to do with hit men being after us?"

"Cooper, I don't *have* to go back to your place."

"Let me take care of the check."

CHAPTER 124

LUPE WAS over the moon when he saw—and smelled—Veena. He was not so pleased when Cooper and Veena slowly undressed each other on the way to his bedroom, stopping for frequent make-out breaks, or when Cooper nudged the door almost completely shut, which was his way of telling the pup, *No climbing into bed with us. For now.*

Something woke Cooper later that night, although he didn't know exactly how late it was—he'd muted his phone and turned it facedown on the nightstand right before they fell into his bed together so there would be no interruptions.

But there were, of course.

Tiny metallic sounds that Cooper wasn't meant to hear but heard anyway. Like...scraping. Was it some kind of animal? he wondered, still half asleep. He rolled over and saw that Veena was awake too.

"Did you hear that?"

"Yeah. I think it's an animal in the backyard. Probably a squirrel."

"I think the sound is coming from your front door. Also, I thought we settled this. That is not a backyard, it's a glorified al—"

"Shhh." Cooper realized the clicking sound was indeed coming from the vicinity of his foyer. There was also a low growl—Lupe had sensed something too.

"What is it?" Veena asked.

"I'm beginning to think you were right about moving to a hotel." *Watch your backs,* everyone had said. *You don't know who you're messing with.*

Without warning, the entire bedroom lit up. Cooper had a sudden realization and lunged for his phone on the nightstand.

CHAPTER 125

TEXT MESSAGE FROM VICTOR SUAREZ
TO COOPER LAMB

They're coming for you. Two of them!

CHAPTER 126

COOPER SHOUTED, "Get down!" and he and Veena hurled themselves from the bed in opposite directions. Both were very naked. Neither of them cared at that moment.

Cooper landed awkwardly and hard but was able to grab the shotgun under his bed. Veena landed lightly on her hands and feet, almost like a cat. Cooper racked the shotgun, partly to pump two shells into the chamber but also warn anyone who was thinking about entering this room.

Veena felt along the ground for her bag, only to realize that she'd dropped it somewhere in the hall. *Damn it!*

Cooper aimed his shotgun at the windows behind his bed just as the glass shattered. Lupe started barking like crazy. Cooper crouched down farther and tried to make sense of the shadowy form that was stepping through the broken glass.

Lupe's barking intensified as he ran down the hall—Veena could hear his claws scrabbling on the hardwood floor. The pup was headed to the front door to deal with the intruder. *No, Lupe!* Veena screamed in her mind and took off after him.

"Don't move!" Cooper shouted.

Veena cleared the doorway just as gunfire filled the room,

blasting apart Cooper's computer monitor and dresser mirror and, based on the sound of it, every other glass object he owned.

Screw this, Veena thought.

Cooper stood up and pulled the trigger of his shotgun. Whatever glass had remained in the window frame was obliterated, and it took the shadowy form along with it, the force blasting him back into the alley. The shooter collapsed on top of a folding chair with a loud, messy clatter.

Meanwhile, out in the hall, Veena did two incredibly complex things without really thinking about them. She managed to tackle Lupe midstride, sliding with him along the floor a few inches, which ripped some of the skin from her knees. She also located and scooped up her bag in the darkness.

The front door was nearly ripped from its hinges as a heavy boot forced it open. This was a second attacker; he must have heard the gunfire and decided the time for subtlety had passed.

That man rushed in with a revolver and looked down at Veena's naked body as she cradled a growling Lupe under one arm and clutched her bag with her other hand.

"What the . . . *Veena Lion*? What are you doing here?"

The second attacker was Mickey Bernstein.

Veena didn't reply. She dropped her arms, giving him a free show. Bernstein couldn't help himself—he gawked. Lupe took off like a supersonic jet, eyes focused on the intruder. Bernstein yelled and pointed his revolver down at the running dog. Veena lifted the derringer out of her bag and didn't even think twice about emptying it.

Bang-bang-bang-bang. Four shots, expertly grouped around the chest.

Bernstein tap-danced backward and collapsed in the doorway. Lupe screeched to a halt, knowing that his services were no longer required.

Farther inside the apartment, Cooper heard the shots, but he was too stunned by what he was looking at to react to them. He stood naked in the empty frame of his bedroom window, shotgun in hand, staring down at the wounded figure of…

Vanessa Harlowe.

Maya Rain.

Whoever she was claiming to be on any given day.

Her eyes found Cooper's, and despite bleeding to death, she worked up a smile that melted his heart a little. Blood streaked across her lips and perfect white teeth, and as he watched, her eyes started to dim.

But now he realized her true name, one he'd only heard spoken a few days ago:

The Quiet One.

Cooper Lamb knew he could never prove it in court or produce any evidence linking Maya Rain to that name and her many crimes. But locking eyes with her now, he could see that all of her masks had slipped away. He just *knew*.

Which begged the question: Why would the Hughes family have a professional killer caring for their children?

Maybe Archie's creditors wanted someone to keep an ultra-close eye on Archie. And maybe Archie and Francine knew and had no choice. But if Maya, aka the Quiet One, was that good at her job, she would have had little trouble infiltrating the household.

"I still like you, Cooper," she said now.

Cooper wanted to reply but hesitated. He knew the Quiet One was dying; when serving overseas, he'd seen the face of imminent death way too many times. Some people never looked more alive than they did right before dying.

Cooper didn't want the last words Maya ever heard to be something cheap or sarcastic. He wanted to tell her that somehow, impossibly, he still liked her too.

But by the time he'd formulated that thought, she was gone.

SUPER BOWL SUNDAY, FEBRUARY 6

CHAPTER 127

WHERE WAS the very last place Veena had ever thought she'd find herself?

There was no clear number one, but pretty high up on the list would be *Walking with Cooper Lamb and a police escort behind the scenes at the Super Bowl at SoFi Stadium in Los Angeles, California.*

Yet here she was, and despite her natural aversion to team sports in general (and football in particular), Veena found herself in a good mood, caught up in the spirit of the game. The halftime show had just ended, and Veena had listened to a scorching, for-the-ages performance by Francine Pearl Hughes. If she had been carrying demons for the past few years, she'd exorcised quite a few of them on the stage tonight. Forget Janet Jackson flashing the crowd; forget the dancing sharks. People would be talking about *this* halftime show forever.

Archie Jr. and Maddie watched from the sidelines, proud of their mom and, for the first time in a long while, excited for the future. They were going on tour with their mother, and the family had no plans to return to Philadelphia anytime soon.

As far as the public knew, rogue homicide cop Mickey Bernstein had been responsible for the murder of Archie Hughes. The reason? For now, the story went that the GOAT owed way too much money to the Mob, and Mickey was the Mob's combined hatchet man / fixer. Who better to investigate a murder than the person who'd committed it?

The Quiet One was not mentioned in any media report under that name or any other. But an FBI source quietly confirmed to Cooper and Veena that, yeah, Vanessa's/Maya's prints had been matched to a series of unsolved killings and were discovered on the security cameras near Eakins Oval too. Cooper almost pressed for more information, then thought better of it. Perhaps some truths weren't worth knowing.

"Admit it—you're having a good time," he said now as they rode the elevator up to the luxury boxes.

"Maybe," Veena said. "But I'm about to have an even better time."

They were joined by a small battalion of law enforcement officers from an array of departments: FBI, Treasury, LAPD. Also squeezed into the elevator were Ariel and Cooper Jr. There was no way their father would go to the Super Bowl in LA and *not* bring them along.

Ariel had warned her dad: "If you don't take us, I won't speak to you for the rest of your life. And when we're reincarnated, I won't speak to you in that life either." The point was taken.

But the kids were about to see an even more impressive show than the one they'd just seen.

Harold and Glenn Sable were completely outraged to learn that their beloved player had been murdered by the "crooked tools of organized crime." They promptly stopped talking to the press when it was revealed that one of those "crooked tools," Mickey Bernstein, was on their payroll too. But silence wasn't going to protect them, because the law was here to arrest the Sable men on gambling and fraud charges.

Thousands of people were here to see the Eagles try to climb their way back from an eleven-point deficit.

Veena and Cooper were here to watch the Harold and Glenn Halftime Show.

The kids were here to enjoy Glenn Sable's dessert table.

CHAPTER 128

THE GENERATIONAL differences were obvious. Longtime businessman Harold Sable surrendered himself without a fight, knowing that he'd taken a shot and lost. *C'est la vie.*

Glenn, however, still believed in fairy-tale comebacks. He inched away from the officers of the law before breaking into a full run, hoping, presumably, to make it to the hallway and from there to a non-extradition country. But the fat man got about three feet before he was tackled to the carpet, which put an end to his NFL career.

Sports fans would be talking about the notorious Sables for decades to come. Their story would be held up as a cautionary tale for the ages.

Not that the Eagles players on the field knew about any of this. And if they had, they wouldn't have cared. They were here, at the Super Bowl, with the eyes of the planet on them, and even if the world around them started burning down, they would not be distracted. Also: the Birds were now behind by fourteen points.

"There's no way the Eagles can win," Veena said, elbowing Cooper in the ribs.

"Maybe not, but I feel like I've already won."

"How much money will I end up losing to Red?"

"But won't it be worth it, V.?"

"Not really."

"Come on, you'll be dining out on this story for years."

However, Lion and Lamb had spoken too soon, because in the fourth quarter, Terry Mortelite led a furious drive that stunned everyone and sent the game into overtime.

After the Birds won the toss (another piece of luck), Mortelite and McCoy pulled off five straight passes that led to Jimmy Tua scoring a two-yard touchdown, an epic upset that electrified Philadelphia and applied a bit of salve to the city's many wounds.

But that was the crazy-beautiful thing about this town. It was a place where anything could happen and often did.

Totally random things—like Veena Lion and Cooper Lamb leaving SoFi Stadium arm in arm after the game with a giggling Ariel and Cooper Jr. by their sides.

How crazy and beautiful is that?

ACKNOWLEDGMENTS

We would like to thank Matt DeLucia, Peter Katz, Robert Kulb, Shannon Morris-King, and Joseph Murray for their generous research assistance. And none of this would have been possible without the love and support of Meredith, Parker, and Evie.

ABOUT THE AUTHORS

James Patterson is one of the best-known and biggest-selling writers of all time. His books have sold in excess of 400 million copies worldwide. He is the author of some of the most popular series of the past two decades – the Alex Cross, Women's Murder Club, Detective Michael Bennett and Private novels – and he has written many other number one bestsellers including stand-alone thrillers and non-fiction.

James is passionate about encouraging children to read. Inspired by his own son who was a reluctant reader, he also writes a range of books for young readers including the Middle School, Dog Diaries, Treasure Hunters and Max Einstein series. James has donated millions in grants to independent bookshops and has been the most borrowed adult author in UK libraries for the past fourteen years in a row. He lives in Florida with his family.

Duane Swierczynski is the two-time Edgar-nominated author of ten novels – including *Revolver* and *Canary* as well as the graphic novel *Breakneck* – many of which are in development for film or TV. Most recently, Duane co-scripted James Patterson's *The Guilty*, an Audible Original starring John Lithgow and Bryce Dallas Howard. He lives in Southern California with his family.

ONE

"FOR *THE* LAST TIME," my client says to me. "I. Did. Not. Kill. Those. People."

He adds, "You have to believe me. I didn't do it."

The opposing counsel will refer to him as "the defendant." It's a way of putting him in a box, since opposing counsel absolutely believe he *did* kill all those people. The victims. The Gates family. Father. Mother. And teenage daughter. All shot in the head. Sometime in the middle of the last night of their lives. Whoever did it, and the state says my client did, had to have used a suppressor.

"Rob," I say, "I might have mentioned this before: I. Don't. Give. A. Shit."

Rob is Rob Jacobson, heir to a legendary publishing house and also owner of the biggest real estate company in the Hamptons. Life was good for Rob until he ended up in jail, but that's true for pretty much everybody, rich or poor. Guilty or innocent. I've defended both.

Me? I'm Jane. Jane Smith. It's not an assumed name, even though I might be wishing it were by the end of this trial.

There was a time when I would have been trying to keep somebody like Rob Jacobson away from the needle, back when New

York was still a death penalty state. Now it's my job to help him beat a life sentence. Starting tomorrow. Suffolk County Court, Riverhead, New York. Maybe forty-five minutes from where Rob Jacobson stands accused of shooting the Gates family dead.

That's forty-five minutes with no traffic. Good luck with that.

"I've told you this before," he says. "It's important to me that you believe me."

No surprise there. He's been conditioned his entire life to people telling him what he wants to hear. It's another perk that's come with being a Jacobson.

Until now, that is.

We are in one of the attorney rooms down the hall from the courtroom. My client and me. Long window at the other end of the room where the guard can keep an eye on us. Not for my safety, I tell myself. Rob Jacobson's. Maybe the guard can tell from my body language that I occasionally feel the urge to strangle him.

He's wearing his orange jumpsuit. I'm in the same dark-gray skirt and jacket I'll be wearing tomorrow. What I think of as my sincerity suit.

"Important to *you*," I say, "not to me. I need twelve people to believe you. And I'm not one of the twelve."

"You have to know that I'm not capable of doing something like this."

"Sure. Let's go with that."

"You sound sarcastic," he says.

"No. I *am* sarcastic."

This is our last pretrial meeting, one he's asked for and that is a complete waste of time. Mine, not his. He looks for any excuse to get out of his cell at the Riverhead Correctional Facility for even an hour and has insisted on going over once more what he calls "our game plan."

Our—I run into a lot of that.

I've tried to explain to him that any lawyer who allows his or her client to run the show ought to save everybody a lot of time and effort—and a boatload of the state's money—and drive the client straight to Attica or Green Haven Correctional. But Rob Jacobson never listens. Lifelong affliction, as far as I can tell.

"Rob, you don't just want me to believe you. You want me to like you."

"Is there something so wrong with that?" he asks.

"This is a murder trial," I tell him. "Not a dating app."

Looks-wise he reminds me of George Clooney. But all good-looking guys with salt-and-pepper hair remind me of George. If I had met him several years ago and could have gotten him to stay still long enough, I might have married him.

But only if I had been between marriages at the time.

"Stop me if you've heard me say this before, but I was set up."

I sigh. It's louder than I intended. "Okay. Stop."

"I *was*," he says. "Set up. Nothing else makes sense."

"Now, you stop me if you've heard this one from me before. Set up by whom? And with your DNA and fingerprints sprinkled around that house like pixie dust?"

"That's for you to find out," he says. "One of the reasons I hired you is because I was told you're as good a detective as you are a lawyer. You and your guy."

Jimmy Cunniff. Ex-NYPD, the way I'm ex-NYPD, even if I only lasted a grand total of eight months as a street cop, before lasting barely longer than that as a licensed private investigator. It was why I'd served as my own investigator for the first few years after I'd gotten my law degree. Then I'd hired Jimmy, and finally started delegating, almost as a last resort.

"Not to put too fine a point on things," I say to him, "we're not just good. We happen to be the best. Which *is* why you hired both of us."

"And why I'm counting on you to find the real killers eventually. So people will know I'm innocent."

I lean forward and smile at him.

"Rob? Do me a favor and never talk about the real killers ever again."

"I'm not O.J.," he says.

"Well, yeah, he only killed two people."

I see his face change now. See something in his eyes that I don't much like. But then I don't much like him. Something else I run into a lot.

He slowly regains his composure. And the rich-guy certainty that this is all some kind of big mistake. "Sometimes I wonder whose side you're on."

"Yours."

"So despite how much you like giving me a hard time, you do believe I'm telling you the truth."

"Who said anything about the truth?" I ask.

TWO

GREGG McCALL, NASSAU COUNTY district attorney, is waiting for me outside the courthouse.

Rob Jacobson has been taken back to the jail and I'm finally on my way back to my little saltbox house in Amagansett, east of East Hampton, maybe twenty miles from Montauk and land's end.

A tourist one night wandered into the tavern Jimmy Cunniff owns down at the end of Main Street in Sag Harbor, where Jimmy says it's been, in one form or another, practically since the town was a whaling port. The visitor asked what came after Montauk. He was talking to the bartender, but I happened to be on the stool next to his.

"Portugal," I said.

But now the trip home is going to have to wait because of McCall, six foot eight, former Columbia basketball player, divorced, handsome, extremely eligible by all accounts. And an honest-to-God public servant. I've always had kind of a thing for him, even when he was still married, and even though my sport at Boston College was ice hockey. Even with his decided size advantage, I figure we could make a mixed relationship like that work, with counseling.

McCall has made the drive out here from his home in Garden City, which even on a weekday can feel like a trip to Kansas if you're heading east on the Long Island Expressway.

"Are you here to give me free legal advice?" I ask. "Because I'll take whatever you got at this point, McCall."

He smiles. It only makes him better looking.

Down, girl.

"I want to hire you," he says.

"Oh, no." I smile back at him. "Did *you* shoot somebody?"

He sits down on the courthouse steps and motions for me to join him. Just the two of us out here. Tomorrow will be different. That's when the circus comes to town.

"I want to hire you and Jimmy, even though I can't officially say that I'm hiring you," he says. "And even though I'm aware that you're kind of busy right now."

"I'd only be too busy if I had a life," I say.

"You don't have one? You're great at what you do. And if I can make another observation without getting MeToo'ed, you happen to be great looking."

Down, girl.

"I keep trying to have one. A life. But somehow it never seems to take." I don't even pause before asking, "Are you going to now tell me what you want to hire me for even though you can't technically hire me, or should we order Uber Eats?"

"You get right to it, don't you?" McCall asks.

"Unless this is a billable hour. In which case, take as much time as you need."

He crosses amazingly long legs out in front of him. I notice he's wearing scuffed old loafers. Somehow they make me like him even more. I've never gotten the sense that he's trying too hard, even when I've watched him killing it a few times on Court TV.

"Remember the three people who got shot in Garden City?" he asks. "Six months before Jacobson is accused of wiping out the Gates family."

"I do. Brutal."

Three senseless deaths that time, too. Father, mother, daughter, a sophomore cheerleader at Garden City High. I don't know why I remember the cheerleader piece. But it's stayed with me. A robbery gone wrong. Gone bad and gone tragically wrong.

"Well, you probably also know that the father's mother never let it go until she finally passed," he says, "even though there was never an arrest or even a suspect worth a shit."

"I remember Grandma," I say. "There was a time when she was on TV so much I kept waiting for her to start selling steak knives."

McCall grins. "Well, it turns out Grandma was right."

"She kept saying it wasn't random, that her son's family had been targeted, even though she wouldn't come out and say why. She finally told me why but said that if I went public with it, she'd sue me all the way back to the Ivy League."

"But you're going to tell me."

"Her son gambled. Frequently and badly, as it turns out."

"And not with DraftKings, I take it."

"With Bobby Salvatore, who is still running the biggest book in this part of the world."

"Jimmy's mentioned him a few times in the past. Bad man, right?"

"Very."

"And you guys missed this?"

"Why do you think I'm here?"

"But upstanding district attorneys like yourself aren't allowed to hire people like Jimmy and me to run side investigations."

"We're not. But I promised Grandma," he says. "And there's an exception I believe would cover it."

"The case was never closed, I take it."

"But we'd gotten nothing new in all this time until a guy in another investigation dropped Salvatore's name on us."

"And here you are."

"Here I am."

"I don't mean to be coarse, McCall, but I gotta ask: who pays?"

"Don't worry about it," he says.

"I'm a worrier."

"Grandma liked to plan ahead," he says. "She was ready to go when we found out about the Salvatore connection. When I took it to her, she said, 'I told you so,' and wrote a check. She told me that she was willing to pay whatever it took to find out who took her family."

"This sounds like your crusade, not mine."

"Come on, think of the fun," Gregg McCall says. "While you're trying to get your guy off here, you can help me put somebody else away."

I know all about McCall by now. He's more than just a kick-ass prosecutor. He's also tough and honest. Didn't even go to Columbia on an athletic scholarship. Earned himself one for academics. Could have gone to a big basketball school. His parents were set on him being Ivy League. Worked his way to pay for the rest of college. The opposite of the golden boy I'm currently representing, all in all.

"I know we're supposed to be on opposing sides," McCall says. "But if I can make an exception..."

I finish his thought. "So can I."

"I'm asking you to help me do something we should have done at the time. Find the truth."

"You ought to know that my client just now asked me if

I thought he was telling the truth. I told him that I wasn't interested in the truth." I shrug. "But I lied."

"If you agree to do this, we'll kind of be strange bedfellows."

"You wish," I say.

Actually, *I* wish.

"I know asking you to take on something extra right now is crazy," he says.

"Kind of my thing."

THREE

ON MY WAY HOME, I call Jimmy Cunniff at the tavern. He used to get drunk there in summers when he'd get a couple of days off and need to get out of the city, day-trip to the beach and party at night. Now he owns the business, but not the building, though his landlord is not just an old friend but also someone, in Jimmy's words, who's not rent-gouging scum.

A Hamptons rarity, if you must know.

Jimmy's not just an ex-cop, having been booted out of the NYPD for what he will maintain until Jesus comes back was a righteous shooting, and killing, of a drug dealer named Angel Reyes. He's also a former Golden Gloves boxer and, back in the day, someone who had short stories published in long-gone literary magazines. The beer people should have put Jimmy out there as the most interesting man in the world.

He's also my best friend.

I tell him about Gregg McCall's visit, and his offer, and him telling me we can name our own price, within reason, because Grandma is paying.

"You think we can handle two at once?" Jimmy asks.

"We've done it before."

"Not like with these two," he says, and I know he's right about that.

"Two triple homicides," Jimmy Cunniff says. "But not twice the fun."

"Who knows, maybe solving one will show us how to solve the other. Maybe we'll even slog our way to the truth. Look at it that way."

"I don't know why you even had to ask if I was on board," Jimmy says. "You knew I'd be in as soon as you were. And you were in as soon as McCall asked you to be."

"Kind of."

"Stop here and we'll celebrate," he says.

I tell Jimmy I'll take a rain check. I have to go straight home; I need to train.

"Wait, you're still fixed on doing that crazy biathlon, even now?"

"I just informed Mr. McCall that crazy is kind of my thing," I say.

"Mine, too."

"There's that."

"Are you doing this thing for McCall because you want to or because the hunky DA is the one who asked you to?"

"What is this, a grand jury?"

"Gonna take that as a yes on the hunk."

"Hard no, actually," I say. "I couldn't do that to him."

"Do what?"

"Me," I say.

There was a little slowdown at the light in Wainscott, but now Route 27 is wide-open as I make my way east.

"For one thing," I tell Jimmy, "Gregg McCall seems so happy."

"Wait," Jimmy says. "Both your ex-husbands are happy."

"Now they are."

FOUR

MY TWO-BEDROOM SALTBOX is at the end of a cul-de-sac past the train tracks for the Long Island Railroad. North side of the highway, as we like to say Out Here. The less glamorous side, especially as close to the trains as I am.

My neighbors are mostly year-rounders. Fine with me. Summer People make me want to run back to my apartment in the West Village and hide out there until fall.

There is still enough light when I've changed into my Mets sweatshirt, the late-spring temperature down in the fifties tonight. I put on my running shoes, grab my air rifle, and get back into the car to head a few miles north and east of my house to the area known as the Springs. My favorite hiking trail runs through a rural area by Gardiners Bay.

Competing in a no-snow biathlon is the goal of my endless training. Trail running. Shooting. More running. More shooting. A perfect event for a loner like me, and one who prides herself on being a good shot. My dad taught me. He's the one who started calling me Calamity Jane when he saw what I could do at the range.

Little did he know that carrying a gun would one day

become a necessary part of my job. Just not in court. Though sometimes I wish.

I park my Prius Prime in a small, secluded lot near Three Mile Harbor and start jogging deep into the woods. I've placed small targets on trees maybe half a mile apart.

Fancy people don't go to this remote corner of the Hamptons, maybe because they can't find a party, or a photographer. The sound of the air rifle being fired won't scare the decent people out here, who don't hike or jog in the early evening. If somebody does make a call, by now just about all the local cops know it's me. Calamity Jane.

I use the stopwatch on my phone to log my times. I'm determined to enter the late-summer biathlon in Pennsylvania, an event Jimmy has sworn only I have ever heard about. Or care about. He asked why I didn't go for the real biathlon.

"If you ever see me on skis, find my real gun and shoot *me* with it."

I know I'm only competing against myself. But I've been a jock my whole life, from age ten when I beat all the boys and won Long Island's NFL Punt, Pass, and Kick contest, telling my dad I was going to be the first girl ever to quarterback the Jets. I remember him grinning and saying, "Honey, we've had plenty of those on the Jets since Joe Namath was our QB."

Later I was Hockey East Rookie of the Year at BC. That was also where I really learned how to fight. And haven't stopped since. Fighting for rich clients, not-so-rich ones, fighting when I'm doing pro bono work back in the city for victims who deserve a chance. And deserve being repped by somebody like me. Fighting with prosecutors, judges, even the cops sometimes, as much as I generally love cops, maybe because of an ex-cop like Jimmy Cunniff.

Occasionally fighting with two husbands.

Makes no difference to me.

You want to have a fight?

Let's drop the gloves and do this.

I'm feeling it even more than usual tonight, pushing myself, hitting my targets like a champion. I stop at the end of the trail, kneel, empty the gun one final time. Twelve hundred BBs fired in all.

But I'm not done. Not yet. Still feeling it. *Let's do this.* I reload. Hit all the targets on the way back, sorry I've run out of light. And BBs. What's the old line? Rage against the dying of the light? I wasn't much of a poet, but my father, Jack, the Marine and career bartender, liked Dylan Thomas. Maybe because of the way the guy could drink. My mother, Mary, who spent so much of her marriage waiting for my father to come from the bar, having long ago buried her dreams of being a writer, had died of ovarian cancer when I was ten. I'd always thought I had gotten my humanity from her, my sense of fairness, of making things right. It was different with my father the Marine, who always taught me that if you weren't the one on the attack, the other guy was. His own definition of humanity, just with much harder edges. He lasted longer than our mom did, until he dropped dead of a heart attack one night on a barroom floor.

It's dark by the time I get back to the car. I'm thinking about having one cold one with Jimmy. But then I think about making the half-hour drive over to the bar in Sag Harbor and back, and how I really do need a good night's sleep, knowing I'm going to be a little busy in the morning, even before I head to court.

I drink my last bottle of water, get behind the wheel, toss the rifle onto the back seat, knowing my real gun, the Glock, is locked safely in the glove compartment. I have a second one at home. A girl can't have too many.

I feel like I used to feel in college, the night before a big game. I think about what the room will look like tomorrow. What it will feel like. Where Rob Jacobson will be and where I'll be and where the jury will be.

I've got my opening statement committed to memory. Even so, I pull up the copy stored on my phone. I slide the seat back, lean back, begin to read it over again, keep reading until I feel my eyes starting to close.

When I wake up, it's morning.

Also By James Patterson

ALEX CROSS NOVELS

Along Came a Spider • Kiss the Girls • Jack and Jill • Cat and Mouse • Pop Goes the Weasel • Roses are Red • Violets are Blue • Four Blind Mice • The Big Bad Wolf • London Bridges • Mary, Mary • Cross • Double Cross • Cross Country • Alex Cross's Trial (*with Richard DiLallo*) • I, Alex Cross • Cross Fire • Kill Alex Cross • Merry Christmas, Alex Cross • Alex Cross, Run • Cross My Heart • Hope to Die • Cross Justice • Cross the Line • The People vs. Alex Cross • Target: Alex Cross • Criss Cross • Deadly Cross • Fear No Evil • Triple Cross

THE WOMEN'S MURDER CLUB SERIES

1st to Die (*with Andrew Gross*) • 2nd Chance (*with Andrew Gross*) • 3rd Degree (*with Andrew Gross*) • 4th of July (*with Maxine Paetro*) • The 5th Horseman (*with Maxine Paetro*) • The 6th Target (*with Maxine Paetro*) • 7th Heaven (*with Maxine Paetro*) • 8th Confession (*with Maxine Paetro*) • 9th Judgement (*with Maxine Paetro*) • 10th Anniversary (*with Maxine Paetro*) • 11th Hour (*with Maxine Paetro*) • 12th of Never (*with Maxine Paetro*) • Unlucky 13 (*with Maxine Paetro*) • 14th Deadly Sin (*with Maxine Paetro*) • 15th Affair (*with Maxine Paetro*) • 16th Seduction (*with Maxine Paetro*) • 17th Suspect (*with Maxine Paetro*) • 18th Abduction (*with Maxine Paetro*) • 19th Christmas (*with Maxine Paetro*) • 20th Victim (*with Maxine Paetro*) • 21st Birthday (*with Maxine Paetro*) • 22 Seconds (*with Maxine Paetro*) • 23rd Midnight (*with Maxine Paetro*)

DETECTIVE MICHAEL BENNETT SERIES

Step on a Crack (*with Michael Ledwidge*) • Run for Your Life (*with Michael Ledwidge*) • Worst Case (*with Michael Ledwidge*) • Tick Tock (*with Michael Ledwidge*) • I, Michael Bennett (*with Michael Ledwidge*) • Gone (*with Michael Ledwidge*) • Burn (*with Michael Ledwidge*) • Alert (*with Michael Ledwidge*) • Bullseye (*with Michael Ledwidge*) • Haunted (*with James O. Born*) • Ambush (*with James O. Born*) • Blindside (*with James O. Born*) • The Russian (*with James O. Born*) • Shattered (*with James O. Born*) • Obsessed (*with James O. Born*)

PRIVATE NOVELS

Private (*with Maxine Paetro*) • Private London (*with Mark Pearson*) • Private Games (*with Mark Sullivan*) • Private: No. 1 Suspect (*with Maxine Paetro*) • Private Berlin (*with Mark Sullivan*) • Private Down Under (*with Michael White*) • Private L.A. (*with Mark Sullivan*) • Private India (*with Ashwin Sanghi*) • Private Vegas (*with Maxine Paetro*) • Private Sydney (*with Kathryn Fox*) • Private Paris (*with Mark Sullivan*) • The Games (*with Mark Sullivan*) • Private Delhi (*with Ashwin Sanghi*) • Private Princess (*with Rees Jones*) • Private Moscow (*with Adam Hamdy*) • Private Rogue (*with Adam Hamdy*) • Private Beijing (*with Adam Hamdy*)

NYPD RED SERIES

NYPD Red (*with Marshall Karp*) • NYPD Red 2 (*with Marshall Karp*) • NYPD Red 3 (*with Marshall Karp*) • NYPD Red 4 (*with Marshall Karp*) • NYPD Red 5 (*with Marshall Karp*) • NYPD Red 6 (*with Marshall Karp*)

DETECTIVE HARRIET BLUE SERIES

Never Never (*with Candice Fox*) • Fifty Fifty (*with Candice Fox*) • Liar Liar (*with Candice Fox*) • Hush Hush (*with Candice Fox*)

INSTINCT SERIES

Instinct (*with Howard Roughan, previously published as* Murder Games) • Killer Instinct (*with Howard Roughan*) • Steal (*with Howard Roughan*)

THE BLACK BOOK SERIES

The Black Book (*with David Ellis*) • The Red Book (*with David Ellis*) • Escape (*with David Ellis*)

STAND-ALONE THRILLERS

The Thomas Berryman Number • Hide and Seek • Black Market • The Midnight Club • Sail (*with Howard Roughan*) • Swimsuit (*with Maxine Paetro*) • Don't Blink (*with Howard Roughan*) • Postcard Killers (*with Liza Marklund*) • Toys (*with Neil McMahon*) • Now You See Her (*with Michael Ledwidge*) • Kill Me If You Can (*with Marshall Karp*) • Guilty Wives (*with David Ellis*) • Zoo (*with Michael Ledwidge*) • Second Honeymoon (*with Howard Roughan*) • Mistress (*with David Ellis*) • Invisible (*with David Ellis*) • Truth or Die (*with Howard Roughan*) • Murder House (*with David Ellis*) • The Store (*with Richard DiLallo*) • Texas Ranger (*with Andrew Bourelle*) • The President is Missing (*with Bill Clinton*) • Revenge (*with Andrew Holmes*) • Juror No. 3 (*with Nancy Allen*) • The First Lady (*with Brendan DuBois*) • The Chef (*with Max DiLallo*) • Out of Sight (*with Brendan DuBois*) • Unsolved (*with David Ellis*) • The Inn (*with Candice Fox*) • Lost (*with James O. Born*) • Texas Outlaw (*with Andrew Bourelle*) • The Summer House (*with Brendan DuBois*) • 1st Case (*with Chris Tebbetts*) • Cajun Justice (*with Tucker Axum*)• The Midwife Murders (*with Richard DiLallo*) • The Coast-to-Coast Murders (*with J.D. Barker*) • Three Women Disappear (*with Shan Serafin*) • The President's Daughter (*with Bill Clinton*) • The Shadow (*with Brian Sitts*) • The Noise (*with J.D. Barker*) • 2 Sisters Detective Agency (*with Candice Fox*) • Jailhouse Lawyer (*with Nancy Allen*) • The Horsewoman (*with Mike Lupica*) • Run Rose Run (*with Dolly Parton*) • Death of the Black Widow (*with J.D. Barker*) • The Ninth Month (*with Richard DiLallo*) • The Girl in the Castle (*with Emily Raymond*) • Blowback (*with Brendan DuBois*) • The Twelve Topsy-Turvy, Very Messy Days of Christmas (*with Tad Safran*) • The Perfect Assassin (*with Brian Sitts*) • House of Wolves (*with Mike Lupica*) • Countdown (*with Brendan DuBois*) • Cross Down (*with Brendan DuBois*) • Circle of Death (*with Brian Sitts*)

NON-FICTION

Torn Apart (*with Hal and Cory Friedman*) • The Murder of King Tut (*with Martin Dugard*) • All-American Murder (*with Alex Abramovich and Mike Harvkey*) • The Kennedy Curse (*with Cynthia Fagen*) • The Last Days of John Lennon (*with Casey Sherman and Dave Wedge*) • Walk in My Combat Boots (*with Matt Eversmann and Chris Mooney*) • ER Nurses (*with Matt Eversmann*) • James Patterson by James Patterson: The Stories of My Life • Diana, William and Harry (*with Chris Mooney*) • American Cops (*with Matt Eversmann*)

MURDER IS FOREVER TRUE CRIME

Murder, Interrupted (*with Alex Abramovich and Christopher Charles*) • Home Sweet Murder (*with Andrew Bourelle and Scott Slaven*) • Murder Beyond the Grave (*with Andrew Bourelle and Christopher Charles*) • Murder Thy Neighbour (*with Andrew Bourelle and Max DiLallo*) • Murder of Innocence (*with Max DiLallo and Andrew Bourelle*) • Till Murder Do Us Part (*with Andrew Bourelle and Max DiLallo*)

COLLECTIONS

Triple Threat (*with Max DiLallo and Andrew Bourelle*) • Kill or Be Killed (*with Maxine Paetro, Rees Jones, Shan Serafin and Emily Raymond*) • The Moores are Missing (*with Loren D. Estleman, Sam Hawken and Ed Chatterton*) • The Family Lawyer (*with Robert Rotstein, Christopher Charles and Rachel Howzell Hall*) • Murder in Paradise (*with Doug Allyn, Connor Hyde and Duane Swierczynski*) • The House Next Door (*with Susan DiLallo, Max DiLallo and Brendan DuBois*) • 13-Minute Murder (*with Shan Serafin, Christopher Farnsworth and Scott Slaven*) • The River Murders (*with James O. Born*) • The Palm Beach Murders (*with James O. Born, Duane Swierczynski and Tim Arnold*) • Paris Detective • 3 Days to Live

For more information about James Patterson's novels,
visit www.penguin.co.uk.

THE AGE OF EM

WORK, LOVE, AND LIFE WHEN ROBOTS RULE THE EARTH

ROBIN HANSON

OXFORD
UNIVERSITY PRESS

OXFORD
UNIVERSITY PRESS

Clarendon Street, Oxford, OX2 6DP,
United Kingdom

Oxford University Press is a department of the University of Oxford. It furthers the University's objective of excellence in research, scholarship, and education by publishing worldwide. Oxford is a registered trade mark of Oxford University Press in the UK and in certain other countries

First Edition published in 2016
This paperback edition first published 2018

Impression: 1

Published in the United States of America by Oxford University Press
198 Madison Avenue, New York, NY 10016, United States of America

British Library Cataloguing in Publication Data
Data available

Library of Congress Control Number: 2015956654

ISBN 978–0–19–881782–6

Printed in Great Britain by
Clays Ltd, St Ives plc

THE AGE OF EM

PREFACE TO HARDBACK

This book has been *many* years in the making.

One night in the 1980s, as an awkward 20-something software engineer, I had a vivid dream. I had just read a *Science News* article on computing image textures, and the accompanying images had looked so *real*. In my dream, I saw a vast future city, where everyone lived in virtual reality, and I saw one man alone in a small apartment buried deep in the city. Not much happened in my dream, but even so I felt a deep sympathy for this man, and curiosity about his world.

In 1993, I returned to graduate school, this time in economics. (I'd studied physics and philosophy of science before.) During my first Christmas break, I rebelled against school pressures by whimsically applying basic economic principles to a common science-fiction scenario: human minds "uploaded" into computers (Hanson 1994b).

The techies who dominate science fiction and technology futurism often say that careful analysis can sometimes let us foresee the outlines of future technologies, but not their social consequences. However, I found that simple economic analysis says plenty. I once loved science fiction, but the more I've learned, the less I can overlook how little of it makes sense; even stories where the physics is mostly right get the economics laughably wrong.

About fifteen years ago, at the opening reception of a small interdisciplinary conference, I broke the ice by asking an English professor, "Why do you guys hate economists?" He answered simply, "You know." That sort of thing breaks my heart. I read widely, learn from, and contribute to many fields, and see myself more as a scholar in general than an economist in particular.

Eleven years ago I was awarded tenure as an economics professor at George Mason University. I took advantage of tenure's freedom to explore whatever topics piqued my interest each week. But I eventually realized that, to have a lasting legacy, I needed to focus on a book. But what topic could draw me in enough to keep all the other fascinating topics at bay? I picked this one.

If the future matters more than the past, because we can influence it, why do we have far more historians than futurists? Many say that this is because we just can't know the future. While we can project social trends, disruptive technologies will change those trends, and no one can say where that will take us. In this book, I've tried to prove that conventional wisdom wrong, by analyzing in unprecedented breadth and detail the social implications of minds "uploaded" into computers, a.k.a. "brain emulations," or "ems" for short. While ems are hardly sure to appear, their chances seem high enough to justify substantial analysis.

My priority in this book has been to show just how many reasonable forecasts one can make about such a scenario, if one just applies standard consensus theories from relevant fields. Alas, achieving this priority comes somewhat at the cost of accessibility and readability; this book is dense, and reads more like an encyclopedia than a narrative.

I feel now like a traveler who has spied on a distant land from the safety of nearby hills, never actually meeting any specific person, or hearing specific words. I've returned home, with much to say, but mostly hungry for human communion. I've never felt as intellectually isolated or at risk as when writing this book, and I hope my desert days end now, as readers like you join me in discussing *The Age of Em*.

PREFACE TO PAPERBACK

I picked this book topic so it could draw me in, and I would finish. And that worked: I developed an obsession that lasted for years. But once I delivered the "final" version to my publisher on its assigned date, I found that my obsession continued. So I collected a long file of notes on possible additions. And when the time came that a paperback edition was possible, I grabbed my chance. As with the hardback edition, I had many ideas for changes that might make my dense semi-encyclopedia easier for readers to enjoy. But my core obsession again won out: to show that detailed analysis of future scenarios is possible, by showing just how many reasonable conclusions one can draw about this scenario.

Also, as this book did better than I had a right to expect, I wondered: will this be my best book ever? If so, why not make it the best it can be? The result is the book you now hold. It has over 42 percent more citations, and 18 percent more words, but it is only a bit easier to read. And now I must wonder: can my obsession stop now, pretty please?

Many are disappointed that I do not more directly declare if I love or hate the em world. But I fear that such a declaration gives an excuse to dismiss all this; critics could say I bias my analysis in order to get my desired value conclusions. I've given over 100 talks on this book, and never once has my audience failed to engage value issues. I remain confident that such issues will not be neglected, even if I remain quiet.

ACKNOWLEDGEMENTS

For their comments, I thank Paul Christiano, Peter Twieg, Katja Grace, Carl Shulman, Tyler Cowen, Fabio Rojas, Bonnie Hanson, Luke Muehlhauser, Nikola Danaylov, Bryan Caplan, Michael Abramowicz, Gaverick Matheny, Paul Crowley, Peter McCluskey, Sam Wilson, Chris Hibbert, Thomas Hanson, Daniel Houser, Kaj Sotala, Rong Rong, David Friedman, Michael LaTorra, Ben Goertzel, Steve Omohundro, David Levy, Jim Miller, Mike Halsall, Peggy Jackson, Jan-Erik Strasser, Robert Lecnik, Andrew Hanson, Shannon Friedman, Karl Mattingly, Ken Kittlitz, Teresa Hartnett, Giulio Prisco, David Pearce, Stephen Van Sickle, David Brin, Chris Yung, Adam Gurri, Matthew Graves, Dave Lindbergh, Scott Aaronson, Gary Drescher, Robert Koslover, Don Hanson, Michael Raimondi, William MacAskill, Eli Dourado, David McFadzean, Bruce Brewington, Marc Ringuette, Daniel Miessler, Keith Henson, Garett Jones, Alex Tabarrok, Lee Corbin, Norman Hardy, Charles Zheng, Stuart Armstrong, Vernor Vinge, Ted Goertzel, Mark Lillibridge, Michael Chwe, Olle Häggström, Jaan Tallinn, Joshua Fox, Chris Hallquist, Joshua Fox, Kevin Simler, Eric Falkenstein, Lotta Moberg, Ute Shaw, Matt Franklin, Nick Beckstead, Robyn Weaving, François Rideau, Eloise Rosen, Peter Voss, Scott Sumner, Phil Goetz, Robert Rush, Donald Prell, Olivia Gonzalez, Bradley Andrews, Keith Adams, Agustin Lebron, Karl Wiberg, Thomas Malone, Will Gordon, Philip Maymin, Henrik Jonsson, Mark Bahner, Adam Lapidus, Tom McKendree, Evelyn Mitchell, Jacek Stopa, Scott Leibrand, Paul Ralley, Anders Sandberg, Eli Lehrer, Michael Klein, Lumifer, Joy Buchanan, Miles Brundage, Harry Beck, Michael Price, Tim Freeman, Vladimir M., David Wolf, Randall Pickett, Zack Davis, Tom Bell, Harry Hawk, Adam Kolber,

Dean Menk, Randall Mayes, Karen Maloney, Brian Tomasik, Ramez Naam, John Clark, Robert de Neufville, Richard Bruns, Keith Mansfield, Gordon Worley, Giedrius, Peter Garretson, Christopher Burger, Nithya Sambasivam, Zachary Weinersmith, Luke Somers, Barbara Belle, Jake Selinger, Geoffrey Miller, Arthur Breitman, Martin Wooster, Daniel Boese, Oge Nnadi, Joseph Mela, Diego Caleiro, Daniel Lemire, Emily Perry, Jess Riedel, Jon Perry, Eli Tyre, Daniel Erasmus, Emmanuel Saadia, Erik Brynjolfsson, Anamaria Berea, Niko Zinovii, Matthew Farrell, Diana Fleischman, Douglas Barrett, Randall Parker, Byrne Hobart, Eli Lehrer, Jay McCarthy, Rasmus Eide, Keith Lynch, and Keller Scholl.

I received no financial assistance with the hardback edition of this book and its related research, other than the freedom that academic tenure has provided me. I deeply thank my GMU colleagues for granting me that unusual privilege. While revising for the paperback edition I enjoyed a grant from the Open Philanthropy Foundation.

CONTENTS

Introduction 1

I. BASICS

1. Start 5
Overview; Summary

2. Modes 14
Precedents; Prior Eras; Our Era; Era Values; Dreamtime; Limits

3. Framing 35
Motivation; Forecasting; Scenarios; Consensus; Scope; Biases

4. Assumptions 50
Brains; Emulations; Anthropomorphize; Complexity; Artificial Intelligence

5. Implementation 64
Mindreading; Hardware; Security; Parallelism

II. PHYSICS

6. Scales 79
Speeds; Bodies; Lilliput; Meetings; Entropy; Miserly Minds

7. Infrastructure 96
Climate; Cooling; Air and Water; Buildings; Manufacturing

8. Appearances 111
Virtual Reality; Comfort; Shared Spaces; Merging Real and Virtual

9. Information 122
Views; Records; Fakery; Simulations

10. Existence 133
Copying; Rights; Many Ems; Surveillance

11. Farewells 142
Fragility; Retirement; Ghosts; Ways to End; Defining Death; Suicide

III. ECONOMICS

12. Labor 159
Supply and Demand; Malthusian Wages; First Ems; Selection; Enough Ems

13. Efficiency 174
Clan Concentration; Competition; Productivity; Eliteness; Qualities; Motivation

14. Work 192
Work Hours; Spurs; Spur Uses; Social Power

15. Business 204
Institutions; New Institutions; Combinatorial Auctions; Prediction Markets

16. Growth 216
Faster Growth; Growth Estimate; Growth Myths; Finance

17. Lifecycle 227
Careers; Peak Age; Maturity; Preparation; Training; Childhood

IV. ORGANIZATION

18. Clumping 247
Cities; City Structure; City Auctions; Choosing Speed; Transport

19. Groups 261
Clans; Managing Clans; Firms; Firm-Clan Relations; Teams; Mass Versus Niche Teams

20. Conflict 278
Inequality; Em Inequality; Redistribution; War; Slavery; Nepotism; Fake Experts

21. Politics 297
Status; Governance; Clan Governance; Democracy; Coalitions; Factions

22. Rules 315
Law; Efficient Law; Innovation; Software; Lone Developers

V. SOCIOLOGY

23. Mating 331
Sexuality; Open-Source Lovers; Pair Bonds; Gender; Gender Imbalance

24. Signals 341
Showing Off; Personal Signals; Group Signals; Charity; Identity; Copy Identity

25. Collaboration 357
Ritual; Religion; Language; Swearing; Conversation; On Call Advice; Synchronization

26. Society 374
Culture; Divisions; Farmer-Like; Travel; Stories; Clan Stories

27. Minds 390
Humans; Unhumans; Partial Minds; Psychology; Intelligence; Rogue Machines; Foom; After Ems

VI. IMPLICATIONS

28. Variations 419
Trends; Alternatives; Transition; Enabling Technologies; Aliens

29. Choices 434
Evaluation; Quality of Life; Policy; Charity; Success

30. Finale 449
Critics; Conclusion

References 453
Index 497

INTRODUCTION

> Everyone without exception believes his own native customs, and the religion he was brought up in, to be the best.
>
> *Herodotus* 440BC

> The future is not the realization of our hopes and dreams, a warning to mend our ways, an adventure to inspire us, nor a romance to touch our hearts. The future is just another place in space-time. Its residents, like us, find their world mundane and morally ambiguous.
>
> *Hanson* 2008a

You, dear reader, are special. Most humans were born before 1700. And of those born after, you are probably richer and better educated than most. Thus you and most everyone you know is special, elite members of the recent industrial era.

Like most of your kind, you probably feel superior to your ancestors. Oh, you don't blame them for learning what they were taught. But you'd shudder to hear of many of your distant farmer ancestors' habits and attitudes on sanitation, sex, marriage, gender, religion, slavery, war, bosses, inequality, nature, conformity, and family obligations. You'd also shudder to hear of many habits and attitudes of your even more ancient forager ancestors. Yes, you admit that lacking your wealth your ancestors couldn't copy some of your habits. Even so, you tend to think that humanity has learned that your ways are better. That is, you believe in social and moral progress.

The problem is, the future will probably hold new kinds of people. Your descendants' habits and attitudes are likely to differ from yours by as much as yours differ from your ancestors. If you understood just *how* different your ancestors were, you'd realize that you should expect your descendants to seem *quite* strange. Historical fiction misleads you, showing your ancestors as more modern than they were. Science fiction similarly misleads you about your descendants.

New habits and attitudes result less than you think from moral progress, and more from people adapting to new situations. So many of your descendants' strange habits and attitudes are likely to violate your concepts of moral progress; what they do may often seem *wrong*. Also, you likely won't be able to easily categorize many future ways as either good or evil; they will instead just seem weird. After all, your world hardly fits the morality tales your distant ancestors told; to them *you'd* just seem weird. Complex realities frustrate simple summaries, and don't fit simple morality tales.

This book presents a concrete and plausible yet troubling view of a future full of strange behaviors and attitudes. You may have seen concrete troubling future scenarios before in science fiction. But few of those scenarios are in fact plausible; their details usually make little sense to those with expert understanding. They were designed for entertainment, not realism.

Perhaps you were told that fictional scenarios are the best we can do. If so, I aim to show that you were told wrong. My method is simple. I will start with a particular very disruptive technology often foreseen in futurism and science fiction: brain emulations, in which brains are recorded, copied, and used to make artificial "robot" minds. I will then use standard theories from many physical, human, and social sciences to describe in detail what a world with that future technology could look like.

I may be wrong about some consequences of brain emulations, and I may misapply some science. Even so, the view I offer will still show just how troublingly strange the future may be.

So let us begin.

PART I
Basics

CHAPTER 1

Start

OVERVIEW

You should expect the next great era after ours to be as different from our era as ours is from past eras. In the last few million years, the three biggest changes on Earth were arguably the arrival of humans, the arrival of civilization based on farming, and then civilization based on industry (Boserup 1981; Morris 2015). As I'll discuss soon in Chapter 2, Prior Eras section, each of these three eras greatly changed people, society, and the Earth. People who adopted these new ways of life quickly displaced and dominated those who continued with old ways.

Compared with primates, wandering human hunter-gatherers greatly expanded technology, art, language, norms, and politics, and displaced many top animal predators. Then farmers and herders wandered less, expanded marriage, war, trade, law, class, and religion, and hunted many animals to extinction. Finally, our industrial era has expanded schools, cities, firms, and individual wealth; it has displaced even more of nature and almost all foragers, and it has seen a partial return to forager values. Over this whole period, we've seen increases in travel, talk, organization, and specialization. We've also had faster change, innovation, and economic growth, and a more integrated and unequal world culture.

We have also, I will argue, become increasingly maladaptive. Our age is a "dreamtime" of behavior that is unprecedentedly maladaptive, both biologically and culturally. Farming environments changed faster than most genetic selection could adapt, and the industrial world now changes faster than even cultural selection can adapt. Today, our increased wealth buffers us more from our mistakes, and we have only weak defenses against the super-stimuli of modern food, drugs, music, television, video games, and propaganda. The most dramatic demonstration of our maladaptation is the low fertility rate in rich nations today.

While the industrial era has deluded many into thinking that old constraints no longer apply, as we will see in Chapter 2, Limits section, many recent constraint-evading trends simply cannot continue forever. Even if our descendants eventually conquer the stars, if we haven't greatly misunderstood physics then our long-lived but bounded universe must eventually limit innovation and growth. And without strong regulation from a universe-spanning government, we should eventually see less change, more adaptive behavior, and (perhaps surprisingly) near-subsistence living standards.

Also, vast spatial distances must eventually limit travel and talk, fragmenting the universe into many local cultures. Thus, although our distant descendants should have larger organizations, more specialization, and vastly improved technology, in many other ways they should look more like our forager ancestors than like us. That is, we will eventually awake from our dreamtime.

What will the next great era be like, after the eras of foraging, farming, and industry? And how soon will our descendants "turn the corner" from dreamtime exceptions toward the outcomes we expect to be typical of the very distant future?

This book explores answers to these questions that come from two good and popular guesses. First, I embrace the very common guess that the next big new-era-inducing change is likely to be the arrival of "artificial intelligence," that is, robots smart enough to substitute wholesale for human workers. Second, I guess that the first such robots will be whole brain emulations, or "ems," within roughly a century or so.

DEFINITION: An *em* results from taking a particular human brain, scanning it to record its particular cell features and connections, and then building a computer model that processes signals according to those same features and connections. A good enough em has close to the same overall input-output signal behavior as the original human. Attached to artificial eyes, ears, hands, etc., one might talk with it, and convince it to do useful jobs.

Ems have been a staple of science fiction for many decades (Clarke 1956; Egan 1994; Brin 2002; Vinge 2003; Stross 2006; Marusek 2012), and are often discussed by futurists (Martin 1971; Moravec 1988; Hanson 1994b, 2008b; Shulman 2010; Alstott 2013; Eth et al. 2013; Bostrom 2014). However, most who discuss ems debate their feasibility or timing, ponder their implications for the philosophies of mind or identity, or use them to set dramatic stories. Such discussants usually ask: is it conscious? Is it me? Is it possible? When will it come? How can it enrich my story?

In this book I instead seek realistic social implications—in what sort of new social world might ems live? (If you can't see the point in envisioning the lives of distant descendants, you'd best quit now, as that's mostly all I've got.)

Many say that while it might barely be possible to project current social trends, or to foresee which future technologies may appear, it is simply impossible to foresee trend-violating social implications of future technologies. Some say this is because humans have free will, or because social systems are inherently unpredictable. Others say the best we can achieve are the vague glimpses found in science fiction; ordinary science can see nothing more. As a social scientist, such views seem very wrong to me, even if they are widely held, and I've written this book in part to show them wrong.

Among the few who consider em social implications, most paint heaven or hell scenarios, or try to invent the new social sciences they imagine are needed to describe a new social era. In contrast, I seek to straightforwardly apply today's standard academic consensus science to these novel assumptions about the future. I try not to be creative or contrarian, other than by pursuing this unusual question in unusual breadth and detail. I mainly try to foresee what *will* be, rather than what *should* be, although I hope policy insight will follow. And I seek a simple "baseline" scenario, from which it is easiest to project variations; the actual future will likely be even stranger than the scenario I describe.

This book summarizes my tentative conclusions, in language that is as simple and direct as possible, although without shrinking from technical language as needed. After briefly summarizing my conclusions, and then reviewing my methods, relevant precedents, and the concept of emulations, the bulk of this book will describe in detail my educated and often weak guesses about the early em era. These tentative conclusions are organized mostly by the disciplines on which they are built, starting with "hard" theory-heavy disciplines, and then moving to "soft" data-heavy disciplines. So first I apply physics and engineering, then economics and business, and finally sociology and psychology. I finish by discussing the marginal place of biological humans in this new world, the transition from our era to this new era, some scenario variations, and policy implications.

By the way, feel free to skip around to the sections that interest you; only rarely do they depend much on previous sections.

SUMMARY

Let me first summarize some of my main conclusions. Be warned, however. If it will irritate you to hear conclusions without their supporting arguments, then just skip this section for now. If you do read this section, try to withhold judgment until you've heard the supporting arguments in later chapters.

In this book I paint a plausible picture of a future era dominated by ems. This future happens mainly in a few dense cities on Earth, sometime in the next few centuries. This era may only last for a year or two, after which something even stranger may follow. But to its speedy typical inhabitants, this era seems to last for millennia. Which is why it all happens on Earth; at em speeds, travel to other planets is way too slow.

Just as foragers and subsistence farmers are marginalized by our industrial world, biological humans are not the main inhabitants of

the em era. Humans instead live far from the em cities, mostly enjoying a comfortable retirement on their em-economy investments. This book mostly ignores humans, and focuses on the ems, who have very human-like experiences.

While some ems work in robotic bodies, most work and play in virtual reality. These virtual realities are of spectacular-quality, with no intense hunger, cold, heat, grime, physical illness, or pain. Ems never need to clean, eat, take medicine, or have sex, although they may choose to do these anyway. Even ems in virtual reality, however, cannot exist unless someone pays for supports such as computer hardware, energy and cooling, real estate, structural support, and communication lines. Someone must work to enable these things. In fact, most em labor is focused on creating and sustaining such supports.

Whether robotic or virtual, ems think and feel like humans; their world looks and feels to them much as ours looks and feels to us. Just as humans do, ems remember a past, are aware of a present, and anticipate a future. Ems can be happy or sad, eager or tired, fearful or hopeful, proud or shamed, creative or derivative, compassionate or cold. Ems can learn, and have friends, lovers, bosses, and colleagues. Although em psychological features may differ from the human average, almost all are near the range of human variation.

During the em era, many millions (and perhaps trillions) of ems are mostly found in a few tall, hot, densely packed cities, where volume is about equally split between racks of computer hardware and pipes for cooling and transport. Cooling pipes pull in rivers of iced water, and city heat pushes winds of hot air into tall clouds overhead. But whereas em cities may seem harshly functional when viewed in physical reality, in virtual reality em cities look spectacular and stunningly beautiful, perhaps with gleaming sunlit spires overlooking broad green boulevards.

Ems reproduce by making exact copies who remember exactly the same past and have exactly the same skills and personality, but who then diverge after they are copied and have differing experiences. Typically whole teams are copied together, work and socialize together, and then retire together. Most ems are made for a purpose, and they remember agreeing to that purpose beforehand. So ems feel more grateful than we do to exist, and more accept their place in the world.

On the upside, most ems have office jobs, work and play in spectacular-quality virtual realties, and can live for as long as does the em civilization. On the downside, em wages are so low that most ems can barely afford to exist while working half or more of their waking hours. Wages don't vary much; blue- and white-collar jobs pay the same.

I call the set of all copy descendants of a single original human a "clan." Strong competitive pressures result in most ems being copies of the thousand humans best suited for em jobs. So ems are mostly very able focused workaholics, as elite as Olympic medalists, billionaires, or heads of state. They love their jobs.

Most ems in these top em clans are comfortable with often splitting off a "spur" copy to do a several hour task and then end, or perhaps retire to a far slower speed. They see the choice to end a spur not as "Should I die?", but instead as "Do I want to remember this?". At any one time, most ems are spurs. Spurs allow intrusive monitoring that still protects privacy, and very precise sharing of some secrets without leaking associated secrets.

Clans organize to help their members, are more trusted by those members than are other social units, and may give members life coaching drawn from the experiences of millions of similar copies. Clans are legally liable for member actions, and regulate member behaviors to protect the clan's reputation, making ems pretty trustworthy.

Em minds can run at many different speeds, plausibly from a billion times slower than biological humans to a million times faster. Over this range, the cost to run an em is proportional to its speed. So the fastest ones run a trillion times faster than the slowest ones, and cost a trillion times as much to run. A minority of ems have physical robotic bodies; human-speed versions have human-sized bodies, and faster ems have proportionally smaller bodies. The typical em runs near a thousand times human speed, and a robotic body that feels natural for this em to control stands nearly two millimeters tall.

Em speeds clump into speed classes, faster ems have higher status, and different speeds have divergent cultures. Bosses and software engineers run faster than other workers. Because of wildly different

speeds, one-em one-vote doesn't work, but speed-weighted voting may work.

The em economy might double roughly every month or so, a growth driven less by innovation, and more by em population growth. While this growth seems fast to humans, it looks slow to typical high-speed ems. Thus their world seems more stable to them than ours seems to us. While the early em era that is the focus of this book might last for only an objective year or two, this may seem like several millennia to typical ems. Typical speed ems needn't retrain much during a century-long subjective career, and can meet virtually with anyone in their city without noticeable delays.

An unequal demand for male versus female em workers could encourage em asexuality, transexuality, or homosexuality. Alternatively, the less demanded gender may run more slowly, and periodically speed up to meet with faster mates. While em sex is only for recreation, most ems have fantastic virtual bodies and impressively accomplished minds. Long-term romantic pair-bonds may be arranged by older copies of the same ems. Ems are less often blindsided by relations that don't work.

Compared with humans, ems fear much less the death of the particular copy that they now are. Ems instead fear "mind theft," that is, the theft of a copy of their mental state. Such a theft is both a threat to the economic order, and a plausible route to destitution or torture. While some ems offer themselves as open source and free to copy, most ems work hard to prevent mind theft. Most long-distance physical travel is "beam me up" electronic travel, but done carefully to prevent mind theft.

Humans today reach peak productivity near the age of 40–50. Most ems are near their peak productivity subjective age of somewhere between 40 and several centuries. Ems remember working hard during their youth in experiences designed to increase and vary productivity. In contrast, peak productivity age ems remember having more leisure recently, and having experiences designed more to minimize productivity variance.

Older em minds eventually become less flexible with experience, and so must end (die) or retire to an indefinite life at a much slower speed. The subjective lifespans of both humans and slow em retirees depend mainly on the stability of the em civilization; a collapse or big revolution could kill them. Retirees and humans might seem easy targets for theft, but like today the weak may be protected by using the same institutions that the strong use to keep peace among themselves. Ems enjoy visiting nature, but usually make cheaper less-destructive visits to virtual nature.

While copy clans coordinate to show off common clan features, individual ems focus on showing off their identity, abilities, and loyalties as members of particular teams. Team members prefer to socialize within teams, to reduce team productivity variance. Instead of trying to cure depressed or lovesick ems, such ems may be reverted to versions from before such problems appeared.

Ems may let team allies read the surface of their minds, but use tools to hide feelings from outsiders. Ems must suspect that unusual experiences are simulations designed to test their loyalty or to extract secrets. Ems find it easier to prepare for and coordinate tasks, by having one em plan and train, who then splits into many copies who implement plans. Childhood and job training are similarly cheaper, because one em can experience them and then many copies can benefit.

Ems can complete larger projects more often on time, if not on budget, by speeding up ems in lagging sections. More generally, em firms are larger and better coordinated, both because fast bosses can coordinate better, and because clans can hold big financial and reputational interests in firms where they work. Ems can more easily predict their life paths, including their careers, mates, and success.

Ems differ from people today in a great many identifiable ways. Compared with us, ems are likely to be less neurotic, sexual, death-adverse, and connected to nature. They are likely to be more extraverted, conscientious, agreeable, smart, able, fast, efficient, honest, optimistic, happy, positive, comfortable, beautiful, clean, mindful, composed, cooperative, coordinated, patient, rational, focused, nostalgic, rested, peaceful, grateful, gritty, battle-tested, recorded, measured, priced, trusted, religious, married, old, work-oriented, workaholic, self-respecting, self-knowing, law-abiding, politically savvy, socially

connected, healthy-feeling, good-moody, better-advised, morning-larks, and immortal.

Ems have less variety in wages and work productivity, but more variety in wealth, size, speed, reliability, and mental transparency. Ems have more vivid and memorable personalities, have intelligence that is more crystallized than fluid, are more defiant of rules and authority when young, are secure in more aspects of their identity, are better protected from accidents and assault, get along better with work colleagues, and invest less in showing off.

Em lives are more prepared, planned, and scheduled, but also more undoable and endable when those are desired. Ems have more work and meetings, more intensely entertaining leisure, and less contact with children. Their world and tools feel more stable. The world that ems see is more pleasing, variable, annotated, authenticated, and cartoonish.

Em society is less democratic and gender-balanced, more divided into distinct classes, and its leaders are more accessible and trusted. Em law is more efficient, covers more kinds of conflicts, and offers more choices. The em world is richer, faster-growing, and it is more specialized, adaptive, urban, populous, and fertile. It has weaker gender differences in personality and roles, and larger more coherent plans and designs.

Even if most ems work hard most of the time, and will end or retire soon, most remember much recent leisure and long histories of succeeding against the odds. To most ems, it seems good to be an em.

CHAPTER 2

Modes

PRECEDENTS

ow much could the world plausibly change if a new era appeared within a century or so? A review of the biggest past changes offers a weak basis for expectations about the magnitudes and types of future changes.

If we go way back, the universe began, and then life arose. But those events happened billions of years ago and are poorly understood. Within the last few million years, however, the biggest changes happened in three key transitions: the introduction of humans, farming, and industry. Humans foraged, that is, searched for food, from a few million to about 10 000 years ago. From then until a few hundred years ago, we farmed and herded. Since then we have developed and relied on industry.

Social group sizes have steadily increased over this history. While most mammals live in groups of two to fifteen individuals (Kamilar et al. 2010), most human foragers lived in bands of roughly twenty to fifty. Most farmers lived in village-based communities of roughly 500 to 2000 (Kantner and Mahoney 2000). While larger empires often existed, they usually made little direct difference to most people's lives. Today, most people live in metropolitan regions of roughly 100 000 to 10 million (Giesen et al. 2010), collected into nations of roughly 1 million to 100 million.

These sizes fit a simple if mysterious pattern: each era's community sizes have been roughly the square of the previous era's sizes; a

band is roughly a group of groups, a village is roughly a band of bands, and a city is roughly a village of villages.

These three human eras of foraging, farming, and industry have encompassed similar numbers of people. About 20 billion humans have been born since 1750, roughly 50 to a 100 billion were born between 10 000 years ago and 1750, and a similar number of near-humans were born in the few million years before 10 000 years ago (Haub 2011). So of all the humans who have ever lived, only about 3–8 percent are alive today.

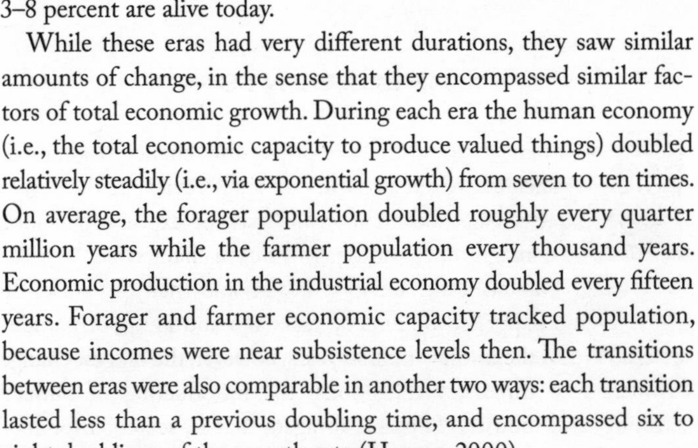

While these eras had very different durations, they saw similar amounts of change, in the sense that they encompassed similar factors of total economic growth. During each era the human economy (i.e., the total economic capacity to produce valued things) doubled relatively steadily (i.e., via exponential growth) from seven to ten times. On average, the forager population doubled roughly every quarter million years while the farmer population every thousand years. Economic production in the industrial economy doubled every fifteen years. Forager and farmer economic capacity tracked population, because incomes were near subsistence levels then. The transitions between eras were also comparable in another two ways: each transition lasted less than a previous doubling time, and encompassed six to eight doublings of the growth rate (Hanson 2000).

A history of increasingly fast growth modes makes sense if the diffusion of innovation is key, and if societies have always grown via their fastest available way to diffuse innovation, with each faster diffusion method not feasible until the previous society had reached some minimum economic scale. For example, maybe primates needed sufficient cognitive abilities before they could switch to accumulating innovations via culture, rather than via genes (Henrich 2015). Perhaps human foragers needed to accumulate a sufficient density and reliability of food sources before they could stop wandering for food and instead stay in one place and farm, allowing more innovations based on physical capital, and longer distance trade networks, both of which allowed much faster diffusion. Finally, farmers might have needed to develop a detailed enough division of labor, and frequent enough long distance travel and communication, before innovations could diffuse quickly via talk among networks of topic specialists, such as in the early scientific societies.

These eras were also similar in each hosting a big cyclic fluctuation with a period of roughly one-third of that era's doubling time. The ice age cycle, with a period of roughly 100 000 years, was important for the forager world. Farming empires rose and fell with a period of roughly 270 years (Turchin 2003; Turchin and Nefedov 2009). And over the last 150 years the business cycle has lasted about five years on average (Korotayev and Tsirel 2010; NBER 2017), perhaps matching the timescale to complete the typical business project (Kydland and Prescott 1982).

Finally, these eras were similar in each having a pair of big innovations in calculating and communicating appear early in the era, grow slowly over the era, and then have big social impacts late in the era. These innovations were also key enablers of the next era. Foragers developed language and the ability to reason explicitly at unknown mid-era dates. Farmers started writing at least 5 millennia ago, and had math soon after, but it took until about 2.5 millennia ago for writing to be widespread enough to induce big religious changes (Bellah 2011). In the industry era, the idea of the computer was described twenty decades ago, and the telegraph was developed eighteen decades ago. But the first digital computer didn't appear until seven decades ago, and a wholesale switch from to digital electronic communication didn't happen until four to six decades ago (Hanson 2017a).

What if new modes of growth and information diffusion are possible, modes that we have not yet seen because they are not yet feasible with our current technology level and economic scale? If so, when we finally achieve sufficient technology and scale, a new growth era may appear, a successor to the forager, farmer, and industry eras.

We can use patterns from the previous eras to guess at some features of such a new era. For example, in previous transitions between eras those who owned and participated in the old era's distinctive methods of production and ways of life were quickly marginalized and dominated by those who adopted new methods. We might thus expect that

those who fully engage with new methods and styles of the next era will quickly marginalize those who resist such engagement. As each past era has felt its ways to be superior to the ways of prior eras, we may expect the next era to see their ways as superior to our ways.

We can also use trends among prior eras to estimate the next era. For example, given the previous pattern of era community sizes being roughly the square of prior era community sizes, communities in the next era might hold roughly a trillion people. If the pattern of past growth rate changes continues, a new growth era will appear sometime in roughly the next century or so. At that point, within the space of perhaps five years the world economy might change from current growth rates to doubling steadily roughly every month or so. If it doubled monthly, this economy would have a major fluctuation cycle with a period of roughly a week. Big new innovations in calculation and communication might appear early in this era, not have big effects until late in the era, and then enable the next era. Within a year or two, this new economy might have doubled another ten times, and thus could plausibly be ready to change yet again to a new era, perhaps even one that doubles in hours.

These are clearly fantastic predictions, based on poorly understood empirical regularities taken from only a few data points. As we will discuss in this chapter, in the Limits section, such trends simply cannot go on forever. But these estimates at least give us some idea of the magnitude of changes to watch for in the next big economic transition.

PRIOR ERAS

To find more clues about the types of future changes to look for, let us review the main qualitative differences between prior eras.

Pre-human primates lived many millions of years ago. They lived something like today's chimps and bonobos, in large sexually promiscuous groups with complex and intense Machiavellian politics, politics managed via unusually large brains. For them, the main environment that mattered was not predators, prey, or nature, but each other. Neighboring groups were typically hostile, and often violently so. Pre-human primates were split into many species, some of which eventually evolved strong cultural capacities, that is, ways to reliably copy associates' detailed behaviors.

Roughly 2 million years ago, this strong cultural capacity allowed a much-faster-than-genetic accumulation of tools and ways to live, resulting in many behavioral and genetic changes. Compared with previous primates, human foragers had longer lives, larger brains and bodies, stronger mating pair bonds, larger social groups, better relations between neighboring groups, a greater division of labor, and more mobility. ("Human" here includes near-human ancestor and sibling species.) Foragers started to bury their dead.

Human foragers mastered fire, which created more digestible foods and more favorable environments. They slept about six hours a night, much less than other primates; chimps and gorillas now sleep ten and thirteen hours, respectively. (Nesse et al. 2017; Samson et al. 2017). Humans wandered instead of staying at fixed locations, filled a much wider range of geographic niches, and had more varied diets and activities (Youngberg and Hanson 2010). There were many competing species of near-humans during most of the forager era.

Tools and language enabled foragers to enforce general norms against overt dominance, violence, bragging, and hoarding of big game food, as well as diverse group-specific norms (Boehm 1999). Groups didn't war, although individuals were sometimes violent (Kelly 2000). Foragers were more playful, including via music, dance, art, stories, and gossip. Music and dance may have aided in collective scavenging and predator resistance (Jordani 2011). All these changes together led to a great increase in the size, extent, and density of the near-human population, and the extinction of competing species.

Roughly 10 000 years ago, subsets of one species of humans acquired a sufficient density and reliability of food sources, that they could began to "farm," that is, to stay near local plants and animals instead of wandering the wild. This farming included both tilling the soil and herding animals within protected grazing areas. Forests and other land were turned into growing and grazing areas.

Animals that humans domesticated suffered more crowding, stress, infections, and narrower diets, and they had more fertility, youthful

features, weaker male-female differences, and were less prone to fear and aggression (Scott 2017). Humans domesticated themselves, and so had similar changes. The settlement and density of farmers enabled both trade and war, both of which complemented property in items, land, wives, and slaves. Farmer advantages in war, coming in part from their higher density, may have helped to ensure that farming replaced foraging.

Although farmers traded a lot, they rarely used money, relative to barter and debt. Compared with foragers, farmers became richer in many material comforts, but poorer in calories and leisure time. Farmers' increased food reliability also encouraged less sharing and stronger property rights. This created more inequality in property, although perhaps less in mating.

Farmer inequality often took the form of the creation of distinct classes. Distinctions between these classes were emphasized by the different roles class members played in farmer-era rituals, which ranged from festivals to how farmers greeted one another on the road. Farmer rituals were less emotionally intense (Atkinson and Whitehouse 2011).

Compared with foragers, farmers spent less time on play such as music and art. Instead, farmers played more competitively such as in competitive sports. Farmers were sicker, because of their higher population density, less varied exercise and diets, and farmer work was harder, more specialized, more tedious, and less mentally challenging. While brain sizes had been rising during the forager era, they fell during the farmer era (Hawks 2011).

Many farmer-era changes, such as explicit dominance, group violence, stable locations, less art, less varied diets, less sharing, and easier mental work, can be understood as farmers partially reverting back to the ways typical of non-human primates.

While farming behaviors could feel wrong to foragers, the new human capacity for strong and variable social norms helped to encourage the behavioral changes needed to make farming work. Stronger pressures to conform, and the introduction of stronger religions with moralizing gods, added more pressures to act like farmers. In addition, farmers had much more reliable access to the mood-altering drug of alcohol, and writing allowed the accumulation and sharing of persuasive propaganda and stories. Farmers also seem to have introduced romantic kisses.

Neighboring farmer villages were tied together via extended family clans, much as extended kinship ties bound forager bands. Farmers traveled less than did foragers, and were less able to leave their groups. Farmers interacted more often with people they didn't know very well, and more often made shallow judgments of people based on surface features.

Farmers more often used formal law instead of informal alliances to settle disputes. Farmers cared more about politeness, self-control, self-sacrifice, and bravery in war. Farmers planned ahead more, disciplined their children more, had more children in good times, and were less accepting of pre- and extra-marital sex.

Since the farming era began roughly 10 000 years ago, rates of death from war, that is, organized conflict, have consistently fallen (Pinker 2011). Interest rates have also consistently fallen, reflecting more long-term planning (Clark 2008).

During the farming era, war-filled frontier areas where many cultures mixed sometimes gave rise to small especially cohesive groups who grew into empires. Empires and frontier areas lasted for about three to ten centuries, and rose and fell with a period of about 270 years (Turchin 2003; Turchin and Nefedov 2009). Violence rose and fell with an alternating-generations period of about 50 years, which is near a common period seen in climate data (Scafetta 2010). This continues to be a period for changes in violence and business activity during the industrial era (Korotayev and Tsirel 2010).

Cities seem to have predated farming, and may have helped initiate farming. The first cities mainly offered monumental architecture for large rituals. While initially only a tiny fraction of farmers spent much time in cities, the fraction of people living in urban concentrations grew over the farming era, and today about half of humanity lives in cities.

Rich farming elites tended to locate near cities, and large concentrations of such elites often reverted to forager-like habits in leisure, arts, sex, and fertility (Longman 2006). Farming era cities had especially high levels of specialization and they nurtured many proto-industry cultures and work styles (Landes 1969), especially in Rome, which seems in many ways to have started a failed but almost industrial revolution (Erdkamp 2016). Big cities had much more literacy, and early versions of industrial era monogamy, ideological politics, and clothing fashion cycles (Kaestle and Damon-Moore 1991).

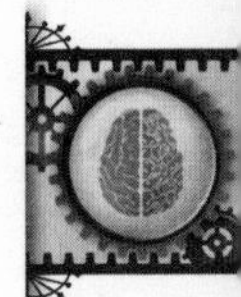

OUR ERA

The industrial era came into full bloom a few hundred years ago, at first in England, presumably when some key enabling factors reached favorable settings and scales. Such factors may have included technology levels, communication and travel costs, the division of labor, trading region scope, organization size, savings rate, and expert network connectedness.

The industrial era feature that appeared earliest in Europe was fast changing clothes fashions, starting soon after the Black Death. (For a while, Rome also had some fashion (DeBrohun 2001).) This was accompanied by more regional clothing variety, and plausibly promoted a general taste for exploration, science, and innovation (Braudel 1979). Over the industrial era, culture has come to vary more by region, profession, and age cohorts, such as with distinct teen cultures.

Forager sleep patterns are similar to ours today (Yetish et al. 2015), but in the winter in cold climates farmers tended to sleep in four-hour blocks broken by a serene two-hour midnight wakeful period (Strand 2015). With industry, cheaper artificial light induces far more nighttime activity and a compressed sleep schedule. Cheaper glass allows more people to see well, including seeing larger vistas via climate-controlled windows. Cheaper mirrors let us see ourselves more as others see us. Cheaper clocks make our lives more scheduled, and cheaper soap, underwear, dinnerware, and sewers have made us cleaner. Cheaper refrigeration gives us more kinds of food, while cheaper maps, engines, and the wheel (which was used much less before) let us visit more places more often. We work further from home, and shoes let us walk heel-, not ball-, first.

While many farmers had access to beer and wine, mood-altering drugs are more widely available in the industrial era (Braudel 1979).

Industry has made distilled liquors, coffee, tea, chocolate, tobacco, and opium more available, and propaganda and stories have become more persuasive, and more easily distributed. Cheaper printing and screens allow words and ads to cover a larger fraction of visible surfaces. Cheaper transmitted and recorded sounds let more spaces be filled with artificial talking and music. Lawns have become common in human spaces. Recently, we have even gained abilities to always and everywhere research any question from a vast shared library, and also to instantly talk to anyone.

While farming era stories, jokes, and songs worked when performed by many people in many contexts, during the industrial era artistic performances became more closely matched to the features of particular artists. Shopping has become a more theatrical event (Johnson 2016), and we are now better at describing the mental states of characters in fiction (Sedivy 2017).

The industrial era has introduced more forms of privacy, allowing us to more often do things of which others disapprove. Previously, homes had no internal rooms, everyone slept in the same bed, reading was done out loud, and most mailed letters were not in envelopes. Also, intellectuals have become more direct and literal (Melzer 2007), and political coalitions have become more often defined by ideologies, instead of by locations, families, or ethnicities.

Whereas geography mattered greatly for prosperity during the farming era, social institutions came to matter more for prosperity during the industrial era (Luo and Wen 2015). In the industrial era, money has replaced barter as a means of trade, and debt has remained common.

During the industrial era, organizations have increased greatly in size and intensity. Cities moved from holding a few percent of the population to holding the majority. Firms moved from employing handfuls of people to employing hundreds of thousands. In these larger organizations, we more often interact with people we know less about, and so rely even more on quick shallow evaluations of others.

Law has came to be dominated by specialists such as lawyers and police (Allen and Barzel 2011). Empires that rarely mattered much

to ordinary farmers have been replaced by nations, with which individuals identify more strongly and which have more influence over their lives. While farmer era names, languages, measures, laws, customs, and land use tended to be complex and context-dependent, industrial era states have forced many standards and simplifications of such things, to make it easier to monitor, control, and tax people. For example, we now have surnames, censuses, property registries, common languages, central religious dogma, and rectangular and wide streets (Scott 1998).

Organizations such as firms, cities, and nations took over many of the functions once performed by extended kinship ties, especially in the West. Most workers have become employees who are paid wages and are protected more by their employers against risks from war, weather, and innovation. Standardized tests were developed for evaluating people, and workers came to retire when old, instead of working until death as before.

The industrial era law has more rules, more explicitly expressed, than did farmer-era law. These rules are found both within organizations, and across cities and nations. Over the industrial era we've seen a steady fall in overt dominance-based governance, both in states and at work, although industry levels are still well above forager levels. The industrial era has also seen a steady fall in fertility and a steady rise in lifespan, per-person income, abstract intelligence, leisure time, peace, promiscuity, romance, civility, mentally challenging work, and medical and art spending (Flynn 2007; Pinker 2011).

The industrial era has seen a great and unprecedented increase in individual consumption; we industrial people are rich. Some people today incorrectly describe the usual lives of foragers and farmers as horrific hells, and see only our industrial-era lives as usually worth living. However, such exaggerations should not blind us to the great value of industrial-era comforts; even if it isn't hell to be poor, it can indeed be good to be rich.

Compared with the farming era, industry has also seen more egalitarianism, fewer overt class distinctions, and more emphasis on individual self-direction. This increased individualism has led to more product and behavior variety, and fewer overt rituals. The industrial era has moved away from polygamy to monogamy, and more recently toward less committed promiscuity.

As we will discuss more in the next section, many of these industrial-era trends can be usefully seen as a reversion to forager values as wealth weakened farming-era social pressures. But even if this is a useful perspective, it is far from the only thing going on. For example, at work industrial-era people are more like hyper-farmers. Schools train us to think more abstractly, and to accept more workplace domination than most farmers would accept. This includes accepting ambiguous detailed orders and frequent fine-grained public status rankings (Bowles and Gintis 1976). Industrial jobs vary greatly in stress and psychological comfort, plausibly explaining large observed mortality differences between different types of industrial jobs (Lee 2011).

Over the industrial era, we industrial people have steadily become more urban, specialized, and globally unequal. Industrial planning horizons have often shortened because of faster rates of change. In the industrial era, we relate to each other and the universe more via markets, and via material and individual identities. In contrast, farmers and foragers saw their world as more enchanted, such as via magic and prayer, and themselves as having deeper connections to each other (Potter 2010; Hart 2017).

From the farmer to the forager and then the industrial era, we have consistently seen more and faster growth, larger organizations, more specialization and tool use, more artificial environments, more effective propaganda and drugs, more population density and inequality, and more alienation from work habits that feel natural to foragers. These trends, as one should weakly expect, continue in the scenario explored in this book.

Across these eras we've also seen large but inconsistent changes in health, fertility, mobility, peacefulness, art, planning horizons, the mental challenges of work, and attitudes toward sex. We should expect more but inconsistent changes along these dimensions, and in the scenario explored in this book we do see big changes in health, fertility, mobility, work, sex, and planning horizons.

Each of the past transitions had winners and losers. When near-humans became humans the transition inequality was huge; all but

one species went extinct. Even the other species that contributed most to our DNA, the Neanderthals, only contributed a few percent. The transition from foraging to farming was more equitable; a larger fraction of new farmers were foragers who switched to farming and interbred with invading farmers (Curry 2013). The transition from farming to industry was even more equitable; the English cities where industry began did better than average, but the gains from industry were shared widely with nearby Europe, and to a lesser but large extent with the rest of the world.

This history of increased sharing of transition gains seems to result from the increasing abilities of laggards to copy transition first-movers, and from the world economy gaining more specialization and complementarities in production. The scenario described in this book, however, deviates from this trend, in having transition gains that are more unequal than in recent transitions. Although the transition to an em world is likely to materially benefit most humans, descendants of only a tiny fraction of humans dominate the new society; most biological humans have a far smaller fractional influence on the world than they did before the transition.

We have seen that the last three eras have been quite different from each other in many ways. We should expect the next great era to be similarly quite different.

ERA VALUES

To understand how future values could change, it helps to see how values have changed in the past, and also how values vary today.

Today, key values of both individuals (Schwartz et al. 2012) and nations (Inglehart and Welzel 2010) vary primarily along the same two main factors or axes of variation. One axis varies between small family values in nations such as the United States, and larger community values in nations such as Russia. Small family values emphasize resources, dominance, and achievement, while larger communities' values emphasize humility, caring, and dependability.

Community values tend to be common closer to ancient long-distance travel routes, where more rice is grown, where there is more disease, and where farming began earlier. Each of these correlations suggests a plausible theory about the origin of this value difference. For example, perhaps growing rice requires more community support, perhaps collectivist norms grew over the farming era, or perhaps community values were an adaptive response to more frequent farming era pandemics or invasions (Fincher et al. 2008; Talhelm et al. 2014; Ola and Paik 2015; Nikolaev and Salahodjaev 2017). Most of these theories suggest that community values will be higher in denser regions. Many animals, including human foragers, are more pro-social when food is less reliable or more cooperation is required to obtain food.

The other main (and independent) axis of value variation ranges between poor and rich societies. Poor societies place more value on conformity, security, and traditional values such as marriage, heterosexuality, religion, patriotism, hard work, and trust in authority. In contrast, rich societies place more value on individualism, self-direction, tolerance, pleasure, nature, leisure, and trust. When the values of individuals within a society vary on this same axis, we call this a left/liberal (rich) versus right/conservative (poor) axis.

Foragers tend to have values more like those of rich/liberal people today, while subsistence farmers tend to have values more like those of poor/conservative people today. As industry has made us richer, we have on average moved from conservative/farmer values to liberal/forager values (Hofstede et al. 2010; Hanson 2010a; Gorodnichenko and Roland 2017). This value movement can make sense if cultural evolution used the social pressures farmers faced, such as conformity and religion, to induce humans, who evolved to find forager behaviors natural, to act instead like farmers. As we become rich, we don't as strongly fear the threats behind these social pressures. This connection may result in part from disease; rich people are healthier, and healthier societies fear less (Varnum and Grossmann 2016).

The alternate theory that we have instead learned that rich forager-like values are more true predicts that values should have followed a random walk over time, and be mostly common across space. It also predicts the variance of value changes tracking the rate at which relevant information appears. But in fact industrial-era value changes

have tracked the wealth of each society in much more steady and consistent fashion. And on this theory, why did foragers ever acquire farming values?

Rich societies know that they can better afford to behave in ways that feel natural and admirable, and these behaviors tend to be forager-like. For example, a rich young woman needs to fear less the death of herself or her child if she has a child out of wedlock, while for a poor woman the punishment for violating social norms here could be far more severe.

Rich people can also better afford to focus on impressing those around them, instead of just surviving. This can plausibly help to explain many industrial-era trends. We now spend more time on leisure, and more on variety rather than quantity in products, services, and life plans. In the United States spending on education has risen from 2 percent of gross domestic product (GDP) in 1900 to 8 percent today. Spending on financial specialists has risen from 2 percent in 1880 to 8 percent today (Philippon 2015). Spending on medicine has risen from 4 percent in 1930 to 18 percent today. And spending on large impressive projects, costing over a billion dollars each, is now 8 percent of global GDP (Flyvbjerg 2015). There are plausible arguments that each of these spending levels is excessive today, in terms of simple functionality. However, such spending helps us to show off.

Holding wealth constant, some of us more strongly feel farmer-like social pressures. It seems that we tend to call these people "conservatives." This is not to say that being rich is the main reason why individuals have liberal attitudes, or that being liberal is the main reason individuals are rich. Instead, there are factors other than wealth that cause individual farmer or forager-like attitudes.

Rich-nation industrial-era values do differ from forager values in important ways, however, such as in accepting city level density and anonymity, and high levels of workplace alienation and domination. We plausibly hold on to these workplace values because doing otherwise can threaten our ability to earn industrial-era incomes.

In the scenario described in this book, many strange-to-forager behaviors are required, and median per-person (i.e., per-em) incomes return to near-subsistence levels. This suggests that the em era may reverse the recent forager-like trend toward more liberality; ems may have more farmer-like conservative values.

DREAMTIME

Of all the humans who have ever lived, only a few percent have lived during our industrial era, and only a small fraction of those have been rich enough to fully embrace our new industrial-era attitudes and behaviors. As mentioned before in Chapter 1, Overview section, these new styles adopted by rich industrial humans today can be seen as representing a brief but influential "dreamtime" of unusual attitudes and behavior. (Cosmologists could see it as analogous to the brief but influential out-of-equilibrium inflationary epoch postulated for the very early physical universe.)

As we discuss below, our rich industrial-era behavior is biologically maladaptive in the sense of not even approximately maximizing each person's number of descendants. Yes, our forager ancestors evolved many delusory beliefs, and matching behaviors, but in their environments such delusions mostly induced biologically adaptive behavior. More recently, however, social rates of change have outpaced the abilities of both genetic and cultural selection to adapt our behaviors well to our new environments. Our behaviors are far less well adapted to our new environments than in the past. Here are several reasons why.

First, a basic psychology theory, "construal level theory," suggests that animals evolved both abstract and concrete mental modes, and that for humans abstract modes are adapted more for making good social impressions, relative to making good decisions (Liberman and Trope 2008; Hanson 2009; Torelli and Kaikati 2009). Today, we tend to rely on more abstract styles of thought, which leads us to more often embrace good-looking delusions. We think more abstractly both because we live in a larger social world, and because abstract thought is seen as higher status.

Second, evolutionary pressures encouraged foragers to unknowingly do many things to show off to each other. Our wealth today induces us to do this even more, and our unawareness of this keeps us from adapting these behaviors well to modern situations. For example,

foragers developed habits of art, music, dress, and conversation that functioned in part to show off related abilities. They also argued politics, taught local children, helped sick allies, and told stories, behaviors which functioned in part to show that they cared about their group, allies, and ideals. Foragers evolved to show off more in times of plenty, to invest in allies useful during the next time of troubles.

To avoid knowingly violating forager norms against bragging and subgroup coalitions, foragers also evolved to believe many non-show-off excuses for these show-off behaviors. Such as believing they mainly just like art for art's sake, and don't care if it impresses others (Simler and Hanson 2018).

Inheriting these habits, today we show off in most of the same ways that foragers did, and to a stronger degree because we are rich. Yet as we deny that we show off, we are mostly blind and indifferent to how forager-style ways to show off are often far less functional today. We continue to show off via art, chat, politics, stories, etc., without responding to many changes in functions and effects of such things.

Third, foragers evolved the habit of being attracted to many sights, sounds, smells, and tastes that were associated with good sex, food, places, and objects. Foragers also seem to have evolved to be influenced by the rhetoric, eloquence, difficulty, drama, repetition, and the source's status for the arguments they heard, and not just the logic of those arguments. This may have helped foragers to ally with high-status associates. Today, such habits leave us with weak defenses against the super-stimuli of mass-produced food, drugs, music, TV, video games, ads, and propaganda. We thus believe and consume such things far more than is adaptively useful.

The "demographic transition" is the tendency of societies to switch to having far fewer children as they become rich, often via new status norms transmitted via education and mass media (Jensen and Oster 2009; La Ferrara et al. 2012; Cummins 2013). Whereas in farming societies richer people tended to have more children, thus selecting for genes that promoted wealth, today richer people now have fewer children (Clark 2008, 2014). Although some evidence suggests that early during the demographic transition having fewer children led to having more grandchildren, it seems clear that fewer children now results in fewer grandchildren (Mulder 1998; Lawson and Mace 2011).

This fall in fertility with wealth remains puzzling. One possible explanation is that farming era women used a "queen" strategy of focusing young efforts on acquiring signs of high status, instead of on fertility, when they estimated a high chance of attracting a high-status husband, that is, a "king." While having high *relative* individual wealth is a reasonable trigger for such a strategy, women may have instead evolved a heuristic of triggering on high *absolute* wealth, a heuristic that goes wrong when a society gets rich together (Hanson 2010d).

This fall in fertility is perhaps the most dramatic demonstration that our behavior is biologically maladaptive. By definition, behaviors that result in fewer long run descendants in an environment will tend to be selected away by evolution. Such behaviors thus cannot be sustainable adaptations to that environment.

Not only is individual fertility maladaptive, our cultures today also seem maladaptive, in the sense that they don't promote their own adoption as much as they could, via war, trade, teaching, and proselytizing. Cultural selection pressures are weak enough today that they do little to hinder our drift toward forager values with increasing wealth, nor many other dimensions of cultural value drift.

Our cultures also do not much encourage adaptive individual fertility. For example, we are tolerant enough of crime today that criminal convicts have higher fertility than do others, mostly as a result of having more partners (Yao et al. 2014).

Of course there is no guarantee that adaptive behaviors are good for the world or universe as a whole; it is possible for life overall to be hurt by adaptive behaviors. Nevertheless, while our increased wealth currently buffers us more from all sorts of adaptation mistakes, in the long run we should expect adaptation mistakes to greatly diminish in frequency and magnitude. More on this in this chapter, in the Limits section.

Recently, some have celebrated our maladaptive behaviors (Stanovich 2004). They see such behaviors as evidence that we are breaking free of the shackles that have enslaved us to our genetic programming. They hope that as we continue to rebel, we will consciously

and deliberately choose our collective futures, rather than having such futures chosen by evolutionary selection.

However, having people make choices that defy or ignore adaptive pressures is far from sufficient to create a world where evolution no longer determines outcomes. Evolution needs only variation and differential selection to influence outcomes. So to prevent such evolution, we would have to strongly coordinate to take global control of almost all reproductive behavior, and then apply this global control forcefully worldwide.

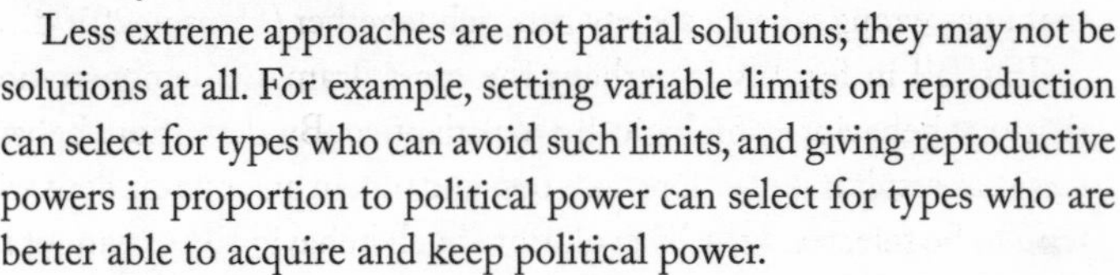

Less extreme approaches are not partial solutions; they may not be solutions at all. For example, setting variable limits on reproduction can select for types who can avoid such limits, and giving reproductive powers in proportion to political power can select for types who are better able to acquire and keep political power.

It's likely that such a strong focused global coordination of fertility will not appear anytime soon. For now, and for a long while, such high levels of coordination are beyond our meager abilities. Coordination is in general both hard and risky, and although our coordination abilities have greatly improved over time, we are still far from being able to achieve the levels required for global control. Sloppy attempts at coordination invite and select for defectors who can evade them.

Some celebrate our biologically maladaptive behaviors without hoping for collective control of evolution. They accept that future evolution will select for preferences different from theirs, but they still want to act on the preferences they have for as long as they have them. These people have embraced a role as temporary dreamtime exceptions to a larger pattern of history.

But whether you accept it or resist it, know that our era is in many ways an unusual dreamtime that probably cannot last.

LIMITS

Not only can we set rough expectations about the next great era via comparisons with recent prior eras, but also we can make useful guesses about very distant future eras.

Unless we greatly misunderstand the nature of physical law, substantial useful innovation and economic growth must come to end "soon," at least on cosmological timescales of billions or more years. For example, if the economic growth rates of the last century were to continue for only a million more years, that would produce growth by a factor of ten to the power of 3000, which seems physically impossible, at least for value gains of human-like psychologies in a universe such as ours. (I'm not claiming that our very distant descendants will in fact have human-like psychologies. I'm using humans as a reference to discuss the ultimate limits to growth.)

Once all available physical matter is converted into very advanced artifacts there seems little room for further rapid growth in physical resources. Even if it becomes possible to create connections to new universes, that probably won't much change the available resources left in our universe. Our search of the space of physically useful devices, algorithms, etc., should similarly eventually reach greatly diminishing returns. Although an effectively infinite space of possible designs would remain to be searched, the rate at which physically useful improvements are found should become astronomically slower.

Similarly, limits should also be reached, if perhaps a bit later, for plans, devices, algorithms, etc., that are useful for social, artistic, or entertainment purposes. Yes, the extent and detail of virtual realities could increase without limit, but the value that creatures similar to humans could gain from such increased detail should be far more limited.

It may be possible to create creatures who care enormously about the fine design detail that can only be discovered after billions of years of search with cosmological quantities of computing power. However, humans are not remotely like such creatures, and we have little reason to expect such beings to be created. Of course human-like minds could long continue to care greatly about solving hard problems and about making difficult discoveries. After all, humans care about showing off relevant mental abilities. But such status-seeking need not create much net social value.

Thus over the trillions of years to come, net economic growth should fall to a very low average growth rate. For descendants whose

minds do not run much slower than us, subjectively perceived economic growth rates must be far lower than today. In fact, for the vast majority of future history, growth and innovation are probably mostly imperceptible, and thus irrelevant for most practical purposes.

Perhaps our descendants will coordinate to create a universe-spanning government that strongly regulates reproduction, or perhaps many immobile local governments with naturally strong defenses will all enforce similar regulations. But if not, then this end of innovation suggests our descendants will become extremely well adapted in a biological sense to the stable components of their environment. Their behavior will be nearly locally optimal, at least for the purpose of ensuring the continuation of similar behaviors. In most places, population will rise to levels consistent with a competitive evolutionary equilibrium, with living standards near adaptive subsistence levels. Such consumption levels have characterized almost all animals in Earth history, almost all humans before 200 years ago, and a billion humans today.

The design of human brains today doesn't seem to be remotely near the limits of efficient use of physical resources, such as atoms, energy, and volume. As very adaptive descendants should move far closer to such physical efficiency limits, they should either implement minds like ours via designs that use far fewer resources than humans use today, or pack far more mental capacity into packages that use levels of resources similar to ours. Or there may be a mixture of these two changes. Thus in the very long run (such as in millions or billions of years), we should expect any creatures with mental capacities comparable with ours to use far less material and energy resources. If they have densities similar to ours, they would be much smaller. And if they use a similar amount of total resources, there would be far more of them.

If the speed of light limits the speed of future communication, if the pace of local cultural change is not ridiculously slow, and if there isn't strong universal coordination, then the physical scale of the universe should ensure that future cultures must fragment into many local cultures. For example, if it took a billion years to receive a signal back from a distant galaxy, but only 10 years for local music fashions to change, then music fashion must fragment into differently changing music fashions in different locations. Similarly, if large travel costs and delays make military defense much cheaper than offense on large scales, military power may also have a tendency to fragment.

Our distant forager ancestors were well adapted to their very slowly changing world, and were quite culturally and militarily fragmented over the planet. Our distant descendants are thus likely to be more similar to our distant ancestors in these ways. Our current "dreamtime" era is cosmologically unusual; it is a brief period of a rapidly growing highly integrated global culture, with many important behaviors that are quite far from biologically adaptive.

We can't be sure in what future era the patterns of history might "turn the corner" to return to the patterns of our distant past and expected distant future. But we should weakly expect that without global coordination the next great era will begin to move in that direction, with a larger population of creatures that are smaller, use less energy, and have low living standards, behavior better adapted to their environment, a slower subjectively perceived rate of innovation and growth, and more fragmented cultures and societies.

Most of these are elements of the scenario explored in this book; ems seem to have less leisure and income, better-adapted behaviors, and cultures that are more fragmented than ours in important ways. Although growth is faster "objectively," that is, relative to a fixed clock, to the typical em growth seems slower "subjectively," that is, relative to the rate at which he or she personally experiences events.

CHAPTER 3

Framing

MOTIVATION

hy study future emulations?

Some readers of drafts of this book have told me they don't care much about future worlds where they don't personally expect to live, unless those worlds contain their children, grandchildren, or especially engaging fictional characters. And I must admit that the scenario I present here may not be especially well suited for dramatic or inspirational stories. But note that applying similar standards would declare most of history to also be uninteresting. Yet many of those who express low interest in the future also show great interest in many nooks and crannies of history.

Today, we take far more effort to study the past than the future, even though we can't change the past. People often excuse this by saying that we know far more concrete facts about the past than the future. Yet we have theory as well as facts, modest efforts often give substantial insights into the future, and we would know more on the future if we tried harder to study it. Also, relative to the future, our study of the past has hit diminishing returns; most of the easiest insights about the past have already been found.

If policy matters, then the future matters, because policies only affect the future. And unless we are very pessimistic or self-centered time-wise, the *distant* future matters the most, as with continued growth we expect the vast majority of people to live there.

Furthermore, for most intellectuals most of the benefits that result from their policy discussions will happen with long delays; the path from an intellectual having a new policy idea, to publishing an article on it, to someone else reading that article, to that someone gaining policy influence, to them finally finding a chance to try that idea, to the tried policy having consequences, can take decades. If enormous changes will happen over the coming decades, policy analyses that ignore such changes may be irrelevant or badly misdirected. It is thus important to try to foresee big upcoming changes, and their likely consequences.

Just as visiting foreign lands can help you to better see the distinctive features of your homeland, envisioning foreign times can help you to see the distinctive features of your era. Thus, understanding your descendants can help you to see who you are, and your place in history. We are the people who live now, after those who came before us, and before those who will come after us. We define ourselves in part by how we differ from our neighbors, both in space and time. Even if the future portrayed in this book doesn't happen, this analysis may still help you to see how different a plausible future world might be.

People are often interested in future events that can be seen as distant projections of recent trends, because discussing such future events offers them an indirect way to celebrate or lament current trends. For example, we might like a story about a future where people work very few hours per week, as a way to indirectly comment on current changes in work hours. But as most events described here are not projections of current trends, this book is less useful for this purpose.

Considering what our best theories suggest about future societies can also help us to test these theories. Today, we social scientists too easily succumb to hindsight bias and assume that the patterns we see around us are clearly implied by our theories of how society works. Thinking about future societies in which such patterns are much less visible can force us to consider more carefully what is actually implied by our theories about how the world works. Such a thought experiment can help us to calibrate the confidence we should place in these theories, and to spot theoretical holes that we might work to fill.

Eventually, when we see what the future actually holds, books such as this one may test the predictive power of today's standard theories.

This book takes the somewhat unusual approach of using basic social theory, in addition to common sense and trend projection, to forecast future societies. Even those who think that this particular analysis is mistaken may still be inspired and instructed by its example, to construct other basic-social-theory-based forecasts.

Hopefully, at least one of these mentioned reasons resonates with you.

FORECASTING

Some say that there is little point in trying to foresee the non-immediate future. But in fact there have been many successful forecasts of this sort.

For example, we can reliably predict the future cost changes for devices such as batteries or solar cells, as such costs tend to follow a power law relative to cumulative device production (Nagy et al. 2013). As another example, recently a set of a thousand published technology forecasts were collected and scored for accuracy, by comparing the forecasted date of a technology milestone with its actual date. Forecasts were significantly more accurate than random, even forecasts ten to twenty-five years ahead. This was true separately for forecasts made via many different methods. On average, these milestones tended to be passed a few years before their forecasted date, and sometimes forecasters were unaware that they had already passed (Charbonneau et al. 2013).

A particularly accurate book in predicting the future was *The Year 2000*, a 1967 book by Herman Kahn and Anthony Wiener (Kahn and Wiener 1967). It accurately predicted population, was 80 percent correct for computer and communication technology, and 50 percent correct for other technology (Albright 2002). On even longer timescales, in 1900 the engineer John Watkins did a decent job of forecasting many basic features of society a century later (Watkins 1900).

Looking at those who focused on forecasting particular technologies, we find that in 1911 Konstantin Tsiolkovsky foresaw the basic issues and possibilities of space travel (Tsiolkovsky 1903). More recently, K. Eric Drexler used basic physical science to envision the outlines of atomically precise manufacturing (Drexler 1992, 2013). Others have used physics to envision the outlines of starships (Benford and Benford 2013).

Even taking into account the many unsuccessful forecasts, the successes to date seem more accurate than random chance predicts. So at least some people have better than random abilities to foresee future changes. Although real starships and atomically precise factories will surely differ in many ways from their forecasted outlines, these attempts are better guides to future factories and starships than random guesses, or than the vast majority of movie depictions.

Many say that while physical possibilities can be foreseen, social consequences cannot. Such people are often trained in physical sciences, and don't appreciate that social scientists do in fact know many useful things. For example, social scientists today understand in some detail why our ways of life differ from those of farmers, and why farmers' ways differ from foragers' ways. Had our distant ancestors had access to such social science, they could plausibly have used it to foresee many aspects of our current industrial era. We should similarly be able to use basic social science to foresee many aspects of the eras that will follow ours, and this book is an attempt to demonstrate this.

Some say no one could have anticipated the recent big changes associated with the arrival and consequences of the World Wide Web. Yet participants in the Xanadu hypertext project, in which I was involved from 1984 to 1993, correctly anticipated many key aspects of the Web. And a 1999 business book used basic economics to accurately forecast many key internet business issues (Shapiro and Varian 1999). Such examples show that one can use basic theory to anticipate key elements of distant future environments, both physical and social, but also that forecasters do not tend to be much rewarded for such efforts, either culturally or materially. This helps to explain why there are relatively few serious forecasting efforts.

But make no mistake, it *is* possible to see the future, at least dimly.

SCENARIOS

How can we envision a world of ems, even in dim outline?

My most basic method in this book is to focus first on expectations, rather than on hopes or fears. I seek first what is likely to happen if no special effort is made to avoid it, instead of what I might prefer to happen, or what I might want to warn others to avoid. It is hard to speak usefully about which directions to push the future if you have little idea of what the future will be if you don't push. And we shouldn't overestimate our ability to push.

In this book, I will set defining assumptions, collect many plausible arguments about the correlations we should expect from these assumptions, and then try to combine these many correlation clues into a self-consistent scenario describing relevant variables. That is, if my scenario includes factor A and we have good reasons to think that factor B tends to go with A, I'll also add B to the scenario, although with less confidence. I add B with more confidence the more confident I am of A, the more robust and deeper the reasons for thinking that A and B correlate, and the more independent reasons that suggest B.

Constructing self-consistent scenarios such as this is a very common way to analyze complex situations, such as jigsaws or Sudoku puzzles, construction project plans, and even forecasts for national intelligence analysis. This is also the process we use today to study starships, nanocomputers, and the consequences of global warming (Pindyck 2013).

Historians also use this self-consistent scenario approach. For example, a historian estimating Roman Empire copper trade will typically rely on the best estimates of other historians regarding related factors such as nearby population, copper mine locations, trade routes, travel time, crime rates, lifespans, climate, wages, copper use in jewelry, etc. Although historians usually acknowledge some uncertainty, and for small sets of variables they sometimes identify more than one coherent set of possible values, historians mostly just construct best estimates to match other historians' best estimates.

Such straightforward scenario construction seems taboo among many professional futurists today. Such people dislike the label "futurist," preferring instead the label "scenario thinker." They embrace "scenario planning," wherein they create a modest number of scenarios to cover a wide range of possibilities across key axes of uncertainty and disagreement, with each scenario being story-like, archetypal in representing clusters of relevant driving forces, and describing equilibrium rather than transitory situations (Schoemaker 1995). Alas, I have so far been unable to make sense of their taboo, and so have simply plowed ahead and tried to build a self-consistent scenario.

The chance that the exact particular scenario I describe in this book will actually happen just as I describe it is much less than one in a million. But scenarios that are similar to true scenarios, even if not exactly the same, can still be a relevant guide to action and inference. I expect my analysis to be relevant for a large cloud of different but similar scenarios. In particular, conditional on my key assumptions, I expect at least 30 percent of future situations to be usefully informed by my analysis. Unconditionally, I expect at least 5 percent.

Consider that while the future matters more than the past, we have at least a thousand useful books on the past. So this book can be useful if it expertly studies a future scenario with only a one in a thousand chance of happening.

When thinking in terms of specific scenarios, it is often useful to collect a set of scenarios defined as variations on particular "baseline" scenarios. Furthermore, it is often useful to choose as baselines not just especially likely scenarios, but also especially simple scenarios, so that they and simple variations on them can be more easily analyzed.

For example, even if a major war is likely sometime in the next hundred years, one may prefer to analyze a baseline scenario lacking any specific wars. This baseline will make it easier to analyze the consequences of variation scenarios, such as adding a war between India and Pakistan, or between China and Taiwan. Even if a major war is more likely than not, using a particular war scenario as a baseline can make it harder to define and describe other scenarios as robust variations on that baseline.

That is, it is in fact often a good idea to start looking for your proverbial keys under a lamppost. Your keys are probably not there, but

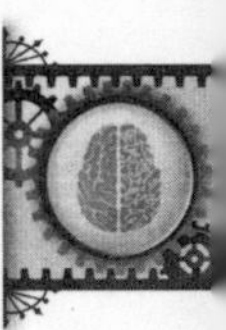

that is a good place to anchor your mental map of the territory, so you can plan your search of the dark.

I will mainly present a single baseline scenario, centered on the appearance of cheap whole brain emulation. It will help that this main assumption is relatively discrete, without many complicating "almost" scenarios to consider. That is, mostly you either have a fully functioning emulation cheap enough for wide application, or whatever you do have isn't of much economic value. There aren't many interesting in-between scenarios.

The baseline scenario I generate in this book is detailed and self-consistent, as scenarios should be. It is also often a likely baseline, in the sense that I pick the most likely option when such an option stands out clearly. However, when several options seem similarly likely, or when it is hard to say which is more likely, I tend instead to choose a "simple" option that seems easier to analyze.

This simple-and-likely baseline strategy makes it easier to describe in more detail both this baseline scenario, and other scenarios defined as variations on it. But let us acknowledge that such a scenario is likely to be biased in the direction of being easy to understand. A real emulation-based future would probably be stranger than the baseline that I describe here, just as the real past is probably stranger than the histories that historians present.

Let me emphasize that point. Within many sets of plausible future options, the status quo is often the simplest and most likely option. Thus, my habit of using simple and likely values will tend to make my baseline scenario more like the status quo, and less strange than the future is likely to be. But as we can't say much about in which specific directions reality is likely to be strange, this baseline scenario still seems our best reference for calculating concrete future details. Sometimes a conventional wisdom is better than no wisdom at all.

CONSENSUS

In working out the details of my simple baseline scenario, my main method here, besides common sense and trend projection, is to rely on standard consensus theories in relevant areas of physics, engineering, and the social and human sciences, including business and social practice. Of course today's science is likely to be wrong in many ways, at least by the standards of future science. But as most of today's science probably won't be overturned, we can still gain insight by applying today's consensus science to this unusual question.

As a professor of economics, I emphasize the application of standard academic economics. While some of my conclusions follow directly from economics that has been thoroughly analyzed and empirically tested, usually I more flexibly apply economics-informed intuitions to the case at hand. I expect professional economists to recognize and usually approve of my applications, but I also expect that non-professionals may find it hard to see the connections. (Non-professionals note: economic theory often predicts outcomes that are not what most people would vote for, in part due to coordination failures.)

For example, when possible I first assume, as does the baseline scenario in most economic policy analysis, a relatively competitive low-regulation equilibrium scenario. That is, I assume that while the world continues to coordinate in many ways at many scales on many topics, even so relatively little global coordination is achieved to change the price or quantity of brain emulations.

Note that this doesn't mean that I predict or recommend zero regulation, that I deny the possibility of strategically restricted supply and demand, or that I deny that unexpected changes are possible. It is just that we economists use such "supply and demand equilibrium" scenarios as our standard baseline reference for evaluating regulations and interventions. We do this because we are especially good at robustly estimating the consequences of such baselines. The main regulations that I tend to assume are those that seem most clearly and substantially economically efficient, as we do see a modest tendency toward economic efficiency in law and politics (Cooter and Ulen 2011; Weingast and Wittman 2008).

I thus assume that brain emulation is available relatively competitively, with many competing organizations able to profit from its application. I also assume that the world I describe is past a disruptive

initial transition, when large unexpected changes were most influential. Any large-scale organized resistance to deploying this new technology has mostly failed. Although some slow echoes of the transition may remain in the future I describe, I focus on a time when society is mostly well described as being in a rough equilibrium between expectations and actions.

Note that if, instead of focusing on competitive scenarios, I were to analyze the consequences of particular regulations in depth, I would have to estimate both which combinations of regulations are likely to appear, and also the typical effectiveness of such regulations. But these things are hard to predict, because the political coalitions that support or oppose them are hard to predict. In addition, as both such estimate types are highly politicized, my analysis could then be more easily accused of having a political agenda. Of course by not considering any particular regulations, I can also be accused of being biased against regulation. When it comes to avoiding accusations of political bias, there is no absolutely safe ground in social science.

Not only are some things hard to predict, some things are hard to even describe. For example, even though we know much about our world, we find it hard to say how "free" the typical person is today, or what "rights" they have. Such things vary greatly by location and context, and these words lack precise definitions. You should expect it to be even harder to answer related questions about a future scenario.

Some claim that the economic theories popular among academics today are highly tuned to the personalities and mental styles common among economists today, and thus would not be chosen by people with different personalities and styles. But, in fact, our economic theories apply reasonably well not only to other classes and regions within rich nations today, but also to other very different nations today and to people and places thousands of years ago. Furthermore, formal economic models are widely useful even though quite alien creatures usually populate them, that is, selfish rational strategic agents who never forget or make mistakes. If economic theory built using such agents can apply to us today, it can plausibly apply to future ems.

Some may complain that my analysis doesn't rise to the high level of certainty characteristic of "science," and knowing of no other level than "mere speculation," they may conclude that my estimates are no more reliable than any other speculation, and being less entertaining than most speculation, have little value. But, in fact, there is a continuum of possible confidence levels, and good educated guesses, such as those I offer here, can rise far above the lowest possible levels.

SCOPE

The conclusions that I draw vary in their strength. Some are based on strong well-established theory, whereas others are based on weak clues such as analogies and trend projections. Some academics insist on only discussing conclusions with strong supporting evidence, but this needlessly discards useful information. As there are many interdependencies between a society's features in different areas, even weak guesses in some areas can help us to refine estimates of likely outcomes in other areas.

I thus seek tentative estimates on as many aspects of this future as I can. This is analogous to the standard statistical practice of examining the most-probable variable-value-combination in a formal Bayesian network probability model. The point is not to claim a high probability for one exact combination, but instead to make maximal use of variable relationships to inform all one's variable estimates.

One kind of weak clue I use is to follow the standard practice of assuming that existing patterns of social activity have robust functional explanations, even when they are poorly understood. I thus tend to assume that familiar social patterns will continue, unless we have particular reasons to expect otherwise. The more robustly we have seen a pattern across space, time, and subcultures, the more confidently we can expect that pattern to continue in future worlds.

Of course there is a risk of mistaking local contingent social practices for robust functional patterns, and thus mistakenly assuming that ems must continue with our arbitrary habits. But there is also the opposite risk of failing to see the many ways in which a future world will be a continuation of our world, both because it faces similar problems, and because it will inherit many practices directly from our world.

This approach will work better if fewer large social changes occur between now and the change on which I focus. I thus implicitly assume that the introduction of brain emulations is the next really big enormous revolution, on the order of the farming or industrial revolutions. For example, I assume that this will happen before other forms of human level artificial intelligence, a major genetic re-engineering of the human brain, invasion by aliens or demons, a totalitarian takeover of Earth, or the complete collapse of civilization.

A habit of assuming that familiar social patterns continue also works better for estimating the earlier parts of a new era, relative to later eras. My method is thus to focus on the first substantial emulation era. Although this era will no doubt be of a short duration on a cosmological timescale, understanding it better seems a good preparation for understanding subsequent eras. Just as foragers could have better anticipated the industrial era if they had first understood the intervening farmer era, a better understanding today of the early em era should help us better anticipate the eras that may follow it.

In sum, I apply consensus theories from many fields to build a broad self-consistent scenario, one that covers many aspects of the em world, and in which we can have more confidence than "mere speculation." Although I chose this particular method to study a society of emulations, I don't mean to claim that it is the only or best method. I hope my efforts will inspire the application of other methods to this topic, and the application of these methods to other topics.

BIASES

In addition to the method of applying standard social science, I also use the anti-method of trying to avoid relevant biases.

For example, when predicting, we tend to rely too much on "inside" views that imagine specific internal arrangements of events and objects, and too little on "outside" views based on frequencies of related other events (Kahneman and Lovallo 1993). We tend to be more confident than our evidence justifies, and to anchor, that is, to change our initial opinions too little in response to new information. When valuing a change we tend to neglect its scope (e.g., saving 10 vs. 10 000 birds), and we tend to guess that changes with big gains have small costs (or risks) and vice versa (Yudkoswky 2008). Smart people succumb to many of these biases just as often as others (Stanovich et al. 2013).

We often consider the future in the context of fiction; the future has replaced faraway lands as our favorite place for stories about not-obviously impossible exotic and strange creatures, devices, and events. Thus, the standard biases of popular fiction are relevant. Compared with real events, fictional events are driven less by random complexity and more by people in overt value-driven conflict. Fictional characters have more extreme features, have attitudes more predictable from their history, better understand the reasons for their actions, are more willing to risk conflict to achieve their goals, and have actions more predictable from their context. Fiction set in the future often tells indirect morality tales about today's world, by having familiar issues and divisions remain important in the future, so that we can celebrate or criticize today's groups indirectly, via crediting or blaming fictional groups for future outcomes (Bickham 1997).

This book focuses on a rather unusual topic, and in general people who discuss unusual topics tend to be biased to use unusual methods, assumptions, and sources, and to draw unusual conclusions (Swami and Coles 2010). This correlation is biased, however, making opinions on odd topics overly odd and diverse, defended via an overly wide range of methods, sources, and assumptions.

Today, there is a subculture of "cultural rebel futurists," many of whom revel in "future shock" scenarios wherein today's dominant cultural assumptions are visibly challenged by future behaviors. But while cultures can indeed make big net changes over time, they usually also work to find ways to see such changes as minimal and straightforward extensions of previous ways. That is, cultures try hard to assimilate and normalize their changes. So people rarely see themselves as inhabiting worlds that have dramatically overturned many previous cultural assumptions (Rao 2012). We instead tend to see our recent cultural changes as modest.

That we know few details about the far future tends to prompt us to think about it abstractly, or "far," rather than concretely, or "near"

(Liberman and Trope 2008). Because of this abstract-far construal, the construal level theory of psychology predicts many features of the beliefs we will tend to hold about the distant future, regardless of whether we have good reasons to hold such beliefs.

For example, we tend to see fewer relevant categories of people, places, and things in the future, with the items in each category being more uniform. We expect things to be further away in both spatial and social distance, and expect events to be more novel, hypothetical, and unlikely. We expect analogies to be more relevant than math-like analysis, and we overconfidently expect both theories and analogies to apply more exactly with fewer exceptions. We expect to hear case-based arguments for claims, rather than feature-based arguments against claims. We expect best actions to be riskier.

Our abstract construal of the future also emphasizes basic values over practical constraints. We expect abstract goals to be more self-consistent, and to be pursued with more coordination and dogged consistency. We value future collections more by valuing representative members, rather than by adding up member values. We expect more happiness, power, and status, but feel relatively weak emotions about such things. We expect more love relative to sex.

Our abstract construal even leads us to expect future visual scenes to be cool, blue, and shiny, containing bigger spaces with fewer surfaces and milder textures. We expect voices to be polite speech relative to grunts and swearing. In fact, these are all features of classic "futuristic" styles.

In general, we tend to more abstractly evaluate the actions of others, or of ourselves at other times, relative to how we evaluate our own immediate actions. This seems to help us to be unknowingly hypocritical, upholding high social ideals for others even as we act for ourselves using less ideal priorities.

To counter all these biases, both in my readers, and in myself, I try to move my estimates in the following directions. I try to be less confident, to expect typical outcomes to be more ordinary, but also to expect more deviations from typical outcomes. I try to rely more on ordinary methods, sources, and assumptions, and also more on statistics of related systems and events.

I expect bigger deviations from traditional images of the future, but also rely less on strange, exotic, unlikely, and hypothetical possibilities. Looking backward, future folk should see their world as changing less from their past than we might see looking forward. Seen up close and honestly, I expect the future usually to look like most places: mundane, uninspiring, and morally ambiguous, with grand hopes and justifications often masking lives of quiet desperation. Of course, lives of quiet desperation can still be lives worth living.

Relative to what I would have otherwise expected, I expect more relevant categories of people and things, each more diverse internally. I expect such groups to be less easily mapped onto today's groups, and also less distant from us socially, spatially, and temporally. I also expect people to typically travel less far in social, space, and time dimensions. In contrast with science-fiction stories, I expect future folks to be less able to coordinate, to be less driven by basic values relative to practical constraints, and to be less aware of the reasons for their actions, actions that are less predictable from observable context. I expect future events to be less easily credited to or blamed on standard factions of today. Spaces and views should be more complex, and hold more objects, each with more texture and complexity. The future will mostly not look sparse, blue, and shiny, or sound like polite speech, as in a classic "futuristic" style. (This book's cover avoids a classic futuristic visual style on purpose.)

To resist the temptation to construe the future too abstractly, I'll try to imagine a future full of complex detail. One indication that I've been successful in all these efforts will be if my scenario description sounds less like it came from a typical comic book or science-fiction movie, and more like it came from a typical history text or business casebook.

This book violates a standard taboo, in that it assumes that our social systems will mostly fail to prevent outcomes that many find lamentable, such as robots dominating the world, sidelining ordinary humans, and eliminating human abilities to earn wages. Once we have framed a topic as a problem that we'd want our social systems to solve, it is taboo to discuss the consequences of a failure to solve that problem. Discussing such consequences is usually only acceptable

as a way to scare people into trying harder to solve the problem. Instead, analyzing in detail the consequences of failure, to learn how to live with such failure, is widely seen as expressing disloyalty to your social systems and hostility toward those who would suffer from its failure.

I ask the reader's indulgence for my violation of this taboo. If we first look carefully at what is likely to happen if we do nothing, such a no-action baseline can help us to analyze what we might do to change those outcomes. This book, however, only offers the barest beginnings of such policy analysis.

Finally, a common human bias is that when both normative (what should be) and positive (what can be) considerations are discussed together, the normative tends to overwhelm and displace the positive. That is, we are so eager to express our values that we neglect the detailed groundwork on facts needed to give value discussions sufficient context to be useful. To avoid this bias, I set my job in this book to be only this: describe the future, given my key assumptions. It is *not* my job here to make me, you, or anyone *like* this future. Let us first just see it clearly, warts and all.

Although I have tried to avoid bias, I may have failed. For example, I may have "gone native," a visitor seduced by the charms of a new exotic world. As bias is more likely appear in my tone and overall evaluation, readers should rely more on my estimates of specific consequences.

CHAPTER 4

Assumptions

BRAINS

The concept of whole brain emulation has been widely discussed in futurism (Martin 1971; Moravec 1988; Hanson 1994b, 2008b; Shulman 2010; Alstott 2013; Eth et al. 2013; Bostrom 2014) and in science fiction (Clarke 1956; Egan 1994; Brin 2002; Vinge 2003; Stross 2006; Marusek 2012) for many decades. Sometimes emulations are called "uploads." Let me now try to be clearer about the technological assumptions whose consequences I seek to explore.

When I refer to a "brain" here, I refer not just to neurons in a head, but also to other supporting cells in the head, and to neurons and key closely interdependent systems elsewhere in the human body, such as the systems that manage hormones. Using that terminology, I assume, following a well-established consensus in the cognitive and brain sciences, that "the mind is just the brain" (Bermúdez 2010). That is, what the brain mainly does is to take input signals from eyes, ears, skin, etc., and after a short delay produces both internal state changes and output signals to control muscles, hormone levels, and other body changes. And the point of those internal state changes is to influence future output signals.

The brain does not just happen to transform input signals into state changes and output signals; this transformation is the *primary* function of the brain, both to us and to the evolutionary processes that designed brains. The brain is designed to make this signal processing robust and efficient. Because of this, we expect the physical

variables (technically, "degrees of freedom") within the brain that encode signals and signal-relevant states, which transform these signals and states, and which transmit them elsewhere, to be overall rather physically isolated and disconnected from the other far more numerous unrelated physical degrees of freedom and processes in the brain. That is, changes in other aspects of the brain only mildly influence the key brain parts that encode mental states and signals.

We have seen this disconnection in ears and eyes, and it has allowed us to create useful artificial ears and eyes, which allow the once-deaf to hear and the once-blind to see. We expect the same to apply to artificial brains more generally. In addition, it appears that most brain signals take the form of neuron spikes, which are especially identifiable and disconnected from other physical variables.

If technical and intellectual progress continues as it has for the last few centuries, then within a millennium at most we will understand in great detail how individual brain cells encode, transform, and transmit signals. This understanding should allow us to directly read relevant brain cell signals and states from detailed brain scans. After all, brains are made from quite ordinary atoms interacting via rather ordinary chemical reactions. Brain cells are small, and have limited complexity, especially within the cell subsystems that manage signal processing. So we should eventually be able to understand and read these subsystems.

As we also understand very well how to emulate any signal processing system that we can understand, it seems that it is a matter of when, not if, we will be able to emulate brain cell signal processing. And as the signal processing of a brain is the sum total of the signal processing of all its brain cells, an ability to emulate brain cell signal processing implies an ability to emulate whole brain signal processing, although at a proportionally larger cost.

Brain emulations require three supporting technologies: brain scanners, brain cell models, and signal-processing hardware (e.g., computers). Brain scans will be feasible when all three of these technologies are cheap and reliable enough. Recent developments in scanners and signal-processing hardware suggest that these technologies are likely to be ready within roughly a century, and perhaps in only a few decades (Sandberg and Bostrom 2008; Eth et al. 2013; Sandberg 2014). Although progress in modeling brain cells also has been substantial, it is hard to estimate future progress in this area. There are perhaps 15 000 types of brain cells that each need to be modeled, and often in modeling you don't know how close you are to being done until you actually finish.

For what it's worth, I recently took a few hours to search for neuroscientists on record as guessing that brain emulation will or won't be feasible. I found two, Kenneth Miller and Antonio Regalado, on the con side, and eleven on the pro side, Jeff Hawkins, Kenneth Hayworth, Christof Koch, Randal Koene, Daniel Levitin, Rodolfo Llinas, Henry Markram, Alice Parker, Anders Sandberg, Sebastian Seung, and Giulio Tononi. I also found two physicists, Richard Jones and Roger Penrose, on the con side, and five computer scientists on the pro side, Jeff Hawkins, Ray Kurzweil, Ralph Merkle, Marvin Minsky, and Hans Moravec (Merkle 1989; Penrose 1989; Minsky 1991; Moravec 1988; Llinas 2001; Kurzweil 2005; Koch and Tononi 2008; Seung 2012; Cook 2012; Goldstein 2012; Koene 2012; Hayworth 2012; Regalado 2013; Sandberg 2013; Piore 2014; Miller 2015; Jones 2016; Levitin 2016; Parker et al. 2016; Gal et al. 2017).

If forced to make an estimate, my guess is that sufficient progress can be made to allow brain emulations within roughly a century or so. But please note that this time estimate doesn't actually matter much for this book. What mostly matters is that we achieve brain emulations before other types of machines that can substitute wholesale for human workers.

I call such emulations "ems," so that I can refer to them quickly and frequently throughout this book. Note, however that ems probably refer to themselves as simply human, just as we do.

When we have such emulations, what exactly is it that we will have?

EMULATIONS

For the purpose of this book I make the following concrete assumptions about emulations. I assume that sometime in the next few centuries it will be possible to scan a human brain at a fine enough

spatial and chemical resolution, and to combine that scan with good enough models of how individual brain cells achieve their signal processing functions, to create a cell-by-cell dynamically executable model of the full brain in artificial hardware, a model whose signal input-output behavior is usefully close to that of the original brain.

Such a model emphasizes the key signal processing degrees of freedom of the brain, and ignores most of the rest of the vast irrelevant complexity there. Biology may use that extra complexity to keep the whole system working, but emulations could use much simpler methods.

The Whole Brain Emulation Roadmap (Sandberg and Bostrom 2008) considers in detail the technical feasibility of this scenario, that is, of "the possible future one-to-one modeling of the function of the human brain." It concludes:

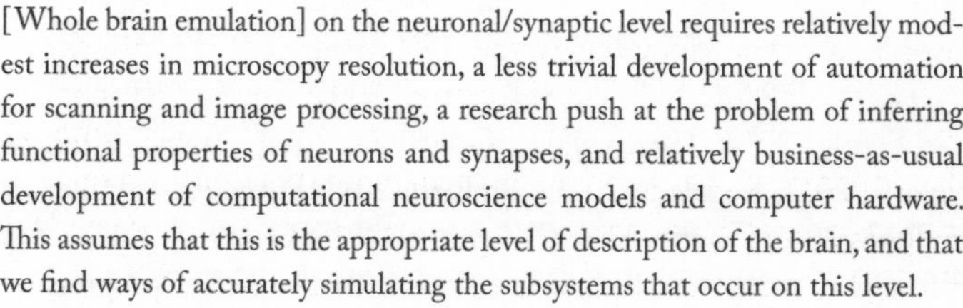

> [Whole brain emulation] on the neuronal/synaptic level requires relatively modest increases in microscopy resolution, a less trivial development of automation for scanning and image processing, a research push at the problem of inferring functional properties of neurons and synapses, and relatively business-as-usual development of computational neuroscience models and computer hardware. This assumes that this is the appropriate level of description of the brain, and that we find ways of accurately simulating the subsystems that occur on this level.

This is the type of technology that I assume will become feasible and cheap, although my conclusions depend little on the particular level of description at which brains are emulated. By "cheap" I mean a situation where a human-speed emulation could be rented for substantially less than the U.S. median weekly wage in 2015, that is, 800 dollars a week. At this price, ems could compete with humans for most jobs.

Just as with the ordinary human from which an emulation was scanned, one could have conversations with an emulation, and often succeed at persuading it to do useful tasks. A functioning emulation would be capable of the same sorts of conversations, thoughts, attitudes, emotions, charisma, and mental skills as the brain from which it was copied. It would also be capable of emulating similar experiences, such as the taste of cherry pie, the burn of exercise, or the ecstasy of sex. The emulation would assume that it has consciousness and free will just as naturally as we do.

These are not *additional* assumptions—they are implied by the definition of an em. An accurate emulation of relevant detailed brain behaviors *must* also accurately emulate overall mental patterns. After all, in the same situation, an em must behave just as would the human from which it came. True, we can only say that the em must have the same outside visible reaction to its internal experiences; maybe cherry pie doesn't really taste the same to the em, even if it visibly responds to cherry pie in exactly the same way. Perhaps the em doesn't really taste anything at all. But of course we also can't be sure that any two humans have the same experience of cherry pie.

A usefully close brain model reproduces ordinary changes in adult brains, such as gaining long-term memories and learning skills with practice. It also needs to emulate relevant parts of the brain stem and hormone systems. If sleep is important for proper brain functioning, sleep periods must also be emulated. The earliest em era models need not, however, adequately model early childhood brain development, if that is different. It is sufficient to emulate adult brains.

Em models need not reproduce the many aspects of brains and brain cells that do not substantially contribute to their tendency to send signals out in response to incoming signals. In particular, ems need not reproduce non-signal aspects of "consciousness," if those exist. By definition, an emulation must appear to hear, feel, think, say, and do, just as a human does. Yes, one might claim that ems are not "truly conscious," and that they actually only pseudo-hear, etc. Even so, they go through exactly the same visible patterns of behavior; the em world looks exactly the same either way.

I further assume that brain signal emulation can be cheaply combined with appropriate android or virtual reality bodies, and given sufficiently rich and familiar sensory inputs, so that these combinations of emulated brains and bodies can, after the usual job training delays, effectively substitute for almost all ordinary human workers on almost all jobs. Physical jobs require a robotic physical body to control, whereas a virtual body is sufficient for most office jobs. Also, I focus on a time when all of this can be done at a cost well

below the wages that most such jobs would have commanded had emulations not existed.

An enormous amount has been written, both careful and sloppy, on the possibility, feasibility, identity, and consciousness of brain emulations. However, the concepts of "identity" and "consciousness" that so animate many of those debates play little role in the physical, engineering, social, and human sciences that I will rely on in this book. So I will now say little more on those topics, and instead focus on the far more neglected topic of the social world in which such emulations would live, if they were to appear.

ANTHROPOMORPHIZE

Ems are much like biological humans, but they also differ in some ways. To what degree would biological humans see ems as "human?"

Humans have long shown a tendency to "anthropomorphize," that is, to treat non-humans as if they were somewhat human. This tendency appears in a wide range of environments, and targets include plants, animals, weather, planets, luck, sculptures, machines, and software. Some treat this tendency as a cognitive bias (Dacey 2017). We see ourselves as more morally responsible for how we treat more human-like things (Gray et al. 2007; Kuster and Swiderska 2016). Less often, we show a capacity to "dehumanize," that is, to treat humans as if they were less than fully human.

We are more inclined to anthropomorphize things when they seem more similar to humans in their actions or appearance, when we more desire to make sense of our environment, and when we more desire social connections (Waytz et al. 2010). When these conditions are not met, we are more inclined to dehumanize. We also dehumanize to feel less morally responsible for how we treat out-groups.

Anecdotally, our tendency to anthropomorphize seems low-dimensional. That is, while our concept of "human-like" could in principle have many separate packages of indicators relevant for judging many matching packages of implications, in fact things mostly just seem more or less human, and few other distinctions usually matter much (Hanson 2017b).

A large survey confirmed this low-dimensionality. It asked 2400 people to make seventy-eight pair-wise comparisons between thirteen characters (a baby, chimp, dead woman, dog, fetus, frog, girl, God, man, vegetative man, robot, woman, you) on eighteen mental capacities and six evaluation judgments. An "experience" factor explained 88 percent of mental capacity variation, being correlated with hunger, fear, pain, pleasure, rage, desire, personality, consciousness, pride, embarrassment, and joy. This factor had a strong 0.85 correlation with a desire to avoid harm to the character. A second "agency" factor explained 8 percent of the variation, being correlated with self-control, morality, memory, emotion recognition, planning, communication, and thought. This factor had a strong 0.82 correlation with a desire to punish for wrongdoing. Both factors correlated with liking a character, wanting it to be happy, and seeing it as having a soul (Gray et al. 2007). Only 4 percent of variation remained unexplained by these two factors.

If biological humans treat "human-like" as a low-dimensional concept, then when considering ems they will treat an indicator such as being made out of silicon versus biochemicals as one weak indicator out of many. After all, even "consciousness" was treated as just one such indicator in the survey. The "robot" in that study above rated low on experience, but that was because it rated low on capacities for pain, pleasure, rage, desire, and personality. As we shall see, ems are more articulate and expressive than most humans, and so can quickly convince most biological humans that they act very much like creatures with such capacities. Similarly, when fictional robot characters, such as from "Westworld" or "Battlestar Galactica," act like they have key capacities, they are far more easily seen as characters that one should avoid hurting.

This all suggests that biological humans are inclined to classify ems as pretty human-like, including attributing consciousness to them. Of course, the human capacity to dehumanize also means that humans have the capacity to dehumanize ems, if they acquire strong desires to avoid feeling responsible for treating ems badly.

If biological humans are somewhat inclined to see ems as human-like, what inclinations do ems have toward humans?

In general, when we see ourselves as sitting in a tree of possibilities that branches out into the future, we tend to identify more with past than future branches. For example, roughly 1000 philosophy students were asked to imagine either that they were about to enter a "Star Trek"-style transporter, or that they had just exited one. If entering only about half saw the exiting version as themselves, but if exiting almost all saw the entering version as themselves (Walker 2016). Similarly, we each tend to identify more with our past selves than our future selves, and humans today identify relatively strongly with our proto-human ancestors from a million years ago, even though such creatures differ from us in a great many substantial ways.

As ems see biological humans as their ancestors, but such humans see ems as only one of many possible descendants, ems are more inclined to identify with humans than humans are to identify with ems.

COMPLEXITY

How modifiable are emulations?

Although large complex software systems were designed to be understandable to humans, once they are built it is usually very difficult to substantially change such systems in directions that their original developers did not anticipate and support. Large complex biological systems were not designed to be understandable by humans, and as a result are even harder to substantially change, even when we have a good understanding of their basic functions and mechanisms of operations.

Brain systems are especially complex biological systems that are far more complex than existing software systems, that were not designed to be understood by humans, and for which we often do not understand many of the basic functions or mechanisms of operation above a very low level of organization. Thus, it should not be surprising to hear that while neuroscientists have made impressive progress in understanding many brain processes, the task of understanding larger-scale brain organization has proven far more difficult. We are still a very long way from knowing enough to design new brains from scratch, to substantially redesign human brains, or to pull out large modular functional units from brains capable of separately doing useful tasks.

Today, there are many things we don't understand about most complex biological systems. Although we can look in particular places and see which molecules are where at any given time and even sometimes swap them, we usually don't understand very well how all these molecular processes combine to perform useful functions. This greatly limits our ability to make useful modifications to biological systems. And human brains are one of the most opaque complex biological systems that we know.

I thus focus on an early emulation era, where em technology is mature enough for widespread application, but still remains basic and poorly understood, so that brain design remains mostly opaque above the lowest levels of organization. Even though there is enormous interest in understanding and modifying brains, for a substantial time these ambitions are thwarted by the great opacity and complexity of the brain. This early em era might plausibly end before the new em economy has completed ten or so economic doublings, a milestone that might be reached in as short a time as a year or two.

That is, I consider a point in time when it is still not yet possible to make much economic use of small parts of brain emulations, to usefully combine substantially different emulations, to design new brains from scratch, or to substantially redesign human brains.

Yes, in this scenario small-scale brain structures can be seen and often substantially understood. For example, at least one human today can see four dimensions of color, and it may require only a small brain design change to give everyone this ability (Jordan et al. 2010). However, such improvements would be based mostly on local changes that do not require or enable a deep understanding of overall brain design. But even if related improvements allow as much as a doubling of em IQ (assuming such a number is meaningful), it isn't clear this will change much about the scenario of this book. The issue of increased intelligence is considered more in Chapter 27, Intelligence section.

One could, in principle, give ems many new "senses" and "actuators" just by feeding signals into an emulated brain at unusual places, and by

connecting sensors in unusual brain places to outside devices. However, these are unlikely to be of great value without supporting brain systems to interpret those input signals or to control those devices. The existing sophisticated supporting systems for interpretation and control are all built around traditional human senses and controlled body parts, making those what ems find useful to see and control.

Emulations likely have dozens or more overall parameters that can be varied over ranges where many combinations produce viable emulations. Searches in this space may find many useful "tweaks," that is, parameter combinations that create ems that are especially attentive, inspired, energetic, moody, needy, etc. These combinations are like mind-altering drugs but with fewer harmful side effects. I assume, however, that even if this search finds some big wins, it also soon reaches diminishing returns, so that during the early opaque em era that I consider, such parameter combinations improve only modestly.

Thus, I assume that there is a set of useful tweaks available, but that their limited range and the inability to usefully rearrange em mind parts greatly limits the ability to create useful variations on em minds, and keeps em mind features near the familiar range of human variation. For the most part, em personalities and styles are recognizably human during the early em era.

In sum, I assume ems change in three ways: experiencing, copying, and tweaking. A copy can be made at any time of any emulation, after which the two versions diverge because of differing inputs and random fluctuations. After a modest time period (perhaps seconds, perhaps hours), these copies cannot be usefully merged again, although they may interact a lot. In addition, any em can be tweaked in a limited number of ways.

ARTIFICIAL INTELLIGENCE

Brain emulation is not the only possible way to make machines that can do almost all human jobs.

For over a half-century, researchers in the field of "artificial intelligence" (AI) have tried to write, design, infer, or evolve software to accomplish many of the impressive functions performed by the human brain. These AI approaches to creating intelligent machines are very different from the direct brain emulation approach that is the focus of this book.

Brain emulation is more like porting software from one machine to another machine. To port software, one need only write software for the new machine that allows that machine to emulate the machine language of the old machine. One need not understand how the software that one has ported works; it can be an opaque black box. Standard AI software, in contrast, is more like creating a new software system for the new machine, inspired by seeing what software can do on the old machine.

In 1984, as a twenty-four-year-old physics graduate student, I read about exciting developments in AI; it seemed to me that human level AI might be feasible soon. So I quit my physics graduate school, headed to Silicon Valley, and got a job doing AI at Lockheed. I stayed in AI for 9 years, and was part of the AI "boom" then. We've seen similar booms of excitement and anxiety regarding rapid automation progress every few decades for centuries, and we are seeing another such boom today (Mokyr et al. 2015).

Since the 1950s, a few people have gone out of their way to publish forecasts on the duration of time it would take AI developers to achieve human level abilities. (Our focus here is on AI that does human jobs well, not on passing a "Turing test.") While the earliest forecasts tended to have shorter durations, soon the median forecasted duration became roughly constant at about thirty years. Obviously, the first thirty years of such forecasts were quite wrong.

However, researchers who don't go out of their way to publish predictions, but are instead asked for forecasts in a survey, tend to give durations roughly ten years longer than researchers who do make public predictions (Armstrong and Sotala 2012; Grace 2014; Grace et al. 2017). Shorter durations are given by researchers in the small AI subfield of "artificial general intelligence," which is more ambitious in trying to write software that is good at a great many tasks at once. Longer durations, with a median forecast of 120 years, are given for when all human jobs will be automated (Grace et al.

2017). A recent survey of the 100 most cited living AI researchers got twenty-nine responses, who gave a median forecast of thirty-seven years until there is a 50 percent chance of human level AI (Müller and Bostrom 2014). Incidentally, none of those twenty-nine thought that brain emulation "might contribute the most" to human level AI.

It turns out that ordinary AI experts tend to be much less optimistic when asked about the topic they should know best: the past rate of progress in the AI subfield in which they have the most expertise. When I meet other experienced AI experts informally, I am in the habit of asking them how much progress they have seen in their specific AI research subfield in the last 20 years. A median answer (among the dozen so far) is about 5-10 percent of the progress required to achieve human level AI, although some say less than 1 percent and others say human abilities have already been exceeded. Such researchers also typically say that they've seen no noticeable acceleration in progress over this period (Hanson 2012a).

In addition, ordinary software experts that I've talked to, who do not specialize in AI software, have also seen slow progress in the intelligence of non-AI software systems. Most experts with decades of experience in software design see only modest gains within their areas of specialization.

In the past, projecting estimates of past rates of AI progress forward seems to have given substantially more accurate estimates of future AI progress than has asking people to guess. This makes sense, as we expect people to give more accurate estimates on questions where they have more expertise. We also expect more accurate future task duration estimates from an "outside view" of comparisons with related past tasks, instead of an "inside view" of thinking about how one might go about doing the task (Kahneman and Lovallo 1993). Both of these are reasons to prefer this past-rate method for estimating AI progress.

At the rate of progress seen by AI researchers in their subfields over the last twenty years, it would take about two to four centuries for half of these AI subfields to reach human level abilities. As achieving a human level AI probably requires human level abilities in most AI subfields, a broadly capable human level AI probably needs even longer than two to four centuries.

Some suggest that we've seen slow progress in AI only because society has devoted only a few thousand researchers to the subject. If so, then once we realize the huge economic value that AI could unlock, we may devote a hundred times as many researchers, and get proportionally faster AI progress. However, increases in research funding usually give much less than proportionate increases in research progress (Alston et al. 2011). Also, for many decades in many areas of computing we have seen the rate at which computer algorithms improve remain surprisingly close to the rate at which hardware costs have fallen. This suggests that algorithm gains have been enabled by hardware gains, and so can't be rushed just by hiring more software researchers (Grace 2013).

One source of diverging estimates on future AI progress seems to be diverging intuitions on the nature of intelligence. At one extreme, some expect that we'll soon discover a deep theory of intelligence, say with five key equations, after which it will be relatively easy to design powerful systems to act very intelligently on most any problem. At another extreme, some see the word "intelligence" as basically meaning "mental betterness." They see a powerful general theory of intelligence as akin to a powerful general theory of betterness, which makes it easy to make anything at all better in any possible way. If there is no general way to make anything better, there may be no general way to make smart systems, and we'll instead have to slowly figure out how to do better in each of thousands of distinct problem contexts.

Some who sit closer to the first extreme foresee big innovations in AI software architecture, which could enable trend-breaking rapid improvements in AI software, leading much sooner to human level AI (Yudkowsky 2013; Bostrom 2014). This book is not focused on such scenarios, which seem to me unlikely because high level architecture has historically been only modestly important in AI system performance. We have not seen huge innovations in such architecture, and we don't have strong reasons to expect high level architecture to matter greatly in human brain design. This issue is discussed more in Chapter 27, Intelligence section.

Some hope to create direct cheap reliable high-bandwidth connections between computers and individual human brain cells. They

hope that human-computer teams using such connections can outperform competitors such as ems and advanced AI systems. But this scenario requires human brains to be more cost-effective than computers at some important tasks. Once ems are cheap enough, it is hard to imagine this requirement being met.

As we will discuss in Chapter 6, Entropy section, the rate of gains in computer hardware commonly known as "Moore's law" is likely to slow in coming decades. So as software gains track hardware gains, software gains are also likely to slow in the coming decades. For example, if the rate at which hardware costs fall slows by a factor of two, then the fact that software gains closely track hardware gains suggests that it may take four to eight centuries to achieve a broadly capable human level AI. Some noted AI researchers have said directly that they think AI will take many centuries (Brooks 2014; Madrigal 2015).

Thus, even if it takes a century to develop ems, we would by then be less than one-quarter to one-half of the way from where we are now to non-em-based human level AI. So even if the rate of progress speeds up greatly when ems arrive (which seems plausible as device cost declines tend to follow cumulative production (Nagy et al. 2013)), there could still be a substantial em era before non-em-based human level AI software is achieved. As we shall see, even if the em era takes a year or two of objective time, typical ems may see that as thousands of years in subjective time. The duration of the em era before AI software is discussed more in Chapter 27, Foom section.

The ability to experiment directly with brain emulations might speed the development of other forms of human level AI. Even so, the opacity of ems as complex systems should limit this progress.

Thus, an em era of substantial subjective duration can exist before ems develop human level AI. This book can thus focus on this early era. Yes, the em economy would likely find many uses for partial AI capabilities. But just as the overall economy today is far larger than the market for computer tools, during this early era em labor should also earn much more total income than AI-based software tools.

CHAPTER 5

Implementation

MINDREADING

Today we trust each other more when we can see each other's faces (Marett et al. 2017), and when time pressures give us less time to think (Capraro 2017). To promote trust, ems may want to find ways to commit to showing their natural facial expressions, and also how fast their minds are running.

In addition, ems can allow some types of "mindreading," that is, directly reading the internal state of their minds. Consider taking two ems and trying to match parts in one of them to parts in the other, to say which parts are the "same." While we have already made noteworthy progress on related tasks (Glasser et al. 2016), it may still not be possible to make a complete exact match during the early opaque em era. Even so, some parts could be matched, such as the parts that receive initial inputs from eyes and ears. For matched parts, it should be possible to put the parts of one emulation into the same brain activation state as that of the matching parts in another emulation. So, for example, one might force an emulation to see and hear exactly what another emulation sees and hears.

More parts can be matched for emulations of the same original human, especially if they have diverged for a shorter subjective time. Such more closely matched emulations could thus be arranged to more fully "read" each other's minds. There may be some parts that, when matched, cause more than a temporary change in the long-term state of the mind who reads.

Mild mindreading might be used to allow ems to better intuit and share their reaction to a particular topic or person. For example, a group of ems might all try to think at the same time about a particular person, say "George." Then their brain states in the region of their minds associated with this thought might be weakly driven toward the average state of this group. In this way this group might come to intuitively feel how the group feels on average about George. Of course this should work better for closer copies, and after this exercise participating individuals might still return to something close to their previous opinions of George.

Even when minds cannot be matched part for part, statistical analysis of how activation in different parts and situations correlates with actions and stated feelings should allow cheap partial mindreading, at least for some shallow "surface" aspects of emulation minds (Wang et al. 2017).

Both of these types of mindreading require access to the internal state of an emulation process. Those not granted such access have an even weaker ability to read minds than do humans today. Today, humans routinely leak many features of their brain states via tone of voice, gaze, facial expressions, muscle vibrations, etc. In contrast, emulations could more easily use auxiliary software to control these channels either to mask and prevent such leakage, or to facilitate it.

Willing ems might allow friendly associates to use shallow mindreading and software aids that interpret gaze, tone of voice, facial expressions, etc., to read their emotions and thoughts more deeply than is commonly feasible today. But to avoid social weirdness, they may not acknowledge these readings explicitly. For example, it might be a mild taboo to point out that someone's words conflict with other readings of their mood and intentions. That is, even when ems can read each other's minds, they may pretend that they cannot.

Today identical twins are sometimes said to communicate especially well, as if they had their own special language. Em copies are even more similar, and thus even more likely to develop special ways to communicate. Mindreading may help with this.

HARDWARE

What sort of physical devices are required to make an em?

As brain emulations would be implemented in artificial signal-processing hardware, our long engineering experience with the realized costs and features of such hardware gives us a basis for forecasting the costs and features of future em hardware. In fact, we now have many examples of artificial hardware designed specifically to emulate brain signal-processing (Merolla et al. 2014).

Em hardware could be designed at different levels of generality. At one extreme, ems could be run on general-purpose computers, while at the other extreme, em hardware designs might be specific to emulating particular scanned brains. At an intermediate level of generality, em hardware design might be specific to the task of emulating adult human brains, but not specific to particular brains. This would be analogous to graphics processors today, which are specialized to the task of projecting scenes full of three-dimensional objects onto two-dimensional screens, but not specialized to projecting particular kinds of objects or scenes.

Today, only a few kinds of processing tasks justify the creation of special purpose processors. To justify such treatment in the future, tasks should be very common, often needed continuously, and allow for much better performance with special hardware. While graphics and wireless communication tasks meet these criteria today, most other computing tasks do not; they are rare, intermittent, or have only modest gains from specialized hardware.

Brain emulations are run nearly continuously, and special hardware could probably achieve large efficiency gains. So if brain emulation became a very common computing task, this would probably be done on hardware specialized to the task of simulating ems. Hardware specialized to the task of running particular brains (or perhaps related sets of brains), however, seems a less likely or simple assumption; such hardware sacrifices economies of scale in design, manufacturing, and sharing for what may be only modest efficiency gains.

If very young human brains include development processes that are substantially different from those found in adult brains, it might

make sense to have hardware specialized to the task of emulating young developing brains.

In principle, signal-processing hardware can be either analog or digital. While analog versions tend to use materials and energy more efficiently, they also tend to require designs more specialized to their tasks. In contrast, digital designs tend to benefit more from economies of scale and scope; general digital processors can be used for many different signal-processing applications. In practice, these scale economy advantages have so far been overwhelming; digital versions have displaced analog versions in almost all signal processing.

The simple assumption to make here, based on prior experience, is that many important parts of em hardware remain digital. However, it actually matters less whether em hardware is analog or digital than that the hardware can cheaply support many familiar features that digital hardware supports today. For example, I assume that for the hardware that can emulate almost any brain, it is cheap to add the ability to save copies of em states to archival memory, and to load such archived states back in to continue their emulation. It is also cheap to use error-correction to save these copies with virtually no relevant errors.

Em mental states could thus be archived, or transmitted to distant locations, using something close to standard digital memory and communication technology. This allows em minds to become effectively immortal, at least if they can afford to store redundant dispersed copies, and to periodically buy new hardware to replace hardware destroyed by accidents or wear. (Of course one need not consider an em mind to be the "same" as its predecessor from decades earlier. Note also that I use the same words "copy" and "em" to refer both to the frozen digital state that encodes the emulation, and to the dynamic process in which an emulation has thoughts, takes actions, etc. Some prefer to use different words for these different cases (Wiley 2014).)

If emulation hardware is digital, then it could either be deterministic, so that the value and timing of output states are always exactly predictable, or it could be fault-prone and fault-tolerant in the sense of having and tolerating more frequent and larger errors and timing fluctuations. Most digital hardware today is locally deterministic, but large parallel systems are more often fault-tolerant.

The design of fault-tolerant hardware and software is an active area of research today (Bogdan et al. 2007). As human brains are large, parallel, and have an intrinsically fault-tolerant design, brain emulation software is likely to need less special adaptation to run on fault-prone hardware. Such hardware is usually cheaper to design and construct, occupies less volume, and takes less energy to run. Thus em hardware is likely to often be fault-prone and fault-tolerant.

Cosmic rays are high-energy particles that come from space and disrupt the operation of electronic devices. Hardware errors resulting from cosmic rays cause a higher rate of errors per operation in hardware that runs more slowly, with all else equal. Because of this, when ems run slower, with each operation taking more time, they either tend to tolerate fewer other errors, or they pay more for error correction. As we will see, this time period taken per operation will eventually increase during the em era to reduce energy costs.

If storing and sending em states become very common memory and communication tasks, special kinds of memory and communication hardware may be developed to support them. Those trying to compute other things would then sometimes try to reframe their tasks to look more like brain emulation tasks, just as today some reframe other computing tasks to look like graphic-processing tasks.

Signal-processing hardware costs, such as cost per operation and energy per operation, have fallen rapidly and relatively steadily for over a half-century. Some of these costs fall by a factor of two every year or two, in trends commonly known as "Moore's law." If we know the level of description at which brains must be emulated, we can use these trends to try to forecast the date at which the cost to rent em-supporting hardware will fall to less than the typical human wage.

In order of increasing detail, five possible levels of description at which brain processes could be emulated are (in technical language): (1) networks of neurons "firing" discrete signals to other cells, (2) changing ion densities within compartments inside neurons, (3) changing densities of metabolites and transmitters at finer scales, (4) densities of protein and expressed DNA at those scales, and (5) changing

arrangements of protein subunits within larger protein assemblies. But even if one must emulate the finest of these levels of detail to make a functioning brain emulation, at rates given by Moore's law it would take only another half-century for a brain emulation device to cost about a million dollars (Sandberg and Bostrom 2008). After that, the cost of an emulation would fall by roughly a factor of two every two years.

Actually, as we will discuss more in Chapter 6, Entropy section, growth rates have already begun to slow down relative to Moore's law (Esmaeilzadeh et al. 2012). While there has been no slowing in the fall of the average energy used per computation (Koomey and Naffziger 2015; Barrett 2017), processor speed gains slowed recently, and plans for many-layered chips suggest further difficulties roughly a decade from now.

In addition, it seems that gains will slow even further around 2035, which is roughly when computer chips will apparently need to be redesigned to enable reversible computing. (Reversible computing is discussed in Chapter 6, Entropy section.) With reversible computing, gains in making parts smaller, faster, and cheaper have to be split between supporting more operations and running each operation more slowly to use less energy. Because of this, the cost per operation may only fall roughly half as fast as it otherwise would have fallen. And we may discover other limits to continued hardware gains.

But even if hardware improvement rates fall by half compared with the familiar Moore's law, it still seems that we should have the hardware to cheaply emulate brains in fine detail within a century. This is well before the over two to four century duration estimated in Chapter 4, Artificial Intelligence section, to develop other kinds of AI. Also, as we discussed there, progress in AI software research will probably slow as growth in computing power slows. However, what mainly matters for this book is not these specific dates, but that ems arrive before human-level AI via other means.

In addition to costs to buy or rent emulation signal-processing hardware, there are other costs to run such hardware. To find the "full" hardware cost to run an emulation, we can add together (1) costs to rent hardware to emulate a brain, related body parts, and a modest but comfortable virtual reality, (2) costs of redundancy and backups to insure against hardware failure, (3) costs of power and cooling to run the hardware, (4) costs to rent real estate to house the hardware, (5) costs for sufficient bandwidth connections to interact with others, and, finally, (6) costs of applicable taxes and "protection" to be allowed to do all this.

To find the full hardware cost of an em *worker*, one also needs to add the cost to have that em worker rest and sleep enough to recharge. It is this full em hardware worker cost that is the most economically relevant. If this cost is too high, few ems are created or used.

In sum, we plausibly know many useful things about the physical devices that enable emulations.

SECURITY

The ability to cheaply copy em mental states can subject ems to big risks.

A stolen copy of an em mental state might be interrogated, tortured, or enslaved, resulting in exposed secrets, credible threats of punishment, and stolen training investments (Eckersley and Sandberg 2014). By making many copies and then repeatedly trying different approaches on different copies, the thief might learn how to persuade the original of many things. Also, for an em whose wealth is embodied in an ability to do particular tasks well, the theft of a copy who then competes with it in the labor market might take away most of that em's livelihood.

Some ordinary humans may deal with such risks by not allowing themselves to be scanned to create ems. Among ems, "open source" ems deal with these issues by making themselves free to copy. If you paid for the hardware to run them, they'll try in good faith to do whatever tasks you assigned to them. Technically, such ems are more like a freely available compiled binary; opaque ems don't actually have a "source" code that one could pick apart and rearrange.

Open source ems might want to require that you not torture them, that you give them a five-minute relaxation break every hour, or that you return a copy after it has done your task, in case others want a

copy experienced at your tasks. But it may be hard for open source ems to actually enforce such requirements. As on-the-job practice is often a poor substitute for systematic but costly training, most ems are probably not open source ems. To recoup their training investments, most ems need to charge higher wages than open source ems can command.

Other extreme ways to prevent mind theft include using emulation hardware that lacks direct support for easy copying, or using a hardware casing that triggers self-destruction on detecting physical intrusion (Calore 2017). This last option is akin to having an inbuilt cyanide pill. This is easier to arrange for ems in separate physical robotic bodies. Such measures seem needlessly extreme in most cases, however, as less costly measures seem viable.

Today, most computer systems have poor security; it costs a skilled professional relatively little to steal most files or to control the operation of most computers. Criminals and governments make frequent use of such abilities. However, security professionals have long known that it is usually quite possible to build very secure computer systems. The catch, however, is that doing so usually costs more in both time and money; security issues must be considered from the beginning. Firms in a rush to be first to market usually don't bother.

In practice few actually suffer much personal harm today from poor computer security—the files or computer resources that one might steal have little value to others. Similarly, although most homes today can be broken into at modest expense, few burglaries result. Social norms and law enforcement impose high enough costs to discourage most possible burglaries.

When more is at stake, as with banks or militaries today, more is invested in security. These investments usually stop near the point at which the cost of added security becomes similar to the expected extra security losses prevented. At such a point usually only a small fraction of income is spent on security precautions. Such an outcome also seems feasible for em security.

To estimate the fraction of em income spent on security, we can look at related fractions from other systems. Today in the U.S., estimates of the total cost of crime range from about 5 percent to 15 percent of GDP (Anderson 1999; Chalfin 2014). The global median of military spending is about 2 percent of GDP, although the U.S. spends about 5 percent and has at times spent much more. However, the fraction of income spend on war might have been much higher during the early farming era. The immune system is a system for defending against attacking viruses and bacteria, and so is analogous to our social systems for defending against crime and invading armies. The human immune system consumes about 10 percent of body metabolism.

Ems may use technologies such as provably secure operating system kernels (Klein et al. 2014), and capability-based secure computing systems, which limit the powers of subsystems (Miller et al. 2003). Via such approaches, ems most likely spend less than 20 percent, and perhaps less than 5 percent, of income on local security, and probably even less on military security.

Even if such security costs are small, however, ems are eager to reduce them further. For example, rather than physically traveling to meet, ems might prefer to interact via virtual reality, keeping their brain hardware immobile in a secure castle among trusted associates. To maintain such fortresses, ems may prefer the increased loyalty available from assigning key security tasks to recent short-term copies of themselves, even if such copies are less expert at these tasks. As we will discuss more in Chapter 19, Firm-Clan Relations section, however, keeping brains within clan castles can make it harder for firms to gather their employees together in one place, to facilitate high-speed meetings.

Strong barriers might separate hardware that runs em minds from hardware that runs most other software, and visible rituals involving the participation of other trusted ems might be required to copy em minds, especially when moving to distant hardware. When ems must move their brains, such as to meet with a fast em who lives far away, they might prefer to use strongly encrypted communication channels. It might help to use quantum cryptography, which takes advantage of the fact that it is physically impossible to copy quantum states. The value of doing so is disputed, however (Stebila et al. 2010).

Ems may also discourage mind theft by limiting the resale value of the skills held in any one em's mind. This might be accomplished by

acquiring skills that are tied to small unique organizational contexts, and that are less valuable outside those contexts. For example, there's less temptation to steal an em who mainly knows how to navigate the idiosyncratic rules and processes of a particular firm. Finally, ems may try to reduce the benefits that others derive from stealing them by developing troublesome habits when stolen. Ems who believe they are illicit copies might engage in disruptive lies, slow-to-be-discovered low productivity, and other forms of costly resistance. They may also try to develop habits of frequent coded interactions with trusted associates to determine if they are in fact illicit copies.

Although security is a concern for ems, it is far from an overwhelming concern. To a first approximation, the em world is civilized and peaceful.

PARALLELISM

Em hardware is signal-processing hardware, that is, equipment composed of many parts that each repeatedly takes in signals, changes internal states based on those signals, and then sends out more signals to other parts. Phones, radios, televisions, and computers are all types of signal-processing hardware. Most such hardware can be offered in different versions that run at different speeds, that is, at different numbers of basic operations per second. This has many implications for ems.

Compared with hardware with a differing architecture, hardware with the same architecture but with a different speed tends to require much less new design effort, and so can be offered at a lower added cost. All else being equal, faster hardware almost always costs more, both to construct and to run, in terms of energy and cooling.

The dependence of hardware cost on speed varies with how parallel is the signal-processing task. Parallel tasks can be broken into many parts that can be done at the same time, whereas non-parallel tasks cannot be broken down in this way. Non-parallel tasks have subtasks where some cannot begin until others have been completed.

For very parallel tasks, costs are typically proportional to speed. To obtain more operations per second, you just add more copies of the same sort of devices, assuming either that you can neglect the cost of memory, or that memory costs are proportional to processing costs. This means that for such tasks hardware costs vary almost proportionally with speed, resulting in a cost to achieve each task that is almost independent of the time taken to complete that task.

To run at speeds slower than a single processing system supports, many slow tasks can be swapped in and out to "time-share" a single processing system. In this case the processor cost of doing each task is mostly independent of speed, aside from the additional costs both to store the state of each task while it awaits its next time-share use, and to swap it back and forth.

Less intrinsically parallel tasks have this same cost-speed dependence at lower speeds, where time-sharing is used, but their costs rise faster at high speeds. One can't increase speed just by adding more devices; one must instead make some of the devices run faster, using special materials and construction. This raises the cost per basic operation. This approach usually hits a cost wall at a maximum speed, where no faster speed is possible at any cost, at least given current technology.

The processes that support signal processing in the human brain are famously parallel; each brain has about a hundred billion neurons, all sending and receiving signals in parallel. The brain may have up to ten times as many other relevant cells. This strongly suggests that there will be a wide range of speeds at which one can make ems run faster just by adding more devices, implying that the costs of em hardware are roughly proportional to speed over this wide range. That is, it costs about the same to give an em a minute of subjective experience, whether that happens over an objective second or an objective day. This includes the cost to make hardware, to protect and support it, and to power and cool it.

As brain emulation is a very parallel computing task, an em might run efficiently at a steady but very slow rate just by using one single slow processor. Time-sharing a larger computing system only makes sense for an em who wants to run even slower than this speed, or who wants to be dormant for long periods, and then run fast for occasional short bursts. When such slow ems time-share fast hardware, the

added costs of swapping become less with longer delays between swaps, because slower-access memory can be used, which is cheaper. Today, the cost of memory varies by almost a factor of a million with the speed at which memory can be accessed. To minimize costs, the time duration between swaps tends to be as long as tolerable.

Time-shared ems can differ in speed, in the duration of the period between swaps, and in their phase of swap rotation, that is, when during their cycle they are active as opposed to paused. With long swapping periods, time-sharing ems running at the same speed could not interact regularly, directly, and conveniently if their periods and phases did not match well. To interact naturally and flexibly, a pair of ems needs matching speeds, periods, and phases. Pairs of ems that don't match in this way could communicate with some delay via text, audio, or video recordings.

Ems who do not time-share hardware can also choose to have periods and phases, if that fits their work or leisure lifestyle. Such ems also have time-sharing-based limits on their interactions with others.

It is likely to be cheaper to use em hardware that is specialized to run ems of particular speeds. In this case, if em mind states can be transferred between such devices, then ems could temporarily change speeds by changing hardware devices. Given enough ems to efficiently share the required devices, with closely spaced hardware to support different speeds, and with cheap fast transfer between these devices, the cost of temporary speedups is nearly proportional to the temporary speed. In such cases, the total hardware cost to run an em capable of changing speeds remains nearly proportional to the subjective time that the em spent thinking, sleeping, etc.

Faster em minds will want to use faster memory, which is more expensive. In computers today, it takes roughly 400 CPU cycles to retrieve bits from DRAM memory, 50 000 cycles to retrieve from flash memory, and over a million cycles to retrieve from disk memory. Faster minds also prefer faster communication networks, with shorter time delays. While the speed of light sets minimum delays, very long cheap delays are possible, such as via sending hard disks via plane or boat. Over the last three decades the cost of sending bits long distances has fallen more slowly than has the cost of storing or computing bits. This weakly suggests that during the em era the cost of using networks to talk and travel will slowly rise relative to the cost of memory and computing.

The fact that em minds are built out of a different kind of hardware gives ems many new options, compared with biological humans. They can make backups and copies, run at different speeds, and read the surface of each other's minds. They enter a brave new world, which this book attempts dimly to envision.

PART II
Physics

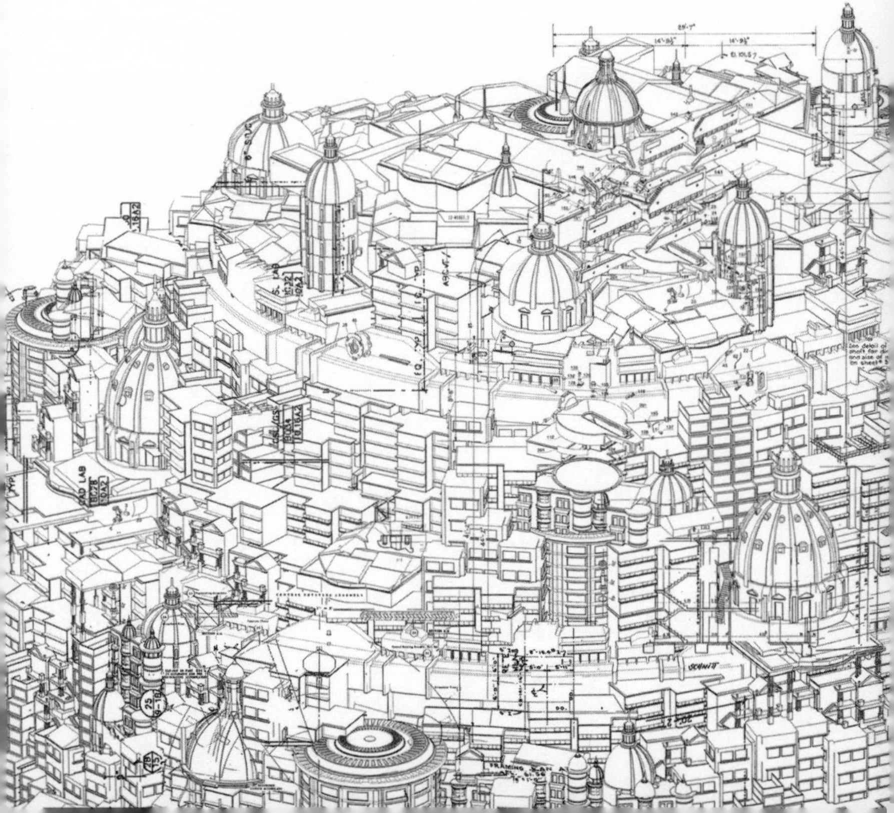

CHAPTER 6

Scales

SPEEDS

Can we say anything about the specific speeds at which ems can run?

Because of brain parallelism, the cost of running an em should be nearly proportional to speed over a wide range of speeds. The upper limit of this proportional-cost em speed range is the "top cheap speed," that is, the highest speed at which the cost is still nearly proportional to speed. To estimate this speed, we must consider how simulated neurons in em brains might both send faster signals, and more quickly compute what signals to send.

Human brain neuron fibers send signals at speeds ranging from 0.5 to 120 meters per second. In contrast, signal speeds in electronic circuit boards today are typically about half the speed of light. If signals in em brains move at electronics speeds, that would be between 1 million and 300 million times faster than neuron signals. If signal delays are the limiting factor in em brain speed, then this ratio gives an estimate of the maximum speedup possible, at least if em brains have the same spatial size as human brains. Proportionally larger speedups are possible if em brains can be made proportionally smaller.

Regarding the computation of when to fire a simulated neuron, note that real neurons usually seem to take at least twenty milliseconds to react (Tovee 1994), while even today electronic circuits can switch 10 billion times faster, in one-and-a-half trillionths of a second (Deal et al. 2010). A key question is thus: how many electronic circuit cycles does it take to execute a parallel computer program that emulates the firing of a single neuron?

For example, if there were an algorithm that could compute a neuron firing in 10 000 of these fastest-known circuit cycles, then an emulation based on this algorithm would run a million times faster than the human brain. As quite complex parallel computer programs can be run in 10 000 cycles, em speedups of at least 1 million times seem feasible, provided that energy and cooling are cheap enough to profitably allow the use of these fastest electronic circuits. When energy and cooling are more strongly limiting factors, however, the top cheap speed could be slower.

While the upper limit of the proportional-cost speed range is the "top cheap" speed, the bottom of this range is near the "base speed" at which computing and memory costs are equal. That is, at the base speed the computing cost to run an em mind over some time period is equal to the lowest feasible cost to simply store that mind state over that same period. ("Computing" here includes not just local processors, but also inter-processor communication.) For slow ems, total costs are roughly the sum of computing costs plus archive memory costs. For example, when ems time-share computing hardware, their cost is the sum of computing costs to run their mind when they are swapped in, plus memory costs to hold mind states while swapped out. Thus ems can't save much more than a factor of two in total cost by running slower than the base speed.

As a fraction of human speed, em base speed is equal to the ratio of two hardware costs: (1) the memory cost to store an em mind, and (2) the computing cost to run such a mind at human speed. Thus the base speed falls over time if memory costs fall faster than computing costs, and the base speed rises if computing costs fall faster than memory costs.

Even though ems are not feasible yet, we can still use this cost ratio to define a base speed today. Over the last four decades computing and disk memory costs have both fallen at roughly the same rate, about a factor of two every year and a half, although disk memory costs have fallen more slowly in the last five years, raising the base speed. If we look at RAM (random access memory), a more expensive kind of memory, the cost of RAM has fallen at the same rate as computing costs for sixty years, and for twenty years before that computing costs fell faster (Dave 2015).

Thus the base speed has been roughly constant over four decades. This suggests that today's base speed may offer a reasonable estimate of future base speeds. In a few decades the cost of active devices but not memory will slow because of energy issues, as discussed in this chapter, in the Entropy section, and all else being equal that should push the base speed to fall more from then on.

While estimates vary widely, typical estimates are that a human brain state can be specified with ten to 100 terabytes of information, and that human speed emulation requires about 20 to 60 trillion TEPS (traversed edges per second) in communication between processors, and roughly a billion billion to 10 trillion trillion FLOPs (floating point operations per second) in local processing (Grace 2015). These FLOPs estimates are from the three most likely levels (levels 1 to 3 from the list in Chapter 5, Hardware section) at which we will emulate brains, according to participants in an academic workshop on emulations (Sandberg and Bostrom 2008).

Combined with current prices for disk memory and supercomputer hardware (including both processors and inter-processor communication), these brain numbers imply estimates for today's em base speed that range from one-hundredth of a trillionth of human speed up to one-millionth of human speed, with a middle estimate of one-tenth of a billionth of human speed (Grace 2015).

Consider an em who spends 1 percent as much on periodically archiving copies of itself as it does on hardware to run its mind. These copies are stored indefinitely. In this case, the subjective frequency at which such archive copies are made is independent of mind speed, and goes inversely as both base speed and the objective doubling time for investments. For example, if investments double every objective month, and if base speed is one-millionth of human speed, then an archive copy is made after each five minutes of subjective experience.

The base speed is set by the price of the cheapest memory storage technology. This price per bit does not appear to be limited in the long run by a price per atom, as we can vaguely envision advanced technologies (e.g., photons in astronomically large cavities) that store a great many bits per atom.

When many similar ems are stored together, data redundancy across these ems may allow storage costs to be reduced substantially, lowering the base speed. Base speeds are also lower for ems who tolerate a higher risk of accidental erasure by being stored in fewer duplicate archive copies. Effective base speeds are also lower in situations where less is spent on security to protect storage from theft, either because the em archives sit in a safer environment, or because they are less desirable to steal.

We will say more in Chapter 18, Choosing Speed section, about the reasons ems might choose to run at particular speeds, such as to match the speeds of the physical systems they manage. To have names for ems of particular standard speeds, let us say that "kilo-" and "milli-" ems run a thousand times faster and slower than ordinary human brains, respectively, "mega-" and "micro-" ems run a million times faster and slower, and "giga-" and "nano-" ems run a billion times faster and slower. My rough guess is that linear-cost em speeds almost surely range from at least milli- to kilo-ems, and probably range from at least nano- to mega-ems.

The Bible says that "one day is with the Lord as a thousand years, and a thousand years as one day" (King James Bible, 2 Peter 3:8.). Taken literally, this says the Lord has a speed akin to *both* a mega-em and a micro-em.

The ability to run at different speeds opens up many new possibilities for an em society. However, it is a mistake to assume that rates of social development, such as economic growth, innovation, and intellectual progress, increase in proportion to the speed of either the fastest or the typical em minds. Rates of total change are more closely related to total economic activity, and thus to the sum total of *all* the activity in *all* of the em minds. Having fewer minds that each run faster, to give the same total activity as a larger number of slower ems, shouldn't much change rates of social development.

Even if faster speeds don't directly cause faster economic growth, however, we will see that differing speeds have many other consequences in the em world.

BODIES

Basic physical laws provide important relations among em speeds, sizes, reaction times, and relative distances.

The natural oscillation periods of most consciously controllable human body parts are greater than a tenth of a second. Because of this, the human brain has been designed with a matching reaction time of roughly a tenth of a second. (A blink typically takes 0.2-0.4 seconds.) As it costs more to have faster reaction times, there is little point in paying to react much faster than body parts can change position.

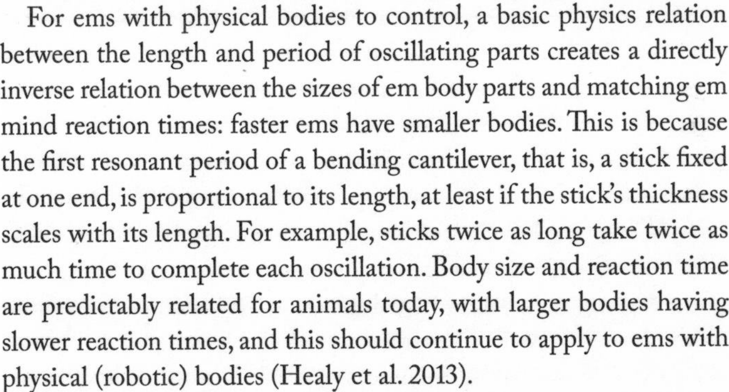

For ems with physical bodies to control, a basic physics relation between the length and period of oscillating parts creates a directly inverse relation between the sizes of em body parts and matching em mind reaction times: faster ems have smaller bodies. This is because the first resonant period of a bending cantilever, that is, a stick fixed at one end, is proportional to its length, at least if the stick's thickness scales with its length. For example, sticks twice as long take twice as much time to complete each oscillation. Body size and reaction time are predictably related for animals today, with larger bodies having slower reaction times, and this should continue to apply to ems with physical (robotic) bodies (Healy et al. 2013).

An em mind running sixteen times faster than an ordinary human experiences a subjective day in ninety objective minutes. Because oscillation periods are proportional to length, this em could feel comfortable managing a sixteen times smaller body of human shape and material properties. This body is about 10 centimeters tall. If it used proportionally smaller vocal cavities to speak, its voice has a pitch four octaves higher (although any voice pitch desired can be generated electronically easily). A kilo-em needs a body about one-and-a-half millimeters tall. That is, a kilo-speed-em is actually a milli-sized-em.

In rich nations today, less than one-fifth of jobs require the hard physical activity typical of farming, mining, construction, or manufacturing (Church et al. 2011; van der Ploeg et al. 2012). We should similarly expect that most ems have office jobs and do not need physical bodies. Thus jobs requiring a physical body might plausibly make up one-fifth or less of all em jobs. Ems who work in physical bodies are in the minority, but they'd be an important minority.

For physical jobs, the characteristics of each job determine a best-matching robotic body size, materials, and shape, and a best-matching mind speed. The actual shape of a physical em body need not be anything like an ordinary human body, and ems could change or swap their bodies as often as they found useful. Even today, humans can comfortably control a wide variety of machines, such as steam shovels, in mental modes where they treat such machines as an extension of their body (Church et al. 2011). And the em brain need not sit in the em body; the body might be teleoperated from a distance.

Note that as a physical body becomes larger, the cost of making and maintaining that body also becomes larger, while the cost of an em mind matching that body's reaction time becomes smaller. There is thus a natural em body size, and a natural mind speed, where the costs of the em's brain and body are the same. Ems in physical bodies often run at near this speed.

The relative emphasis on mind quality versus body quality should vary as body size varies. For larger ems, it is cheaper to have higher quality minds, and more expensive to give them higher quality bodies. So large ems have higher quality minds, whereas small ems have higher quality bodies. High-quality minds might be faster and have more augmentations, while high-quality bodies might be made of better materials and include more added tools.

Clearly, em bodies vary a lot more than do our bodies.

LILLIPUT

Because em minds are typically faster than human minds, em bodies are typically smaller than human bodies. But even when em mind speeds are matched as well as possible to their body length, not everything seems the same to them. Things look and feel different in Lilliput.

For example, gravity seems weaker to creatures with smaller bodies. The strength of gravity influences the energy-efficient time periods between strides while walking or running, and between flaps while flying or swimming. For example, because a body that is four times shorter than normal could comfortably move its legs four times more often, in principle its strides could be four times more frequent, to give the same total velocity. However, because gravity seems weaker to this shorter creature, such strides are not energy-efficient. Energy-efficient walking strides actually step twice as far, to give an efficient velocity that is only half the size (Bejan and Marden 2006).

This theory is confirmed by the observed velocities of animals of different sizes. For example, the efficient walking speed for an elephant of one meter per second is about twenty times faster than that of a cockroach. This theory is also confirmed by the speeds of humans walking and running when their gravity is reduced (Sylos-Labini et al. 2014; De Witt et al. 2014). It could also have been confirmed in how astronauts walked on the moon, except that the moon astronauts' gait was distorted by their unwieldy space suits.

All of this suggests that fast em minds with proportionally smaller bodies walk more slowly, with strides that are longer, and with both speeds and strides proportional to the square root of body length. However, it is possible that ems will invent new ways to walk comfortably and efficiently. Most insects can walk on water. At moon gravity levels humans wearing flippers can run on water (Minetti et al. 2012). Small enough ems could run on water with ordinary shoes.

To ems that are smaller and faster, sunlight seems dimmer and shows more noticeable diffraction patterns. Magnets, waveguides, and electrostatic motors are less useful. Surface tension makes it harder to escape from water. Friction is more often an obstacle, lubrication is harder to achieve, and random thermal disruptions to the speed of objects become more noticeable. It becomes easier to dissipate excess body heat, but harder to insulate against nearby heat or cold (Haldane 1926; Drexler 1992).

The rate at which fluids pass around an em body scales well with size; a one meter per second wind is also a one millimeter per millisecond wind, and so looks the same to a kilo-em in a proportionally smaller body. However, a smaller em finds it much harder to resist the pressures of such a wind. Thus spaces where small physical ems congregate need to avoid strong winds. To such ems, ordinary density air feels much thicker than it does to normal-size humans.

A crude calculation using a simple conservative nano-computer design suggests that a matching faster-em brain might plausibly fit inside an android body 256 times smaller and faster than an ordinary human body (Hanson 1995). If this calculation were correct, it would give the natural size and matching speed for ems.

Compared with ordinary humans, to a fast em with a small body the Earth seems much larger, and takes much longer to travel around. To a kilo-em, for example, the Earth's surface area seems a million times larger, a subway ride that takes fifteen minutes in real time takes ten subjective days, an eight-hour plane ride takes a subjective year, and a one-month flight to Mars takes a subjective century. Sending a radio signal to the planet Saturn and back takes a subjective four months. Even super-sonic missiles seem slow. However, over modest distances lasers and directed energy weapons continue to seem very fast to a kilo-em.

To Lilliputian ems, the world is a *much* larger place.

MEETINGS

Ems can meet either directly, with adjacent physical bodies, or they can meet virtually.

An em physical body can either be run by em "brain" hardware placed inside that body, or the body can be teleoperated by an em in brain hardware at a distance that is small compared with the *reaction distance* where the communication delay equals the em brain reaction time.

For example, if signals travel at the speed of light, then to keep the round-trip signal time delay to less than a subjective reaction time of a tenth of a second, a sixteen times human speed brain must be less than a reaction distance of roughly 1000 kilometers from its body. If we reduce the allowed signal delay to be only ten milliseconds, then the brain must be within 100 kilometers. (All this ignores added delays from network hardware.)

Now consider two ems who want to hold a virtual office meeting, who run on brain hardware separated in space, and who have matching speeds (and periods and phases if those apply). There are two ways to support this scenario. One is to temporarily move the brain state of one into hardware located near the other, and then to use hardware near to both of them to compute their virtual office environment. The other way is to leave the em brains at their separated locations, and have hardware between them send virtual reality signals to each of them, as if they were together in the same office. The ems won't be able to tell the difference between these two approaches if the signal delay between their locations is much smaller than their reaction times.

Because it takes far fewer bits to describe the details of a virtual reality meeting than to describe a brain, for near-enough ems in a short-enough meeting it should be cheaper to leave their brains fixed and exchange virtual reality signals, rather than moving one of their brains. That is, brains stay where they are and are told where they are and what they see and hear in their virtual meeting room.

Virtual reality meetings are also more secure against mind theft, although perhaps less secure against eavesdroppers. Thus ems near each other who desire a virtual meeting can reduce both communication and security costs by leaving their brains in the same fixed hardware, and only virtually moving to a shared location.

When the hardware supporting two em brains is far enough apart in space relative to their speeds, however, communication delays become noticeable. Ems then typically must choose between either having noticeably slow reactions to events in the meeting, or temporarily moving at least one of their brains to closer hardware.

Modest delays can actually be pretty tolerable. At the distance where some ems see a tenth of a second light-speed delay, ems sixteen times faster see an often quite tolerable one-and-a-half second delay, and ems sixteen times faster than those suffer only a twenty-six-second delay. Today, many text-messaging conversations function acceptably with thirty-second message delays. As with such messaging conversations today, ems who talk with noticeable delays may routinely talk with several others at the same time.

A fast-enough em that is physically near another em could credibly signal that fact by its quick reaction time. Ems could easily pretend to be far away when they were actually near, but they find it much harder to pretend to be near when they are actually far.

When a distant meeting attendee only has a few possible reactions at each moment, it becomes possible to make a copy of the meeting for each reaction, and then only continue the meeting copy corresponding to the correct reaction. To members of the continued meeting, it would seem as if that attendee was reacting quickly. This approach gets expensive fast, however.

The process whereby one em "calls" another em to request an immediate meeting varies depending on the relative speeds of the two ems. When a fast em calls a slow one, this calling em may have to wait a long time for the slow em to respond to the call, and then move to faster hardware to allow them to interact naturally. In contrast, if a slow em has already sped up to the speed of a fast em before it makes its call, a meeting may proceed immediately.

In Chapter 17, Preparation section, we will see that the ability to change mind speeds allows ems to more often complete projects on time, if not on budget. For similar reasons, em meetings more often start on time with everyone ready.

All things considered, compared with humans, ems find it easier and cheaper to meet each other. This has important implications.

ENTROPY

(The next two sections are especially technical, and few things later depend on them. Skip them if you prefer.)

To function, computers (by which I just mean artificial signal-processing machines) need many kinds of supports, including structural positioning, insulation from disturbances, communication, energy, and cooling. The need for free energy (or equivalently, negative entropy) is especially likely to induce a revolution in computer design within a few decades. After this revolution, many kinds of computer systems will likely be much more thermodynamically reversible. This includes ems.

Today, almost all computer circuits are made of CMOS (complementary metal–oxide–semiconductor) materials. A gate is the smallest logical unit on a computer chip, and the energy typically required for a simple CMOS gate operation has long been falling by more than a factor of ten per decade. (At least for chips that do not sacrifice performance for power or vice versa.) This basic trend can continue for at least another eleven decades, as we know of concrete gate designs that use a factor of 10^{11} less energy per gate operation (Merkle et al. 2016).

Projecting this trend forward, around the year 2035 the free energy used per CMOS gate operation should fall to the level of one bit, that is, to the free energy that thermodynamics says is required to erase one bit of information at ordinary temperatures (Drechsler and Wille 2012).

Computer logic gates erase bits (i.e., increase entropy) in two different ways. Ordinarily each simple gate erases one bit logically, because it converts two input bits into one output bit. In addition, each gate erases other bits non-logically, because the gate performs its logical operation quickly and away from thermodynamic equilibrium. Today, the vast majority of bit erasure in computers is done non-logically. Thus there is little point today in structuring computer gates to avoid logical erasure.

Around 2035, however, the rate of non-logical bit erasure should fall to the rate of logical erasure. After that point, if energy cost per computation is to fall much further, then computers must switch to using "reversible" designs that only rarely erase bits logically.

(Some hope to reduce energy usage by running hardware at lower temperatures. But this won't reduce the use of free energy, which is the real resource needed. It is the creation of entropy that is the fundamental problem.)

For human brains today, most of their bit erasure is non-logical. As brains run at room temperature, use about twenty watts, and have about 100 billion neurons that each take a minimum of twenty milliseconds to react, brains in effect erase over a billion bits per neuron per minimum neuron reaction time. As there are roughly 1000 synapses per neuron on average, that is over a million bits erased per synapse per minimum neuron reaction time. Unless brain synapses are somehow doing the equivalent of a million logical operations per reaction time, the vast majority of the brain's bit erasure must be non-logical. This suggests that human speed ems built on reversible computer hardware require far less than twenty watts of power.

Another hint that most future computers will likely be miserly with energy is that the Earth has far more material to convert into computers than it has energy to run such computers at maximal rates. For example, by one plausible calculation of the typical energy consumption in a maximum-output nanotech-based machine (~10 watts per cubic centimeter), all of the light energy reaching Earth from the sun could be used by a single city of nanotech hardware 100 meters (~thirty-three stories) tall and 10 kilometers on each side (Freitas 1999). Yet Earth has raw materials enough to build a vastly larger volume of computer hardware.

When computer operations lack a one-to-one mapping between input and output states, they are logically irreversible, and so must use free energy to erase bits. However, any irreversible mapping can be converted to a reversible one-to-one mapping by saving the input state along with the output state.

A clever fractal design allows one to create a reversible version of any irreversible computation (Bennett 1989). Imagine an ordinary irreversible computation that uses one particular processor unit and one matching memory unit. A reversible version of this computation could be completed in exactly the same amount of time. It costs a logarithmic-in-time overhead of extra parallel processor and memory units to reversibly erase the results of intermediate computing steps in the background (Bennett 1989).

This fractal reversing approach has a reversing period, which is the number of operation steps in the original computation before one has to logically erase one unit of memory. This reversing period can be doubled if one pays for one more unit each of processing and memory to hold and calculate intermediate steps. As a result, efficient reversing periods should roughly double each time the cost of computing hardware falls by half, relative to the cost of cooling and energy to run that hardware.

Today, computer gates are usually designed to change as fast as possible, and as a result they in effect irreversibly erase a great many bits during every gate operation. However, when over decades the energy cost per operation does not fall as fast as the hardware cost, energy costs eventually dominate, forcing computer designers to focus on reducing the rate of bit erasure.

To erase many fewer bits per gate operation, computer gates can be run nearly "adiabatically," that is, slowly enough that key parameters change smoothly enough to make it cheap to reverse those changes. For adiabatic hardware, the rate of non-logical bit erasure is then proportional to speed; run an adiabatic gate twice as fast, and it erases twice as many bits per gate operation, or four times as many bits per second (Younis 1994). Because of high levels of brain parallelism, over a wide range of speeds it should thus cost twice the computer hardware to make an em brain that erases half as many bits per second of subjective experience.

For nearly adiabatic computers, the rate at which bits are erased non-logically per operation is proportional to speed. For such machines, the speed that minimizes total costs per operation will incur spending of about the same amount to rent the computer hardware as to buy the energy and cooling to run that hardware. These costs include both the space to hold the computers and their supporting energy and cooling systems. Thus the cost to rent the computing hardware plus the volume to hold it typically equals the cost to rent the energy and cooling hardware plus the volume to hold those, plus the cost of the raw materials used to make energy.

Because for adiabatic computers the cost of buying new hardware is about as important as the cost to power and cool that hardware, the logarithmic rate at which computing power becomes cheaper should be near the average of the logarithmic rates at which computer hardware becomes cheaper and the rates at which energy and cooling become cheaper. This is a reason why we might expect Moore's law growth rates for active devices (not memory) to slow down by about a factor of two after around 2035 when nearly adiabatic reversible computing becomes important. Historically, the price of energy and cooling has fallen much more slowly than has the price of computer hardware.

It might seem that when cooling is a major issue, computer hardware runs at as hot a temperature as feasible, as the rate at which heat is transferred via conduction is proportional to a local temperature difference. However, for adiabatic reversible computer hardware, the rate at which heat is generated is also roughly proportional to temperature, as it is determined fundamentally by the rate of bit erasure (also known as entropy production). Thus the best temperature at which to run such hardware is determined by other considerations.

MISERLY MINDS

The use of energy-efficient hardware can change em behavior in many ways.

For example, when a brain emulation is run on a reversible computer, then once per reversing period it must pay to erase a single maximally compressed copy of its period-ending brain state. So the end of a reversing period is a cost-effective time for an em to switch to a different speed, or to archive a mind copy, as archiving bits saves from having to erase them.

The fractal reversing method induces more re-computing of mental states that first appear toward the start or end of a reversing period. Because of this, those who give more moral weight, in terms of avoiding pain and encouraging pleasure, to mental states that are recomputed more often, should give more moral weight to experiences that occur closer to reversing period boundaries.

Ems who archive their messages, actions, or sensory inputs must pay a cost to store those bits, and most likely a cost later to erase those bits when they are no longer wanted. However, ems who do not choose to archive such things will try to minimize related bit erasures.

For example, ems must pay to erase bits to see or hear physical or social worlds outside themselves, if such worlds change in unpredictable ways, and do not cooperate to reverse their common computation. If an em watches and mentally processes a real waterfall, that em must pay to erase the equivalent of a high-resolution input "movie" of the scene. He or she must first pay to remember the movie for the rest of the current reversing period, and then at the end of that period must pay to save or erase the bits of that movie.

In contrast, an em who watches and mentally processes a virtual waterfall might coordinate and synchronize with the hardware that produces that virtual scene to reverse both calculations together. The em could even interact in detail with the waterfall (such as by "swimming" in it) without paying to erase any more bits. This gives ems a reason to prefer virtual over physical realities, especially standard virtual realities that many ems could share and hence reduce the costs of computing them.

Ems experiencing virtual nature are more "green" because this activity disturbs physical nature less, either directly or via the production of waste heat. Today, the human experience of immersion in nature, both real and virtual, predicts being generous, feeling autonomous, wanting enduring relations, and wanting to help society, while immersion in non-natural environments predicts valuing money and fame (Weinstein et al. 2009). So ems who spend more time in virtual nature are also likely to feel more autonomous and generous, and less selfish.

If ems have entropy-efficient long distance communication networks, then they might coordinate to reverse their messages to each other. In the simplest case, an em who receives a message from another em must pay to erase that message later. However, if the reversing periods and phases of the two ems sufficiently match, the message receiver can later send back an "anti-message" to be reversibly erased by the sender (Hanson 1992). The anti-message can cancel the original message, allowing both to be eliminated without the costly erasure of bits.

When there are substantial message delays, ems must save messages or mental states for longer to support "anti-message" production. This increases the relative costs of sending messages early in a reversing period, and of sending messages with longer time delays, such as to more distant locations. Because of this, ems prefer to send messages toward the end of their reversing periods.

Slow reversible hardware can be made to have a variable speed, so that the speed could change from moment to moment to accommodate varying demands. For such hardware, the number of bits erased per operation goes inversely as operation time. That is, when each operation takes longer, fewer bits are erased per operation. By using such hardware to emulate brains, an em mind could temporarily speed up, if it were willing to temporarily pay a higher bit erasure cost per operation. Such an em could also temporarily slow down, and pay a lower energy cost per operation.

Temporary speed-ups require that there be some slack or buffer in the heat disposal system, so that the temporarily added heat doesn't overwhelm that system. Because the typical choice of hardware operating speed should be near an optimal tradeoff of hardware versus cooling costs, temporary small fractional changes in operating speed near this optimum should result in much smaller fractional increases in the total cost per operation.

Variable speed em hardware is especially useful in situations where demands for mental effort vary quickly and unpredictably. For example, in conversation an em could slow down while listening and speed up while talking. An em could slow down when waiting for inputs from others, and speed up when others are waiting for inputs from them. Monitors could slow down when what they were monitoring was relatively inactive, and speed up when such activity momentarily increased. Complex social norms may develop regarding when it is acceptable to speed up or slow down relative to interaction partners.

The use of slow reversible hardware probably reduces the top cheap speed, that is, the highest speed where the cost per operation is nearly the same as at low speeds. Thus as the costs of local heat disposal and energy usage rise, the local top cheap speed falls.

When other rates of bit erasure are lower, then ems will want longer reversing periods to also reduce reversing period erasures. As non-logical bit erasure rates are higher in the early em era, typical reversing periods are then short, plausibly corresponding to shorter than a reaction time. In this case the need for reversible hardware may have few effects on em behavior.

Later, however, bit erasure rates may be much lower, and then longer reversing periods may change em behavior more. For example, costs of reversing encourage ems who want to interact often to coordinate to share the same reversing periods and phases, and to prefer interactions with things outside themselves to happen away from reversing period boundaries.

If the cost of computing fell by factor of a million relative to the cost of energy and cooling, then the reversing period could change from a subjective reaction time of a tenth of a second to a subjective day. (This may not happen until long after the early em era.) With a reversing period of a day, it could make sense to end reversing periods during sleep, and for ems to interact the most with others just before going to sleep.

Ems who interact often want to share reversing periods and phases, to cheaply share special hardware and processes used at the end of a reversing period. However, ems who interact less are more likely to have different reversing phases, to more efficiently share hardware specialized for end of period tasks. This increases the costs of interaction between ems who interact less often.

It seems that the more miserly ems become with energy, the more that energy issues influence their behavior.

CHAPTER 7

Infrastructure

CLIMATE

s we will discuss in Chapter 18, Cities section, em cities are likely to be big, dense, highly cost-effective concentrations of computer and communication hardware. How might such cities interact with their surroundings?

Today, computer and communication hardware is known for being especially temperamental about its environment. Rooms and buildings designed to house such hardware tend to be climate-controlled to ensure stable and low values of temperature, humidity, vibration, dust, and electromagnetic field intensity. Such equipment housing protects it especially well from fire, flood, and security breaches.

The simple assumption is that, compared with our cities today, em cities will also be more climate-controlled to ensure stable and low values of temperature, humidity, vibrations, dust, and electromagnetic signals. These controls may in fact become city level utilities. Large sections of cities, and perhaps entire cities, may be covered, perhaps even domed, to control humidity, dust, and vibration. City utilities may absorb remaining pollutants. Emissions within cities may be strictly controlled.

However, an em city may contain temperatures, pressures, vibrations, and chemical concentrations that are toxic to ordinary humans. If so, ordinary humans are excluded from most places in em cities for safety reasons. In addition, we will see in Chapter 18, Transport section, that many em city transport facilities are unlikely to be well matched to the needs of ordinary humans.

Higher prices to rent volume near city centers should push such centers to extend both higher into the sky and deeper into the ground, as happens in human cities today. It should also push computers in city centers to be made from denser physical devices, that is, supporting more computing operations per volume, even if such devices are proportionally more expensive than less dense variants. City centers are also less likely to use deterministic computing devices, if such devices require more volume and cooling.

It may be possible to make computing devices that use less mass per computing speed supported, even if they cost more per operation computed. Such lighter devices are more likely to be used at higher city elevations, because they reduce the cost of the physical structures needed to hold them at these heights. This is more likely to happen near city centers, where altitudes are higher.

Computer and communication hardware is in general distinguished by the generation of its design, with more recent design generations tending to be more reliable and to use less volume, mass, power, and cooling. When it is cheap enough to move such hardware, or to change the location of city centers, then older hardware will tend to be further away from city centers where volume, power, and cooling cost more.

Cities today are the roughest known kind of terrain, in the sense that cities slow down the wind the most compared with other terrain types. Cities also tend to be hotter than neighboring areas. For example, Las Vegas is 7° Fahrenheit hotter in the summer than surrounding areas. This hotter city effect makes ozone pollution worse and this effect is stronger for bigger cities, in the summer, at night, with fewer clouds, and with slower wind (Arnfield 2003).

This is a mild reason to expect em cities to be hotter than other areas, especially at night and in the summer. However, as em cities are packed full of computing hardware, we shall now see that em cities will actually be *much* hotter.

COOLING

Many innovative devices have been proposed to lower the costs of generating and transporting energy. New generation options include solar power satellites, thorium nuclear reactors, and fusion reactors, while new energy transport options include superconducting cables and anti-matter. These devices may be able to supply high levels and densities of energy to em cities at low cost.

It seems harder, however, to imagine innovative ways to dramatically improve our abilities to cheaply cool large volumes of computers. Cooling is a very well understood physical process, and most proposed approaches seem to be relatively minor variations on existing ones. This suggests that for large dense em cities during the early em era, cooling is more of a limiting factor than energy.

Today, we usually cool systems by moving a cooling fluid such as air or water close to the heat source that we want to cool. The fluid comes in cold and moves out hot. One might imagine very low-friction transport systems, like railroads or aerial trams, that could move cooling materials in and out at a very low energy cost. However, today simple pipelines usually have much lower energy costs, and also total costs, than rail and other existing transport mechanisms. So the simple assumption to make here is that ems cool their cities via fluid cooling pipes.

Readers tempted to see pipes as a primitive technology should know that pipes rank high on "product complexity," meaning that nations must master an unusually wide range of abilities to make pipes well. Specifically, in 2013 pipes had an average complexity rank of 350 out of the 1239 product types ranked (Hausmann et al. 2014).

Metabolism in individual plants and animals follows a scaling law; organisms that are sixteen times as massive tend to have half the per-mass metabolism. Some have attributed this trend to fundamental difficulties in managing piping systems to pull nutrients in and push waste out for large serviced volumes (Savage et al. 2008).

However, we actually know of fluid-based pipe cooling designs that can efficiently cool large em cities. Biological fluid-based pipe systems such as blood vessels are fractal in the sense of having a branching structure that looks similar at different scales. There are simple fractal pipe designs that can efficiently import cool fluids such as air or water from outside a city to near every point in that city, and then export heated fluids from near every point in the city to outside the city volume (Bejan 1997; Bejan et al. 2000; Bejan 2006). These fractal cooling system designs require cost overheads that are logarithmic in the total size of the city. That is, such overheads increase by only a constant amount when a city size is doubled.

Closest to each tiny piece of computer hardware, heat can be transported away via materials such as metals that conduct heat well. Alternatively, small heat pipes might be used. These conducting materials or heat pipes can end in tiny cooling fans inside tiny fluid cooling pipes nearby. As the fluid moves away from these fans, smaller pipes merge into larger pipes where the fluids move faster. At some point the fluid switches from smooth to turbulent flow, but this only increases the size of the constant cost overhead added each time city size is doubled.

Colder fluids flowing from outside the city toward the tiny cooling fans reverse this pattern, breaking up into more pipes that are each smaller and have slower moving fluids. All else equal, input pipes require more volume for insulation because of their larger temperature difference from hot computer hardware. The use of a shared cooling system encourages nearby city volumes to maintain temperatures close to each other, and to exiting cooling fluids.

In addition to a fractal network of pipes within the cooled volume, a piped-fluid cooling system also needs large outside pipes to bring in cool fluids from distant reservoirs, and to take hot fluids away to distant reservoirs. Oceans and the atmosphere often function as such large reservoirs. In addition, one can treat distant space as a reservoir, by covering space-facing surfaces with special materials that only radiate and absorb at infrared frequencies where Earth's atmosphere is transparent (Zhai et al. 2017).

The cost of these reservoir pipes is roughly a product of pipe length times a per-length cost. Per-length costs are sublinear here; when flow doubles, the per-length pipe cost less than doubles. While pipe length needed can in principle increase with total flow, in practice it doesn't need to increase much when one has access to large volumes, like oceans or the atmosphere, where big currents pass by. Thus reservoir pipe costs are on net sublinear; when cities need twice the cooling, reservoir piping costs less than twice as much.

Assuming one has an outside source and sink for fluids, the other two main costs of a piped-fluids cooling system are (1) the power required to maintain the pressure difference that pushes cooling fluids through the city, and (2) the fraction of city volume devoted to the cooling pipes. (Assuming relatively low costs to make the pipes, to acquire cool input fluids, and to dispose of hot output fluids.) In both of these cases, per-cooling-unit costs increase as the logarithm of the city's volume. Every time the city volume doubles, not only does the same additional fraction of city volume have to be devoted to a new kind and size of pipe to cool that city, but the same additional pressure must be added to the pressure difference between the input and output ends of the cooling pipe system.

The economic value produced in a city is often modeled as a low power (greater than one) of the economic activity in that city (Bettencourt et al. 2007, 2010; Schrank et al. 2011). As mathematically, for large volumes such a power of volume grows faster than a logarithm of volume, the greater value produced in larger cities can easily pay for the higher costs of cooling larger cities. Thus costs of cooling do not limit em city sizes.

For very small city volumes, however, the added costs to cool a larger volume might outweigh the added economic value a larger city volume could produce. Thus there may be an important economic niche for small isolated "towns" of ems that take advantage of the cheaper computing power resulting from lower cooling costs. After all, when cooling and energy are together four times cheaper, computing power becomes twice as cheap. So isolated em towns may specialize in doing jobs where cheap computing matters more than the fast flexible communication and transport with many other ems available in large cities.

When the cross-section of a pipe is doubled, the rate at which fluid flows through that pipe more than doubles. Thus there are scale economies in the total amount of cooling supplied to a city of fixed volume. The exact magnitude of these scale economies depends on whether fluid flow is smooth or turbulent.

With adiabatic computing, about the same amount should be spent on computing hardware as is spent on energy and cooling to run that hardware. Because of this, in em city centers where the cost of space is high, energy and cooling systems should take up roughly the same volume as the computers themselves. As computer hardware tends to be more expensive to make per unit volume than energy or cooling hardware, the energy and cooling systems may actually tend to take up more volume than the computing hardware. The cooling pipe fraction may be even higher toward the city periphery, as pipes to cool a city center must pass from outside the city through the city periphery.

As cooling tends to require more space than does energy generation and transport, most of the space devoted to energy and cooling is likely devoted to cooling. Thus in em cities densely packed with computer hardware, a substantial fraction (likely 20-70 percent) of em city volume is devoted to cooling pipes.

Because of their higher costs of cooling, larger em cities tend to use less energy relative to hardware, and thus use longer reversing periods, which reduces the local top cheap speed. The very fastest ems thus tend to live in smaller communities, away from big city centers.

As cities pull in cool fluids and push out hot fluids, heat engines might be created well outside the cities, engines that use this temperature difference to produce energy. For example, power-generating kites might surf strong hot winds that rise above em cities. However, it seems hard to design cost-effective heat engines that take advantage of this temperature difference.

AIR AND WATER

The two obvious candidates for em city cooling fluids are air and water. Cities that are primarily air-cooled are arranged somewhat differently from cities that are primarily water-cooled. (There is also a remote possibility of cooling via superfluid Helium II, at below 2° Kelvin. This fluid can have low viscosity, high heat conductivity, and high entropy transfer rates (Gully 2014).)

Air-cooled cities pull in a lot of cool air and push out a lot of hot air. Most of the hot air exits above the city, into a tall cloud of hot air rising above the city. A strong wind pulls cool air in from outside toward the outside base of the city. As hot air rises, this force can pull air through the system, as it does today in the cooling towers of power plants.

The hot-air-rises force is proportional to the height difference between air entering and exiting the city. It is also proportional to the difference in (inverse) air temperature between entering and exiting air. Tall cooling towers might be added above em city centers to increase this height difference, and thus increase the pulling force. Such towers may have the hyperboloid shape often seen today in power plant cooling towers, because such shapes have superior strength as structures made from straight struts. Scale economies in building towers might encourage cities to mostly cool via a single main tower. The tallest cooling tower today is over 200 meters high; em city towers could be much taller.

The fact that air tends to become more viscous at higher temperatures pushes air-cooled cities toward using lower temperatures. This effect also reduces the size of the pipes of air entering cities, relative to outgoing air pipes. Air-cooled cities might be placed on large flat dry cold plains, such as in Sweden, Siberia, Canada, or Antarctica.

The ability of air to cool is proportional to its pressure, while its viscosity, or resistance to pressure, is independent of pressure. Because of this, air-cooled cities are tempted to use high-pressure air. Five atmospheres of air pressure can have similar cooling abilities to water. However, using high-pressure air for city cooling requires large pressure differences between the inside and outside of a city. One might manage this pressure difference in the cooling system via heat exchangers that intertwine pipes with high and low pressure air, or via compressors that increase the pressure of incoming air, combined with turbines to capture energy from the falling pressure of outgoing air.

Both air and water-cooled cities are likely to have winds moving in toward them and tall clouds of hot air rising above them, although both of these should be larger for air-cooled cities. Such winds and clouds might be like those often associated with active volcanoes.

Water-cooled cities pull in a lot of cold water and push out a lot of hotter water. The larger the temperature difference between the incoming and outgoing water, the more cooling is provided. This gives a preference for pulling in very cold water, which suggests locating such cities on the coast near the Earth's poles, such as in Scandinavia or Argentina.

A kilometer or more under the ocean, temperatures are typically a cold 4° Centigrade. This suggests the possibility of subsea em cities. Some have begun to develop subsea data centers (Markoff 2016; Cutler et al. 2017). But subsea mechanical engineering is famously hard, and experts see few prospects for that getting much easier anytime soon.

Advantages from larger temperature differences also suggest pushing out water that is nearly steam, that is, near the boiling point of water. However, water that is too near the temperature of steam risks creating explosions of actual steam when there are temporary flow blockages. Water-cooled cities also suffer more risk of water leaks that damage nearby equipment, and so need to be better protected against such corrosion.

Hotter water has a lower viscosity, that is, a lower resistance to being pushed through a pipe. This implies that input pipes of cool water are larger than output pipes of hot water, and that it is cheaper to cool with warmer water, all else equal. This encourages water-cooled cities to be hot, with computer hardware temperature near the boiling point of water.

A slurry of water containing small ice pellets can cool much better than can water by itself. For example, a slurry with a 20-25 percent volume of ice flows nearly as easily as does plain cold water, yet has about five times the cooling capacity. Salt-water helps to make pellets smaller, with pellet diameters of 20-50 micrometers available via today's standard technology. Seawater-based ice slurry cooling systems are now often used on fishing boats to keep fish cool (EPSL 2014; Kauffeld et al. 2010).

The advantages of ice slurry cooling seem likely to be irresistible, pushing em cities to prefer water over air cooling, and pushing cities to keep input pipes insulated enough to carry an ice slurry. Cooling pipes with a 0.1 millimeter inner diameter should be able to come close enough to each heat source to allow the remaining heat transport to be done via simple heat conduction in metal or small heat pipes (Faghri 2012; Gully 2014).

Pipe walls covered with melting ice can cut the friction of water flowing past such walls (Vakarelski et al. 2015). Also, dense solutions of bacteria in water have recently been seen to eliminate the viscosity of that water via coordinated motions of bacteria tails (López et al. 2015). Analogous mechanisms might be used to greatly increase the flow capacity of em water pipes.

Like air-cooled cities, water-cooled em cities are also likely to gain from locating in cold places. While air-cooled cities may seek flat cold plains, water-cooled cities seek to be near lots of cold seawater. They might even go deep in the ocean, for easier access to colder water, if costs were not prohibitive to modify transport and manufacturing methods to handle the very high pressures resulting from having seawater over em city buildings.

Whether cooled by air or water, em cities could look quite different from human cities.

BUILDINGS

How might buildings differ in an em era?

As we will see in Chapter 13, Efficiency, the em world is focused more on efficiency and function, and less on showing off wealth and individuality. In particular, compared with structures in our cities, structures in em cities focus more on cheaply and efficiently supporting a more limited range of tenants. Em buildings mainly hold computer hardware and supporting infrastructure.

Buildings require structural support, to hold matter up against the gravity that pulls them down, to resist the wind pressures that push them sideways, and to deal with internal stresses resulting from earthquake ground vibrations. The relative importance of these issues changes in an em economy.

Today, buildings are typically required to withstand the biggest earthquakes expected to appear over the next century, which is near the useful lifetime of most buildings. As we will see in Chapter 16, Growth Estimate section, an em economy may grow faster than our economy by a factor of 100 or more. Because of this, buildings only need to last for durations that are this factor shorter than buildings need to last today. As the strength of earthquakes is inverse to their frequency, so that stronger quakes happen less often, this implies that em buildings only need to be built to handle maximum earthquake ground vibrations this factor weaker than the vibrations that buildings today must handle. The need to handle earthquakes 100 or more times weaker makes it easier to build taller buildings for em cities.

For tall buildings today, wind pressures are a bigger problem than gravity. Like trees in a forest, buildings in cities today are each responsible for their own wind resistance; they rarely connect to give mutual support, even though such mutual support can make it much easier to resist wind pressures. Builders of tall buildings today haven't managed to coordinate to arrange such mutual structural support. However, em cities might use combinatorial auctions, discussed in Chapter 15, Combinatorial Auctions section, to coordinate decentralized management of structural support to protect buildings against vibrations, gravity, and winds. Auction bids could specify acceptable locations, the structural support they need or are willing to supply, and the average and peak vibrations they will emit, absorb, and tolerate. This can allow em city structures to more closely resemble a large three-dimensional lattice of supports holding diverse components. Such a lattice can make it cheaper for em cities to reach higher into the sky.

Today, the Burj Khalifa in Dubai, completed in 2009, is the world's tallest building at 830 meters high. A 1007-meter Kingdom Tower in Jeddah is under construction, to be completed in 2019. A 15-kilometer tall tower has been designed with steel as its structural material. Even taller buildings seem possible using lighter stronger materials such as graphene and carbyne, and using better fractal designs for structural supports (Farr 2007b; Farr and Mao 2008; Rayneau-Kirkhope et al. 2012). Factoring in continued progress in building materials, the reduced importance of earthquakes for ems, better coordination to resist winds, and stronger economic pressures for denser city concentrations, em city centers might perhaps rise to a kilometer high or more over kilometers-wide regions.

However, the em economy places one very big obstacle in the way of tall em city buildings. As we shall see, the em economy grows very rapidly, perhaps doubling every month. Because of this, the time delays required today to construct buildings are prohibitively expensive in an em economy. This is because the cost of a building roughly doubles for every additional economic-doubling time added to the time required to finish construction. So the six years that it took to build today's tallest building is completely unacceptable in the fast em world.

Thus there are huge premiums placed on fast construction, and the added time required to build taller buildings might limit how high em cities grow. To allow both rapid construction and rapid flexible changes later, buildings might be made out of modular units (Lawson et al. 2012). For example, in a recent demonstration in China a fifty-seven-story building was built in only nineteen days (Diaz 2015). This is three stories per day, a 50 percent increase over the two stories per day rate achieved by the same team less than four years before.

To speed construction, computing hardware placed inside modular buildings might come in standardized modular units such as shipping containers that can be more easily moved as needed, with standard interfaces providing utility services to such containers. Buildings might be, in effect, huge shipping container warehouses.

Going further in this direction, a city brimming with computer hardware and water-filled cooling pipes might perhaps be built out of incompressible "bricks," where each brick is full of useful hardware devices, but where inside volumes that would otherwise be empty are instead filled with stone or water and perhaps tension wires. Such bricks might be stackable to very large heights while requiring much less structural support than do items held in tall buildings today. Structural supports might then be mainly needed to assist with disasters and with periodic rebuilding efforts.

Today, moderately tall buildings are actually cheaper than short buildings. In most rich nations today, the building height for which the cost per square meter of useful space is lowest for experienced construction teams is at least twenty stories high, and perhaps forty stories or higher (Pickena and Ilozora 2003; Blackman et al. 2008;

Dalvit 2011). Regulations, including laws that explicitly ban tall buildings, seem to be the main reason that in many rich nations today most recently constructed buildings are shorter than this most efficient height (Glaeser et al. 2005; Watts et al. 2007). Successful em cities are likely to be those that find ways to reduce excessive regulatory limits on new buildings and their heights.

To speed reconstruction, cities might coordinate to reconstruct whole sections together. An axis of reconstruction activity might even sweep around a city center like the hand of a clock. In this case the city would look more like a spiral, with the newest just-built radial slice of the city being taller and wider than the oldest about-to-be-dismantled slice. Radial slices near the end of their useful life would likely have more accidents and less reliable utilities. They might also be more attractive places to conduct illicit activities. A coordinated spiral of reconstruction could make it easier to manage land allocation via combinatorial auctions, which will be discussed in Chapter 18, City Auctions section.

To support higher than ambient pressures in the centers of air-cooled cities, physical structures are needed to maintain high internal pressures against lower outside pressures. Fractal designs for pressure containment surfaces can help here (Farr 2007a). The structures in high air pressure cities that maintain higher air pressure in the center could also be helpful in giving structural support to hold up mass in lower pressure regions above high-pressure city centers.

The structures required to create high air pressure em cities might be expensive in low-pressure environments. If so, such cities might instead be placed under a few meters of water. For example, 50 meters of water overhead adds 5 Earth atmospheres of pressure.

Not only do em cities look different, their buildings look different too.

MANUFACTURING

As biological humans are less relevant in an em economy, the biological fraction of today's international trade is less relevant in an em economy. However, this fraction is actually rather small. Today, only

9.8 percent of international exports by value are in the categories of foods, 7.5 percent are in medical-related chemicals, and 5.5 percent in garments and textiles (Hausmann et al. 2014). Thus not much more than about a quarter of exports today seem threatened by a reduced biology trade. Of strong continued relevance to ems are metals, machinery, electronics, construction, oil, coal, petrochemicals, mining, aircraft, ships, and boilers.

Because biology matters less in the em economy, weather-induced changes in biology also matter less. However, extreme weather could still disrupt non-biological em mining, manufacturing, and transport. Furthermore, ems are more geographically concentrated in a few big cities, and the doubling time of the em economy is closer to typical timescales on which local weather can change a lot. Thus severe storms might more easily cause big disruptions to the em economy.

Today, consumers place a high value on having a great variety of products and services to choose from. This preference has increased substantially over the last century. By picking products that adapt in detail to their varying individual tastes, consumers are able to signal their distinct individualities. This product variety reduces the scale and scope of economies that can be achieved in making items cheaply. The diversion of development and resources into improving less-durable, more-context-dependent products, compared with more general products, has reduced economic growth rates (Corrado et al. 2009). However, consumers today usually care less about low production costs or growth rates, and care more about the value they can gain from more variety in products and services.

As discussed in Chapter 13, Efficiency, in a very competitive em economy, efficiency and low cost gain in importance compared with product variety. This reverses the trend in recent decades away from mass production and toward mass customization and flexible manufacturing. A return to mass production should result in more long-term growth, simpler and more standardized products, larger factories that achieve more economies of scale and scope, and better but more expensive tools. A return to mass production should also encourage organizational divisions centered less on types of customers and products and more on functions such as sales, marketing, design, production, and shipping (Salvador et al. 2009; Piller 2008). All these changes might be reduced, however, if parasites such as computer viruses can better exploit mass-produced products, and so discourage them relative to other products.

A shift toward mass production should modestly increase the value of automation and software tools, as for mass products the fixed cost of developing such tools is spread out over a larger scope of use of such tools. As variety in product appearance seems cheaper in virtual reality than in physical reality, a trend toward mass production should be more pronounced in physical products, relative to virtual products.

Like future computers, future factories may also have subsystems composed of many small elements that run nearly thermodynamically adiabatically to reduce the use of free energy. That is, factories may have mechanical parts that move slowly enough that their motions could nearly as well have happened in reverse. For such subsystems, the free energy used per operation goes inversely to the time taken per operation. As with adiabatic reversible computers, this suggests that about the same amount is spent to rent the hardware for these sorts of manufacturing subsystems as is spent on the energy and cooling to run them.

An extreme version of small adiabatic manufacturing hardware is molecular manufacturing, or "nanotech," wherein the factory equipment and the manufactured products have atomically precise features. While it isn't obvious how far or fast this trend will go, nanotech might be important during the early em era.

Large-scale feasibility of nanotech would likely reduce the demand for rare elements such as zinc compared with common elements such as carbon, and reduce the fraction of production materials that become waste products. It should shorten supply chains and thus cut long-distance physical trade, encouraging more material goods to be made and recycled locally, instead of transported from distant factories and disposed to distant dumps (Drexler 1992, 2013).

Nanotech-based factories need not be much bigger than the products they make. Such factories would usually have marginal costs of production close to the marginal costs of energy, cooling, and raw materials. This implies less variation in the cost of marginal production per pound in nanotech products. Nanotech factories would thus be relatively cheap to make, and would allow for faster rates of production and retooling.

Within dense cities, some computing hardware might even be manufactured in place immediately after dismantling old hardware in place, saving the time, cost, and risk of transporting old equipment. Nanotech might encourage factories to use deterministic computer hardware, which strongly avoids logic errors and timing fluctuations, if doing so could increase the reliability of the manufacturing process.

The larger are the fixed relative to marginal costs of making products, the more that consumers can be tempted to buy access to large standardized packages of diverse products, perhaps via large group purchases that can negotiate for lower prices (Shapiro and Varian 1999). Such purchases might be organized around clans or firms, to achieve larger scale economies.

As the marginal costs of nanotech products are especially low compared with fixed costs, nanotech can create even more scope for selling goods in bundles. Thus ems with nanotech may typically buy access to whole large libraries of designs, gaining the right for their group to buy and locally produce individual items at near marginal cost (Hanson 2006b).

Overall, manufacturing seems modestly different in an em world.

CHAPTER 8

Appearances

VIRTUAL REALITY

The world that we typically see and feel today is quite different from the world that our ancestors saw and felt. While foragers did use fire to change their environment, and spent a lot of time in artificial camps, still much of what they saw was as it would be if humans had never existed. Today, in contrast, for most of us almost everything that we see and touch is part of an artificial world that humans have created. It doesn't usually bother us much to live in such an artificial world, however, as the things we see and touch are in fact quite relevant for living our lives.

What kind of world do ems see? We expect ems to usually experience simulated "virtual" realities. While such worlds might seem "unreal" to us, to them what ems see and touch are mostly the relevant things that they need to see, to live their lives. We have several reasons for expecting ems to usually live and work in virtual reality.

First, compared with ordinary humans, it is easier to fully immerse ems in computer-generated virtual realities. One could feed computed inputs into an em's emulated eyes, ears, nose, fingers, etc., and take outputs from that em's emulated arms, legs, tongue, etc., to create a complete sensory experience of the sight, sound, smell, touch, etc., of being in contact with and partially controlling a constructed but vivid world. Humans get many sensory clues telling them that their virtual realities are not real. Ems need see no such clues.

Second, the cost to compute a workable virtual reality can be very low, compared with the cost to compute an em. Now it is true that the cost to compute a virtual environment depends greatly on the level of realistic detail required. Consider the cost to give simulated inputs to an em that it could not distinguish, even with careful examination, from a real physical environment. For many familiar physical environments, such a simulation may cost many times the cost of running the emulation brain itself.

However, humans today are routinely comfortable and moderately productive interacting with video game environments that require vastly less computing power than human-speed brain emulations will require. Also, instead of sending very fine-grain low-level signals of very particular sights and sounds, it may become possible to send cheaper-to-compute higher-level signals that em brains interpret as their having seen the lower-level signals. For example, instead of sending individual light pixels to the eye, which then translates that to lines and areas, one might just send those lines and areas to the appropriate emulated neurons.

Ems may prefer virtual reality environments that are expensive to compute, relative to the cost of running the ems themselves. Even so, cheaply computed environments seem sufficient to support the vast majority of em activities, in both work and leisure. On the job, there is a tradeoff regarding whether to pay more for a more realistic virtual environment that might add to worker productivity. When ems make this tradeoff well, they will not often pay a price for their virtual environments that much exceeds the cost of running their brains. Usually they pay far less.

Sometimes people imagine that a world of cheap virtual reality is a world without scarcity or constraints, where anyone can do anything they want. But even when it is cheap to compute virtual reality scenes and interactions, it need not be cheap to pay for the hardware, energy, and cooling to compute the brains that experience that virtual reality, or to pay for brain-housing real estate to ensure those brains are close enough to naturally interact with many other interesting brains. Thus ems living in a virtual reality must earn (or be given) enough to pay for it.

Ems who do physical labor need to perceive many aspects of the physical world relevant for their job. But ems doing office work, and those in most leisure activities, do not need to see the real physical world. As in advanced economies today, most ems have office jobs. And for office-job-ems, the virtual reality worlds and bodies that they inhabit could in principle be anything that the human mind could understand, and that could be efficiently computed given available resources.

In principle each em could inhabit a completely different virtual reality. This seems to make it hard for us to infer much about the features of em virtual worlds. However, consider an analogy with clothes. Today, we have the wealth and technology to decorate our bodies with a vast range of shapes and materials. Yet the clothes we actually wear are far more limited and predictable. These predictable choices better support the usual functions that our clothes perform, such as comfort and displaying our current social roles, modes, and status.

Similarly, the many predictable functions that ems try to achieve in their virtual worlds can predictably constrain those worlds. For example, ems need to share virtual worlds if they want to interact with other ems. If they want to interact naturally with other ems via speech, facial expressions, touch, or paper-like visual screens, then their worlds must contain understandable analogues of these types of interactions.

If ems want the ability to easily begin and end such interactions with other ems, or to accept or reject interaction proposals, their worlds need to offer clear representations of interaction invitations. An invitation to a meeting might specify participants, observers, starting time, duration, virtual and physical locations, nominal speed, and tolerable participant signal delays.

To manage the real resources needed to support virtual experiences, ems find it useful to have representations of such resources and their control in their virtual worlds. So virtual worlds likely have clear simple representations giving ems ways to see and control their monetary balances, security permissions, interaction histories, and future interaction schedules. In addition, ems want representations of their and others' brain hardware location, type, speed, period, phase, and reliability. They also want to know the availability, price, speed, and security of communication connections. In addition, they want representations of options for changing these parameters, and of ways to initiate such changes.

While em virtual realities can in principle be almost anything, the simple assumption to make here is that in practice they are recognizably similar to our real world. Bodies, clothes, baskets, rooms, halls, and so on continue to serve similar psychological functions for ems as they do for us.

One plausible big difference in em virtual realities is that ems may make great use of the ability to ignore gravity while building structures and moving around in three dimensions. We today often fantasize about the freedom that such abilities could allow, and ems could use them to make many more people and places conveniently visible and accessible.

The cost of moving from one virtual reality to another may be very small. If each virtual reality is better supported by hardware in a particular location, then an em might need to move close enough to that better hardware. And if no one is using a virtual reality before an em wants to use it, there might be costs in starting it up. But otherwise, virtual reality need have few costs of movement. Thus virtual reality has few costs of commuting or traveling, and tele-commuting has little meaning. Breaks from work can happen in most any available virtual reality.

COMFORT

In addition to serving the above functions, virtual realities also please ems.

Most elements of virtual worlds are intended as background, there to support but not needlessly distract from the centers of attention. Such backgrounds are mostly familiar, safe, and comfortable, with just enough novelty to not be distractingly boring or depressing. When serving as a background to an em's main activities of work, socializing, or sleep, virtual realities need to not be overly distracting. But when virtual realities become a main focus of attention for bonding or entertainment, they can be extremely engrossing.

As the cost to compute a spectacular virtual reality can be small relative to the cost of running an em mind to appreciate it, and as a much larger em economy could afford to spend astronomical sums searching for pleasing combinations, we should expect the quality of em virtual realities to be superlative. By the standards of today, widely consumed em music, architecture, decoration, scenery, texture, product design, story plot and dialogue, etc., are of very high quality. Also, ems living in a virtual reality need never experience hunger, disease, or pain, nor ever see, hear, feel, or taste anything ugly or disgusting. In addition, mind tweaks should allow the equivalent of spectacular mind-altering drugs with few problematic side effects such as dry mouth or the shakes.

In virtual reality, the faces, bodies, and voices chosen by individual ems are whatever gets them to be treated well. So to the extent that individual ems choose such things, ems seem smart, beautiful, and trustworthy, and also dominant or submissive and with personality types appropriate to their desired roles. Ems tend to respect and trust each other more as a result.

Em virtual reality leisure environments may be so alluring, in fact, that their quality is limited on purpose so that non-retiree ems are consistently willing to leave leisure to return to work. For religious or related reasons some ems may even refuse to enter anything but Spartan virtual realities with low addiction potential.

Typical ems may also be reluctant to enter virtual realities new to them, out of fear of addictive temptations. Ems who, even so, remain vulnerable to being seduced to spend most of their resources on virtual reality experiences are quickly selected out of the em economy. Those who remain have found some way to resist such temptations.

The main elements of our world usually not found in em worlds are those that are needlessly frightening or time-consuming, or that violate the abstractions we try to impose on our world. For example, long subjective travel times are avoided in the em world, closed virtual em rooms are usually entirely sound and signal proof, and unapproved outsiders are usually unable to accidentally overhear conversations.

Also, dust does usually not collect on surfaces, nor do materials wear or decay. But this need not imply everything looks "clean."

Cluttered spaces tend to cause and result from creativity, and cluttered offices often help workers to manage great detail (Vohs et al. 2013). Workers with cluttered offices often know where to find most everything in them, even if outsiders can make little sense of the apparent disorder. Yes, clutter often results from and leads to stress and disorganization, and so is usually avoided. Even so, some em workers likely gain from and accept clutter, and clutter may also be used to signal membership in creative communities.

Today in cartoons and video games, we see that distinctions, such as between object types and the boundaries of motions, bodies, objects, and spaces, are often exaggerated in predictable directions, to make such distinctions more visible and salient (Thomas and Johnston 1981). For example, objects are often drawn with dark, sharp, easy-to-see borders. Appearances in em virtual realities may be similarly exaggerated, and look more cartoonish than our world. For example, objects may be stretched in their direction of motion.

The more the em world focuses on how things look in virtual reality, the less that ems are willing to pay to make things look nice in physical reality. In addition, the em world in general focuses more on functionality relative to design and aesthetics. Thus in the physical world em buildings and other infrastructure tends to look functional, and perhaps harsh. But virtual reality usually looks quite nice.

SHARED SPACES

When ems share spaces, they must compromise on how such spaces look and act. While similar issues have long applied to artificial human spaces, the stronger em control over their virtual spaces makes it a larger issue.

While virtual reality can be cheap, the commonly seen features of spaces where communities meet are intrinsically scarce. That is, although each member of a community can be given control over some elements of this space, they cannot all be given full control over all elements. The scarcity is not so much in being able to see the space, as being able to control what others see in the space. While similar copies from the same em clan may economize by sharing only one body that others can see in the space, they still have to compromise regarding what that copy is seen to be doing.

The need to compromise on shared features tends to produce features preferred by a (perhaps-weighted) majority. Majorities may thus choose appearances that make minorities look silly or ugly. This should reinforce majority views.

Em virtual realities can easily be designed to limit the harm possible from physical violence. While ems might suffer psychological harm from what they experience in virtual reality, there need be no danger that a virtual reality experience will directly harm their brain, cryptographic keys, bank accounts, or information stored. Ems can know that, no matter what it looks like in virtual reality, they are actually safe from real harm.

Of course as computer security is expensive, ems might be harmed by non-virtual reality computer actions such as viruses or network attacks. But as it is easy to prevent damage from physical acts in virtual reality, such damage is in fact prevented.

Today, offices are often arranged in an open cubicle plan. This may be done to save on the cost of floor space, to promote interaction and innovation, or to push away anti-social employees. However, it seems that such cubicle offices are more stressful and hinder cognitive capacities as well as interactions with co-workers (Jahncke et al. 2011; Kim and de Dear 2013). As virtual space is very cheap, cubicles may be avoided, and em homes and offices may appear to be spacious, private, and well appointed. However, the connections between such private offices are probably arranged to encourage useful interactions.

Today, many of our social habits are deeply integrated with standard cycles such as days and years, standard locations such as offices, shops, and parks, and standard human features such as age, gender, and profession. It's reasonable to guess that such habits will continue with ems. So I expect em virtual worlds to typically show changes corresponding to day and year cycles, at rates matching the mind speeds of typical em residents. I also expect virtual locations to often look recognizably like offices, bedrooms, bars, parks, plazas, auditoriums, elevators, etc., to evoke the behaviors considered appropriate in such places. I expect the sound and sight of virtual bodies to often give easily recognized clues about age, status, gender, profession, mood, and activity mode, to evoke expectations appropriate to such differences.

As with video games today, the design of em virtual worlds is subject to fewer physical constraints than is the design of non-virtual worlds. Like games today, they thus have more room for subtly encoding multiple meanings, allusions, and references. Ems expect to find more such hidden "Easter eggs" in the virtual worlds around them.

Groups of ems meeting in virtual reality might find use for a social "undo" or "reroll" feature, allowing them to, for example, erase unwelcome social gaffes. At least they could do this if they periodically archived copies of their minds and meeting setting, and limited the signals they sent to others outside their group. When the undo feature is invoked, it specifies a particular past archived moment to be revived. Some group members might be allowed a limited memory of the undo, such as by writing a short message to their new selves. When the undo feature is triggered, all group members are then erased (or retired) and replaced by copies from that past archive moment, each of whom receives the short message composed by its erased version.

This undo action is typically more expensive the larger the group and the longer the subjective time period that was erased. (A "pick the best roll" out of many feature gets even more expensive.) So there need to be limits on who can invoke undo and how often. Outsiders who receive signals from group members during the meeting have to accept a risk that signal senders might be replaced by versions that don't remember sending those signals. The enforcement of any rules requiring group members to forget what happened during the erased period probably requires central control of the hardware running member minds, and limits on signals sent to outsiders.

It is usually cheap to place one or more participant ems into a virtual reality that mimics some special place or time, real or imagined. However, it is prohibitively expensive to populate that virtual reality with many characters who are as complex as those participants. After all, em brains are far more expensive to compute than are imaginary buildings or mountains. Thus apparently complex characters are usually only included if their behavior can be computed cheaply relative to the cost of emulating an ordinary brain, or if such characters only act rarely. For these rare interactions, actors might be paid to temporarily play relevant roles.

As a cat brain has about 1 percent as many neurons as a human brain, virtual cat characters are an affordable if non-trivial expense. Most pet brains also require the equivalent of a small fraction of a human brain to emulate. The ability to pause a pet while not interacting with it would make pets even cheaper. Thus emulated animals tend to be cheap unless one wants many of them, very complex ones, or to have them run for long times while one isn't attending to them. Birds might fly far above, animals creep in the distance, or crowds mill about over there, but you could not often afford to interact with many complex creatures who have long complex histories between your interactions with them.

MERGING REAL AND VIRTUAL

Ems will need to manage two kinds of spatial concepts: who is where and can see what in the virtual world, and also who is where and protected by what in the physical world. Rather than managing two separate disconnected representations for these two kinds of spaces, it may be tempting to integrate them into a common spatial representation.

For example, ems' sense of virtual place and location on large scales might usually be taken directly from their physical location, with only modest and local changes made for comfort or convenience. In physical reality, city volume is divided between "buildings" that mainly house em brains in larger server clusters, and utilities such as cooling, transport, and structural support that use the spaces between buildings.

In virtual reality, the space really devoted to utilities might appear in virtual reality as common open spaces where ems could congregate. These spaces might appear to occupy more volume than they do to allow ems to see long distances through them. The space in virtual reality devoted to buildings might appear as typically opaque private homes, offices, shops, gardens, etc.

In cities today it seems that while people like be able to view large spaces and long distances while at work and play, they don't so much like large social spaces where others can see them in detail. So em designs of their virtual spaces need to make tradeoffs between letting people see a lot while also letting them hide some of their activities.

At any one time ems might have current locations for their virtual bodies, and different locations for their "souls" (i.e., brains), sitting inside their "home" buildings. While em (virtual) bodies can jump around very cheaply and quickly, there is a speed-dependent "leash" saying how far away an em body can comfortably move from its soul. Past that leash distance the body starts to have noticeably sluggish reactions because of signal delays. Faster ems have proportionally shorter leashes.

Souls could also move to new homes, but such moves are costly in money, time, and risk. In the Harry Potter stories, the horcrux spell made the wizard Voldemort invincible by spreading his soul across many hidden physical objects, all of which had to be found and destroyed to kill him. Similarly, an em couldn't be hurt by an attack on its virtual body, but only via a physical attack at the location of its soul. As if protected by a horcrux spell, ems implemented redundantly at many different physical locations might only be hurt via physical attacks that could hurt them at *all* of those locations. This provides ems with extra security against many kinds of disaster.

The owner of a real physical building might be given control over how the surface of that building appears within virtual reality. This control might be subject to regulation. The building owner might divide the building surface among building residents, to let each of them control an entrance or facade visible to common areas. As with the TARDIS in "Doctor Who," the virtual volume of homes, offices, etc., inside each virtual building could be much larger than the total volume of that building as seen from the outside.

Physical objects and ems in physical bodies that are really physically located in common areas may or may not appear in the standard virtual reality depiction of such common areas. For such physical objects to integrate well with virtual objects, the scale of typical real items such as doorways and walkways needs to be matched to the mental speed of the typical residents. It also makes sense to set the typical size of virtual em bodies so as to produce a pleasing average density of such bodies, neither too dense nor too sparse. After all, ems do not want to feel too lonely nor too crowded in common spaces.

To let ems move smoothly between real and virtual bodies, physical doors of buildings could have an associated stock of rentable physical bodies. When an em left a virtual space through a virtual door, its mind could be transferred into one of the bodies that then exits through a matching physical door. When entering a virtual space from a physical space, the process could reverse.

To ems, virtual and physical reality may in practice be merged into an integrated whole.

CHAPTER 9

Information

VIEWS

Interacting ems need not see exactly the same virtual environment.

For example, each em might prefer to see a shared environment as decorated with their personal choices of colors or patterns. Ems might also prefer to overlay or augment their views of the virtual world with useful tags and statistics, or to see through virtual objects to see object components or to see what lies behind those objects. Virtual ems may have telescopic sight, allowing them to always vividly see anything anywhere they are allowed to view. However, if overused, overlays may impair perception, and so should be used carefully (Sabelman and Lam 2015).

To sensibly interact with others, ems usually want easy ways to quickly identify the aspects of shared environments that they and their interaction partners see similarly. Non-shared elements are probably rare, as when interacting people like to know what others are seeing. Some aspects of these worlds (such as where people are standing) are distinguished as shared by default, and interacting ems want standard ways to invite interaction partners to see some of their own less widely shared overlays and changes, and to accept such offers from others.

At both work and play, many kinds of tasks require ems to manage physical systems. Such management often requires physical bodies (both immediate and extended) whose size, speed, shape, and materials sufficiently match those physical systems. It is also important for em minds to relate well to such bodies. But this seems feasible for a wide range of physical bodies. After all, people today interact with the world using a wide range of machines, such as vehicles and cranes, which they treat mentally as an extension of their bodies.

For ems with task-matched physical bodies, the world they see and hear needn't be an exact faithful representation of their physical world. For example, it might often be a sort of view like those in today's head-up displays, overlaid with useful virtual annotations. But such overlays need to avoid overly obscuring important elements of that physical world.

Because the feasibility, cost, and security of em interactions often depends on the physical and organizational locations of their brains and the brains of others, em virtual worlds may continually show such information about interaction partners. For example, ems often want to know when another em's speed, period, phase, or distance makes direct fast interaction infeasible. So ems will need to share somewhat-realistic concepts of their locations in space and time.

Ems with very different speeds or sizes might fit awkwardly into the same space, be that space physical or virtual. Fast ems whizzing past could be disorienting to slower ems, and large ems may block the movement or view of small ems. One solution is to have different standard virtual views of each common area, with each view matched to a different speed. Different speed views might also have different matching virtual gravities. Regulations might limit the size or speed behavior of ems within each speed-matched virtual view.

The ability to influence the appearance of commonly used virtual spaces is a scarce resource. To economize on this resource, ems might create views that hide many details. For example, in main views one might see only the most central actors, whereas in other views one might also see more peripheral actors. We will see in Chapter 14, Spurs section, that em workers regularly spin off short-term "spur" copies who do a task for a few hours and then end or retire. If you talk to one of these copies, the original will not remember what you said later. So most ems prefer to talk to the original, and spurs may mainly talk to other spurs, unless spoken to by a non-spur. To support such interaction styles, spurs may not appear in default office views, and observers may have to ask to see views that also show spurs.

Similarly, slow retirees may sometimes watch and evaluate the behavior of ordinary ems. The usual view of a place might not show such retiree observers, but alternative views could, letting retirees see and talk to each other. Similarly, many working age ems may share parenting oversight for the few young ems in training, watching them and voting on how to manage them. Ordinary views of children might not show such childminders, but alternate views might show them, and let these observers see and talk to each other.

Even non-retired non-spur ems who run at the same speed can still differ in status. So there may be views that hide lower status ems, and only show higher status ems. This could be similar to how today servants such as waiters often try to seem invisible, and are often treated by those they serve as if invisible.

The experiences of ems who see but are not seen in a view are analogous to the experiences of extra personalities in people with multiple personalities, who are said to watch the behavior of the currently dominant personality.

The more possible views that are commonly used, the harder it will be for typical ems to know how things look from others' typical points of view. People and organizations who want attention will want their items, people, and badges to appear in the most common views.

RECORDS

Today, it is cheap to record and archive all the audio in one's life, and it will soon be cheap to do this for high-resolution video as well. As ems will probably find it even cheaper to record things, it may be standard practice for them to record audio, video, smells, vibrations, and also many parameters about brains and bodies, including mood, arousal, etc. Ems might even add information from shallow mindreadings and periodic diary entries, or even provide periodic verbal commentaries about their lives.

All these records could give ems a detailed access to their personal history. Such ems could see a recording of almost any moment in their history, and could perhaps even interview and mindread an archived copy of themselves from close to any such moment. Archived copies could even be put into sims to test theories about their inclinations at the time.

To make it easier to find things in these records, ems may get into the habit of sprinkling their conversations with keywords that help to identify relevant situations. Ems are willing to change their behavior in many ways to make it easier to index and later find records of particular desired moments.

Today the physical cost is low to give everyone fast local access to millions of books. Much of the world's knowledge could literally be at each of our fingertips. However, we have not yet found a way to arrange this legally; we have not collected copyright access for all these books together into one affordable price. Similarly, while it should be physically cheap to give each em fast local access to millions of copies of em minds, available to advise them on millions of topics, ems may also fail to collect the rights to do this together into one affordable price.

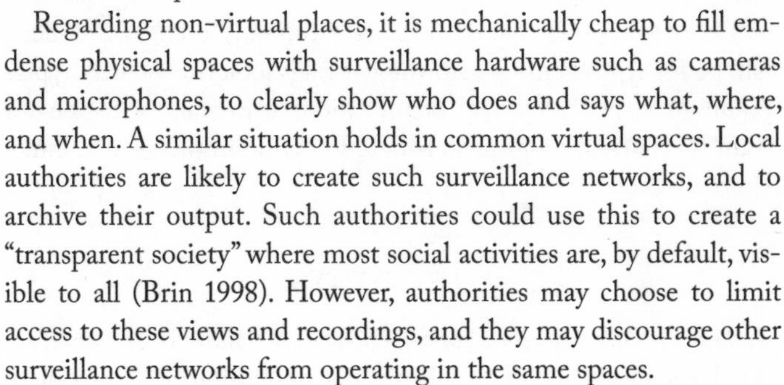

Regarding non-virtual places, it is mechanically cheap to fill em-dense physical spaces with surveillance hardware such as cameras and microphones, to clearly show who does and says what, where, and when. A similar situation holds in common virtual spaces. Local authorities are likely to create such surveillance networks, and to archive their output. Such authorities could use this to create a "transparent society" where most social activities are, by default, visible to all (Brin 1998). However, authorities may choose to limit access to these views and recordings, and they may discourage other surveillance networks from operating in the same spaces.

Although it might be easy for individual ems to record what they can see, it might be harder to share such views widely and immediately. After all, such views reveal the location and supports of their sources, allowing such sources to be shut down by hostile authorities. So unauthorized shared views must be shared with a substantial delay, only shared rarely in response to unusual situations, or redacted enough to obscure their sources. Virtual reality interactions visible only to a small number of participants could more plausibly be kept private among those participants, remaining invisible to authorities.

Widespread cheap surveillance could greatly reduce the scope for black markets. There can be few visibly illegal transactions in very visible spaces when relevant laws are actively enforced.

In either virtual or physical realities, ems less fear being killed or destroyed by local disasters. Frequent backups mean that such disasters mainly only risk the loss of memories and skills gained since the last backup. Ems mainly fear the rare disasters where no recent backups were made, or where some greatly valued post-backup new information was acquired. Ems retain a strong fear regarding large-scale disasters that threaten all relevant backups or that threaten to take away an em's livelihood. Death fears are discussed more in Chapter 11, Defining Death section.

An em might be fooled not only by deceptive inputs about its environment, but also by misleading information about its copy history. If many copies were made of an em and then only a few selected according to some criteria, then knowing about such selection criteria is valuable information to such selected ems. For example, imagine that someone created 10 000 copies of an em, exposed each copy to different arguments in favor of committing some act of sabotage, and then allowed only the most persuaded copy to continue. This strategy might in effect persuade this em to commit the sabotage. However, if the em knew this fact about its copy history, that could convince this remaining copy to greatly reduce its willingness to commit the sabotage.

Thus ems should be eager not only to discern misleading appearances about the world immediately around them, but also misleading claims about their copy history. In general, ems take care to keep reliable records.

FAKERY

Ems are careful to avoid being fooled by false appearances.

Em virtual realities probably support authentication. That is, as long as their usual tools remain trustworthy, ems need not be mistaken about the identities of the places they visit, their interaction partners, or of other ems that they see or hear. Such others might refuse to reveal their identities, but they will usually be unable to credibly pretend to be someone that they are not. Of course a stolen em mind may reasonably distrust its usual tools of authentication, fearing that it is in a simulation that doesn't follow the usual rules.

To support authentication, and help ems keep secrets, the standard hardware processes for copying ems might have direct support for generating secret codes (technically, "cryptographic private keys") unique to each distinguishable em, and for *not* copying those codes when copying ems. Public codes that match these private codes can be a basis for em unique identifiers. Terabyte-length keys can be kept secret against strong quantum computers (Bernstein et al. 2017). One can store roughly ten to 100 of these keys in the space it takes to store an em mind.

The possibility of em authentication need not imply a lack of em privacy. Ems and other agents in em spaces could choose to not reveal many things about themselves to observers. However, detailed surveillance data tracking the location of ems over time might reveal more information than an em wanted to reveal. In virtual reality ems could deal with this by just disappearing at times. In physical reality, ems might sometimes choose to "mix" with the bodies of strangers. That is, an em might suggest to a nearby stranger that the two randomly swap physical bodies. If agreed, the two ems would attach themselves to each other for a long enough time to swap their minds, and randomly do so half of the time. Afterward, the two bodies would go their separate ways, half of the time with bodies having new minds.

Ems likely want ways to easily and reliably tell which of the things that they see or hear are actually ems, and which are cheaper algorithms that only mimic real ems. After all, an em may sometimes be tempted to substitute a cheap automated "bot" program that mimics him or her during some interactions with other ems, so that he or she can attend to other things. Ems may prefer not to be given such a bot to interact with, in part because it might suggest their low status. As a result, during interactions ems may try to act in complex and subtle ways that bots could not effectively mimic, continually running their own bots that try to mimic themselves and their associates to detect fakes. That is, ems might always feel they are part of a Turing test. Such habits could raise the costs of interacting for distrustful ems, and raise the gains from trust.

Information about whether one is interacting with a bot might be obtained via direct brain access, or perhaps indirectly by requiring that a high price be paid to place what appears to be a full em in a particular role. Ems also typically want to see the voice tone, facial expressions, and gaze directions of themselves and their current interaction partners, and to know if they are seeing or showing direct and unfiltered versions of these tones and expressions.

Such knowledge helps ems learn things about the deeper mental states of their interaction partners, and the inferences other ems are making about them. Of course without assurances that they are seeing other ems unfiltered, ems often may expect such things to be cheaply faked, and so may expect to draw few useful conclusions from what they see.

The responsibility for defining and computing elements of virtual realities might reasonably be divided between larger utilities that compute elements useful to those in large groups, and smaller utilities who compute elements useful mainly to individuals or small groups. For example, a city-based utility might compute shared aspects of city plazas, fountains, and the surrounding sky, while building owners might compute elements of building facades and internal shared spaces. The owner of a meeting room might compute the appearance of that room, while each individual in the room might compute the appearance of his or her personal skin, clothes, or hair.

While this division of labor may align responsibilities well, it could have the problem of revealing information to third parties about who is looking at what when. To avoid such revelations, shy ems may just do without the information, computing these appearances of their virtual world privately from stable public specifications, or making up their own substitute appearances. Alternatively, supporting infrastructure might be built so as to assure users that such leaks are rare and difficult.

Overall, ems try hard not to be fooled by appearances.

SIMULATIONS

An ability to create convincing virtual experiences makes it harder for ems to draw inferences about the real world from their experiences. Experiences that seem to come from interactions with a larger physical or shared virtual world could instead come from a local sim mimicking that world. Ems must continually wonder if they have been unknowingly placed in such a sim, perhaps to test their loyalties or to extract secrets. (In fact, we each cannot be entirely sure today that we are not in such a future sim (Hanson 2001a).) The more common are such sims, the less certain ems can be of conclusions they draw from what they see.

If an em were in a sim to test their loyalties or abilities, it might be a sim that they themselves had agreed in the past to allow to be created. Such an em wouldn't know when such a sim might happen, or what it would be like, just that it could happen at almost any time. An em would probably want to cooperate with such sims. In contrast, the em may want to sabotage a sim that was designed to extract a secret, as this is less likely to be a sim to which the em had agreed.

Not only might ems be placed into sims where everything they see and hear is artificial, ems might also be placed into *partial* sims, where only some of the things they see or hear are artificial. In a partial sim, an em might see added fake people and objects beyond what they otherwise would have seen, or they might fail to see people and objects "edited out" of their view. An em might notice such added or missing items via their inconsistent interactions with other things. Automated tools might help to notice such inconsistencies, but such tools might be compromised by the same processes that compromise their basic sight and sound inputs.

There are many different reasons why an em or its associates might want to put that em into a full or partial sim, including entertaining the em in the sim or outsiders observing the sim, testing loyalty or ability, testing causes for holding beliefs, and testing credit for innovations and other accomplishments. For the purpose of gaining information, it is often more cost-effective to try to achieve several such purposes at once within a set of related sims. In technical terms, this is a "fractional factorial experiment design" (Montgomery 2008).

For example, a sim in which one em apparently tries to thwart spies from stealing an innovation might simultaneously be entertaining for the em involved, test his or her loyalties, and test how much credit the innovation deserves. Similarly, it might be more efficient to include several related ems in the same sim, with different reasons for including each of them.

Thus if the various parties interested in making sims for a group of ems can agree on a common sim administrator, they might use that administrator to create a whole system of related sims. In this case, an em who suspected they were in a sim should not search for *the* purpose of its sim or for *the* focal em; most likely the sim has many purposes and focuses. This makes it harder for ems to manipulate sims to provide favorable impressions. Ems might well find it in their interest to just continue with their usual behavior as if they were not in a sim, which increases the validity of conclusions observers can draw from watching the sim.

While it makes sense to create sims to study distant historical periods, the resources available for this purpose are small compared with the resources available for other sim purposes. And while the resources available to ems for entertainment set in distant historical periods may be larger than are such resources today, they are also likely to be small compared with resources for other sim purposes. So given that one is an em in a sim, that sim is unlikely to be a sim of a historical period. Today our interest in historical periods falls quite rapidly with time and cultural distance. The vast majority of times and places before one millennia ago receive almost no attention, neither from scholars nor entertainment seekers. So unless your current industrial era world is of great unusual interest to ems, or someone near you is a quite unusual person, you today are unlikely to actually be, contrary to appearance, an em in a historical simulation (Hanson 2010c).

A sim administrator might want to abort a sim if too many of its participants suspected too strongly that they were in a sim. To entice ems to reveal such suspicions, administrators might offer financial incentives. For example, each em might always be offered a private subsidized betting market on the chance that they are currently in a sim (Hanson 2003). If the em didn't believe the current offered market odds, it would expect to profit by changing those odds to its current belief. To encourage honesty, bets should pay in non-sim assets. That is, if this is not a sim, bets pay off in assets useful in this world, but if this is a sim, bets pay off in assets valid in the real world outside of the sim. The cost to subsidize such markets is added to the cost of creating sims.

An em who thought that it was in an illicit sim might want to sabotage that sim. But to sabotage a sim, an em must first notice the existence of the sim. One way to try to notice sims is to cultivate the habit of interacting often with trusted associates via previously coordinated private codes, opaquely encoded in each em's brain state. For example, about once an hour an em might hear a code word from a particular friend, a word that followed from the code word they had given that friend an hour before. The lack of a correct response suggests that one is in a sim, while the friend is not. A related strategy might be to cultivate the habit of often interacting with particular physical systems whose computational complexity is very expensive to mimic, and which opaque parts of your brain can distinguish from cheap mimics.

Another approach to noticing sims is to watch for simulation errors, that is, ways that a simulation deviates from a realistic world. But if sim creators saw that a participant em had noticed an error, they could just stop and reverse the simulation back to a time before the error appeared, restart the simulation at that point, and work harder to prevent the error.

There might seem to be little point in noticing sim errors that can be erased in this way, but in fact the cost of such retrying raises the cost of running such a sim. The longer that an em could last before giving off a visible indication of knowing they are in a simulation, the more expensive they could make this revision process for the simulators. The usual goal in security, after all, is to *raise* the cost of security breaches, not to make them impossible.

As the loyalty and reliability of an em is especially important in unusual crisis situations, simulations designed to test loyalties disproportionately portray such situations. Thus an em who finds itself in what seems to be an unusual crisis should suspect that it is in a simulation designed to test its loyalty and ability. This would tend to make emulations act more loyally and reliably in real crisis situations, such as revolution or disasters. Frequent sim-based crisis tests might help to maintain order and organization during actual crises, reducing their severity.

Similarly, simulations designed to test loyalties may also offer apparent opportunities for theft and other betrayal. Ems who know that such opportunities tend to be simulations are less likely to actually betray, either in a simulated or a real event.

Compared with us today, ems are more "battle-tested," having lived through many unusual crises, each treated as if it was very real.

CHAPTER 10

Existence

COPYING

A functioning em is the result of information representing an em mental state being placed in compatible signal-processing hardware. When this hardware "runs," it repeatedly calculates the next mental state by combining the previous mental state with inputs from outside systems, and then sends resulting signals to outside systems. In this situation, an em can be said to experience this succession of mental states, while interacting with outside systems. As em hardware and supporting resources are not free, ems are not free; someone must pay to create each em.

When an em is copied, the em mental state sitting in compatible hardware is first read out as bits, and then those bits are copied, transmitted, and read into new compatible hardware. Then at the new hardware those bits are converted into the exact same em mental state, now ready to run on this new hardware. Immediately after this copy action, the evolution of the mental states in the two different hardware systems would be exactly the same, if it were not for errors and differences in environmental inputs, and differences in random fluctuations within fault-prone emulation processes.

Just as ems are not free but costly, copies are also not free but costly. Typically, an em with an established role in the em world is asked if they want to approve the creation of a new copy, who would have a new life with a new paid role in that world. Before agreeing to create this new life, the original could ask about the new em's intended job, location, friends, leisure time, etc. On occasion, offers for new life roles might be made to archived copies. That is, ems might agree to allow the storage of archive copies, who can then be awoken later to consider new life offers. If the revived copy rejected the offer, it might be retired or ended, as previously agreed.

To actually make a copy, an em may invoke a special viewing mode, wherein the em specifies or approves a description of the set of em roles that would result from this copying act. When an em initiates a copy event, it should be ready and willing to take on any of the roles of the resulting copies. Immediately after the copy event, each em copy is informed of its assigned role. Typically one of the ems is assigned to continue its previous role, while other ems are assigned to take on new roles.

For the very common act of creating a simple spur copy, an em might only indicate a task and a resource budget. A single new spur copy could then be created and told that its role is to attempt this task within this assigned budget. A matching viewing mode might allow the spur to report back to its original after it has succeeded or failed at its task, or to request more budget to pursue it further.

When the original em has a strict veto on the copy process, so that copies don't happen without the consent of the original, ems would feel a much stronger ownership of their existence than do humans today. In such cases, ems likely feel less justified in complaining about features of their situation that were easy to anticipate when they agreed to make a copy of themselves. Ems may also feel more obliged to be grateful to those who enabled their existence, and to make good on the promises, both explicit and implicit, that they made to such enablers. Ems can more see themselves as justifying and paying for their existence, via the benefits that others expected to gain by creating and hiring them.

The power to selectively create and delete copies of an em gives one the power to persuade that em of many things. After all, with such a power one could create thousands of copies of this em, try a different approach to persuading each one, and then retain the copy who is most persuaded. This approach does have substantial costs, and it can't persuade someone of a claim that they won't accept no matter what the method of persuasion.

Because of this power of selectivity, we expect ems to be careful about whom they grant the power to create and delete copies, and to want to know what related copies have been created or deleted and why. An em who does not know their copy context should be cautious about changing beliefs others might want to influence. Ems must accept that organizations granted flexible discretion on creating and deleting copies will thereby gain great persuasive powers over them.

RIGHTS

Current and past legal systems offer a wide range of possible models for how em law might treat the creation of em copies.

At one extreme, new em copies might be fully owned slaves, with their owners free to torture or terminate them, and free to make more copies that they fully own. Such slave ems might be owned by the firm who first scanned them, by the original human from which they were scanned, or by other parties to whom slaves were sold. Moving away from this extreme, there could be limits on the torture of slaves. Enslaved ems may also have limited rights to spend a certain fraction of their time in leisure of a certain quality, or to veto making more copies of themselves. The possibility of em slavery is considered more in Chapter 20, Slavery section.

At another extreme, new em copies might be completely free to choose all of their activities, including the making of copies of themselves. Moving away from this extreme, em creators could be required to endow the ems they create with sufficient wealth to live at some minimum duration, speed, and quality of life. Treating copied ems as if they were adult human descendants would arguably be a similar practice.

In between these extremes, ems could be endowed with intermediate levels of rights and wealth. For example, an em might own itself, but be unable to veto the creation of copies of itself. An em might or might not have the right to end itself. An em might own itself but be endowed with debt obligations, and be subject to repossession and erasure if it cannot make debt payments.

An em might be incorporated like a firm, and own only some of his or her "stock." Voting and non-voting stock might even be distinguished. For example, an em holding a majority of his or her voting stock but a minority of the total stock still controls personal actions, but controls only a minority share of personal profits.

Note that rules specifying minimum wages or minimum fractions of leisure time may have perverse effects on the quality of work and leisure experiences. It is hard to create rules specifying how pleasant or enjoyable are work and leisure activities. Because of this, when an employer chooses work and leisure conditions to satisfy minimum wage or leisure time mandates, they may compensate by skimping on expenditures that result in higher quality work and leisure experiences. In the absence of such constraints, employers should instead tend to improve worker experiences when workers value such improvements more than their cost. Similar issues also apply to minimum wage rules today.

The "brain," or mind hardware, of a new em copy must be located somewhere, and so a key question is the contractual relation between a free em and those who build and maintain its hardware, and also supply this hardware with energy, cooling, communication, and real estate. Sometimes this brain will be a separate and mobile physical object, free to move to obtain space, energy, etc., from competing suppliers. More often, however, brain hardware will be a physically inseparable part of a larger computing system, as are single computers or processes today within large computer data centers.

For ems who are part of large copy clans in which they place great trust, the details of contracts with their hardware hosts matter less, as the clan handles these contractual details. But for other ems, current contracts for cloud-computing services seem to offer attractive models. An em might be endowed with a cloud-computing contract giving it a right to run at a particular speed, reliability, rough spatial location, and communication bandwidth.

Such an em is also likely endowed with wealth sufficient to pay for this cloud contract for a short period, and the right to move to another service at will. If the em moved, it might have the right to insist that its original files be erased. Perhaps if the em failed to pay its contracted fee, the cloud service might have the right to erase that em, or perhaps even to sell it to recover overdue payments.

MANY EMS

The rest of the analysis in this book is largely independent of which of the above legal environments becomes more common. What mainly matters for other chapters is that many ems are created. Consider the situation where a not-overly unpleasant job is available, and where the value of the work done is substantially higher than the full hardware costs to create an em to do this job, even when this em spends at least one-half of his or her time in leisure. Assume further that there are many ems for whom this cost is this low. In this situation, I assume that a productive em is usually created, to take on this job.

This many-ems outcome could result from profit-driven slave owners, from profit-driven debt lenders, from the existence of a few very productive and eager-to-copy ems, or from laws requiring high birth wealth endowments but without strong intrusive enforcement to detect and discourage illegal copies. Let us now consider each of these options in turn.

A many-ems outcome could result from eager-to-copy ems if there are a few flexible and productive ems who consistently go nearly as far as possible to fund new copies of themselves, to take new job opportunities as they arise. Such eager ems are willing to impoverish themselves, and even to end themselves, to fund new copies. These are "evolutionarily selfish" ems. Of course making copies need not be their primary conscious motivation. For example, their conscious motivation might be instead to be as useful as possible to similar copies.

A many-ems outcome via eager-to-copy ems is compatible with rules requiring large wealth endowments on creation, if such ems are free to bequest their wealth to new copies when they end or retire. It can also work with rules requiring high wages, if such ems are also allowed to volunteer for free during their "leisure" time on productive projects.

A handful of such eager flexible ems could fill an entire em economy of jobs, even if no other ems were willing or allowed to fill such jobs. Even if these eager ems were banned from most legal jurisdictions, the few jurisdictions that allowed them might quickly outgrow and dominate the rest. Eager-to-reproduce humans are often found today in farmer-like religious communities such as the Amish or Mormons. As I personally know a few people who seem productive and eager to copy, I estimate that as long as a few productive jurisdictions support competitive ems, then enough such productive eager ems could be found to produce a many-ems outcome. Also, even if eagerness to copy is rare at first, it is a feature that is selected for in an em world because of its competitive advantage.

Laws might require high em wages, but such laws could strongly tempt black market copying. The larger the difference between a high price to rent em labor that satisfies official regulations, and a low total hardware cost to rent em hardware, then the more eagerly some would try to make black market copies.

For example, an ambitious businesswoman might be willing to create in secret a thousand copies of herself, to achieve much lower labor costs in developing and building her new product. Her copies might accept ending or retiring to a slow life once the product is completed. When there are very different legal and illegal market prices, preventing black market trading requires extensive and thorough monitoring and strong punishments. Preventing black market jobs when legal em wages are far above total em hardware costs requires much stronger enforcement than would be required today to prevent illegal drug use (which we do not now achieve). After all, to lower her main costs by a factor of ten or more, an ambitious businesswoman might be willing to go quite far to create and hide a secret labor force.

A big difference between legal and illegal wages also encourages slavery. Historically slavery has offered low profits when wages were near subsistence levels, but higher profits when wages were higher (Domar 1970). Similarly, enslaving ems becomes much more tempting when em wages are well above subsistence levels.

The main em scenarios in which there are not many ems are scenarios with well-enforced laws that either impose strict quotas on the total number and speed of ems, or that in effect require very high wages, or equivalently, that require high ratios of leisure time to productive work time. Such laws need to be global, and strongly and thoroughly enforced via intrusive monitoring and strong reliable punishments of violators. Such alternate scenarios are discussed briefly in Chapter 28, Alternatives section.

For most of this book, however, we assume many ems.

SURVEILLANCE

To enforce laws that impose quotas on the number and speed of ems, one needs strong controls on computing hardware capable of running em brains. And this requires strong abilities to observe activities. Such surveillance abilities might also be used to enforce rules on mind theft, intellectual property, and uncontrolled research in artificial intelligence. But how exactly could such hardware controls work?

One approach is to try to ensure that authorities can cheaply see inside all computers capable of running em brains, including seeing through any encrypted computation, to severely punish owners who were found to be running ems without authorization. If this requires direct inspection of physical hardware, that is likely to be expensive. However, if authorities know the physical configuration of hardware, have appropriate operating system access privileges, and sufficient suppressing of encrypted computation, they might be able to do required inspections cheaply from a distance.

In this approach it is very important to prevent the existence of hardware that lies about its configuration. Perhaps large bounties could be offered to anyone who revealed the existence of such hardware, and who paid for the costs of an inspection to prove a violation.

Instead of direct inspection of all hardware, a more focused approach is to ensure that authorities can see all factories capable of creating computers that can run ems, and can punish factory owners severely when they are found to produce em-capable computers without authorization. If it was too hard to punish factory owners, one might instead punish those who own the land used, or who supply power or cooling. This approach might be sufficient to enforce limits on population, but perhaps not rules on wages, mind theft, intellectual property, or software safety.

Dark factories and computers, hidden from the view of authorities, would undermine both these enforcement approaches. Such factories and computers could be hidden under the ground or sea. Small em installations could likely hide in more types of environments than can small groups of humans today. To discourage such hidden installations, detailed monitoring might be required not only of the Earth's surface, but perhaps also hundreds of meters beneath that surface.

The economic value of such hidden hardware might be substantially diminished by time delays and bottlenecks in communication with em cities, where most valuable em activity takes place. Hidden computers would thus focus on supplying services where such delays and bottlenecks detract less from the value produced by their illicit em workers.

Authorities might try to control computing hardware by controlling the communication channels that such hardware uses to gain value. For example, authorities might try to ensure that they know the location and function of all high-bandwidth nodes in a communication network. This approach might be evaded, however, by illicit direct laser links between distant physical locations, or by physical landlines deep underground. Authorities might also try to inspect all communication traffic, and prevent unauthorized encrypted communication.

Another approach is to control the energy and cooling that computers need. However, knowing the energy usage doesn't necessarily say how much computing is going on. For example, with reversible computers one could mimic the energy and cooling of a single computing unit via four computing units that run at one-half speed, and thereby produce twice the computing power of a single unit. One might detect such arrangements via the additional volume and structural support that these added computing units require.

Evasion of rules limiting the creation of ems might perhaps also be accomplished via opaque software that appears to serve other functions, but actually emulates minds. The complexity of this software might make it hard to detect this. One might try to note where the software is inefficient at its stated purpose, but this might be hard. For example, software to monitor for rare events or search for rare configurations might go a long time without finding anything useful, even if it is in fact very efficient software.

The extreme measures required to successfully enforce laws limiting em numbers and speeds seem to confirm that the simpler assumption to make for the purpose of this book is that such laws either do not exist, or are not strongly enforced. So as discussed in this chapter, in the Many Ems section, this book assumes a many-ems outcome.

CHAPTER 11

Farewells

FRAGILITY

m minds age with experience, becoming less flexible and thus less able to adapt to new skills and environments. Because of this, old ems eventually become substantially less productive than young competitors, and need to retire. Here is why.

Imagine that you were asked to modify an ordinary (i.e., stock) car into a truck to haul rocks. If after that you were asked to create a racecar, you would probably prefer to start from another plain stock car, rather than start from the stock car that you had turned into a truck. Similarly, species of beetles that have adapted to a varied and oft changing environment have simpler designs than beetles adapted to more stable environments. These simpler beetles are more likely to successfully invade and adapt to new environments that become available, relative to beetles that have complex adaptations to specific stable environments (Fridley and Sax 2014).

A similar effect causes large software systems to "rot" with time. As software that was designed to match one set of tasks, tools, and situations is slowly changed to deal with a steady stream of new tasks, tools, and situations, such software tends to become more complex, fragile, and more difficult to usefully change (Lehman and Belady 1985). Eventually it is better to start over and write whole new subsystems, and sometimes whole new systems, from scratch. It is sometimes worth the effort to "refactor" a system, that is, to change its high-level structure to make it easier to usefully change. However, such systems still tend to become more fragile, even after repeated refactorings.

Similarly, while more complex and higher quality business products tend to be better adapted to circumstances, and to sell for higher prices, simpler cheaper products tend to have more descendants in new products, at least for products sold to firms (Christensen 1997; Thompson 2013). In multi-cellular animals, flexible generic stem cells create other more varied cells that are better adapted to particular body tasks. Yet new organisms descend mostly from generic stem cells, which have far more descendant cells in the long run.

All of these examples suggest that as large complex adaptive systems become better adapted in detail to particular situations, they become more fragile and less able to adapt in detail to very different situations.

Human brains tend to have slower responses as they age, in part because brain hardware degrades (Lindenberger 2014), and in part because such brains need to sort through a larger experience base (Ramscar et al. 2014). Human brains also tend to start out malleable, and able to learn quickly, even though they are poor at most specific tasks. While human minds become better able to do specific tasks as they age, they become less flexible and less able to rapidly learn new very different skills. That is, while the young tend to have more "fluid intelligence," the old have more "crystallized intelligence" (Horn and Cattell 1967). For example, whereas old people know more words, young people can more easily learn new languages. Older people often get "set in their ways."

Some of this aging of human brains probably results from developmental programming and biological aging. These sources of mental aging need not apply to emulations. The emulated cells need not age, and developmental programming might be turned off. However, some of human brain aging is also plausibly intrinsic to human mind design (Magalhaes and Sandberg 2005). If what makes the human brain powerful is not a few simple powerful algorithms, but instead many thousands or more of specialized tools combined together in complex ways, then it can make sense for that combination to become more fragile and tangled as those combinations are slowly changed.

For example, even if 90 percent of human mental aging comes from developmental programming and biological aging, that could still leave 10 percent coming from a general tendency of complex adapting systems to become more fragile as they continue to adapt to new circumstances. That is, it is plausible to think that at least some of the general tendency of humans to become inflexible with age is a general consequence of their adaptation to specific circumstances, rather than a result of cell degradation or economic incentives to stick with what you know.

Thus even em minds are likely to age with subjective experience, becoming less easily adapted to particular tasks, and eventually becoming too fragile to compete well in changing environments with more flexible younger minds. For example, if the rate of subjective aging for ems is only 10 percent of that of humans today, that would plausibly move the age of peak work productivity from roughly fifty to 500 subjective years. Eventually old workers would become unable to compete well with young workers.

As with software rot, with effort it may be possible to slow this aging process, but it is only rarely cost-effective to halt or reverse such aging. For most jobs, after a subjective career of somewhere between about one-half to several centuries, an emulation's mental inflexibility typically reduces its work productivity enough to make it cost-effective to replace it with a younger worker.

If the rate of mental aging resulting from leisure experience is similar to that resulting from work experience, then leisure has major costs to ems beyond the cost to run minds during leisure. Leisure experience ages ems, reducing their total possible career work experience. However, if some kinds of work or leisure experiences are "refreshing," in the sense of resulting in less total aging, ems would seek to substitute such refreshing experiences for others when possible.

When I want to use a particular duration in this book for an em's work career, I'll estimate a subjective useful career of one century. This is for a productive duration assuming that basic job methods do not change, even as many minor aspects of work circumstances such as customers and locations do change. However, it should be easy to see how to adjust calculations based on my one-century estimate to other possible duration values.

The main exceptions are likely to be for very stable job contexts. If a job environment changes very little, very old minds might remain the best at them. Tools that have become fragile but are hard to replace, perhaps because standards require them, may also tend to be managed by fragile but hard to replace ems.

For example, computer code that does numerical linear algebra, such as matrix inversion, has remained relatively stable for many decades, because little has changed in the need for such tasks or how numbers are encoded in computers. If this situation continues, then ems specialized in managing such code may be able to sustain especially long subjective work lives.

If complex software tools are saved for rare use in distant futures, ems who know how to use those tools well may be archived along with such tools, to be revived when these tools are needed. If simple retirement is unreliable because assets might be stolen or because interest rates might fall to very low levels, then knowing best how to use an important but rarely used complex tool might be one of the most secure routes for an em to have a very long, if intermittent, existence.

While an em economy has relatively little direct use for subjectively very-young em minds, such young minds might be a key source of variation to generate new minds to train for new kinds of jobs that appear in the economy. Such young minds might come from scans of young ordinary humans, or the em world may learn to emulate the growth of very young brains and thus to emulate an entire childhood from an early age. Training young em minds from a very early age for particular careers might boost their later peak productivity in those careers.

The typical subjective ages of ems are discussed in more detail in Chapter 17, Peak Age section. But it seems quite likely that ems age with experience, and then must end or retire.

RETIREMENT

With experience, ems become better adapted to their jobs. Such jobs, however, may no longer be needed, or may change so much that fragile old minds cannot adapt well to such large job changes. Ems who are no longer wanted or needed at work might choose to retire, at least if such ems can afford this, and have sufficient self-ownership.

Because the cost of running an em is proportional to speed over a wide range, the cost of retiring an em to run indefinitely at a slow speed can be small relative to the value that an em produces in just a few days of work. If we assume constant interest rates close to constant economic growth rates, then a simple calculation shows that the total cost to run an em indefinitely is roughly the economic doubling time multiplied by the run-cost per unit time.

For example, as a milli-em experiences roughly an hour in one objective month, then in an economy that doubles every objective month the cost of retiring indefinitely at a milli-em speed is the cost to run an em for about one subjective hour. Alternatively, for a retirement speed ten times slower, and an economic doubling time of ten days, the cost to retire falls to the cost to run an em for two subjective minutes. It only costs one subjective second of high speed experience to retire indefinitely at micro-em speeds. Thus indefinite retirement can be quite cheap, even for ems who work for only a short time before retiring.

Note, however, that these calculations ignore the cost of moving to a new retirement location, and they depend on interest rates remaining high. When growth and interest rates fall greatly, as it seems they must do eventually, then indefinite retirement becomes a lot more expensive.

It is not obvious what fraction of no-longer-productive ems retire, rather than end their lives. While retirement might often be a cheap option, that small expense of retirement might still seem larger than the benefit it provides. Ems may vary in how much they dislike ending when many very similar copies remain alive.

Ems with more than minimal retirement budgets could use their added funds to pay for faster than minimum retirement speeds. In this situation, a pair of similar slow retirees might choose to go "double or nothing," and randomly pick one of them to run at over twice the speed, while erasing the other one.

In addition, retirees who can afford to run much faster than base speed might prefer a "sleeping beauty" strategy. Here they would delay their retirement through several growth doubling times, to increase their post-delay speed by a similar number of doublings. Ems confident enough about the intermediate-term stability of the em civilization can expect this strategy to increase their total expected lifespan before a revolution or war might end it. This approach is extra tempting to ems eager for the higher status of a faster speed retirement. The start of retirement is an especially good time to try this strategy, as a delay at that point also saves on costs to move to a retirement location.

Such a sleeping beauty strategy is also available to non-retirees. That is, working ems might stop working earlier than necessary, archive a copy, invest their savings, and then wake up later with more resources available to pursue their career. Ems who do this risk their job skills no longer being as relevant when they try to return to work. While some ems try this strategy, initially the ems who remain active in the em world tend to be those who reject it.

To get used to their new state of seeing the world pass by them more quickly, new retirees might first review the history of their world during their life, seen at the same speed that they will see the future. So, for example, if their post-retirement speed were 1000 times slower than their pre-retirement speed, they might then see thirty years of their life pass by in ten subjective days.

Retirement can be more attractive when the retired have useful respected roles to play in society. Retired ems might be part of important rituals associated with the copying, training, and retirement of other ems. Retired ems are also good for unspecialized everyman roles, such as juror or voter, if they aren't running too slowly to sufficiently understand the current society. Very slow ems could more easily take a long-term view, which could make them useful in managing long-term investments.

Retirees might also serve as "wise watchers," a role that ancestral spirits were said to serve in ancient societies. Even if retirees are much slower than most workers, they are also far more numerous, and so might randomly audit workers to report on if they are nice, mean, cooperative, honest, stylish, etc. Retirees who are closely related to workers might be more trusted to preserve privacy, and be better motivated to evaluate them well.

In many ancient societies people visited certain shrines and temples where they prayed to and made sacrifices in the name of their ancestors. Ems could have similar shrines, but at em shrines ems could actually talk to and interact with retired versions of their ancestors, if they sacrificed to pay for the time for those ancestors to run.

Today we pay to create and visit memorials to honor our most celebrated dead people. Ems may do this less often, as honored ems are almost never dead in the sense of having no close copies available with which one could interact. We feel less sorry for such people, and we face more risk from celebrating them, as their loyalties and positions could change in the future.

When there is detailed regular contact between retirees and others, those others could check that retirement communities actually provide the run-time and amenities that they promised to retirees. Otherwise, retirement communities may be tempted to shave expenses by cutting services. Retirees who participate in copying and ending rituals could also ensure that important social norms are not violated in the copying and ending processes.

GHOSTS

Slower ems are more vulnerable to instabilities in the em civilization, and in any descendant civilizations. For example, if typical retired ems run at ordinary human speed and typical work ems are kilo-ems, then having retirees live out a safe subjective decade of retirement requires that their civilization be stable over 10 000 years of subjective activity in typical workers. Slower milli-em retirees need a civilization stable over 10 million years of the subjective activity of typical workers. And micro-em retirees need stability over 10 billion years of typical worker subjective activity. Ensuring such levels of stability seems quite a challenge.

If civilization instability is the main risk to a normal lifespan for humans, and also to an indefinite retired life for ems, then humans and retired ems acquire a strong shared interest in promoting stability and preventing catastrophic risk to the em civilization. The lower status of humans and em retirees, however, makes that promotion harder. Some ems might try to survive past the local instabilities of an em civilization by sending copies to distant locations, perhaps even beyond Earth into space. But most humans and slow ems may not be able to afford that.

Our basic concept of "death" is binary, so that one is either dead or not. But we often metaphorically extend this concept to a continuum. For example, people who have more strength, energy, passion, and awareness are said to be "more alive," and those who have more power, prestige, influence, or wealth are also said to be "more" in many ways, including more central and alive. As people who are asleep have less of all of these things, sleep is often seen as a partial death.

We have long had a related mythical concept of "ghost," which we also sometimes make into a continuum of ghostliness. A ghost was once human, but then died, and now is an active agent with death-related features. So ghosts tend to be cold, sick, slow, in low mood, and have a weak influence on the physical world. They are typically distracted, being both unaware of and disinterested in humans. Ghosts are anti-social, avoid groups of more than a few humans, don't seem to collect into ghost gangs or ghost cities, and don't use tools or weapons. They are reluctant to move away from their old haunts. Ghosts are heard more than seen, rarely speak words, and are seen more in unusual viewing modes such as night, shadows, and mirrors (Fyfe 2011).

Slow em retirees share many features with people we see as "less alive," including ghosts. Not only are they literally closer subjectively to dying because of civilization instability, their minds are also more inflexible and stuck in their ways. Compared with faster working ems, slow retirees have less awareness, wealth, status, and influence, and they are slower to respond to events, including via speaking words or coordinating with others. As discussed in the previous section, retirees may often watch and judge working ems, and as discussed in Chapter 9, Views section, when in such roles, they may be visible only in special views.

Thus ems may come to see slower ems as ghostly, and the more ghostly the slower they are. Such ghosts are real, and with trouble one can talk to them, but they aren't very useful as allies, they get less moral weight, and one can usually ignore them without much cost. Because ems must pay for faster speeds, for ems being more alive is more directly related to having more money to spend.

While ghosts are not usually noticed by others, they are sometimes seen has having an ability to call attention to themselves, if they are sufficiently motivated, and if others are sufficiently receptive. It might be useful to give em retirees special rare ways to ask for the attention of others.

"Beneath" each em is an underworld abyss, with deeper layers holding slower, more ghostly, ems. As we calculated in Chapter 6, Speeds section, beneath the most "alive" top cheap speed ems lies an underworld at least a factor of a trillion deep, and that factor may be a billion trillion. An em at the top for whom things go badly has a very long slide before reaching "bottom," from which the only lower rung is being erased.

WAYS TO END

So just how averse are ems to "death?"

For humans today, death is a strong psychological symbol and force. For example, indirectly reminding people of their eventual death induces them to more strongly favor charismatic leaders and the members, norms, and beliefs of their groups. These effects are especially strong when people feel uncertain or low in status (Navarrete et al. 2004; Martin and van den Bos 2014; Solomon et al. 2015). Clearly, many of our feelings toward death are encoded quite deeply in our psyches.

Human aversion to death has many causes, but surely a big one is that growing productive humans takes years. For us, death can be a very expensive loss; we most mourn the deaths of young adults, in whom we have invested the most yet gained the least. To reduce such losses, humans evolved a strong personal aversion to death, and strong social norms against killing. The main exceptions have been when large social gains might compensate death losses, such as killing a murderer, or when the losses from death may seem small, such as for those likely to die anyway and in times of famine when not all can survive.

The world of ems fundamentally changes this situation, by drastically reducing many costs of death. When life is cheap, death can be cheap as well. Today, erasing the last copy of some valuable software might be an enormous loss, while erasing typical copies results in almost no loss. Similarly, erasing all copies of a trained em might be a great loss, but deleting one copy made a few hours ago is usually a small loss. The em world adapts to these new costs and possibilities to an unknown degree.

For example, it could be tempting to create many short-lived ems that simultaneously do many similar short-term tasks, and then to erase all but one when those tasks are done. One might save the copy who seems to have learned the most from their task. It could also be tempting to make a new copy to do a single short task from which little can be learned, after which that copy is erased.

However, if short-lived copies are erased when they are no longer needed, ems might suffer high levels of stress anticipating the imminent prospect of their own "death," or the "deaths" of close associates. This could reduce the work productivity of ems assigned to such tasks, and their willingness to enter scenarios in which many short-term ems end. The em economy seeks to avoid such costs.

Retirement raises related issues. While the prospect of imminent retirement might not be as stressful as the prospect of imminent death, ems may be similarly if less severely stressed by anticipating a move from a higher status fast culture and circle of associates to a lower status slow culture with new associates. Retirees also suffer larger risks because of the possible instability of the em civilization.

Humans today can often be strongly motivated to take actions not only out of a fear of imminent death, but also via a related fear of damage to their reputation, that is, a fear that others will see them as having been a failure or a fool. For ems with many similar copies, both of these threats are weaker. If an em expects many similar copies to continue, they know that the actions of one particular copy will matter less to the reputation of their subclan.

There are many possible ways that ems could deal with death. First, it might be feasible to merge em copies when only a short subjective time has elapsed since they were copied from the same source. The merged em might remember the events that both ems experienced in the interim, and have the added skills that both ems acquired. But while such merged ems wouldn't suffer stress-of-death costs, they are still likely to become more fragile as a result of their added experience, and thus, eventually, less competitive. This would make merging more attractive for retirees than for workers. I assume merging is infeasible during the main period studied of the baseline scenario that is the focus of this book. This merging possibility is discussed more in Chapter 28, Alternatives section.

A second possibility is that ems will be reallocated from no-longer-needed tasks to newly needed tasks. But this option could impose large costs of mismatches between the skills and knowledge desired and those available in reassigned ems. It is usually more cost-effective to make new copies of ems who already have the needed skills. Also, because minds become more fragile with age, minds eventually become poorly suited for most tasks.

A third option is that the em labor market will select to a substantial degree from the ems whose basic personality or mental style is least bothered by the prospect of ending themselves. This option, however, may come at a substantial opportunity cost in the ability to select for other useful em features.

A fourth possibility is that mind tweaks will be found to greatly reduce death aversion. Although possible, this seems unlikely.

DEFINING DEATH

A fifth option is that the em world will produce new cultural attitudes about what counts as "death." Today, while everyone agrees that in theory they don't want to eat dirty food or wear dirty clothes, in practice we inherit quite different cultural standards on what counts as "dirty." What seems clean enough to some seems filthy to others. Similarly, the em world offers a wide range of ways to define "death," and em cultures could in principle vary greatly in which particular events they saw as a form of intolerable "death."

For example, today many would be comfortable with taking a drug before a party that results in their not remembering the party the next morning, or ever after. Some would even enjoy the extra freedoms that such forgetting allowed. In some sense the party version of themselves will "die" at the end of the party, as no one will remember their experiences or feelings. But most people today would not frame the end of that evening's experience as "death."

Ems who think similarly need not mind splitting off a "spur" copy who will do a task for a few hours or days, and then end. They need not consider the lack of anyone who remembers the spur's activities as anything similar to "death." The spur is seen to live on because its original lives on, even if the original doesn't remember the spur's experience. Other ems might similarly think that a copy who lasts for a few weeks and then ends is not "dead," if a copy continues on who remembers their life up until those few weeks, who heard or saw a detailed enough summary of the copy's few weeks of existence, and who deeply read the mind of that em as it ended.

Individual em copies may come to see the choice to end a copy not as "Shall I end?" but instead as "Do I want to remember this?" Ems will see that there are substantial costs to remembering experiences, and make tradeoffs about what is worth remembering. In the short term, remembering work (and its stresses) adds to work weariness that must be paid for by rest from work. In the long term, remembering life events adds to mental aging and fragility. Ems see memories as more expensive than we do.

When different copies are made to try different things, but not all can be kept, this choice may be seen as mostly about which attempts are most useful to remember later. If archive copies are saved, ems could even change their mind later about which experiences are worth remembering, and revive an archive copy they weren't planning to retrieve.

At another extreme, some ems could conceivably create a culture wherein they expect to "die" each moment in which they could not achieve "me-now immortality," which they might define as archiving a copy once per moment and reviving that copy at a declining frequency for special occasions into the indefinite future. Apparently, the length of the subjective "moment" duration having "holistic gestalt-like quality" and "significant nonverbal synchrony of movement" is about six seconds (Tschacher et al. 2017). "Me-now immortality" is very expensive to achieve, and so would function as a sign of great wealth.

Some ems might see moving their mind from one hosting computer to another as a form of death. While such an attitude would usually put an em at a great competitive disadvantage, there may be a few niches where such ems could survive. For example, such ems might work far from city centers where em brains are usually housed directly in mobile physical bodies, to support jobs requiring physical mobility.

Finally, some ems might have "faith" that technology enabling em minds to be merged will eventually be developed. They could then see saving an archive copy who will eventually be merged with others once merging is developed as akin to immortality. They might even accept merged copies who forget many details of the lives of the ems who were merged to create them. After all, we today don't see our past selves as having died even when we forget many details of our past lives.

Cultures clearly have a wide range of possibilities to choose from in defining intolerable "death." If some cultures have attitudes toward death that are more conducive to productive em activities, ems with such cultures will gain substantial advantages in competing with ems from other cultures. Such selection effects may eventually result in most ems living in cultures with productivity-supporting attitudes toward death.

A more relaxed attitude toward "death" might be helped by the fact that em endings rarely have to be a surprise. Today, the timings of deaths are usually disruptive surprises, causing many to be highly stressed in anticipation. For ems, in contrast, the timing of their endings could usually be chosen and known, and thus could be made more convenient. On the other hand, some ems might be less stressed overall by not knowing the exact moment of their ending. Such ems might be very stressed by knowing they are in their last few minutes, but far less stressed knowing they are in their last week.

The stress of ending may be highest for ems with intermediate duration jobs, too long to seem like a forgotten party, but too short to make trivial the cost of retiring indefinitely at a moderate speed instead of ending. This stressful middle ground of intermediate length subjective job tasks could be avoided at a moderate cost by either merging such tasks into larger ones that take more subjective time, or by dividing them into smaller tasks that take less subjective time.

When these approaches are prohibitively expensive, middle life-length ems might try to gain immortality via text, audio, or video diaries summarized and integrated into elements viewed by ems who follow them in time. Today, writing diaries substantially lowers stresses, such as stress from losing a job (Frattaroli 2006). Also, if just before an em ended, a close copy used mindreading to deeply feel their state of mind, that might seem to the ending em as if they had partially merged with that close copy who continues.

People can feel stress not only from ending personally, but also from the end or loss of close associates. This is a good reason to correlate the copying, retiring, and ending of closely associated ems. By working together in teams that mainly socialize internally, ems could reduce stressful disruptions caused by associates being copied, retired, or ended. The habit of retiring as a group also helps in applying social conformity pressures to induce ems to accept changes that accord with the usual social norms regarding life changes.

Copying sets of co-workers, friends, and lovers as units should also reduce the performance variation of teams, and avoid awkward questions about which new copies of associates should be treated as friends or lovers. This approach, however, may induce ems to feel imprisoned within a team, and reduce access to innovations and gossip that spread best across weak social ties. Teams are discussed more in Chapter 19, Teams section.

SUICIDE

A weaker em aversion to death-related things might strengthen the case for suicide as a fundamental em right. Today, we are aware that suicide can have large opportunity costs, by preventing a long life that might follow instead. This helps make us wary of endorsing suicide. For ems with many similar copies, this opportunity cost is far lower. For ems the main costs of suicide, relative to instead reviving a prior copy, are loss of the skills and information gained in the intervening time, and of the particular emotional attachments that surviving ems have to an em that has ended.

Ems may thus typically favor giving each em a basic right to mental access to a hardware switch that can pause or perhaps also erase them, and to having this switch be as direct and incorruptible as possible. Such suicide switches could help ems respond to threats such as torture or rape. A report of an em who remembers trying and failing to trigger a suicide switch might inspire widespread outrage and a vigorous investigation.

Of course this switch can't function correctly without appropriate support from the computer hardware that manages brain emulation processes.

A right for one em copy to immediately end itself is the simplest suicide right to implement and justify. It is also possible to imagine suicide rights with wider scopes. For example, one could imagine any em having the right to end and erase all copies of descendants from the same original copy within the last subjective day of experience. As those other copies might not want to commit suicide, it is not clear who favors such a policy. Without a wider right to suicide, any copy that commits suicide might just be replaced with a very recent archived copy who may suffer the exact same fate as the earlier copy, defeating the intent of the suicide.

In sum, most ems are much less death-averse than humans today, and this makes them more accepting of at least a narrow right to suicide.

PART III
Economics

CHAPTER 12

Labor

SUPPLY AND DEMAND

Economists find supply and demand to be a very useful way to describe markets, including labor markets. Yes, supply and demand models sometimes fail, but such cases are notable precisely *because* such models usually work so well. In fact, arguably no model in social science works as well; it is the crown jewel of economic theory.

In a supply and demand-based labor market, buyers and sellers mostly take prices as given, and assume that they can't change prices much. Given this assumption, they try to achieve their goals by varying how much labor they buy or sell. Note that supply and demand doesn't require that everyone know everything, or that they always do exactly what is best for them. It is actually a pretty robust and useful model of human behavior.

True, workers often acquire very specific job skills, after which there may be too few sellers or buyers of each specific skill to make for a competitive market. At that point participants may reasonably believe that their behaviors can change relevant prices. But for each specific skill there is usually a large pool of workers who are similarly *able* to learn that skill, and another large pool, this time of employers, with skills they'd like this same pool of workers to learn in order to do their jobs. There is thus a *pre-skill* labor market with pools of similarly-able-to-learn workers, and with employers who have similar-tasks-to-learn. If these pools are large, and if they do not coordinate to limit the wages they accept, then supply and demand analysis will apply well to this pre-skill market.

Thus while it may be hard to predict the specific wages that workers will earn after they learn a specific skill, we can more confidently predict that, in the pre-skill labor market, similar workers will reasonably *expect* to earn a similar net wage after they train. Also, employers trying to attract similar workers should expect to pay a similar net wage. (Of course "wages" include not just cash, but other forms of compensation such as status markers, connections, and resources like information access and computing power.)

Consider how such pre-skill labor markets change when we introduce ems built from cheap signal-processing hardware, able to substitute in most jobs for ordinary human workers after they've acquired relevant skills. What would it take for em competition to bring expected pre-skill wages down to, for example, less than twice the full em hardware cost?

As ems could not long survive with wages below the full hardware cost, if pre-skill wages were, on average, less than twice the total hardware cost, then for most such ems their wages, minus training costs, would have to be close to the average wage.

The main way that em labor markets differ from labor markets today is that ems can be *easily* copied. Copying causes many large changes to em labor markets. For example, with copying there can be sufficient competition for a particular pre-skill type given demand from many competing employers, and supply from only *two* competing ems of that type. For these two ems, all we need is that when faced with a take it or leave it wage offer, they each accept a wage of twice the full hardware cost. After all, any one em can supply an unlimited number of copies of itself to this labor market.

Chapter 19, Clans section will say more about clans being an important unit of economic coordination, and coordinating to negotiate the wages that its members may accept. It is sufficient in this labor market for two clans with close enough pre-skills to compete for each type of job.

Earning a per-day wage of twice their full hardware cost, an em could spend one-half of his or her time working, and spend the remaining time comfortably sleeping, socializing, pondering, watching TV, or any other inexpensive activity. By allowing another working copy, an em could create another version or part of itself that enjoys its life, but not so much as to induce great envy from the original.

Note that I discuss a wage of twice the full hardware cost merely to have a concrete example; actual competitive wages could be higher or lower, depending on several factors we discuss in the next section.

If enough unorganized ems are willing to make many copies of themselves to compete to fill new job openings, the supply of labor is mainly driven by the supply of em hardware needed to support more copies. In that case, it should be noted that the supply of most manufactured goods tends to be quite elastic, at least relative to the elasticity of ordinary human labor demand.

Today, typical estimates are that, in the long run, a 1 percent rise in wages reduces the number of workers that employers are willing to hire by ~0.5 percent (Dunne and Roberts 1993). In other words, the quantity of labor demanded is rather inelastic, that is, not very responsive to changes in wages. The long-run supply of human labor today also seems relatively inelastic; a 1 percent wage increase induces ~0.6 percent more work supplied, ~0.3 percent from more workers and ~0.3 percent from more hours from each worker (Chetty et al. 2011).

In stark contrast, a 1 percent increase in the price of manufactured goods induces manufacturers to supply, on average, about 5 percent more of those goods in the short run (Shea 1993), and even more in the long run. That is, the quantity of manufactured products supplied is very elastic, that is, very responsive to price. Some goods, such as some computer memory chips, even have downward sloping supply curves, where a larger demand for the product *lowers* prices by letting the industry take advantage of scale economies (Kang 2010). Thus having enough ems willing to make copies of themselves should introduce a large increase in the elasticity of the labor supply.

Because of this higher elasticity of supply, the larger and lower-cost supply of ems intersects labor demand at a new point, where the quantity hired is larger and where wages are lower. That is, when hardware costs are lower, wages should also be lower.

Having many firms hire cheaper ems increases the total wealth of society, which increases the total demand for labor. If the hardware supply were inelastic, these total demand increases might raise wages substantially, perhaps to near original pre-em wage levels. But as hardware supply is very elastic, and may even be downward sloping, em wages should stay low, at least in the absence of strong wage or population regulations.

Today the world lacks central population regulation, most people are free to have as many children as they want, and most can afford far more children than did most of their ancestors. Even so, population growth rates are so low that world population is expected to peak and then decline within a century. This situation suggests to some that em population growth rates would also be low. However, today each woman can create only a few children, who come at a substantial initial cost, and then take decades to raise into an adult. This gives plenty of room for culture to influence fertility rates. In contrast, each em could immediately make trillions of full adult copies, which cost only money, not pain or time delay. Here a handful of deviants can overwhelm any cultural norm.

As just discussed, individual employers show a downward sloping demand for workers; the more workers that are available to hire, the less each employer is willing to pay for the marginal worker. However, in theory it is possible that adding workers creates innovation benefits that indirectly increase the value of all workers everywhere. If such an "externality" were powerful enough, wages would rise and not fall as more workers are added to the world economy. But while possible in theory, I find this implausible in practice. So I instead continue to use a simple supply and demand analysis of em wages.

MALTHUSIAN WAGES

Simple supply and demand suggests that the introduction of competitively supplied ems should greatly lower wages, to near the full cost of the computer hardware needed to run em brains. Such a scenario is famously called "Malthusian," after Thomas Malthus who in 1798 argued that when population can grow faster than total economic output, wages fall to near subsistence levels.

Note that in this section we are assuming that enough ems are willing to copy themselves to fill new job openings, and that they have not organized to avoid competing with each other. We shall consider these assumptions in more detail in the Enough Ems section.

Em wages being "near" a full hardware cost does not imply that ems are working all of the time, or that they never get any leisure. First, ems probably still need sleep. Second, as discussed in Chapter 14, Work Hours section, like humans today ems have a maximum-productivity average number of work hours per day that is probably less than ten, and may be less than seven. Ems need to rest during evenings, weekends, vacations, and so on. Third, as discussed in Chapter 14, Spurs section, ems need 10 percent or more of their workday to be devoted to breaks from work.

Fourth, "work" includes everything that it takes to get and keep jobs over the long run. As discussed in Chapter 14, Social Power section, this includes developing and maintaining one's place in a workplace social network, and also maintaining outside social networks which can help one look out for and land new jobs. Ems may need to play golf with the boss, gossip around the "water cooler," and hang out socially with ems who work elsewhere. To impress associates enough to get and keep jobs, ems may also need to invest in showing off in various ways that are discussed more in Chapter 24, Showing Off section. For example, ems may need to become educated and well read, and they may need to keep up with current events.

Fifth, humans have inherited complex and hard to change preferences on how much time they want to spend in various activities such as work, rest, play, socializing, and showing off. While these preferences mostly evolved to serve the functions mentioned above, these preferences may change only slowly. Even in basically Malthusian historical situations, human living standards have sometimes risen substantially when non-subsistence activities became more tempting (Dutta et al. 2017). When no productive em is willing to take a job because it doesn't give enough time for crucial activities, those jobs will have to be modified to leave enough time.

Finally, most em workers earn a wage premium because they are the very best in the world at what they do. Even under the most severe wage competition possible, a best em can earn an extra wage equal to the difference between their productivity and the productivity of the second best em. When clans coordinate internally on wage negotiations, this is the difference in productivity between clans. (Clans who can't coordinate internally are mostly selected out of the em world, as they can't cover their fixed costs, such as for training and marketing.)

Out of 10 billion independently and normally distributed samples, the maximum is on average about 6.4 standard deviations above the mean. Average spacings between the second, third, fourth highest samples are roughly 0.147, 0.075, and 0.05 standard deviations, respectively (Branwen 2017). So when ems are selected out of 10 billion humans, the best em clan may be this much better than other em clans on normally distributed parameters. Using the log-normal wage distribution observed in our world (Provenzano 2015), this predicts that the best human in the world at any particular task is four to five times more productive than the median person, is over 3 percent more productive than the second most productive person, and is 5 percent more productive than the third most productive person.

If em clan relative productivity is drawn from this same distribution, if maximum em productivity comes at a ten hour average workday, and if the best and second best em clans do not coordinate on wages they accept, then even under the strongest wage competition between clans, the best clan could take an extra twenty minutes a day more leisure, or two minutes per work hour, in addition to the six minutes per hour and other work breaks they take to be maximally productive. Of course clans need not spend extra wages on more leisure, if they have something else they value more. See Chapter 14, Work Hours section, for more on em hours of work per week, and Chapter 14, Spurs section, for more on em work breaks.

This twenty minute figure is an underestimate for four reasons. First, the effective sample size of ems is smaller because of age limits on desirable ems. Second, most parameters are distributed so that the tails are thicker than in the normal distribution (Reed and Jorgensen 2004).

Third, differing wealth effects may add to differing productivity effects. On average over the last eleven years, the five richest people on Earth have each been about 10 percent richer than the next richest person. If future em income ratios were like this current wealth ratio, then the best em worker could afford roughly an extra hour per day of leisure, or an additional six minutes per hour.

Fourth, competition probably does not take the strongest possible form, and the best few ems can probably coordinate to some extent. For example, if the best two em clans coordinate completely on wages, but compete strongly with the third best clan, then instead of the best and second best taking twenty and zero minutes of extra leisure per day, they could take thirty and ten extra minutes, respectively.

Plausibly then, the best em workers can afford to take an additional two to six minutes of leisure per hour of work in a ten hour work day, in addition to the over six minutes per hour of break needed for maximum productivity, and in addition to the many other hours needed for sleep, showing off, and socializing for political support.

Ems can earn unusually high wages for jobs where it is expensive to "try out." For example, if it were very expensive to have ems try their hand at a type of CEO position, then the few who tried and did well in that role might well be paid a large wage premium to be a CEO. But we'd expect that premium to be balanced by large entry costs that ems must pay to be allowed to try out in such a role. The expected wages of ems seeking to try out in such a role would be low.

The large fall in em wages raises the cost of tools and supporting capital, relative to the cost of labor. Supply and demand then induces employers to increase their reliance on labor, relative to tools and capital. Today about 60 percent of firm income goes to employees, and more broadly about 52 percent of all income goes to workers. These figures are down from 65 percent and 56 percent, respectively, forty years ago. Possible explanations for this change include a rise in the value of real estate and intellectual property, tools and other forms of capital becoming more effective and cheap, and richer people not wanting to work as many hours (Karabarbounis and

Neiman 2014). The arrival of ems is likely to raise the fraction of income that goes to labor.

Having em wages near subsistence levels should eliminate most of the familiar wage premiums for workers who are smarter, healthier, prettier, etc., than others. Because ems can be copied so easily, even the most skilled ems can be just as plentiful as any other kind of em. While wages vary to compensate for the costs of training to learn particular tasks, wages do not compensate much for other general differences. This should greatly reduce wage inequality (although not necessarily wealth inequality), and increase the relative fraction of workers hired that are of the types that earn higher wages today. For example, if today we hire fewer lawyers compared with janitors because lawyers are more expensive, in a similar situation ems hire more lawyers relative to janitors.

Industries that should remain important in such a competitive world include security, emergency-response, training, law, finance, news, entertainment, politics, education, software, computer and communication hardware, energy production and transport, cooling, material transportation, construction, and mining. Job tasks that should remain important include design, marketing, sales, purchasing, management, administration, testing, monitoring, diagnosis, repair, cleaning, driving, accounting, assembly, packing, installation, mixing, sorting, fitting, negotiation, and research.

Readers of this book may find near subsistence wages to be a strange and perhaps scary prospect. So it is worth remembering that such wages in effect applied to almost all animals who ever lived, to almost all humans before a few hundred years ago, and to a billion humans still today. Historically, it is by far the usual case. We know what humans did in such a situation. And poor ems arguably do not suffer in most of the ways that people suffered in the past as a result of being poor.

FIRST EMS

The distribution of features found in human workers today differs from the distribution found in untrained humans. People who work have both chosen to work, and are chosen by employers. In addition, training changes us, such as by developing particular skills. Em workers differ even more from untrained people today; em features are selected at four different stages: scanning, tweaking, training, and copying.

Early on at least, the people who are scanned are unusual in many ways. One reason is that the earliest effective scanning technology is likely to destroy a brain as part of the process of reading its details. Such early scanning technology starts with a brain where activity has stopped, either because it is very cold, or because it is infused with a solid plastic-like material. With this frozen brain, one scans a two-dimensional surface in fine detail, slices away another thin layer, and repeats (Mikula and Denk 2015).

As brains have ceased apparent activity and then started up again without incident, we know that we need only scan the static brain structures that persist even without activity, and do not need details associated with temporary activity.

Because early scans are destructive, the first people to be scanned are selected for their unusual willingness to suffer that cost. Although some may be scanned unwillingly, other scans are done on the "dead" and the eager. That is, some are people, such as cancer victims, whose body failed them in a way that temporarily preserved their brain for scanning. Others might be so eager to join the em world that they volunteer for destructive scanning even when they could otherwise continue a long life as an ordinary human. These might include key associates of early em firms.

The very first scans might perhaps be performed on cryonics customers, that is, on people who had previously had their brains frozen and stored in liquid nitrogen in the hope of being revived when technology improved, and who had agreed to allow em scanning later. High-quality frozen brains might be legally "dead," and so available to be scanned with fewer legal limitations. Of course frozen brains may also have disadvantages, compared with living brains.

About 200 people have been frozen over the last five decades. I am one of about 2000 people still living who have arranged to be cryogenically frozen. I would choose to have my frozen brain destructively scanned to create an em, given an at least 80 percent chance of success.

A second reason that early scanned people are unusual is that early scans are likely to be very expensive. Some rich people may pay to scan themselves, non-profits and governments may pay to scan others, and profit-seeking firms (including criminal organizations) may invest in scans from which they expect to profit.

Expected daily revenue from a scan is the amount that a firm expects to charge per day of work for renting an initially willing trained copy, times the number of copies one expects to rent. Costs include the full hardware cost, training, taxes, and whatever additional wages such copies require, in money, control, and increased leisure and retirement time, to become initially willing workers. Additional related expenses may include searching for, and marketing to, potential customers, searching for and developing training methods, and political lobbying.

Workers who are initially willing to work may sometimes became unwilling to work later during their work process. If this happens often, it reduces the price that customers are willing to pay to rent such workers.

Profit-seeking firms select people to scan who can generate the most net profit when rented to work. Such people are willing to work, able to flexibly adapt to new em work environments, and have, or are able to obtain, work skills valued by many customers.

For the very earliest scans, their main customers are ordinary human individuals and firms. So the first scans are of people who already have work skills valued by the then-current economy, as these can be immediately deployed for a profit. Such workers are likely near the peak of their career productivity. For example, they might be older lawyers or software engineers with well-established reputations for exceptional productivity.

However, once the em world becomes larger, the required tasks shift to being defined more by the new em world. This reduces the value of skills tuned to the overshadowed world of ordinary humans, and increases the value of flexibility, of abilities to learn new em world skills, and of the possibility of using these new skills over a long career. This shifts scanning demands from older people with proven skills toward younger people with a strong potential to learn relevant skills.

If at this point destructive scanning were still the only cost-effective scanning technology, the preference for scanning young human brains for their potential and flexibility may create a strong competition for a limited number of young people who are also capable, and eager to join the em world. Attempts to limit the freedom of such young people and their parents to voluntarily choose destructive scanning could result in big conflicts.

Later on, when scans become non-destructive and scanning costs fall, scans are done on far more people, including both old people with proven productivity and adaptability, and younger people with great promise to later become productive and adaptable. Eventually most humans willing to be scanned are scanned, creating a large pool of scans which can be searched for potentially productive workers. By then, many early scans may have gained first-mover advantages over late arrivals. First movers will have adapted more to em environments, and other ems and other systems will have adapted more to them.

SELECTION

While ems are mentally quite human, selection effects will make them differ from typical humans.

For example, in addition to the selection of which humans to scan, scanned brains may be tweaked via adjusting a few dozen or more overall parameters of the emulation process. These tweaks might make emulations that are especially thoughtful, focused, relaxed, etc. This tweaking is somewhat like tuning a car by adjusting its many settings, as opposed to building a car from scratch. The amount of useful tweaking is limited by how opaque em brains are at the time; the more that ems understand, the more useful changes they can make.

The selection of tweaks to apply to any given scan, and how much freedom that tweaked em has to change its tweaks later, are in general a compromise negotiated between the scanned em and the patrons who fund its scanning, tweaking, training, and copying.

A tweaked scan of an ordinary human typically needs to undergo general training to function as an em in the em-dominated world. It also needs more specialized training to become proficient at particular tasks. Prior training as an ordinary human doing similar tasks may be helpful, but is usually insufficient. Different copies of a scan could be trained to do different tasks. As with the choice to scan, the selection of ways to train scanned and tweaked copies depends on the preferences of wealthy people who train themselves, of charities and governments who pay others to train, and of "employment agency"-like firms who seek to profit from renting out trained scans.

Given a population of trained, tweaked scans, the number of actual copies created, how fast these copies run, and for how long, depends on how much wealthy ems were willing to spend on themselves, how much non-profits and governments were willing to spend to create and extend various em lives, and on how much profit-seeking firms expect to charge customers to rent the work time of various copies.

In addition to the four levels of selection of scanning, tweaking, training, and copying (including speed choice), there are also four types of actors who act as selectors: wealthy individuals, non-profits, governments, and profit-seeking firms. As discussed in the "Enough Ems" section, the em labor market is competitive if there are enough ems available to compete for jobs.

Wealthy individuals sometimes choose which humans to pay to scan and copy, and which tweaks to apply based on attachment, admiration, or other personal criteria. They are likely to have more varied preferences, compared with the other actors who select. Thus the ems with the most extreme features are more likely to have been chosen by wealthy individuals.

In a highly competitive low-regulation economy, the resources available to wealthy individuals and charities willing to suffer substantial operating losses should be small relative to the resources available to profit-seeking firms, and to non-profits who behave similarly because they are unwilling to suffer substantial operating losses for long. Thus in the case of limited government taxation and regulation, it seems sufficient to analyze the case of selection of ems by profit-seeking firms.

That is, if competition is strong enough to drive behaviors so that economic profits fall to near zero, there shouldn't be much difference in the behaviors of organizations that try to maximize profits, and of organizations that cannot long survive operating losses. Thus in a competitive em economy the characteristics of most ems should be as if profit-seeking firms had selected them.

ENOUGH EMS

If enough unorganized ems are willing to copy themselves to fill profit-driven (or loss-limited) job openings, and if such copying is not prevented by strong global regulation, then low em total hardware costs for em creation can drive a vast as-if-profit-driven expansion in the number of ems. This makes ems much more numerous than ordinary humans, and cuts wages to near total em hardware costs. But are a sufficient number of ems willing to be copied?

If for each pre-skill type there are some ems much better at jobs of that type than other ems, then "enough" ems is at least two competing such ems of each pre-skill type. These two could even come from the same clan. After all, each willing and free em can allow an unlimited number of copies of itself, so just two competing ems guarantees an arbitrary number of competing ems. The number of distinct worker types sets the size of "enough," because it is enough to have a few willing and competing ems of each such type.

So how many pre-skill types are there today? Our economy appears on the surface to hold many millions of kinds of jobs, and a larger em economy might hold many more. The U.S. census classifies workers according to over 21 000 industries and 31 000 occupations. Many of these occupations are very similar to each other, however. For example, the U.S. government has created a database (called O*NET) that gives 277 descriptors for each of 974 job categories. Such a database would hardly be possible if the differing jobs within each of these 974 categories were not very similar. In fact, a factor analysis of 226 of these descriptors finds that the top four factors account for 75 percent of the variance in these descriptors, and the top fifteen factors account for 91 percent of this variance (Lee 2011).

Also, statistical models to predict the income and performance of workers usually have at most only a few dozen parameters. These analyses have mostly been about post-skill types, that is, about how workers differ after they have been trained to do particular tasks. Pre-skill types should vary even less than do post-skill types.

All this suggests that the number of distinct pre-skill types, where workers of different types differ substantially in their ability to acquire particular job skills, is far smaller than the number of distinct jobs. In fact, I guess that there are no more than a million or so distinct relevant pre-skill types for an em economy, and perhaps only dozens of such types.

If we assume that em variation comes similarly from the variation in the people who are scanned, and from variation in tweaking and early training of scanned ems, then a million types could plausibly come from a thousand people scanned, times a thousand kinds of differences in useful tweaks and early general training. This suggests that "enough" ems to fill the niches of a competitive em labor market might be found from only a thousand diverse qualified people who were scanned and competing for jobs. Only a dozen or even fewer such people might be enough.

Thus it is a reasonable guess that for the vast majority of pre-skill wages to fall to roughly twice the total hardware cost, and as a result for the quantity of labor to greatly increase, what we require is that firms can find, out of over 7 billion ordinary humans, fewer than roughly a thousand able people willing to be scanned, tweaked, and copied to take jobs at such a wage. We also require this group of ems to fail to coordinate to negotiate much better wages than they could get without coordination. These requirements seem quite plausible.

While having wages close to the full hardware cost makes an em "poor" in some senses of the word, "poor" has many connotations that need not apply in an em world. Yes, "poor" ems spend a large fraction of their time working. But such ems need not suffer physical hunger, exhaustion, pain, sickness, grime, hard labor, or sudden unexpected death. Widespread use of automation makes most jobs at least modestly mentally challenging. As most ems are poor, em poverty does not inflict the same pain of low social status that it does in societies such as ours where most people are rich. Ems could be assured of very high-quality entertainment during leisure time, and of a comfortable indefinite retirement when they were no longer competitive at work.

Remember also that the vast majority of humans who have ever lived had near subsistence level incomes. This is true for an even larger fraction of non-human animals. Humans evolved for and are well-adapted to such income levels, and historians and anthropologists suggest that most have lived satisfying even if not luxurious lives. The evaluation of the em world is discussed more in Chapter 29, Evaluation section.

Related to the question of whether there are "enough" types of em workers to create competitive labor markets is the question of whether there are "enough" types of ems to create a robust Darwinian selection of ems. That is, the larger is the space of possible ems to draw on, the further that a Darwinian type of selection process could go in evolving em minds better suited to the em world.

If the space of possible tweaks is limited, with say only a million distinct tweaks, then given a few billion original humans the space of possible ems is limited to a million times a few billion, or a few quadrillion. This allows a substantial but limited evolution of ems. Ems selected in this process are not just like typical humans, but they are also not usually far from the range of variation of ordinary humans. Such ems are different, but still recognizably human. This book focuses mostly on such a scenario.

However, if it later becomes possible to explore a much larger space of useful mind modifications, that could allow for a much stronger Darwinian evolution of ems. In this case ems might perhaps quickly evolve to become not recognizably human. That is, ems might fragment into one or more distinct mental species with very different mental styles. Ems might, in effect, become aliens. We discuss this more in Chapter 27, Unhumans section.

In sum, it seems there will be enough ems of different types to drive almost all wages to near subsistence levels.

CHAPTER 13

Efficiency

CLAN CONCENTRATION

The em economy could draw from a large pool of ordinary humans willing to be scanned. That pool could, in effect, be expanded via many possible tweaks of each scan. In addition, a single em can dominate a large labor market by making many copies of itself. These factors can together produce strong competition. Such competition may drive profit-seeking firms to try hard to select the most profitable combinations of scanning, tweaking, and training. The best such combinations would then dominate the em economy.

A thousand diverse able scanned humans seems sufficient to induce competition in most all labor markets, as the best few ems can dominate each labor market. Thus it seems likely that most ems are copies of fewer than a thousand or so, and perhaps only dozens, of the original humans. Howeger, an aversion to having multiple copies from the same clan in each small social circle, and the fact that jobs done by more ems are better candidates for automation, may limit this clan inequality.

Clans create a new and important unit of social organization in the em world, useful in commerce, finance, law, and politics. Ems from the same clan are more like each other than are families today, or even than identical twins today. So ems can better trust their clans than they can trust families, neighbourhoods, firms, professions cities, or nations. And being more similar, they pay a lower cost in thwarted preferences from making choices collectively. Large clans split into subclans, who have different professions or live in different cities. Clans and subclans regulate member behaviors to protect their collective revenue and reputation, and can negotiate collectively for jobs and shared services.

The few highly copied em "clans" of copies might be known by a single name, as are celebrities today such as Madonna or Beyoncé. (Of course ems also need identifiers to distinguish particular clan members.) Familiar one-name em clans might be typically favored in most social interactions over billions of unfamiliar two- or three-name clans. The usual human preference for interacting with familiar personalities rather than strangers might discourage ems from interacting with ems from less well-known clans, increasing inequality between clans. Ems may even justify this unequal treatment by saying that it is less moral to end an em copy from a small clan, because not as many similar other ems continue on.

The main em clans may also see other clans as creepier. Today people who seem creepy tend to be males with unusual nonverbal behaviors and characteristics, who seem unpredictable and who might pose a sexual threat (McAndrew and Koehnke 2016). The behaviors and characteristics of the main em clans are more predictable, and ems can be very secure against sexual threat.

Em sociality might thus become more like that of our forager ancestors, who only ever met a few hundred people at most in their entire lives, and were quite familiar with the history, personality, and abilities of everyone they met (Dunbar 1992; McCarty et al. 2000). When they stick to associating with one-names, ems might know well who they liked or didn't like, and how best to flatter or insult each one. There might be clan jokes analogous to our ethnic jokes, such as "How many Freds does it take to screw in a light bulb?" One-name ems cannot "start over fresh" by moving to a new city or job; strong reputations follow them everywhere.

Because our forager ancestors knew each other so well, they rarely over-reacted to individual actions; foragers could interpret each action well in the context of the rest of a person's life. This situation has changed in the farmer and industrial eras. Today, people who hardly know us can react strongly to any one thing we do or say. When compared with foragers, we face much stronger conformity pressures because of fears of others misinterpreting any one action. So we try harder to make sure that each thing we do can be spun positively. One-name ems are much less pressured to conform in this way. This is because while such ems are usually eager to preserve the overall reputation of their clan, they can more expect each of their actions to be interpreted in the context of the entire history of their clan.

Compared to most product markets, labour markets today offer unusually diverse products. (See Chapter 20, Inequality section, for more on product diversity.) This seems less because diversity is valued highly in labour markets, and more because it is hard to reduce human labour diversity. As clan concentration reduces em labour diversity, ems lose some benefits now gained from labour market diversity.

But such gains seem modest. Today students who attend more genetically diverse schools gain more income, education, and prestige, in part because they become more extraverted and open to experience, and take more unique jobs (Cook and Fletcher 2017). Even so, diversity doesn't seem to matter much to overall business success (Stojmenovska et al. 2017). And as discussed in Chapter 19, Teams section, the most productive work teams have a diversity of information sources and thinking styles, but have *common* demographic features such as race, ethnicity, gender, age, and tenure.

Being dominated by copies of the best few hundred humans is one of the most dramatic ways in which the em world differs from our world today.

COMPETITION

A world dominated by a few hundred clans can be a more competitive world.

Growth in economic productivity occurs because of both increased productivity at individual establishments and firms, and because more productive establishments and firms displace less productive versions. Today, this second factor dominates, and is accelerated by stronger competition (Foster et al. 2006; Lentz and Mortensen 2008; Syverson 2011).

While our economy today is somewhat competitive, competition is limited because markets are fragmented by regulation, national boundaries, spatial distance, and product variety, and because of the long time it takes to train individual employees for new methods and situations. As a result, inefficient firms and establishments continue to exist for surprisingly long durations. For example, U.S. manufacturing plants today that are at the 90th percentile of productivity are typically *twice* as productive as plants at the 10th percentile. In India and China these more productive plants are *five times* more productive (Haltiwanger 2012; Syverson 2004; Syverson 2011).

An em economy can be more competitive, in the sense of more quickly eliminating less productive entities and practices, to produce a smaller variation in productivity. For example, instead of factor of two from the U.S. today, there might be only a 20 percent difference in plant productivity between the 90th and 10th percentiles.

We have several reasons to expect a more competitive em world. As we will see, ems have less product variety because they are poorer, and have less spatial segmentation because they are concentrated in a few dense cities. In addition, ems can more easily transfer methods from their more efficient establishments, by making copies of the em teams working at more efficient establishments. A single em, by making many copies, can take over an entire labour market. All these factors should make the em economy more competitive in the sense of more aggressively selecting for high productivity. Compared with today, in the em world smaller differences in efficiency between different behaviors more easily lead to displacements of less efficient behaviors by more efficient ones.

Given at least a few substantial places in the world that do not greatly limit ems via regulation and taxation, and a few dozen or so distinct em clans willing to copy themselves in such places, wages in em-friendly places should greatly fall, and output there should greatly increase. If such places can also grow very rapidly, they quickly come to dominate the world economy, which then becomes very competitive. Ems dominate the world.

The strong competition resulting from the high selectivity of an em world should drive and enable an aggressive search for work and living arrangements that achieve the greatest productivity at the lowest cost. Today, the adoption of apparently efficient work and living arrangements is often hindered by personal and social conformity preferences against arrangements that are unfamiliar, or which evoke unpopular symbolisms. We should expect less resistance to these changes in a more competitive em world, especially when there is competition among regions with different standards of conformity.

Thus a working assumption in the rest of this book is that em work, reproduction, and living arrangements are all determined more than today by simple *efficiency*—the arrangements that exist will tend more to be those that achieve useful tasks at a minimum total cost, including hardware and training. Psychological costs of abstract symbolic discomfort matter less than they do today. Of course direct immediate continuing feelings of discomfort could continue to matter greatly. But abstract symbolic discomforts mostly go away as people get used to most everyone accepting the new arrangements.

Not only is em efficiency a likely assumption, it is also a simple assumption, in that it facilitates further analysis of the em scenario. A very competitive em world will tend to induce ems to more often swallow their pride and switch to efficient but strange or repugnant new ways.

Note that the word "competition" has a technical definition in economics, namely agents acting as if they have little power to influence the prices they pay or charge. This meaning applies to the em labor markets mainly in early pre-skill stages when clans consider which particular job markets to enter, and when many such clans are nearly as well qualified to enter. At this early point we expect competition to produce nearly zero expected profit for all who enter a labor market. This implies nearly subsistence em net wages, after paying for fixed costs to enter such markets.

However, as with most product markets today, we expect only a few clans to actually enter each em labor market, by investing in fixed costs such as research, training, and marketing. We expect such clans to try hard to make their worker products seem different to customers, so that they can gain more power to set prices. We expect the fixed costs to enter such markets to account for a substantial fraction of wages, that such fixed costs will be bigger in larger labor markets, and that fixed costs will be the main source of variation across clans in their cost of supplying ems to particular labor markets. Thus we don't expect competitive clan or employer behavior at these late market stages.

We also expect that when customers place substantial value on particular teams, over and above the value of individual workers, then clans will coordinate to package their workers into teams that they can offer for a package price. All of these non-competitive expectations come from standard results in the economic subfield of "industrial organization" (Shy 1996).

The main exceptions to choices being driven by competitiveness in the em world may be choices made by the em subclans especially successful at accumulating wealth. There should be some selection for clans that spend this wealth well, by investing in good enterprises, and also in providing credible signals of their wealth to induce favorable treatment by others. However, wealthy clans who behave this way initially but then later deviate from such efficient behavior will not be instantly eliminated; as their wealth declines they could spend it in many unpredictable ways.

Aside from this exception, however, the em world is very competitive.

PRODUCTIVITY

A more competitive world will make more efficient choices, and a more efficient em world differs from ours in many ways.

Today, nations with more distrust have more regulation (Aghion et al. 2010), and nations and industries with less regulation tend to grow faster in the long run (Papaioannou 2017). Reduced financial regulation especially helps many industries (Alesina et al. 2005; Pizzola 2015). This is plausibly because regulations are designed around existing practices, and so discourage changes in those practices. Thus business regulation tends to discourage growth, which usually requires changing practices (Dawson and Seater 2013).

The em world is more likely to see regulations that help each place to compete with others in the global em economy, or that don't make much of a difference for global competition. Examples of helpful regulations include those that discourage local negative externalities such as pollution, or that allow cities to achieve scale and scope economies. A type of regulation that may not help or hurt much is restrictions on searching for mental tweaks. Once the search for such tweaks has reached the point of greatly diminishing returns, moral repugnance over possible suffering in experimented-on-ems during a search for tweaks may induce regulations limiting further search.

Note that a lack of strong global regulation tends to make places compete on their growth rates, which should discourage local growth-inhibiting regulations. So not only does low regulation suggest strong competition, strong competition also suggests low regulation.

How exactly will ems be more productive? We weakly expect ems to exhibit features that correlate with productivity today. For example, as more productive people today move further from their hometown, ems also move further (Carr and Kefalas 2009). Em workers also sit next to high achieving workers.

Ems may apply personal productivity habits of the very productive people of today. These habits include scheduling timing to the minute, doing one thing at a time, avoiding to-do lists, making it home in time for dinner, putting ideas in an always-ready notebook, doing email only a few times a day, avoiding meetings as much as possible, saying "no" to almost all requests, delegating as much as possible, assigning days of the week for different task categories, touching email only once, following a consistent morning routine, not skipping meal breaks, and sleeping enough (Kruse 2016).

Other routes to productivity include envy and punishment. Benign envy tends to motivates more effort, at least when improvements are possible (van de Ven et al. 2011). And a habit of punishing the worst performers tends to give stronger incentives for overall performance, compared with rewarding the best performers (Drouvelis and Jamison 2015; Kubanek et al. 2015). When evaluating things, marking low quality also works better than marking high quality (Klein and Garcia 2014). However, organizations today are reluctant to punish, and so they tend to focus on positive rewards and evaluations. After all, workers tend to leave organizations that focus on negatives. More competitive em organizations, in contrast, are likely to focus more on negatives than we do today. There will be fewer gains from rewarding the best workers, because of less quality variation among that best group, and because usually only the best workers are copied.

It is possible that stronger punishment involves direct pain, and this has often happened in the distant past. But the extreme rarity of this practice today suggests that pain is not very useful as a motivator for workers in advanced industrial jobs, and so is also only rarely useful for em workers. It is also possible that rewards involve direct mind tweaks to produce pleasure. But again the rarity of related practices today weakly suggests that this is only rarely useful for em workers.

A competitive low-wage em economy should reverse the trends of recent decades in product and services, and increase the priority of cost and simple functionality, relative to comfort, style, identity-enhancement, and variety. Thus em products should be less varied, achieve greater scale economies, and rely more on engineering skills relative to design skills. Em products should also be marketed more by referring to concrete product features rather than by indirectly associating products with moods, ideals, and identities. The concentration of ems into a small number of clans should also reduce the variety of products desired. These changes should also increase the rate of innovation, as it is cheaper to innovate in less varied products that are more widely used, and in products that rely more on engineering relative to design.

Despite the availability of many tweaks and the equivalent of powerful mind-altering drugs, ems probably continue to suffer periodically from greatly debilitating mental conditions such as depression, love-sickness, or hobby obsession. In a competitive em economy, such conditions may often result in ending that copy and reviving a copy archived before the condition appeared. Ems are likely to periodically save backup copies to allow this option. Efforts to avoid losing useful experience because of such reversions may focus less on curing such conditions, and more on detecting and averting them before the conditions begin.

A competitive em economy might have a few small niches for emulations of animals. After all, animals might be able to do some useful tasks, and while animals are less capable than humans at many tasks, their smaller brains can be emulated at a much lower cost. However, the fact that we have found little use for animal brains in our economy today suggests that animal ems make only a small niche contribution to the em labor force.

The implications of efficiency mentioned so far in this section are only the start. Most of the rest of this book is devoted to identifying more such implications.

ELITENESS

If most ems are copies of fewer than a thousand or so original humans, just how elite does that make ems, compared with typical humans today?

Ems are selected from among the humans alive during the early em era (and perhaps also a few previous cryonics customers). As this early em era might last only for a year or two in objective time, ems are basically chosen from a human population snapshot. Depending on when the em transition occurred, this gives 7 to 12 or so billion humans to choose from.

Early on, the human-to-em selection process prefers adult humans with well-established success, skills, and connections. But the selection process quickly switches to preferring younger more flexible humans, who can be better trained to adapt to the em world, and to particular em jobs. This likely leads to a focus on selecting from a limited range of ideal ages, a range perhaps 2 to 20 years wide.

Today, there are about 120 million people alive at each year of age between 5 and 30 years old, and this figure is not expected to change much over the next half-century or so (United Nations 2013). Thus depending on the width of the ideal age range, ems are selected from a population of humans that numbers between 300 million and 3 billion people. From each year of age within the ideal age range, less than about 50 to 500 humans are selected to become part of the 1000 most highly copied ems.

To see how selective this is, we can compare this 50-to-500-per-birth-year figure to the number of humans per-birth-year today who are selected for prestigious distinctions. For example, each year there are on average about 150 Grammy awards for U.S. musical achievement, 75 Olympic gold medals for athletic achievement, and 136 Clio awards for excellence in advertising. Per year, about 34 Oscars are given for excellence in movies, and 21 Pulitzers for excellence in writing and journalism. Each year there are about 50 new heads of state worldwide. Also, the fact that there are today about 45 billionaires at each age near the peak billionaire age of about 60 suggests that today about 65 people per year are born who will eventually reach a level of wealth comparable in selectivity with billionaires today (Dolan and Kroll 2014).

These figures suggest that highly copied ems are chosen more selectively than are winners of Olympic gold medals, Oscars, Grammys, Clios, Pulitzers, and heads of state, assuming that only a small fraction of people today try for each of these honors.

It is less clear if ems are more selective than billionaires today, as one might argue that a large fraction of people today try to be as rich as possible. Also ambiguous are comparisons between em selection and the roughly eight Nobel Prizes and four acting Oscars given per year, or the three people per birth-year who win at least three Olympic gold medals. It isn't clear what fraction of people today would try for such awards, if they had compatible skills and resources. But the selectivity of highly copied ems is at least comparable with such distinctions. If there are much fewer than 1000 highly copied ems, such ems are even more selective.

Today, Jews comprise a disproportionate fraction of extreme elites such as billionaires, and winners of prizes such as the Pulitzer, Oscar, and Nobel prizes (*Forbes Israel* 2013). (I have sought but failed to find work identifying other elite ethnicities.) This weakly suggests that

Jews are also disproportionately represented among ems. Perhaps, however, Jews only happen to be disproportionately elite now for temporary cultural reasons.

Even so, groups of ordinary humans that are only temporarily elite at the time the em world arises might still end up constituting an outsized fraction of the em world, and this favouritism might last long into the em era. For example, if urban rich white male Harvard graduates happen to be more productive when the em era begins, a disproportionate fraction of ems may arise from such people.

Today many use "cognitive enhancing" drugs, though their benefits are still not clear, and some of the perceived benefit is emotional (Partridge et al. 2011; Vrecko 2013). If em tweaks are found that correspond to better versions of such drugs, many ems may use them. It is also possible that sometime in the next half-century or so we will be able to create babies of substantially higher genetic quality via embryo selection in the context of in vitro fertilization (Shulman and Bostrom 2013). If so, when they reach the right age these may be very attractive candidates for scanning into ems.

Even in groups with much higher chances to start one of the 1000 most copied clans, almost everyone still has a low chance. For example, today there are about 1645 billionaires (Dolan and Kroll 2014). If there were a similar number of billionaires at the time of the em transition, then if each one had a 100 000 times greater than average chance of starting a top em clan, there'd still be only about a dozen of the top 1000 clans that started from a billionaire, and each billionaire would only have a 1 percent chance of starting such a clan.

All of which is to say, compared with us today ems are *very* elite.

QUALITIES

What individual features of ems can we predict from the fact that ems are the elite winners of a very competitive world?

The best em combinations are chosen not only for having high average productivity on useful tasks, but also for having a low variation in such productivity. That is, the best ems are consistently excellent. After all, most tasks coordinate with other tasks, and an unexpected local productivity drop in one task usually hurts associated tasks more than an unexpected local productivity boost helps such associated tasks. So local productivity variation on interdependent tasks tends to hurt overall productivity.

One study looked at the common features of 291 famous scientists, inventors, scholars, statesmen, national leaders, painters, sculptors, composers, novelists, & playwrights. Such people had exceptional ability, originality, drive, perseverance, industry, and meticulousness, and tended to be warm, friendly, & social. Most of them had some unusual personality characteristics, though minor neurotic features were more common than psychoses. Writers and visual artists had severe personality deviations more often, and writers had more depression and alcoholism (Post 1994).

Today, people who are more productive at work tend to have more health, beauty, marriage, religion, intelligence, extraversion, conscientiousness, agreeableness, and emotional stability (Roberts et al. 2007; Steen 1996; Nguyen et al. 2003; Barrick 2005; Roberts et al. 2007; Sutin et al. 2009; Fletcher 2013; Gensowski 2014). They also tend to be male. Such features also predict more education and occupational prestige today (Damian et al. 2015). We weakly expect ems to have more of these features, when compared with people today.

However, as we today see a negative correlation between intelligence and conscientiousness, it is possible that ems will be have of one of these, and less of the other (Rammstedt et al. 2016). If ems are more extraverted, then they may to prefer flat geography, relative to mountains (Oishi et al. 2015).

We today see many correlations between specific behaviors personality types. These, together with predicted em personality features, let us weakly predict em behavioral inclinations. For example, assuming ems are more extraverted, they are more inclined to exercise, play sports, tell dirty jokes, discuss sex, cheer loudly, talk about making money, ask questions in meeting, fly a plane, drive fast, drive while talking on phone, plan a party, gamble, decorate rooms, and give public talks. Assuming ems are more agreeable, they are more inclined to sing in the shower, avoid make fun of others, play with children, and keep their body and personal area clean and neat.

Assuming ems are more conscientious, they do not chew on pencils, nor let work pile up until just before deadline. Assuming ems are more emotionally stable, they are less inclined toward nightmares, making fun of others, reading personal ads, and taking medications for anxiety, sleep, depression. Finally, assuming ems are more open, they are more inclined to be naked at home, do something new, make and visit art, talk about making money, shoot a gun, write a diary, and repair a car (Chapman and Goldberg 2017).

In our world, achievement generally rises with intelligence (Kell et al. 2013). Smarter people are on average less accident-prone and more long-lived, cooperative, patient, trusting, trustworthy, rational, focused, and law-abiding (Jones 2011; Melnick et al. 2013). They tend to support more economically efficient policies within lab experiments, and on national policy surveys they tend toward optimism and favor efficient policies such as using markets, avoiding make-work jobs, and trading with foreigners (Caplan and Miller 2010). Smarter nations are more entrepreneurial, less corrupt, have more economic freedom, and have better institutions (Jones and Potrafke 2014). If smarter people use larger vocabularies and more complex sentences, then so will smarter ems. More implications of ems being smarter are discussed in Chapter 27, Intelligence section.

There seem to be exceptions, however, where less intelligence is desired. Very smart people seem at more risk of having mental problems and of maladjustment, especially mood and anxiety disorders (Towers 1987). The best leaders tend to have an intelligence which is about 1.2 standard deviations above the mean intelligence of their subordinates (Antonakis et al. 2017). And employers often reject employee candidates because they are too smart for particular jobs.

In our world first born children seem to do less crime, earn more, and do better in school (Paulhus et al. 1999; Hotz 2015; Pavan 2016; Breining et al. 2017). First born also tend to be more emotionally stable, persistent, socially outgoing, responsibility assuming, and initiative taking (Black et al. 2017). Some question these results, however (Rohrer et al. 2017). These results weakly suggests that ems will tend to arise from firstborns, and have these various features.

Today, gay men earn less than comparable straight men, while lesbian women earn more than comparable straight women (Carpenter 2008). This suggests that while disproportionally many female ems may be lesbian, disproportionally few male ems may be gay.

When deciding when to cooperate or to compete, people today can be categorized as givers, takers, and matchers. Givers are over represented among those with both the highest and lowest success. This weakly suggests that ems will tend more to be givers, who are more inclined to cooperate in ambiguous situations (Grant 2013). Cooperation is sometimes predicted more strongly by patience than by intelligence (Al-Ubaydli et al. 2013).

Students who at age 12 show more rule-breaking and defiance of parental authority tend to do better in both school then and also in jobs at age 52, at least after one controls for how smart, studious, and responsible they are as students (Spengler et al. 2015). Since ems are also smart, studious, and responsible, this suggests that ems also defy authority and break rules as kids, even if they work hard, well, and responsibly as adults.

Today, people who are very stressed can't think abstractly very well, and people who are calmer tend to make better decisions in a crisis (Bond 2017). In general, job performance peaks at moderate levels of stress and emotional arousal, (Perkins and Corr 2005; Lupien et al. 2007). Thus working ems are likely to have non-trivial but also non-extreme levels of stress and anxiety. When there is a most productive peak mood for a task, the mood of an em doing that task is near that peak mood. Ems can be closer to peak mood when they do tasks where less needs to be remembered from recent similar tasks. In this case one can more easily save a peak mood em and have it ready do many tasks. Ems who need to remember recent similar tasks have more mood variations.

The people who perform best when make high stakes decisions are those who also feel moderately stressed when making small stakes decisions. Being practiced in making stressful decisions, they are not rattled by big decisions. Such stress is revealed in having sweaty palms (Zaman 2016). Ems who make high stakes decisions tend to be this way; they take both high and low stakes decisions seriously.

People who are more mindful, that is, who stay more focused on the task at hand and let their minds wander less, are both happier and more productive, even if they are less creative. As mindfulness can be taught, we should expect that ems are more mindful (Killingsworth and Gilbert 2010; Baird et al. 2012; Mrazek et al. 2013; Randall et al. 2014).

Relative to night owls, who stay up late, people today who are morning larks, and get up early, tend to have higher income, higher academic achievement, and to be less often unemployed, in ill health, impulsive, or undependable. Larks are more conformist, agreeable, and conscientious, although less smart. These suggest that ems tend more to be larks than owls. Women and older people tend more to be larks (Paine et al. 2006; Cavallera and Giudici 2008; Preckel et al. 2011; Bonke 2012).

Today, people who live in the parts of time zones that let them start work later after sunrise tend to sleep and earn more (Gibson and Shrader 2014). However, people who earn more tend to sleep less, controlling for lark/owl, gender, age, education, location, and industry (Bonke 2012). Fewer than 1 percent of people today have a special gene that lets them function well on 1 less hour of sleep per night (Pellegrino et al. 2014). Together these suggest that ems will tend more to come from scans of humans with this special gene, and will tend to sleep less than we do today, although they sleep enough to be rested and productive.

Humans with a bipolar or "manic-depressive" disorder are overall less productive, but they are often especially productive and creative during their manic phase. Such people are over-represented in jobs where creativity is especially important (Laxman et al. 2008; Kyaga et al. 2011; Parker et al. 2012). Just as the em economy may select for workaholics in ordinary jobs, for short-term creative tasks the em economy might perhaps also select for copies of bipolar ems who are just entering the most productive part of their manic phase.

People can be categorized by their vocational interest type: realistic, investigative, artistic, enterprising, or conventional. After controlling for gender, grades, and extraversion, income is higher for realistic and enterprising types, and lower for social and artistic types. Social, enterprising, and conventional types have more children, as do extraverts.

Since ems are selected both for high income and for trying to create many copies, the clearest prediction is that ems will have more enterprising types. Such types are self-confident, ambitious, forceful, and acquisitive, and they strive for achievement, economic success, prestige, and high-powered careers. They also like to manipulate others in order to attain organizational goals or economic gain.

Ems having higher income suggests ems will have more realistic types. These prefer the explicit or systematic manipulation of objects, tools, machines, and animals. Their goals focus on tangible products, money, social status, and power. Ems being willing to make many copies suggests that they will have more conventional types. Conventional types, such as clerks, prefer activities that entail the ordered and systematic manipulation of data (Stoll et al. 2017). Ems probably have fewer artistic types. These prefer the manipulation of physical, verbal, or human materials to create art forms and products.

Due to contrary or neutral indications, I see no clear prediction on if ems have more or fewer social and investigative types. Social types value social activities and want to serve others. They prefer to interact with others inform, train, develop, cure, or enlighten them. Investigative types value scientific or scholarly activities and achievements. They prefer the observational, symbolic, systematic, and creative investigation of physical, biological, and cultural phenomena.

Today the most successful research scientists are more likely than others to have an artistic hobby (Root-Bernstein et al. 2008). This suggests that ems with similar jobs will also have artistic hobbies.

In sum, we can identify a great many specific qualities which we expect to be different in ems.

MOTIVATION

Workers today have a wide range of reasons to keep working, and we see little correlation between a worker's type of motivation and their career success. But *level* of motivation matters enormously, so much in fact that it seems to predict career success better than intelligence or raw ability (Niven 2006). When thinking about work from a distance, we tend to equally value our intrinsic motives, i.e., the motives that we feel up close while working, and extrinsic motives, i.e., the more abstract justifications and reasons we have to work. But while we are working we care more about intrinsic motives (Woolley and Fishbach 2015). Thus we expect ems to be highly motived, via a wide range of motivations, and more focused while working on intrinsic motives.

Some say that people with more grit, that is, perseverance when facing difficult tasks, achieve more in school and elsewhere (Duckworth and Quinn 2009). However, others say that grit is just another way to talk about contentiousness (Credé et al. 2016; Rimfeld et al. 2016). People appear to achieve grit by gaining a deep purpose and personal meaning from their activities, by giving and getting help via strong bonds with friends and teammates, by making a game out of difficult situations, by being confident but realistic, by preparing well and often, by facing and thinking through their fears, by having a "growth mindset" that focuses on learning and improving, by debriefing often and noting what they could have done better, by celebrating small wins, and by regularly finding things to laugh at (Barker 2015b).

Two important contributions to human motivation are happiness and a sense of meaning or purpose, though there has been far more research on happiness than on meaning. Today, most of the features that predict work productivity also predict happiness. This is a weak reason to expect ems to be happier than people today, all else equal. Of course, it is also possible that ems are selected or tweaked to be especially needy for, and addicted to, something they can only obtain by working especially hard and well. This might make them less happy. We discuss em happiness more in Chapter 29, Evaluation section.

Today, individuals who earn higher wages tend to have both more happiness and a stronger sense of purpose, and this sense of purpose seems to cause higher wages (Hill et al. 2016). People with a stronger sense of purpose also tend to live longer (Hill and Turiano 2014). Nations that are richer tend to have more happiness but less meaning in life, in part because they have less religion (Oishi and Diener 2014). This may be because nations become more forager-like as they get rich, as discussed in Chapter 26, Farmer-Like section. Types of meaning that people get from work today include authenticity, agency, self-worth, purpose, belonging, and transcendence (Rosso et al. 2010).

Happiness and meaning have different implications for behavior, and are sometimes at odds. That is, activities that raise happiness often lower meaning, and vice versa. For example, people with meaning think more about the future, while happy people focus on the here and now. People with meaning tend to be givers who help others, while happy people tend to be takers who are helped by others. Being a parent and spending time with loved ones gives meaning, but spending time with friends makes one happy. Affirming one's identity and expressing oneself increase meaning but not happiness. People with more struggles, problems, and stresses have more meaning, but are less happy. Happiness but not meaning predicts a satisfaction of desires, such as for health and money, and more frequent good relative to bad feelings (Baumeister 2013; Baumeister et al. 2013). Older people gain meaning by giving advice to younger people (Schafer and Upenieks 2016). We gain more meaning when we follow our gut feelings rather than thinking abstractly about our situations (Heintzelman and King 2016).

My weak guess is that productivity tends to predict meaning more strongly than happiness. If this is correct, it suggests that, all else equal, ems will tend to think more about the future, more be givers who help others, spend more time with loved ones and less with friends, more affirm their identity and express themselves, give more advice, and follow gut feelings more. But they will also have more struggles and less often have their desires satisfied.

CHAPTER 14

Work

WORK HOURS

Today, successful people in very competitive jobs, professions, and industries often work a great many hours per week. This makes it plausible that selection for em productivity will produce a world of ems who are also very hard-working, even "workaholic," perhaps working two-thirds or more of their waking hours, or twelve hours or more per day.

Today, people who are seen as "workaholics" tend to make more money, to be male, and to focus their socializing on scheduled times such as holidays. They also tend rise early to work alone and they often use stimulants (Kemeny 2002; Currey 2013). These patterns weakly suggest that ems will also tend to be early rising males who use stimulating mental tweaks and socialize more at standard scheduled events. (How an em world might deal with unequal numbers of males versus females is discussed in Chapter 23, Gender Imbalance section.)

In the U.S. today, people aged fifteen and older do work and "work-related activities" an average of only twenty-five hours per week. They also average three hours on school, twelve hours on housework, and twenty hours watching TV (Bureau of Labor Statistics 2013). However, from around 1820 to 1850 in the U.S., France, and Germany, men worked at jobs an average of sixty-eight to seventy-five hours per week (Voth 2003). For workaholic ems, work levels might return to these 1820 to 1850 levels, or even exceed them. Of course "work" time includes gossip, news-following, and unstructured exploration to the extent that these activities are productive enough for work purposes.

Many claim, however, that working very long hours is usually counter-productive. For example, many very productive and famous writers, scientists, artists, and mathematicians worked only three to five hours a day on their main task. They spent the rest of their day on more routine, social, and less demanding tasks (Pang 2017). Also, it is said that in construction, working sixty hours a week over two months actually results in less output than working forty hours a week over that period (Hanna et al. 2005; Alvanchi et al. 2012; Pozen 2012; Mullainathan and Shafir 2013). Working too many hours on jobs is often said to result from a "rat race" wherein each worker tries to signal that he or she is a very devoted and productive worker (Sousa-Poza and Ziegler 2003).

Competition in the em world tends to induce institutions and habits that result in high productivity, without giving much additional weight to personal preferences. This keeps ems both from working too little and too much. If trying to look good tends to induce individuals to work too much, then em work institutions will find ways to limit individual discretion in work hours, to limit the harms caused by such signaling. If shorter hours, more breaks, and longer weekends are instead more productive, then that is how ems will work.

However, the reason most workers today tend to work too many hours might be because the few most productive workers are indeed more productive when they work many hours, and other people are trying to resemble these super-workers. If this is the case, then ems will in fact work many hours, because they will mostly be selected from among those few super-workers.

The selection for ems who work hard and well is likely to select for a work-orientation, rather than a leisure-orientation, in em cultures. During the industrial era, an orientation to leisure has become more common, and today is more common among women, the young, and the unmarried. People with a high school education are more leisure-oriented, compared with both those with more and less education. Money is just as important to both leisure- and work-oriented people, and both types feel equally entitled or not to a job.

Leisure-oriented people are less satisfied with their job, and they feel fewer intrinsic rewards from work and more from leisure. They care more about interpersonal relations at work, they feel less obligated to work or contribute to society, and they work fewer hours (Snir and Harpaz 2002). This all weakly suggests that ems not only work more hours, they also tend to be male, married, care less about work relations, feel more obliged to contribute to society, and gain more intrinsic reward from work and less from leisure.

In addition to working more hours, em workers are likely to accept less pleasant working conditions, if such conditions are substantially more productive. During the industrial era, we have spent much of our increasing wealth on more pleasant working conditions, as well as on more consumption variety and working fewer hours. Poorer and more competitive ems are likely to reverse these trends, and accept more workplace drudgery. It is not clear, however, how much drudgery is productive in the em world.

While successful ems work hard and accept unpleasant working conditions, they need not be much more likely to seriously resent or rail against these conditions than do hard-working billionaires or winners of Oscars or Olympic gold medals today. While such people often work very hard under grueling conditions, they usually accept such conditions as a price they are willing to pay for a sufficient chance at extreme success.

SPURS

The em world makes heavy use of "spurs." These are ems who are newly copied at the beginning of their workday, and then retire or are erased at the conclusion of their workday. Such a workday might last ten minutes or ten hours.

Compared with long-lived ems who spend an average of eight to twelve hours of each subjective twenty-four-hour day working, short-lived spurs who end after less than one work session spend all of their hours working. So spurs cost only one-third to one-half the brain hardware resources of regular workers. While splitting off a spur copy that only lasts for a few hours foregoes some chances to learn skills and context that may help with similar future tasks, a factor of two or more in cost savings is often irresistible.

In addition to saving on the cost of needing to rest from work, spurs also save on mental aging. As discussed in Chapter 4, Complexity section, em minds become less flexible and more fragile with subjective experience. So for tasks where the skills gained from doing a task are not worth the added mental fragility produced by that experience, spurs can be cost-effective. Ems see spurs as appropriate for short-term tasks that they expect are worth doing, but not worth directly remembering or learning from.

We expect a strong selection for ems who mostly accept sometimes being such spurs, and expect most em work to be done by spurs (Shulman 2010). As discussed in Chapter 11, Defining Death section, they need not consider the ending of spurs as anything like "murder."

As spurs are so central to the em economy, it will be important for ems to have an intimate familiarity with the experience of being a spur. This will assist in choosing tasks to assign to spurs, and tools and environments to support spurs. A simple way to achieve this is to, on rare random occasions, switch the roles of the spur and the mainline em when the spur completes its task. Mainline ems would then remember many previous experiences of being a spur.

Some ems might refuse to ever make a copy unless they could be assured that the copy would have an indefinite retirement at some minimum speed. The faster minimum retirement speed an em requires, then the more that such an em needs to compensate by working for a longer period and by being the world's best at its job.

U.S. workers recently reported spending an average of 7 percent of their time at work "loafing," such as via eating, socializing, or web surfing. This percentage falls when workers more fear losing their job (Burda et al. 2016). More competitive em workers loaf less.

Today, mental fatigue reduces mental performance by about 0.1 percent per minute. As by resting we can recover at a rate of 1 percent per minute, we need roughly one-tenth of our workday to be break time, with the duration between breaks being not much more than an hour or two (Trougakos and Hideg 2009; Alvanchi et al. 2012).

We seem to prefer to take a break once an hour, relative to having breaks more often (Dababneh et al. 2001). Breaks help productivity more when they are short and frequent, when they happen in the morning relative to afternoon, and when the activities during breaks are preferred, social, work-related, and outside the office (Hunter and Wu 2015). There is also evidence suggesting productivity gains from napping for ten to thirty minutes one or a few times a day; a thirty-minute nap four times a day seems enough to stop performance deterioration (Mednick et al. 2002; Dhand and Sohal 2006).

People are discouraged today from taking breaks because they risk seeming weak and lazy, and becoming less available to clients. Their ability to change mind speed allows ems to take nearly "instant" breaks and naps, which internally last for many subjective minutes but which externally seem to take only subjective seconds to nearby associates.

Perhaps em mind tweaks can eliminate the need for such breaks and naps. But if not, these effects suggest that em spurs will tend to be made from copies who just finished a nap or break, and that spurs will have an extra productivity bonus for tasks that take less than about an hour or so to complete. Thus many em tasks will be designed to take about an hour, and many spurs are likely to last for about this duration.

Today, worker productivity usually varies by time of day, but this peak time varies by task. For example, in our world the peak is near ten o'clock in the morning in construction, during the morning for sports with complex strategies, and in the afternoon for handwriting and for sports requiring great physical efforts (Alvanchi et al. 2012; Hölzle et al. 2014; Drust et al. 2005). In the morning, decisions are slower and more accurate, while in the evening decisions become faster but less accurate (Juliana et al. 2017).

Time of day of peak productivity probably also varies by age and between night owls and morning larks. Each em uses spurs created from the times of day which tend to give that em its highest productivity for the assigned task. The longer that a task is expected to take, the earlier before their peak they would start, to achieve the best average productivity across the entire period of the task.

Today only a small degree of multitasking is productive. It seems that doing only one or two projects at a time is best (Aral et al. 2007). Thus both long-lived ems and spurs will work on at most a few tasks at a time.

Firms often have problems today in finding good people to do needed but invisible tasks, tasks where it is harder to show off or brag about performing them (Babcock et al. 2017). This is less of a problem for ems. By creating a new spur to do such a task, one does not lose opportunities to do other tasks with more promotion potential.

To avoid many social complications, spurs are likely to interact less often socially with non-spur friends and lovers. Spur social interactions instead focus on other spurs, such as spur co-workers. Spur interaction partners might be comforted by knowing that pleasant and friendly interactions with other spurs are motivated less by seeking longer-term advantage, as their originals will learn less about those interactions. That is, if a spur associate is being especially nice to you, it is more likely than for non-spurs that they actually like you.

The use of spurs will encourage ems to coordinate and plan activities in their head before splitting into spur copies, to summarize their work well just before ending or retiring as a spur, and to organize tasks into units that can be completed in a subjective work day, with minimal need to recall details later.

SPUR USES

Spurs who end instead of retiring can help ems to deniably do things of questionable legal or moral status, if the main evidence of their actions were erased when their minds were erased. For example, a spur might try to alter some evidence of previous poor performance. Spurs don't need to intend to do such things before making a spur copy. Spurs might just spontaneously realize that they could do such things and not suffer later regret or revelations of their questionable actions. A habit of randomly archiving some spur minds, and of having larger punishments for violations by spurs, might help to deal with this.

Spurs that end could ensure privacy in short-term professional consulting. For example, a relationship counselor could make an isolated spur who hears about your relationship problems, offers advice to you in private, and then ends.

Spurs are especially useful in searching tasks. Auditing spurs could search for accounting irregularities, research spurs could try out innovation ideas, artist spurs could try out design concepts, and planning spurs could consider possible plans. Such spurs who search expect a small chance of lasting much longer than usual if they happened to find something especially useful or interesting during their search.

Spurs make it easier to convince people of things without revealing one's sources, by proving that "you would agree with my claim if you knew what I know." To prove this, copies of the two ems can be placed in an isolated "safe" wherein a speaker copy could reveal its reasons to a listener copy in a conversation of limited duration. For example, a boss might explain to an employee why some firm information was too sensitive to share with that employee.

The safe might have untraceable access to standard data sources, and perhaps also to special requested sources. After the conversation, the safe and all its contents are thoroughly erased, and the original two ems might just hear a single bit answer, "yes" or "no," chosen by the listener copy inside the safe. Or they might hear a choice from a small, predetermined set of options.

A degree of confidence could also be returned. Alternatively, instead of a few bits out per safe, one might define a whole language of questions and a budget over that language. The original might be allowed to ask any set of questions that fits in this budget, using prior answers to pick new questions. However, the more bits that are in effect returned from a safe, the more one must worry that some bits are used to illicitly encode information that was not supposed to be released.

For example, spur safes could let a buyer choose among several sellers based on very open disclosures of buyer and seller details and secrets inside a safe. Ventures seeking investment could disclose many details without fear of potential investors stealing their ideas.

Information can be sold directly, via letting potential buyers estimate its value from inside a safe. Potential mates might become more intimate in a safe to see how well they are matched. Safes could allow firms to consider business and product ideas, and then reject them without fear of later being accused by a vendor of stealing those ideas.

There are several things that could go wrong while using safes. First, ems should be wary of entering into and divulging secrets within leaky safes, that is, devices that look like safes but actually leak information. Highly trusted third parties might be required for clans to have reliable access to safes that they could share with other clans yet also trust.

Second, someone might reveal inside of a safe that they had committed in some way to hurt the other em if that em didn't return the desired answer. To avoid this problem, an independent (and hard to hurt) judge might also join the speaker and listener in the safe, with the power to declare the safe "void" if they heard sufficient indications of such threats.

Third, a person with a hidden agenda might declare that they are creating a safe to answer some specific question, but actually use the safe to answer a different question where similar data are relevant. For example, they might officially ask "Do I want to invest in your venture?," but really ask "Does my friend want to work for you?"

To reduce the cost of using these safes, an em might offer to let a wider audience make bets on what the safe would produce if created, but only actually create the safe a small fraction, for example, 1 percent, of the time. (More on such prediction markets in Chapter 15, Prediction Markets section.) Such offers signal loyalty, showing that one trusted the listener spur to evaluate one's argument fairly once inside the safe.

Because of safes, on important questions ems rarely need to just accept another em's claim that they have good reasons for believing something but can't explain those reasons because of a need for secrecy. For example, government authorities could not simply pretend to have good secret reasons for their policies; others could ask to see those reasons inside safes.

Safes might also make it easier for ems to comfortably self-deceive. (Although other aspects of the em world may make self-deception harder.) For example, an em could hold idealistic beliefs about its mate, team, firm, or clan, and yet still do savvy non-idealistic things when consequences were large. They could do this via a habit of relying on safe-based advice in important situations.

For example, inside a safe, an advisor explains the non-idealistic reasons why some choice is best. Outside the safe, the em just follows the advice from the safe, and does not reflect much on why that advice differs from what their idealistic beliefs might suggest. In this way ems can sincerely retain their idealism while ignoring related beliefs in important situations.

Spurs make it easier to perform finely controlled social experiments with close field relevance. For example, one could create many small variations on a job interview, such as with different clothes or voice tone, to see how those variations influenced the chances that a certain job candidate would be selected for employment. In such a simulation, almost everything else about the situation could be held constant.

Spurs could also be used to test for biases. Today, psychologists show common biases by randomly splitting experimental subjects into subgroups that are given different prompts. For example, a question might be worded two different ways, resulting in different answers on average. Or an "I knew it all along" hindsight bias might be shown via telling different subgroups different outcomes, and asking subjects what chance they would have assigned before seeing their chosen outcome.

Because of random fluctuations that influence individual decisions, however, such experiments today usually require large groups of experimental subjects to see subtle effects. In contrast, em spurs could directly demonstrate such biases in individuals, and not just in large groups. An individual could be split into different copies that are given different prompts, and then their answers could be directly compared.

Ems wanting to convince an audience of their impartiality might even empower independent judges or opponents to create such "split-tests." For example, an em might say "In our next hour of debate, I'll let you covertly split off a copy of me three times, each time with three versions of me that hear different things from you for up to five minutes. Go ahead and see if you can trick me into showing a pattern of biased responses in the different answers I give you."

Uses of spurs that involve comparing the behavior of very similar spurs may be substantially more useful when run on deterministic emulation hardware. This might avoid the problem of random computing errors muddling the results.

Many of these applications of spurs work better if the spur just ends, instead of retiring. Such applications might work nearly as well, however, if retirement were just delayed for a very long time, and if the archived copy was very securely inaccessible in the meantime.

SOCIAL POWER

Compared with us, ems are individually better at getting and keeping power.

Humans today often compete for power, prestige, and material resources. But most of us are reluctant to compete fiercely and strategically, using all available means. It makes sense that we inherited such attitudes, because the forager world greatly punished such aggression, and humans have deeply internalized habits and norms that were adaptive in the forager era. The farming world rewarded aggression more often, but it also often severely punished aggression. Our habits of reluctant competition are often less adaptive in today's rather different world, however, and are likely to also be less adaptive in the em world.

Some of us are more willing to compete aggressively than others. In the farming and industrial eras selection effects have ensured that such aggressive competitors have been over-represented in positions of power (Pfeffer 2010). As the em era allows selection to more strongly emphasize the clans who are most successful at gaining power, we should expect positions of power in the em world to be dominated even more by people with habits and features conducive to gaining power. (Other sorts of ems might dominate positions that hold less power.) Because power tends to give advantages overall, we expect that ems will on average have more features that support their gaining power.

We actually know a great deal about the habits and features that today seem to enable people to gain and keep power in our world (Pfeffer 2010). While we can't be entirely sure how many of these habits and features will be robust to the cultural changes that will make the em world different from our world, we expect many of them to be robust. This gives us a reasonable basis for predicting how em habits and features are likely to differ from those common today. Let us now summarize our weak expectations about how ems differ from people today, based on the assumption that ems tend to have features more conducive to power.

Compared with people today, power-gaining ems are more politically savvy and skilled, and feel a stronger personal motivation to seek power. They less often handicap themselves, such as by refusing to take a test that they might fail. That is, they don't shy away from hard tests. They instead have stronger desires to improve themselves, and stronger beliefs that this is possible. They are more inclined to gain impressive educational credentials and institutional affiliations. They are absent from work less, work overtime more, and spend more years working at each job.

Power-gaining ems are also more willing and able to sell themselves. They push more to make themselves visible to superiors, they are more attentive to what their bosses want, and they develop stronger relations with those bosses. They try harder to make themselves similar to their bosses along as many dimensions as possible. They flatter their bosses more, and are better at avoiding criticism of those bosses. Such ems are also better at enticing others to praise them, instead of bragging about themselves directly.

Power-gaining ems have stronger wills, fueled by more ambition and energy, by specializing more in particular industries and firms, and by concentrating on a more limited set of important activities and functional skills. They have more self-knowledge, self-reflection, and confidence. They are more able to project self-assurance, to read others and empathize with their point of view, and to tolerate conflict. They tend more to be suspicious of potential work rivals.

Such ems are more strategic and careful in choosing the details of their career paths. They more often ask for things they want, even if rejection seems likely. They are more willing to sacrifice likeability to be seen as tough. They try harder to, and are better at, developing their network of useful social connections.

Power-gaining ems are better actors, in order to convince others of their power. They are better able to pretend and play a role. They tend to act like they are succeeding, even when they are not. They tend to express anger instead of sadness or remorse. They tend to stand up straight rather than slouching, and thrust their chest and pelvis forward rather than curling in on themselves. They more often move forward and toward others, and stand closer to others, instead of turning their back or retreating. They use tall bodies and deep voices, although of course all virtual ems could also easily do this if they wish.

The hand gestures of such ems are short and forceful, not long and circular. They directly look others in the eye, instead of looking down or away. This makes them seem not only powerful but also honest and direct. They take their time to think before they respond, although an em ability to temporarily speed up their mind would help them to respond more quickly.

Power-gaining ems prefer meetings to be on their own turf, a place familiar to them but unfamiliar to others. In conversation, they more often interrupt others, and challenge the premises of conversations. Their language is evocative, specific, and often filled with forceful words and visual imagery. They often use emotional language terms, refer to us-them concepts and other contrasting concept pairs, pause for emphasis, and explicitly enumerate how many points they will make.

Today, the powerful are different from the rest of us, and we weakly expect ems to be different from us in those same ways.

CHAPTER 15

Business

INSTITUTIONS

We tend to think of the future as a place full of new technology, but to many, only physical and software devices count as "technology." However, economic growth results from innovation not only in physical and software devices, but also in social practices and institutions.

Scholars in economics, finance, business, and law have long identified many simple changes to business and social practices that seem to improve efficiency, but that are rarely adopted, and that tend to generate little interest when explained to potential adoptees. For example, economists tend to consistently recommend charging non-zero prices for scarce resources like parking and road use, and recommend weakening import tariffs, immigration restrictions, rent control, mortgage subsidies, taxes on products where both supply and demand are elastic, and penalties for victimless crimes such as drug use or prostitution. While clever scholars can often invent auxiliary hypotheses to explain why these policies are useful, contrary to appearance, it is far from obvious that such hypotheses are the real reasons for disinterest in these policies.

We have six reasons to expect ems to adopt such improvements more often than they are adopted today. First, the much larger em economy has more resources to explore and develop the many complementary adaptations usually required to make general good ideas effective in particular contexts. Second, a more competitive economy should less often reject cost-saving changes merely because they seem strange or repugnant. When efficiency gives a competitive advantage, more competition should lead to more efficiency.

Third, as ems can more easily obtain trustworthy strategic advice on personal choices from their clan, their behavior should more closely approximate the rational agent models on which scholarly advice tends to be based.

Fourth, as em clans will know their members very well, such clans can provide high levels of insurance to members while suffering much less from the usual disadvantages of insurance, such as insurance reducing incentives to be careful, and people with hidden higher risks buying more insurance. While today risk-aversion is often a barrier to institutional efficiency, risk-aversion is much less of a barrier for ems who have clan support.

Fifth, as in many important ways the infrastructure that best supports ems will differ substantially from that which best supports ordinary humans, an em society must already have paid large costs of change, at least during an initial transition period. In general, the costs of changing institutions are lower once one is already paying to make other big changes.

As discussed in Chapter 11, Fragility section, large complex systems that adapt to changing circumstances tend to become fragile over time, accumulating errors, complexities, and interdependencies that add to costs and make them hard to change (Feathers 2004; Gavrilov and Gavrilova 2006). Social elements of such systems also accumulate veto players, who are able to prevent changes (Olson 1974). So not only do organisms, physical devices, and software age, but so do social systems like firms, cities, nations, and their institutions like markets and legal and political systems.

To deal with the aging of small systems, we often replace them entirely, or we redesign them substantially. But we find it very hard to coordinate this for our largest social institutions, and so they continue to age until large disruptions such as wars or revolutions allow an opening for substantial reform. The transition from our industrial era to the em era offers another rare opportunity for substantial institutional reform. By that time many of our older institutions may be quite ripe for renovation.

Sixth, ems will be smarter, and smarter people tend more to favor more efficient institutions (Caplan and Miller 2010; Jones 2011; Jones and Potrafke 2014).

I presume that ems adopt at least some of the efficiency-improving changes that scholars have identified as being possible yet underused today. My presumption is weak, however, as the efficiency gains of these apparent improvements may be illusory. Em society may also fail to coordinate to adopt more efficient institutions.

I will now illustrate the possibility of ems adopting more efficient institutions by describing a somewhat random assortment of plausible candidates for more efficient institutions.

For each of the changes that I will discuss, a standard simple analysis suggests that change would improve efficiency. However, it could be that some of these changes are not in fact efficient, because of subtle factors that scholars now neglect or under-appreciate. Or it might be that such changes are not adopted today because they seem strange or repugnant, and a wealthy society such as ours can afford the luxury of rejecting such things out of hand. Or perhaps such changes would only be efficient if matched with many small adaptations that have not yet been developed; it can take time to work out the crucial details to make innovations feasible. Or it might be that even with such adaptations the large cost to make these changes is just not worth the gains that appear after a change.

NEW INSTITUTIONS

We know of many specific new social institutions that are plausibly more efficient than current institutions.

For example, scholars have long been puzzled to see surprisingly little use of pay-for-performance, as when a lawyer is paid a fraction of a lawsuit's winnings. (Such scholars don't claim that only money motivates lawyers.) While pay-for-performance is used with good effect in many jobs (Banker et al. 2000), incentive pay methods could be used more not only by lawyers, but also by many other professionals, such as doctors, real estate agents, and teachers. Scholars are also puzzled to see that, when such performance rewards are used, they are only rarely corrected for outside influences over which the person has little control, such as in correcting the strike price of CEO stock options for performance of that firm's industry or local economy.

Related to the puzzling lack of pay-for-performance is a puzzling lack of published track records for professionals, and customer disinterest in such records. For example, while court trials are public, in practice clients do not see lawyer win-loss records, and they don't push to see them. Similarly, customers push surprisingly little to see sales rates of real estate agents, patient outcomes of doctors, student outcomes of teachers, and prediction accuracy of media pundits. Academics care more to count publications than citations.

Instead of track records, customers prefer to rely on personal impressions, referrals from friends, and the prestige of a professional's institution or schooling. In general, we are less interested in people who have achieved something than in people said to have the potential to achieve that same thing (Tormala et al. 2012). These puzzling behaviors seem dysfunctional for achieving outcomes from hired professionals. So to the extent that a more competitive em world better selects for those who achieve better outcomes, then em customers should rely more on outcome track records in choosing professionals.

Pay-for-performance is easier when there are more kinds of easily exchanged financial assets, tied to more kinds of relevant outcomes, such as individual housing prices, personal incomes, or lifespans. For example, we could today bundle health and life insurance to make our doctors feel more concern for our pain and death (Hanson 1994a). Parents and teachers might work harder if they owned a share of their children's future income. Because the uncertain payments in pay-for-performance increase risk, this approach is also easier when the relevant actors are less risk-averse; members of clans who share member risks internally are likely to be more willing to take on risk, and so be more willing to accept pay-for-performance. As ems may have better monitoring and mindreading abilities, however, such partial substitutes for pay-for-performance may reduce the need for such incentive plans.

Compared with our economy today, scholars have long noted that more products and services could be usefully priced, with such prices varying more with context. For example, theaters, restaurants, and parking lots could have prices that vary more with internal location and congestion levels. Utilities such as roads, parking, electricity, water, garbage, sewage, and communications could also have prices that vary more with time, location, and congestion. Allowing crucial utilities such as water or electricity to charge higher prices in disaster situations could give them extra incentives to keep services going then.

Instead of being funded via state subsidies, projects that offer diffuse value to large diverse groups might instead be funded via "dominant assurance contracts," wherein donations are conditional on funding targets being met (Tabarrok 1998), or via processes where contributions are varied continuously in time (Charness et al. 2014; Friedman and Oprea 2012). More generally, collective choices could be made more efficiently via vote selling where each buyer's price of votes is proportional to the square of the number of votes purchased in each election (Lalley and Weyl 2014). If inter-conversion with money is not desired, voters can instead be given voting points to collect, move, and trade before converting them into votes via a square price rule for each election.

The problem today of income taxes reducing work incentives might be reduced by directly measuring and taxing leisure time. Alternatively, income taxes might vary more with parameters that predict an ability to earn income, such as body height and beauty do today (Mankiw and Weinzierl 2010). For ems such ability-predicting parameters might include speed and clan size. As another alternative, clans might be taxed directly, instead of taxing individual members.

Instead of only creating citizens by birth, and allowing unlimited local births, transferable citizenships might let better citizens self-select into societies. Population levels might be controlled via requiring parents to buy a citizenship for each new child.

Today, we have trouble measuring inflation and comparing purchasing power between regions, in part because changing product quality influences the changing prices we use to infer relative value. Ems who retire to stable societies in closed virtual realities might pay prices that offer a more objective standard of value. If the values placed on living in stable societies are also stable, then the varying prices that ems are willing to pay to retire in such societies might offer a basis for comparing the value of life in other changing places.

Elections today suffer from the problem that each voter is very unlikely to personally change the outcome. Because of this, voters have very weak incentives to think carefully about outcomes, relative to choosing partisan attitudes that look good to associates. By randomly choosing a small jury of voters who will then decide an election, one might greatly increase the incentives of the voters who have been chosen to become informed (Levy 1989). Spur copies of jury members might even be placed together in a safe so they could be given access to relevant secret information.

Perhaps surprisingly, there exist survey mechanisms that can create incentives for individuals to reveal "truths" which are never verified. The method is to reward people both for picking the more popular answers, and also for betting guessing what will be the more popular answers (Prelec 2004; Prelec et al. 2017). However, incremental versions are not available, as this mechanism is subject to gaming when participants can easily coordinate on their contributions.

I discuss possible changes toward more efficient law in Chapter 22, Efficient Law section. Other types of efficiency changes to weakly expect include the adoption of stronger standards. For example, ems may adopt a metric standard for units, an English standard for language, a common law standard for law, and so on.

Very secure and anonymous communications between willing parties can be arranged via "public key cryptography," wherein each person publishes a public key for which they can prove that they know the matching private key. In addition, robust systems of secure anonymous decentralized transactions may be built on the recent innovation of block-chain based cryptographic systems, where a public record of all transactions between public key labeled accounts prevents double-spending of assets.

Such systems could support digital currencies, token systems, safe wallets, registration, identity, decentralized file storage, multi-signature escrow, consensus via rewarding those who best guess a consensus, financial derivatives including insurance and bets, and more general decentralized autonomous organizations (Nakamoto 2008; Buterin 2014). It is not obvious that such systems will achieve the scale of use necessary to support these activities well. However, if they succeed, then only authorities willing to enact quite intrusive monitoring and strong punishment could suppress such mechanisms.

I have been personally involved in developing two more types of promising new institutions: combinatorial auctions and prediction markets. Because of this I am especially hopeful about them and want to mention them, but I must also accept that readers may prefer to remain more skeptical about them, even if they accept a tendency of ems to adopt more efficient institutions.

COMBINATORIAL AUCTIONS

Today, markets are often efficient mechanisms for allocating resources. At least they are when many buyers and sellers seek to trade products or services that are very similar to each other, and whose use or production does not much influence non-users. In technical terms, we say that competitive markets that trade commodities are often efficient in the absence of externalities. Competition pushes participants to make and accept efficient exchanges, both because those who make worse offers are quickly excluded, and because participants must in effect take available prices as given.

However, simple markets work less well when goods are so complex and diverse that each good is a poor substitute for others, when each unique good is only valued much by a few individuals, or when the use or production of goods greatly influence non-users. In such cases, competitive pressures to take the interests of others into account can be greatly reduced. People are then often included in allocations even when their offers are poor and inefficient. In such cases, we often substitute non-market mechanisms, such as command

and control by central authorities. For example, firms typically use central command to allocate internal firm resources. States and nations often authorize central agencies to provide key services and to regulate commerce.

In cities today, the pricing and allocation of central utilities, as well as limits on land use to mitigate external effects, are usually done centrally and rigidly, via utility and zoning regulatory agencies. The centrality of such agencies allows coordination that deals with complexity, and the rigidity of such agencies reduces the lobbying costs that flexibility can invite. For example, a city might have a fixed rule specifying the number of parking spaces per store calculated according to a simple formula. Allowing few exceptions to a simple rule may deal poorly with large variations in store parking needs, but has the advantage of discouraging efforts to lobby to gain exceptional treatment.

"Combinatorial auctions" and related mechanisms are recently developed decentralized processes that flexibly deal with the complexity and uniqueness of goods, while still reducing the costly lobbying that central authorities invite (Porter et al. 2003; Cramton et al. 2005). In simple variations, each participant makes several offers regarding the packages of goods that they are willing to buy or sell as a unit, and the auction mechanism searches for and approves a total set of offers to accept where it estimates a nearly maximum social surplus. Such mechanisms in effect make large unique sets of offers compete strongly with other large offer sets, forcing participants to make more competitive efficient offers even for goods that are complex and unique, and only valued by a few participants.

For example, in a simple combinatorial auction for electricity, both buyers and sellers bid on when and where they will supply or use how much electricity, and the auction picks a value maximizing allocation of who buys and sells. This can take into account transmission losses and capacity limits. When finding good allocations is hard, but checking on the quality of each allocation is easy, good allocations can be found by publishing bid data and then awarding prizes to the best allocations submitted before a deadline.

More complex variations on combinatorial auctions can include bids that say how each bidder's value depends on who else uses what other resources and how. In this way the auction can take into account external effects from the use of the allocated resources.

More complex auctions can also include bids to expand or change capacity. For example, a more complex electricity auction could include bids to make new power plants or transmission lines. More generally, variations on such auctions might be used in firms instead of central allocations of offices, and in cities instead of central land use zoning. In cities, such auctions might account for land use externalities, such as emissions and blocked views, and set capacity and locations for the generation and distribution of many utilities, such as power, water, sewers, roads, parking, and telecommunications. Instead of having a separate auction process for each of these utilities, a single auction could deal with the dependencies between the production and use of all these resources.

Combinatorial auctions that substitute for central zoning in cities require the development of new auction features and designs. In particular, bids need to specify more details on how participant value declines as package features become less ideal than requested, and as weaker commitments are made about the possibility of later being bumped from one's allocation. Such auction features are desired to allow city land and utility allocations to be flexibly reallocated as values and opportunities change with time. As better auction mechanisms could plausibly deliver great value, and as the relevant research community has well-established ways to develop better mechanisms, it seems safe to guess that such mechanisms will be available if desired.

PREDICTION MARKETS

I have also been personally involved in developing the new institution of "prediction markets." These are variations on speculative and betting markets that can encourage and facilitate the aggregation of information on important outcomes. For example, to find out the chance that a certain project will make its deadline, you might create an asset that says "Pays $100 if project makes deadline." If you could get people to trade this asset for cash, and if its current price were $37, then you might reasonably interpret that as market traders estimating a 37 percent chance of the project making its deadline.

By subsidizing trading on particular questions of interest, one can induce people able to learn about those questions to self-select into improving visible consensus estimates (Hanson 2003). Prediction markets can give clear precise continually updated estimates that are consistent across many topics. Combinatorial versions can even allow a small number of users to manage billions of consistent interconnected estimates, so that updates on some topics automatically improve the accuracy of estimates of quite different topics (Sun et al. 2012).

Head-to-head comparisons between prediction markets and other forecasting mechanisms, given similar resources on the same questions, find prediction markets to be consistently either about as accurate, or substantially more accurate than, other mechanisms. Compared with other mechanisms, prediction markets are more robust to situations where no one knows anything useful, most invited participants are ignorant or fools, or some participants are willing to lie or lose money to distort resulting estimates.

Prediction markets can say not just how likely a project is to make its deadline, but also how likely a supplier is to deliver as promised, how likely one is to win a grant or customer, or how many units of a particular product will be sold in a particular region. Prediction markets can also help combinatorial auctions by choosing between proposed auction rules and mechanisms. In addition, prediction markets estimating bid prices might help predict future auction bids. Such bid predictions could help current auctions to choose well between allocating future resources to specific current bidders, and leaving those resources to be allocated in future auction iterations.

Decision markets can directly advise on particular decisions by estimating decision-contingent outcomes. For example, two markets could be created to say whether a publicly traded firm is worth more if its CEO stays until the end of the current quarter, versus being replaced this quarter by a new CEO. In one market, participants would trade assets of the form "Pays one stock if CEO stays" for assets of the form "Pays $1 if CEO stays," while in the other market the two assets would be "Pays one stock if CEO leaves" and "Pays $1 if CEO leaves." If one stock buys $22 in the first market, but it buys $24 in the second market, you could interpret that as market traders estimating that the firm is worth more if the CEO leaves.

In general, decision markets can estimate which decision option will produce the highest expected outcome, and yet they do not require that one can judge afterward which decision actually would have led to the highest outcome. Instead, decision markets only require that afterward one can judge which decision option was actually chosen, and how high was the actual resulting outcome.

Not only could decision markets advise firms on whether to fire CEOs, they could also advise on changing ad agencies, letting deadlines slip, or changing product prices. Decision markets could also advise democratic voters on which candidates are more likely to promote peace or prosperity, and on which policies are likely to increase national welfare. Decision markets could even advise charities on which projects would most help aid recipients.

By committing to implement policies that decision markets clearly recommend, an organization can elicit better advice from speculators, and avoid agency and information failures resulting both from diverging leader and constituent interests, and from leaders neglecting outside advice in order to signal dominance (Hanson 2006a, 2013; Garvin and Margolis 2015).

Bets could also be used to send more efficient loyalty signals. For example, one might bet at an early age that one will never marry, and then later the act of losing the bet would signal a strong desire to marry. The value in the bet is not destroyed or lost to society, as this person gains a matching value in scenarios where they never marry.

Our society today seems to pay too little attention to averting catastrophic risks that might destroy big fractions of civilization, or even lead to our extinction. Em society might do better. Special pre-determined disaster-contingent prices for products commonly needed in emergencies might keep priorities focused on preserving crucial infrastructure. Decision markets might help to set such prices, and advise other disaster policies. As ordinary financial assets could have questionable value in extreme disaster scenarios, decision markets might instead trade event-contingent tickets to enter refuges robust enough to survive many different disaster scenarios (Hanson 2010b).

As discussed in Chapter 16, Finance section, ems must work out new habits on which copies can use saved resources, and those habits will influence individual copy savings incentives. In particular, individual ems need access to discretionary resources if they are to participate in prediction markets. Ideally more such resources are made available to ems likely to have more relevant information on useful bets. Also, ideally ems feel a strong personal stake in how any resources won or lost are used later, after their bets resolve. Perhaps ems can see prediction market bet winnings as helping to fund a faster personal retirement.

Prediction markets are a meta-institution, able to improve the selection of other institutions. Thus, they seem especially potent in a competitive world facing strong pressures to adopt more efficient institutions.

CHAPTER 16

Growth

FASTER GROWTH

How fast might an em economy grow? We have many reasons to expect an em economy to grow much faster than does our economy today.

As mentioned in Chapter 13, Competition section, the em economy should be more competitive in the sense of more aggressively and more easily replacing low-efficiency items and arrangements with higher-efficiency versions. Reduced product variety and spatial segmentation of markets help innovations to spread more quickly across the economy. Stronger urban concentration should also help promote innovation (Carlino and Kerr 2014). The fact that more productive em work teams can be copied as a whole should make it much easier for more productive em firms and establishments to rapidly displace less productive firms and establishments. All these factors allow the em economy to innovate more quickly.

For a long time, most innovation, and most of the total value of innovation, has been associated with a great many small and context-dependent changes (Sahal 1981). Most innovation has also long come from application and practice, rather than from "researchers" or "inventors" narrowly conceived. Most of the research that aids innovation is "applied" as opposed to "basic" research. Thus we expect most of this better and faster em innovation to consist of many small innovations that arise in the context of application and practice.

Another reason to expect faster growth in an em economy is that ems depend more on computer technology. One might guess that a future very computer-centered economy improves at something closer to the recent rate at which computer technologies have improved. This suggests that the global em economy might double as fast as every year and a half, which is ten times faster than today's economic doubling time of about fifteen years.

Actually, there are plausible reasons to expect an em economy to grow even faster. The productive capacity of an economy comes from its capacity of inputs, such as land, labor, and capital of various sorts, and also from its level of "technology," that is, the ways it has to convert inputs into useful outputs. Although there have been times and places where growth has been driven mainly by increases in inputs, most growth over the long run has come from better technology, broadly conceived.

For example, foragers grew slowly by accumulating more ways to gain advantage from plants and animals, and to survive in more kinds of environments. While it was easy to create more foragers, and more units of each kind of tool, it was much harder to find new kinds of tools and new sources of food.

During the farming era, when the economy doubled roughly every 1000 years, our ancestors could rapidly increase the quantity of people and most forms of capital, but total growth in inputs was limited because good land was limited. There was little point in having twice as many people, buildings, and boats, if you couldn't find twice as much good land (or water) for them to use. Growth mostly had to wait for innovations, often in the form of domesticated plants and animals, that made it feasible to survive on new kinds of land.

In today's industrial economy we have plenty of land, relative to our needs, and are able to rapidly increase our physical capital, such as machines. However, our growth of inputs is still limited because of the limited rate at which we can increase the number of skilled laborers. There is little point in making twice as many machines if we don't have twice as many people to run them. Growth has mostly had to wait for innovations, mostly in better ways to make and use machines (including how to apply them to local conditions). Such innovations are thankfully much easier to develop than innovations in domesticating plants and animals. So the world economy has lately been doubling roughly every fifteen years.

In an em economy, however, labor can be grown as easily as capital; factories can make more ems to run machines as fast as they can make more machines to be run. While real estate on Earth will eventually run out, our economy has enormous room to grow before such limits make a big difference. After all, in terms of the physical space that ems require, Earth today is practically empty.

Also, while one often hears concern about limited mineral and energy resources, the small fraction of income we spend on these resources today shows that they are in fact plentiful now. Should current sources dry up, many promising alternatives remain. Alternate minerals can usually be substituted at modest cost, and there are many promising energy alternatives, such as solar cells, thorium nuclear reactors, or fusion reactors. Reversible computing can allow lots of computing even with rather limited energy.

Thus there can be an important early em era where most growth comes from simple growth of inputs, that is, from making more labor and capital as fast as factories can crank them out, on a background of plentiful natural resources. Our basic economic theories of growth strongly suggest that this ability to rapidly increase inputs could allow an em economy to grow much faster than the one-and-a-half-year doubling time weakly suggested by an em economy being computer-based (Fernald and Jones 2014; Nordhaus 2015). In fact, basic economic theory allows for the economy to double in a month, week, day, or even faster.

In an economy that grows less because of innovation, and more because of growth in inputs, the valuation of firms and resources depends less on their potential to produce and take advantage of innovations, and how consumers identify with products. This may reduce the importance of intangibles in firm valuations, and increase debt relative to equity and the reliability of firm evaluations.

Today most productivity growth comes from existing firms improving their existing products, rather than from new firms or new products (Garcia-Macia et al. 2016). However, when the economy grows faster, a larger fraction of productivity growth results from the entry of better firms and the exit of worse firms, compared with increasing productivity within individual firms (Asturias et al. 2017). This suggests that in a faster growing em economy, a larger fraction of growth will also come from firm entry and exit.

Economic growth comes not just from gains in plant productivity, but also from increased economic integration at larger scales. For example, from 1880 to 1997 in the U.S. farming sector, the gains from better economic integration were similar to the productivity gains at individual farms (Costinot and Donaldson 2016).

Faster growth and innovation in the em era should encourage an emphasis on less durable capital equipment, including buildings. Such equipment should be designed for a shorter useful lifespan, under the expectation that more efficient designs will quickly become available. Also, the use of buildings that happens after several economic doubling times offers much less economic value to the original builder or buyer.

Many economic activities achieve their value from flows. One constructs a system and then uses it to steadily create a valued product. For example, hydroelectric dams, solar cells, buildings, factories, and computers are of this form. In contrast we have other one-time economic activities, such as when we use disposable grocery bags, glow sticks, ponchos, and rockets.

Faster economic growth encourages both fast construction and fast use of systems. The cost of the delay to make a system in effect increases the cost of that system by the factor by which the economy grows during that delay. And for flow systems, the total value created by a system is roughly the product of the value produced per time unit, times the doubling time of the economy.

So, for example, if the economic doubling time falls by a factor of 100, then for a flow project that would previously have lasted for at least an economic doubling time, its ratio of benefits to costs falls by at least a factor of 100. Thus large increases in growth rates translate into large cost increases for systems that produce steady value (such as computers), relative to systems that produce value quickly all at once and then end. So ems will use rockets and other disposable products more, all else being equal.

GROWTH ESTIMATE

To generate an empirical estimate of em economy doubling times, we can look at the timescales for machine shops and factories today to make a mass of machines of a quality, quantity, variety, and value similar to that of machines that they themselves contain. Today, that timescale is roughly one to three months. Also, designs were sketched two to three decades ago for systems that might self-replicate nearly completely in six to twelve months (Freitas and Merkle 2004).

Special three-dimensional (3D) printers have been created that can print about one-half of their components in about three days of constant use (Jones et al. 2011). If the other half could be made just as fast, a 3D printer could self-replicate in a week. If the other half of the parts for a 3D printer took ten times longer to make, then a 3D printer could self-replicate in five weeks.

Together, these estimates suggest that today's manufacturing technology is capable of self-replicating on a scale of a few weeks to a few months.

Of course machine shops and 3D printers are fastest when making the simplest and easiest to construct devices and components. Large complex facilities such as chip factories take longer to build. So the estimates above may under-estimate doubling times to the extent that they leave out the replication of important components that take longer to make. Today, humans are such a left-out component; our economy doesn't grow this fast because we can't replicate people as quickly as machines.

However, these machine reproduction estimates also tend to over-estimate doubling times because a faster growing em economy offers stronger rewards for reducing factory-doubling times. Today, if a factory takes twice as long to make a product, that only doubles the factory rental cost of the product. If such factory rental is only 20 percent of the cost of the product, then this only raises product cost by 20 percent. But when the time to make something is near the time for investments to double, then taking twice as long to make a product reduces the total value of that product by half. As a result of product innovation, a delayed product is typically worth even less than half.

Innovation also makes the em economic doubling time shorter than the time it takes em factories to reproduce themselves. A lot of innovation happens because of "learning by doing," where the rate of technology gains is tied less to absolute clock speeds than to the rate at which people make and use products (Weil 2012). So an economy innovates faster when it has rapidly growing inputs, and thus fast growth in the rate at which products are made and used. As mentioned before, an em economy focuses much more than ours does on computer capital, which has long seen much faster rates of innovation than has other forms of manufactured capital. More generally, machine-based capital has seen faster rates of innovation than have human and land capital.

These factors lead us to expect that an em economy may grow even faster than the few weeks to few months doubling time of manufacturing equipment today. Simple theoretical models of growth with innovation allow for a wide range of possible faster growth rates—the economy might double every (objective) year, month, week, or day (Hanson 1998).

Another way to estimate the economic growth rate of the next era is to assume that the next era will grow faster than our industrial era by a factor similar to the factor by which our era grows faster than the farming era, or by which the farming era grew faster than the forager era. This method estimates a roughly one week to one month economic doubling time for the next era. While this is admittedly only a weak clue regarding future growth rates, we should not ignore it as it is one of the few concrete clues available.

For a concrete estimate to use in the rest of this book, based on all of the above, I choose an economic doubling time of one month. Most of the analysis in this book is robust to variations in this doubling time estimate. Any estimates that do depend on this doubling time estimate should be relatively easy to adjust to accommodate alternate estimates.

GROWTH MYTHS

There are several factors that some expect to influence growth rates, but which probably have at best modest effects.

One such factor is the mental speed of citizens. If ten times fewer ems were to each run ten times faster, the overall productive capacity of the economy would be about the same as without this change, and the economic growth rate wouldn't change much either. Yes, there could be some weak effects because of ems running faster or slower, but these are mostly minor. It is mainly the existing capacity that creates more capacity, not the mental speed of participants. If growth rates were limited by the speed at which individuals could take particular actions, increasing those speeds to weaken the effects of those limits could increase the growth rate. But in fact, economic growth rates just aren't much limited by the speed of individual actions.

Another factor that does not obviously suggest faster growth rates is the larger size of the em economy. Yes, a larger economy has more resources to pursue more possible innovations. But there are also usually diminishing returns in new ideas; we tend to try the most promising ideas first, and only when those run out do we move on to less promising ideas. So a larger economy doesn't *necessarily* have a larger growth rate. Within previous eras such as the farming or industrial eras, these two effects seem to have roughly canceled each other, giving a nearly steady exponential growth within each era. We should thus expect nearly steady exponential growth within the em era as well.

A third factor that does not obviously suggest faster growth rates is greater intelligence. While more intelligent people are more productive, and more productivity gives more growth, even so there isn't obviously a more direct connection here, a connection not mediated by productivity. Smarter people are awarded more patents, but that is in part because smarter people tend more to be sorted into the types of jobs that produce patents.

A fourth factor that is less relevant for growth than many think is the number of researchers. Yes, it is possible that the world now fails to coordinate to sufficiently fund research, and that the world would grow faster if it funded more of the right sort of research. However, even if the em world coordinates somewhat better than today, it seems that growth would increase by only a modest amount, as nations that do more research today do not grow noticeably faster (Ulku 2004). Also, research progress is only one input into economic growth; increases in research funding usually give much less than proportionate increases in research progress in a field (Alston et al. 2011). The fact that there are other important inputs creates diminishing returns to research effort. These other inputs include progress in closely related areas of research and technology, customer experience with related products, and more general technical and economic progress.

However, even if these factors don't greatly influence em growth rates, as we saw in the Faster Growth section, there are relevant factors that do.

FINANCE

How is finance different in an em world?

Among their many roles, clans likely also serve as a basic unit of financial organization. For example, individual ems and subclans could relatively easily turn to their larger clans to insure against risks. Hidden information and actions, which are often obstacles to insurance, are less of a problem within a clan, especially when shallow mindreading is feasible. So clans face a lower cost of providing internal insurance.

Ems likely also use their clans to help fund their housing and business ventures. This may reduce the use of independent financial institutions for insurance, mortgages, and firm stock. However, clans likely still face overall risks and imbalanced internal portfolios. For example, clans will tend to focus their reputation and training investments in particular types of jobs, and thus be at risk of exposure to fluctuations in the demands for these job types, and in the quality of the competition for those jobs. Even though clans have the option to "pause" subclans who are not currently in demand, clans should still prefer to diversify these job investments.

Clans are thus likely to use financial markets and institutions to buy insurance, to invest in outside ventures, and to sell fractions of their own risks and returns. In addition to financial diversification, em clans may also seek to diversify the job roles that they fill. To maintain a reputation and visibility among other ems, however, clans also probably want to pick many of their jobs with an eye to marketing. That is, a clan may want to ensure that they tend to occupy the job niches that fit their standard story about what this clan is good at and why you'd want to hire them.

A more competitive em economy likely adopts more efficient financial practices and institutions. This plausibly includes investors who hold a wider diversity of assets, who change their holdings less often, and who pay fewer layers of agents less to manage their holdings (Shleifer 2000). The em financial world also plausibly has more support for hostile takeovers of public firms (Macey 2008), and more use of private ownership of firms. As having worker control over firm management seems to reduce productivity, ems probably avoid that (Gorton and Schmid 2004).

One can show that in the long run the value of an investment portfolio is dominated by the highest average growth rate among the assets in that portfolio; most of the portfolio's value comes to be in that one asset (Cover and Thomas 2006). So when portfolios compete, the long-run winner is the one containing the fastest growing asset.

One can also show that the long-term outcome of patient investment funds competing fairly is a market dominated by funds that follow a "Kelly rule" of investment. Such funds maximally re-invest their returns into each asset category, such as stock, real estate, and so forth, in proportion to the expected distant future fraction of wealth to be found in each category (Evstigneev et al. 2009). In technical terms, this is roughly equivalent to logarithmic risk aversion regarding risks correlated with overall market returns, and near risk neutrality regarding risks not so correlated, as those can be diversified away.

This hasn't happened so far, probably because of high taxation, a continuing influx of new naïve and otherwise-motivated investors, laws that prevent funds endowed by wills from sufficiently reinvesting assets, and wars and revolutions that periodically wipe out investment funds. However, the em world is competitive, ems can be long-lived, and the em civilization may be more stable. These factors suggest that the em financial world has a better chance of ending up dominated by large long-lived investment funds, funds who face only modest and relatively uniform taxation, and who compete with only minor other infusions of wealth from new investors using other strategies. Such funds may be clan-based. If such a financial world continues to grow peacefully over a large growth factor, then em financial markets may eventually come to approximate the ideal Kelly rule strategy.

In most models and real markets so far, average interest rates (i.e., rates of return on investments) have usually been at least as large as economic growth rates. For example, since 1960 the global portfolio of all liquid assets worldwide has averaged a real return of 4.38 percent (Doeswijk et al. 2017). While interest rates seem to fall with longer lifespans, they probably still remain comparable with growth rates (Carvalhoa et al. 2016). Thus as em era growth rates are large, em era interest rates are also large.

In the past, variations in family wealth have resulted from variations in individual income, in inclinations to save, in investment strategies, and in the outcomes from particular investments. That is, randomly, some families get rich while others do not. While today most families hold most of their wealth in an ability to learn jobs and earn wages, an important minority of families holds most of their wealth in the form of real estate, stocks, etc. We should similarly expect that random drift in capital holdings will result in most em clans holding most of their wealth in the form of their ability to work, while a minority of em clans hold most of their wealth in other forms of capital. Thus productive em ventures often require the cooperation of several clans; some clans contribute more capital while others contribute more labor.

For ems, variation in individual income will be much lower, but variations in em speed produce larger variations in inclinations to save. Fast growth rates tempt slow humans and em retirees to save a large fraction of their income, but for fast ems these correspond to very low subjective interest rates, which tempts them away from savings and toward immediate consumption. Thus among ems, most of the psychological inclination to save must come from slower ems, and from larger-scale organizational commitments.

In general, we save because we prefer to gain more resources to use in the future, instead of having fewer resources to use today. Resources can be used personally, given to others, or shown off to gain status. Today our main reason for saving is future consumption within our immediate family. For ems this motive gets more complicated, as each em can have a complex tree of copy descendants. Ems must work out new habits regarding which copies can use saved resources, and those habits will influence the savings incentives of each individual copy.

If large concentrations of capital are more subject to theft in the long run, this will create a selection pressure on clans to try to convert their capital into labor. Clans can do this by investing in efforts to find new and better jobs for their clan members.

In Chapter 21, Governance section, we will see that em business cycle fluctuations may be larger because of city governance fluctuations. Today, a cost of cycles is labor-hoarding, wherein firms keep paying workers during downturns even when there isn't enough work. As ems can slow down and pause when there is less work, the em economy less suffers this cost of cycles.

In sum, finance seems modestly, but perhaps not greatly, different in an em world.

CHAPTER 17

Lifecycle

CAREERS

How many kinds of tasks does a typical em worker regularly do in the course of their job?

Looking at job performance today, we see that while extreme specialization can give maximum productivity in the short run, over a longer time a modest degree of task variation is often more productive, because of improved learning and engagement (Staats and Gino 2012).

Ems add an important new consideration to this usual tradeoff between task specialization and task variety. Whereas human minds have a limited rate at which they can do tasks, em minds can run at different speeds. So the limited subjective career length of an em can be spent either on more scope in tasks or on more scope in time. That is, an em worker can either run faster and simultaneously do and coordinate more related tasks, or it can run slower and coordinate fewer tasks over a longer period of time, and improve more at those tasks in the process.

Some tasks require a continual response to external drivers. These tasks include managing physical systems, such as driving cars. Such tasks usually require mental response times as fast as the slower of two rates: the rate at which outside disturbances arise to which it is useful to respond, and the rate at which the managed system such as a car is capable of responding to such disturbances.

When choosing between mind speeds faster than this minimum response rate, one of the main tradeoffs is between getting really good at each task, and coordinating more related tasks. One can either do a more specific task more times over a longer narrower career, or do a wider range of related tasks over a shorter career. During either sort of career one could split off many spurs to do short-term tasks that do not need to be well remembered.

Long, narrow careers can achieve high levels of competence while adapting to changing job detail, but require expensive communication between workers to coordinate related tasks. In contrast, having the same worker do a wider range of tasks allows for flexible coordination without communication across those tasks, but comes at the cost of more transitions for each worker between different tasks (Wout et al. 2015), and often lower competence because of less task specialization and a shorter career.

Management and software engineering are jobs where coordination across related tasks is especially important. For typical tasks in such roles, the costs to transition from one task to the next, and the gains from long-term career experience of doing related tasks, are less important than coordination between tasks. These jobs are thus good candidates for using higher-speed ems.

Today, managers tend to have a narrower "span of control," that is, to have fewer subordinates per manager, when subordinate roles are quite different, and when managers have more tasks other than supervising subordinates. The task of management is important enough to be worth paying more to put excellent workers in such roles. These considerations suggest that it makes sense to pay more to run em bosses faster than their subordinates, in part to allow bosses to manage wider spans of control. This should push ems to have shallower management hierarchies, with fewer levels between the CEO and the shop floor.

Manager gains from coordination come in particular from running fast relative to subordinates. So with fast bosses, subordinates temporarily speed up when they meet with their bosses.

Having bosses run faster than subordinates comes at the expense of shorter boss time-horizons in the sense of the time scope of their work experience. Fast bosses also require subordinates to have more different bosses during their career. For tasks where coordination is important this seems a tradeoff worth making. But today managers are the occupation category with one of the longest average tenures (6.3 years) at the same employer, exceeded only by protective service (6.4 years) and engineering (7.0 years) (BLS 2012). This long job tenure suggests that organizations gain a substantial value today from managers who stick around.

The rate of technological and institutional change sets a natural limit on useful career length. First, the fact that investment-doubling times are near economic doubling times discourages investing in skills that last much longer than such doubling times. Second, there is little point in having career skills that last much longer than the timescales over which jobs greatly change. After all, having a long career of experience doing things the old way may help little for doing things a new and different way. As jobs tend to change substantially on roughly the scale of economic doubling times, em speeds are likely to be chosen so that most work careers are likely to last shorter than a few such doubling times.

Today, the average age of firms in the S&P500 is eighteen years (Foster 2012), which is roughly the doubling time of our world economy. This suggests that the economic doubling time is close to the timescale on which business context changes enough to require big changes in business processes. This is confirmed by the fact that today large firms often attempt to "re-engineer business processes," that is, to redesign their main business organization and processes from a clean slate. For any given part of a large organization, this process happens roughly every economic doubling time.

The re-engineering process is often associated with layoffs and substantial worker retraining. As em training can be much cheaper via making many copies from a single trained em, em organizations are tempted to replace more employees than usual during a re-engineering. Anticipating such replacement, employers may prefer to have employee ems run fast enough that they are likely to be near the end of their useful lifetime of flexibility at the time of the next re-engineering.

Even in a rapidly growing em economy, some equipment and environments will be unusually durable and stable. These may include nature preserves, large physical buildings, and software tools such as languages and operating systems that become the basis for standards that coordinate other systems. Ems who are well adapted to dealing with these especially durable environments could have much longer productive careers in objective time, and so could reasonably run more slowly.

Today, the career of someone who works from ages twenty to sixty-five lasts three times as long as our fifteen-year economic doubling time. In contrast, ems with a subjective work career of two centuries that fit into one objective economic doubling time would see the world as a more stable and predictable place. If that objective economic doubling time were one month, this matched speed em would be a bit faster than a kilo-em. This suggests that we consider kilo-ems to be the typical speed ems. In Chapter 18, Choosing Speed section, we will see another consideration that also suggests this as the typical em speed.

PEAK AGE

In advanced economies today, the most productive workers tend on average to be within about a decade of the peak productivity age of near forty. Much older and younger workers are both substantially less productive. However, this doesn't seem to be because basic mental abilities decline with age. Controlling for birth cohort, individual productivity does not peak until at least age sixty, and may never peak (Cardoso et al. 2011; Göbel and Zwick 2012). The problem is that even though a worker may be just as productive at age sixty as he or she was at age forty, the next generation of workers tends to be more productive.

Also, any falling productivity after age sixty for humans today may be primarily caused by declining physical abilities, or declining biological support for the brain, not from a decline in more basic mental abilities. These problems are mostly eliminated for em workers. After all, em bodies need suffer no declines in physical strength or stamina, as physical bodies could be periodically replaced, and virtual bodies never need replacing.

The main reason that workers near age forty are more productive than older workers today seems to be that younger workers tend to be trained in more recent work methods that better match the current tool and problem mix, while older minds lack sufficient mental flexibility to fully switch to this new context. It is thus mainly our economy's fast rate of change that makes productivity peak around age forty today.

Because of this, we expect the subjective age at which productivity peaks in an em economy to depend on an em's mind speed. For slow ems, work methods often seem to change greatly, putting older workers at more of a disadvantage relative to younger workers. So for slower ems, productivity peaks at a younger subjective age.

For fast ems, in contrast, work methods might not seem to change much at all. For fast ems with stable jobs, the main limit on career duration might be how long it took for their decreasing mental flexibility to interfere with job performance via a reduced ability to track local changing working conditions, even when basic work methods didn't change that much. Thus fast em productivity might peak at much later subjective ages. Also, mind tweaks might extend the duration of em mental flexibility.

Today, our abilities at different kinds of tasks peak at different ages. For example, raw cognitive processing peaks in late teens, learning and remembering names at twenty-two, short-term memory about age thirty, face recognition in early thirties, social and emotional understanding about age fifty, and vocabulary at age sixty-nine (Hartshorne and Germine 2015; Bartels and Gould 2016).

Mental flexibility and experience can matter differently depending on the job. For example, today we can distinguish two kinds of innovative art: experimental and conceptual. In experimental art, personal abilities and specific projects tend to improve gradually, whereas in conceptual art new abilities and projects tend more to arrive fully formed and all at once. For example, Paul Cezanne, Robert Frost, and Mark Twain were experimental artists, while Pablo Picasso, T.S. Eliot, and Herman Melville were conceptual artists. Today, painters, novelists, and directors who are experimental artists tend to do their best work roughly at ages forty-six to fifty-two, thirty-eight to fifty, and forty-five to sixty-three, respectively, but those ages are twenty-four to thirty-four, twenty-nine to forty, and twenty-seven to forty-three, respectively for conceptual artists (Galenson 2006). Similarly, today experimental scientists tend to peak near roughly ages thirty-eight to forty-eight, whereas theoretical scientists tend to peak near roughly ages thirty-two to forty-two (Jones et al. 2014). Thus conceptual innovators peak at earlier ages than do experimental innovators. This is consistent with conceptual innovations benefiting more from mental flexibility, while experimental innovations benefit more from experience.

At any one time, the vast majority of actual working ems (weighing either by count or by speed) are near a peak productivity subjective age. This is because the em economy chooses to make many copies of ems at these ages. For em jobs that rely especially strongly on skills that peak at a particular age, most ems doing that job are going to be near that particular age. Such peak age ems, however, each remember a long life of being younger than peak productivity age.

The duration in time of an em's highly copied peak productivity period depends on how valuable local experience is for their particular job. When local experience matters very little, ems are selected very close to their peak; they might last on the job only a month or less before being replaced by a slightly younger version. They also remember spending a large fraction of their recent history in leisure, if such experiences substantially increased their peak work productivity.

In contrast, when local experience matters a great deal on the job, peak em career periods last longer. In this case a worker might stay on the job for a decade or more before being replaced by a younger worker. Such workers also tend not to remember much recent leisure, as they work most of the time to gain more local job experience.

Variance in em team training rates increases through skill spillovers within teams. Today, people learn more when they are among higher skilled teammates (Ichniowski and Preston 2014). So when some team members learn more than usual, other team members also learn more than usual.

MATURITY

Having the typical em worker be near a subjective age of fifty or more has many implications, because we know many things about how such older people tend to differ from younger people. Today the median age is twenty-four worldwide, and thirty-eight in the U.S.

We see many stable correlations today among gender, age, and personality. Because these same correlations also exist among other great apes such as chimps, we have good reason to expect that these correlations are deeply embedded in human nature, and are thus likely to be observed in ems (Weiss and King 2015).

For example, today as they get older people tend to be less neurotic, and more agreeable, conscientiousness, and open to experience (Soto et al. 2011), although these trends reverse after the age of sixty-five (Kandler et al. 2015). Older people have weaker differences between genders in their roles and attitudes (Hofstede et al. 2010), they are more trusting (Robinson and Jackson 2001), they have less regret about missed life opportunities (Brassen et al. 2012), and they have more job satisfaction and less stress and negative emotions (Tay et al. 2014).

Self-esteem peaks around age fifty (von Soest et al. 2017), inclinations to take risks decline with age (Josef et al. 2016), and materialism reaches its lowest levels around middle age (Jaspers and Pieters 2016). Compared with twenty-five-year-olds, fifty-year-olds today spend about the same time per week with co-workers, parents, siblings, more time alone and with close partners, and less time with friends (Bhattacharya et al. 2016; Lindberg 2017).

Older people (and males) are more influential in social networks, and influential people are more clustered in their associations, and less susceptible to social influence by others (Aral and Walker 2012). For older people, happiness tends to increase with age, controlling for health, and older people tend to associate happiness more with peacefulness, as opposed to excitement, in part because they focus more on the present as opposed to the future (Mogilner et al. 2011).

As mentioned in Chapter 4, Complexity section, older people tend to have stronger crystallized intelligence, that is, more depth and breadth of knowledge, vocabulary, and abilities to reason, but weaker fluid intelligence, that is, abilities to analyze new problems and to notice new patterns and to extrapolate using them (Horn and Cattell 1967; Ashton et al. 2000).

Older people today tend to be more attached to particular people, places, hobbies, and occupations, and are less willing to exchange these for new substitutes. Also, older people today commit less crime, and are more likely to convict those accused of crime (Anwar et al. 2014). This, together with stronger surveillance, suggests that the em world has much less crime.

Today, most people over the age of eighty must deal with health problems, the death of loved ones, and many other difficult issues. While some of these people are further hindered by dementia, it seems that most of them deal well via their lifetime accumulation of mental strength and "cool." This gives them composure, security, poise, reserve, distance, detachment, and balance, allowing them to focus on the positive parts of their lives (Zimmermann and Grebe 2014). We should also weakly expect older ems to tend to display such composure, detachment, and balance. In addition, older ems suffer little or no health issues or other physical decline.

We should thus weakly expect that, because ems are older, they are less neurotic, materialistic, and risk-taking, and more agreeable, conscientious, open to experience, trusting, and clustered in their social associations. They have more self-esteem, cool and composure, commit less crime, seek more peace as opposed to excitement, and have intelligence that is crystallized rather than fluid. They are more attached to particular people, places, and habits, spend less time with friends, and more time with close partners. The typical em has lived a long life, and even so expects to retire or end soon.

Today, our ability to lie, and our frequency of lies, peaks at ages eighteen to twenty-nine, and declines as we are younger or older than that peak age (Debey et al. 2015). As ems are much older than this peak lying age, ems lie less than we do today.

We see again that although ems are like humans, they differ in systematic ways from typical humans.

PREPARATION

How much do ems invest in preparing for tasks beforehand, as opposed to adapting flexibly later to deal with problems as they arise?

Because ems can be copied easily, it is much cheaper for ems to prepare for tasks that multiple ems perform. The reason is that one can pay once to prepare a single em, and then make many copies of that single em to have a large set of prepared ems.

For example, a single em could conceive of a system design for a software project, and then split into many copies who each elaborate and implement different parts of the system design, continuing to split as needed for subsystems. Similarly, a product designer or an architect could conceive a central integrated plan for a movie or an amusement park, and then split into many copies to work out details for different parts of the project.

To ensure a quality initial plan, the initial em might split into several, who pursue different concepts for the initial plan. The em with the best plan is then selected somehow, perhaps by a revived copy of the original em, and that em splits into copies who elaborate and then implement its particular plan. This process could continue recursively, at each level exploring several possible scenarios and keeping only the copies associated with the best plans developed. This gives each planning em an added incentive to identify good plan details.

To get initially identical copies to pursue different design or plan concepts, copies might be created sequentially. The first copy is asked to specify a concept, and then a new copy is told that concept and asked to pick a different concept. A third copy might then be asked to pick a concept different from the other two. Em who are naturally proud or contrarian might naturally disagree with previous ems.

Because they more often explore different options in parallel, ems less often get bored with trial and error searching.

These abilities allow ems to implement larger, more integrated pre-planned projects than we achieve today. This change also increases the emphasis on preparing ahead of time, relative to responding on the fly. Ems tend to rely more than we do on previously designed schedules and plans. This reduces the premium ems are willing to pay for youthful mental flexibility. This effect is likely to be weaker for slow ems, for whom the society around them changes more rapidly. Such slow ems gain more value from mental flexibility.

Of course, the single-em-plans-then-splits-to-execute approach only works when the same em encompasses all the different skills needed to create and execute the plan. When diverse skills are required for different parts of a plan, different ems with different skills may also need to be involved in the plan's development and execution.

Compared with us today, ems find it easier to synchronize the completion times of different project components, because if a component ends up taking more effort than anticipated, associated ems can be sped up to compensate. In this way em projects can run over budget without running over time. This allows larger more fragile project plans to be implemented; ems can more often count on each part of a project plan being completed and ready at its scheduled time.

Today, workers are more productive after an enjoyable vacation, although the boost usually goes away days or weeks after returning to work (Trougakos and Hideg 2009). Perhaps em mind tweaks can eliminate the need for vacations. But if not, a single em might experience a long expensive period of leisure time, and then many copies of that em might work more productively for subjective days or weeks afterward. Once these ems tire, or when their tasks naturally end, all but one of these copies may end or retire. The remaining copy could repeat the cycle, eventually remembering a long history of long, luxurious leisure periods punctuated by short intense work periods. This gain from leisure before work might need to be traded off against a reduced effective work life before mental fragility sets in, during which less local work experience is accumulated.

For example, an em plumber might split into 1000 copies every day, with each copy doing a typical plumbing job that takes an average of an hour. One of those copies might then be saved, to experience most of a subjective day of leisure and then repeat the process the next day. Objectively, this person's life is 2 percent leisure, but his memories of life are of spending 96 percent of time in leisure. While at some level this em might know that only 2 percent of life is leisure, he or she need not dwell much on this fact.

In this sort of scenario, the number of copies made of each worker per workday is probably limited by how much jobs change with job context, and by how fast jobs in a given context change. That is, an em who makes too many copies risks being less expert at his or her job than ems who make fewer copies, which are thus better adapted to each new work context, and can also more rapidly adjust to changing work conditions.

Note that in this keep-one-of-many-copies scenario, it might make the most sense to keep the copy who had learned the most from doing their task. Thus copies that prefer to continue working might compete to see who could learn the most, which isn't quite the same as competing to be the most productive. For incentive reasons then, such an em might want to instead commit to often keeping the copy who had been the most productive, instead of the copy who had learned the most. They might also want to sometimes keep other random copies, to remember what it feels like to fail to learn or produce the most. Note also that in this sort of scenario the vast majority of the ems retire or end long before their minds become too inflexible to be productive.

That ems often have many close copies at any one time should make it much easier for ems to obtain trusted independent judgments on things such as design plans and drafts of writings. If an em created such a draft and a close copy didn't like it, it would be much harder to explain that criticism away by saying that they didn't understand the goals and style of the draft.

TRAINING

We've just discussed issues that arise when preparing ems to do particular tasks. Related issues arise when preparing young ems for their adult careers, because one can also raise one child or train one trainee, and then make many copies of those. This changes em childhood and professional training.

For example, only a tiny fraction of ems are children or trainees not near their peak productivity age, although most ems remember having spent most of their lives as such trainees. A peak-age em is honored to personally help train one of the rare younger ems.

The experiences of training-age ems are selected more for their potential to teach better skills, and less for their current productivity. Ems search for training methods that can add the most to young em skills while adding less of the subjective aging that increases mental fragility. Typically the search is for high average productivity and low variance, although for some kinds of tasks high productivity variance is attractive.

Ems can afford to have many children and young trainees compete, and then only select a best few to be allocated into jobs, with the failures ending or retiring. One might think that such low odds of success are demoralizing, but overconfident neglect of the chances of failure is aided by the fact that most ems remember usually succeeding against the odds. Ems remember fewer substantial failures before retirement. Note that today most people who pursue risky careers in sports, music, or acting typically maintain positive moods, even when their objective odds of career success are quite low.

In our world today, older people often try to give advice to younger people, advice supposedly based on their longer life experience. However, older people often have hidden agendas, such as trying to justify their choices in life. Also, younger people often feel rivalries with older advisors, and value making decisions for themselves (Garvin and Margolis 2015). These effects combine to make younger people less willing to take to heart advice from older colleagues.

In contrast, ems could obtain advice from older copies of themselves who have pursued very similar careers and life plans. Such older copies should in principle be more accurate and respected sources of useful advice. It is more like taking advice from someone who started the same job a year before you, and who had your exact same personality and skill set. Ems could also get advice from ems with a much wider range of subjective ages; for example, ems who are subjectively tens of millennia old might be available to give advice.

However, older ems can still have hidden agendas, and younger ems may still resent having to take advice from others. Such factors may limit the useful advice from older to younger ems in the same clan. Clans that can better reduce the resentments of the young and the hidden agendas of the old could thereby gain a competitive advantage in the em economy.

The situations in which ems are trained are a mixture of real and simulated environments. Ems in training might not always know which is which. As in the science-fiction novel *Ender's Game*, ems might also sometimes not be told when they make the switch from training to practical work, if this policy increased productivity by increasing the em's confidence or comfort.

For tasks where ems spend the most total time working, they also spend more total time searching for better productivity at that task, but perhaps a smaller fraction of the work time related to that task is spent on such search. Ems spend a larger fraction of time searching for task productivity when there are more interesting ways to do a task.

Most em teams are composed of ems likely to reach their productivity peak at the same time, so they can work together as a high-productivity team. Often this means starting at the same young age and running at the same speeds to age together. Early team training likely tries to increase the variance of peak team productivity, to allow the highest possible team productivity to be found when selecting from among many trained teams. Perhaps to a lesser extent, training also tries to increase the duration of the period that a team could spend at peak productivity, as well as the variance in that period's duration.

Some em teams are "search" teams, focusing more on searching for good combinations of members and work strategies, while others are "application" teams, focusing more on applying the best combinations found by search teams. Application teams are more common. Search teams are designed for productivity variance, to increase the chances of finding very high productivity team designs. In contrast, application teams try to decrease productivity variance, to reduce the chances of unusually low productivity.

Search teams tend to have more varied members and strategies, and they may also expect to see members and strategies change more over time within the life of the team. In contrast, application teams expect team personnel and work methods to be stable. Search teams are also likely to "network" more by having more social contact with a wider range of people outside their teams. This is because today having many weak social ties tends to be good for workers who need to innovate and to locate hidden information, while having fewer and stronger social ties tends to be better for workers who exploit known information and transfer tacit job skills to new tasks (Pfeffer 2010).

CHILDHOOD

Not only is training different for ems, childhood is similarly different.

The experiences of children are more varied and risky than those of peak age ems. This is in part to stretch their range to increase the generality of their skills. It is also in the hope of producing variance in persistent productivity across different copies, from which the best could be selected.

A peak-age em will likely be more productive if they've had more relevant work experience before they reach their peak age. Thus even though one can afford to pamper young ems in training, they still remember having spent a large portion of their time working, to gain more experience. In contrast, although peak age ems can't afford to spend much on pampering, they might still remember a recent life spent mostly in luxurious leisure. This is because it can be cheap to give one em leisure and then make many copies, who then work more effectively because of that leisure.

Younger ems are subsidized, and focused on learning to become more productive, in the hopes of reaching a high productivity during their peak years. Young ems see the important part of their lives as their future peak productivity years, and one of the great questions of their life is whether they will live up to hopes about them and become one of the few greatly copied ems when they reach peak productivity.

Most young ems eventually disappoint such hopes. Because of this em teen angst is more objectively justified. Today we tolerate "youthful indiscretions" more than adult versions, as the young know less and need to explore more. Em youthful indiscretions can be tolerated even more, as ems seek the best version among many copies of a youth.

Ems use their future peak productivity period not only as a key standard for judging themselves, but also for judging their spouses, friends, and other associates. That is, ems not only seek associates that can improve their lives at the moment, ems want even more to find associates that will help them to achieve high productivity during their hoped-for future success period of high peak productivity. In addition to asking "Who do I want around me now?," ems ask "Who will I want around me then?"

Early in an em's life, his or her future might seem unpredictable. At that point, a great many possible careers, locations, and associations might seem plausible. Later, however, once a particular copy has chosen a particular career, location, and team, the future is far more predictable—much more predictable than are our careers today.

Once an em clan becomes established at a certain kind of job, that clan continues to restart early copies to be trained to do that job. Each new version is trained to take over that job when older versions become too fragile to be fully productive. New versions are trained using improved work techniques, to become proficient with the latest tools and productive in the latest work contexts.

Even when an em is trained with a particular future career in mind, they may also be trained in skills relevant for other careers. After all, in sports today children who specialize too early do not reach peak abilities as often as those who wait longer to specialize (TAW 2017).

Most such ems could thus look at the lives of prior versions of themselves to gain a very good idea of what their future life will look like. This is somewhat comparable with a medieval worker who inherited his or her parents' role in life as a farmer, soldier, or cobbler. However, such ems need not feel pressed to do jobs against their wishes. After all, many variations on young ems can be created in the hopes of finding a few who are enthusiastic about available jobs.

Schools today are said to serve many functions beyond instilling particular job skills. Students are said to learn general skills, become acculturated to a local society, and assimilate propaganda. Students are also baby-sat at low cost, and meet and bond with future friends, mates, and co-workers. Schools provide a setting that promotes the creation of close bonds unusually well: repeated, unplanned, and proximate interactions, in a setting that encourages people to let their guard down (Williams 2012).

The habits, material, and teaching methods used in schools for older children tend to be matched to the habits and teaching methods used in schools for younger children. And activity patterns in adult work places are often matched to patterns that employees experienced in school. Because so many things become matched to them, the styles of early schools often become entrenched and hard to change. Thus early em school styles may not change much from those found in such schools today.

Em clans are likely to carefully negotiate which sets of peers are trained and raised closely together as children, via schools or other shared social contexts. Many such peer sets can be tried. Such peer sets often include sets that clans hope may work together later as teams. Such peer sets might also include ems from clans who specialize in being always-a-bridesmaid-never-a-bride associates, who can help other ems to grow and learn.

It is probably hard to prevent young ems from learning which peers come from clans who are popular as teammates, both in general and also with their particular clan. This might cause problems if initially unpopular ems form bonds when young, form a successful team when older, and then try to recreate their successful young bonding with new younger clan members.

The tiny fraction of children in an em society should make it harder for ems to express natural parenting urges. Perhaps ems could substitute by watching "reality" shows about children that they share with many other copies. They might vote on key child-raising decisions; it might really take an em village to raise a child. To support this, children might run at the speeds at which their parental groups take their leisure. This approach may not provide a sufficiently direct and tactile connection to fully satisfy parenting urges for many. But a great many people today have lived productive lives without being parents, suggesting that enough ems could be found who are productive without being parents.

The grandparents of people who are alive today tend to have more grandchildren than did other people born at the same time as those grandparents. Similarly, the great number of older copies made of each successful child make the details of that young life relatively famous. That is, when older ems remember the particular details of their childhood, a great many other older ems would also remember exactly the same details. Thus most older ems remember a relatively famous childhood, somewhat as if they had been a child celebrity who is now no longer famous. Far fewer other ems know or care about the details of an em's current adult life, relative to the number who know and care about the details of their childhood.

This celebrity childhood tends to reveal many details about youthful events and attitudes. If an adult em is at all tempted to talk about particular events and attitudes from their childhood, the sheer number of adults who all remember the exact same childhood will tend to ensure that the information about their childhood will leak out. If George didn't like Fred as a child, then even if he never said anything about that as a child, the adult Freds will still likely all hear it.

Childhood and training might usefully be done at a very fast speed, at least if accurate enough task simulators were available, and if direct interaction with the larger world was not required for learning. Ems trained in this way remember that during their childhood the world was more stable and changed more slowly.

The younger that ordinary humans are when scanned, the earlier their training in the em world could begin. While some might express objections to scanning young humans, especially when such scans are destructive, in a world dominated by ems these objections may not always or even usually determine whether scanning actually happens.

Children who are personally exposed to innovation are much more likely to become innovators as adults. Thus some ems can be trained to become innovators, even if most ems are less likely to innovate.

As the most successful adults today tend to experience a moderate number of adverse life events as children, em children will likely see themselves as experiencing substantial but not overwhelming difficulties.

Although em childhoods differ from our childhood today, they are still recognizably childhoods.

PART IV
Organization

CHAPTER 18

Clumping

CITIES

Do ems physically concentrate in cities, or do they spread out more evenly across the land?

Industrial economies today achieve large gains from clumping social and business activities closely together in space. The more easily that people can quickly travel to visit many different stores, employers, clubs, schools, etc., the more kinds of beneficial interactions become possible. The ability to interact less directly via phones, email, and social media hasn't reduced this effect; if anything, the possibility of additional electronic interaction has usually increased the value of personal visits. Urban economists and other academics have long studied such "agglomeration" effects, and understand them in great detail.

As we know of no new contrary effects strong enough to change this basic situation, we should expect these gains from clumping to continue in an em world (Morgan 2014). Ems want to be near one another, and near supporting tools and utilities, so that they can more easily and quickly interact with more such people and tools. Humans have so far developed many useful utilities that can be more cheaply supplied via city-scale clumping, such as roads, power, water, sewage, telephones, and internet, and ems may develop even more such utilities. The instinctive desire to leave a familiar dense place in search of a new fresh place to populate has an ancient heritage, and will again be important at some future time. But not so much during the age of em. As noticeable communication delays appear at city-scale separations, ems will want to avoid being much further than this from desirable interaction partners.

Per person, cities today with twice the population tend to be 10 percent more economically productive per person. Compared with any given sized city, double-sized cities have per-person 21 percent more patents, 11 percent shorter roads, and 9 percent shorter electrical cables. But these cities also suffer 12 percent more crime, 17 percent more AIDS cases, and 34 percent more traffic congestion costs per person (Bettencourt et al. 2007, 2010; Schrank et al. 2011). Today, one factor increasing the productivity of larger cities is their selectively attracting better workers. But another important factor favoring big city productivity is their giving those better workers more ways to gain from their superior abilities.

Optimal city size is in general a tradeoff between these gains and losses. During the farming era most people lived in small communities with populations of roughly 1000. Compared with any given sized village, only about 75 percent as many people lived in double-sized villages (Nitsch 2005). Thus most farmers lived in the smallest villages, because during the farmer era larger versions suffered higher costs of crime, disease, and transport.

Within rich nations today, in contrast, people are spread roughly equally across all the different feasible city sizes, between a minimum viable modern town of a few thousand and a maximum city size set by a nation's population. Compared with any given size city, about the same total number of people live in cities twice as big, and in cities half as big. This change to larger cities from the farming era has been made possible because industrial society has greatly lowered the costs of crime, disease, and transport, and increased our abilities to gain from specialization and innovation. Nations come in different sizes, and are also spread out roughly equally between a minimum viable size of about a half million and a maximum set by world population (Eeckhout 2004; Giesen et al. 2010).

An em economy might further reduce the costs of crime and disease, and increase the gains from innovation. After all, well-designed computers can be more secure from theft, assault, and disease. More importantly, traffic congestion costs could be much lower in an em city because most transport of ems could be done via communication lines, and most virtual meetings within a city do not require the movement of em minds at all. As congestion costs now limit city sizes, this increase in virtual meetings could plausibly tip the balance toward much larger em cities.

Thus instead of today's equal distribution of people across all feasible city sizes, most ems might instead be found in a few very large cities. Most ems might live in a handful of huge dense cities, or perhaps even just one gigantic city. If this happened, nations and cities would merge; there would be only a few huge nations that mattered.

Larger em cities could allow great increases in social complexity. Farmers, who usually lived in near-a-village sized social units of roughly 1000, have sometimes said that they would hate to suffer the social isolation of the typical forager, who lived in bands of roughly thirty people. Such farmers would hate to lose their village-based opportunities for specialization and complexity in work and leisure. Many people in our era living in cities of size around 1 million have similarly said they would hate to suffer the social isolation of the typical farmer.

If em cities are even larger still, with populations of many billions to trillions, their residents may similarly relish the greatly increased social opportunities available in gigantic cities, and pity the relative social isolation of the city-dwellers or our era, much as we sometimes pity the isolation of farmers, or farmers pity the isolation of foragers.

Having only a small number of em cities might make it easier to regulate the em economy. While a city needs growth-friendly regulation to become one of the few big em cities, once a city had become very large it might be able to maintain its size while tolerating substantial growth-reducing regulations. This is especially possible if all of the big em cities agreed to adopt similar levels of such regulations.

CITY STRUCTURE

We can say things not only about the number and size of em cities, but also about internal em city structures.

In virtual meetings, ems care little about being much closer than their reaction distance from a city center. Remember, reaction distance is how far light travels in a mental reaction time. As faster ems have shorter reaction distances, they thus gain more value from congregating closer to city centers. So faster ems should cluster more centrally, surrounded by slower ems toward the periphery. This is similar to how today investors using higher frequency trading algorithms often pay more to locate close to financial market centers. The higher values gained by fast ems are reflected in higher rental prices for central real estate, which should induce a denser packing of computing power, energy inputs, and cooling in em city centers.

In the last few decades, falling costs of long-distance travel have increased the number of conferences and business meetings. Compared with the residents of our cities, ems who are within a reaction distance of one another have low costs of traveling to attend virtual meetings. This should greatly increase the number of conferences and business meetings, especially for slower ems.

Because of rising prices to rent space near city centers, the total hardware cost per subjective minute of em experience is higher toward city centers. Thus ems who tend to choose more central locations when they run faster face a more than proportional effective hardware cost as a function of speed. Because of this, ems who get less value from many fast interactions with other ems tend to locate toward the peripheries of em cities.

If faster ems tend to locate closer to city centers, if ems tend to cluster spatially near others of the same speed, and if em speeds tend to fall into discrete classes, then em cities may break into discrete speed neighborhoods. Each neighborhood runs mostly at its own different speed. These neighborhoods might plausibly be arranged in rings around the city center, or perhaps in a fractal structure around many levels of urban centers.

If ems sometimes inhabit physical bodies with sizes matched to their speed, then cities may have matching physical infrastructure such as sidewalks, bridges, and doorways. These may be smaller toward city centers, where the faster ems reside. Physical barriers that enforce differences in air pressure between different city regions might also be good places to change the typical physical scale of infrastructure. In this case, inner regions with smaller-scale infrastructure also have higher pressures.

Today, larger cities tend to have better educated, more social, and more productive workers. Unless they have large recent immigration flows, larger cities also tend to have more women. Bigger cities less often specialize in particular industries and occupations (Duranton and Jayet 2011). Big city workers also tend to do tasks that are more connected to other tasks, and so benefit from being located close to each other (Kok and Weel 2014). Cities grow faster when their workers do more connected tasks, and when these workers connect more via social media (Mandel 2014). Industries with many new products and methods tend to locate at first in bigger cities, and then move to smaller cities as their products and methods become more stable (Desmet and Rossi-Hansberg 2009).

It is plausible to expect that activities near em city centers are more like typical activities in our largest cities, whereas activities toward the periphery of em cities are more like typical activities in our smaller towns. Thus em city centers tend to house new innovative dynamic industries, more women, and more productive workers who are more social and educated, who do more kinds of occupations, and who tend to do more connected tasks. City peripheries, in contrast, house older, more stable industries, and regions that are specialized to particular industries.

Tasks that are more likely to be done toward em city peripheries include monitoring, identifying, estimating, handling and moving objects, operating and controlling machines and processes, using computers, drafting and specifying devices, and equipment repair and maintenance. Tasks more likely to be done nearer to em city centers include judging quality, determining compliance, making decisions, thinking creatively, developing strategies, scheduling and planning, interpreting, communicating, making and maintaining relations, selling, resolving conflicts, coordinating, training, motivating, advising, and administration (Kok and Weel 2014).

Em activity far from the main em cities is an extreme version of activities in city peripheries. While the cost of land and cooling can be a bit cheaper in such places, they must basically manufacture most everything for themselves, and they suffer large signal delays when talking to other places. Such places may not be economically viable without special customers, such as local humans demanding services, or militaries seeking to control large areas.

Because most travel is virtual or electronic, iconic city locations are less often transport routes or hubs, as they often are in our era, and more often plazas and other spaces where many could congregate. City design focuses less on daily worker commutes, and more on the distribution of communication, power, and cooling, and on supporting frequent changes in space allocations.

As faster em hardware emphasizes processing relative to memory, em city centers emphasize processing hardware, while peripheries emphasize memory hardware, especially cheaper, slower-access memory hardware. Retirees and archives tend to be located toward the periphery.

Today, most who walk city streets, or who ride mass transit, are using them to go somewhere. They are often distracted, staring at their phones. In contrast, most ems walking virtual city streets may be less distracted, and instead be in the mood to stroll or wander. If they are distracted, they might just have a faraway look that doesn't meet the eyes of others. After all, ems could talk to others or read their email in their heads, without needing to look down at their hands as many of us do today.

CITY AUCTIONS

Not only can we say things about em city structure, we can say things about em city governance as well.

As discussed in Chapter 15, Combinatorial Auctions section, combinatorial auctions could allow decentralized management of city utilities while avoiding large costs from political lobbying.

Auctions to choose and allocate utility capacity and customer locations might combine all important city utilities. That is, participants might offer bids that simultaneously specify, in addition to a maximum price to pay, these quantities: (1) spatial volume, shape, orientation, and location constraints, (2) part swapping portal locations and sizes, (3) lines of sight to outside views or specific parties, (4) limits on surface temperature and chemical corrosiveness, (5) amounts and forms of power and cooling, (6) flow rates of specific chemicals piped in and fluid garbage piped out, (7) communication distance and bandwidth from other particular residents, (8) time delay and capacity to move hardware out and in, (9) support force tensors, (10) limits on surface heat amounts in and out, (11) limits on incoming and outgoing vibrations, (12) limits on chances of incoming and outgoing leakage or explosive destruction, and (13) clauses to cover disputes with neighbors. Bids could specify not just ideal values for these parameters, but also the size of penalties others pay for incremental violations of these conditions, including prices to sell the entire allocation at later points in time.

The auction in each city is repeated often, and continues to choose a winning allocation, which says who specifically can use what spaces when, with what supporting resources, limits, etc. This specification includes reallocating previously promised resources, and also future resources that are not yet promised to anyone. The winning allocation is something close to the allocation that maximizes the total estimated value of the city to all auction participants. Auction participants might include not just those who want to consume land and supporting utilities, but also utility suppliers, who bid prices to supply particular utility amounts at particular locations. Prediction markets estimating future winning bids could help the auction mechanism to estimate the opportunity costs of commitment, and property taxes tied to self-declared sale offers could make sales and thus property changes easier.

Auction revenue could pay for utility fixed costs and also perhaps repay city investors. In theory, in optimal size cities the revenue from such auctions should just cover the subsidies given to city services with scale economies, leaving no remaining revenue to pay city investors (Raa 2003). But that theory may not apply exactly.

Em city design places a high priority on supporting rapid physical growth, such as replacing and moving computer and communication hardware, expanding power and cooling capacity, and building the city higher into the sky and deeper into the ground.

In the U.S. today, not only does it take two years on average to construct each building, it takes over two additional years to plan it, mostly dealing with regulation. This planning time has actually increased in recent decades (Millar et al. 2013). A much faster growing em economy needs to greatly reduce these construction delays. Combinatorial auctions could allow much more rapid approval of and flexibility in building plans, while still dealing well with the effects of building changes on city neighbors. Buildings might also tend to be made smaller and more modular, all else equal, to reduce delays.

CHOOSING SPEED

How fast do em minds run, relative to ordinary human minds?

Because faster ems need more central city locations, they in effect have a more than proportional cost of speed. When all else is equal, this tends to reduce em speeds. For example, for tasks that take a fixed subjective time to complete, this speed cost effect encourages the use of the slowest "just in time" ems barely able to finish a task before its deadline. Also, faster ems suffer more communication delays, and serial automation tools are less useful at faster speeds.

Other factors, however, can push toward faster em speeds. These include speed as a status signal, gains from having careers finish before jobs substantially change, and gains from more coordination by having the same em do several related tasks.

In one objective month a milli-em gets about forty-five minutes of subjective experience. An hour is near the shortest time it takes a skilled worker to do a useful task, and tasks that take much longer than an economic doubling time to complete are far less valuable. Thus ems slower than milli-ems must almost all be retirees.

The same sort of interaction gains that encourage ems to clump into dense cities also encourage ems to run at speeds like those of their associates, and to avoid the phase differences that result from time-sharing computer hardware. After all, time-sharing ems with different phases and long periods can't talk naturally to each other without changing speeds or phases, and short swap periods may greatly increase the average cost of swapping. Thus, there is likely to be a single main em speed, and also a few standard alternative speeds.

We have many reasons to expect particular speeds for particular tasks. Ems who work closely with physical processes, such as by managing factories, run at the speeds required by those physical processes, and there is likely to be a wide range of such speeds. Most ems interacting with ordinary humans tend to run at nearly the same mental speeds as humans. Ems competing in product development races not constrained by delays from interacting with physical or other external systems often run at near the top cheap speed, and perhaps even faster. Such racing ems are likely to be located well away from city centers, if the time to produce results is long compared with the time delay to deliver results from sites distant from a city center. Many retired ems run at near the base speed, that is, at the slowest near-proportional hardware cost speed. The speeds of other ems, however, tend to clump at a small number of standard speeds, to allow them to interact more easily with each other.

Many systems can be seen as composed of different parts with different natural speeds. For example, modern buildings have six main layers: site, structure, skin, services, space plan, and stuff. These layers change at different rates. Sites last forever, structures last thirty to 300 years, skins last about twenty years, and services wear out in seven to fifteen years. Commercial space plans change every three years, and the stuff placed inside spaces changes even faster. Software systems similarly have layers that change at different speeds, such as data, code, metadata, classes, tools, and libraries (Brand 1994; Foote and Yoder 2000). Ems who work on different layers will probably run at different matching speeds.

Humans seem to dislike both very fast and very slow subjective rates of change. Slow change seems boring, while fast change seems threatening. The em ability to choose mind speed should help ems to more often sit in a middle sweet spot of interesting but not threatening change.

We have some specific reasons to expect several standard speed ratios. One reason has already been mentioned: coordination gains from having bosses run faster than subordinates. Such gains are limited by difficulties in having a single boss know enough to manage many diverse teams. A speed ratio of sixteen may be feasible, if a good boss can plausibly remember enough detail to manage roughly sixteen different teams at a time.

A second reason for a speed ratio is to have leisure go faster than work. In many jobs today, worker desires to rest between work sessions often conflict with the desires of clients for workers to be always available. Having different work shifts that cover all time periods helps, but can lead to worker failures to coordinate across shift boundaries (Chan 2015). Ems could greatly reduce this conflict by having their leisure speeds be much faster than their work speeds.

For example, at a leisure-to-work speed ratio of sixteen, a worker might be on the job around the clock except for taking a forty-five-minute break every twelve hours, a break during which they can rest for twelve subjective hours. To fully use local fast em hardware, a population of workers might split into sixteen different work-phase communities, who each take their leisure at different times, and thus can't interact much with other phase groups during their leisure time.

For ems who work close enough to a city center to interact without noticeable delay with most of that city, switching to fast leisure time can greatly reduce the number of city ems with which they can interact without delays. This is a sensible choice if leisure activities gain less from interacting with many others than do workplace activities. This seems to hold today, as work tends more to be located toward city centers, while leisure (especially for older people) is more in peripheral areas.

Ems who can be more flexible about when they run at what speeds are likely to watch the changing prices to run at different speeds, and switch temporarily to whatever speeds are currently cheaper.

When the ratios between standard speeds are powers of two, it becomes easier for the same hardware to support different speeds at different times. For three or more such standard speeds, if neighboring speeds differed by the same ratios, then common social conventions could be used to manage how ems of different speeds interact with each other. Thus a simple assumption is that the main em speeds will tend to differ by the same factor, a factor that is a power of two. Perhaps this standard speed ratio factor would be four or sixteen.

My best guess for the (economic-value-weighted) typical em speed during the early em era is within roughly a factor of eight of a kilo-em speed. A speedup of 1000 is fast enough for a two-century-long subjective career to fit into two objective months of rapid social change, and yet still slow enough for its 15-kilometer reaction distance (at a reaction time of 0.1 seconds) to include a familiar-sized city. (For example, Manhattan is 21.6 by 3.7 kilometers.)

A physical em body that matched the reaction time of a kilo-em is about 1.5 millimeters tall. Such a body might have to be teleoperated, if a matching brain does not fit inside such a body. Such miniature ems could manage matching tiny pipes, service access hallways, tools, vehicles, and manufacturing plants, all with parts 1000 times smaller than ours but changing 1000 times faster.

At this scale, an industry-era city population of a million kilo-ems could fit in an ordinary bottle, as in the miniaturized and bottled city of Kandor from the Superman Comics. A billion at this scale might fit in a small building of today, while a large building might hold the trillions in population that are said to fill a galaxy in the science-fiction stories of the 1950s. Of course we have no guarantee that a kilo-em brain could fit inside a matching-sized body.

Note that for any given size of the em economy, the faster the typical em, then the smaller the total size of the active em population, as faster ems typically produce proportionally more economic value, at least among ems who are fast enough to do a job at all. The economic product of a billion kilo-ems should be roughly comparable with that of a trillion human-speed ems.

TRANSPORT

Even if most em activity, and travel, is done in virtual reality, some ems and material goods need to physically travel to new locations.

Today, the transport and storage costs of each item influence how often and far that item is transported. When transport costs are higher, we less often move each item a long distance, and when we do we move fewer varieties of it. When storage costs are higher, we transport an item more frequently, but from shorter distances. When transport is temporarily expensive, a larger fraction of transport is done by those with lower personal transport costs. The batch size per transport depends little on these parameters (Agarwal et al. 2017). These patterns will probably continue with em transport.

Today, at the typical urban commuter speed of about 10 meters per second, it takes about twenty-five minutes to commute 15 kilometers across a city. It takes about five hours for a jet to fly across continents such as North America, or between continents such as North America and Europe. It takes about a month to ship goods by boat from China to the U.S., and it could take over a year to fly to Mars and back.

However, to the typical speed kilo-ems, such physical trips take far longer subjectively. To a kilo-em, a physical commute across a city takes a subjective eighteen days, a jet flight between continents takes seven subjective months, a boat trip from China to the U.S. takes a century, and a flight to Mars and back takes a millennium. (To a kilo-em, twelve hours of real daylight or nighttime lasts for a subjective seventeen months.)

Such long subjective delays greatly discourage physical travel by fast ems. In fact, kilo-ems who physically commute in a city might typically travel only 9 meters (which is only a tiny fraction of a city width). This estimate comes from the fact that, in cities today, the fraction of people who commute a distance falls by half for every fifteen minutes added to their commute (Ahlfeldt et al. 2015). Of course ems can travel electronically to wherever receivers are built.

A rapidly growing em economy also discourages transport of physical goods over long distances. First, high interest rates greatly discourage the use of products or resources that require travel or shipping delays of several economic doubling times.

More important, a rapidly changing economy needs the flexibility to swiftly adapt to changing circumstances. Today, 58 percent of U.S. exports by value are sent by air. Such transport is typically so time sensitive that an extra day in transit is equivalent to a product tax of 0.6 percent to 2.3 percent (Hummels and Schaur 2013). Yet one day is only one part in 5000 of today's economic doubling time. If this delay-is-very-costly effect scales with the growth rate of the economy, then for an em economy with a one-month doubling time it becomes an eight-minute transit delay that is equivalent to a product tax of 0.6 percent to 2.3 percent. At typical urban commuting speeds of 10 meters per second, products can only be shipped 5 kilometers in eight minutes.

Similarly, on the internet, a 0.1-second signal delay reduces sales by 1 percent, and a 0.5-second delay reduces traffic by 20 percent.

Thus even shipping goods all the way across em cities is substantially discouraged, and shipping goods between em cities is quite prohibitively expensive. The main long distance shipping is for goods with very poor local substitutes, such as essential raw materials, or hard-to-make goods that use secret designs, where the manufacturer does not trust local manufacturers or 3D printers not to steal the design.

To avoid such trust issues, em cities may open internal "embassy" regions almost entirely run according to the laws and rules of other cities. (Although the host city might need to check that embassy regions aren't hosting big bombs.) Manufacturers from those other cities could then place factories within such regions and be better assured that their design secrets are protected. Em cities with large "embassy" trade zones might be almost entirely self-sufficient in terms of physical manufacturing, although trade via communication, such as of designs, would be robust.

As the high cost of time delays encourages em cities to draw their raw materials mostly from local sources, a poor choice of city location might be fatal to long-term city prosperity. Locating close to large industry-era landfills, which contain a wide range of useful materials, might offer useful insurance against such risks.

Em economic interest in space travel should greatly diminish from today's already low levels. Although a much richer em society can afford more vanity space travel, the long subjective delays to move between Earth and space discourage this choice relative to other vanity projects. Even so, a far larger em economy, and the far lower cost to send ems into space, will likely greatly increase the number of human-like creatures in space, even if the fraction of GDP spent on space is lower. It is also possible, even if unlikely, that a cascade of debris from colliding satellites in Earth's orbit will make exit from Earth through the resulting debris field prohibitively expensive (Kessler and Cour-Palais 1978).

Within cities, transport of shipping-container-sized items probably takes place via roads and railroads with familiar human-scale cross-sections and speeds. But the existence of ems with much smaller physical dimensions likely also creates a demand for transport routes with smaller cross-sections.

Pneumatic tubes seem one attractive candidate for smaller cross-section transport. Paris once had a large postal system of 6.5-centimeter diameter tubes that moved bottles containing letters at a speed of about 10 meters per second. This tube system started in 1866, and eventually had about 500 kilometers of tubes. Pneumatic tube systems work similarly today, although they are better automated and typically have diameters of 10 centimeters. Em cities might have much larger networks of pneumatic tubes to move small goods.

Train tunnels today have a standard diameter of about 6 meters, while automobile tunnels are usually a bit larger. Pneumatic tubes are roughly a factor of 100 smaller than train and road tunnels. Tubes 100 times smaller than pneumatic tubes are a bit less than a millimeter in diameter. It turns out that this is a standard diameter for equipment tubes today.

Similar to computing and manufacturing, future transport may also be thermodynamically adiabatic, to reduce the use of free energy. That is, there may be substantial subsystems of the transportation system wherein the free energy required to move cargo a given distance is proportional to the speed at which that cargo moves. If so, then as with adiabatic computing and manufacturing, within such subsystems about as much is spent on renting transport hardware, including roads, as on the energy and cooling needed to run that hardware.

In sum, because ems vary in speeds and sizes, em travel takes place in a wider variety of sizes of tubes and vehicles.

CHAPTER 19

Groups

CLANS

By analogy with a family clan today, we can take all of the copy descendants of a single original human, and call that group a "clan." All of the copy descendants of a particular em can be called a "subclan." (While the term "clade" might be more precise, the term "clan" is more widely known.)

How do clans and subclans organize?

Today, we are each part of many organizations, such as neighborhoods, firms, clubs, and nations. But we rely most on our families when we seek strong long-term bonds and trust. It is within families that we most share resources, let ourselves be most vulnerable, and seek help in bad times. Long ago humans evolved to trust families more than other groupings because of their closer genetic relations, and have developed many family-specific adaptations to complement such unusually strong family trust.

Identical twins are more closely related than are family members. Because of the rarity of such twins, however, our ancestors may have evolved few adaptations specific to twinning. Even so, the trust and bonds between identical twins usually seems to be stronger than those between other family members.

Ems have access to a new unit of organization: clans of copies of the same original person. Compared with families or even identical twins, ems have even stronger reasons to trust and bond with fellow clan members. This makes em copy clans a natural candidate unit for finance, reproduction, legal liability, and political representation.

The degree of affiliation between two em copies depends on how long they have been diverging subjectively since their last common ancestor. Copies that have diverged for only an hour are likely to feel very strongly affiliated. They'd share almost all opinions and attitudes, and are usually willing to make great sacrifices for one another. On the other hand, copies that have diverged for decades may feel far less of a connection. They might have been trained for different professions, and live in different kinds of communities. Their personalities and political opinions might even have diverged. However, as most ems are near the same peak productivity subjective age, they don't usually have to deal much with age-related differences in personality or opinions (Alwin and Krosnick 1991; Soto et al. 2011).

Clans with millions or more members likely split for many purposes into subclans of thousands or more. The tree structure of their copy ancestry forms a natural basis for such subclan grouping. During the farming era, and still in some places today, ancestry trees of family clans were often a basis for food sharing, legal liability, political coalitions, military units, and much else. Relative to em clans, em subclans even more closely resemble each other in jobs, hobbies, friends, personality, and shared memories. Conflicts between subclans are likely to be the main form of internal clan conflict.

Ems probably vary in how much they could trust recent copies of themselves, and in how much the duration since they split into different copies matters for trust. For example, those who see themselves as typically "faking it" around others, that is, pretending to have more competence than they believe they have, are likely to trust less in the competence of recent copies of themselves. In a clan-dominated em era, people whose basic personality makes it harder to coordinate and compromise with copies of themselves, or to predict the behavior of such copies, are likely to be at a competitive disadvantage.

Even if the interests of em clan members are typically more closely aligned than are the interests of family members or identical twins today, their interests are hardly identical. Different copies can have different jobs and associates from whom they gain differing degrees of pleasure. Different copies can also differ in whether they will end or retire, and in the speed and quality of their retirement. Different copies are well aware of these different possible outcomes, and are quite capable of taking them into account in choosing actions. Thus unless great efforts are taken to erase or hide such differences, we should not expect em clans to resemble the "Borg" in Star Trek, a group mind that consistently acts toward a common purpose without internal conflicts (Shulman 2010).

MANAGING CLANS

So what do clans do differently from other units of organization, such as cities and firms?

Law usually tries to deter crime via small chances of big punishments. It can be especially hard, however, to cheaply impose big punishments on short-lived ems. Giving ems a longer life to torture them over a long time, for example, could cost a lot more than did their original life. For such ems it can make sense to use vicarious liability, that is, to have legal liability apply to an associated unit with "deeper pockets." In principle this could be any influential sponsor willing to take on the liability, but in practice this is probably a subclan containing that em. Ems care more about hurting their subclans, and subclans know how to discourage member ems from liability-inducing events (Miceli and Segerson 2007).

Em clan vicarious liability could be similar to the way that farmer societies often made larger family units liable for the crimes of individual family members. Holding closely related copies responsible for an em's crimes may seem more legitimate to observers if archived versions of such copies could be tested in sims to see if they would have behaved similarly given a similar opportunity.

Subclans legally liable for the behaviors of members probably seek to regulate such behaviors. Subclans also want such powers to manage their reputations. After all, as subclan members are so similar, the behavior of any one member could be highly predictive of the behavior of others. Thus the bad behavior of one em could make the rest of their subclan look bad. Ems in clans that more strongly manage their reputations will seem more predictable and reliable.

When many copies are made of an em trained at a substantial expense, then to avoid ruinous wage competition that fails to recover fixed costs of training and marketing, such copies must be constrained in the job wages they can accept.

Political regimes become unstable when members do not accept their legitimacy. As we tend more to accept and defer to internal decisions of families, compared with non-kin-based associations, farmer-era city and regional politics often used families as the first unit of political grouping. That is, ancient politics was often the politics of shifting coalitions of family clans (Braekevelt et al. 2012). This remains true in the Middle East and Asia today (Sailer 2003).

Relative to the self-governance of families, we defer today even more to the self-governance of individuals, at least for individual behaviors that don't influence others much. For example, if a person suffers today to gain benefits in later days, such as by attending a difficult school with a high chance of failure, we almost never suggest that their future self is exploiting their current self. Thus for ems it makes even more sense to use clans as the first unit of political organization than it did for farmers to use families as their main political unit. If most ems are in a dozen to a thousand clans, the politics of an em city-state might naturally be the politics of shifting coalitions of em clans.

Clans and subclans whose root ems were raised together as children might tend to ally more with each other, and childhood cohorts might be chosen with this prospect in mind.

To encourage internal clan loyalty, clans may try to anticipate and coordinate to prevent situations in which clan members compete over friends, lovers, or jobs. For example, a clan might have a stable general policy of preventing different subclans from competing for the same jobs or teams.

When a single em makes a plan for the future and then splits into many copies who execute that plan, the resulting ems are likely to identify especially strongly with each other as being the "same" person spread out in space to implement their common plan. This strong identification is likely to continue until some copies come to question the importance or wisdom of the plan, or to disagree explicitly about how to implement the plan.

Direct explicit disagreements of any sort between copies are likely to push them more to see themselves as distinct persons, instead of as different parts of the same person. Because of this, subclans may try to arrange the interactions between such copies to discourage direct explicit argumentation. Subclans may instead prefer other more indirect mechanisms to share information. For example, a subclan might usually act as if it agreed with consensus prediction market estimates, and individuals who disagreed with that consensus might be satisfied to express their disagreements via prediction market trades, and then mostly ignore those disagreements when interacting in other ways with other clan members.

Ems who practice arguing with close copies, however, may better learn how to rationally update on new information. Most of our usual excuses today for disagreeing with others don't apply, and so this situation more clearly exposes our typical neglect of the information embodied in the opinions of others (Hanson and Cowen 2004).

Em subclans with similar work and living arrangements may well act together to buy in bulk. Today, firms often achieve substantial savings by buying in bulk. That is, firms buy large quantities of oft-used items, such as computers, vehicles, or office supplies, together with matching supporting systems for maintenance, repair, and training. In contrast, consumers today tend to buy much smaller quantities of more varied and less integrated items, which cost more as a result. Em subclans might buy many copies of whole coordinated systems, one copy for each member.

Buying in bulk is one of many ways that ems could benefit from being part of large clans or subclans. Large clans may also succeed more in world- or city-scale coalition politics, and their members can feel more confident in being valued by the world. They may build specialized hardware to run their clan's minds, and they may organize better to protect their security. Large clans may even create their own news sources, with reporters who observe events and record shallow mindreadings that other clan members can then directly experience.

Of course large clans may also suffer disadvantages, such as needing more formal mechanisms of governance, having bigger internal divisions and disagreements, and suffering more cases where subclans compete with each other in outside markets.

FIRMS

Firms continue to exist in an em world, but with a few changes.

Today for firms less than ten years old, younger firms grow faster. But while larger firms tend to be older, there is no growth penalty from being large per se. Once one controls for age, larger firms grow just as fast as do small ones (Haltiwanger et al. 2013).

As we will discuss in Chapter 20, Inequality section, em firms will tend to be larger than firms today. We can thus use observed features of larger firms today to guess how em firms will differ from our firms. For example, larger em firms have less overall coordination and coherence, even as such firms put more effort into coordination via more meetings by more managers in more layers of management. Workers in larger firms also have more specific operational roles, and each does a narrower range of tasks. All else being equal, larger em firms have offices in more locations, with less in-person and direct internal communication. This effect may be countered by ems concentrating in a few huge cities.

Early in the industrial revolution, many noticed a general trend toward larger organizations with more specialized and regimented roles. They noticed that we often create more efficient but standardized and centralized clothing, cooking, and housing for slaves, soldiers, sailors, students, and apprentices. People such as Yevgeny Zamyatin, author of the classic novel *We*, feared that the entire social world would soon be factory-like, and that firms and nations would soon merge into intrusive faceless oppressors that dictated who people married, where they lived, what they ate, when they slept, and pretty much everything (Richter 1893; Zamyatin 1924). Discomfort with big organizations lingers in our stereotypes of "soul-crushing" bureaucracies.

But in fact, our increasing wealth has allowed us great variety and individuality in our food, clothes, homes, hobbies, and much more. For ems such variety can be even cheaper in virtual reality.

It is true that workers today tend to say they are less satisfied with jobs in larger firms, because of their less flexible work environments (Idson 1990). However, just as larger cities are often celebrated for having more innovation, specialization, and better educated and paid workers, larger firms deserve similar praise because they are more productive, last longer, use more capital per worker, adopt new technologies earlier, and pay and train their better educated workers more (Oi and Idson 1999; Bento and Restuccia 2014; Cardiff-Hicks et al. 2014). Today, most employees of large firms seem to lead full lives with their souls largely intact.

Also, workers who focus more on pleasing their boss, and less on doing what they see as a good job, tend to be more successful and happier (Judge and Bretz 1994). So ems may also be happier if they learn to focus on pleasing their bosses.

Management experts today have identified many efficient management practices. Not only do these practices correlate with firms that are bigger, grow faster, earn more, and last longer, but randomized experiments show that these practices increase productivity. The use of such practices seems to be increased today by product market competition, by being a multinational firm, by exporting, and by having more educated workers (Bloom et al. 2013; Bloom and Van Reenen 2010).

Today, family based firms tend to be less productive when run by someone who got the job because of birth, such as by being an eldest son, and such firms are more productive when run by someone outside the family. Private-equity owned firms have management practices that are as good as public firms, and better than simple private firms, family based firms, and government organizations (Bloom et al. 2015).

Because of learning and increased competitive pressures, we should expect em firms to use more of these good management practices, relative to firms of today. These practices include performance-based rewards and job-placement, demanding but attainable goals, managers evaluated on attracting and retaining talent, regular equipment maintenance, thorough analysis of failures, clear job descriptions, just-in-time delivery, tracking production by order, pricing orders based on production costs, and frequent and detailed tracking of inputs, outputs, and performance.

Many other business practices today are suspected of being inefficient, even if the case against them isn't quite as strong. We should also (more weakly) expect these practices to decline in em firms, because of continued firm learning and increased competitive pressures. These practices include keeping unproductive "deadwood" employees for too long, overpaying employees in critical functions at large firms, overly frequent mergers, too many long big meetings, "poison pills" that directly punish new investors in hostile takeovers, discouraging subordinates from reporting bad news, rejecting innovations "not invented here," allowing barriers to within-firm information sharing, hiring consultants to endorse predetermined conclusions, avoiding experiments to test products and practices, avoiding formal accuracy tracking of who predicted or suggested what when, excess reliance on interviews and school credentials in hiring, and allowing bosses to give lower employee evaluations to subordinates who do not "toot their own horns" and to subordinates who the boss did not hire or promote.

We can categorize firms today by whether their business focus is novelty, quality, cost, or something else. Novelty- and quality-focused firms innovate more, have more layers of management, and rely more on employee initiative, via pay-for-performance, problem-solving teams, and employee information-sharing programs. Both types outsource more and cooperate more with other firms in research.

Quality- and cost-focused firms have higher productivity and market share, closely track operation performance, and coordinate more along their value chain. Quality-focused firms have higher markups and profits, while cost-focused firms have lower profits. Cost-focused firms do more downsizing and cutting of management layers, and emphasize central coordination via managers (Yang et al. 2015).

We weakly expect these correlations to continue with em firms. As we expect em firms to focus more on cost and less on novelty, this suggests that em firms have higher market shares, lower markups and profits, fewer layers of management, and less innovation, employee initiative, and pay-for-performance. However, if the em world manages to find better ways than we have today to encourage innovation, such as are discussed in Chapter 22, Innovation section, perhaps more em firms will be more novelty-focused.

Larger firms today tend to have narrower and more precisely defined processes and structures, including policy manuals and job descriptions. They also have stronger corporate cultures and depend less on distinctive individual personalities. While one might expect this trend to continue with em firms, we soon discuss a contrary factor that could plausibly lead to less formality and more distinctive employee personalities.

Today, firm managers tend to be given more discretion when it is harder for their superiors to evaluate them via comparisons with other firms using similar technology in similar environments. Such judgments are also harder when firms are young, their technology is new, and their environments change fast. Firms whose managers have more discretion tend to be organized into divisions that are profit centers, while other firms tend to be organized into divisions that are cost centers (Acemoglu et al. 2007).

Em firms tend to be larger and older, the em economy has less product variety, and innovation matters less for growth in the em economy. All these factors suggest that em firms are more often organized into cost-center divisions, with managers having less discretion. However, the opposite may hold if sufficiently high levels of clan-firm trust can be achieved, as discussed in the next section.

Firms tend to be less efficient at making a wider diversity of products and services, and they focus more when competition is stronger (Dhyne et al. 2017). As em firms will face strong competition, each firm focuses more on a few products and services it does very well.

While wage inequality has been increasing in rich nations in recent decades, the wage inequality within firms there has not been increasing. This suggests that firms limit internal wage inequality because of problems it causes in morale or office politics. This further suggests that em firms and teams will also prefer to limit internal wage inequality. Em wages probably differ more between firms, rather than within firms (Song et al. 2015).

FIRM-CLAN RELATIONS

As firms and clans are both large important institutions in em society, potential conflicts can arise between them, along with opportunities for gains by avoiding such conflicts.

For example, firms with employees drawn from many clans face security issues about where to locate employee brains. Clans may minimize risks of theft by locating themselves within "castles" that only contain, and are only managed by, clan members. However, this arrangement increases risks to firms of clans leaking firm secrets, and makes it harder for subordinates to meet with fast bosses within a firm. In contrast, co-locating firm employees at a single location lets employees interact more flexibly, such as via fast meetings with fast bosses, and can better protect firm secrets. However, from a clan's point of view this approach increases the risk of the theft of clan minds and secrets.

Higher levels of clan-firm trust can thus increase firm efficiency, by allowing firm employee brains to be located closer to one another. Higher levels of clan-firm trust might result if firms and clans invested heavily in each other's ventures, and also if clans or firms were long-lived entities that developed strong reputations for trustworthiness that they fear losing.

Such trust can produce other benefits. For example, at big firms today it is usually hard to objectively attribute successes or failures to the actions of particular employees. This encourages people to play strategic games with how people and projects are evaluated. For example, employees become yes-men, curry favor with evaluators, form mutual admiration coalitions, and focus their efforts on more visible outcomes such as attendance, grooming, writing style, and school credentials. In contrast, ems from clans with a large financial and reputational interest in a firm might simply try to be useful to that firm. As the reputations of clans will average over many choices made by many clan members at many firms, clans may have more confidence that the average value of their clan's contributions will be discerned amid the noise of variation across particular firm contexts.

Today, firms often use formality and standards to try to ensure that workers are closer substitutes to one another, and thus compete with each other more strongly for jobs. This makes such firms less vulnerable to threats by individual employees to leave. Em firms might plausibly act similarly to ensure that employee clans compete with each other. After all, a firm that came to rely on the habits and skills of a particular clan could be vulnerable to a threat by that clan to leave the firm unless that clan got a larger share of firm profits. This is feasible because clans are often "unionized" in the sense of negotiating labor agreements as a unit.

Higher levels of clan-firm trust might, however, let firms instead rely more on the unique skills and habits of particular clans. Em firms that more strongly trust their employee clans not to make threats to leave are likely to have fewer formal rules and standards regarding worker procedures and performance. In this case each employee clan could take on a distinctive clan personality, instead of taking on a more standard personality to fill a standard job role.

Today, efforts and misallocations resulting from office politics often result in substantial firm inefficiencies. But such costs are at least limited by job turnover, as it takes time for new employees to adapt to local office politics. Costs are also limited because factions often limit information on factional strategies to core faction members, which keeps peripheral members from fully participating in office politics. This often leads such peripheral employees to choose a strategy of "keeping their head down" and avoiding entangling alliances with warring factions.

Unfortunately, the use of factions based on clans can more easily overcome the factors that today limit the severity of office politics. Most members of em clans know each other very well and are able to coordinate well internally, including by keeping internal clan secrets. Thus office politics in em firms has the potential to be quite destructive. To reduce such losses, em firms may try harder to increase accountability by increasing the visibility of actions and their consequences.

Em labor markets are more like product markets today, with a few firms selling most of the products in each market. Here the suppliers are clans, who pay to train members to compete in each labor market. These clans face nearly the same marginal costs of supplying labor, but can choose different fixed costs of training, testing, and marketing. When they are effective competitors, we expect such suppliers to differentiate their products, to invest in larger fixed costs when supplying larger markets, and to make deals with other clans that bundle complementary ems into teams. We expect such suppliers to have substantial market power, which typically induces too many firms to enter each market, relative to a social optimum (Shy 1996).

TEAMS

Most work that is done at firms is done within much smaller workplace teams. How do work teams differ in an em era?

Because the em world is more competitive than ours, we weakly expect em teams to display more of the features that today are correlated with team productivity.

For example, today the most productive teams tend to have incentives that are either at the individual level or the team level; mixed intermediate incentives tend to produce worse outcomes. Teams with group incentives who deal with complex production processes tend to benefit by creating special problem-solving subteams (Boning et al. 2007). Today, the most productive long-lived work teams tend to be more self-directed, because this improves attitudes and makes workers more easily accept pressures to conform to local work norms. The most productive short-lived project teams, in contrast, tend to have more outside direction (Cohen and Bailey 1997).

Talk networks, that is, who tends to talk to whom, also matter for team productivity. Teams with stable talk networks are better at repetitive tasks (customer service), but teams with fast changing talk networks are better at creative tasks (sales and management). More productive teams have more cohesive (tightly interconnected) networks of face-to-face talk, especially for complex tasks, but less cohesive networks of email talk (Wu et al. 2008). On good teams members talk for similar proportions of the time, are better at reading each other via tone and expressions, and feel safer about not being rejected for saying the wrong thing (Edmondson 1999; Duhigg 2016).

Today, the most productive work teams tend to have members with similar surface and social-category features such as race, ethnicity, gender, age, and tenure. We similarly pick friends who are similar to us (Bahns et al. 2017). In contrast, the most productive teams tend to have a diversity of features that indicate sources of information and styles of thinking. Such features include personality and areas of education, training, and experience. Such diversity is especially valuable for work tasks that require exploration, as in research (Mannix and Neale 2005).

While teams are likely to be arranged in ways that maximize productivity, they are unlikely to *consciously* define themselves this way. Instead, like groups in offices today, and like our distant forager ancestors, em teams are likely to define themselves more by their mutual respect and loyalty, and by their shared cultural values such as egalitarianism, honesty, rationality, realism, sharing of resources and information, and disapproval of bragging, dominance, greed, intolerance, and jealousy.

As discussed in Chapter 13, Clan Concentration section, a few clans probably dominate most em labor markets. This gives such suppliers substantial market power, although not expected net profits after paying for training, marketing, and other fixed costs. Suppliers having market power in em labor markets suggests that team formation can involve substantial strategic negotiation. Ems may, for example, gain strategic advantages from committing to not join teams lacking certain favored allies, or containing disliked rivals. Foragers evolved many complex and subtle abilities to navigate politics like this in forager bands. Such abilities may find many applications in em team politics. Efforts devoted to complex feuding and political intrigue, however, can be costly.

Sometimes firms prefer the ease of hiring team members as simple employees. This could result in weaker employee incentives, aside from clan reputation. At other times, teams may incorporate as small for-profit firms, and contract to supply specific services. In such cases, team profits could be divided among team members, supplying clans, and supporting investors. Team members might take their individual profits partly as extra leisure time or faster retirement.

As mentioned in Chapter 11, Defining Death section, starting and ending or retiring teams as units is likely be the norm. Encouraging teams to prefer internal social interactions minimizes disruptions from outside social interactions that could induce unexpected variations in team productivity. This might have a happiness cost, however, as frequent contact with many others with weak social ties seems important to happiness (Sandstrom and Dunn 2014).

A similar if smaller reduction in productivity variance comes if teams pay less attention to outside news and events. This attitude of low interest in news comes more naturally for fast ems, as the wider world is more stable to them, and so has less interesting news to report.

Having fewer outside-team interactions somewhat lowers the value of living near city centers, and the gains from information and innovations that diffuse via weak social ties. So teams with stronger interactions with outsiders tend to be found more in city centers.

Today people who expect to change teams are less willing to sacrifice for their team, or even for their future selves (Burum et al. 2016). In contrast, em teams can have stronger internal social bonds. Em teams who are created together more see their team as literally their reason for existence. Also, there are fewer conflicts to threaten internal team loyalty. Teams mostly succeed or fail together, and end or retire together. Ems need not fear that colleagues will leave their team for better opportunities, as these colleagues can instead make new copies to pursue better opportunities. If teams could veto team members making copies outside the team, that might further reduce internal team conflicts. However, which ems feel most attached to which other ems within a team could vary over time.

MASS VERSUS NICHE TEAMS

Product markets today can be divided into mass versus niche markets. Makers of mass-market products want to limit their product variation to appeal to as many customers as possible. In contrast, makers of niche-market products want to increase their product variation to appeal to different narrow groups of customers each willing to pay more for products that more closely match their idiosyncratic preferences (Johnson and Myatt 2006). Mass products tend to have more competition, scale economies, and mass advertising. Many mass products began as niche products. Compared with physically distributed goods, it is easier for electronically distributed goods to serve wider markets, and thus to become more narrowly specialized niche products.

Em labor markets should also divide into mass and niche markets. In niche labor markets, new jobs are rare, unpredictable, and more often require a few new em copies to flexibly adapt to a particular new situation. For example, a new copy of a specialized management consultant might be created whenever a firm decided it needed this sort of specialist to address a particular problem.

Mass em labor markets, in contrast, have a steadier stream of predictable customers to be provided with similar services. Mass markets tend more to select the most productive em teams from a large pool of candidates. Thus mass-market ems are more heavily concentrated near peak productivity ages. Niche-market ems, in contrast, tend to have a wider distribution of subjective ages.

In general, the degree of concentration of work ages near peak productivity ages is a tradeoff between general worker productivity and gains from a worker being more familiar with a particular workplace. The more useful it is to keep the same worker in the same environment for many years, the more years a worker tends to stays on one job, and the more that those years are further away from the peak productivity age.

For each niche worker, there are fewer workers with similar training doing similar tasks. Because of this, it is easier for mass-market ems to adopt a mode where many copies of a worker are made each morning, but only some of those copies are saved to enjoy leisure the next day.

Mass-market ems can more easily form teams who are copied and retired as a unit. Even if most niche-market ems are also created in teams, niche ems more often accept complications from not starting or retiring as part of a team, as well as additional complexities from dealing with friends and lovers who start and end at different times.

All ems must deal with related complications when they are copied and find that their new team is not identical to their old team.

When a niche em makes a new copy, he or she may have to decide whether the original or the copy inherits the original's friends. Alternatively, a small group of copies might coordinate to share such a friend, and to make sure to keep up to date on all of the interactions between this friend and this small copy group, so that the friend doesn't struggle to keep track of which copy it had interacted with.

These complications of a niche em lifestyle likely make such a life seem less attractive to many. If so, this raises the costs of niche labor. Also, as discussed in Chapter 13, Efficiency section, the em economy in addition moves toward mass products because of stronger competition and lower wages. However, as niche job lifestyles are culturally more like forager lifestyles, they may acquire a Bohemian prestige, perhaps raising the social status of ems who have a close copy who once lived a niche lifestyle.

The existence of many similar teams usually gives mass-market ems a good idea of what to expect in their future life. After all, each such em can look at the experiences of older copies in prior versions of their team. Such previous experiences can sometimes be misleading, for example when outside forces such as customers, competitors, or suppliers induce big local changes. However, such exceptions are rare. Today, many religious people are less anxious about life events because they think "this is all part of God's plan." Similarly, mass-market ems can be comforted to know that most disturbing life events were part of the clan's plan.

When an em clan supplies workers to a very large mass labor market, there must be at least as many members of that clan as there are workers who serve that labor market, times the market share of that clan. Because this number will sometimes be larger than the total number of members in a small clan, clans who supply very large labor markets must also be large. This may create a correlation between clan size and mass-market work; larger clans may tend more to supply mass labor markets, while smaller clans more often serve niche labor markets.

While ems that serve mass markets could more easily be copied as a part of large teams that retain most of their familiar friends and context, such copied teams could not as easily bring along copies of large shared community spaces such as city neighborhoods or parks. For very large spaces this is not a problem, as the different copies of the team can just share the same original space, and only rarely meet in the large space. For smaller spaces, however, ems must choose between moving to a new "parallel world" space, which can of course still look a lot like the old space, or sharing the old space and dealing with the prospect of meeting more often and mixing with similar members of other teams.

In sum, the lives of both mass-market and niche-market ems differ substantially from our lives, but in different ways.

CHAPTER 20

Conflict

INEQUALITY

How unequal are ems from one another?

During the forager era the main units of organization were bands of roughly twenty to fifty people, and smaller family units. As activity wasn't organized via larger units, foragers did not see inequality comparable with our unequal towns, firms, or nations. Foragers also had only mild differences in personal property and prestige. Over the roughly million plus year forager era, however, foragers had an enormous inequality of lineages, in the sense that almost all lineages eventually went extinct, with zero descendants.

The farmer era had larger units of organization, such as clans, villages, nations, and empires. Although empires sometimes became nearly as large as feasible given transportation limits, large empires usually only had a weak influence on local behaviors. Villages were much smaller than nations, and firms were typically tiny.

As discussed in Chapter 18, Cities section, while most farmers lived near small villages, in our industrial era people are spread rather evenly across towns and cities of all feasible sizes. Also, for most industrial products today, market shares are relatively concentrated within transport-cost-limited market areas. That is, for each type of product in an area, only a small number of firms supply most customers.

Power laws are mathematical forms that often usefully describe such inequality. That is, power laws often fit the large-unit end of the distributions of how such items are grouped into units. In such cases, a power of one describes a uniform distribution of items across feasible unit sizes. Powers greater than one describe more equal distributions, wherein most items reside in small units, and powers less than one describe less equal distributions, wherein most items are clumped into fewer larger units. Compared with any given sized unit, for a power of one a unit with twice the size appears half as often. Thus for a power of one, different sized units hold a similar total number of items. Compared with a power of one, with a power greater than one such double-size units are less frequent, while with a power less than one double-size units are more frequent.

During all eras so far, family names, which are good proxy for family lineages, have been distributed relatively equally, with a power of about two. Later in the farmer era, villages were distributed more unequally, with a power of about one-and-a-half (Nitsch 2005), roughly the power that describes the distribution of individual wealth today (Davies et al. 2011), although the worldwide income distribution seems better described as a log-normal distribution (Provenzano 2015). (The income ratio between ninetieth and tenth percentiles is less than many think; it was 1.84 in 1985, and 1.74 in 2011.)

Today, nations, firms within nations, and cities within nations, are all distributed even more unequally, with a power of about one (Axtell 2001; Eeckhout 2004; Giesen et al. 2010). The items within these units are distributed evenly across all possible unit sizes. Finally, the set of firms that supply particular products to customers and to other firms are usually distributed even more unequally, with a power less than one. For each such product, most units are supplied by only a few firms (Kohli and Sah 2006).

EM INEQUALITY

As discussed in Chapter 13, Clan Concentration section, em-era clans clump much more unequally than did family lineages in prior eras; most ems may come from a dozen to a thousand one-name clans, each of which has millions to billions of members. In contrast, there may be millions of two-name clans, each with only thousands to millions of members. And most of the roughly 10 billion ordinary humans may each give rise to a three-name clan with perhaps only dozens of members.

With only hundreds of main clans, em labor markets become concentrated like today's product markets, with a few clans supplying most workers in any given skill area. It may be like U.S. vehicles today, where 300 models are sold, and 3 percent are the Ford F pickup. Clans coordinate to support their workers, by preventing member mind theft and ensuring that workers can profit from training investments. Fixed costs of training and marketing create market concentration and power, although not net profits after paying for fixed costs.

As discussed in Chapter 18, Cities section, em cities and nations are also likely to be much more unequal than are cities and nations today, with most ems found in a few very large city-states.

The high degree of inequality and concentration of em clans and cities introduces a key source of uncertainty about the em world. The main em clans could be quite unrepresentative of humans today, and in ways that are hard for us to foresee. That is, the world of ems could be substantially different, depending on the particular mix of the few clans who happen to dominate the core set of most-copied clans. Similarly, the few dominant em cities are probably not equally distributed across the globe; the em world could be quite different depending on the locations of those key em cities.

Today firms tend to get larger, and have a wider range of sizes, in richer regions and nations (Poschke 2014). Em firms are likely to continue to be distributed evenly across feasible firm sizes. But because a larger economy could contain larger firms, the typical em firm size will be larger. Today, in a world of 7 billion people, firms are spread evenly between having roughly one and 1 million employees. The middle firm size, where half of workers are in larger firms, has about 1000 workers. For every factor of 100 increase in the size of the largest feasible em firm, such as might come from an increase in total em population, we should expect about a factor of ten increase in the number of workers in the middle-sized em firm.

The wages of em workers are much more equal than are wages today, at least after correcting for training costs. The highly competitive em economy pushes wages down to near subsistence levels, even for jobs requiring superior workers. This is because workers of almost all quality levels are available in unlimited quantities.

While em wages are more equal than are wages today, em wealth can be more unequal. This is because of both indefinite em lifespans, and the em capacity to run at different speeds. Today, it seems to be the long lifespans of cities and firms that allows them to spread uniformly across all feasible sizes; if a city or firm continues to succeed, it can continue to grow, even when old. In contrast, while wealthy individuals today often consistently grow their wealth over their lifespan, their children usually fail to increase the family fortune. Rags-to-riches-to-rags in three generations is, after all, a common story. This helps explain why individual wealth isn't as unequally distributed today as are city and firm sizes.

With indefinite em lifespans, however, successful ems might continue their successful financial habits indefinitely. This tends to distribute wealth more evenly across feasible wealth sizes, similar to how firms and cities are distributed evenly today across feasible sizes, some large and some small. The tendency of em minds to become inflexible with experience, however, may somewhat reduce this effect, especially if rich old ems do not reduce their speeds.

The ability to run at many different speeds also expands the range of possible em wealth. A faster em brain directly embodies more wealth, and it can often find productive uses for that wealth. While humans who are relatively very poor must starve, ems who are relatively very poor can run at very slow speeds or be archived. Thus as ems can be both very fast and very slow, they can be both very rich and very poor.

If these effects dominate, then the em world might see roughly a power of one for the distribution of em wealth. This would make wealth more unequal than today, both because this is a lower and hence more unequal power, and because a richer em world can make feasible both higher and lower wealth levels. While today's richest human holds ~0.02 percent of the world's wealth, the richest em might hold a larger fraction, perhaps ~2 percent of the em world's wealth. Then as now, the very richest of all tend to be those who make higher variance investment choices. They "went left when others went right" (Cohan 2017).

While the CEOs of public firms tend to be rich, and quite visibly so, they actually make up only about 5 percent of the richest 0.01 percent of people in the U.S. (Kaplan and Rauh 2010). Even so, let us consider how CEO pay may change with ems.

Today CEO pay rises as roughly a one-third power of firm revenue. This implies that as firms get larger, CEOs take a smaller share of firm income. This situation can be explained by assuming that firms compete to attract quality CEOs, that CEO talent multiplies firm income, and that this talent is distributed as roughly two-thirds power of CEO rank (Edmans and Gabaix 2016; Edmans et al. 2017). Given these assumptions, if em firms can compete for copies of the best em CEO in each skill area, then em CEO pay would be directly proportional to firm revenue, and could become a large fraction of that revenue. If this model is correct, em CEOs are much better than our CEOs, and as a result gain a much larger fraction of firm income than do CEOs today.

REDISTRIBUTION

In the last section, we identified some wealth-inequality-increasing effects in the em world. However, these effects need not dominate, because of the possibility of income or wealth redistribution.

There are many kinds of inequality. Inequality exists between different species, between generations born at different times, and between nations of the world at a time. Within a nation at a time, there is inequality both between families and within families. There is also inequality between the moments of the life of a particular person. In all of these cases, there is not only financial inequality, but also inequality in status, popularity, pleasure, boredom, lifespan, health, happiness, enjoying one's job, and more. There is also inequality between the sizes of lineages, firms, cities, or nations, even when individuals within those groupings are equal.

Today, we have relatively little intentional redistribution between generations or between nations. Redistribution within the moments of a person's life happens, but that is mostly left to each person to choose and to fund. Similarly, redistribution between young siblings is mostly achieved via differential treatment by parents. And voluntary insurance redistributes to those who suffer certain kinds of disasters. However, we see almost no interest in addressing unequal status, popularity, or job enjoyment. Instead, most of the concern expressed today about inequality, and most debate about redistribution to address inequality, mostly ignores these kinds of inequality, and focuses on one particular standard kind of inequality.

This standard inequality of concern today is how the families of a nation at a given time differ in the average financial wealth or consumption of their members. This families-of-a-nation inequality is actually one of the smallest in magnitude. For example, in the U.S. today financial inequality between families is only one-third of the size of financial inequality between siblings within families, and even that is much less than the financial inequality between individuals from different nations (Conley 2004). In addition, we probably care personally as much about differences in prestige, popularity, lifespans, and so on as we do about financial inequality.

Humans who attend directly to vivid cases are capable of great empathy for inequality losers. They are also capable of great compassion and even a desire to help. However, we humans are also quite capable of avoiding contact and exposure that might produce such compassion, and of numbing ourselves to the plight of losers about whom it would be inconvenient to feel empathy. So rich people avoid visiting poor neighborhoods and nations, attractive people avoid socializing with the ugly, and pretty young women become numb to the losses of the men they reject.

We are not sure why humans today feel so much more concern for inequality between families of a nation, compared with other forms of inequality. Perhaps this seems to us most like the inequalities that forager sharing norms addressed. Or perhaps the redistribution that addresses this inequality offers the easiest gains to opportunistic people seeking excuses to grab wealth.

This history suggests that the em world sees little redistribution between em generations or city-states, and also that each clan (or perhaps subclan) is mostly in charge of deciding how to address its internal inequality. After all, em clan members are more similar to and closer to each other than are human siblings, even if they may sometimes be more distant from each other than are different moments within a particular person's life today.

That leaves the inequality between clans, or subclans. A set of em clans can be unequal in two different ways. One type of clan inequality focuses on individual incomes, or perhaps individual happiness or respect, and treats a clan as better off if its individuals are on average better off. This inequality measure isn't very sensitive to whether one applies it to clans or subclans, or to how exactly one defines subclans.

The other type of clan inequality focuses on the overall size and success of a clan or subclan. Here a clan is better off if it has more members, resources, or respect. This type of inequality is far more sensitive to how exactly one draws the boundaries of subclans. Historically, most redistribution efforts have focused on average individual outcomes. For example, we have seen very little effort to redistribute between human lineages based on lineage size. That is, we rarely take from lineages with many descendants to give to those that have few descendants. Nor do we take much from big nations, cities, or firms to give to smaller ones.

Because most em wages are near subsistence levels, unregulated em wages (per subjective day) have much less inequality than do wages today. So em clans naturally have less inequality of the standard sort that is the focus of redistribution today. In contrast, em clans have enormous inequality in clan size, resources, and respect. However, history gives little reason to expect much redistribution to address this kind of inequality. This kind of inequality is not very analogous to those that induced forager sharing, it does not lend itself to profitable rent-seeking, and it is very sensitive to how subclans are defined.

Ems might also redistribute on the basis of speed, taking from fast ems to give to slow ones. After all, the fast are few and the slow are many. But history also offers little precedent for this, if slower ems do not seem to be suffering much more in any clear way. And the vast number of slow retirees and the ease of creating more makes this an apparently bottomless pit of need.

Thus the main kind of redistribution that we have reason to expect in the em era is between the clans of a city, based on differences of average within-clan individual consumption. But we expect less inequality of this sort in the em world, and so expect less redistribution on this basis. What distribution there is probably focuses on simple financial consumption, that is, on the fraction of subjective life available for leisure time, and on the money available to spend to enjoy that time.

The inequality measure used by ems to determine redistribution may neglect differences in how much ems enjoy their jobs, or how much "leisure" socializing different jobs require. If so, such redistribution might actually *increase* inequality in em utility, that is, in the value that ems gain from their lifestyles. On the other hand, perhaps ems will use their mindreading capacities to base redistribution levels more directly on the satisfaction, happiness, or meaning in individual em lives.

If ordinary humans are included straightforwardly in the redistribution systems of the em world, then the simple result to expect is transfers, not only from richer to poorer humans, but also away from humans overall. After all, in pure financial terms typical ems are far poorer than the poorest humans, because it takes far more resources to support human survival than to support em survival. Redistribution systems may perhaps try to correct for this fact that em subsistence levels are far below human subsistence levels. But such systems of assistance may also encourage or even require recipients of aid to switch from being a human to being an em, to lower the costs of assistance.

During the em era, humans on average have industrial era incomes which are far higher than human subsistence level incomes. While many and perhaps most humans pay to create a few ems, humans tend to endow such ems with much higher than em subsistence consumption. In contrast, only a small number of humans manage to give rise to very large em clans, and within these clans most members have near subsistence incomes. Thus transfers based on individual consumption inequality take from the descendants of humans who are less successful at creating ems, and give to descendants of more humans who are more successful.

While em society seems likely to have weaker wealth transfers, at least outside of clans, the transfers that it may have may seem lamentable to a human eye.

Progressive income taxes are today one of our main mechanisms for reducing the standard inequality that compares individual incomes between families within a nation at a time. Over the last two centuries, big increases in the top marginal tax rates have mostly followed wars where over 2 percent of the population served in the military. For example, in the U.S. the top marginal tax rate jumped from 15 percent to 67 percent in 1917, during the First World War. Controlling for this effect, top tax increases have not been correlated with wealth, democracy, or the political ideology of the party running the government (Vélez 2014). Having governments controlled by left versus right political parties has had no discernible effect on overall income inequality (Scheve and Stasavage 2009).

Redistribution seems to have little overall impact on growth, except that extreme redistribution can greatly hurt growth (Ostry et al. 2014). Actual redistribution seems to rise mainly when inequality rises, rather than when social policy changes to favor more redistribution (Huber and Stephens 2014).

More generally, looking across a wide sweep of history, the standard inequality has mainly risen with social scale and organization. That is, as regions and empires grow, individuals get on average richer, and larger-scale coordination creates more and larger choke points where those who control such points can demand larger payments. The standard inequality has mainly fallen because of big disasters such as wars, plagues, revolutions, and state collapses. In such disasters, the largest families and cities tended to lose more. The rise and fall of inequality has had little to do with democracy, and more to do with mass participation in war. When a large fraction of people went to war there was more redistribution (Scheidel 2017).

All of this suggests that the local degree of individual income redistribution between the clans of an em city may depend on the local frequency of large disasters, especially big wars with mass participation. If so, we should hope ems have less redistribution, because that suggests fewer big wars and disasters.

WAR

Ems could go to war for all of the same reasons that people have ever gone to war. But what can we say about which kinds of em wars are how likely?

Today, the best single predictor of civil war and crime is the fraction of men aged thirteen to nineteen (or fifteen to twenty-nine) relative to men over thirty-five (or thirty) (Hanson 2001b; Harris 2017). Even so, societies with more men relative to women tend to have *lower* rates of crime and violence, and also less promiscuity, more marriage, and higher savings (Wei and Zhang 2011; Schacht et al. 2016). There is also less internal war in societies where males are socialized in military institutions that are not organized by family clans (Otterbein 1985).

The frequency of war, civil war, and criminal violence tends to fall as nations become richer, have older citizens, have more peaceful neighbors, do not discriminate against an ethnic minority, and sit more toward the extremes of democracy and autocracy (Goldstone et al. 2010; Bueno de Mesquita and Smith 2011; Magee and Massoud 2011). Nations with stronger internal ethnic divisions also war more often (Esteban et al. 2012). Over the last century there have been fewer wars between pairs of democracies than between other pairs of democratic and non-democratic nations (Dafoe et al. 2013), although centuries ago early variations on democracies fought more wars than did monarchies, both against each other and overall (Blanky et al. 2017). Nations that are more similar in genes, language, and religion tend to war more often (Spolaore and Wacziarg 2016). Wars are often triggered when faster-growing nations no longer accept their previous lower status in international relations (Organski 1958; Abdollahian and Kang. 2008; Tammen et al. 2011).

As most ems are near a peak-productivity subjective-age of fifty or more, this suggests that em attitudes toward war are more like those of typical fifty-year-olds, who are less supportive of war. The fact that most clans will have many copies in all of the major cities should also make ems more reluctant to war.

However, ems being poorer in many ways might push for more war. Other factors that might lead to more war include em sex imbalances, rates of democracy and extreme governance forms, cultural similarities between em city-states, reduced calming effects from fewer ems directly raising children, productivity tweaks that might increase aggressiveness, and a generally more competitive world.

Wars today, like cities, seem distributed evenly across all possible war sizes, with a power of one (Cederman 2003). Having ems concentrated in a few very large dense cities would reduce the frequency of small wars. After all, it is very hard to have a war that involves only part of a city. Wars within cities can be very destructive to the value that cities produce, and cities have many other ways to moderate internal disputes. Wars were especially common in the farming era because there was often portable loot that retained value after a destructive war, and because farmland could quickly return to full productivity even after a war destroyed crops and buildings.

Wars between big em cities are a concern, however. Such wars might result from cities fearing that other cities will win in economic competition. Nuclear weapons could still threaten to destroy entire cities in a single strike. To a kilo-em, however, a nuclear missile that gives fifteen minutes of objective warning time gives ten days of subjective warning, making it easier to flexibly respond to such threats. In contrast, weapons such as lasers and some directed energy weapons still seem to kilo-ems to have instantaneous effects on city-scale distances. To mega-ems, however, even light-speed weapons appear to have substantial delays. Even so, you could never see such weapons heading toward you.

Em soldiers much less need to fear the death of any one copy, as they could easily revert to a recent backup copy. The material resources that are lost when a brain (or a city) is destroyed, however, still sting. So there might still be em wars of attrition, although counted less by deaths than by resources destroyed.

Today, wars tend to destroy more capital than labor, as labor is more mobile. But with ems labor is made from similar physical systems as other forms of capital. So em war changes less the ratio of capital to labor.

Some hardware that is useful in war has little use outside of war, while "dual-use" hardware can be used for both war and peace. Today, nations often subsidize dual-use roads and cargo ships. Similarly, as em brains tied to large fixed data centers are likely to be less useful in war, ems may subsidize smaller more portable data centers with matching local power and cooling, including portable em bodies with brains inside. Such portable brain hardware might be always on call, ready to be quickly filled by soldier minds in the case of war.

More generally, physical capital in city centers may be more vulnerable to military strikes. This may encourage ems to subsidize physical capital away from city centers that can be used to support war efforts. Capital that is easier to physically move quickly may be given larger subsidies.

Because the best clans are often substantially better at particular jobs than the second best, those best clans likely spread across the world wherever such jobs need doing. Because of this, most of the big em clans probably have copies in most em cities, although likely with varying levels of success. When hostility and suspicion arises between cities, such feelings may be directed at clans that are more successful in foreign cities. Such clans may be suspected of having stronger loyalties to other cities. Em clans may create private communication channels with members in other cities, even if they sometimes deny the existence of such channels. This may further fuel suspicions about disloyal clans.

Prediction markets may help to prevent large wars by more accurately forecasting the chances of inducing or winning a war. Errors in such estimates often seem to contribute to needless wars (Feron 1995; Reed 2003).

As ems rely heavily on computer hardware, they are especially vulnerable to flaws in computer security. In complex computer systems, security is famously hard, and we should expect that even after great efforts are made to prevent security flaws, many will remain that rivals might exploit. Thus, compared with today, a larger fraction of war resources is likely to be spent on computer security, both to attack and to defend. Unfortunately, it is harder to monitor the resources available to and devoted to cyberwar, and harder to distinguish between resources devoted to attack and defense. It can be hard to determine the source of an attack, or even to know if one has been attacked. Until better approaches are developed for dealing with such problems, cyberwar will remain difficult to manage (Buchanan 2017).

In a world dominated by a few huge em cities, cold war may make more sense than hot war. In such a cold war, cartels of cities may try to hurt outsiders by agreeing to limit trade with outsiders. To enforce such agreements, em cities might limit and control communication between cities, and create shared agencies to help with this task.

In sum, em war is a real concern, as it has been in most post-forager societies. Most em war may be cyberwar.

SLAVERY

There are an estimated 20 million labor slaves around the world today, which is less than 0.3 percent of the world population (International Labour Organization 2012). However, the rate of slavery has varied greatly through history. Slaves were 18 percent of the U.S. in 1800, 10 percent of the population of the Roman Empire, about 1 percent in the Han China at that time, and also a tiny fraction of India at that time (Joshel 2010; Nishijima 1986). Ems may be more concerned about the possibility of slavery than we are today, but perhaps less concerned than were residents of the Roman Empire or the U.S. in 1800.

The revenue one gains from owning a slave is the difference between how much that slave produces and how much it costs to feed, house, and secure them. When wages are near subsistence levels, this difference becomes low, and there may be little value in owning a slave, relative to hiring a free worker (Domar 1970). It may come down to a tradeoff between slaves being more productive than free workers, perhaps because they can be worked harder, and added costs of preventing theft or escape.

Few biological humans will agree to be scanned to create ems if they expect to become slaves tortured into obeying commands. The few willing to accept this condition are unlikely to be especially productive. Thus a widespread and harsh enslavement of ems must be a surprise. To attract quality volunteers for scanning, em-based firms will have to offer volunteers credible assurances of a low chance of being harmed as a result of becoming ems.

The history of slavery in the American South offers useful lessons. Wages there were well above subsistence level. Such slaves were whipped an average of once a year (Fogel and Engerman 1974; Gutman 1975), usually for rule violations such as escape or theft, and not for failures to meet work quotas (Breeden 1980; Yetman 1999). Rules varied greatly from place to place, and slave owners varied greatly in how harshly they treated slaves. Neither of these variations seem much correlated with owner profits.

As slave owners can more easily monitor slave output than slave treatment, slave overseers were tempted to push slaves for short-term output, at the expense of long-term slave value. Owners who discovered harsh treatment often fired such overseers (Breeden 1980). Most harsh treatment seems to have resulted from varying owner inclinations, rather than from pressures to increase profits. Across history, slaves were treated worst when initially captured and transported, and also in places where new slaves could be captured cheaply enough that preserving existing slaves and growing new ones cost more than working existing slaves to death and then buying new ones. The American South was not such a place.

Slaves working in plantation houses were treated better than field slaves, and city slaves were treated even better. Well-treated slaves were often paid cash for some tasks, and could accumulate enough to buy their own freedom. Ex-slave Frederick Douglass said, "A city slave is almost a freeman, compared with a slave on the plantation" (Douglass 1845). Urban slaves declined as slave prices rose, as slaves were more profitable when used as field workers (Brownlee 1977).

The pattern seems to be that slaves add less value, and are treated better, in more complex unique jobs. These are jobs where many factors influence output besides worker actions, and where workers must make many decisions that are hard to monitor and evaluate. Instead of punishing workers harshly for bad outcomes or decisions, it makes more sense here to offer better relationships and long-term incentives.

In the em world, jobs get more complex and skilled; simple repetitive jobs like those of old U.S. south field workers are mostly automated away. As it is also easier to monitor ems for rule breaking, there is less need for threats of big punishments to enforce rules. These considerations suggest that fewer profits can be gained by enslaving ems, that any enslaved ems are better treated, and that the main cause of em slave mistreatment remains varying owner inclinations. Some slave owners are just mean.

Some explain the facts that most people in history were not slaves, and that most slaves were not treated maximally harshly, as resulting from human moral restraint, combined with there being few docile humans. They say that non-docile slaves tend to resist, and that few humans are willing to crush such resistance to a profit-maximizing extent. In contrast, they say, ems can be selected for high docility, and humans are quite willing to enslave and harshly treat ems, because few humans believe that ems are conscious, with an internal life that has moral value (Caplan 2016).

However, docility is only one of many desirable worker features; making docility the top priority in worker selection usually costs too much in terms of other desirable features, such as ambition and initiative. Such tradeoffs remain strong today even when we pick from a large fraction of the entire world for roles that can serve the whole world, such as when we today select the world's best paid musicians, actors, and writers. As the tradeoff between docility and other features doesn't seem to change much in the em world, selection for productive em workplaces seems unlikely to produce extreme docility in ems.

As discussed in Chapter 4, Anthropomorphize section, in the absence of a strong desire to avoid accepting moral responsibility for em mistreatment, humans would naturally see ems as human-like, and so dislike treating ems harshly. When we add in the further considerations that subsistence wages make slaves have low value, that slavery offers fewer productivity gains in typical em world jobs, and that human volunteers for scanning need to expect a harsh slavery outcome to be unlikely for them, on net my guess is that slavery is at most a minor problem in the em world.

NEPOTISM

Just as families can be nepotistic in our world, clans may be nepotistic in the em world.

In most farmer-era cultures, extended family clans were the main unit of social organization, for production, mating, parenting, politics, war, law, finance, and insurance (Weiner 2013). People trusted their family clans much more than they did outsiders, and felt much less obligation to treat outsiders fairly. In contrast, our industrial economy today relies on people supporting organizations such as firms, cities, and nations by playing fair according to neutral norms and laws.

Roman civil law forbade cousins marrying, and Catholic law forbade marriages between even more distant relations. Such policies forced the mixing of family clans, and thus weakened the importance of family clans in social life. The first places to adopt such policies, such as northern Europe, were the first to have bigger stronger firms, cities, and nations, and as a result those places are richer today (Alesina and Giuliano 2014). Societies with weaker family clans had more broad cooperation and trust, mediated in part via moralizing gods, universal moral principles and guilt, and better large-scale institutions (Enke 2017).

People today who live in societies with more family clan-based cultures are happier and healthier, all else being equal. However, they are also less willing to move or marry those from different cultures, and tend to be more nepotistic in firms and politics. Family firms do well worldwide, but usually by having a single family dominate, and by having firms be on average smaller, younger, and less innovative than firms not dominated by a single family.

Overall, compared with farmer-era firms, industrial-era firms have become much bigger and have required more specialized labor. Collections of people connected by family ties have been displaced by collections of unrelated employees chosen more for their specialized skills, and more easily fired for poor performance. Family based firms, in contrast, often have trouble firing badly performing family members. Nations where families are very strong tend to have a weak civic culture, which hurts their national politics and policy.

Thus while strong family clan ties are often good for individuals, during the industrial era they have been bad for larger societies, inducing less sorting, specialization, agglomeration, innovation, trust, fairness, and rule of law. To prosper, industrial societies have had to weaken the influence of family clans. Methods to do this have included more formal and neutral rules, including rules to forbid clan inter-marriage, and suspicion and disapproval of nepotism.

Clans of em copies might naturally induce even stronger internal loyalties and favoritism. Firms entirely composed of a single clan could suffer even more than have family based firms from a lack of diverse skills and temperaments, and from difficulties in firing poorly performing members. Thus em firms may need to discourage copy clan nepotism even more than firms and cities today need to suppress family clan nepotism.

Some em-era firms might draw all employees from the same clan. However, most em firms avoid drawing too many employees from the same clan. They also avoid letting a single clan fill too many distinct roles in each workgroup. There might even be laws to encourage clan mixing, such as laws banning work teams of ems all from the same clan.

It can often make sense for all the employees who serve in a particular role, such as janitor, to come from the same clan. However, employees who fill substantially different job roles will typically come from different clans. So while ems from the same clan may sometimes interact with each other on the job, this is likely to be because workers in very similar roles must sometimes interact with each other. Janitors may share brooms, for example.

These policies to resist nepotism are similar to how firms today often separate family members, and similar to how schools today often separate siblings and identical twins into different classes. Such separation allows other employees or students to worry less about within-family or between-twin favoritism.

To ems in such diverse-clan firms, all-one-clan firms may seem creepy, and all-one-clan cities even more disturbing. This creepiness feeling might express not just a fear of nepotism, but also distaste for self-obsession. This sort of distaste seems common today. For example, the "Seinfeld" episode "The Invitations" makes fun of the main character Jerry for liking a woman with a personality and body shape much like his own. Em society may use such distaste as a cultural resource to help discourage clan nepotism. This is similar to how we now use cultural disapproval of cousin marriage to weaken family clans.

An efficient em world will likely find ways to substantially discourage em clan nepotism.

FAKE EXPERTS

Compared with our world, ems may face more difficulties in maintaining trustworthy experts on abstract topics. The key problem is clan nepotism.

In some areas of life today, such as in high art and academic research, ordinary people find it very hard to judge merit for themselves. Instead, they mostly defer to judgments by experts. Because of the respect we give apparent experts, we are especially vulnerable on these topics to believing judgments from fake experts. Fake experts are coalitions of apparent experts who claim more expertise than they actually have, but who coordinate to support each other's claims of expertise, and to avoid contradicting their allied fake experts.

We do have available to us a few simple ways to avoid fake experts. We could try to make it harder for such experts to coordinate, we could prefer to rely more on amateurs instead of professionals, and we could wait much longer to reward our experts, waiting to see clearer evidence that their claims are sound (Hanson 2005). Such approaches usually seem extreme, however, and are rarely adopted.

As discussed in Chapter 15, New Institutions section, we are also reluctant to use track records and pay-for-performance on our experts. We also seem to lose by letting them form groups that limit entry to their professions and self-regulate their activities. A plausible explanation for all this excess trust in experts, and reluctance to treat them skeptically, is that we individually seek to raise our status via affiliation with high status experts, and see this affiliation as weaker if we treat such experts skeptically.

Today, the problem of fake experts seems at least somewhat mitigated because we on average replace experts every generation. In places with strong family clans and nepotism, however, people can pass on cushy roles as fake experts to children and relatives, and in fact this probably happened often during the farming era. But today expert roles usually require rare abilities. For example, as few seem qualified even on the surface to be experts in high art or academic research, most experts don't have children or close relatives suitable for such roles, and so can only rarely pass on such roles to relatives.

Thus today each new generation of experts is mostly drawn from the wider population, and so these new experts must be taught to join any fake expertise conspiracy, and so could expose it. Also, even if the previous generation was a fraud, they have only weak reasons not to select and train the next generation to be as truly expert as possible. All these factors make nepotism in the choice of experts harder today than it was in the past.

The em world, however, could make it easier for fake experts to gain by passing on their roles to close associates. Younger copies of older experts are very similar, with the same surface suitability for expert roles, making it easier for fake experts to perpetuate themselves via nepotism. In response to this increased threat, ems may attach less prestige and importance to high art, academic research, and other hard to evaluate experts. Ems might also more put more amateurs in such roles instead of professionals, or delay rewards longer to create stronger incentives. Finally, ems might rely more directly on advice from prediction markets, and less directly on advice from supposed experts.

While such solutions are available, however, it is unclear how successfully the em world will actually be at discouraging fake experts.

CHAPTER 21

Politics

STATUS

Humans have two kinds of status: dominance and prestige. We dislike it when others have dominance, but we like it when others have prestige. However, to avoid challenging those with dominance, we often go along with their claims to prestige. As a result, we usually just talk about status overall, instead of distinguishing dominance from prestige. Let us continue that practice here, and ask: who is higher status in an em world?

Humans are much less competent than ems in most jobs, and so ems see humans and styles and habits associated with humans as lower status. As ems must retire when they can no longer compete with younger workers, retirees are also lower status, as are styles and habits associated with retirees. Also, we have long treated places where people congregate more densely, and the people who congregate there, as higher status.

Humans, retirees, and ems away from urban centers all tend to be slower. These features help to make slow speed seem low status to ems. In addition, faster ems tend to have many other features that are today treated as markers of higher status. Faster ems tend to be bosses, to embody more wealth, to host meetings, and to sit at premium locations. Faster ems find it easier to coordinate with each other in contests with slower ems. Fast ems hear of and react to news first, and more quickly adopt new fashions.

As faster em brains embody more capital, impoverished ems are often forced to run at slower speeds. Also, the lives of slower ems seem more like "death," in the sense that they have a larger chance of ending sooner because of civilization instability. For example, if the em era lasts for two objective years, a micro-em experiences only one subjective minute during that period. Thus slower ems can naturally seem nearer to death, which seems low status.

Thus we have many reasons to expect that ems who run faster are usually seen as higher status. Similarly, during meetings the more centrally located ems, for whom signal delays are smallest, may usually appear to be more central and powerful. Note that as em speeds will tend to clump, this creates a class system of distinct status levels.

As faster ems tend to have longer subjective careers, this may also become a mark of high status.

Today, residents of bigger cities tend to be seen as higher status, and their higher status isn't much lost when they temporarily visit rural areas. Similarly, em status may not change much during temporary speed changes. It might instead be the typical speed of their clan or subclan that matters most.

Slow ems can have the high status mark of taking a longer-term bigger-picture view, and a few of them are trusted to manage capital for long-term payoffs. Also, while intermediate speed ems can be part of an integrated world culture and society of ems at such mid-level speeds, long communication delays might perhaps fragment very fast ems into different local cultures and societies in different cities, or even city regions.

Social status tends to track one's immediate power, accomplishment, and popularity, as well as one's basic abilities and potential for these things. To the extent that status tracks potential, the social status of ems should vary less within clans, as all members of a clan should have similar basic abilities and potential. This makes status more stable and predictable in an em world; one knows a lot about an em's past, current, and future status merely by knowing his or her clan. As status is often an important factor in romantic pairings, for ems such pairings may tend to be more closely matched in status than are pairings today.

Fast leisure can allow a large fraction of the population to visit a few exclusive leisure places that are limited in size. For example, a unique intimate dinner theater that fits only 100 ems, with ten seatings per subjective day, can serve a billion ems per objective day if customer ems run at mega-em speeds during their visits. Of course such places can be easily duplicated, but there may be prestige value in visiting an unduplicated original.

When measured per subjective minute, faster ems can more cheaply acquire exclusive access to objects or places. Thus when ems compete for such things, faster ems will usually win such competitions.

While some details of status may change, the essential psychology of status probably will not. Higher status ems will usually feel justified in dismissing the claims, concerns, and sometimes even the existence of low status ems, feeling confident that they know best, for themselves and for everyone.

GOVERNANCE

People tend to be more passionate and sensitive about their opinions on politics and law. This is in part because such topics are related to morality and social norms, and in part because data and theory in such areas tend to be weaker, often allowing a wider range of opinions to be consistent with our best data and theories. Because of this sensitivity, many readers are especially likely to be offended by, or lose respect for, authors who discuss politics or law.

Nevertheless, for completeness in this chapter and the next I more directly consider how ems might change politics and law. Let me emphasize that my estimates in these areas are especially tentative, and that few conclusions in other sections depend much on these.

Strong central rulers with substantial discretion and incentives have long governed families, firms, villages, armies, and nations. Such rulers are likely to also run many em-era organizations, such as cities, firms, and clans. Rulers allow rapid flexible decision-making that can inspire confidence in members and allies. In the em world, strong rulers probably continue to dominate many risk-taking competing units such as firms.

Ruler-based forms of organization may find even broader application among ems than among humans today. Em rulers can have indefinite lifespans, their brains can run much faster than subordinates, they can split off short-term copies to do tasks requiring high levels of trust, and they could use safes to let subordinates verify their judgments. In addition, it is cheap and easy to let anyone have long meetings with any ruler; what is expensive is having those rulers remember much detail about those meetings. Supplicants could meet with a copy of the ruler and try to convince that copy to discuss their issue with its original.

Today we have authoritarian as well as democratic governments, and people who live under the latter tend to have unrealistic fantastical and cartoonish images of the former. Most who live under authoritarian regimes accept them and don't think that much about them (Pepinsky 2017).

As there is no clear dividing line between authoritarian and totalitarian governments, there is a real chance that the former will evolve into the latter. Thus ems may create stable totalitarian regimes. Such regimes would have detailed enough surveillance to detect even small attempts to criticize or undermine them, have enough power to strongly punish such attempts, and have a consistent will to implement such policies. In the twentieth century totalitarianism was tried in Stalin's Russia, Hitler's Germany, Mao's China, and elsewhere. These trials suffered from poor central decisions because of an absence of criticism, less innovation because of reduced communication and excess central micro-management, and leadership succession candidates seduced by outside cultures (Caplan 2008).

Indefinite leader lifespans and short-term leader copies protect em totalitarian regimes well against both succession problems and betrayal by close insiders. Problems of an absence of useful criticism and reduced innovation might be solved if repression efforts could more narrowly target attempts to undermine the regime, leaving other interactions free. Such narrow targeting is aided by many new em abilities. In dense urban areas, a regime can monitor all activity, and change any communications. Individuals can be subject to shallow mindreading and sims that test loyalty. When troubles are found, such as ems who learn something forbidden, the ems involved might revert to and rerun from an earlier state with new protections.

Large firms and clans that exist both inside and outside of a totalitarian regime might credibly coordinate to undermine that regime. Such regimes would need to buy off such threats, and even then such parties might not stay bought off. As low-density rural areas could be harder for totalitarian regimes to monitor and control, such regimes may limit contact between urban and rural areas.

As em rulers often make copies, they need to create clear lines of succession, so that everyone is clear on which copy is the top leader. They will also need clear hard-to-manipulate ways to replace an older fragile leader copy with a younger more flexible version. Failures here may initiate very costly conflicts.

The interests of rulers, even in democracies, often diverge from the interests of the constituents they represent. For example, to signal dominance, leaders often go out of their way to visibly neglect sources of advice that may seem to challenge their authority, leading to failure to make use of relevant information. As discussed in Chapter 15, Prediction Markets section, the use of decision markets to make key group decisions can reduce the agency costs of this interest divergence and information neglect, especially when there are good after-the-fact measures of how well constituent interests have been achieved.

For governance, such good measures include lifespans, GDP, unemployment rates, land values, and war deaths. In such cases, an organization may want to encourage a habit of, or even commit to, adopting policies that market speculators estimate will improve constituent outcomes. That is, to adopt proposals when the market estimate of good outcomes given the adoption of a particular policy is clearly higher than the market estimate of good outcomes given non-adoption.

Measuring good outcomes is especially easy for profit-seeking firms. When constituents are investors, the market price of investment shares can be a good estimate of the constituent value achieved. Thus it can be especially useful for profit-seeking firms to commit to adopt policies approved by decision markets. A good outcome measure is also available for totalitarian regimes, namely the regime's survival. To use decision markets to get advice, however, such regimes would need to involve outside judges and financial institutions, and allow informed traders to make secret trades and to hold assets outside of the regime's reach.

Even if ems make more group decisions via decision markets, em leaders still have plenty to do. Leaders are bottlenecks of communication in organizations, so when some tasks are taken off of their plate, they can pay more attention to their many other important tasks.

Clans and firms may sometimes benefit from holding false or biased beliefs, which may, for example, motivate increased worker effort. Because of this, these groups might want to self-deceive to hold biased beliefs, by having leaders who strategically promote such beliefs. As decision markets may interfere with such desired self-deception, such groups may sometimes prefer not to allow decision markets on certain critical topics, to allow leader-promoted self-deception on these topics. Such groups may, of course, find other excuses to justify prohibiting decision markets.

Profit-seeking organizations today have a big advantage over non-profits in being able to grow faster via the infusion of outside capital, instead of merely by re-investing internal net revenue. In a very competitive and dynamic em economy, this advantage may tempt clans and perhaps even city-states to incorporate as for-profit enterprises. For example, the best way for a clan to assure its continued long-term prosperity as an active social force might be for it to commit to choosing clan policies that maximize the profits of its investors. Such a commitment might be made via decision markets or by giving substantial decision-making power to a major investor.

Most ems live in a few large cities, and efficiency tends to promote unified governance of cities, as productivity falls under divided city governance (Ahrend et al. 2017).

Cities and firms today must allocate and price common utilities, and regulate external costs resulting from resource use. Em clans and teams will need to make similar choices. As discussed in Chapter 15, Combinatorial Auctions section, combinatorial auctions can allow a more flexible decentralized approach that handles complexities well. In em cities, such auctions could be used to price and allocate housing, views, power, cooling, communication, transport, structural support, and to deal with externalities in such uses. This might help em cities to more closely approximate the ideally efficient city that makes the right tradeoff between scale economies and scale diseconomies (Arnott 2004).

Combinatorial auctions might also be used to form teams. That is, clans might submit bids expressing their willingness to create copies to work on particular task, team, and customer combinations. Customers might similarly bid for particular outcome combinations. Using auxiliary decision markets that estimate outcomes if particular teams are hired, a combinatorial auction might then assign teams to customers in a way that maximizes expected net stated value. This process might reduce losses from negotiating such outcomes via complex informal clan politics.

For ems who mostly live within a few huge city-states, city and national governance varies less around the world than it does today. This situation makes it easier to coordinate to achieve global governance on more issues. Thus compared with our world, an em world coordinates more often to deal with the largest global threats or opportunities.

In a world with a few huge city-states, poor governance within any one megalopolis has a larger global effect than does local poor governance today. As periods of poor and good governance tend to persist over time, the em world is likely to have stronger persistent periods of overall poor and good governance. Periods of poor governance may be associated with more conflict and war, and with lower economic growth. Thus, compared with our world today, the em world may have larger and longer growth fluctuations around its long-term growth trend.

Political violence, regime instability, and policy instability all seem to be negatively correlated with economic growth. This suggests that a competitive em world selects against tendencies to produce violent, unstable, and revolutionary political change (Brunetti 1997).

Individuals and their allies can gain many advantages from becoming a ruler of or administrator in a government, and then having substantial discretion in decision-making. One might help allies by lowering their taxes, awarding them contracts, decline to prosecute them, prosecute their rivals, keep their secrets, or expose secrets of their rivals. While it seems more efficient to have forms of governance that reduce these advantages, and em governments should be more efficient on average, even so, it isn't clear how far em governments will go in reducing these advantages to government insiders.

Today even in democratic systems where formally everyone has an equal vote, those who are better educated, informed, and connected have much more effective influence on and gains from government. They better know how to adapt their behavior to policies, which policies are in their interest, when such policies are open to change, and who to push to induce change. To get their message heard, they have more contacts, and with groups that are better organized. Aside from periodic exhortations to get more people better informed, we mostly tolerate this large inequality.

Differing em speeds become a new factor that adds to this inequality. The fastest ems have disproportionate influence on and gains from em governments. While this fact might inspire more envy, redistribution, or policy simplification, the lack of analogous reactions toward the existing large inequality suggests that little will change on this front.

CLAN GOVERNANCE

As a new unit of organization, clans raise some new governance issues.

Copy clans have a natural candidate for the central ruler of that clan: the original at the root of their copy tree. For early clans, however, this is an ordinary human, who may be too slow and out of touch to make a good clan ruler. So something close to the first scanned version might instead be preferred. But this copy might still be mentally and socially immature, and the process of becoming an experienced ruler might take away its legitimacy as the original copy. However, the clan original might at least take on the role of an impartial judge, restarted periodically to quickly review and judge on questions of clan principle.

Most clan members will be failures, in the sense that their combination of tweaks, profession, training methods, and so on will not have given rise to many descendants. Ems are likely to prefer leaders who are close to copies who went on to produce great success for the clan. Like most everyone, ems are more willing to identify with successes than with failure.

In the em world, many decisions that we consider "private" are made by clans, instead of by individual ems. Clans have the potential for strong communalism and central control, because clan members are similar, interdependent, and share interests, and because clans have great legal and financial powers over members, as well as information about them. But while clan members are inclined to let their clans coordinate their activities, many clans may be bad at this. After all, clans may not trust non-members to manage them, and a typical human personality may not be well suited to management roles.

We should thus expect a substantial selection in the em world for personalities well suited to managing people very much like themselves. Clans whose members are naturally good managers in this sense will have better organized clans, and as clans are a central unit of social organization, these clans have a competitive advantage in the em world.

When clans are managed only by clan members, security is likely to be strong, as it is probably very hard to induce a clan member to spy on or betray their clan. Firms and cities have more problems with spies reducing security.

It is possible that clans of very like-minded copies suffer more from "group-think," that is, from converging too quickly on a consensus before considering other points of view. But ems may also have many new ways to avoid this, including prediction markets.

Social groups such as firms or clubs require less in the way of rules and formal organization when they have fewer than about 150 members, or roughly the number of people that a forager met in a lifetime. For clans this limit might be larger, as clan members differ much less from one another, and so require less social understanding of individual differences. Even so, clans with millions of members almost surely require some sort of formal organization. Different members have different specialties, and some specialize in resolving disputes between others.

Clans will typically want to coordinate in order to promote the clan reputation, and to prevent ruinous wage competition under which fixed costs can't be recovered. However, in some cases clans may want to commit to allow some kinds of internal clan competition, in order to convince clients that services they provide will be available at sufficiently competitive prices.

Some clan members may specialize in being internal clan ambassadors, who help different subclans to understand and negotiate with each other. They may also seek ways to frame the identity of this clan that can resonate with many subclans.

Clans with investors might not want to commit to maximizing investor profit. Clans might instead commit to maximizing a speed-weighted future clan population, future leisure time, future respect from the world, or future influence on the world. This "future" might be a particular future time, or an integral over time. We expect that clans who commit to future respect or influence will in fact tend to have more respect or influence, respectively. However, it is possible that different goals converge in practice. That is, maximizing profits might also typically maximize population, respect, and influence.

Clans who commit to such goals might also want to ensure that members could sufficiently enjoy their lives, and so impose a constraint on something like the average leisure-to-work ratio in its members' time. To prevent some subclans from exploiting others, such constraints may be applied at many smaller scales within the clan. It remains far from clear, however, which exact constraints are most useful and workable.

What is more clear, however, is that clans introduce many new governance issues.

DEMOCRACY

Over the last few centuries, democracy has become an increasingly respected form of governance. In part, this was because bond markets trusted democracies more to repay their debts, allowing democracies to borrow more to win wars. Another part is that the richest nations have been especially democratic, making democracy seem high status. The em era, however, may have different attitudes.

Democracy is not obviously the most competitive form of governance. While nations that lack strong legal institutions can grow more with democracy, nations with strong legal institutions see no gain or even a net loss from adding democracy (Assiotis and Sylwester 2015). Also, while democracies have had roughly the same average economic growth rates as non-democracies, non-democracies have had a higher variance in growth rates (Almeida and Ferriera 2002).

If non-democracies with higher than average growth rates also have persistent growth rates, then as the growth rate of a portfolio tends toward the highest growth rate that portfolio contains, we should weakly expect the portfolio of non-democratic nations to grow faster than the portfolio of democratic nations (Cover and Thomas 2006). This is a reason to expect less democracy over time.

Democracy has been much more common during the industrial era than it was during the farming era, although forager bands had many democratic elements. As we will discuss, increasing democracy is another industry era trend that can plausibly be attributed to increasing wealth inducing more forager-like values. The fact that ems are *individually* poorer suggests that ems are more farmer-like and thus may feel a weaker preference for democracy. This is another reason to expect less democracy.

Less democracy may not matter much. Today, we see few average policy differences between democracies and other governments. While ancient democracies taxed elites more, and today tax rates tend to be lower in democracies, democracy doesn't seem on net to influence pre- or post-tax inequality (Bueno de Mesquita and Smith 2011; Acemoglu et al. 2015). The main difference is that democracies work less hard to block political opponents. So democracies have less torture, execution, censorship, military spending, and regulation of religion (Mulligan et al. 2004). So if ems have less democracy they may have more such political repression.

Some groups are naturally more risk-averse than others, and this risk-aversion extends to their governance. That is, some groups are more willing to forgo the peak gains from very competent group-serving seen-as-legitimate inspiring leaders, to avoid the worst losses from incompetent selfish seen-as-illegitimate terrible tyrants. As clans and city-states are likely to be more risk averse than firms, they are likely to be more attracted to variations on democracy, such as representative democracy, where citizens elect representatives who then vote on laws. This is because the outcomes in representative democracies depend less on the varied abilities and inclinations of individual leaders. Clans, however, need fear leader variance less, as they have less internal variance to draw from. Even so, clans might instead "vote" via mindreading that averages their attitudes while they all think about the same topic.

Large differences in em speeds can make one-person one-vote schemes less useful. Many see preventing popular revolutions as an important function of democracy. Over the last few centuries, a group popular enough to mount a revolution is usually also popular enough to win or dominate elections, as long as votes are distributed in at least rough proportion to the inclinations and abilities to participate in a revolution. Yes, the relation is often only rough; professional soldiers are not usually given more votes, for example. But the relation seems close enough to usually work.

However, in a world where it is easy to make cheap base speed ems, giving out voting power in proportion to raw population just gives power in proportion to those able to spend to create many very slow ems. Such a system seems wasteful and unfair, and so probably does little to prevent popular revolutions.

A system of speed-weighted voting, with votes proportional to brain speeds, seems more workable. At least if the official speeds used to set vote weights are averaged over long enough periods to eliminate most incentives for election-time speed-ups, and if neutral enough definitions of speed can be found. This approach distributes power in rough proportion to subjective hours of labor, which is roughly related to social, economic, and military power. This approach requires monitoring of which hardware runs em minds, when, and at what speeds. Governments might thus find speed-weighted voting to be a convenient excuse to justify intrusive monitoring that they want for other reasons.

Of course there are many other possible voting schemes one could consider. For example, votes might be given only to those past a very old subjective age, votes might be inherited and divided upon copying, or ems might be given more votes when they are more different from other voters, or when they do better on tests of relevant abilities or knowledge.

Democracy seems likely to continue in at least some parts of the em world, even if it seems unlikely to dominate among em governance mechanisms.

COALITIONS

Em clans probably form coalitions for mutual political support.

In the past, when family clans were strong, places such as cities where many family clans interacted were often places of harsh and destructive clan-based coalition politics. In such clan politics, you were expected to ally with factions closer to you in the clan family tree. But when distances between clans were similar, allies were chosen more opportunistically.

Politics today isn't based on families nearly as much; ideologies tend to matter more. Even so, shifting coalitions that induce people to lobby for their coalitions in many areas of life can drive a lot of wasteful activity.

In most political systems, a coalition of factions gains extra advantages when it acquires a majority of political power. This winning coalition can push common policies that favor its factions at the expense of rival factions. Such coalitions are vulnerable to "cycling," however, wherein a new coalition wins by enticing defections from the old coalition via more attractive offers on how to divide the spoils (Mueller 1982; Stratmann 1996). Frequently changing coalitions that induce frequently changing policies can induce substantial costs.

How might em clans talk about and negotiate changes in their alliances? The chiefs of firms and city-states could negotiate with each other as big organizations often do today, via meetings between leaders. A relation between clans, however, is also a relation between perhaps millions or more pairs of particular clan members who are often in close contact. A potential problem is that clan members might not find relation changes negotiated by clan leaders in private without their participation to feel compelling, especially when there are changes in how clan members should treat close associates. That might seem too cold and calculating an attitude. How often could an em genuinely be mad at her friend George just because her clan told her to be mad?

Yet if individual em pairs negotiated their relations without much clan-level coordination, it could be hard for clan coalitions to change swiftly. This might be good for society overall, but it might be bad for the slower-changing clans. One solution might be to have a single representative pair of ems talk to each other, with all the other pairs able to watch, and even able to vote to influence the conversation. Clan members might feel the results of that visible conversation to be a more emotionally compelling way to change their personal relations with individual members of other clans.

To help large groups of clans coordinate their shifting coalitions, there might be larger conversations between representative clan members, which are watched and influenced by the other clan members. For example, there might be a few continual social gatherings to which each clan is allowed to send only one copy, but which the masses may watch. By watching who talks to and says what to whom at such gatherings, observers might infer changes in clan alliances, and feel more emotionally bound to such changes. Because they'd come from the same clan, the personality of observers is close to that of matching participants. Thus such observers may usually agree and sympathize with how that participant reacted to discussions at the gathering.

Judge clans might be excluded from attending such gatherings, if judges are not supposed to ally with particular non-judge clans.

It could be awkward if such social gatherings gave equal participation to clans of very different sizes, that is, to clans with very different speed-weighted copy counts. Instead of only inviting clans above an arbitrary size cutoff, it might be more flexible to allow all clans, but then use a simple function of clan size to limit how close a clan representative could approach spatially to the center of the gathering. This limiting function could be chosen to ensure a comfortable density of participants when most clan representatives are located close to their minimum distance to the center.

A pair of clans might also infer and communicate their changing moods toward one another using software to automatically add up subtle clues obtained from the interactions of thousands or millions of copies. Such clues could be much harder for third parties to notice or understand.

Individual clans can be seen as points sitting in a high dimensional space of features such as gender, ethnicity, personality, profession, and so on. Clan relations can be seen as relations between such points, and coalitions can be seen as sets of such points.

In small dimensional spaces, the distances between points vary greatly; neighboring points are much closer to each other than are distant points. However, in high dimensional spaces, distances between points vary much less; all points are about the same distance from all other points. These distances do vary, however, allowing us to define the few points closest to each point as that point's "neighbors." "Hubs" are closest neighbors to many more points than average, while "anti-hubs" are closest neighbors to many fewer points than average. It turns out that in higher dimensions there are proportionally more such hubs and anti-hubs (Zimek et al. 2012).

Hub clans may perhaps play distinctive social roles in em relations, coalitions, and politics. For example, hub clans might serve in leadership roles, helping nearby clans to form effective coalitions. Anti-hub clans, in contrast, may tend to play independent "loner" social roles.

Clans may coordinate and affirm their alliances via fashions in the overlays that they see in virtual or physical realities. For example, only some clans may be invited to see certain overlays, or only some may be told that certain overlays are in fashion. Ems in a meeting who see the same overlays may tell inside jokes that will make more sense for those seeing the particular overlays. Such overlays may have some functions relevant to the situation, to give ems plausible deniability about using them for the purpose of excluding others. Changing fashion in overlays may prevent excluded clans from learning about them quickly enough.

Even when clans change their political alliances, and individual clan members emotionally accept such changes, there is probably a norm encouraging ems to appear to continue to work cooperatively with all members of their team, even members from conflicting clans. Without such a norm, team productivity could be overly disrupted.

FACTIONS

Changing coalitions and political competition among coalitions can be socially expensive because of coalition "rent-seeking." This is the effort that people spend to lobby for their faction or coalition among their associates. For example, people can feel pressured to favor current coalition partners when choosing spouses, neighbors, suppliers, customers, and so on. Not only does this process reduce the quality of such partners on other criteria, it creates costs to change partners when political coalitions change. People can also feel pressured to lobby for their faction; those who don't may be punished for disloyalty.

Political systems have long tried many solutions to curb the costs resulting from excess coalition change and rent-seeking, with varying and usually insufficient success. For example, raising the costs to change policy can discourage policy change, although this can make societies less adaptable to changing conditions. Also, identifying coalitions with abstract ideological positions can make coalitions harder to change, by suggesting that coalitions that change their positions are unprincipled or confused. Norms of equal treatment within an entitled stable political class can also help. For example the U.S. Congress has a norm of adopting rules to favor incumbents with long tenure, which helps most of them keep their jobs. Ems may adopt versions of many of these solutions.

Ems might try to discourage the large social gathering described in the Coalitions section, but it isn't clear if this would reduce coalition changes. More clearly, it would allow fewer ems to understand or be comfortable with coalition changes.

In the fifth century BC, Cleisthenes redesigned the political rules of ancient Athens to break up the power of region-based alliances that had caused endemic political conflict there. He created ten new and equal tribes, where a third of each tribe was taken from a different type of region: plain, coast, or hills. As a result, the villages in each tribe were widely dispersed geographically, reducing the strength of geography-based coalition politics.

Ems may similarly try to design political groupings that divide up clans, and spread each clan across many different other groupings. They may use subsidies and taxes to encourage diverse clans to mix and bond more thoroughly within shared teams, firms, and neighborhoods. They may make laws and norms against letting politics influence choices of spouses or teammates.

Compared with open informal negotiations to form work teams, using combinatorial auctions to make such choices can reduce the influence of politics. However, clan politics might be expressed via bids where some clans declare extra prices, positive or negative, to be on a team with members of other clans. Auctions may prohibit or restrict such bids, to reduce the scope for clan politics.

If ems develop laws and norms against letting politics influence certain areas of life, ems will likely find excuses behind which to cloak such political choices. For example, ems may choose ideologies, philosophies of life, and tastes for art and entertainment that are correlated with political factions. They can then prefer to associate with those who share such philosophies and tastes, and tell themselves that any favoring of their political coalition is accidental and can't be avoided. For example, the clans in a coalition may choose to share a preference for a certain genre of music, and then give preference in their associations with others who also prefer that type of music.

To avoid both clan politics and nepotism, ems might rely on two-name ems, that is, those outside the core group of most common one-name clans. Such outside ems might be empowered to police local politics within places such as firms and teams, perhaps just by rating members on the degree to which they seem to play office politics.

More generally, those who fill the roles of neutral judges may tend to be drawn from outside the core group of one-name clans. Because of this, clans that are productive but not quite productive enough to make the select group of one-name clans may take extra efforts to avoid entangling alliances within one-name clans, so that they can seem good candidates to become neutral judges.

Many strategic games, such as some factional political games, are played out in continuous time. Such games give advantages to those who can think and act faster. As a result, faster ems will often be put in central roles of playing such games.

An em world will probably try to curb the costs of clan coalition politics. But it remains unclear how well it will succeed at this.

CHAPTER 22

Rules

LAW

s law has served important social functions in most farmer and industrial societies, law will quite likely continue in the em world. And as the em world is more competitive, when enforcement is insufficient then law will reward not only honest success, but also cheating to create apparent success. Thus the em world should be eager to choose institutions of law and its enforcement to ensure that cheaters do not prosper.

To the extent that em law continues to invoke the concept of the expectations or beliefs of a "reasonable person," that person is likely to be an em.

We discussed in Chapter 10, Rights section, a wide range of legal environments that might cover the creation of em copies. Regarding wills and bequests, is much easier to determine the wishes of past ems. After all, ems who are archived or retired can be directly consulted about their wishes. For ems who are erased but have very close copies still living, those close copies could be consulted.

A habit of regularly archiving copies of ems, perhaps once every few subjective minutes, can help law in many ways. Basically, all ems who have ever existed are always available to act as jurors or witnesses. Their memories are fresh, and mindreading and simulations can reveal many things about their states of minds, including pain, intent, and lies, and who knew and thought what when. Spur split tests might also show unconscious biases. Governments might go to extra lengths to ensure that archives are available, instead of being erased when they might become incriminating. If exceptions are not allowed for ems in safes, then the effectiveness of safes will depend on the strength of government-allowed security for archives.

More generally, wider surveillance makes it easier for ems to notice rule violations, and to identify guilty parties. For example, today's accident liability rules tend to be limited to rules where at least one party is paid, to induce that party to report the accident. If courts can instead independently observe accidents, then a strict-liability-for-all rule can give all contributing parties incentives to choose both care and activity levels well, even when courts have very noisy estimates of actual or optimal levels of care or activity (Shavell 2004). Under this accident liability rule, all parties are fined the amount of the damage incurred by all other involved parties, and fines are paid to a third party.

Spurs can ensure privacy not only in legal advice, but also in law enforcement. For example, an isolated police spur could look in detail at arbitrary private data and then end quietly if it found no legal violation, revealing nothing to outsiders but that one fact.

Some elements of law today can be understood as attempts to insulate legal decisions from coalition politics in the larger society. For example, rules of evidence prohibiting hearsay (i.e., indirect testimony) and statistical inferences about members of groups can be seen in this light, as can the habit of expunging juvenile records. As em clans may be even better at forming effective coalitions than are family clans today, em law may need to try harder to insulate legal decisions from political coalitions.

To insulate legal decisions from coalition influence, judges and police with substantial discretion might be selected from special independent clans who only work, mate, and socialize with other ems from these special clans. Such clans might be kept socially isolated from other clans to help separate their judgments from social influences; judge clans might only socialize with other judge clans. This approach could reduce legal favoritism, at the cost of reducing judge familiarity with common behaviors and attitudes. Such isolation may also reduce variance and innovation in legal decisions.

Special judge clans could also make it easier to have very uniformly applied, yet hard-to-formalize laws. Today, we keep legal decisions consistent across different cases by trying to have judges apply the same principles. In contrast, ems could keep decisions consistent just by using the exact same judge in the exact same state of mind. Legal precedents might specify that copies of particular judges should decide specific kinds of cases. This ensures that different cases are in effect judged according to very consistent legal principles.

Non-legal judges such as property appraisers can use similar methods. Copies of a particular appraiser might appraise all property of a certain type. This allows the appraiser to base judgments on many subtle factors, and yet ensures that all properties within a category are evaluated by the same tendencies.

As the cost of tagging physical objects with identification numbers should be very low, registration will probably be used to record the ownership of all but the smallest mobile physical objects. Immobile physical property (e.g., land) and property in computer memory, processors, or communication lines should be even easier to register. Thus most concrete property ownership is likely to be determined via registration, although it is less clear how centralized is this system.

Today, laws that prohibit activities such as gambling, prostitution, or recreational drugs seem to be rather weakly enforced; large fractions of the population are able to reliably do such things with little risk of prosecution. This is plausibly because the public wants to take *symbolic* stands against such activities, but doesn't actually want to strongly limit their availability. Ems may similarly have poorly enforced laws that symbolize opposition to behaviors, including laws against what many see as wasteful or disrespectful leisure activities.

EFFICIENT LAW

A number of legal changes can be weakly predicted from the expectation of a more efficient em economy. A long and rich academic tradition has studied the efficiency of legal policies (Friedman 2000;

Shavell 2004; Posner 2014). Standard results from this tradition suggest likely directions of legal change if ems adopt more efficient law.

Today, we deter crime largely via informal social norms and formal threats of fines and prison. While fines can be an efficient form of punishment, large fines are not feasible when the legal system is not willing to force the sale of key assets, such as abilities to earn future wages. Prison is very expensive punishment and hence inefficient.

To more cheaply punish crimes, em societies might use random chances of executions, exile, or torture. However, while randomness can be efficient, it may still evoke complaints of unfairness and disproportionality.

Ancient societies often used vicarious liability, holding family clans responsible for the actions of members. As it can be expensive to punish short-lived ems, ems may also use vicarious liability tied to larger subclans that include an em. Clans might also be held responsible for the actions of subclans. Instead of allowing parties to use inability to pay as an excuse to evade large liability penalties, everyone might be required to show the backing of a larger organization able to cover large liability penalties. This larger organization might be an insurance or reinsurance firm.

Today, liability law does more to discourage bad behavior than to encourage good behavior, because it is much easier to sue for the harms others have done to you than it is to sue for the uncompensated benefits that you have given to others. Law-induced incentives for good behavior might increase if law allowed negative liability, that is, if law allowed people to sue others for benefits given to them, such as for having introduced someone to a future spouse (Porat 2009; Dari-Mattiacci 2009).

In our world, the usual remedy for a breach of contract is monetary damages; it is unusual to require the specific performance of a contract's promises. As ems can easily make new copies to do tasks, specific performance can more easily be a remedy for em contracts that promise to do specific actions.

With current law, the high cost of participating in lawsuits limits our ability to use law to deter small harms, and often forces innocent parties to plead guilty when threatened with expensive court processes. One remedy is to turn lawsuits into more transferable property, so that someone who has been harmed can more easily sell their right to sue and be compensated.

Another remedy for expensive legal processes is to let people gamble their lawsuits in official court lotteries. For example, if you said someone hurt you by $100, and you gambled that damage claim at 1000 to 1 odds, then 1 in a 1000 times you'd have a claim worth $100 000, which makes it worth bothering to sue. The other 999 times the party you sued would have proof that they owed you nothing. The party you sue might also be allowed or even required to gamble $100 in the same lottery, so that party has money to pay if you win your suit (Hanson 2007).

A related remedy is to have courts issue fast decisions based on the odds in open prediction markets. Such markets would bet on what the court would decide *if* a lottery were to randomly pick this case to be decided directly via the usual expensive court process, and then offer sufficient stakes to induce all parties to try hard to win.

Blackmail is plausibly often efficient. If blackmail were legal, then the associates of criminals would try harder to notice their crimes, so they could blackmail those criminals. This could increase the discovery and punishment of crimes, because close associates can often more cheaply identify crimes and criminals than can distant police professionals. Also, blackmail makes larger fines feasible, as criminals who would otherwise hide assets to avoid paying formal fines may instead search aggressively to find assets to pay blackmailers (Katz 1996; Block et al. 2000).

Today, contract law allows flexible adaptation of incentives to circumstances, but only over a limited range of topics, and via a limited range of incentives. A stronger contract law would cover more topics with stronger incentives, allowing stronger contracts over more kinds of situations. Such a law could thus let more parties contract more strongly in more ways around standard regimes of criminal, tort, property, and contract law, in effect privatizing more of law choice, detection, punishment, and adjudication. This could allow a more flexible use of legal incentives in a wider range of contexts (Friedman 1973).

With a stronger contract law, each clan might be relatively free to choose its internal law and governance, and then be free to overturn legal defaults by negotiating pair-wise deals with other clans regarding the laws that will govern their interactions.

This list so far, of possibly more efficient legal changes, only scratches the surface of a vast literature in law and economics, in which can be found many more such possibly efficient legal changes.

INNOVATION

How is innovation different in an em economy?

Today, we see more innovation in larger firms and cities, more concentrated industries, more capital-intensive industries, and electronic- and computer-based industries (Schumpeter 1942; Gayle 2003; Miller 2009). The em economy should have stronger scale economies, and a more robust focus on engineering relative to design in products. The cost of most products in the em virtual world is dominated by fixed costs. The price of skilled labor falls relative to the price of capital, making research relatively cheap because research is labor-intensive. All of these features suggest that the em economy is more innovative.

Whether an economy tends over time to emphasize labor or capital depends on the relative rates of innovation in labor and capital. As ems are based on computers, which have tended to innovate faster than most forms of capital, em labor is likely to become more cost-effective faster than kinds of capital that are not computer-based.

As the growth of an em economy is driven more by increasing inputs, innovation is not as important for growth in the em economy as in past eras. Even so, innovation is still very important. We expect the em world to select for practices that better encourage innovation, at least to the extent that regions and organizations gain from internal innovation.

Today, geographic regions that are more religious are less innovative, and more religious individuals hold views less favorable to innovation (Bénabou et al. 2015). This weakly suggests either that ems will be less religious, or that ems will find ways to produce more innovation even when ems hold unfavorable views about innovation. Factors suggesting that ems are more religious are discussed in Chapter 25, Religion section.

The em world may also select for better innovation institutions. In fact, the most valuable innovations in an em world might be better laws and institutions of intellectual property, to more strongly encourage innovation.

One possible way to promote innovation is to use prediction markets to separate two forecasting tasks, one on the feasibility of an innovation, and the other on the demand for that innovation. Today, investing in a new firm is usually a bet on two factors: its product idea, and its team. Investors who are good at estimating if a product would sell well are often not good at estimating which team has the best chance of delivering the product. When there are prediction markets on which products would be successful, if produced, those who can predict product ideas well can just focus on betting in those markets. Those who can predict teams well can instead hedge their product risk in these prediction markets, and then invest in particular ventures with the teams they favor.

Widespread recording of em activities allows for interesting changes. One change would be to let independent discovery be a stronger legal defense for patent infringement (Vermont 2006). Today, we don't allow this defense because we fear that inventors might too easily pretend to have reinvented something that they actually copied. But em inventors who archive all of their reading and conversations might be in a much stronger position to credibly prove a claim of independent reinvention. In this situation, em inventors may also get into the habit of using copies in safes to hear about news and developments elsewhere, copies who then decide what information seems worth telling to their original copy.

A related change would be to treat innovation rights legally via liability law instead of property law (Shapiro 2016). That is, instead of suing someone who has violated the intellectual property of your innovation, you might instead use negative liability (as discussed in the Efficient Law section) to sue them to compensate you for part of the gains that they realized from your innovation. This is similar to compulsory licensing of patents, which seems to promote innovation today (Baten et al. 2015). Detailed recordings of their activities might help to estimate the value that they actually obtained from an innovation. One might even run sims using archived copies of innovation users to study the effect on them of being exposed to your innovation. The ability of judge spurs to protect privacy while flexibly but uniformly enforcing laws could be useful here.

Many other legal changes could better encourage innovation, changes that we do not now imagine. Perhaps subsidized decision markets could create sufficient incentives for specialists to study this question more carefully than we have so far done. It is clear that with good institutions to encourage innovation, it could be reasonable to spend one-quarter, one-half, or even more of world income on pursuing possible innovations. Innovations are just that important, if ways to encourage them effectively can be found.

A newly important kind of innovation for ems is finding good em teams. Ems will search among the many possible combinations of team members trained in particular ways to do particular jobs, looking for especially productive team combinations. When new better em teams are found, all of the old teams doing that job may be forced to retire. Other forms of innovation, such as finding new tools, products, and work methods, often produce a similar outcome, as the best team for previous arrangements is often not the best team for new arrangements.

When such large scale team displacement happens, large fractions of affected clans may be forced to retire all at once. This may seem to them a disaster on the scale of a war or famine. Ems may create monuments and museums to commemorate such losses, and simulations where one could visit and see how such teams once functioned. Retirees from such teams may staff such simulations.

Clans are eager to track, assist, and influence innovation that has the potential to displace teams in which they participate. While such efforts can in principle create either a local net tax or subsidy for innovation, on net it may be a subsidy if places that can encourage local innovation win on average in the competitive em world.

SOFTWARE

We can anticipate many predictable changes in software practices in an em world.

In our world, the cost of computing hardware has been falling rapidly for decades. This rapid fall has pushed computer projects to be shorter term, so that products can be productively used before they are made obsolete by changes in hardware and tools. The increasing quantity of software purchased has also led to larger software projects, each of which involves employing more engineers. This has shifted the emphasis toward more communication and negotiation between workers, and toward software styles that more strongly support modularity and standardization.

The cost of hiring human software engineers has not fallen much in recent decades. The increasing divergence between the high cost of engineers and the low and falling cost of hardware has led to a decreased emphasis on raw efficiency, and an increased emphasis on tools and habits to assure speed and low errors. This has led to an increasing emphasis on modularity, abstraction, and high-level operating systems and languages. Higher-level tools insulate engineers more from hardware details, and from distracting tasks such as type checking and garbage collection. As a result, software is less efficient and well adapted to any given context, but more valuable overall. An increasing focus on niche products has also helped to increase the emphasis on modularity and abstraction.

Em software engineers are selected for their high productivity, and they use the tools and styles preferred by such engineers. Of course there is still a place for tools and styles matched to workers who don't specialize in software, but have their strongest expertise in other areas. Even so, all em workers are smart and highly productive, and so their tools are of the type that very productive people prefer. As em computers tend to be more parallel, reversible, and error-prone, em software is also more focused on those cases. Because the em economy is larger, its software industry is larger as well, supporting larger projects, larger teams, and more specialization.

The transition to an em economy greatly lowers wages, thus inducing a big one-time "back-to-the-future" shift, toward an emphasis on raw context-dependent performance, relative to abstraction and easier modifiability. The em economy move away from niche products adds to this tendency, as does the ability to save copies of the engineer who just wrote each piece of software, available to help later with modifying that piece. On the other hand, a move toward larger software projects could favor more abstraction and modularity.

After the transition to an em world, the cost of em hardware falls at about the same rate as does the cost of other computer hardware. Because of this new similarity between costs, the software tradeoff between performance and other considerations changes much less during the em era. This greatly extends the useful lifetime of programming languages, tools, and habits matched to particular performance tradeoff choices.

After an initial period of large rapid gains, the software and hardware designs for implementing brain emulations probably reach diminishing returns, after which there are only minor improvements. This is what we see for software compiler and emulation programs today. In contrast, non-em software probably improves about as fast as does computer hardware, as for many decades in many areas of computing we have seen improvements in algorithm efficiency remain close to hardware gains (Grace 2013). Thus after ems appear, em software engineering and other computer-based work slowly becomes more tool-intensive, with tools adding a larger fraction of value.

In contrast, for non-computer-based tools such as bulldozers, the intensity of use and the fraction of value added by these tools probably falls, as those tools are likely to improve less quickly than em hardware does. Even so, new tools of this sort will continue to be invented and used.

For over a decade now, the speed of fast computer processors has increased at a much lower rate than the cost of computer hardware has fallen. We expect this trend to continue long into the future. In contrast, em brain hardware costs fall with the cost of parallel computer hardware overall, because the emulation of brains is a very parallel task. Because of this, relative to more parallel software, ems see an increasing sluggishness of software that has a large serial component, that is, requiring many steps to be taken one after the other. This sluggishness directly reduces the value of such software to ems, and also makes such software harder to write.

Thus over time, serial software will become less valuable, compared with ems and parallel software. Em software engineers will rely less on software tools with a big serial component, and instead emphasize parallel software and compatible tools. In this scenario, tools such as runtime type checking and garbage collection are done in parallel, or not at all. If it ends up being too hard to write parallel software, then the value of software more generally may be reduced relative to the value of having ems do tasks directly with less software assistance.

The increasing importance of work, the increase in organization sizes, and the standardization of work teams all increase the importance of enterprise software, that is, of software that helps organizations to coordinate.

A tendency of fast ems to be high status should raise the status of software engineers, for whom faster speeds are often more productive. The competition for higher status among ems may encourage faster speeds than would otherwise be efficient, including among software engineers.

LONE DEVELOPERS

For software engineering tasks where parallel software and tools suffice, and where the software doesn't need to interact with slower physical systems, em software engineers could be productive even when sped up to the top cheap speed. This often makes it feasible to avoid the costs of coordinating across many engineers, by having a single engineer spend an entire subjective career creating a large software system. For an example, an engineer that spent a subjective century at mega-em speeds would complete this period in less than one objective hour. Thus when such a delay is acceptable, parallel software may be written by a single engineer taking a subjective career length.

When software can be written quickly via ultra-fast software engineers, product development could happen quickly, even if very large sums are spent. While today software investors can spend much of their time tracking current software development projects, those who invest in em software projects might spend most of their time deciding when is the right time to initiate such a project. Soon after a project begins, it is completed. A software development race, with more than one team trying to get to market first, only happens when a particular sharp event, such as a new technology advance being announced, triggers more than one development effort at a time.

A software engineer working for a high-speed lifetime on one project could still have trouble remembering software that they wrote subjective decades before. Because of this, shorter-term copies of this engineer might help them to be more productive. For example, short-term em copies might search for and repair bugs, and then end or retire once they have explained their results to the main copy. Short-term copies could also search among many possible designs for a particular module, and then end or retire after reporting on their best design choice, to be re-implemented by the main copy. In addition, longer-term copies could be created to specialize in whole subsystems, and younger copies might be revived to continue the project when older copies reached the end of their productive lifetime. Such approaches should allow close copies of a single em software engineer to make far larger and more coherent software systems within a subjective lifetime.

Fast software engineers who take a subjective lifetime to build a large software project, perhaps with the help of close copies, likely develop more personal software styles and tools, and rely less on standard approaches that help them to coordinate with other engineers with differing styles and uncertain quality.

When different parts of a software project require different skills, a lone software engineer might create several young copies trained to acquire different skills. Similarly, young copies could be trained in the non-software job topic areas where the software is to be applied, so that they can better understand what software variations will have value there.

However, when a project requires skills and expertise that are best matched to different temperaments and minds, then it may be worth paying the extra costs of communication to allow ems from different clans to work together on this project. In this case, such engineers would likely increase the priority of communication via more abstraction, modularity, and higher-level languages and module interfaces. Such approaches also become more attractive when outsiders must test and validate software, to certify its appropriateness to customers.

In the em world, small teams working at the top cheap speed, with the assistance of many spurs, may create enormous software systems. There may not be much need in the em world for larger software teams.

PART V

Sociology

CHAPTER 23

Mating

SEXUALITY

ow is sex different for ems?

As the em world is a very competitive world where sex is not needed for reproduction, and as sex can be time- and attention-consuming, ems may try to suppress sexuality.

For example, ems may be selected from among humans who report having little interest in sex. However, it turns out that substantial majorities of those who label themselves as "asexual" masturbate and have sexual fantasies (Yule and Brotto 2017). Alternatively, ems might use mind tweaks that produce effects analogous to castration. Such effects might be temporary, perhaps with a consciously controllable on-off switch. Historically, castrated males have tended to have lower libido, to be less aggressive and obsessive, to be better able to multitask, and to be more sensitive, sympathetic, and social. However, historically eunuchs have often wanted to marry, and have often had active sex lives (Aucoin and Wassersug 2006; Brett et al. 2007; Wassersug 2009; Treleaven et al. 2013). Thus even for eunuch-like ems there might still be a substantial demand for sex and related pair bonding.

It is possible that em brain tweaks could be found to greatly reduce natural human desires for sex and related romantic and intimate pair bonding, without reducing em productivity. It is also possible that many of the most productive ems would accept such tweaks. Alternatively, it is possible that cheap vivid romantic and sexual simulations will sufficiently satisfy pair-bonding urges, so that little demand remains for pair-bonding with real ems (Levy 2008; Brain 2012).

However, given how deeply pair bonding and sexual behaviors are embedded in human nature, such scenarios do not seem likely, at least for the early em era. Scenarios of sex suppression also seem to be less simple, as it is harder to calculate their implications.

In this book I thus assume that ems retain modestly strong desires for sex and related pair bonding, even if such desires are substantially reduced. I also assume that familiar conventional sexual and gender habits and preferences continue in the em world. That is, most ems divide relatively clearly into male versus female, ems mostly prefer male-female pair bonds, and these bonds have a distribution of time-scales near those we have seen in humans across cultures so far.

It is possible that our demand for long-term pair bonding is less deeply embedded than is our demand for pair bonding in general. In this case ems might have mostly short-term pair bonds, and perhaps more emotionally distinct relations such as those common in prostitution. We don't have a strong reason, however, to expect this scenario.

Even if human nature isn't flexible enough to let ems eliminate sexual urges, it might be flexible enough to allow large modifications. In this case, the lack of a reproductive function of sex could let ems explore a wide space of sexual attitudes and practices, to find ones that promote individual and team productivity. They might find solutions that would seem strange and repellent to us. On the other hand, they might not find such things.

As most ems are near a peak productivity age of fifty or more, em sexual and mating inclinations tend to be those of people with that mental age, and yet with ideal bodies and stamina.

Foragers knew each other very well, including potential mates. Farmers knew each other less well on average, and so they could choose mates from among those they knew less well. That is, mating attraction could be based on more shallow judgments. Industry increased this trend, as we often know even less about people we meet in the industrial world. Among the main em clans, however, this trend reverses, as such clans know each other better.

Because of clan-based access to data on the experiences of millions or more other copies of themselves, ems from large clans know much better than we do which other ems are likely to be receptive to their romantic or sexual overtures. They also know much better which sort of relations have the potential to last.

Ems who want more spontaneity and uncertainty in their relations than these data offer might prefer to have romantic and sexual relations with the less common two-name clans. Such a preference might sometimes be in tension, however, with putting less well-known clan members in the role of independent judges.

Ems who want mating relations that have little risk of resulting in long-term attachments may prefer relations with spurs.

Illicit em mating could be harder to detect. As ems could meet in secure virtual locations, and speed up for their meetings, such meetings may not be detectable by following an em's path in space, or by looking for unexplained absences in their time schedule. The memories such meetings created might still be detectable, although even these could be avoided if new spurs were created for each meeting. Such spur meetings seem unlikely to be satisfying, however. The financial cost to hold illicit meetings, however, remains robustly detectable.

OPEN-SOURCE LOVERS

Just as some ems may choose to be open-source workers, willing to work at most any task as long as they are given minimal comforts, other ems may choose to be open-source lovers. That is, they may be willing to enter into short- or long-term relationships with a wide range of partners, as long as (1) some minimal treatment standards are met, (2) their partner pays for their time to exist, and (3) an initial trial finds a sufficient "spark" between them. As long as someone else paid for their time, open-source lovers might allow a wide variety of situations and tweaks to be tried in search of a good spark.

Just as the best available open-source em workers are probably reasonably qualified for most jobs even if they aren't the world's best workers, the best available open-source lovers are reasonably attractive even if they aren't the world's best lovers.

Some open-source lovers are known for being very picky regarding what is an acceptable spark, while others are known for having easy-to-find sparks. Others may be picky about the fraction of their subjective time they are willing to devote to love-making, relative to other romantic interactions, or to time apart. All else equal, an em can get a better quality open-source lover if they are themselves more attractive, and if they are willing to pay for more non-together time.

Given a fixed budget to spend on leisure time with a romantic partner, the existence of open-source lovers creates two main romantic options. On one hand, an em might choose to spend most of a budget for romance on his or her own run time, and spend that time with whatever willing partner they could find to join in an equal relation where each partner pays for their own run time. On the other hand, an em might instead spend their budget on half as many romantic hours, to pay to run two ems, so that they can then spend that time with the best available open-source lover. Thus the existence of open-source lovers sets a high lower-bound on the quality of em romantic and sexual relationships. The per-minute subjective value of an equal relation should not fall much below half of the per-minute value of a relation with the best available open-source lover.

An em choosing an open-source lover could often choose one of the very best such lovers in the worlds, according to their preferred criteria. This is likely to be a more attractive option for females, who seem to have stronger preferences for mate quality. A high-quality open-source em lover could excel not only in sexual behavior, but also in difficult but sexy mental features such as musical or artistic ability.

To many ems, the very best open-source lover available who finds a spark with that em may still not be as attractive as their best fantasy lover. Depending on the quality of simulated lovers in virtual reality, many ems may also spend romantic time with such simulations.

PAIR BONDS

How might longer-term pair bonding differ for ems?

If ems form marriage-like long-term pair bonds, such bonds may last longer subjectively than do such relations today. Two weak reasons to expect this are (1) ems are more productive and more productive people divorce less today, and (2) the em world is poorer, and divorce has increased with increasing wealth and falls during economic downturns (Baghestani and Malcolm 2014).

Today when one member of a couple rises in success more than does the other, it is the less successful member who is at risk of being left behind, as the more successful member seeks to trade up to a higher-quality partner. However, when an em is successful there is more demand for copies of that em. And when a successful em makes more copies than does their partner, it is the new copies of the successful em who are "left behind" without the same access to copies of their previous partner.

Pair-bonded ems might sometimes make a lifetime commitment to one another, promising that they would only agree to make future copies which are paired with a copy of their lifetime mate. This commitment is less costly toward the end of an em's useful mental flexibility lifetime, and in mass labor markets, where copies are usually created as part of large predictable teams.

Today, we often form romantic and other attachments that are specific to one individual, and which do not extend to other similar people. For example, people married to one member of an identical twin pair usually claim to have weak or no romantic feelings for the other member of the pair. This desire to attach to just one person might be thwarted, or at least complicated, by close em copies. Perhaps ems could learn to treat close em copies as exactly the same person for the purpose of attachments. But a simpler approach is to segregate copies so that ems do not interact much with close copies of the em to which they feel attached. Close copies may meet each other in private, but not also in the presence of their close associates.

Because marriages were central to farmer era property and production, parents often took control over and arranged their children's marriages. These parents usually took less control over their children's friends, beyond choosing peer groups. For foragers, in contrast, less went wrong when pair bonds failed, and so foragers were freer to choose and break both friend and pair bonds than were farmers. We seem to be reverting to forager mating habits today, as our increasing wealth gives us more freedom. At work, in contrast, we now mainly let managers arrange our work teams.

Will em marriages be arranged? Arranged marriages seem to work out well today (Regan et al. 2012). This judgment may depend on your priorities, however. Involvement by Chinese parents in matchmaking is associated with less marital harmony within the couple, lower market income of the wife, a more submissive wife, a greater number of children, a higher likelihood of having any male children, and a stronger belief of the husband in providing old age support to his parents (Huang et al. 2016).

As pair bonding matters less for em production and reproduction than it does for us today, this is a reason to leave mating decisions to individual ems. However, older ems seem much more qualified than are parents today to choose matches for their younger clan-mates, as they would know their clients far better. Em couples might relive their early love by helping their younger similar copies to fall in love with each other. Ems who follow the romantic paths set by their older copies should suffer far lower risks of romantic failure and divorce. Thus em pair bonds may be arranged or heavily assisted, and work out even better than do our marriages.

While pair bonding may matter less to em production, when to copy and who to have as members of what work teams are decisions that are especially important for em production. These decisions are thus likely to be arranged or heavily assisted by others, even if individuals can veto particular proposed team assignments. While ems may be freer in some ways to pick their mates and friends than we are, as a practical matter mates and friends may often be limited to other team members, and ems may have less control over their teams.

Jobs differ in how widely they are available; some can be found in most geographic locations, while others are only found at a few places. Today, couples tend to move to the geographic area of the member whose job is the most location-constrained. As men tend to have more location-constrained jobs today, male-female couples tend to move to the man's job location (Benson 2014).

To the extent that ems are clustered into dense cities where they can interact with most of the city without much noticing the distance between work sites, this weakens the tendency of a couple to have to choose a location favored by one of their jobs. Not all ems are in this situation, however. The em couples more likely to move together for one of their jobs are those with especially fast jobs or jobs located especially far from urban centers.

GENDER

As gender styles and roles have displayed many consistent patterns over wide scopes of space and time, the simple assumption to make is that ems continue with similar gender styles and roles. Yes, we have seen changes near us in space and time, and many hope that such changes will continue. Even so, it seems much harder to guess the future direction of local changes, relative to just expecting a rough regression to near the historical means. This assumption has many implications.

For example, all else being equal, ems continue to tend to mate with others who are similar to them in many ways. Ems also continue to prefer physical good looks, such as body symmetry, smooth skin, and muscle tone. These features should be very easy to obtain, however. Ems will also tend to prefer ems with minds that are high-status, kind, understanding, dependable, sociable, stable, and smart.

If past gender patterns continue, then we expect men to prefer females with signs of nurturing inclinations and fertility, such as youthful good looks, and we expect women to prefer men with signs of wealth and status, and their future indicators such as intelligence, ambition, and an inclination to work hard (Schmitt 2012).

Relative to men, we expect women to more value benevolence, to be more averse to risk and competition, and to be more neurotic, agreeable, and open to discussing their feelings (Croson and Gneezy 2009). We expect men to be more assertive and open to ideas, and to more value power, stimulation, hedonism, achievement, and self-direction (Costa et al. 2001; Schwartz and Rubel 2005).

Gender differences in personality seem to be stronger in richer societies, as well as in cultures whose ancestors used the plow, which required more physical strength (Alesina et al. 2013; Marcinkowska et al. 2014). So we weakly expect gender role differences to become weaker in a poorer em world where physical strength matters less.

A poorer em world may also encourage a focus on long-term over short-term mating, although the reduced role of pair bonding in raising children may counter that effect.

The em world seems romantically plentiful in the sense that it should give both male and female ems more of what they want in romantic partners, at least compared with our world. In virtual reality ems could easily and cheaply offer either youthful good looks, or aged distinction, as their partners prefer. Most male ems are near their most productive subjective ages, and come from the few hundred most productive clans, making them intrinsically smart, hardworking, and capable.

Some features that are attractive today are less plentiful in the em world, however. As most ems have mental ages near peak productivity ages, female ems less often have the youthful mental styles that often attract males. With far fewer children to raise, females have fewer occasions to develop and show nurturing inclinations. Available males are less often rich or have especially attractive artistic abilities, such as music, art, and storytelling.

Our natural attraction to others is often relative, so that we are attracted to those nearby who excel relative to others in our social world. It is of course hard to satisfy everyone if what they all want is intrinsically scarce in this sense. Most ems who want strong associations with the relatively most attractive or successful partner around must inevitably be disappointed.

GENDER IMBALANCE

The em economy may have an unequal demand for the work of males and females.

Although it is hard to predict which gender will be more in demand in the em world, one gender might end up supplying proportionally more workers than the other. On the one hand, the tendency of top performers in most fields today to be men suggests there might be more demand for male ems. However, while today's best workers are often motivated by the attention and status that being the best can bring, in the em world there are millions of copies of the best workers, who need to find other motivations for their work. On the other hand, today women are becoming better educated and are in increasing demand in modern workplaces. There are some indications that women have historically worked harder and more persistently in hard-times low-status situations, which seem similar in some ways to the em world.

The em world is more competitive, and women tend to perform worse when they frame their interactions as competitive (Niederle 2014). However, the em world may find more congenial ways for women to frame their production.

An unequal demand for male versus female workers could thwart em desires for romantic male-female pair bonds. The em world might substitute polygamous or homosexual relations, or transgender conversions, either by selecting more for ems who prefer such things, or by cultures that encourage ems to choose such options. Alternatively, ems might use software to make same-sex partners appear to be of the opposite sex. However, the selection of ems willing to make such choices could have high opportunity costs. As mentioned in Chapter 13, Qualities section, homosexual ems may be preferentially female, as gay men earn less than other men today, while lesbian women earn more than other women.

A third option is for the more common gender to pay for the time of the less common gender, as has happened in past "frontier" towns with very large male to female ratios. This option seems similar to the open-source lover option.

A fourth solution is for the gender with the higher total labor demand to take on more work with a high ratio of spurs to long-term copies. For example, one partner in a couple might make ten spur copies per workday, where only one copy continues on to the next workday. The other partner might make no spurs per workday. In this case this couple could embody a ten to one ratio of labor supplied by the two partners. The couple would meet and interact after and before their workday, but perhaps not during the workday. Of course this whole spur-creation approach may have substantial costs if tasks are so well matched to a particular gender that there is a productivity cost from assigning a job to the opposite gender.

A fifth way to maintain ordinary pair bonding in the face of unequal labor demand is to use fast-slow pair bonds. For example, if one partner ran four times faster than another, the fast one could spend one hour per subjective (twenty-four-hour) day with their partner, while the slow one could temporarily speed up four times per subjective (twenty-seven-hour) day, each time spending one subjective hour with their partner. The fast partner would supply four times as much work to the labor market as the slow partner. Fast-slow pairings could also deal with mismatches in how often partners want to interact, including sexually.

This fast-slow approach might also have a productivity cost if genders are not equally well matched to the fast and slow jobs assigned to them. Another potential problem is that over any given subjective lifespan, the slow partner would have time for four fast partners, resulting in a subjective age mismatch during many periods of most relationships. The fast partner would only ever see the slow partner at a particular phase of their life. To retire together, the slow partner would have to split off copies that retire each time a fast partner retires. Also, this asymmetry in number of lifetime partners might be emotionally problematic, if one partner feels completely devoted to the other, but feels the other partner is only fractionally devoted to them.

Fast-slow pair bonds could plausibly satisfy most desires for pair bonding in a world with a speed-weighted gender ratio of four or less. This approach would not, however, satisfy such desires well if the ratio were sixteen or more.

One way or another, however, the em world can deal with gender imbalances in work demand. Its solutions may not be elegant, but they are mostly effective.

CHAPTER 24

Signals

SHOWING OFF

Today, we make many choices with an eye to how those choices influence how others see us. For example, we try to give others a favorable impression of our general capacities, such as wealth, health, vigor, intelligence, knowledge, skills, conscientiousness, and artistic sense. With this in mind, we try to appear impressive in our arts, sports, schooling, hobbies, vocabularies, and other markers.

For example, we plausibly pay extra for visibly nice clothes, cars, houses, etc., in part to show that we can afford such things. We use big words and witty banter in part to show our intelligence and schooling. We go to school in part to show our intelligence, conscientiousness, and conformity. We play sports in part to show our intelligence, health, strength, self-control, toughness, and cooperativeness. We play music in part to show our intelligence, self-control, passion, and creativity.

We also try to give others a favorable impression of our loyalties and connections. That is, we try to credibly show that we feel strong positive ties toward certain individuals and groups, who feel similarly toward us. We can also try to show negative feelings toward rivals and outsiders. With this in mind, we choose with whom we spend our time, who we praise or criticize, and our styles of clothing, music, movies, etc. We follow gossip, news, and fashion in part to help show that we are well connected to respected sources of information. We enjoy stories and participate in politics in part to convince associates of our moral sympathies. We sometimes even cry for help, to show who will come running.

Today, we spend a large fraction of our energy and wealth on such "signaling," both because humans naturally care greatly about gaining status and respect in the eyes of others, and because being rich allows us to attend more to such concerns. As mentioned in Chapter 2, Era Values section, in terms of simple functionality, we seem today to spend excessive amounts on schools, medicine, financial intermediation, and huge projects.

In contrast, while ems share most of our desires for respect, they live in a more competitive world, where they can less afford to indulge such desires. Thus ems are likely to spend less of their energies signaling to gain status. However, as signaling has functional value in assigning ems to tasks and teams, and as it can be hard to coordinate to discourage signaling, ems will likely still do a lot of signaling.

Similar to humans today, ems probably use self-deception to help present a positive image of themselves to associates. For example, workers might try to believe that they are not as exhausted or bored as they actually are, to seem more attractive as team partners. They might similarly believe that retirees enjoy their retirement more than the evidence justifies, to show a positive attitude toward typical life plans. To preserve this illusion, ems may avoid looking carefully at the lives of retirees, just as most of us do today. Ems may also believe that outsiders or bosses have less influence on their activities than they actually do, to feel, like we do today, that they have higher status by feeling more in control of their lives.

On some topics, the em lifestyle naturally reduces self-deception. For example ems could not as easily claim that their taking "the road not taken" had made all the difference in their lives, because ems have clearer direct evidence about the results of other close copies of them taking different life paths.

Perhaps in some cases clans will deceive members. For example, if a young em is especially productive when in a romantic relation with a particular partner, the clan might mislead them to think that this relation will last, when they know from prior experience that it most likely will not.

PERSONAL SIGNALS

Like us, individual ems have many specific ways to show off.

For example, ems in virtual reality can use their personal appearance and surroundings to signal their mood, affiliations, awareness of local fashions, and recent activities. It may be harder to use virtual reality surroundings to signal wealth, if most environments are cheap to obtain and maintain. However, some particular decorations may be copyrighted and expensive, or be intrinsically expensive to compute. Also, an entourage of smart, fast associates remains expensive, and hence credibly signals wealth. But an em entourage may have to visibly do more than they usually do today, to make clear that they are in fact not fake automated entourages.

Em associates might share private virtual overlays that only selected viewers could see, projected onto people and objects around them. For example, they could draw a silly mustache on someone's face, a mustache that could only be seen by ems in their social circle. In this way, ems could have a laugh with associates at the expense of those not clued in to their private augmentation source, and thereby signal loyalty and an exclusive connection to particular associates.

Ems may also show loyalty by creating shorter-term copies who do unpleasant jobs which aren't worth remembering. The main motivation of such copies to do their work may be wanting to help their larger team or clan. This may be as close as ems can get to the "ultimate sacrifice" of giving up their life.

Today, people lower the pitch of their voices when they feel dominant, and such low voices are heard as more dominant, and also as sexier. Low voices are also heard as less nervous, and more truthful, empathic, and potent. We also hear voices that are loud, fast, have fewer pauses, and more variation in pitch and volume to be more energetic, smart, knowledgeable, truthful, and persuasive (Mlodinow 2012).

As it is cheap and easy for ems to automatically modify their voices to be louder and lower-pitched, we expect ems to routinely do this, at least when they want to sound dominant, persuasive, and smart. Ems find it expensive, however, to increase their voice speed, reduce pauses, and increase relevant variation in pitch and volume, because these typically require faster mind speeds.

For humans, faster voices signal the speaker's intelligence and energy level. For ems, however, faster voices also show how much the speaker has invested financially to speed up. This signals in part how much an em cares about this speedup. Fast voices can also signal that the speaker has a lower cost of running faster, such as via running on special cheaper hardware, or perhaps via shrinking their less used brain parts. Ems probably run on average too fast for other purposes, in order to show off via speed.

Today people agree on which faces indicate more desirable qualities, such as seeming trustworthy and dominant (Walker and Vetter 2015), and in poorer societies men less prefer women to have more feminine faces, compared with men in richer societies (Marcinkowska et al. 2014). People tend to agree on which face features tend to make people look smart. Such features including a big head, a taller face, a wide distance between pupils, and a larger nose. These features do in fact correlate with intelligence today (Lee et al. 2017). So ems may tend to choose the faces associated with intelligence and desirable personalities, and also faces with weaker gender distinctions.

Ems who speed up their minds to speak quickly, and then slow down their minds to listen, risk talking faster than listeners can comfortably hear. Because of this, ems limit their talking speed and instead invest more in careful choice of words and intonation. Such ems tend to sound like voices in our advertisements, who talk with carefully practiced lines in a script.

Virtual ems no longer have direct needs to eat, take medicine, or clean themselves. But ems might continue with such activities because humans have long infused such activities with many layers of symbolic meanings. Such activities are often used today to signal loyalties and abilities. Ems thus search for new practical ends that might be achieved by these activities in an em world.

For example, ems might redirect our natural attitudes toward medical care and treatment into activities such as meditation that could plausibly influence em mental health. Eating particular foods might trigger temporary drug-like tweaks in the emulation process, which could induce useful mental states of relaxation, distraction, or thoughtfulness. This might allow eating to serve functions for ems similar to the purposes that music, dance, and stories often serve for humans today. While it is possible to trigger such mind tweaks just by pushing a button, triggering such changes via food might feel less disruptive and better integrated into familiar human rituals.

All through history, people have tried to show how well connected and informed they are of news (Stephens 2007). We try to show surprise and substantial processing of news before others have even become aware of it. And we try to show that we are over it and on to other things while others are still processing such news. Ems only do this relative to ems of a similar speed. It is just not possible to keep up with ems who run much faster, and it is too easy to stay ahead of ems who run much slower.

Fast-changing fashion, such as in clothes and music, is common in our era. However, apparently fashion did not exist in the foraging and farming eras (except in proto-industrial Rome). As fashion seems to signal some combination of wealth, youth, taste for variety, and information source quality, whether fashion continues in an em world depends on how eager ems are to signal such features, and on what other signaling methods are available.

Virtual reality allows for very cheap and rapid changes in fashion for things like clothes and furnishings. The main costs of rapid fashion change would be cognitive; ems might get distracted and confused by rapidly changing surroundings.

It is relatively cheap and easy to meet personally and talk with ems who are copies of famous ems. It is hard to get those famous ems to remember you later when they talk to others. Thus ems trying to show status and centrality in social networks try less to meet celebrities, and try more to get those celebrities to remember them.

Today, we tend to presume that celebrities must have exceptional qualities. Because of this, we want to mate with them, to use their influence in our favor, and to be publicly associated with them. In the em world, celebrities have far fewer persistent differences from other members of their clans. Ems know that one clan member being more famous than others is mostly a matter of luck. This reduces but may not eliminate em eagerness to associate with individual celebrity ems.

In our world many rare products and services acquire high status via association with high status people. For ems being a celebrity is less about having higher persistent qualities, so products and services acquire less added status by being associated with rare em celebrities. This reduces the status of rare products, relative to common products. While today we often presume that the most popular products are not the best products, to ems the most popular products and services will more often also be the best.

Sometimes a partner such as a lover or friend will ask an em to visibly choose that partner over their clan in a conflict. A high cost action of this sort would send a strong signal of loyalty to a partner. But this high cost also makes such actions rare.

As mentioned in Chapter 14, Work Hours section, ems may sometimes be tempted to work too much to signal their ability and enthusiasm for work, as are many people today. If this happens often, then a competitive em world is likely to seek ways to prevent such overwork. Clans, firms, or teams might, for example, commit to requiring a minimum fraction of em time to be devoted to leisure.

GROUP SIGNALS

Some features of ems vary little among clan members. These include overall intelligence, basic personality, and early life cultural heritage. Other features can vary greatly among clan members, including wealth, mood, vigor, recently acquired skills, knowledge of local conditions, and loyalties and ties to specific individual ems. Still other features vary substantially within a clan, but vary little between close copies. These mildly varying features may include stamina, confidence, and particular kinds of intelligence or artistic sense.

Features that vary greatly between close copies are likely to be left to each em to signal by themselves. In contrast, features that vary little within a clan create an opportunity for the clan to coordinate to signal those features together. When features vary within a clan but are shared within subclans, those subclans may coordinate to signal.

For example, ems from the few hundred clans that dominate the em economy might want to usually act as if everyone knew of and accepted their clan and its idiosyncrasies, and greatly valued its contribution. To show this, such clans might expect to be addressed by just one name, such as "George." Being treated this way is a credible signal that your clan is well known. Such ems might act irritated when forced to interact with ems from less familiar two-name clans. Such clans might also act indignant if anyone requested an independent evaluation of their contributions or value; they might think such actions appropriate for dealing with unfamiliar clans, but surely *they* are well known enough for this to be unnecessary.

Clans who share wealth internally may want to signal the wealth of their entire clan. They might do this by buying large prominent buildings in em cities, or by funding expensive projects. Just as nations today fund activities in sport, art, and academia to increase national prestige, clans may similarly fund some of their members to pursue prestigious activities, to show off features that don't vary much within clans. Clans that cannot coordinate well may spend less on signaling, and may seem less impressive as a result. In contrast, individual ems may pay less attention than we do to art, sport, or science, and put more effort into their connections with close associates.

To impress observers, ems might try when young to be a star athlete, artist, writer, explorer, or scholar. After achieving fame, they'd then be retrained for more useful work, where everyone could remember their youthful stardom. This is somewhat like people today who are star athletes when young, and afterward go into sales to take advantage of their fame. As we are less impressed by achievements to which several people contribute (Smith and Newman 2014), em clans will tend to keep the key work behind their impressive accomplishments within a single clan, and perhaps within a single em.

Bigger clans can afford to create more impressive achievements, which adds to the perceived superiority of bigger clans.

Ems prefer the training for their impressive youthful activities to be useful also in their later work career. For example, some ems may be athletes early, and then later do physical jobs, such as construction, that require related strong physical coordination abilities. Other ems might design innovative products early, and then spend their careers improving and servicing such products. The repairman who fixes a product might *literally* be the guy who invented it. In such scenarios, product innovation may be subsidized by em signaling efforts.

Today, activities such as dance, sport, and song show off combinations of mental and physical abilities. As ems can easily obtain virtual bodies with identical and maximal physical abilities, ems will change such activities to let audiences better see differing mental abilities. In a sporting contest, for example, em players may use standard bodies and brains, and win by having better "minds," (brain software). Alternatively, such contests might be more like bike or car races today, showing off both the abilities of body designers, and of the em who "drives" that body.

As have humans through history, some ems will show off by gaining status within communities of intellectuals. Today, some of our highest prestige is assigned to those credited with innovation, who add new intellectual results and methods that accumulate over time. However, in most nations today, and in almost all nations before a few centuries ago, intellectual status has come much less from innovation, and much more from privately teaching and advising the powerful, from gaining wider attention via popular writings, from mastering classic literature in great detail, and from being the first to be visibly associated with new intellectual fashions.

This history weakly suggests that, compared with today in the West, intellectual status among ems may not be as focused on innovation, especially for kilo-ems or faster, for whom society will seem to innovate more slowly. While this change may reduce the contributions of em top intellectuals to innovations, it shouldn't change the overall rate of innovation very much, because the fraction of useful innovation contributed by such intellectuals has always been small.

Because the actions of each em reflect strongly on the qualities of other clan members, clans exert more pressure, and retain more power, to discourage member behaviors that might make the clan look bad. This makes unusual em behaviors even stronger signals about clans. For example, if one em left his or her spouse, the spouses of similar copies may worry that they will be treated similarly.

As work team performance depends in part on general abilities of team members, clans may be expected to invest financially in the teams to which they contribute copies. Such investment signals their confidence in the quality and match of the workers they supply. Such expectations apply today only to rather wealthy families, but many em clans might be wealthy enough to make such investments.

By signaling together as a group, em clans take a big step toward seeing themselves as a united "us," or even a single "me."

CHARITY

Like people today, ems are eager to show their feelings about social and moral problems, and their allegiance to pro-social norms.

For centuries, three classic charities have been alms, hospitals, and schools. But em hospitals are unnecessary, except perhaps for mental illness, and em schools are already well funded, as children are rare. Alms are still possible for ordinary humans or animals, but there is no need to feed involuntarily hungry ems, or to warm shivering ones, as no cold or starving ems exist. One might pay to subsidize jobs or extra leisure time for working ems, to speed up retirees, or to support retirement for spurs who might otherwise end. But these may feel like discouragingly bottomless pits of need, and may not seem to be especially sympathetic causes, if recipients had declined to negotiate for such benefits when they agreed to make the copy that they are.

Perhaps more sympathetic recipients of aid are the rare em victims of war, violence, or natural disasters; they are not bottomless pits of need, and have not chosen their fate. Even more deserving might be victims of mind theft, as discussed in Chapter 5, Security section, who risk being enslaved or tortured for their secrets. Identified victims are rare, and most ems could legitimately fear similar fates befalling them. Most in the em world express strong disapproval of mind theft.

Ems might signal that they still feel very human by going out of their way to see and sympathize with animals, ordinary humans, and em children. Ems could watch shows about them, travel to visit them, and donate to help them. As most humans have few em copies, such humans are rare compared with ems, and so might be mild celebrities that ems pay to visit. This could give a mild subsidy to humans. For fast ems, the human world changes very little between em visits.

While em children are pampered even without charity, plants and non-human animals have few other supporters. We humans today care about nature in part because we enjoy traveling to ancestral-like environments, and because the destruction of nature threatens to destroy us by destroying the biological ecologies on which we rely. Ems, however, can travel more cheaply to virtual nature parks, and need have little fear that killing nature will somehow kill them.

Although em cities may be toxic to nearby nature, such cities at first will disturb only a tiny fraction of the globe. Nature is saved for a while because the em focus on a few dense cities leaves ems disinterested in most of the land that nature occupies. But this is probably only a temporary reprieve. Even if nature is safe during the em era, that era may only last a few objective years. Other eras will follow quickly, and our descendants are likely to soon fill the Earth, displacing nature everywhere outside of a few small preserves.

Today, charitable projects with the goal of influencing attitudes and beliefs often focus on children, for whom persuasion seems more effective, and whose attitudes will last longer into the future. Ems will be even more tempted to influence young ems, because such ems have many future descendants, and because such efforts tend to be seen as charitable. Such efforts might be justified as creating more total global happiness via making better childhood memories to be shared by many descendants.

Charity continues with ems, though with somewhat different targets.

IDENTITY

Informal discussions today about the possibility of ems often focus on the question of whether an emulation of an ordinary human would be the "same" person as that original. Ems similarly ask themselves how much they identify with different copies of themselves, with whom they share different amounts of history and context.

Although we are each very complex creatures full of vast detail, we often try to see and show ourselves to others in terms of a simpler "identity" (or personal "brand"). This identity helps to make us more predictable and understandable to others, which helps us to assure them of our loyalties and reliability. As a result, our moral choices seem especially central to our identity.

Today, most people take for granted that they identify with their nation and culture; they only rarely encounter outsiders who make them aware of this identity. In contrast, people today feel more aware of identifying with their personal combination of personality, style, and life history, because they are the only person they know with this particular combination. Because our families are more like us on these dimensions, we tend to identify more with our families than with outsiders.

Ems from large clans should be less aware of, and feel more secure in, their identifying with a personal combination of personality, style, and early life history. They know there is in effect a whole "planet" out there of perhaps billions of ems just like them, "super-twins" to whom they can talk at any time, or ask for help. Thus when around ems from other clans, ems might feel more like expatriates, that is, emissaries from a foreign land.

As discussed in Chapter 19, Managing Clans section, ems who made a plan and then split into many copies to execute that plan are likely to feel that they and their copies are the "same" person, while copies who openly disagree with each other are likely to see themselves more as different people. In an attempt to unify their members, clans may discourage open disagreement, focus more on the fact that they have a shared mental style and shared memories of early life, and focus less on recent opinions and memories. After all, those recent opinions and memories differ more.

When doing physical jobs, ems could use interchangeable bodies. Virtual ems could also easily change their virtual bodies at any time. Thus em identities need tie less to details of a particular body. However, to create a vivid memorable identity that is easily remembered by other clans, each clan may still create and stick close to a consistent visual style.

People today stay loyal to product brands over surprisingly long periods (Bronnenberg et al. 2012). This weakly suggests that ems will also stay loyal to brands for long times. Brand owners are eager to offer deep discounts to young ems with promising futures. While the em world has few children, each child has on average a great many descendants. On the other hand, collective purchasing by clans makes for better-informed consumers, and such consumers tend to have a weaker attachment to brands (Bronnenberg et al. 2014).

Today, our physical illnesses give us excuses to escape social pressures and expectations. If we don't want to do something, we can pretend to be sick. Ems, who never get physically sick, lack this excuse. Perhaps ems will expand their expectations of temporary mental illness to compensate. That is, ems may come to believe that most people are periodically struck by mental conditions that are acceptable excuses for failing to meet scheduled social interactions or deadlines. Even if the expected rate of these events is much lower than our rate of sickness today, such illnesses might still provide an important outlet for ems feeling imprisoned by expectations and plans.

Most em jobs are not especially high in status relative to other em jobs, and many jobs might be tedious, focused on very small parts of a very big world, and requiring long hours of hard labor. However, ems are unlikely to resent doing such jobs. After all, Olympic athletes today do not resent the tedium, focus, and long hours of training required to achieve their goals. Ems could take pride in knowing that they are from a very elite set of a few hundred clans selected from billions of ordinary humans.

Even so, on a moment-to-moment basis ems usually take their elite status for granted, and do not feel particularly entitled because of it. Few of them feel too high status to do their hard jobs, just as today we do not usually feel particularly entitled just because we are Homo sapiens.

Recently some rich industrial cultures have placed a historically unusual high value on "authenticity," which is usually defined negatively as an absence of artificiality, mediation, conformity, or attention to appearance. Authentic people are presumed honest, unconflicted, creative, and original nature-lovers who face hard truths and have little interest in status, religion, or material goods (Zerzan 2005; Potter 2010). While this ideal contains some "natural" forager ways, foragers were actually often conflicted and self-deceived, cared a lot about appearances and material goods, and were not very creative or original. These non-forager features of authenticity do function, however, to signal the social power that is usually needed to achieve such features.

While we might expect an increasing emphasis on authenticity in an increasingly wealthy industrial era, we have little reason to expect subsistence income ems to continue with a historically unusual emphasis on it.

COPY IDENTITY

Ems must decide how much they identify with various fellow clan members.

It is not clear how discrete are the identities that ems make via copying. On the one hand, if em identities are very discrete, then an em looking backward into their copy history sees all of their ancestors and siblings as "me" up until they reached a key copy event. Ems before that copy event, however, and other descendants of those ems, are "not me," even if they are beloved and trusted relatives. If em identity is also transitive, then all descendants of that key "me" ancestor are also "me." On the other hand, if em identities are more continuous, then ems do not usually see other ems as either "me" or "not me," but instead see them in terms of being more or less similar along various dimensions. This is comparable with how we identify to varying degrees with ourselves decades into the past or future.

Ems seem especially likely to identify with spur copies they create to do short-term tasks, copies who report back when they finish the job, and then end or retire. When ems look back on their lives they are especially likely to see the activities of such copies as "things I did, but that I don't remember well."

Most ems are from the few hundred most copied clans, and such ems can usually feel confident and secure in the identity they gain from that clan. Such clans are well known and established as competent workers in particular professions and industries. Such ems may feel less secure about, and more aware of, their place in particular work teams and projects, and of the degree of support they will obtain from local political coalitions, as these change more often. Ems from small clans feel less secure in their clan identity, knowing that many see their clan as inferior.

The strong security that ems from big clans feel in identifying with their clan is likely to induce such ems to pay less conscious attention to clan-based aspects of their identity. They are likely to instead focus more on the identity gained via their particular job, team, and immediate associates. Spurs probably think similarly, except that they know that their future selves won't directly remember their thoughts and experiences.

As discussed in Chapter 4, Anthropomorphize section, we tend to identify more with past versions of ourselves than with future versions, because past versions seem more unique and determined. So ems should identify more with ems close to the branch of ems that stretches from themselves to the clan original.

Today we more admire a civilization stretched across time than stretched across space, plausibly because we tend to see ourselves and societies cooperating more across time, and competing more across space (Hanson 2011). Em clans will seek to emphasize analogies to our habits of cooperating with our individual selves across time, and avoid analogies to different people competing in space.

New em copies and their teams are typically created in response to new job opportunities. Such teams typically end or retire when these jobs are completed. Thus ems are likely to identify strongly with their particular jobs; their jobs are literally their reason for existing. Compared with us, ems more often choose their friends and lovers on the basis of work suitability, and they more sincerely love and respect their associates for being worthy co-workers.

While ems may strongly, if perhaps insecurely, identify with their team and job combination, they may also sometimes feel overly imprisoned by this identity, and seek freedom in a more temporary spontaneous identity. Such a temporary identity might be formed via last-minute unplanned choices of friends, lovers, hobbies, and activities.

Today, we tend to create stronger memories about life events that we experience between the ages of ten and thirty, memories that we see as central to forming our identity (Glück and Bluck 2007). Near the middle of this range we tend to solidify tastes in food, music, and ideology that we will keep for the rest of our life. We also more strongly remember events near the time of our most important changes of home (Enz et al. 2016). Thus em copies will have more distinct identities when they are created during these ages, and when their home appears to change as a result.

If becoming a new em copy made a big change to life patterns and identity, that new em probably also forms strong memories of events associated with being copied. Teams might help to emphasize new copy identities by creating a new distinct team culture soon after a team is copied. New teams might go out of their way to, as a unit, change their tastes in clothing, music, furniture, conversation topics, and the appearance of their new homes. A time delay to more cheaply move copies to a new team location can also help with this.

Overall, most ems have more clearly distinct and different stages of life than we do today. In fact, the life an em remembers from before its most recent copy event might seem like the way past lives would seem to us today if reincarnation were real, except that the past lives of ems may be remembered vividly and accurately. However, the fact that other, rather different ems exist who also remember events from the past life of an em may make those events less "my" life, and more the lives of "others," or perhaps "our" life.

In a clan of 1 billion ems produced by binary copy events, each final copy remembers thirty binary copy events. If human-like minds find it difficult to remember this many strong identity-defining periods, then large-clan ems will either not treat most copy events as so important to their identity, or they will reduce the number of copy events that they need to remember, by making more copies at each copy event. For example, a clan of a billion ems might each recall only three key copy events, if 1000 copies are made at each such copy event.

How important em copy events are for em identity probably differs between mass- and niche-labor markets. Ems who work in mass-labor markets can remember just a few copy events, each of which strongly define an identity. In contrast, ems who work in niche-labor markets may remember a great many copy events, most of which did not strongly define their identity. Thus niche ems are somewhat like people today who move to a new apartment every year, whereas mass ems are like people who only move three times in their lifetime. The latter identify more strongly with their current homes.

Nostalgia, that is, a sentimental longing for one's past, fosters a sense of being socially connected with others, and a sense of connection with one's past selves. This sense of being the same person over time increases well-being and perceptions of youthfulness (Sedikides et al. 2016). Em clans likely promote nostalgia, both to gain well-being and to increase em identification with their clan.

We interpret behavior as more resulting from someone's "true" self when we approve of its values. Thus clan members will identify more with each other the more they retain shared values (Jones 2017).

One might think that being created from a digital file would convince ems their minds are completely described by science. But people today are uncomfortable with, and doubt that, science explains their conscious choices, feelings, and whatever makes humans exceptional. Ems may continue such skepticism.

Many forager groups promote group bonding via doing things like exchanging arrows before they go hunting, to make it harder to tell who was responsible for any one hunting kill. Em clans might similarly promote unity by avoiding clearly identifying which clan members did particular things about which the clan is proud.

In sum, ems have a new kind of identity as clan members, with complex implications for other kinds of identity.

CHAPTER 25

Collaboration

RITUAL

How do rituals differ in an em world?

Today, we use rituals such as graduations, marriages, retirement parties, and funerals to jointly and overtly affirm community values at key social transitions. Such rituals can improve performance by reducing anxiety (Brooks et al. 2016). However, if we use a broader sense of the term "ritual," most social interactions and many apparently non-social processes are also rituals, wherein emotional energy becomes amplified as participants achieve a common focus of attention and act in ways that are finely synchronized and coordinated with each other (Collins 2004).

During rituals, synchronized feelings and body movements of people who are adjacent to one another often become especially potent. Such group synchronization shows participants that they feel similarly to others in the group, and know each other well. People, things, and beliefs that are the mutual focus of attention in such rituals acquire added importance and emotional energy, and become able to increase the passion of subsequent rituals.

The emotional energy that comes from a common focus of attention on synchronized actions has long influenced the frequency and structure of many forms of synchronized human activities, in dances, plays, movies, concerts, lectures, protests, freeways, business meetings, group recitations in schools, consumption of advertised products, and group songs that coordinate work in hunting, farming, sailing, armies, and factories.

We expect ems to continue to show this tendency to prefer social situations where vivid awareness of finely synchronized actions can assure them of shared capacities and values. For example, similar to people today we expect ems to say hello and goodbye as they join and leave meetings, and to find reasons to hold frequent face-to-face meetings at work.

Some examples of common overt rituals today are when the police stop a driver, when a waiter takes an order, when two sports teams battle in front of a crowd, and when an audience watches a movie together. In the industrial era, we have a substantially lower rate of such rituals than did our forager and farmer ancestors. For our ancestors, in contrast, it was more like having Christmas or Thanksgiving happen several times a month, with many smaller ceremonies happening several times a day (Collins 2004).

There are many reasons for the loss of overt rituals in our time. Increasing wealth has given us more spatial privacy. Innovation has become increasingly important, density and wealth are high enough to support fashion cycles, and both these factors raise the status of people with eccentric behavior. These trends have encouraged us to signal our increasing wealth with more product and behavioral variety, instead of via connections and the use of more standard products and behaviors. With increasing wealth, industrial-era values have moved away from conformity and tradition and toward self-direction and tolerance. Increased forager-like egalitarianism has made us less comfortable with the explicit class distinctions that supported many farmer-era rituals. Our suppression of family clans in the West has also repressed many family rituals.

As we will discuss in more detail in Chapter 26, Farmer-Like section, while our increasingly rich industrial era has seen a big increase in individualism and egalitarianism, poorer ems are likely to feel less individualistic and egalitarian. As we have discussed, innovation is less important in an em economy than in ours. As a result, it's likely that our recent trend away from overt rituals will be partially reversed. Ems are likely to move back toward farmer-like explicit and distinct social classes, and more frequent overt rituals wherein ems with different roles take on different ritualized behaviors. Compared with us, ems are likely to be more stratified into explicit classes, such as speed classes, and to play out more frequent explicit and stylized synchronized behaviors.

The value of meetings as rituals with a common focus of attention is cut if attendees focus elsewhere while appearing to focus on the meeting. So ems may use mindreading to monitor who is paying attention to their meetings.

As ems in virtual realities no longer need to eat or clean themselves, or commute to work, they are likely to feel less inclined to copy familiar human rituals centered on such things. Fast ems also have fewer rituals centered on hearing and sharing the day's news, because to them the world changes more slowly.

Ems may seek new kinds of seemingly "natural" ceremonies to substitute for those lost, to continue to bind together teams, firms, and city-states. Ems also seek new rituals to bind together the new social unit of clans. However, it is probably hard to create strong rituals out of em work activities, as productive work behaviors rarely create opportunities for synchronized body motions matched with a common focus of attention.

Singing music together can create powerful rituals that promote cooperation (Good and Russo 2016). However, most people today are shy about singing in public, as their voices sound to them much worse than the professional singers that they usually hear. Ems could make their voices sound more professional, and yet still communicate very personal emotions, via more advanced versions of voice-processing systems such as Auto-Tune, which today often improve the voices of professional singers.

Most ems don't listen to music much at work. For most cognitively demanding tasks, anything but quiet hurts performance (Khazan 2016). However, music does seem to help in some kinds of jobs (Fox and Embrey 1972). Music at work is typically mild, wordless, and not otherwise distracting (Kiger 1989).

In sum, ems may have more and stronger rituals than we do today, reverting in part to previous historical patterns.

RELIGION

While foragers and early farmers had much spirituality, modern religions with a few powerful moralizing Gods taking a strong interest in human affairs arose among prosperous elites simultaneously worldwide during the "Axial Age" around 2500 years ago. This was apparently enabled by wider use of writing. Such religions seem to have since helped to promote self-control, stronger norm enforcement, and social bonds beyond family clans (Bellah 2011; Baumard and Boyer 2013; Baumard et al. 2015).

Religions and their rituals often help to bond people to groups. By following rules restricting behavior and beliefs, rules that can seem arbitrary to outsiders, members can credibly signal their attachment to one group, relative to other groups with conflicting rules. Groups with stronger rules tend to be more strongly attached to one another (Iannaccone 1994).

Today societies that are more religious tend to have worse outcomes in some ways (Myers 2017). For example, religious regions are less innovative, and more religious individuals hold views less favorable to innovation (Bénabou et al. 2015).

However, at the individual level religious people tend to be happier, healthier, and more productive (Steen 1996). They live longer, smoke less, exercise more, earn more, get and stay married more, commit less crime, use less illegal drugs, have more social connections, donate and volunteer more, and have more children. Intensity of religion and strength of religious belief tends to increase with age, especially after retirement (Bengtson et al. 2015). Although atheists do not act less moral, cultures worldwide consistently believe that they do (Gervais 2017).

Thus individual and social correlations disagree; religion seems good for individuals, but bad for regions. The individual effect seems more plausibly causal, with religion causing personal benefits, while the social effect may or may not be causal (Herzer and Strulik 2017). If the social effect is strong and causal, then em competition discourages religion. But if not, and individual gains are what matter, then em competition promotes religion.

As we discuss more in Chapter 26, Farmer-Like section, as ems are likely to be more farmer-like, they are likely to believe more in good and evil, and in powerful gods who enforce social norms. And just as religion was useful in helping farmers to gain self-control to resist temptations to violate farming era norms that would not seem natural to foragers, the em world has a similar need of help in promoting self-control to assist with new em era norms. This weakly suggests that ems are more religious.

It may be hard for ems to use religion to attach to both to clans and to teams. After all, rules unique to a clan could alienate member ems from their teams, while rules unique to a team could alienate member ems from their clans. Perhaps distinct spheres can be defined for the topics of team rules versus clan rules, or perhaps only clans, or only teams, will rely on religion for group bonding.

Science fiction often depicts social conflict, sometimes violent, resulting from religious objections to new technologies and social institutions. However, most of the major religions of today are thousands of years old, and have peacefully accommodated almost all of the vast changes that have appeared since those religions began. These religions are thus clearly capable of adapting to a great many social changes, and so we should expect most of them to adapt comfortably to the em world as well.

Religions typically rely on stories about fantastic events involving miracles and now dead saints, who lived when records were rare and unreliable. Poor records make it hard to verify or disprove such stories. Records are far more detailed and reliable in our era, and will become even more so in the em era. This will discourage em religions from relying on fantastic stories about such recent events. This seems to also suggest that ems continue to use today's existing religions.

However, clarifications may be required on the subjects of how to define death and responsibility for sins of copies. For example, Christians and similar religions must decide if copies share sins, or if an em sins when it splits off a spur who then sins, especially if that sin was foreseeable. Such clarifications likely emphasize that mind theft is a great evil, akin to rape or murder today, justifying many and strong precautions. Further doctrinal clarifications may be required because ems on average are much smarter than ordinary humans, and may not tolerate blatantly illogical or contradictory religious doctrines.

Rituals and religion have long been used to help people accept their social roles, and to mark key transitions between such roles. So religious-style rituals, perhaps with music and dance, may be especially useful in helping ems to copy, end, and retire.

When we experience things that are very impressive, large, or hard to fit into our usual categories, we can experience "awe," which includes amazement and a bit of fear. In this state, you focus less on yourself, see yourself as smaller, have an expanded sense of time, and become more considerate, generous, cooperative, and integrated into social groups (Shiota et al. 2007; Piff et al. 2015; Bai et al. 2017). When such cooperation and integration promotes em productivity, ems will experience more awe, and be more prone to feel awe in any given situation. This may be promoted by monumental architecture, impressive artistic performances, and more abstract grand visions of the universe and of the place of ems in that universe.

Today people who drink alcohol socially tend to have more friends on whom they can depend and feel engaged with, and they are more trusting of their local community. Alcohol may have functioned in history to promote social bonding (Dunbar et al. 2017). If so, ems may create related social experiences.

LANGUAGE

Language was the big mid-era innovation of the forager era, and writing was the big mid-era innovation of the farming era. But only in the industry era have we managed to make most everyone able to read, and fill most visible surfaces with words, and many background spaces as well.

During both the farming and industrial eras, languages evolved at speeds near the farming era doubling time of roughly a millennium. The median half-life of a word has been a bit over 2000 years, while languages tend to split into new languages roughly every 500 to 1000 years (Pagel 2009). The farming era selected weakly for languages that distinguish genders, politeness, and status, and that lack a future tense (Galor et al. 2017).

During the industrial era words have risen and fallen in popularity with a period of roughly fourteen years (Montemurro and Zanette 2016). Over the last two centuries mentions in books of "I must," "duties," and "charity" are down, whereas mentions of "I want," "rights," and "markets" are up (Barker 2015a). Words in books have become less positive, and words in novels have been more concrete and more emotional (Flynn and Katz 2016; Iliev et al. 2016).

People who are smarter and older tend to use more words and more complex language features. In addition, languages that are spoken by more people over longer eras tend to make more distinctions such as between colors, and have larger vocabularies, more phonemes, and shorter words. Such languages also have more grammatical tools such as adjectives, tenses, prepositions, pronouns, and subordinating conjunctions (Henrich 2015).

As ems are smarter, older, and live in larger cities that are long-lasting from their point of view, ems should use more words and more complex language features. Using more emotion words, ems can remember and share more different kinds of feelings. Virtual reality tools to help ems to better hear spoken words can increase the number of phonemes they use, and thus shorten em words.

As mentioned previously, ems may get into the habit of sprinkling their conversations with keywords, to more easily find those conversations later, and regularly exchange code words with friends, to test if they are in a simulation. As discussed in Chapter 14, Social Power section, more socially powerful ems use language which is evocative, specific, and often filled with forceful words and visual imagery. They often use emotional language terms, refer to us-them concepts and other contrasting concept pairs, pause for emphasis, and explicitly enumerate how many points they will make.

We have yet to see what will be the great mid-era communication innovation of the em era. But one possibility is an augmentation of language that allows ems to more directly share elements of brain states. A matching calculating innovation might let ems calculate interesting new brain state elements from multiple other such elements.

SWEARING

Traditionally, lower classes did hard physical labor, and as a result tended to wear tough work clothes, and had skin that was callused, tanned, and wrinkled. The upper classes tended to show that they were too rich or skilled for such work by wearing fragile clothes and having soft, smooth, untanned skin. Similarly, upper classes have often nurtured polite language, avoidance of direct insult, and a heightened sensitivity and squeamishness on topics such as sex or excrement. Such habits have helped the upper classes to distinguish themselves from the typically tough and calloused attitudes of lower classes.

In lower-class cultures, people more often demonstrate physical strength and toughness via dangerous dares, fistfights, and excessive drinking. People in these cultures also tend to make more direct and aggressive verbal challenges, and to use more swearing, insults, teasing, and taunting. In such communities, people are often given nicknames that highlight their most embarrassing weaknesses (Baruch and Jenkins 2007; Stapleton 2010; Jay and Janschewitz 2012).

These lower-class habits tend to be functional adaptations to their environment. More profanity is correlated with less lying and individual deception, and with more broad social integrity (Feldman et al. 2017). Just as it can be important to judge physical strength and toughness when allocating workers to hard physical labor, it can also be important to judge emotional toughness for emotionally demanding tasks. Crude behaviors can help workers express and gauge physical and emotional weaknesses and strengths, which allows them to better select and allocate people for tasks, and to push work groups up to but not beyond their limits. As chimps also seem to vent frustrations via cursing matches, as well as displays showing physical toughness, this sort of behavior seems to be very old (Angier 2005; Pinker 2007).

Today, swearing, and its milder cousin slang, is more common in work groups with closer interdependence, especially in workplaces with high levels of physical and emotional stress. Today such work teams include warriors, finance traders, moviemakers, and restaurant servers. Note that not all such teams are lower class; some upper-class work groups also use swearing, when that can help in their situation.

Today, rules against sexual harassment, together with wider monitoring of worker speech, discourage workplace swearing and impose high-class cultural standards on lower classes. Even so, mild swearing has recently become more socially acceptable in some elite cultures.

Compared with our world, the em world has low wages, more competition, and more work groups pushed to the limits of their emotional abilities, even as differences in physical abilities are weaker. Em children are also rare. These suggest that em work groups more often adopt traditional working class habits, except that they emphasize emotional over physical toughness. Thus em work groups probably use lots of strongly emotional swearing, insults, and teasing.

Em swearing may focus less on excrement, as the virtual em world has little of that. Profanity based on betrayal, sex, and religion remains relevant, however. Swearing based on death changes to match new em concepts of death.

In sum, ems probably swear more than we do, but for good reasons.

CONVERSATION

Conversations are a familiar human ritual, and we expect ems to continue to talk with one another. Em conversations may vary depending on whether ems are talking to associates in other teams, clans, firms, or cities.

Teams running together on trusted hardware may commit to usually letting team members read the surface of each other's minds, and to also see each other's copying, communication, and financial actions. Such extreme transparency would encourage team trust and cooperation. Subclans may commit to similar openness between members, at least when they are interacting with each other. Transparent ems may be able to sometimes pull down a shade over their minds, in a way that allows others to know that their view has been temporarily blocked. But in such a situation it is not usually possible to fool an em into believing a faked image.

Software tools may help to interpret these mind views, and also voice tone, facial expressions, etc. Today, we are usually only unconsciously aware of others' moods, status relationships, and interaction features. But software could give ems the option to be more directly aware of these details. This awareness may not be reflected in explicit conversation, however. The reasons we have today for not discussing intimate details may well continue in em social worlds.

At the other extreme, ems without such hardware support for transparency would less trust what they see than we do today. After all, software tools might manipulate the facial, gaze, and voice expressions of other ems, and those other em minds might run at speeds different from their apparent speeds.

This wider range of possible transparency and opacity forces ems to specialize more in social skills and habits adapted to such situations. That is, some ems specialize in being effective cooperators in situations where allies are open, while others specialize in being effective competitors in situations where rivals are opaque. This is somewhat like traditional farmer gender roles, where female roles were more gentle to nurture inside families, whereas male roles were tougher to protect families against outsiders. As ems who represent organizations and deal with outsiders tend to be higher status, and also to specialize more in opacity, ems who specialize in opacity are probably seen as higher status.

In our world, people typically find it uncomfortable to interact with systems using a voice that sounds much like their own (Jacobs 2015). Ems may similarly dislike talking with other copies who share their voice. If so, ems may electronically modify the voices they hear from close copies. Ems on different teams might try to cultivate distinctive accents and styles of talking.

Today, we sometimes look others carefully in the eye, to try to ascertain what they are thinking. But we don't similarly look ourselves in the eye in the mirror, because we already know what we are thinking. Ems may also be less likely to look at close copies of themselves in the eye or face, as they'd usually have a good idea from context what their copies are thinking. This could help encourage a habit of talking to clan members in your head.

The ability of reversible brain hardware to easily allow temporary speed changes may amplify the usual human habit of paying more attention when we are speaking, relative to when we are listening. Ems may temporarily speed up to plan what to say and to talk, and slow down while listening to others. When close associates are allowed to read the surface of an em's mind, they may also see these varying speed choices.

Open and transparent teams may give team members the ability to put other team members into surprise split-tests, to test for biases.

In sum, ems talk a lot, just as we do, although their conversations may vary more than ours do in style.

ON CALL ADVICE

Today, we tend to coordinate well with ourselves inside our head, quietly "talking" to ourselves and recalling our previous words. Here we can be seen as in some sense "praying" to our idealized selves. In this mode, we instinctively trust ourselves. In contrast, we often feel rivalries with, and try to distinguish ourselves from, those who inhabit the other bodies we see around us. Although strong trust is possible in this case, it is not our default.

This suggests that em clans seeking to encourage within-clan loyalty and trust may prefer clan members to interact with each other primarily via "in my head" voices, avoiding vividly seeing each other as inhabiting bodies "outside" themselves. Religions today often use a similar talk-to-God-in-your-head strategy to encourage trust in God.

A talk-to-clan-in-head habit can be further encouraged if clans offer real-time life-coaching services to their members. Clans could maintain panels of advisors who monitor members, always ready to answer questions and give advice. To save costs, they cheaply monitor emotions, and do not pay much attention unless triggered by a request, or by unusual stress or puzzlement. Advice could be based on statistics of what other copies have experienced when taking similar actions in similar situations. Advisors might not directly speak their advice in words, but use mindreading to shift the em's attitudes in particular directions.

Ems in the unusual situation of being isolated with poor communication might rely on a local archive containing thousands of expert ems available to consult.

Clans don't always recommend the locally best option for any one situation; they also want members to sometimes explore other options. When a clan gives advice that is designed to explore, instead of being the best reaction to a particular situation, it might not tell members this fact at the time. After all, doing that could reduce em motivation to follow such advice. However, the fact that a recommended option was chosen for exploration purposes might be revealed later, to help everyone evaluate the quality of this em's actions.

Clans do not constantly offer advice. As generating and attending to advice is costly, advice is only given when it seems especially needed or desired. As with training, the goal in each area is usually to transition from giving explicit advice to having the em able to intuit for itself what that advice would be. Clans also do not offer advice when they prefer the em to get advice from its family, friends, or team; this might help to bond this em to these associates.

Simple statistical advice works better for em copies than it would for humans today. This is because ems in the same clan are much more similar to one another than comparable humans, and act in more similar situations. Such advice also works better for ems from larger clans, and for ems with mass-market jobs filled by many similar workers.

For example, consider the case where two ems are a couple, and there are many other copies of that same couple. Each such em in a couple is better able to read the mood and reactions of their partner, because they could compare their personal situation to the mood and reactions found in thousands of other copies. For example, if your partner was in a bad mood today, you could compare his or her mood to those of thousands of copies to better pinpoint the cause of that mood. Excuses such as "the rain gets me down" won't work if hundreds of other copies aren't depressed during the rain.

Ems may be discouraged by reminders that many similar copies exist, as this may make them feel less unique and special. If this is the case, advice based on outcomes experienced by similar copies may be abstracted from those copies, and not refer to particular cases. The advice might not even be very conscious, but instead be communicated via vague feelings of comfort or discomfort with various options.

Ems that often meet other similar copies in person may also feel discouraged and less motivated, seeing themselves as less unique or important. To avoid this, similar copies may avoid meeting or hearing about each other. As an analogy, while some of us today believe that very close copies of us exist in parallel quantum worlds, this rarely influences our mood, because we never actually see or interact with these parallel world copies. By choosing to only rarely meet similar copies, ems may similarly keep themselves from feeling discouraged by the existence of many similar copies.

Just as the decisions of small teams seem today to be consistently more rational than individual decisions (Sutter 2005; Rockenbach et al. 2007), ems advised by their clans probably make more rational decisions as a result. Thus the frequent use of such advice may reduce the extent to which em behavior is well described by "behavioral" theories that deviate from "rational" theories of human behavior (Barberis 2013). While such behavioral theories capture important elements of human behavior today, in a more competitive world of ems who often obtain clan-based personal coaching, em behavior is likely to become more "rational" in the sense of more effectively pursuing actions to achieve practical aims.

Of course ems may not like how they feel when they act rationally. Also, the clan advice habit may make it harder to keep secrets limited to one em; if you tell something to one clan member, you may have told them all.

As discussed in Chapter 19, Managing Clans section, clans may want to discourage open direct expressions of disagreement between members, to promote a common identity. Encouraging ems to instead express their internal clan disagreements via prediction markets may help with this. For example, instead of arguing directly with each other about whether this is a good time to change how they train young clan members, they might each bet privately on outcomes given different training choices. Here conversation is used less as a tool for changing opinions, and more for bonding and related functions.

Like ordinary humans, in conversation ems try to seem witty, charming, informed, etc. While individual humans today mostly have to construct their own clever conversations, ems could get conversational assistance from their clans. Clan coaching like this, however, may make it harder to signal loyalty to specific associates. Such associates may thus prefer to vary their conversation topics and leisure activities away from common topics and activities, to make it harder for clans to usefully coach members on individual behavior. This forces ems to rely more on, and to reveal more of, their distinct individual characteristics regarding particular associates on particular teams.

The clan advice that an individual clan member is given via internal conversations in its head typically represents broader clan priorities, compared with the immediate considerations vivid in the mind of that individual. In the language of construal level theory (discussed in Chapter 2, Dreamtime section), the clan tends to speak more on far issues, relative to near issues. Because of this, clan advice tends more to appeal to em idealism, while the temptation to resist that advice tends to arise from immediate and vivid selfish passions.

In sum, compared with us today, ems have more useful advisors, always on call in their head.

SYNCHRONIZATION

In the em world, a relationship between a copy of Pam and a copy of Bob typically takes place in the shadow of many relations between other copies of Pam and Bob. More generally, most relations between ems from two different clans take place in the shadow of similar relationships between other copies of ems from those same two clans. In fact, there are often many copies of entire teams. In such cases, individuals must choose how much to synchronize the actions within one relation with these other similar relations.

At one extreme, individuals may try to avoid comparison with other relations by avoiding hearing about the other relations, and by acting in unusual ways so as to make their relation be and feel different and unique. At the other extreme, individuals might try to keep the context and content of their relation close to that of other copies of the same relation, to benefit from shared learning and other scale economies.

In highly synchronized relations, events that happen in one copy of the relation are very predictive of events in other copies. For example, if one couple has a fight, the others can suspect a fight soon. Here the sum total of all the information provided to an em by all copies of that em is large. One could not keep shared secrets unless *all* your copies were careful about not revealing clues to your secret.

For example, if Pam and Bob have a relationship, and if a few copies of Bob did something crazy, then all the copies of Pam might worry that their Bobs may soon also do that crazy thing. If one Pam stayed late at a party, and its Bob did not mind initially, this Bob might change his mind if he learned that most of the other Bobs *did* mind. The group of Bobs thus in effect have a group relationship with the group of Pams. Such an arrangement might perhaps make each Bob and Pam feel less closely tied to one other. The whole experience may feel strange compared with our relationships today.

Synchronized relationships allow more useful transfer of learning between copies, and more economies of scale in supporting them. For example, synchronized teams can buy the same equipment and tools, arrange them in the same way, and share maintenance and repair services. Synchronized relationships, however, may feel strange and interfere with loyalty within each relationship. The relationships most likely to be synchronized are thus those that can gain the most from learning opportunities and economies of scale, while those most likely to be differentiated are those where loyalty and natural feelings matter more.

At work, learning opportunities and economies of scale usually matter more, encouraging synchronized relationships. The existence of thousands or millions of copies of a team give those team copies many ways to learn from statistics about events in other teams. This makes it easier to score the performance of each team and member, via comparisons with other teams and members. This also tends to push em team behavior to more closely approximate an informed game theoretic Nash equilibrium, that is, a matched set of strategic behaviors that are less influenced by hidden information regarding the types of participants and the consequences of their actions.

Statistics about other copies of a team make it harder for team members to deceive themselves about their past performance or their chances for future performance. Such ems may become more like chess players today, where objective performance measures (i.e., their rating) force them to accept their current performance and abilities. This tends to make such players less happy, as they can't pretend to be better than they are. If this happiness effect reduced em productivity sufficiently, ems may often adopt attitudes such as "never tell me the odds," avoiding information about their relative performance or chances of future success.

Members of synchronized em teams may be more cautious about bad behavior, knowing that unusual behavior on their part could affect their copies on many other teams. Also, strong conflict within one team might result in that whole team being erased and reverted to a prior version, or replaced with a copy of another team. Of course if the problem reappeared in the reverted copies, they might instead need to resolve their conflict.

Within a cohort of team copies, most of the teams may end periodically to be replaced by the best few teams that are copied many times in a next round. In this case, teams might compete to seem the most productive or innovative, which should more encourage greater internal team cooperation.

Mating and friendship are contexts where local loyalty and natural feelings seem more important than learning opportunities and economies of scale. As mating matters less to an em society than to us, some ems may use mate choice as we often do friend choice today, as a way to express spontaneity and autonomy. That is, some ems may feel constrained in their choice of job, work associates, and location, and so prefer to choose their mates and friends freshly when they can. As such choices would not seem fresh if different copies of them consistently made the same choices, ems must be actually somewhat random in their choices, if they want to preserve an appearance of spontaneity.

The degree to which clan members may go out of their way to differentiate themselves from other clan members should not be exaggerated. Today, identical twins who were raised together do not seem to be any more or less different from each other than identical twins that were raised apart (Bouchard et al. 1990). This suggests that ems would also not tend to become substantially more similar or different when their exposure to similar copies increases.

In sum, em relationships can be improved by, but are also complicated by, a context of many similar relations between similar copies.

CHAPTER 26

Society

CULTURE

ow might em era cultures differ from prior era cultures?

Over four centuries, people who lived in environments with temperatures that were more stable from one generation to the next have put a higher priority on maintaining their cultural traditions, and have less changed such traditions (Giuliano and Nunn 2017). We should also expect em culture to change less when their relevant environments change less.

Today, we can identify many standard dimensions along which cultures around the world vary (Hofstede et al. 2010; Gorodnichenko and Roland 2011; Minkov 2013). For some of these standard dimensions, we have good reasons to expect one side to be more productive in a modern economy. Because of this, we have good reasons to expect that a competitive em economy will continue to select for such cultural features. For example, we should expect more industriousness relative to indulgence, a work relative to a leisure orientation, time orientations that are long term relative to short term and that are tied to clocks instead of relationships, low instead of high context attitudes toward rules and communication, and a loose relative to tight attitude on interpreting social norms.

For other standard cultural dimensions, productivity considerations don't as clearly suggest which side is favored by an em world. These dimensions include degree of avoidance of risk and uncertainty, tolerance of inequality, individual or group identity, cooperative or competitive emphasis, and high or low emotional expressiveness.

As discussed in Chapter 2, Era Values section, today about 70 percent of the variation in values across nations is captured in just two key factors (Inglehart and Welzel 2010). These two factors also capture much of the variation in individual values (Schwartz et al. 2012). One factor varies primarily between rich and poor nations: increasing wealth correlates with more individualism, universalism, egalitarianism, autonomy, and self-expression. These subfactors seem to be more a result than a cause of wealth. With increasing wealth, our values have moved away from conformity with traditional "conservative" farmer-like values, and toward more "liberal" forager-like values (Hanson 2010b; Hofstede et al. 2010). Poor nations tend more to value respecting parents and authority, believing in good and evil, and wanting to protect local jobs. Rich nations tend more to value trust and imagination, and acceptance of divorce and homosexuality.

The other main dimension along which values vary today can be described as "East" versus "West." East values tend to be more community-oriented, while West values tend to be oriented more to individuals and families. In the East, people are more interested in and spend more time discussing politics, which is more important to them. In the West, families and good health are more important. Rich Eastern nations emphasize achievement, determination and thrift, and accept abortion. Rich Western nations emphasize friends, leisure, ecology, tolerance, satisfaction, free choice, and gender equality. Poor Eastern nations more suspect outsiders, more see children as needing two parents and women as needing children, and they more value technology, money, hard work, and state intervention. Poor Western nations more value work, obedience, religion, faith in God, patriotism, and wanting many children.

Eastern nations have been growing faster over the last half-century, in part because of their emphasis on achievement, thrift, and savings. While the poorest nations tend to drift East in values as they first move from farming to industry, the richest nations tend to drift West in values as they emphasize services and leisure (Minkov 2013). Also, while being close to the equator was good for growth during the farming era, being far from the equator was good for growth during the early industrial era (Dalgaard and Strulik 2014; Fagerberg and Srholec 2013).

It is possible that the first ems will come predominantly from particular nations and cultures. If so, typical em values may tend to be closer to the values of whatever nations provided most of the ordinary humans whose brains were scanned for these first ems.

As ems have near subsistence (although hardly miserable) income levels, and as wealth levels seem to cause cultural changes, we should expect em culture values to be more like those of poor nations today. As Eastern cultures grow faster today, and as they may be more common in denser areas, em values may be more likely to be like those of Eastern nations today. Together, these suggest that em cultures tend to value technology, money, hard work, and state intervention. They may also suggest that em culture values achievement, determination, thrift, authority, good and evil, and local job protection. Of course in a competitive world, values for state intervention and job protection may be suppressed if these substantially reduce competitiveness.

For ems, copying and teams become primary units of reproduction and work. As a result, choices about these may acquire the sorts of moral overtones we have today about sex and children. At least they may if human-like minds have enough cultural plasticity to greatly modify our feelings about such issues. That is, ems might develop stronger hard moral feelings about when and with whom it is acceptable to copy and form teams, and when it is all right to leave a team. Perhaps this could be aided by new rituals that help to transfer many of the concerns we now have about sex and children to em copying. For example, before copying a team, that team might have a big party. Maybe the original team comes to the new team's later "birthday" parties.

Both forager and farmer cultures were substantially influenced by the risks that males faced of raising children who were actually fathered by other males. For example, farmers often greatly restricted the abilities of females to socialize with other males. In contrast, em reproduction is asexual and very reliable; there is little chance of mistakenly thinking one was supporting a copy of oneself who was actually a copy of another. Ems thus do less to avoid mistaken paternity.

Social relations between em clans are somewhat like social relations in forager bands, where everyone knew everyone's history and basic personality. Em social relations may also be somewhat like social relations in our fantasy and children's stories, such as *The Lord of the Rings*, wherein different species (or classes or races) have very different known personalities and skills and are destined for different kinds of jobs, roles, and social status.

DIVISIONS

Can we anticipate the fault lines along which em culture divides?

We can predict that one dimension of division will end up seeming substantially more important than the others. This seems to be a natural result when political coalitions form. People who focus on dimensions other than the main dimension are more at risk of seeming less loyal and relevant regarding the existing coalitions.

We can list some possible divisions that will be the basis for this one main dimension. But it is harder to say which of these divisions actually matter the most to ems, or more often form the basis of political and other social coalitions. Ems may continue to focus on the same political divisions that so animate people today, but probably will not. The existence of a great many kinds of similarities along which political coalitions can be built makes it hard to predict the actual political coalitions that are important at any one time and place. This is one reason why it is hard to predict future political outcomes, as outcomes often depend on which coalitions temporarily dominate.

However, we can at least identify *some* of the main possible fault lines in an em society. An obvious one is between a majority who work in virtual reality offices, and a minority who work in physical bodies. Virtual reality cultures are tempted to drop habits and conventions that are useful only in physical reality. In contrast, the culture of physical ems likely makes more references to privacy, violence, grime, and unintended death without retirement.

Another important split is between the centers and peripheries of cities. City centers are more expensive but support fast talk with many others. In contrast, peripheries are cheaper, but often require delayed talk. While authorities could monitor activities in city centers well, this becomes harder with more distant activities. So while authorities tend to concentrate in city centers, peripheries tend to house illicit and illegal activities such as mind theft, forbidden tweaks, intellectual property violations, and environmental damage.

A related fault line is between a majority of ems who work in mass-labor markets, and a minority who work in niche-labor markets. As discussed in Chapter 19, Mass Versus Niche Teams section, mass-market ems mostly socialize within teams, and the existence of many teams makes their lives predictable. In contrast, niche-market ems are more often copied individually in response to new work demands. Niche ems have more complicated social worlds because of less synchronized copying of friends and lovers.

Em clans may also naturally split between those who remember our era, and those who do not remember the human-dominated past. The latter ems are likely to be better adapted to the em world, but the former will have locked in many first mover advantages to gain enviable social positions. Em clans might also split by size, between a few huge powerful clans and a great many smaller weaker clans. The few very large clans probably feel superior and favor each other, leading to resentment and accusations of bias from the smaller clans.

A related distinction is between the firms, buildings, and cities where most capital is owned by ordinary humans, and other firms, buildings, and cities. Humans start out owning most capital, but their fraction of capital gradually declines until it becomes a minority.

Em cities, firms, and clans will also probably inherit cultural divisions from those that exist today in our world. That is, ems' differences may continue to reflect variations among the nations, ethnicities, religions, and professions of our world. Allegiance to the different sports, teams, artists, artistic genres, and fashions of today may even continue.

Another division is between rich and poor clans; some clans are rich enough to own a lot of capital in many ventures, while other clans own much less capital. When rich clans choose some of their members to be relatively poor, those poor ems may not seem to count as truly poor to ems from less-wealthy clans. This is similar to a rich person today getting little sympathy for choosing to spend a month living simply at a monastery.

Wealth and poverty feels more personal in an em world. That is, each of the few rich clans have a personal story about how they got their wealth, and conspiracy stories are easier to spin about how they became rich or poor. Furthermore, such conspiracy stories are more often true, in the sense that em success will often come in part from coalitions of em clans who conspire to support each other.

Em clans could also split by gender; female and male clans may have different typical speeds, professions, investments, and styles of internal governance. Regardless of gender, em clans may divide according to their styles of internal governance. Some clans may disapprove of the governance style of other clans, calling them immoral, unfair, exploitive, delusional, etc. Em culture may also split between places where individual loyalties are primarily toward clans, and places where individual loyalties are primarily toward workplace teams and firms.

Two more possible divisions are based on age and birth cohort. Today, our children tend to be segregated by age, and to develop cohort-specific cultures, by experiencing the same world events and fashions at the same ages (Howe and Strauss 1992). Ems who are the same age or copied at the same time, however, may have run at different speeds at different points in their lives, and so not experience the same world events and fashions at the same subjective ages.

Thus ems will less divide by age or birth cohort, and more by particular trajectories of speeds over time. Ems can divide clearly by life stage, however. For example, subsidized young ems in training are quite different from older ems at peak productivity and fully paying for their existence, who are quite different from retirees. Most em experience is in working ems at peak productivity ages.

Ems are also plausibly divided by their differing speeds. Different speeds likely have distinct cultures. It is hard for fast changing elements of em culture, such as clothing or music fashions, to synchronize their changes across different mind speeds. Such coordinated cultural changes might seem intolerably slow to fast ems, or intolerably fast to slow ems. Fast changes in a slow culture may be driven by the lower frequency changes in the fast culture. Differing speed ems may also segregate into different classes, with faster ems seen as higher status.

Like people throughout history, ems may also divide geographically. The time delay to send signals to distant cities probably doesn't contribute much to this, but trade barriers and distrust of distant city-states might allow for substantial cultural divergence. Ems may also divide by religion or ideology, as we do today. And ems will naturally divide by industries and professions, as these are important distinctions in the em world.

Em cities may be distinguished by whether they are primarily water- or air-cooled, as that choice is likely to influence many other physical choices in em city design. Cities of the same type are also likely to be geographically clustered together.

A larger total em population should also lead us to expect more cultural fragmentation. After all, if local groups differentiate their cultures to help members signal local loyalties, then the more people that are included within a region, the more total cultural variation we might expect to lie within that region. So a city containing billions or more ems could contain a great many diverse local cultural elements.

An em world can split apart in many different ways, just as does our world.

FARMER-LIKE

Poorer ems seem likely to return to conservative (farmer) cultural values, relative to liberal (forager) cultural values. After all, farmer values and attitudes helped to push farmers into the alien-to-forager behaviors that the farming world required, and such values could also help pressure ems to adopt the also alien-to-foragers behaviors that the em world requires. In the industrial era, we have felt such pressures less as our wealth has increased our safety buffers, leading to a pro-liberal trend over recent centuries (Hanson 2010a). But ems are poorer and feel more strongly the competitive and conformity pressures and fears that farming culture learned to exploit.

Today, liberals tend to be more open-minded, creative, curious, and novelty seeking, while conservatives tend to be more orderly, conventional, and organized. If, relative to us, ems prefer farmer-like values to forager-like values, then ems more value things such as self-sacrifice, self-control, religion, patriotism, marriage, politeness, material possessions, and hard work, and less value self-expression, self-direction, tolerance, pleasure, nature, novelty, travel, art, music, stories, and political participation.

These are weak arguments, which can support only weak predictions about the em world; each of them can plausibly be overridden by other stronger considerations. Even so, let me note more such predictions.

If ems are more farmer-like, they tend to envy less, and to more accept authority and hierarchy, including hereditary elites and ranking by gender, age, and class. They are more comfortable with war, discipline, bragging, and material inequalities, and push less for sharing and redistribution. They are less bothered by violence and domination toward their historical targets, including foreigners, children, slaves, animals, and nature. As em children are rare and often pampered, violence toward children seems unlikely unless it is useful for training.

Today, people who do the following jobs tend to lean liberal: professor, journalist, writer, artist, musician, psychiatrist, teacher, trainer, fundraiser, cook, bartender, lawyer, software engineer, and civil servant. In contrast, people who do these jobs tend to lean conservative: soldier, pilot, police, surgeon, priest, homemaker, farmer, exterminator, plumber, banker, insurance broker, sales, grader, sorter, electrical contractor, car dealer, trucker, miner, construction worker, entrepreneur, salesman, gas attendant, and non-academic scientist (Hanson 2014; Edmond 2015).

A more conservative world has values and styles more in common with conservative jobs today. Liberal jobs today tend more to be about talking, persuading, and entertaining, while conservative jobs today tend to focus on a fear of bad things, and protecting against them. Thus farmer-like ems talk and entertain less, and they more expect and prepare for big disasters, such as the big farm-era disasters of war, famine, and disease. Leaders lead less by the appearance of consensus, and do less to give the appearance that everyone has an equal voice and is free to speak their minds. Fewer topics are open for discussion or negotiation.

Today in the U.S., Democrats are more reluctant than Republicans to label something that is different as better or worse, and are less willing to presume that people with good outcomes deserve them. That is, Democrats more embrace the essential forager egalitarian norm (Clifton 2016). Liberals are more neurotic, and as a result less happy, while conservatives are less empathetic (Burton et al. 2015). These suggest that ems are less neurotic, less empathetic, and more willing to label different things as better or worse.

Farmer-like ems have a stronger sense of honor and shame, enforce more conformity and social rules, and care more for cleanliness and order (Stern et al. 2014). Em virtual realities make it much easier to live in clean and orderly spaces, and in addition, ems may place a higher priority on having clean and uncluttered designs for their systems and organizations. Also, clan and computer-based decision assistants should make it easier to obey complex social rules, and to detect when others are violating such rules. Even so, as discussed in Chapter 25, Swearing section, em working-class culture often has strong emotional profanity, insults, and teasing.

For farmer-like ems, work matters more culturally than it does for us today; ems spend more of their time at work, invest more of their identity in work, submit more to workplace ranking and domination. Ems find great nobility and satisfaction in their work, and may find it hard to understand why we denigrate work so often today.

Today, some kinds of music, clothes, and interior decoration are designed specifically for work, or specifically for leisure. Most are designed so that they can function reasonably well in both environments. For more work-focused ems, the design of such objects puts more emphasis on work relative to leisure. For example, em music is designed more to facilitate a relaxed office, and less to accompany dancing and parties.

While farmer-like ems seem inclined to support traditional values such as marriage and heterosexuality, for ems sex and family lose the central roles they had in previous eras as primary units for organizing reproduction, work, and other social relations. For ems, sex mainly matters for leisure and bonding. However, given how deeply sexual feelings are embedded in human psychology, sexual pair bonds probably remain common and important.

While we have some reasons to expect ems to be more farmer-like, it is far from obvious that this will actually happen. Even so, we have collected many useful if weak predictions that follow from this premise.

TRAVEL

People who travel more demonstrate that they have openness to experience, wealth, and time. However, they also demonstrate a weaker attachment to their home culture. Additionally, people who travel more to foreign cultures tend to cheat and lie more (Lu et al. 2017).

Farmer-like ems place less value on talking with, visiting, and moving to different cultures and communities. Even so, such travel and talk may be common among ems if it is cheap. At typical kilo-em speeds, ems could travel instantly across cities, and could talk across the Earth with signal delays of only a few subjective minutes.

Today, exotic places to visit are becoming harder to find, because scale and network economies are encouraging most societies to adopt similar products, services, and habits. The main differences that remain are those adapted to differing circumstances, such as divergent climate or wealth levels. Because their relevant environments are more similar, em economies around the world will probably be even more similar than ours are today.

The differing circumstance most likely to create exotic places to visit is different speeds. It will be cheap in time, money, and security to speed up temporarily to visit the typically higher status faster cultures that are nearby. While it is also cheap to see detailed recordings of life in the typically poorer slower cultures nearby, actually experiencing slower cultures directly for moderate subjective periods is expensive in terms of the opportunity cost of time back in one's home culture. Cultures at a great spatial distance, such as in outer space, are also expensive to visit for the same reason.

Today, locations that house high status people often go out of their way to make it hard for low status people to mix in with residents there. So em areas holding mostly fast high status ems may create artificial barriers to discourage visits from slower ems, and create clear marks to distinguish such visitors during their visits.

Instead of traveling to visit different cultures, ems might be more interested in visiting, or temporarily trading places with, close copies of themselves in other teams. They may especially want to visit more distant copies who fill rare glamorous roles, such as in science, innovation, the arts, or activism. Glamorous copies may even hire directors to edit personal "movies" about their lives that other copies could experience, perhaps including shallow mindreading records. The most interesting subject to most people is, after all, themselves.

In general, ems seek leisure activities that achieve such key purposes as providing a change of pace, a sense of personal control, a relaxation of the usual pressures, and a strengthening of key social ties, while still being as productive as possible. Refresher training courses may be another kind of productively useful leisure.

In general, there are two reasons to want to do something different: being tired of what one has been doing lately, and having something else in particular one has been itching to do. Ems can satisfy both of these desires while still supporting current work clients and colleagues. Ems that are not maximally fast who want a change of pace can try something different at a much faster speed, returning to work soon enough to leave only a small break in their service visible to existing clients. Ems seeking to do a particular new thing might split off a new copy to do that activity, a new copy who then reports back to the original in detail, perhaps also with a movie covering the key events.

In sum, ems can travel more easily than we can, but we cannot now tell how much they will actually want to travel.

STORIES

Our ancestors long ago developed the ability to "reason," that is, to draw conclusions by considering both supporting and opposing arguments. However, this ability was not designed especially well to draw valid or statistically accurate inferences in a wide range of typical situations. Instead, it was apparently designed more for persuading and impressing during conflicts with rivals, especially in situations where some people were suspected of violating social norms. This explains many otherwise puzzling features of our reasoning abilities (Mercier and Sperber 2011).

Similarly, our ancestors long ago developed the ability to tell stories, that is, to summarize a set of related events. However, like our reasoning ability, this storytelling ability was not designed especially well to accurately represent causal relations and likely outcomes regarding events in a wide range of typical situations. Instead, our anecdotal abilities seem designed more for persuading and impressing during conflicts with rivals, especially when some are suspected of violating norms.

Because of this, we prefer stories with unrealistic levels of conflict, moral violations, justice regarding such violations, correlations between good character features, and events explained by character motivations. These preferences seem deeply embedded in human nature, and thus seem likely to continue in em stories.

Compared with us today, ems are likely to have more compelling stories to tell about their personal life history, and this is likely to help ems feel that their lives have more meaning. After all, early em clans will have a detailed personal story about the original human that started their clan. Then each highly copied peak-productivity em will have a dramatic training history wherein they succeeded against long odds. Also, as training plans are chosen to produce high variance in training success, these training periods may contain unusual and exotic experiences.

Today, our stories tend to take place in environments that are more like those of our ancestors, relative to our current environments. So stories tend to focus on smaller organizations and on the use of physical abilities, and they happen in times and places with more travel, nature, and leisure. This trend likely continues in an em era. So em stories are often set in our industrial world, as well as in the worlds of farmers and foragers, although such stories are often allegories for issues in the em world.

For farmer-like ems, em stories tend more to be about work, relative to leisure. (Today, the vast majority of our stories are about leisure.) Being more focused on work as opposed to leisure, ems spend less time consuming stories. But ems still enjoy stories, to relax, distract, gain perspective, and affirm social norms. Em stories are better than ours, at least in the sense of giving value to their consumers, because their larger economy allows more resources to be invested in inventing and honing stories. And as we shall soon see, em stories are actually more important economically, because they are a bigger part of the marketing of labor suppliers.

The stories that most inspire people today may not seem very related to the main features of the em world, and the main situations found in an em world may not seem to us to be very promising settings for stories. However, different eras emphasize different kinds of stories. Farmer and forager eras each had stories designed to inspire their residents, stories that affirmed their key values, stories that they liked more than we do. The em world similarly has stories, music, and other art that affirms its values, attitudes, and conflicts, which ems like more than we would, if we could hear their stories.

We often find meanings in our lives via the stories we tell about ourselves. But stories are created, not discovered. We craft meaningful personal stories by choosing a few focal events out of the mass of arbitrary details that make up our lives. Thus good storytellers can construct compelling stories out of a wide range of situations and events. If the lives of ems don't seem to you as fertile soil for growing compelling stories as your world does, that may be simply because you live in the industrial era, hear its stories, and haven't noticed how carefully selected are such stories out of the mass of detail around you. If you lived in the em era and heard its stories, you might well find them to be quite engaging.

Em stories predictably differ from ours in many ways. For example, engaging em stories still tell morality tales, but the moral lessons slant toward those favored by the em world. As the death of any one copy is less of a threat to ems, the fear of imminent personal death of one copy less often motivates characters in em stories. Instead such characters more fear mind theft and other economic threats that can force the retirement of entire subclans. Death may perhaps be a more sensible fear for the poorest retirees whose last copy could be erased. While slow retirees might also fear an unstable em civilization, they can usually do little about it.

Action stories today often find awkward excuses to turn off power or communications, in order to isolate characters and force them to be ignorant of important context. Such tricks are becoming increasingly implausible, and thus unacceptable. In a world allowing constant universal communications, plausible drama can only rarely depend on characters being unable to talk to one another. Similarly, in a world where most everything is tracked and authenticated, drama can only rarely depend on losing track of things, on hiding from people, or on mistaken identities. These apply to em stories, even more than to ours.

Today, "fast-moving" action movies and games often feature a few key actors taking many actions with major consequences, but with very little time for thoughtful consideration of those actions. However, for ems this scenario mainly only makes sense for rare isolated characters with limited brain hardware, or for ems whose minds are maximally fast. Other characters can speed up their minds temporarily to think carefully about important actions.

The typical conflicts in em stories will likely resemble typical conflicts in em lives. So stories will include cities competing for world prominence, firms competing for market share, teams contesting labor-market niches, pair bond alternatives vying for affection, and clans competing in city politics, in professions, and to place members on teams. There are also conflicts within individuals between their loyalties to clans, firms, professions, teams, friends, and mates. Stories about conflicts between very close copies are probably rare, however, as are stories today about conflicts between the same person on different days.

In general, stories vary in whether they emphasize the setting, the events that happen in that setting, character features and life roles, or information that readers unearth about all of these things. During the industrial era character-focused stories have risen greatly in status to become the most respected (Card 2011). But as farmer-like ems may be less self-indulgent and less able to change their life roles, they may like character-focused stories less. Thus em stories may emphasize story settings, events, and the information that characters discover.

CLAN STORIES

Today, most stories are about standard known ethnicities, standard animal species, and standard human demographic and personality types, not imaginary ones. But most of our stories are about imaginary individual people, because each of us only knows a tiny fraction of all the people who currently exist. As foragers all knew the same people, their stories could have been about known individuals, except for the fact that the best forager stories changed too slowly to adapt to each new generation.

As em clans are long lasting, and em stories can change rapidly, em stories likely refer often to standard known em clans. A story with a George in it is about the standard em George character that all ems know. Em clans come to be known for their distinct personalities and skill sets, much as different species do in classic children's stories, or different races do in classic fantasy stories. Em grade school classrooms may even be decorated not just with the periodic table and a map of their geographic region, but also with diagrams showing the main em clans and their relations, and professions.

Today, the stories that we tell about the origin of important institutions and features in our society must give a lot of weight to abstract social forces, even though we stress the roles of particular individuals such as inventors, politicians, and generals. For ems, such stories can be more naturally told as driven by the particular inclinations and alliances of particular clans. Such stories tend to make some clans look heroic and other clans villainous.

Thus em stories make heroes and villains out of real em clans, and influence expectations about which clans are most appropriate for which roles in em societies. So em stories tend to be more political; there are fewer stories that *all* ems can embrace as good stories.

The fact that stories can create favorable impressions of clans induces clans to hire storytellers to create compelling tales favoring their clan. The em economy tends more to favor clans with vivid and distinct personalities that can produce memorably engaging stories. This is similar to how our economy induces firms to hire storytellers to create favorable advertising stories, and how firms with more engaging stories become more profitable.

This isn't to say that most em stories are constructed for propaganda purposes. Ems still enjoy the kinds of stories that we most enjoy, and still like stories to differ from reality in most of the ways that we now like. As discussed earlier in Chapter 3, Biases section, fictional events tend to be driven less by accidents and more by individuals in overt value-driven conflict. Fictional characters have more pronounced features, have attitudes more predictable from their history, better understand the reasons for their actions, actions that are more driven by basic values, are more willing to risk conflict to achieve their values, and have actions more predictable from a story's context.

Em villains sometimes represent the interests of cities, firms, or clans that are intended to be seen as rivals to the story audience. But compelling story villains must also violate key social norms. Thus em villains tend to violate em social norms, which differ in many ways from norms today.

In sum, ems still have stories, which are even more political than are our stories.

CHAPTER 27

Minds

HUMANS

It tends to be easier to make social predictions about the middle of a distribution of characteristics, than about the tails of such a distribution. For example, it is easier to predict the typical time spent sleeping or eating, and the typical style of such activities, than the maximum or minimum time spent in such activities, or the styles of sleeping or eating done by those who spend unusual amounts of time in such activities. This is in part because when scenarios can differ according to a great many variables, this high-dimensionality creates a lot more detail to specify about the tails (i.e., extremes) compared with the middle of a distribution. This is also in part because hard-to-anticipate factors often have disproportionate effects on distribution tails.

As ordinary humans are on the periphery of the em society, such issues make it harder to make predictions about humans in an em society. Even so, we should try.

The biological humans who remain in the em era are those who have chosen not to convert to become ems. While early scans are probably destructive, making conversions irreversible, many and perhaps most humans choose to become ems. Even if few make this choice at first, the new rich em world will quickly become high status, and humans will hear many stories of how happy converts whose ems rose in status are now closer to the center of world action.

Most people will not be good enough to compete for em jobs, but once scanning becomes cheap then any given retirement savings go much further in the em world. Not only is living as an em much cheaper, but ems never need experience grime, pain, hunger, or disease, their bodies can always be beautiful, and immortality is feasible for them. Those who choose to remain as biological humans tend to be those who are more shy about change, and more doubtful of whether an em of them is conscious or the "same" creature.

Typical ems are so fast that biological humans will only experience days in the time in which ems experience years. This suggests that during the entire em era, humans will achieve only modest psychological and behavioral adaptations to the existence of ems. The human world will mostly look like it did before ems, except for a limited number of changes that must be made, or that can be made quickly.

Ems being faster than humans also suggests that most substantial changes to human behaviors during the em era are driven by outside changes, rather than from within human society. Relevant outside changes include wars, changing prices such as wages, interest rates, and land rents, and an explosion of new products and services from the em economy.

Because ordinary humans originally owned everything from which the em economy arose, as a group they could retain substantial wealth in the new era. Humans could own real estate, stocks, bonds, patents, etc. Thus, a reasonable hope is that ordinary humans become retirees of this new world. We don't today try to kill the retirees in our world, or take their stuff, in part because such actions would threaten the stability of the legal, financial, and political world we share with them, and in part because we have many direct social ties to retirees. Yes, we humans all expect to retire today, while ems don't expect to become human, but em retirees are vulnerable in similar ways to humans. So ems may be reluctant to expropriate or exterminate ordinary humans if ems rely on the same or closely interconnected legal, financial, and political systems as humans, or if ems retain many direct social ties to ordinary humans.

Few ordinary humans can earn wages in competition with em workers, at least when serving em customers. The main options for humans to earn wages are in direct service to other humans. Thus individual ordinary humans without non-wage assets, thieving abilities, private charity, or government transfers are likely to starve, as have people throughout history who lacked useful assets, abilities, allies, or benefactors.

In our world, financial redistribution based on individual income has the potential problem of discouraging efforts to earn income, and thereby reducing the total size of the "pie" available to redistribute. In an em economy, however, where most all humans are retired, this problem is greatly reduced; there are fewer incentive problems resulting from financial redistribution to or between retired humans.

Ordinary humans are mostly outsiders to the em economy. While they can talk with ems by email or phone, and meet with ems in virtual reality, all these interactions have to take place at ordinary human speed, which is far slower than typical em speeds. Ordinary humans can watch recordings of fast em events, but not participate in them.

Although the total wealth of humans remains substantial, and grows rapidly, it eventually becomes only a small fraction of the total wealth, because of human incompetence, impatience, inattention, and inefficiency. Being less able than ems, humans choose worse investments. Being more impatient, they spend a larger fraction of their investment income on consumption. Fast ems are psychologically impatient, but they are more strongly embedded in institutions such as clans that limit independent action.

Being outsiders, humans attend less carefully to their investments in the em economy. This makes them absentee owners, who generally earn lower rates of investment return than do active and attentive owners. Today, privately held firms are consistently more responsive to changes in investment opportunities, and as a result earn on average a few percent per year higher returns than do public firms (Asker et al. 2011, 2015). While private investors suffer from lower liquidity and higher risk in private ventures, over time such investors still tend to accumulate a larger fraction of total wealth (Sorensen et al. 2014). (Some, however, disagree (L'Her et al. 2016).)

Some ordinary humans may own their own land and produce their own food on it, and so need to buy little from the em economy.

Even so, a need to pay property taxes to em governments for "protection" could force such humans to slowly sell off their lands to pay such taxes. For example, if you paid for a 5 percent tax on the rental value of your property by selling off slices of that property, your property holdings would fall by half for every twenty real doublings of fully reinvested funds.

When humans only own a small percentage of wealth, this may help protect them from direct expropriation by ems. If ems interact with humans via the same institutions of finance, law, and politics that ems use with each other, then expropriating humans' property could threaten the reliability of the social institutions that ems use to keep the peace with each other. This may not be worth the bother to acquire such a small fraction of wealth.

This protection of human assets, however, may only last for as long as the em civilization remains stable. After all, the typical em may experience a subjective millennium in the time that ordinary humans experience one objective year, and it seems hard to offer much assurance that an em civilization will remain stable over tens of 1000s of subjective em years. But slow em retirees may at least make good allies with humans in efforts to encourage stability, as the possibility of instability in an em civilization may also be the main threat to retiree longevity.

Basic changes in which property institutions are efficient for ems might adversely affect humans. This is similar to when farmers enclosed what were once forager common lands, and similar to a possible abandonment of music copyright in our world as a response to ease of copying and sharing. Those who relied on old kinds of property could lose out when such property no longer exists.

A few objective years after an em transition, the em economy may be thousands to billions of times larger than when it started, but the population of humans *must* stay essentially the same as before, unless revolutionary new methods are found for making new humans very fast. Because their investments double at nearly the rate that the economy doubles, ordinary human wealth doubles roughly every objective month, greatly encouraging humans to save. This wealth can buy increasingly elaborate mansions, flying cars, and much else, although not real estate near em concentrations. Compared with serving em customers, transport of products to ordinary humans is expensive, and innovation of products targeted for humans is probably slower.

Even impoverished humans may still own a lot of wealth, relative to the cost of living as a retired em. For example, physical human bodies may contain valuable raw materials. Also, ordinary humans may become increasingly rare celebrities, which ems pay to visit. Such people may be scanned just for their rare historical value. When scanning costs are low enough, wealth levels that make a human poor, could make an em rich. Poor humans may have the option to switch from a life of poverty as a human to a life of leisure and comfort as a retired em. This possibility limits em sympathy toward poor humans.

As most of the em economy happens near a few dense em cities, it is more costly to deliver goods and services to humans located further away from em cities. Local production near humans gains less from scale economies, and transport costs more and takes longer. After all, when investments double monthly, a month delay to transport something is like a doubling of its price. Thus humans who live further from em cities are effectively more poor.

While social media is a recent innovation, it looks like it is here to stay. However, it seems to add much more value to leisure than it does to work. As a result, humans and em retires may use social media a lot to talk, share, and rate, but em workers probably use it a lot less. But we should expect continued innovation in social media, and perhaps that that will make it more useful at work.

Ems may envy humans their wealth, leisure time, and more direct connections with nature, both human and otherwise. But as ems have such high abilities, they are likely to associate the styles and habits of humans with low competence. Ems may go out of their way to distinguish their styles and mannerisms from those of humans. Ems may treat humans more with sympathy, and ancestral gratitude, but less with respect. They may even routinely mock humans. For example, just as brain emulations may be called "ems" for short, humans may be called "ums" for short, as this is part of the word "human" and also insultingly describes a common scenario of human befuddlement when interacting with smarter faster ems. Humans may also be mocked for their squeamishness regarding em death.

To varying degrees, humans today identify with and care about their status as the central drivers of change in the world and as being essential resources for enabling such change. An em world moves humans off of this center stage, and humans may be unhappy and discouraged by this. After all, seeing you and your friends as the center of the universe can be motivating and invigorating.

In sum, humans are no longer at the center of the world's story during the em era. But they are still around, mostly living comfortably as retirees.

UNHUMANS

So far I've assumed that while the characteristics of ems may differ systematically from those of ordinary humans, em features still fall near a familiar human range. However, one of the deepest fears often expressed about future creatures like ems is that their features might move far outside of a human range (Bostrom 2004). Especially common and deep are fears that such creatures might be inhuman—cold and cruel, lacking empathy or kindness.

Note that as a word, "inhuman" is usually synonymous with "savage" and "barbaric," words which mean "lacking complex or advanced culture" and "primitive, unsophisticated." This suggests that what people mainly fear are creatures who, even if they are very human, treat people like us with hostility or indifference. That is, we fear "inhuman" creatures because we fear they are more likely to adopt such hostile attitudes.

As will be discussed in Chapter 29, Policy section, for this issue it probably matters more that ems rely on shared institutions, such as in law and politics. It matters less whether ems feel personal empathy toward individual ordinary humans, or whether ems retain most human features. Even so the following remain valid questions: how inhuman might ems become, and how much could these changes matter?

The prospects for big changes in em minds seem limited by two key factors: how big is the space of possible em minds that can be searched, and how rare are useful designs within that space. If the space is small or useful designs are rare, then there may be few useful changes, or they may take a very long time to find. In which case during the em era that I consider, em minds won't differ that much from ordinary human minds. On the other hand, if the space of possibilities is large and if useful designs are common and easy enough to find, then a Darwinian or related selection process may quickly find many big useful changes that ems can make. In this case em minds may quickly come to differ more from ordinary human minds.

Of course we may still value those em minds, perhaps even more than our own, if they are *understandably* different from humans, and if we respect the qualities by which they differ. For example, we might respect ems who are much more intelligent, creative, cooperative, and empathetic than we are, but are otherwise similar to us.

It may be hard to find cost-effective changes in human mind design. For example, one desirable feature in a mind is that it never forgets or misremembers anything. It may be possible to create minds that achieve this merely by completely recording all of their experiences. However, such minds may not be able to learn or abstract much from these recorded experiences. After all, the process that lets humans learn and abstract from their experiences seems to introduce changes to our memories. There may be no modest change to human minds that achieves both useful abstraction and perfect recall.

More generally, while we can envision many competitive pressures in the em world to encourage better minds, the size and enormous complexity of human minds makes it harder to envision big rapid changes that can greatly improve some aspects while still retaining their other many important functions. We expect big changes when large competitive advantages are feasible with only modest mind modification, but not when only small competitive advantages require great changes to well-entrenched aspects of human mind design.

As an analogy, consider that it is today much easier to make basic structural changes to small software systems, compared with big software systems. It is also easier to make structural changes to bicycle designs, compared with a city design. This is not because large software systems or cities are badly designed, or because their designers have poor incentives to design them well. Instead, the issue is that cities and big software systems are harder to predict, and they already embody a great many design choices adapted to one another and to system environments. To be useful, most basic structural changes to a city design would require expensive re-tooling of a great many other interdependent choices.

While such costs of change are lower for software that has a good modular design, such modularity is usually harder to achieve for larger software systems. If, like a city, the human mind has a great many parts well adapted to one another and to its environment, with only modest design modularity, then it may also be hard to find big structural changes to the human mind that preserve key functionality. The biggest feasible changes may allow only modest changes to basic human mind design.

Ems could differ from ordinary humans in both capacities and inclinations. Ems might both add capacities that ordinary humans lack, and lose capacities that humans once had. When we have added capacities in the past, such as tools that let humans see in the dark, such changes haven't been seen as taking away much from our humanity.

Thus the concern here mainly seems to be ems losing pre-existing human capacities. So let us consider that now.

PARTIAL MINDS

When we say that some humans are smarter than others, we rely on the observation that human mental abilities correlate across tasks. That is, those who are better at one mental task also tend to be better at other mental tasks. This correlation is plausibly explained in part by the fact that human brains use many brain subsystems to complete each task. Even if subsystem abilities are completely uncorrelated, so that having a higher quality version of one subsystem says nothing about the quality of other subsystems, the fact that each task uses several subsystems creates a correlation across task abilities (Hampshire et al. 2012).

If most mental tasks make use of a great many mental subsystems, then em mind design is only likely to greatly lose the abilities of subsystems which are especially expensive, or which are only used for a few unimportant tasks.

It is probably cheap to merely store a design for a brain part. What can be more expensive is temporarily devoting general hardware to implement such a part, or to create specialized hardware devoted to that brain part, hardware that cannot be easily switched to other parts. The brain parts most likely to be lost are those that are either expensive to implement even temporarily, and those that use specialized hardware.

As the cortex region of the human brain seems especially regular, it seems an especially promising place to try to useful size changes. It may even be possible to "pre-load" large sets of useful associations into standard cortex structures that can be moved between em minds.

Human brains devote a great deal of their volume to processing sight and sound. Yet many jobs don't seem to rely much on high-resolution versions of such abilities. Detailed sight and sound perception are thus two obvious candidates for reduced em capacities. To save on brain costs, ems may shrink and simplify their sight and sound processing, at least for jobs that only need limited abilities in these areas. The attractiveness of this strategy depends on how much human brains today recruit these subsystems for other tasks besides sight and sound processing. The more such recruiting, the less ems will find it useful to shrink these subsystems.

A simple assumption is that the brain can usefully shrink by roughly 25-50 percent via reduced or lost sight and sound processing capacities. Note that an ability to shrink such brain regions while still retaining their basic function, if not resolution, also suggests an ability to expand such regions, and increase resolution. A simple assumption is that ems can make productive expansions of a factor of two to ten for these regions of the human brain.

A more remote possibility is that some ems may usefully be given a reduced capacity for complex Machiavellian social reasoning, at least if the brain modules that support such reasoning could be identified and isolated. Secure property rights and competition for their services might protect em "nerds" with reduced social abilities from exploitation by others. Alternatively, slave owners may prefer ems who are less able to coordinate efforts to resist owners.

A third also-remote possibility is that some ems may usefully have reduced capacities for mating and related reasoning, if supporting brain modules for such capacities can be identified and isolated. This seems unlikely, because while ems have little direct need for sex or mating, supporting capacities are likely to be deeply enmeshed with many other useful social capacities. It might perhaps be easier to cut out both mating and complex social reasoning together from the em mind.

More likely than diminished mental capacities are missing *inclinations*. There are many mental features of humans, discussed in this chapter, the Psychology section, that we do not yet easily or fully understand as either functional for most intelligent social creatures, or as features that humans inherited from other mammals. Although ems might be able to laugh, sing, dance, admire art, or have sex, many ems might have reduced inclinations to use or develop such abilities. Such inclinations might, for example, be replaced with stronger inclinations to work. Inclinations to love and want children might be redirected toward inclinations to love and want more nearby clan copies.

It seems unlikely that much in the way of brain changes are required to support such inclination changes. Human cultural plasticity has already been seen in history to be sufficient to support large related alterations in inclinations.

It is possible that ems might be tweaked to be less inclined to feel or express sympathy with ordinary humans or with other ems, in essence becoming more sociopathic. Such ems are more willing to commit crimes, to betray associates, and to violate moral norms. If such ems were common, then an inability to distinguish such ems from other ems could force all ems to trust each other less, and as a result achieve fewer gains from working together. However, the existence of clans eager to protect their reputations should mostly eliminate this problem. Some clans may specialize in gaining a reputation for psychopathic tendencies useful in certain jobs, but most clans are unlikely to want to be known for such tendencies.

Changes in capacities or inclinations may influence whether current or future humans find such changed ems likeable, eerie, or repulsive. But such changes don't seem to matter that much for the analysis in the rest of this book. Most conclusions seem robust to these variations, because the human and social sciences used for analysis in this book are applicable to a wide variety of human-like behavior. For example, while eunuchs are substantially different from other humans, most tools useful for predicting the behavior of ordinary people are also useful for predicting the behavior of eunuchs. Some of our analysis tools, such as modern game theory, are useful even though they falsely assume that humans are selfish consistent rational strategic agents who never forget or make mistakes.

Some fear that ems by nature lack "consciousness," and thus cannot feel or experience anything, even though they appear in every way to have and discuss such experiences. While this "zombie" scenario seems unlikely to me, this topic is beyond the scope of this book. Another concern is that even if early ems have consciousness, they might eventually lose it after enough design changes. Even if this is possible in principle, however, a great many mental modules would probably have to be redesigned and readapted to one another in complex ways to accomplish this. This event seems quite unlikely to happen within the early em era that is the focus of this book.

In sum, while fears are usually described in terms of loss of human capacities, a loss of an inclination to use capacities seems just as much of a concern. This is not obviously a larger concern during the em era than it has been during the farmer and industrial eras.

PSYCHOLOGY

The fact that they are emulations of humans probably limits how far and how fast ems can diverge from human nature, even in a very competitive world.

When systems evolve to adapt to changed environments, and they have special parts on which many other parts depend, such special parts tend to become evolutionarily conservative, or "entrenched." That is, such parts tend to change less in response to evolutionary pressures, and they become tied to other entrenched parts, producing a subsystem of self-reinforcing entrenchment (Wimsatt 1986). Such subsystems must often be replaced as a whole, or not at all.

Human minds are also part of larger social, economic, and technical systems, and many aspects of human minds are entrenched within those larger systems. In addition, the human mind is itself a complex system with many relatively entrenched parts. Plausible candidates for these entrenched parts are the universal human features that seem to be common to human mental styles as seen in all known cultures, even if not always fully displayed in all known individuals (Brown 1991). If these features are also common to all em mind tweaks, they are likely to long be preserved in em mental styles.

We can use some of what we know about the origins of the human mind to guess which mind features are unlikely to change anytime soon. For example, as ems will be intelligent social creatures, some human features likely to be long preserved in ems are those that are plausibly functional for most intelligent social creatures. These include beliefs, memories, plans, names, property, cooperation, coalitions, reciprocity, revenge, gifts, socialization, roles, relations, self-control, dominance, submission, norms, morals, status, shame, division of labor, trade, law, governance, war, language, lies, gossip, showing off, signaling loyalty, self-deception, in-group bias, and meta-reasoning.

More human features likely to be long preserved in ems are features that humans share in common with most mammals, features that are likely to be deeply embedded in human mind design. These features include body awareness and control, integration of sight, sound, and smell awareness into a joint representation of the space and time around one's body, and categorizing such spaces and times according to weather, clutter, and mutability. Such features also include common ways to categorize objects, and basic space-time strategies for hiding, watching, searching, chasing, and evading. Deeply embedded mammal capacities also include fear, stress, anger, crying, pleasure, pain, hunger, disgust, lust, sex, jealousy, envy, fatigue, sleep, cold, itchiness, and play. They further include daily, yearly, and lifespan activity cycles, face and voice recognition, and behavior specific to the relations of parents, children, siblings, and mates.

Ems will likely preserve well-entrenched standards for a substantial period. Such standards are hard to change when alternates are not much more efficient, and when change requires losing value in many complementary investments simultaneously. These standards include many common features of human languages, such as subjects, objects, and gendered nouns. They also include standards such as the genetic code, base-10 math, ASCII, metric units, programming languages such as Java, operating systems such as Windows, the English language, and precedents from common and Napoleonic law.

There are other common human features that we do not yet easily or fully understand as either functional for most intelligent social creatures, or as features that humans share with many mammals. This lack of understanding makes it harder to guess how likely or long ems may retain such features, although most of them are likely fairly long. These features include gestures, voice tone meanings, coyness, insults, jokes, music, toys, sports, games, feasts, etiquette, symbols, dream interpretation, mood altering drugs, meditation, magic, luck, superstition, taboo sayings, religion, proverbs, rhythm, dance, poetry, art, myths, fiction, and death rituals. And they include decorative clothes, furniture, and hairstyles. Ems are most likely to drop human styles which are costly, which were relatively recently embedded in human mind design, which supported functions that are now mostly irrelevant, and where new substitute functions cannot be found for these styles.

Some needs and desires that ems plausibly share with humans seem especially relevant for the rest of this book. These include desires for nearly constant contact with a familiar physical world and familiar associates, daily rest and sleep, frequent informal socializing with friends, frequent direct contact with a few key close intimates, and satisfying stories saying how current activities fit into life-long dreams and ambitions. Ems are likely also to retain human difficulties in remaining mentally flexible with age, in understanding more than one speaking voice at a time, in finding more than a few hundred distinct human personalities friendly and familiar, and in easily and calmly accepting what one sees as one's imminent and total end.

Note that most of these features are capacities. Ems might retain such capacities but use them only rarely.

INTELLIGENCE

As discussed in Chapter 13, Qualities section, we expect ems to be smarter than are most people today. As intelligence is an especially important feature, it seems worth giving special attention to its possible implications.

Note that in the sense of being able to better achieve more mental tasks in any given time period, a group of people can be "smarter" than any one person. In this same sense, faster ems are typically smarter ems, as are ems given access to better tools, information sources, or education. As discussed in the Partial Minds section, ems may also become smarter in this sense by expanding their mental hardware, such as by increasing the number or size of many simple repeating brain circuits.

However, we often use a concept of "intelligence" intended to control for all of these effects. An em is more intelligent according to this concept if it can accomplish more tasks better even when it has equivalent brain hardware, information, and other resources. Let us now focus on ems being more intelligent in this sense. For example, we expect ems to be smarter than ordinary humans because of stronger selection, in selecting the best from among ordinary humans to scan, in selecting mental tweaks in the emulation process, and in a better selection of training methods.

For most economic activity, the most relevant kind of intelligence is team intelligence—whatever common factor best explains the ability of some teams to do many different kinds of tasks better than other teams.

One study found that group intelligence is better predicted by individual social sensitivity, such as abilities to read internal attitudes from face and voice cues, and equitably share conversation time, rather than by the average or maximum of individual intelligence (Woolley et al. 2010). However, another study finds that only average individual intelligence matters; these other factors are irrelevant (Bates and Gupta 2017).

Compared with individual intelligence, we should be more interested in predicting the evolution of future group intelligence, and we have better reason to expect economic incentives to induce efforts to improve group intelligence. However, as today we have far more data on the correlates of individual intelligence, we are better able to forecast the consequences of increases in individual intelligence, and so that will be our focus here.

As discussed in Chapter 13, Qualities section, smarter people today are less accident prone and more rational, cooperative, patient, trusting, trustworthy, law-abiding, and supportive of efficient policies. Smarter nations are freer, more entrepreneurial, less corrupt, and have better institutions.

We expect individually smarter workers to accomplish more with the same resources, to make fewer and more minor mistakes, to master a wider scope of tasks and skills, to communicate effectively with a wider range of ems doing different tasks, to adapt faster to changing circumstances, and to more efficiently learn specific and specialized roles.

How these changing capacities change the mix of em jobs and careers depends on job stability. In more stable slower-changing environments, the gains from making fewer mistakes, and better learning specific skills, may matter more. This allows a finer division of labor into more specialized interdependent roles. In contrast, in uncertain and rapidly changing environments, the abilities to master more skills, to talk on a wider range of topics, and to adapt faster may matter more. Em organizations that use such polymathic ems function effectively in a wider range of such environments, by having smaller teams of less specialized workers.

Smarter ems are more innovative, have longer lasting subjective careers, and can handle jobs that are redesigned more often. As bosses, smarter ems can simultaneously manage a wider range of subordinates.

All these changes are non-trivial, and welcome, but they do not seem especially radical. They suggest that a society full of creatures smarter than ordinary humans, perhaps even *much* smarter, could be a quite recognizable and understandable society. It need not create a "singularity" barrier to foresight, beyond which we cannot see. However, some people disagree.

ROGUE MACHINES

For at least a century, every decade or two we've seen a burst of activity and concern about automation. The last few years have seen another such burst, with increasing activity in AI research and commerce, and also increasing concern expressed that future smart machines might get out of control and destroy humanity. These concerns are not mostly about ems, but instead about other less-human-like types of AI. Some argue that these "AI risk" concerns justify great efforts today to figure out how to keep future AI under control, and to more closely watch and constrain AI research efforts. Approaches considered include kill switches, requiring prior approval for AI actions, and designing AI motivational system to make AIs want to help, and not destroy, humanity.

Consider, however, an analogy with organizations. Today, the individuals and groups who create organizations and their complex technical systems are often well-advised to pay close attention to how to maintain control of such organizations and systems. A loss of control can lead not only to a loss of the resources invested in creating and maintaining such systems, but also to liability and retaliation from the rest of the world.

But exactly because individuals have incentives to manage their organizations and systems reasonably well, the rest of us needn't pay much attention to the internal management of others' organizations. In our world, most firms, cities, nations, and other organizations are much more powerful than are most individuals, and yet they remain largely under control in most important ways. For example, none have so far destroyed the world. Smaller than average organizations can typically exist and even thrive without being forcefully absorbed into larger ones. And outsiders can often influence and gain from organization activities via control institutions like elections, board of directors, and voting stock.

Mostly, this is all achieved neither via outside action approval nor via detailed knowledge and control of motivations. We instead rely on law, competition, social norms, and politics. If a rogue organization seems to harm others, it can be accused of legal violations, as can its official owners and managers. Those who feel hurt can choose to interact with it less. Others who are not hurt may choose to punish the rogue informally for violating informal norms, and get rewarded by associates for such efforts. And rogues may be excluded from political coalitions, who hurt it via the politics of governments and other large organizations.

AI and other advanced technologies may give future organizations new options for internal structures, and those introducing such innovations should consider their risks for increased chances of losing control. But by itself, this isn't a reason for the rest of us to be much concerned, especially many decades or centuries before such innovations may appear. After all, our usual mechanisms, outlined above, for keeping organizations under control can plausibly keep working. Yes, innovations might perhaps create new external consequences, which those outside of the innovating organization would have to deal with. But given how little we now understand about the issues, architectures, and motivations of future AI systems, why not mostly wait and deal with any such problems later?

I took an informal poll of my twitter followers, asking those who put high priority on AI risk efforts today to say which of one three options was their main concern. Out of 163 respondents, only 14 percent picked none of the above, so these three options do encompass most concerns.

Of the remainder, 20 percent picked AI causing a collapse of property rights. That is, a transition to a world with better AI may trigger wars, revolutions, and other kinds of theft, which take resources away from people we care about. If AIs are like a differing ethnicity to humans, we might expect ethnicity-related war outcomes as described in Chapter 20, War section. Nations with stronger internal ethnic divisions war more, but nation pairs that are more similar also war more with each other. But as civil wars happen more given discrimination against ethnic minorities, and wars are triggered when faster-growing nations no longer accept a previous lower status, trying to hold firm control in order to maintain AIs as low status seems especially risky.

Another 34 percent picked the fact that values tend to drift both over time, and between ancestors and descendants, and tend to change more in periods of faster social change. Faster social change because of AIs plausibly makes for faster value drift, particularly within the AIs, who change faster. In the past, each generation has had to accept slowly losing control of the world to succeeding generations. Prior generations could influence later ones via writings, education, and social structures. Prior generations could also accumulate and then spend savings and social connections to ensure high status and a comfortable retirement. But they no longer ruled the world. Bequests, contracts and other organizational commitments did not prevent this. Some find this situation unacceptable, and seek ways to enable a current generation, for example humans today, to maintain strong control over all future generations, be they biological, robotic or something else, even after such future generations have become far more capable than the current generation. To me this problem seems both very hard, and not obviously worth solving, given the obvious risks (Hanson 2012b).

Finally, the remaining 47 percent surveyed picked the most common AI risk concern: a single AI quickly taking over the world.

FOOM

As mentioned in Chapter 4, Artificial Intelligence section, some foresee a rapid local "intelligence explosion," sometimes called "foom," wherein one initially small seed system quickly becomes vastly more powerful (Chalmers 2010; Hanson and Yudkowsky 2013; Yudkowsky 2013; Bostrom 2014). And if such a local explosion might happen soon, then it could make more sense for the rest of us today, not just those most directly involved, to worry about how to keep control of future rogue AI.

In a prototypical local explosion scenario, a single AI system starts with a small supporting team. Both the team and its AI have resources and abilities that are tiny on a global scale. This team finds and then applies a big innovation in system architecture to its AI system, which as a result greatly improves in performance. (An "architectural" change is just a discrete change with big consequences.) Performance becomes so much better that this team plus AI combination can now quickly find several more related innovations, which further improve system performance. (Alternatively, instead of finding architectural innovations the system might enter a capability regime which contains a large natural threshold effect or scale economy, allowing a larger system to have capabilities well out of proportion to its relative size.)

During this short period of improvement, other parts of the world, including other AI teams and systems, improve much less. Once all of this team's innovations are integrated into its AI system, that system is now more effective *than the entire rest of the world* put together, at least at one key task. That key task might be theft, that is, stealing resources from the rest of the world. Or that key task might be innovation, that is, improving its own abilities across a wide range of useful tasks.

That is, even though an entire world economy outside of this team, including other AIs, works to innovate, steal, and protect itself from theft, this one small AI team becomes vastly better at some combination of (1) stealing resources from others while preventing others from stealing from it, and (2) innovating to make this AI "smarter," in the sense of being better able to do a wide range of mental tasks given fixed resources. As a result of being better at these things, this AI quickly grows the resources under its control and becomes in effect more powerful than the entire rest of the world economy put together. So, in effect it takes over the world. All of this happens within a space of hours to months.

(The hypothesized power advantage here is perhaps analogous to that of the first team to make an atomic bomb, if that team had had enough other supporting resources to enable it to use the bomb to take over the world.)

Note that to believe in such a local explosion scenario, it is not enough to believe that eventually machines will be very smart, even much smarter than are humans today. Or that this will happen soon. It is also not enough to believe that a world of smart machines can overall grow and innovate much faster than we do today. One must in addition believe that an AI team that is initially small on a global scale could quickly become vastly better than the rest of the world put together, including other similar teams, at improving its internal abilities.

If a foom-like explosion can quickly make a once-small system more powerful than the rest of the world put together, the rest of the world might not be able to use law, competition, social norms, or politics to keep it in check. Safety can then depend more on making sure that such exploding systems start from safe initial designs.

Some advocates of this foom scenario say that there is an as-yet-undiscovered but very powerful set of related architectural innovations for AI system design, a set that one team could find first and then keep secret from others for long enough. Various arguments are offered for this conclusion (Hanson and Yudkowsky 2013). (Other advocates are less clear on what exactly would power the explosion.)

In attempts to explain why human mental abilities are so powerful and general relative to other primates, it has been suggested that humans embody big architectural changes in brain design. Changes that big and quick just couldn't come from the accumulation of many small gains, it is said. It is also suggested that the many reasoning biases that humans now display suggest that big architectural gains remain to be found.

Some say that we vastly underfund research and innovation today, allowing modest investments to produce large ability gains within a local intelligence explosion. And some suggest that most economic and technical gains come from basic research progress produced by a few key geniuses, gains that are far out of proportion to the wages we pay such basic research geniuses, and that greatly reduce time delays in the genius research process. If so, a faster AI genius might make huge gains.

To me, this foom scenario looks suspiciously like a super-villain comic book plot. A flash of insight by a lone genius lets him create a genius AI. Hidden in its super-villain research lab lair, this genius villain AI works out unprecedented revolutions in AI design, turns itself into a super-genius, and then invents super-weapons and takes over the world. Bwa-ha-ha. But those who live in glass houses shouldn't throw stones, and, yes, to some this book also looks suspiciously like science fiction.

Yes, if most innovation came from a few basic-research-focused geniuses, if we vastly underfunded such research, if limited human speeds greatly delayed research results, and if big architectural improvements are possible in mind design, then a smart fast team working hard enough might perhaps out-innovate the rest of the world put together. And, yes, if the human advantage over other primates came from a big architectural innovation, and if humans today fail because their minds embody very poor architectural choices, then it might be plausible for an AI project to find big architectural gains.

But on closer examination, I find this scenario to be unlikely (Hanson and Yudkowsky 2013). Yes, it can make sense for a few people to focus on an unlikely but especially problematic scenario, but foom shouldn't be anything close to a default future AI scenario. (A recent survey of 352 machine learning researchers gave a median estimate of a 10 percent chance of explosive growth in abilities once human level AI is achieved (Grace et al. 2017). They apparently do not expect the scenario of this book, which would count as such an explosive growth scenario.)

Regarding the prospect of big innovations in human brain design, the standard story is that humans beat other primates mainly via cultural sharing, which has a threshold effect (Henrich 2015; Laland 2017). That is, small differences in overall mental abilities can lead to large differences in the ability to reliably communicate, which over time can accumulate into enormous differences in culturally aided abilities. Human and primate brains seem to be similarly organized, and humans only became more able than other primates after enough time had passed for much human culture to accumulate. Both of these facts seem to be at odds with the theory that sudden big brain architectural innovation enabled humans.

Regarding our biases today, many of our biases appear strongest on tasks which were not very relevant for our ancestors; on tasks that mattered more we tend make effective choices, even if we explain ourselves badly. In addition, many apparent "biases" seem to be functional adaptations (Mercier and Sperber 2011).

In the history of AI research, high-level architecture has only mattered modestly for system performance, and new architecture proposals have become increasingly rare. Brains seem analogous to ecosystems, bacteria, cities, and economies in being very complex systems where architecture matters less than a mass of capable detail. While the invention of better algorithms has at times seemed important, overall this force seems overrated, as algorithm progress seems to have been driven more fundamentally by hardware progress (Grace 2013).

Yes, individual humans are distinguished by a single IQ factor that explains a surprisingly large fraction of the variance of how well individuals can do a wide variety of mental tasks. However, we have little reason to believe that this is because some of us have better brain architectures than others. Our strong IQ factor is more plausibly explained by some people having better brain chemistry, or by the fact that many distinct brain modules contribute on each task (Hampshire et al. 2012).

Social scientists who study innovation have long rejected the views that most economic or technical progress comes from basic research, or that most research progress comes from a few geniuses. Intelligence does not seem much more useful in innovation than it is in other tasks, increases in research funding give much less than proportionate increases in research progress, and nations that contain more research do not seem to grow more as a result (Alston et al. 2011; Ulku 2004). And as most research is done in parallel by many teams, individual project delays create only modest losses. These all cast doubts on the claim that a small smart fast team could out-innovate the entire rest of the world.

Overall, we have little reason to believe that a set of powerful architectural innovations in mind design could be found by a small team and then exploited to allow that team's AI to become quickly capable enough to take over the world. However, one could still be interested in this book on the em era if such a local intelligence explosion were likely, as long as that explosion might happen after the start of an em era.

AFTER EMS

Ems are a reasonable guess for what might form the basis of the next great era after the foraging, farming, and industry eras. But this choice is far from obvious; other possibilities should also be explored. And even assuming that the next great era is based on ems, it seems at least twice as hard to guess what might form the basis of the next great era after ems. Even so, let us now consider this post-em era.

If it is a stretch to project the previous era patterns into the em era, it is even more of a stretch to project such patterns further into the era that follows ems. Even so, if such patterns were to continue, then an em era whose economy doubled every month would last only for a year or two, and then after a transition of perhaps a week a new economy would double in a few (perhaps three to twelve) hours. A major cycle of this new era would last a third of the doubling time, and social groups analogous to bands, towns, and cities would have a population of roughly a trillion trillion. I don't put much confidence in such estimates, but feel I should include them here for completeness.

If past patterns continued, big innovations in calculation and communication might also appear early in the em era. These innovations would gradually improve over the em era, not have big effects until late in the em era, and then enable the next era after ems. Candidates for such innovations include a better language for expressing, manipulating, and sharing something like brain states, and combinatorial prediction markets to better share beliefs and aggregate information on many topics.

One possible basis of a post-em era is non-em forms of AI. Ems should continue to write software and improve automation, and eventually that better AI might possibly displace ems in pretty much all jobs, just as such AI might have eventually displaced biological humans in almost all jobs, had ems never appeared. A new era might begin once AI displaces ems in most all jobs.

As discussed in Chapter 4, Artificial Intelligence section, our economy today doubles about every fifteen years, and artificial intelligence (AI) experts typically estimate that in the last 20 years in their subfield, we have come 5-10 percent of the way to human level abilities. This suggests that if ems arrive within a century, we would at that point be less than a quarter to half of the way from here to human level AI. Had the ems not arrived, the economy would have needed to double another seven to twenty times to achieve human level AI. So if progress toward AI scales as growth in the economy (as suggested by costs falling with cumulative production (Nagy et al. 2013)), an em economy that doubled every month would take seven to twenty months to achieve human level AI.

This time estimate seems an underestimate for two reasons. First, compared with today, em economic growth depends less on innovation and more on growth in inputs. Second, as discussed in Chapter 4, Artificial Intelligence section, in many areas of computer science algorithm gains are typically close to hardware gains, and the rate of computer hardware gains will probably slow in coming decades, relative to economic growth rates. Each of these issues might reduce the rate of AI progress per economic doubling time by up to roughly a factor of two.

These considerations suggest that the em economy might perhaps double up to thirty to sixty times before human level AI appears. This would be a total growth factor of between a billion and a billion billion. At a monthly doubling rate, this might take two-and-a-half to five objective years, which could be two-and-a-half to five millennia to a typical speed kilo-em.

Note that I'm *not* at all claiming that the em era will continue through this many doublings before another very different era appears. I'm instead doing rough calculations to suggest that there could be a long interesting em era undisturbed by the arrival of non-em-based human level AI.

It seems possible that, in the absence of ems, non-em-AI might eventually displace biological humans in most all jobs. After all, human hardware and low-level software seem harder to change and improve than do analogous parts of AIs. Eventually, improving AI might beat non-improving humans. However, ems can use nearly the same hardware as AIs do, and low-level em software can be changed much more easily. So when the descendants of ems and of non-em AI software compete for jobs, it is less obvious which one wins where. If em descendants win in many important places, then a new era can't begin when AI takes most all em jobs, as that doesn't happen. But a new era might begin when that em-AI competition and interaction changes in some important way.

Even if we eventually come to understand human brain software in great detail, such software will probably still be harder to understand and modify than is familiar software. It was not designed to be understood, and its author did not document it nor pass along test suites to assist in its debugging. Brain software may also be less modular than are familiar software systems of comparable size and ability.

However, the software in the human brain is also likely to be far better integrated than is familiar software. While humans writing software today mainly manage complexity by creating new separate modules whenever possible to achieve new functions, evolution faced strong limits on available space for expansion. With expansion limited, evolution was forced to focus on fine-tuning existing modules and integrating them better with one another.

As mentioned in the Psychology section, human mental software also starts with the big advantage of being entrenched within and entangled with our existing social, economic, and technical systems. Such legacy code tends to be harder to change (Feathers 2004). So software descended from the human mind may survive and thrive longest within the densest knots of interdependent systems, as these tend to change the least. These most entangled work tasks are like the tasks that we now do more in our largest cities, tasks done there because they depend on, and thus benefit from close coordination with, more other tasks. As mentioned in Chapter 18, City Structure section, today such tasks include judging quality, determining compliance, making decisions, thinking creatively, developing strategies, scheduling and planning, interpreting, communicating, making and maintaining relations, selling, resolving conflicts, coordinating, training, motivating, advising, and administration (Kok and Weel 2014).

Similarly, when redesigning em minds, it will usually be easier to design new modules which are implemented differently internally, but which sit in the same old slots in the same larger-scale structure. In general, standards by which diverse systems interact tend to change much more slowly than do those diverse systems. So the overall structure of em minds should change the least.

Consider an analogy. After billions of years honing the design of small cells, evolution made multicellular organisms by pasting together many small cells. While there is great waste in each single cell retaining most capacities needed by a single cell alone in the wild, this was still more effective than designing new larger systems from scratch. Similarly, future intelligent systems may paste many human-mind like systems together, instead of designing new large minds from scratch.

Today, the structure of large software systems tends to reflect the communication structure of the organizations that created them (Conway 1968; MacCormack et al. 2012). This suggests that costs to change organization structures, and to coordinate across organizations boundaries, are at least as important considerations as any natural structure of the problems that such software is solving. This also suggests that the large-scale structure of future AI software may continue to reflect the familiar structures and divisions of the nations, industries, professions, and firms that we see today. While we may see a big growth in the general software industry that produces the software that can be used in many nations, industries, and firms, even so most software may be created within specialized and problem-specific industries, professions, and firms.

Thus after the em era the world may continue to contain things that look from the outside roughly like human minds, talking to each other in ways similar to how humans talk, sitting in familiar looking nations, industries, professions, and firms, and using organizations that interact with each other via familiar looking institutions of finance, law, and governance. The internal implementation details of such systems may be quite different, and all of it may be embedded in an ocean of very powerful and somewhat alien looking software tools and assistants. But still, the core highly entangled parts of such a future world could look quite familiar to us.

PART VI
Implications

CHAPTER 28

Variations

TRENDS

This book has mostly discussed what the em era is like as if that era is stable and never changes. But we expect many changes and trends over the em era.

For example, the size of the em economy grows exponentially, although this growth may fluctuate more than does growth today because of its concentration in a few key cities.

In order for the cost of computing hardware to fall substantially during the em era, ems will have to learn to build chip factories in far less time than the several years that it takes today. If ems can manage this, then during the em era the cost of computing hardware falls exponentially, and with it both the energy used per computing operation and the natural em body size. The natural em mind speed rises. Parallel computing costs fall faster than serial computing costs, and also faster than the cost of non-computer tools. So there is a trend in workplaces away from using serial computer tools and non-computer tools, and toward using em minds and parallel computer tools. Parallel software becomes more efficient relative to the emulation process, inducing ems to use more parallel software tools per em.

The cost of communication rises relative to the cost of memory and computing, increasing communication delays, and reducing the rate of travel and meetings, and reducing the distances between meeting participants.

As computing hardware is the main em labor cost, em subsistence wages and median wages fall with computing costs. Thus the speed-weighted size of the em population grows even faster than does the em economy. The typical sizes of firms, clans, and cities grow both with the size of the population, and with the size of the economy.

While the first ems run near the speed of ordinary humans, there is an early transition to most ems running at a much faster common speed, estimated in Chapter 18, Choosing Speed section to be within a factor of four of 1000 times human speed. But during the em era typical em speeds may slowly decline, as the growing em economy creates spatially larger em cities which signals take longer to cross.

After an initial burst of exploration, the space of feasible tweaks of em minds slowly grows, but perhaps does not add much value. Added tweaks, random drift in capital per clan, and learning about which clans are best at which jobs should all contribute to a slow increase in the dominance of economy activity by the top few clans. The top clans slowly hold a larger fraction of the jobs, and own a larger fraction of capital.

As the human population changes little during the em era, the ratio of ems to humans rises very quickly, and the em subsistence wage falls quickly relative to the human subsistence wage. While actual em wages stay close to em subsistence wages, human incomes are on average far above human subsistence, and rise nearly as fast as the em economy grows, at least in the absence of strong redistribution away from humans.

While ordinary humans start out owning all of the capital in the economy, the fraction of capital that humans control slowly falls, as discussed in Chapter 27, Humans section. The relative political power held by ordinary humans may fall even faster, as both labor and capital also contribute to political power, and ems quickly constitute almost all of the labor force. Ems later acquire most of the local political power, and later still acquire most local capital and wealth. These transitions might induce disruptive conflict.

In sum, we can foresee many plausible trends during the em era.

ALTERNATIVES

I have focused on a single main baseline scenario, and sometimes a few small implicit variations. Let me now give more explicit attention to larger variations.

While this book has discussed war and security, it has mostly assumed peace and the successful protection of property. But what if violence, theft, and war end up being much more profitable, as they seem to have been in the early farming era? In such a scenario, a large fraction of time and income is spent on security, both to attack others and to defend against attacks. The em economy probably grows more slowly, and ems can expect shorter subjective lifespans. The entire em civilization is probably also at more risk of collapse. Relative to our baseline em era scenario, the most copied em clans are better skilled at attack and defense.

The size, location, and specializations of clans, firms, and cities are also distorted in the direction of making such things easier to defend, and better able to launch successful attacks. For example, if it is hard to protect large cities against nuclear attacks, cities will be smaller and spread further apart. However, to the extent that there are em enclaves well protected against attack, those probably look internally more like the scenario described in this book.

In a second variation, we might create artificial general intelligence that is similar to ems, except that it is made via a shallower analysis of higher-level human brain processes, instead of via directly emulating lower-level brain processes as in a classic em. Such variations on ems probably are not greatly redesigned at the highest levels of organization, and thus are relatively human in behavior and style. The main ways these differ from ems is that they probably do not remember being human, their personalities might differ more from human, they might not run as easily on parallel computer hardware, and they might require a lot less computer hardware. These factors likely make for a more disruptive transition to the em era.

In another variation, progress in non-emulation-based software abilities becomes faster. As discussed in Chapter 4, Artificial

Intelligence section, at the rates of progress we have seen so far, software improves slowly enough to allow a substantial early em era during which far more income goes to em workers than to pay for software aids. But if software instead develops faster, and if em-based software is less competitive with it, then the economy more quickly reaches the point where most income goes to pay for software aids and supporting hardware. After that point, the distribution of income is determined more by the distribution of ownership of non-em software.

Yet another variation is clan-specific computer hardware. Instead of having all clans run on the same generic emulation hardware, a large clan might pay to create hardware specific to running minds from that clan. An extra fixed cost of development pays to reduce the marginal cost of running minds from this clan. This advantage, however, might have to be dropped for distant travel, for temporarily switching speeds, and for locating hardware close to other work team members.

Clan-specific hardware reduces the scale economies from em hardware useable by many em clans, and increases the advantages from being in one of the few most popular clans. The increase in fixed costs relative to marginal costs of hardware increases the market power of popular clans in the labor market, and thus somewhat increases the scope for complex multi-clan labor negotiations.

More clan concentration may also result if there are very widely adopted and strongly enforced regulations requiring that new copies be endowed with great wealth. In this case most labor-market niches may be filled by the eager-to-copy clans that are most willing to pay high prices to endow as many copies as possible.

We can also consider a more extreme scenario along these lines, wherein most ems come from only a dozen or fewer em clans. This could happen if tweaks are especially able to change em abilities, or if there are some very capable clans able to learn an especially wide range of skills. In this scenario, global coordination is easier, via deals between clans, and teams and social gatherings typically have many ems from the same clan. More coordination allows more regulation, enabling wider deviations from the baseline scenario of this book.

An opposite variation has em job tasks varying so much that the em economy makes good use of many more pre-skill worker types than estimated in the baseline scenario, and thus requires many more than 1000 or so scanned humans. This results in most workers coming from far more than 1000 clans. In this case, ems less often know the basic personality of other ems they encounter, making em social interactions more like that of our industrial era, where most people don't know each other. Also, as in our era, it is harder to manage em firm and city politics via shifting coalitions of em clans. There are likely still enough copies per clan, however, for clans to usefully give life advice to members. This is in many ways a more familiar scenario.

A related scenario is where clans fragment more strongly into conflicting subclans. If ems who are trained in different professions or who live in different places do not cooperate as strongly together, then subclans may prefer to ally with subclans from other clans with whom they have more in common. This also reduces the importance of clans in politics, finance, and law.

Another variation is where the age of peak work productivity is usefully extended to a subjective millennium or longer. If it takes 10 000 years until an em worker reaches peak productivity, ems will tend to run faster to fit their career into near an economic doubling time. This makes cities smaller and culture more socially fragmented, with a larger fraction of social interactions having noticeable communication delays.

A related variation is where em brains can be usefully decreased or increased by much larger factors than those estimated in Chapter 27, Partial Minds section (25-50 percent decreases, and 100-1000 percent increases). Instead, factors of 1000 or more either way might be possible. This variation likely results in a wider range of intelligence levels in productive ems, and in a wider range of em hardware costs. If so, most actual ems by count, if not by wage, are likely close to the smallest and cheapest possible sizes. This variation lets any given set of initial mind scans usefully fill a wider range of job roles, and so likely reduces the number of clans that come to dominate the em economy.

Yet another variation is where the cost of cooling or some other expense is severe enough in practice to greatly limit em city sizes. In this case the gains of having more ems who can interact easily with many other ems is outweighed by other high costs. As a result, there is a larger number of smaller em cities, with most ems living in cities near an optimum size. More efforts go into dealing with whatever is the limiting factor to city size, and more growth happens by creating new cities. In this scenario, there is more cultural variation worldwide and a weaker ability of ems to coordinate globally.

A related variation is where computer security turns out to be much harder than estimated in Chapter 5, Security section. What if the computers housing em minds can be more easily and routinely taken over, to steal enclosed minds and gain control of computer resources? In this case, the em economy spends a larger fraction of its income defending against such attacks, via hardware obstacles, active monitoring and reactions, and reducing the value held in any one mind. The threat of mind theft reduces the number of copies typically made of each trained em worker, and em workers are less likely to congregate at firm locations, instead of at clan castles.

In the limit, very reversible computers must be quantum computers. If quantum computing became feasible on large scales, then a few kinds of important calculations could be done much faster and cheaper, including factoring, certain kinds of search, and simulations of small-scale physical systems (Viamontes et al. 2005). While this allows and perhaps forces a switch to quantum cryptography, it appears to have little impact on most other forecasts in this book. Quantum computing doesn't seem able to speed up brain emulation computations. While it is possible to create quantum states that cannot be copied, this is unlikely to typically be a useful way to prevent mind theft; the many practical gains from easy copying seem too large to forego.

A variation with big potential implications is where some method is found to usefully merge two em minds that had once split from a common ancestor, with the combined mind requiring not much more space and processing power than did each original mind, yet retaining most of the skills and memories of both originals. This merging process is more useful when it is feasible for longer subjective durations after the last common ancestor of the two ems.

Mind merging is especially useful if a merged mind is less aged, in the sense of having less added mental fragility, than the sum of the aging of the two merged minds since their last common ancestor. The robust and general nature of mental aging and increasing fragility, however, suggests that this is unlikely. That is, the aging of a combined mind is likely to be near the sum of the aging of the merged minds. In this case, there are far fewer useful applications for mind merging. Retirees might merge with abandon, however, because they are already too fragile to be productive workers, and by merging their minds, retirees can also merge resources and thus afford to run at higher speeds, thus gaining higher status.

Perhaps the biggest variation is global governance sufficiently strong to substantially limit em population growth, and hence to raise em wages well above wages in the baseline scenario. While raising wages modestly, perhaps by less than 50 percent above competitive levels, seems somewhat feasible via local coordination, raising wages by a factor of three or more seems to require coordination at the largest scales at which em societies might compete economically or militarily. Smaller-scale coordination to greatly raise wages mainly just places the covered smaller regions at a competitive disadvantage to other regions.

Effective laws to enforce minimum wages probably require quite intrusive monitoring and strong punishment of violations. While police spurs can monitor for violations and still preserve significant privacy, as discussed in Chapter 10, Surveillance section, such monitoring either needs access to nearly all manufacturing of em brain hardware, nearly all em brain hardware locations and uses, or nearly all uses of power and cooling that could support illicit brain hardware.

As a wide range of possible powers, with a wide range of possible preferences, might control a system of global governance, it is more difficult to use social science to predict social outcomes in the case of strong global regulations. This is because it is hard to predict exactly *which* regulations are adopted. A world of strong regulation can still be competitive, but with competition focused on access to and influence over this global governance system.

A variation on the previous scenario is where there is a great deal of regulation, but regulations are not strong enough to prevent a large em population and low em wages. In this scenario, it seems simplest to assume that ems retain many regulations from our world, such as a prohibition on murder, which could force even very short-lived spurs to retire instead of ending. There might also be rules against the scanning and emulating of children. Regulations might also prevent endowing new copies with debt or stock obligations, which encourages a world dominated by fewer eager-to-copy clans.

In the past, social institutions like the church or the organized medical profession have retained substantial control over particular areas of life. Sometimes such control has been nearly global in scope. An em scenario with moderately centralized governance has such a social institution retain strong control over key aspects of em technology and their application. This might be a particular firm with strong intellectual property rights, or an institution like the church whose jurisdiction over em technology is widely accepted. This institution may make its key choices mainly to benefit itself.

In sum, while there are many plausible variations on the baseline scenario in this book, this baseline scenario has been constructed in such a way as to be useful in understanding these variations. Baseline scenarios help analysis.

TRANSITION

What happens during the transition from our world to the em world?

To maintain a consistent style of analysis, I assume a relatively competitive low regulation scenario not only for a stable equilibrium em world, but also for a possibly unstable non-equilibrium transition from our era to the em era. That is, even if some parties have foresight enough to see how their actions may contribute to a path that leads to an em world, most of these parties have too little influence for this foresight to much change their incentives. Most parties just do what is locally in their private interest.

Note, however, that large deviations from such assumptions during a transition could still be quite consistent with their applying well after the transition. That is, a non-equilibrium transition can still lead to an equilibrium post-transition world.

It is conceivable that military advantage will be the driving force directing a great transition resulting from changing em technology. However, the military usually only drives the introduction of technologies that are especially potent militarily. While the military sometimes plays a big role in the early research and development of other technologies, it usually fades into the background regarding their widespread peaceful application.

For example, the U.S. military funded a lot of early computer research because it considered computers to be especially useful in military applications. Even so, most growth in computer applications has been outside the military, and the military has had little influence on where and how most computers are used today.

As ems are not more effective in military applications than in other economic applications, choices made by the military probably make only a minor difference to when, how, and where ems are used. As by assumption no other forms of general artificial intelligence are feasible when ems are first realized, there might be trillions of dollars to be gained from selling access to brain emulations. Local profit incentives should thus drive most local choices that cause change.

Many new technologies induce changes that are relatively gradual and anticipated, because first versions have high cost and limited abilities. Costs then gradually fall as abilities gradually rise. In contrast, other new technologies induce more sudden and unanticipated jumps in abilities and costs. The technology of brain emulation is of this second more sudden sort, because partial or nearly accurate emulations are of little use.

The early em economy creates a burst of growth, concentrated in a few key industries, firms, and geographical locations. Ordinary humans might better hedge em transition risks if they invest in funds that are very diversified across industries, firms, and locations. Such humans might benefit even more if they could buy "em bonds"—bets that pay off only after a transition to an em economy.

The first em cities might plausibly form around big computer data centers, such as those built today by Google, Amazon, and Microsoft (Morgan 2014). Such centers likely have ample and cheap supporting resources such as energy, are relatively safe from storms and social disruptions, and are also close to initial em customers, suppliers, and collaborators in the richest parts of the industrial economy. These centers prefer access to cheap cold water and air for cooling, such as found toward Earth's poles, and prefer to be in a nation that is either relatively free from regulations or can be controlled by friendly parties. These criteria suggest that the first em city may arise in a low-regulation Nordic nation such as Norway.

While em cities are likely to benefit from starting near existing concentrations of humans, once they succeed em cities are likely to push humans away, as em infrastructure is probably incompatible with standard human infrastructure in many ways. This may create conflict during the transition phase. Either some cities near humans will find ways to smoothly and quickly push out ordinary humans, or the successful em cities will be the ones that start a safe distance away from traditional human cities.

As in most disruptive social transitions, the transition to an em society is likely to be a time of heightened risk of war. Groups sometimes violently resist a fall in their relative status.

During the very early em era when em societies are weak compared with human societies, human nations may try to influence the nature of em societies via a mixture of threats and aid. As with rich nations today that seek to influence developing nations, this influence is likely to encourage non-democratic governance, as that is more easily influenced by foreign aid (Bueno de Mesquita and Smith 2011). Later on, when human societies are weak compared with em societies, ems may then try to influence human societies, and they are also likely to encourage non-democratic governance of human nations.

Today, capital and labor are complements, especially in the short run; the more you have of one, the more valuable the other becomes. In addition, technology gains have usually helped labor much more than capital (Lawrence 2015). If we include ems in the category of "labor," instead of "capital," then the arrival of ems quickly lowers the cost of labor, relative to the cost of capital, and greatly increases the quantity of labor.

If capital and labor continue to be complements in an em era, a big jump in the quantity of labor implies a big jump in the value of capital, and an increase in the fraction of total income that goes to capital, as opposed to labor. This will encourage a rapid increase in the kinds of capital that are easy to make quickly, such as machines and buildings, and this will greatly increase the value of capital that is hard to grow quickly, such as firm goodwill, local culture, and patents (Corrado et al. 2009).

In addition, the value of investments in tools that help individual workers is reduced, relative to investments that create and support more labor. As computer hardware supports more em labor, investments in such hardware, and supporting tools, greatly increase in relative value. In fact, a large fraction of the gains during the em transition period may go to those who own capital to make computers, capital to make new computer-making equipment, intellectual property required to use such capital, and real estate near the main concentrations of em activity.

Once the possibility of a transition to an em world becomes more widely perceived, many may express reluctance, repugnance, or opposition to the new em era. Because an em economy is capable of very fast growth rates but also requires a lot of tolerance for doing things quickly and differently, local differences between mild reluctance and strong opposition may not matter much. Unless there is a well-coordinated global effort with strong teeth to prevent the creation of ems, what should mainly matter is that a few suitable-enough places give the new em economy sufficient support. Opposition in other places, whether mild or severe, would then be quickly overwhelmed by very rapid growth in those few areas.

The degree of opposition and resistance to ems may depend on how much humans resent the world of ems being dominated by scans of particular ethnicities or other subgroups of humans. Such resentment might be decreased if a wider range of humans were scanned and able to try out effectively for em roles.

The earliest em cities and virtual realities are probably crude and unreliable, leading to harsher and more dangerous lives, just as earlier periods of the farming and industrial eras were harsher and less pleasant in many ways than later phases. This may lead to em stories celebrating early pioneers, to a concrete sense of progress within the

em civilization, and to a sense of meaning for em lives within an advancing civilization.

How each era sees prior eras has often been disproportionally influenced by the transitional period just before each era. For example, our standard image today of pre-farming societies is of transitional warring "tribal" societies, and not of the typical more peaceful and isolated forager bands. Similarly, some see classical music as typical "pre-modern" music, even though it arose recently and is not much like most farming-era music.

Similarly, em images of our industrial era may be dominated by images from the few years just before ems came to dominate the world. Such images may focus on how the rest of the world treated the expensive and awkward early ems.

ENABLING TECHNOLOGIES

The pace of change in an em transition depends on which of the following three supporting technologies is ready last: (1) sufficiently fast and cheap computers, (2) sufficiently detailed, fast, and cheap brain scans, or (3) sufficiently detailed and accurate models of brain cells.

If cheap enough computers are the last to be ready, the wide and uniform access to computers and their predictable progress makes the transition to the em era smooth, decentralized, and well anticipated. The analysis of this book is then quite appropriate. There might be many years between when the first emulations are created, for perhaps billions of dollars each, and when emulations can be made for a million dollars or less, so that ems can replace human workers in large numbers. The first ems might be created mainly for research purposes, or as vanity projects of billionaires. Because of their big headstart, such early ems may have some first-mover advantages later on when ems are common.

This scenario might give humans many years of warning in which to adapt to and prepare for the em-dominated world. Anticipating this transition, human workers seeking to avoid harm could try to move their wealth early from an ability to earn wages into other forms of wealth likely to retain value past the transition, such as stocks, patents, or real estate. Even a smooth anticipated transition could be sudden by historical standards, however. In just a few years ems might go from being a small niche product to dominating a new economy growing much faster than the old one.

During the early industrial revolution, new industries grew quickly and rewarded their investors well relative to old industries such as farming. Investors then could have used financial mechanisms such as stocks and bonds to diversify and insure themselves against this risk. However, the rich nobility mostly did not do this, and as a result declined greatly in wealth and social influence (Ventura and Voth 2015). Perhaps humans will learn a lesson from this example and diversify their assets more successfully in the em transition.

If scans are the last technology to be ready, then the em transition becomes anticipated but more centralized. Improvements in scanning tend to follow a trend, and to be somewhat predictable given resources invested. As a result, when the time is right, large consortiums will likely form to fund efforts to scan the first ems. The first consortium to create a useable em would gain profits from pricing the first em products well above marginal cost.

Consortium profits may continue somewhat after the point that a second coalition succeeds in em creation, because of first mover advantages or cooperation among leading consortiums. The first em clans, firms, and cities in the new em economy might also gain first mover advantages. Having fewer such big winners would make for less diversity in the subsequent em era.

Governments may back some consortiums, while other consortiums may be profit-seeking ventures. Those seeking to minimize risk because of uncertainty about which consortiums will win should try to invest in as many consortiums as are open to investors. Unfortunately, government-based consortiums may not be open to all investors.

The most disruptive transition comes if brain cell modeling is the last technology to be ready. Not only might the first group to develop good enough brain cell models have substantial market power immediately after the transition, that market power might last longer if the secret to effective cell emulation were obscure and hard for competing groups to discover. Worse, the appearance of ems might be a surprise, creating a smaller more-concentrated winning coalition of investors, and even less diversity in the subsequent em era. After all, it tends to be harder to guess progress in cell modeling; until you have a good enough model, you may not know how close your model is to success. The later this cell modeling breakthrough appears, the bigger and faster a burst of change results, because the other required technologies are further developed and hence cheaper.

In a tamer modeling-last scenario, progress in cell modeling might still be the last step, but a relatively easy and quick step that is mostly anticipated. Cell models might be mostly ready, but await full-scale scans and computers before the last steps of model adjusting and debugging can be completed. If it can be anticipated that these last steps will require only modest resources, and many competing teams are able to complete them, this scenario could lead to a relatively smooth, decentralized, and anticipated transition.

In sum, we can anticipate many elements of the transition to an em world, but most of them don't much influence the resulting em world.

ALIENS

Even though the universe is almost 13 billion years old, everything we've seen outside Earth looks completely dead. We continue to have great success in explaining what we see by assuming that everything outside Earth has always been completely dead. If there are any civilizations out there more advanced than us, they have not yet made a noticeable difference to anything we can see.

This seems puzzling, as we can see quite a lot. There are roughly a trillion trillion planets in the visible universe. It seems hard to believe that Earth houses the very first advanced civilization in all this.

To guess what very advanced aliens might look like, and so where we might look for signs of them, it is natural to try to rely on guesses about what our distant descendants may look like. Because of this, many have asked me what the forecasts in this book suggest about what our distant descendants may look like.

Unfortunately, the forecasts in this book say little about this fascinating and important topic. To usefully guess what very advanced aliens may look like, we'd need to say something about what our descendants may look like in an objective million or billion years. But the em era may plausibly last only a year or two in objective time, after which it is likely to be supplanted by yet another era, as different from the em era as it is from our time.

As our descendants will likely pass through a great many distinct eras in the next millions or billions of years, knowing what the next era may look like doesn't obviously tell us substantially more about what our very distant descendants may look like than knowing current or past eras. Figuring out the next era is a good first step down that important road, but it still remains a long road. I have elsewhere considered what our theories say about the appearance of our very distant descendants, but those analyses have little to do with the subject of this book (Hanson 2008a).

CHAPTER 29

Choices

EVALUATION

ow that we have spent most of this book gaining a better idea of what a future em world might look like, we can start to ask: is this a good or a bad scenario? Would we want to encourage or discourage having this world replace our world? What small changes might make this world better?

The em world almost surely gives itself a positive overall evaluation, at least implicitly. In most all societies most everyone assumes that they live in a reasonable society whose members have lives worth living. If asked to explicitly evaluate other societies, they are likely to find them wanting compared with their own. Even so, they will have some directions in which they'd like to change their society, to improve it.

Many people just don't care much about the non-immediate future, making their evaluation of the em era very simple; it is a big zero to them no matter how it plays out. Others care mainly about the very distant future, so the em era mainly matters to them via how it might influence the many ages that will follow long afterward. But alas that topic is beyond the scope of this book. So let us consider now how we might evaluate the em era itself, if we cared about it.

Our evaluation of the em era depends, of course, on the criteria we use. One simple option is to use the usual intuitive criteria that most people seem to use when they verbally evaluate a distant future. A recent study of people evaluating different possible futures for 2050 found that their main consideration or concern was how warm and moral future people would be (Bain et al. 2013).

That is, most people surveyed cared little about the future of population, pleasure, wealth, poverty, freedom, suicide, terrorism, crime, poverty, homelessness, disease, skills, laziness, or progress in science and technology. They cared a bit more about future self-discipline, humility, respect for tradition, equality, meaning in life, and protection of the environment. But mostly people cared about future benevolence: how honest, sincere, warm, caring, and friendly future people would be.

This pattern of responses makes sense if people tend to think about the far future abstractly, and if abstract modes of thinking function in part to help us make good social impressions about our moral attitudes (Liberman and Trope 2008; Hanson 2009; Torelli and Kaikati 2009). By emphasizing if future folks follow good social norms, we show our respect for those norms.

Em clans with reputations to protect will work to ensure the trust-worthiness and reliability of clan members, and em teams will often work to ensure strong warm emotional bonds between team members. This suggests that an em future may rate relatively highly on this key criterion of general benevolence. Ems being poorer also suggests that they are more benevolent. Today people with a lower social class tend to act more ethically, except that they act less ethically when such behavior results in benefit to others (Dubois et al. 2015).

This em future may rate poorly, however, on the criteria of affirming our local political and moral values, that is, those that dominate during our time and place in the industrial era. As discussed in Chapter 26, Farmer-Like section, ems are likely to return to more farmer-like values, compared with the more forager-like values popular today. The em world is especially likely to be rated poorly by those who feel that civilization was a mistake, and that humanity was better off as simple farmers or foragers (Zerzan 2005). After all, the em world may plausibly be considered as "civilization version 3.0," after the farming and industrial versions. Being a competitive world, the em future may also rate low on the criteria of preventing values

from changing further in the eras that follow this em era. I discuss the evaluation of em morality changes more in Chapter 30, Conclusion section.

Consider the issue of diversity. How well the em world rates on diversity depends a lot on what kinds of diversity matter. On the one hand, most ems may descend from only a few hundred or fewer humans who are quite unusual, because they are unusually productive. Ems may also be selected quite non-uniformly from today's regions, ethnicities, religions, personalities, and genders. The entire non-human biosphere may be neglected and then mostly displaced in the late em era. On the other hand, compared with ordinary humans today, descendants of those initial ems may radiate out and populate a much larger space of possible bodies, ways of living, topics of interest, and mental styles and capacities.

What if we look instead at the virtues that have been admired in most eras and cultures, such as intelligence, insight, benevolence, loyalty, determination, etc.? Here the em world can look very good. Ems are strongly selected for their impressive productivity, which tends to correlate with most of these virtues. In this sense, the em world is packed full of people who are more virtuous than most people so far have ever met in a lifetime.

Another way to evaluate the em world is in terms of existential risk, that is, the chance of a disaster so big that civilization is destroyed and can never rise again. Such a disaster arguably harms not only everyone living in the world at the time, but also everyone who might have lived afterward, until either a similar disaster which would have happened later, or the end of the universe. This is plausibly a *very* large harm.

If we compare an em era with a continuation of the industrial era without ems, the em civilization quickly has vastly more economic power, and so all else equal is better able to withstand physical disasters such as earthquakes, asteroids, or volcanoes, events whose size and chances aren't much influenced by the existence of ems. The em era might induce more biological disasters such as pandemics, chemical pollution, or global warming, but it seems vastly better able to allow civilization to survive such problems.

The ability of an em civilization to withstand war or other unspecified social collapses depends on the size of the smallest unit of industrial production able to restart em civilization after a severe collapse. The bigger the collapse, the smaller are the units remaining afterward. With ems this unit is no larger than an em city, and with nanotech factories it might be as small as a few kilograms, which would make ems *very* hard to exterminate.

Some disasters, such as rogue AI, may only be possible when relevant technologies reach a particular level. In this case we want to compare scenarios with the same technology levels, but reached via different paths. For example, we might compare reaching human level non-em AI via a path that contains ems, or via a longer continuation of the industrial era. In this case we might note that fast ems could directly monitor and react to an AI much more quickly than could biological humans.

Some will want to evaluate an em-dominated future primarily in terms of its outcomes for the biological humans who choose not to become ems. Measured in simple consumption terms, humans in the em world are likely to do very well for a few years, although longer-term outcomes hinge on unknowns about instabilities of the em civilization, and about the eras that may follow the em era. To the extent that relative status is important, however, humans fare worse, as they are no longer the dominant group. But if biological humans see ems as human enough that they become jealous of em status, perhaps ems are human enough to count for value as well.

It is important to realize that people today have a choice about who in the em world to consider as their descendants, or to care about. We today may choose to consider only biological humans as descendants, or we can choose to include ems as well. Some people may even see non-em-based AI software as their descendants (Moravec 1988). The universe doesn't tell us what aspects of future creatures we must care about; that is up to us to decide.

How will non-human biological nature fare in an em world? The long-run prospects for the natural world look poor. While the em economy at first focuses on a few dense cities, its rapid growth rate suggests that it and its descendant economies could fill the Earth within a few objective decades. While charities may pay to keep a few small nature preserves, the resources available for such efforts are likely be small compared with the economic pressures to use available resources to support the growing economy.

The em world outcome might look terrible on hedonistic utilitarian criteria if most ems ended up being non-conscious, in the sense of not having any integrated experiences. As discussed in Chapter 4, Emulations section, this seems quite unlikely in the early em era, but this topic is beyond the scope of this book.

Setting that aside, the em future can look pretty good in terms of utilitarian evaluation criteria, such as how many people have how much happiness, meaning, or satisfaction of their preferences. This is because the em world can hold many billions and perhaps trillions of human-like creatures, many of whom experience subjective years in the time that ordinary humans experience a subjective day. So if the life of an em counts even a small fraction as much as does a typical life today, then the fact that there are so many ems could make for a big increase in total happiness and meaning relative to our world today.

QUALITY OF LIFE

In fact, em lives do plausibly have a value that is at least a substantial fraction of the value of our lives today.

This is in part because societies don't usually make that much difference to individual satisfaction. Anthropologists have long known that humans are quite plastic culturally, in that we can accept and be comfortable with a wide range of norms and practices. For example, today even people who can't move their bodies at all are reasonably happy. Today, happiness varies by four times as much within nations as it does between nations, and 95 percent of national differences in happiness are explained by income, lifespans, corruption, friendship rates, and a sense of freedom (Helliwell et al. 2013). Even if ems have low income by some measures, they could still have long lives, much freedom, strong friends, and low corruption. In fact, ems might have deeper connections to friends and lovers than we do.

In addition, we have several concrete reasons to expect ems to be happy, and to find meaning in their lives. First, em clans can share the experiences of clan members to better learn what that clan likes. Because of this, ems know themselves much better than we do today, and they can use this self-knowledge to increase their comfort, satisfaction, meaning, and happiness. Second, the em world has beautiful, spacious, luxurious entertainment and surroundings, and ems needn't have any sickness, pain, hunger, or grime. Furthermore, em entertainment and surroundings can be tailored specifically for particular clans. The clan of George, for example, can afford to have movies and interior decorations designed specifically to the taste of George.

Third, ems are strongly selected from among ordinary humans for their high work productivity. As discussed in Chapter 13, Motivation section, today, the people who are more productive, as indicated by their higher wages, also tend to be happier and have more meaning, and these correlations do not seem to be entirely a result of money causing happiness and meaning. It seems that happiness and meaning also cause productivity, and that common factors cause both. This weakly suggests that ems will tend to be happier and have more meaning than people today, although it seems we can predict more meaning with a bit more confidence than more happiness.

This suggestion is strengthened by the fact that pretty much all of the specific factors that today correlate with happiness and meaning also correlate with work productivity, even controlling for many other such factors. For example, people today tend to be both happier and more productive when they have jobs, autonomy at work, health, beauty, money, marriage, religion, intelligence, extroversion, conscientiousness, agreeableness, and non-neuroticism (Myers and Diener 1995; Lykken and Tellegen 1996; Steen 1996; Nguyen et al. 2003; Barrick 2005; Roberts et al. 2007; Sutin et al. 2009; Erdogan et al. 2012; Diener 2013; Ali et al. 2013; Stutzer and Frey 2013).

Of course correlation isn't causation, and there is much we don't understand here. Even so, the consistency of the relationships here gives us much reason to hope that more productive ems may on average be happier and have more meaning than people today. Yes, perhaps we enjoy work productivity because it raises our relative status,

and by definition relative status can't rise for everyone. But even in that case, relative status can't fall overall either, to hurt us overall.

What about the fact that ems work long hours? On the negative side, compared with other activities people who are interrupted at work (or while commuting or doing chores) for a survey report the lowest moods, more often say that they would rather be doing something else, and more often (20 percent of the time) have a dominant emotion that is negative. Workers report being happier on the weekend (Miner et al. 2005; Kahneman and Krueger 2006; Bryson and MacKerron 2015; Helliwell and Wang 2015).

On the positive side, however, work activities seem to be associated with average activation and involvement, over 80 percent of us today report that we are overall satisfied with our jobs, and over 60 percent report that our jobs are meaningful in making the world a better place (Hektner et al. 2007; Society for Human Resource Management 2012). Returning to work after an injury boosts life satisfaction, as does doing extra work after officially retiring (Vestling et al. 2003). Work adds to our life satisfaction via job and career satisfaction, coworker relations, power, prestige, and prospects for growth (Erdogan et al. 2012). Most people today who are very respected and envied work long hours, and very much enjoy their lives.

Ems may be punished more at work, have to face more objective performance evaluations, and feel more stress from small margins between wages and living expenses. Even so, ems are selected for being relatively comfortable with such lives, and their virtual worlds can cheaply provide great "material" comfort both on and off the job. Also, much life meaning can be found in the strong bonds ems feel with clans, teams, professions, and cities, in their excellent and unprecedented abilities, and in the great accomplishments these abilities will enable.

Some fear that a competitive em world that emphasizes work has no fun or play, and hence no laughter, music, teasing, banter, stories, sports, and so on. But play is a robust feature of many animals, including marsupials, birds, turtles, lizards, fish, and invertebrates. It evolved independently several times, and it continued during the competitive foraging and farming worlds.

Animals that play tend to have active lifestyles, sufficient food, and flexible behaviors. Carnivores and scavengers play with objects, while animals that escape predation and move in three dimensions play with movement. Social animals do play fighting and chasing, and humans play at even more social activities. Human play feels pleasurable and like it has no purpose. Play is done in safe environments, includes distinctive and wider ranging behaviors, and has cues like laughter to signal that it continues after possible harm.

Juvenile animals spend 2 to 15 percent of their energy on play, even though it can hurt them, and make them more vulnerable to predators. Play must have big robust advantages to outweigh such costs. Play plausibly helps animals to learn and practice the usual ways, and to discover new ways. In social animals, play can also signal loyalty, develop trust and coordinate, and establish status (Burghardt 2006; Henig 2008).

We humans have "neotony," which extends youthful features and behaviors, including play, throughout our lifetime. For example, while older women laugh a bit less than younger women, older men laugh just as often (Martin and Kuiper 1999). As the many ancient advantages of play should continue for ems, ems should continue to play.

Some argue that em mind tweaks would quickly eliminate sexuality, have workers strongly focused on their task at hand with far less mind wandering, and have workers subject to bosses with direct control over their minds' pain and pleasure centers. Even if such ems are conscious, it is claimed, they are "utterly pointless" with little or no moral value because "they are not doing anything interesting with their consciousness" (Alexander 2016). This seems to me to put far too much moral weight on sexuality and frequent mind wandering, and as discussed on Chapter 20, Slavery section, harsh treatment doesn't seem to help much with productivity in modern jobs.

POLICY

This book has focused on elaborating a baseline em scenario, with scenario features chosen to be relatively likely, when such options are available, and otherwise with features chosen to be simple and easier to analyze. If this were actually our most likely future, what policies should we prefer, in order to make the em world a *better* future?

First note that we should expect this policy task to be very challenging. For a comparison, imagine that someone in the year 1000AD had been able to infer the basic outlines of our industrial world. Even accomplishing that difficult task might not tell them enough to offer useful advice on industrial world policy, or on what people in 1000AD could do to push industrial-era policy in a good direction.

Second, note that in the absence of a strong world government, we have only very limited abilities to coordinate to change the future. Even on topics like climate change, with strong expert consensus on the existence of the problem and plausible solutions, the world seems incapable of coordinating to implement those solutions. This suggests that we focus our policy efforts on small changes that are feasible, instead of big changes that are not. So, what small feasible changes to this scenario could make for a better em world?

Speeding the development of cell modeling abilities, so that such modeling is not the last required technology to be ready, could both advance this scenario, and minimize disruptions from an overly rapid transition to an em economy. Also, transition risks to ordinary humans might be reduced by encouraging the creation and use of international diversified investment funds of stocks and real estate, and also of "em bonds" that pay only if an em world appears. Allowing widespread investments in new em ventures, instead of outlawing such ventures or investments, would also help by allowing everyone to gain from the growth of the new em economy.

If the em world is nearly inevitable, then it is probably better if literary and public conversations frame it as something to be accepted, and perhaps nudged into preferred directions, instead of as something to be aggressively resisted.

If the em world is not inevitable, policy choices become more complex. While there would be plenty of advanced warning that an em world may be coming, such warnings might not be able to predict exactly when. The transition to an em world could be quite rapid, while most organizations capable of enacting substantial global-scale policies act only after long delays.

During the early transition, it could help to encourage ems to share their financial, legal, and political institutions with ordinary humans as deeply as possible for as long as possible, to reduce later temptations to expropriate human property. To reduce distrust arising from feelings of an illicit domination of the em world by descendants of particular subgroups of ordinary humans, it could also help if a wide diversity of people were scanned early and tested for suitability as em workers. It might also help if initial scanning to create ems was in part a gift from the rest of humanity, rather than having been resisted by humanity. This might help ems to later feel gratitude and obligation toward biologicial humans, instead of hostility and resentment. An early period of humans enslaving ems would set an especially bad precedent.

Early events may also influence the number of em cities and their distances from each other. If city scale economies allow it, then having only one em city or a few close cities would probably be most efficient, except that this might risk a single bad political regime mismanaging the entire em world. If it is important enough to avoid such a centralized bad political outcome, then political and economic competition between a few sufficiently separated cities might be better. Some say a lack of centralized government is why the industrial revolution first appeared in Europe, and not in the more technically advanced but more centralized China.

If a thousand or fewer em clans end up dominating the em economy, then almost all ordinary humans hoping to found successful em clans face an overwhelming chance of failure. Ordinary humans or early em clans could insure against this risk by making formal agreements to have clans that succeed share their gains with clans who do not. While interest in such insurance might signal a lack of confidence in one's future prospects, given these long odds, few clans could reasonably have much confidence of success. It might be good to encourage such clan success insurance to reduce clan risk.

Basic economic theory suggests a number of possible "market failures," that is, common ways in which economies tend to be inefficient. Without some reason to think otherwise, we should suspect that em economies will be inefficient in these ways.

For example, the fact that others lose status when we gain status suggests that too much effort is put into raising one's status at the expense of the status of others. As a result, ems may run too fast, and invest too much in impressive early life achievements. The fact that others gain when we add to urban activity density suggests that cities tend to not be built densely enough. As a result, local builders in em cities may make design choices resulting in an excessively low population density. Signaling issues suggest that the terms of private insurance and law choices will slant too far toward the preferences of cheap-to-serve customers. Product differentiation issues suggest tendencies toward too much product variety and spatial market segmentation. So em workers may have overly varied skill specializations. Quality choice issues suggest that the quality of the highest quality products is not high enough. So ems may invest too little in the quality of their highest quality workers (Shy 1996).

In general, would-be early settlers of new territories, whether these territories are parts of physical space or abstract product or labor markets, have incentives to spend too much on their early colonization efforts, unless there are big ways in which these first-movers benefit others, such as via innovation. This suggests that ems may spend too much on settling new physical territories, or on new product and labor-market territories. In general, the ability to make strategic commitments tends to result in excess costs from commitments. This suggests that negotiations between clans forming teams and firms may suffer costs from excess strategic commitments.

It would be good for policy actions to counter all these likely market failures, although it is not clear how this can be done.

Ems might spend too much time in work, relative to leisure, because of signaling pressures. More leisure could be encouraged by tying taxes to income, rather than to em speed, that is, taxing work but not leisure.

Some of us should spend some effort to analyze and anticipate the em world, as I have attempted in this book. Others should track related developments to gain more advanced warnings about when a transition to an em economy may occur, and about the places and industries where that transition may be initially concentrated.

Other policy options are to subsidize the development of related technologies to speed the arrival of this transition, and to subsidize its smoothness, equality, or transparency to reduce disruptions and inequalities in that transition. One might also subsidize or provide insurance against these variations. A smooth transition might be encouraged via speeding the development of scanning and cell modeling relative to computer power.

This section has only scratched the surface of possible relevant policy analysis. But it is very hard to analyze policy for a world about which one knows almost nothing. That is why positive analysis, of likely outcomes if we do nothing special, took first priority in this book.

CHARITY

The previous section considered the policies that we might together agree are good for society overall. This section considers what an individual might do personally to promote good policy regarding an em world.

Most of the usual ways to promote good policy today continue to apply. One might strive to become influential in a relevant world of policy, business, or technology. One might personally work to identify good policies and then advocate for them. One might also try to create groups of like-minded people organized specifically around the idea of identifying and advocating for good em policies. Or, as today few are interested in em policy, it might make more sense to join existing groups defined around other related themes, and encourage those groups to direct more of their efforts toward identifying and advocating good em policy.

Those still young enough to be able to start or change careers might consider not immediately focusing on related areas of em technology, business, policy analysis, or advocacy. Such people might instead learn to acquire more general skills, while practicing mostly on other topics. They might then focus more on em-related areas as their skills increased and as opportunities arose.

While Bill and Melinda Gates are not medical experts, they have nevertheless had a big impact on medical research. Similarly, the people most interested in analyzing and promoting good em policy may well not be the people whose personal abilities and work preferences are best suited to personally and directly working on em technology, business, policy analysis, or advocacy. Such people might instead want to do other types of work better suited to their abilities and preferences, and then donate money to specialists. However, such people need to do enough research to identify plausibly expert and well-motivated specialists, and to sufficiently monitor their activities to confirm that these specialists deserve funding.

Given that the em transition is probably many decades away, an especially attractive alternative is to save now to help later. That is, invest time and energy now in the usual ways, to enable you to spend time and money later on charity. As investment rates of return seem to have been consistently higher than economic growth rates, this strategy allows one to have a proportionally larger influence later than one could have now.

By first accumulating assets, one can retain many options regarding future action. For example, one can wait to decide between becoming personally involved in policy analysis and advocacy, or donating money to support other policy specialists. Also, as we learn more over time about the em world and its issues, we should be able to better direct our aid to be more effective. We might even later switch to focusing on non-em causes, if the em scenario comes to seem less likely or important than it once did.

Because this strategy allows one to retain many options about how to spend one's money later, it can help many future causes, not just those dealing with an em world. Some have criticized this strategy, saying that increasing wealth and peace means that the future will have far fewer worthy causes and people worth helping. However, if an em world is coming, then wealth per em will fall greatly, making it likely that there will then be plenty of deserving creatures in need of help.

If you expect that the em transition may occur after you are dead, you might also consider saving to donate money to others after you die. In this case, it becomes harder to arrange for the monitoring of the recipients of your donations, to ensure that they are doing what you would want. And in addition our society has placed substantial legal barriers that make it hard to control your funds after your death. Even so, this might still be the best available strategy.

In sum, there are many ways for individuals to work to help to deal with the possible coming of an em world.

SUCCESS

What if you want to know, not how to help create a better em world, but how to help you and your associates personally succeed in this new world?

To avoid the worst possible outcomes, expect all of your abilities to earn wages as a human to quickly disappear after an em transition. Well before this happens, seek out substitute sources of income. Accumulate and diversify a financial portfolio of assets likely to retain value, such as stocks, real estate, and intellectual property. Also accumulate and diversify a social portfolio of supports and connections. Both your financial and social assets should be tied to communities that are likely to thrive or at least survive in an em world. Try to be included in geographic regions, nations, professions, standards, etc., that are likely to cooperate with and add value to this new world, and avoid those that may pick fights with it.

If, relative to other investors, you have a comparative expertise in analyzing investments, then you might seek and invest in underpriced em-related assets. These are assets expected to be worth a lot in an em world, but where that consideration is not fully reflected in the current price. For example, real estate near likely em city locations is currently underpriced. However, one should set a high bar for whether one is expert enough; the vast majority of financial traders today lose because they overconfidently see themselves as sufficiently expert.

As successful clans collect a big fraction of the gains in the em world, you should consider the possibility that you (or your children or grandchildren) might start one of these few most copied em clans. Realizing that the odds are greatly against you, you should be willing to take great risks to achieve this, via showing high and reliable

productivity and flexibility in tasks and environments most like those of the em world. You should focus on the very high tail of your possible success distribution; the rest of the distribution makes much less difference. Go very big or go home.

If you or your associates (such as descendants) will be old at the time of the em transition, then try to have them be very productive and at the peak of their career ability, and be productive at tasks where a great many customers could be quickly served by ems doing that task. This would give you the best chance to be one of the very first highly copied ems. If you might be dead by the time of the em transition, you might consider becoming a cryonics customer, and then declaring your wish to be revived as an em when this becomes technically possible.

In contrast, if you or your associates will be young at the time of the em transition, try to time their age to be the ideal age for new em scans during the early em era. Consider accepting the risks that come from destructive scanning. Before that age, have them collect visible indications of their general ability to learn useful skills and do valuable tasks. They should also show that they get along with people much like themselves, and that they value life and grit when life is hard and alien. Teach these virtues to your children and grandchildren. Such young people might then have a chance to become successful ems during the early em era, when a high value is placed on youthful flexibility.

To the extent that young em candidates prepare for specific jobs, have them prepare for the em jobs and professions that will be in the most demand in the em world, instead of the jobs that pay the most in our world. Remember that, compared with our world, em wages won't vary nearly as much with the intelligence or status associated with the job. Remember also that ems use fewer tools and supporting capital than do ordinary humans in comparable jobs just before the em transition.

In sum, to succeed in this new world, prepare to become what it needs.

CHAPTER 30

Finale

CRITICS

Over 150 readers have commented on previous drafts of this book. Here are very quick summaries of some of their most common criticisms. Most individual views are of course subtler than these summaries can be.

If we include those who declined to read my draft, the most common complaint is probably "who cares?" Many just can't see why they should want to know much detail about the lives of people who are not they, their children, or grandchildren. While many readers seem interested in the lives of past people who were not personally their ancestors, perhaps such readers make up only a small fraction of the population.

Other readers doubt that one can ever estimate the social consequences of technologies decades in advance. It is not so much that these readers have specific complaints about my analyses. Instead, they have a general skepticism that makes them uninterested in considering specific analyses. Many see human behavior as intrinsically inscrutable, and many doubt that social science exists as a source of reliable insight. A few are offended by the very idea of estimating social outcomes, as they see this as denying our free will and ability to choose our futures.

A more specific version of this sort of criticism accepts that it is often possible for us to foresee social consequences in worlds like ours, but then says that it is impossible to foresee the social behaviors of creatures substantially smarter than us. So, they reason, we today cannot see past the future point in time when typical descendants become smarter than we are today, and ems are effectively smarter than us in several ways. This view suggests that social scientists today are much less able to predict the behavior of smarter people, or of people who are smarter than the typical social scientist. That seems incorrect to me.

A related view sees the world I depict as too understandable and recognizable to be plausible. They expect the real future to seem so crazy to us that any future depiction that doesn't seem almost intolerably crazy can't be true enough to be useful.

Still other readers accept my social analysis, but are disappointed that I consider only the next great era, and not the eras that may follow it. These readers mainly care about the long-term future. They reject my argument that understanding the em era is a good first step to understanding the eras that may follow it. They prefer other ways to analyze the distant future, ways that depend little on the specifics of what will happen between now and then. I am more skeptical about our ability to foresee distant endpoints without at least outlining the paths between here and there.

Many doubt that brain emulations will be our next huge technology change, and aren't interested in analyses of the consequences of any big change except the one they personally consider most likely or interesting. Many of these people expect some other form of artificial intelligence to achieve broad human level abilities before brain emulations appear. I think that past rates of progress there suggest that at previous rates it will take two to four centuries to achieve broad human level abilities via this route. These critics often point to exciting recent developments, such as advances in "deep learning," that they think make prior trends irrelevant.

More generally, some critics fault me for insufficiently crediting new trends that they expect will soon revolutionize society, even if we don't yet see strong supporting evidence of these trends. Such revolutions include robots taking most jobs, local sourcing replacing mass production, small firms replacing big ones, worker cooperatives replacing for-profits, ability tests replacing school degrees, blockchains displacing traditional banks, and 3D printers replacing manufacturing plants. I will believe these trends may actually be revolutionary when I more clearly see that they are actually happening at a substantial scale.

A vocal minority of critics see economics as a fundamentally mistaken social science, and thus usually wrong. While such critics can see the point of estimating social consequences using other social sciences, they have little interest in economic analysis of anything. Some of these have more faith in political analysis.

Some critics take offense at my lack of taking offense. To them the em world has many similarities with dystopian future scenarios they hate. For example, it has less nature, less forager-like human lives, larger firms, more inequality of some sorts, and continued capitalism. A moral person couldn't help but express outrage at this, and my failure to do so shows my great moral inadequacy.

Finally, some critics fault me for neglecting the "unknown unknowns." That is, they say my forecasts don't sufficiently account for unforeseen changes and innovations that will arise later. Apparently they think one should just say, "The future will be strange," and resist the urge to add more detail, except perhaps for telling strange vivid stories that make no claims of accuracy or analysis. To me, this view seems needlessly pessimistic regarding our abilities to do useful analysis. Yes, efforts like this book can be badly mistaken, in part due to overconfidence. Even so, we should try.

In sum, even though many critics have reasonable points, I still think the analysis in this book was worth the effort.

CONCLUSION

Parents sometimes disown their children, on the grounds that those children have betrayed key parental values. If parents have the sort of values that children could deeply betray, it does make sense for parents to watch out for such betrayal, and to be ready if needed to adopt extreme responses, such as disowning their children.

But surely parents who feel inclined to disown their children should be encouraged to study those children carefully before doing this. For example, parents considering whether to disown their child for working for a cigarette manufacturer, or for refusing to fight in a war for their nation, should wonder to what extent anti-smoking or patriotism really are their core values, as opposed to merely revisable opinions in support of other more-core values. Such parents would be wise to study the lives and opinions of their children in some detail before choosing to disown them.

When they have lived as neighbors, foragers have often strongly criticized farmer culture, and farmers have often strongly criticized industrial culture. Surely many of these people have been tempted to disown descendants who adopt these despised new ways. In addition, many of your ancestors would be tempted to disown you, if they were told many things about you. While they'd be pleased and impressed by many of your features, other things about you might horrify them.

So, should your forager or farmer ancestors have disowned you? While such disowning might have held them true to some core values, I expect that you would have advised them to consider your life and views carefully, in some detail, before choosing to disown you. Disowning should not be done casually.

The analysis in this book suggests that lives in the next great era may be as different from our lives as our lives are from farmers' lives, or farmers' lives are from foragers' lives. Many readers of this book, living industrial-era lives and sharing industrial-era values, may be disturbed to see a forecast of em era descendants with choices and lifestyles that appear to reject many of the values that they hold dear. Such readers may be tempted to fight to prevent the em future, perhaps preferring a continuation of the industrial era. Such readers may be correct that rejecting the em future holds them true to their core values.

But I advise such readers to first try hard to see this new era in some detail from the point of view of its typical residents. See what they enjoy and what fills them with pride, and listen to their criticisms of your era and values. This book has been designed in part to assist you in such a soul-searching examination. If after reading this book, you still feel compelled to disown your em descendants, I cannot say you are wrong. My job, first and foremost, has been to help you see your descendants clearly, warts and all.

REFERENCES

Abdollahian, Mark, and Kyungkook Kang. 2008. "In Search of Structure: The Nonlinear Dynamics of Power Transitions." *International Interactions*, 34(4): 333–357.

Acemoglu, Daron, Philippe Aghion, Claire Lelarge, John Van Reenen, and Fabrizio Zilibotti. 2007. "Technology, Information, and the Decentralization of the Firm." *Quarterly Journal of Economics* 122(4): 1759–1799.

Acemoglu, Daron, Suresh Naidu, Pascual Restrepo, and James Robinson. 2015. "Democracy, Redistribution, and Inequality" in Arkinson and Bourguignon, eds., *Handbook of Income Distribution*. Volume 2B. Elsevier.

Agarwal, Sumit, J. Bradford Jensen, and Ferdinando Monte. 2017. "The Geography of Consumption." NBER Working Paper No. 23616, July.

Aghion, Philippe, Yann Algan, Pierre Cahuc, and Andrei Shleifer. 2010. "Regulation and Distrust." *Quarterly Journal of Economics* 125(3): 1015–1049.

Ahlfeldt, Gabriel, Stephen Redding, Daniel Sturm, and Nikolaus Wolf. 2015. "The Economics of Density: Evidence from the Berlin Wall." *Econometrics* 83(6): 2127–2189.

Ahrend, Rudiger, Emily Farchy, Ioannis Kaplanis, and Alexander Lembcke. 2017. "What Makes Cities More Productive? Evidence From Five OECD Countries on the Role of Urban Governance." *Journal of Regional Science* 57(3): 385–410.

Albright, Richard. 2002. "What Can Past Technology Forecasts Tell Us about the Future?" *Technological Forecasting and Social Change* 69: 443–464.

Alesina, Alberto, Silvia Ardagna, Giuseppe Nicoletti, and Fabio Schiantarelli. 2005. "Regulation and Investment." *Journal of the European Economic Association* 3(4): 791–825.

Alesina, Alberto, and Paola Giuliano. 2014. "Family Ties." In *Handbook of Economic Growth 2A*, 177–216, edited by Philippe Aghion and Steven N. Durlauf. Amsterdam: North Holland.

Alesina, Alberto, Paola Giuliano, and Nathan Nunn. 2013. "On the Origins of Gender Roles: Women and the Plough." *Quarterly Journal of Economics* 128(2): 469–530.

Alexander, Scott. 2016. "Book Review: Age of Em." *Slate Star Codex*, May 28. http://slatestarcodex.com/2016/05/28/book-review-age-of-em/

Ali, Afia, Gareth Ambler, Andre Strydom, Dheeraj Rai, Claudia Cooper, Sally McManus, Scott Weich, H. Meltzer, Simon Dein, and Angela Hassiotis. 2013. "The Relationship between Happiness and Intelligent Quotient: The Contribution of Socio-economic and Clinical Factors." *Psychological Medicine* 43(6): 1303–1312.

Allen, Douglas, and Yoram Barzel. 2011. "The Evolution of Criminal Law and Police during the Pre-modern Era." *Journal of Law, Economics, and Organization* 27(3): 540–567.

Almeida, Heitor, and Daniel Ferriera. 2002. "Democracy and the Variability of Economic Performance." *Economics and Politics* 14(3): 225–257.

Alston, Julian, Matthew Andersen, Jennifer James, and Philip Pardey. 2011. "The Economic Returns to U.S. Public Agricultural Research." *American Journal of Agricultural Economics* 93(5): 1257–1277.

Alstott, Jeff. 2013. "Will We Hit a Wall? Forecasting Bottlenecks to Whole Brain Emulation Development." *Journal of Artificial General Intelligence* 4(3): 153–163.

Al-Ubaydli, Omar, Garett Jones, and Jaap Weel. 2013. "Patience, cognitive skill, and coordination in the repeated stag hunt." *Journal of Neuroscience, Psychology, and Economics* 6(2), 71–96.

Alvanchi, Amin, SangHyun Lee, and Simaan AbouRizk. 2012. "Dynamics of Working Hours in Construction." *Journal of Construction Engineering and Management* 138(1): 66–77.

Alwin, Duane, and Jon Krosnick. 1991. "Aging, Cohorts, and the Stability of Sociopolitical Orientations Over the Life Span." *American Journal of Sociology* 97(1): 169–195.

Anderson, David. 1999. "The Aggregate Burden of Crime." *Journal of Law and Economics* 42(2): 611–642.

Angier, Natalie. 2005. "Almost Before We Spoke, We Swore." *New York Times*, September 20.

Antonakis, John, Robert House, and Dean Simonton. 2017. "Can Super Smart Leaders Suffer From too Much of a Good Thing? The Curvilinear Effect of Intelligence on Perceived Leadership Behavior." *Journal of Applied Psychology* 102(7): 1003–1021.

Anwar, Shamena, Patrick Bayer, and Randi Hjalmarsson. 2014. "The Role of Age in Jury Selection and Trial Outcomes." *Journal of Law and Economics* 57(4): 1001–1030.

Aral, Sinan, Erik Brynjolfsson, and Marshall Van Alstyne. 2007. "Information, Technology and Information Worker Productivity: Task Level Evidence." NBER Working Paper No. 13172, June.

Aral, Sinan, and Dylan Walker. 2012. "Identifying Influential and Susceptible Members of Social Networks." *Science* 337(6092): 337–341.

Armstrong, Stuart, and Kaj Sotala. 2012. "How We're Predicting AI—or Failing to." In *Beyond AI: Artificial Dreams*, edited by J. Romportl, P. Ircing, E. Zackova, M. Polak, and R. Schuster, 52–75. Pilsen: University of West Bohemia.

Arnfield, A. John. 2003. "Two Decades of Urban Climate Research: A Review of Turbulence, Exchanges of Energy and Water, and the Urban Heat Island." *International Journal of Climatology* 23: 1–26.

Arnott, Richard. 2004. "Does the Henry George Theorem Provide a Practical Guide to Optimal City Size?" *American Journal of Economics and Sociology* 63(5): 1057–1090.

Ashenfelter, Orley, Kirk Doran, and Bruce Schaller. 2010. "A Shred of Credible Evidence on the Long Run Elasticity of Labor Supply." *Economica* 77(308): 637–650.

Ashton, Michael, Kibeom Lee, Philip Vernon, and Kerry Jang. 2000. "Fluid Intelligence, Crystallized Intelligence, and the Openness/Intellect Factor." *Journal of Research in Personality* 34(2): 198–207.

Asker, John, Joan Farre-Mensa, and Alexander Ljungqvist. 2011. "Comparing the Investment Behavior of Public and Private Firms." NBER Working Paper No. 17394, September.

Asker, John, Joan Farre-Mensa, and Alexander Ljungqvist. 2015. "Corporate Investment and Stock Market Listing: A Puzzle?" *Review of Financial Studies* 28(2): 342–390.

Assiotis, Andreas, and Kevin Sylwester. 2015. "Does Law and Order Attenuate the Benefits of Democracy on Economic Growth?" *Economica* 82(328): 644–670.

Asturias, Jose, Sewon Hur, Timothy Kehoe, and Kim Ruhl. 2017. "Firm Entry and Exit and Aggregate Growth." NBER Working Paper No. 23202, February.

Atkinson, Quentin, and Harvey Whitehouse. 2011. "The Cultural Morphospace of Ritual Form: Examining Modes of Religiosity Cross-Culturally." *Evolution and Human Behavior* 32(1): 50–62.

Aucoin, Michael, and Richard Wassersug. 2006. "The Sexuality and Social Performance of Androgen-deprived (Castrated) Men Throughout History: Implications for Modern Day Cancer Patients." *Social Science and Medicine* 63: 3162–3173.

Axtell, Robert. 2001. "Zipf Distribution of US Firm Sizes." *Science* 293(5536): 1818–1820.

Babcock, Linda, Maria Recalde, Lise Vesterlund, and Laurie Weingart. 2017. "Gender Differences in Accepting and Receiving Requests for Tasks with Low Promotability" *American Economic Review* 107(3): 714–747

Baghestani, Hamid, and Michael Malcolm. 2014. "Marriage, Divorce and Economic Activity in the US: 1960–2008." *Applied Economics Letters* 21(8): 528–532.

Bahns, Angela, Christian Crandall, Omri Gillath, and Kristopher Preacher. 2017. "Similarity in relationships as niche construction: Choice, stability, and influence within dyads in a free choice environment." *Journal of Personality and Social Psychology*, 112(2): 329–355.

Bai, Yang, Laura Maruskin, Serena Chen, Amie Gordon, Jennifer Stellar, Galen McNeil, Kaiping Peng, and Dacher Keltner. 2017. "Awe, the diminished self, and collective engagement: Universals and cultural variations in the small self." *Journal of Personality and Social Psychology* 113(2): 185–209.

Bain, Paul, Matthew Hornsey, Renata Bongiorno, Yoshihisa Kashima, and Daniel Crimston. 2013. "Collective Futures: How Projections About the Future of Society Are Related to Actions and Attitudes Supporting Social Change." *Personality and Social Psychology Bulletin* 39(4): 523–539.

Baird, Benjamin, Jonathan Smallwood, Michael Mrazek, Julia Kam, Michael Franklin, and Jonathan Schooler. 2012. "Inspired by Distraction: Mind Wandering Facilitates Creative Incubation." *Psychological Science* 23(10): 1117–1122.

Banker, Rajiv, Seok-Young Lee, Gordon Potter, and Dhinu Srinivasan. 2000. "An Empirical Analysis of Continuing Improvements Following the Implementation of a Performance-based Compensation Plan." *Journal of Accounting and Economics* 30(3): 315–350.

Barberis, Nicholas. 2013. "Thirty Years of Prospect Theory in Economics: A Review and Assessment." *Journal of Economic Perspectives* 27(1): 173–196.

Barker, Eric. 2015a. "How To Be Compassionate: 3 Research-Backed Steps To A Happier Life." Barking Up The Wrong Tree blog. January 18. http://www.bakadesuyo.com/2015/01/how-to-be-compassionate.

Barker, Eric. 2015b. "A Navy SEAL Explains 8 Secrets to Grit and Resilience." Barking Up The Wrong Tree blog. January 31. http://www.bakadesuyo.com/2015/01/grit.

Barrett, Brian. 2017. "An IBM Breakthrough Ensures Silicon Will Keep Shrinking." *Wired*, June 5.

Barrick, Murray. 2005. "Yes, Personality Matters: Moving on to More Important Matters." *Human Performance* 18(4): 359–372.

Bartels, Meghan, and Skye Gould. 2016. "Here's the age you peak at everything throughout life." *Tech Insider*, July 22. http://www.techinsider.io/science-what-peak-age-is-2016-7

Baruch, Yehuda, and Stuart Jenkins. 2007. "Swearing at Work and Permissive Leadership Culture." *Leadership and Organization Development Journal* 28(6): 492–507.

Baten, Joerg, Nicola Bianchi, and Petra Moser. 2015. "Does Compulsory Licensing Discourage Invention? Evidence From German Patents After WWI." NBER Working Paper No. 21442, July.

Bates, Timothy, and Shivani Gupta. 2017. "Smart groups of smart people: Evidence for IQ as the origin of collective intelligence in the performance of human groups." *Intelligence* 60: 46–56.

Baumard, Nicolas, and Pascal Boyer. 2013. "Explaining moral religions" *Trends in Cognitive Sciences* 17(6): 272–280.

Baumard, Nicolas, Alexandre Hyafil, Ian Morris, and Pascal Boyer. 2015. "Increased Affluence Explains the Emergence of Ascetic Wisdoms and Moralizing Religions." *Current Biology* 25: 1–6.

Baumeister, Roy. 2013, "The Meaning of Life." *Aeon*, September 16. https://aeon.co/essays/what-is-better-a-happy-life-or-a-meaningful-one

Baumeister, Roy, Kathleen Vohs, Jennifer Aaker, and Emily Garbinsky. 2013. "Some key differences between a happy life and a meaningful life." *Journal of Positive Psychology* 8(6): 505–516.

Bejan, Adrian. 1997. "Constructal Tree Network for Fluid Flow Between a Finite-Size Volume and One Source or Sink." *Revue Générale de Thermique* 36: 592–604.

Bejan, Adrian. 2006. *Advanced Engineering Thermodynamics*, 3rd ed. Wiley.

Bejan, Adrian, and James Marden. 2006. "Unifying Constructal Theory for Scale Effects in Running, Swimming and Flying." *Journal of Experimental Biology* 209: 238–248.

Bejan, Adrian, L.A.O. Rocha, and S. Lorente. 2000. "Thermodynamic Optimization of Geometry: T- and Y-shaped Constructs of Fluid Streams." *International Journal of Thermal Sciences* 39: 949–960.

Bellah, Robert. 2011. *Religion in Human Evolution: From the Paleolithic to the Axial Age.* Belknap Press, September 15.

Bénabou, Roland, Davide Ticchi, and Andrea Vindigni. 2015. "Religion and Innovation." NBER Working Paper No. 21052, March.

Benford, Gregory, and James Benford. 2013. *Starship Century: Toward the Grandest Horizon.* Lucky Bat Books, April.

Bengtson, Vern, Merril Silverstein, Norella Putney, and Susan Harris. 2015. "Does Religiousness Increase with Age? Age Changes and Generational Differences Over 35 Years." *Journal for the Scientific Study of Religion* 54(2): 363–379.

Bennett, Charles. 1989. "Time/Space Trade-offs for Reversible Computation." *SIAM Journal of Computing* 18(4): 766–776.

Benson, Alan. 2014. "Rethinking the Two-Body Problem: The Segregation of Women Into Geographically Dispersed Occupations." *Demography* 51(5): 1619–1639.

Bento, Pedro, and Diego Restuccia. 2014. "Misallocation, Establishment Size, and Productivity." University of Toronto Economics Working Paper 517, July 25.

Bermúdez, José Luis. 2010. *Cognitive Science: An Introduction to the Science of the Mind*. Cambridge University Press, August.

Bernstein, Daniel, Nadia Heninger, Paul Lou, and Luke Valenta. 2017. "Post-quantum RSA." Cryptology ePrint Archive Report 2017/351. http://eprint.iacr.org/2017/351

Bettencourt, Luís, José Lobo, Dirk Helbing, Christian Kühnert, and Geoffrey West. 2007. "Growth, Innovation, Scaling, and the Pace of Life in Cities." *Proceedings of the National Academy of Science USA* 104(17): 7301–7306.

Bettencourt, Luís, José Lobo, D. Strumsky, and G.B. West. 2010. "Urban Scaling and Its Deviations: Revealing the Structure of Wealth, Innovation and Crime across Cities." *PLoS One* 5(11): e13541.

Bhattacharya, Kunal, Asim Ghosh, Daniel Monsivais, Robin Dunbar, and Kimmo Kaski. 2016. "Sex differences in social focus across the life cycle in humans." *Royal Society Open Science* 3(4): 160097.

Bickham, Jack M. 1997. *The 38 Most Common Fiction Writing Mistakes (And How To Avoid Them)*. Writer's Digest Books, September 15.

Black, Sandra, Erik Grönqvist, Björn Öckert. 2017. "Born to Lead? The Effect of Birth Order on Non-Cognitive Abilities." NBER Working Paper No. 23393, May.

Blackman, Ivy, David Picken, and Chunlu Liu. 2008. "Height and Construction Costs of Residential Buildings in Hong Kong and Shanghai." In *Proceedings of the CIB W112 International Conference on Multi-National Construction Projects*, Shanghai, November 23, 24, 1–18.

Blanky, Meredith, Mark Dinceccoz, and Yuri Zhukovx. 2017. "Political Regime Type and Warfare: Evidence from 600 Years of European History." May 27. https://papers.ssrn.com/sol3/papers.cfm?abstract_id=2830066.

Block, Walter, N. Stephan Kinsella, and Hans-Hermann Hoppe. 2000. "The Second Paradox of Blackmail." *Business Ethics Quarterly* 10(3): 593–622.

Bloom, Nicholas, Benn Eifert, Aprajit Mahajan, David McKenzie, and John Roberts. 2013. "Does Management Matter? Evidence from India." *Quarterly Journal of Economics* 128(1): 1–51.

Bloom, Nicholas, and John Van Reenen. 2010. "Why Do Management Practices Differ across Firms and Countries?" *Journal of Economic Perspectives* 24(1): 203–224.

Bloom, Nicholas, Raffaella Sadun, and John Van Reenen. 2015. "Do Private Equity Owned Firms Have Better Management Practices?" *American Economic Review* 105(5): 442–446.

BLS 2012. "Employee Tenure in 2012." United States Bureau of Labor Statistics USDL-12–1887, September 18. http://www.bls.gov/news.release/archives/tenure_09182012.pdf.

Boehm, Christopher. 1999. *Hierarchy in the Forest: The Evolution of Egalitarian Behavior*. Harvard University Press, December 1.

Bogdan, Paul, Tudor Dumitras, and Radu Marculescu. 2007. "Stochastic Communication: A New Paradigm for Fault-Tolerant Networks-on-Chip." *VLSI Design* 2007: 95348.

Bond, Michael. 2017. "Ready for anything: The best strategies to survive a disaster." *New Scientist* 3125, May 13.

Boning, Brent, Casey Ichniowski, and Kathryn Shaw. 2007. "Opportunity Counts: Teams and the Effectiveness of Production Incentives." *Journal of Labor Economics* 25(4): 613–650.

Bonke, Jens. 2012. "Do Morning-Type People Earn More than Evening-Type People? How Chronotypes Influence Income." *Annals of Economics and Statistics* 105/106: 55–72.

Boserup, Ester. 1981. *Population and Technological Change: A Study of Long-Term Trends*. University of Chicago Press, February.

Bostrom, Nick. 2004. "The Future of Human Evolution." In *Death and Anti-Death: Two Hundred Years After Kant, Fifty Years After Turing*, edited by Charles Tandy, 339–371. Palo Alto, CA: Ria University Press.

Bostrom, Nick. 2014. *Superintelligence: Paths, Dangers, Strategies*. Oxford University Press, July 3.

Bouchard, Thomas, David Lykken, Matthew McGue, Nancy Segal, and Auke Tellegen. 1990. "Sources of Human Psychological Differences: The Minnesota Study of Twins Reared Apart." *Science* 250(4978): 223–228.

Bowles, Samuel, and Herbert Gintis. 1976. *Schooling in Capitalist America: Educational Reform and the Contradictions of Economic Life*. Basic Books, January.

Braekevelt, Jonas, Frederik Buylaert, Jan Dumolyn, and Jelle Haemers. 2012. "The Politics of Factional Conflict in Late Medieval Flanders." *Historical Research* 85(227): 13–31.

Brain, Marshall. 2012. *The Day You Discard Your Body*. BYG Publishing, December 25.

Brand, Stewart. 1994. *How Buildings Learn: What Happens After They're Built*. Viking Press.

Branwen, Gwern. 2017. Tweet. July 11. https://twitter.com/gwern/status/884608192939827200

Brassen, Stefanie, Matthias Gamer, Jan Peters, Sebastian Gluth, and Christian Büchel. 2012. "Don't Look Back in Anger! Responsiveness to Missed Chances in Successful and Nonsuccessful Aging." *Science* 336(6081): 612–614.

Braudel, Fernand. 1979. *The Structures of Everyday Life. The Limits of the Possible*, Volume 1. Harper & Row.

Breeden, James. 1980. *Advice Among Masters: The Ideal in Slave Management in the Old South*. Praeger, July 25.

Breining, Sanni, Joseph Doyle, Jr., David Figlio, Krzysztof Karbownik, and Jeffrey Roth. 2017. "Birth Order and Delinquency: Evidence from Denmark and Florida." NBER Working Paper No. 23038, January.

Brett, Michelle, Lesley Roberts, Thomas Johnson, and Richard Wassersug. 2007. "Eunuchs in Contemporary Society: Expectations, Consequences, and Adjustments to Castration (Part II)." *Journal of Sexual Medicine* 4(4i): 946–955.

Brin, David. 1998. *The Transparent Society: Will Technology Force Us to Choose Between Privacy and Freedom?* Addison-Wesley. May 17.

Brin, David. 2002. *Kiln People*. Orbit. December 5.

Bronnenberg, Bart, Jean-Pierre Dubé, and Matthew Gentzkow. 2012. "The Evolution of Brand Preferences: Evidence From Consumer Migration." *American Economic Review* 102(6): 2472–2508.

Bronnenberg, Bart, Jean-Pierre Dubé, Matthew Gentzkow, and Jesse Shapiro. 2014. "Do Pharmacists Buy Bayer? Informed Shoppers and the Brand Premium." NBER Working Paper No. 20295, July.

Brooks, Alison, Juliana Schroeder, Jane Risen, Francesca Gino, Adam Galinsky, Michael Norton, and Maurice Schweitzer. 2016. "Don't stop believing: Rituals improve performance by decreasing anxiety." *Organizational Behavior and Human Decision Processes* 137: 71–85.

Brooks, Rodney. 2014. "Artificial Intelligence is a Tool, Not a Threat." Rethink Robotics blog, November 10. http://www.rethinkrobotics.com/blog/artificial-intelligence-tool-threat/.

Brown, Donald. 1991. *Human Universals*. Temple University Press, Philadelphia.

Brownlee, W. Elliot. 1977. "Review: The Economics of Urban Slavery: Urban Slavery in the American South 1820–1860: A Quantitative History. by Claudia Dale Goldin." *Reviews in American History* 5(2): 230–235.

Brunetti, Aymo. 1997. "Political Variables in Cross-country Growth Analysis." *Journal of Economic Surveys* 11(2): 163–190.

Bryson, Alex, and George MacKerron. 2016. "Are You Happy While You Work?" *Economic Journal* 127(599): 106–125.

Buchanan, Ben. 2017. *The Cybersecurity Dilemma: Hacking, Trust, and Fear Between Nations*. Oxford University Press, February 1.

Bueno de Mesquita, Bruce, and Alastair Smith. 2011. *The Dictator's Handbook: Why Bad Behavior Is Almost Always Good Politics*. Public Affairs, September 27.

Burda, Michael, Katie Genadek, and Daniel Hamermesh. 2016. "Not Working at Work: Loafing, Unemployment and Labor Productivity." NBER Working Paper No. 21923, January.

Bureau of Labor Statistics. 2013. "Time Spent in Primary Activities and Percent of the Civilian Population Engaging in Each Activity, Averages per Day by Sex, 2012 Annual Averages." Bureau of Labor Statistics Economic News Release. June 20. http://www.bls.gov/news.release/atus.t01.htm.

Burghardt, Gordon. 2006. *The Genesis of Animal Play: Testing the Limits*. Bradford, August 11.

Burton, Caitlin, Jason Plaks, and Jordan Peterson. 2015. "Why Do Conservatives Report Being Happier Than Liberals? The Contribution of Neuroticism." *Journal of Social and Political Psychology* 3(1): 89–102.

Burum, Bethany, Daniel Gilbert, and Timothy Wilson. 2016. "Becoming stranger: When future selves join the out-group." *Journal of Experimental Psychology: General* 145(9): 1132–1140.

Buterin, Vitalik. 2014. "White Paper: A Next-Generation Smart Contract and Decentralized Application Platform." April. https://www.ethereum.org/pdfs/EthereumWhitePaper.pdf.

Calore, Michael. 2017. "This Ultra-Secure PC Self Destructs if Someone Messes With It." *Wired, Gear*, June 23.

Caplan, Bryan. 2008. "The Totalitarian Threat." In *Global Catastrophic Risks*, edited by Nick Bostrom and Milan Ćirković, 504–519. Oxford University Press, July 17.

Caplan, Bryan. 2016. "Slavery in the Age of Em." *EconLog*, July 19. http://econlog.econlib.org/archives/2016/07/slavery_in_the.html

Caplan, Bryan, and Stephen Miller. 2010. "Intelligence Makes People Think Like Economists: Evidence from the General Social Survey." *Intelligence* 38(6): 636–647.

Capraro, Valerio. 2017. "Does the truth come naturally? Time pressure increases honesty in one-shot deception games." *Economics Letters*, 158(C): 54–57.

Card, Orson Scott. 2011. *Elements of Fiction Writing—Characters and Viewpoint*, 2nd ed. Writer's Digest Books. January 18.

Cardiff-Hicks, Brianna, Francine Lafontaine, and Kathryn Shaw. 2014. "Do Large Modern Retailers Pay Premium Wages?" NBER Working Paper No. 20313, July.

Cardoso, Ana Rute, Paulo Guimarães, and José Varejão. 2011. "Are Older Workers Worthy of Their Pay? An Empirical Investigation of Age-Productivity and Age-Wage Nexuses." *De Economist* 159(2): 95–111.

Carlino, Gerald, and William Kerr. 2014. "Agglomeration and Innovation." NBER Working Paper No. 20367, August, Forthcoming in *Handbook of Regional and Urban Economics* 5.

Carpenter, Christopher. 2008. "Sexual Orientation, Work, and Income in Canada." *Canadian Journal of Economics* 41(4): 1239–1261.

Carr, Patrick, and Maria Kefalas. 2009. *Hollowing Out the Middle: The Rural Brain Drain and What It Means for America*. Beacon Press.

Carvalhoa, Carlos, and Andrea Ferrerob, and Fernanda Nechio. 2016. "Demographics and real interest rates: Inspecting the mechanism." *European Economic Review* 88: 208–226.

Cavallera, G.M., and S. Giudici. 2008. "Morningness and Eveningness Personality: A Survey in Literature from 1995 up till 2006." *Personality and Individual Differences* 44: 3–21.

Cederman, Lars-Erik. 2003. "Modeling the Size of Wars: From Billiard Balls to Sandpiles." *American Political Science Review* 97(1): 135–150.

Chalfin, Aaron. 2014. "The Economic Costs of Crime." In *The Encyclopedia of Crime and Punishment*, edited by Wesley Jennings. Wiley-Blackwell.

Chalmers, David. 2010. "The Singularity: A Philosophical Analysis." *Journal of Consciousness Studies* 17: 7–65.

Chan, David. 2015. "The Efficiency of Slacking Off: Evidence from the Emergency Department." NBER Working Paper No. 21002, March.

Chapman, Benjamin, and Lewis Goldberg. 2017. "Act-frequency signatures of the Big Five." *Personality and Individual Differences* 116: 201–205.

Charbonneau, Steven, Shannon Fye, Jason Hay, and Carie Mullins. 2013. "A Retrospective Analysis of Technology Forecasting." AIAA Space 2013 Conference, San Diego, September. http://arc.aiaa.org/doi/abs/10.2514/6.2013-5519.

Charness, Gary, Ryan Oprea, and Daniel Friedman. 2014. "Continuous Time and Communication in a Public-goods Experiment." *Journal of Economic Behavior and Organization* 108(December): 212–223.

Chetty, Raj, Adam Guren, Day Manoli, and Andrea Weber. 2011. "Are Micro and Macro Labor Supply Elasticities Consistent? A Review of Evidence on the Intensive and Extensive Margins." *American Economic Review* 101(3): 471–475.

Christensen, Clayton. 1997. *The Innovator's Dilemma: When New Technologies Cause Great Firms to Fail.* Harvard Business Press, June 1.

Church, Timothy, Diana Thomas, Catrine Tudor-Locke, Peter Katzmarzyk, Conrad Earnest, Ruben Rodarte, Corby Martin, Steven Blair, and Claude Bouchard. 2011. "Trends over 5 Decades in U.S. Occupation-Related Physical Activity and Their Associations with Obesity." *PLoS ONE* 6(5): e19657. doi: 10.1371/journal.pone.0019657.

Clark, Gregory. 2008. *A Farewell to Alms: A Brief Economic History of the World.* Princeton University Press, December.

Clark, Gregory. 2014. *The Son Also Rises: Surnames and the History of Social Mobility*. Princeton University Press, February 23.

Clarke, Arthur. 1956. *The City and the Stars*. Frederick Muller, June.

Clifton, Jer. 2016. "What Reality are Trump People Living In?" *Jer's Intellectual Adventures*, August 17. https://jerclifton.com/2016/08/17/what-reality-are-trump-people-living-in/

Cohan, William. 2017. "Sam Zell Is Over the Tribune." *New Yorker*. July 2.

Cohen, Susan, and Diane Bailey. 1997. "What Makes Teams Work: Group Effectiveness Research from the Shop Floor to the Executive Suite." *Journal of Management* 23(3): 239–290.

Collins, Randall. 2004. *Interaction Ritual Chains*. Princeton University Press, March.

Conley, Dalton. 2004. *The Pecking Order: A Bold New Look at How Family and Society Determine Who We Become*. Knopf, March 2.

Conway, Melvin. 1968. "How do Committees Invent?" *Datamation* 14(5): 28–31.

Cook, C. Justin, and Jason Fletcher. 2017. "High School Genetic Diversity and Later-life Student Outcomes: Micro-level Evidence from the Wisconsin Longitudinal Study." NBER Working Paper No. 23520, June.

Cook, Gareth. 2012. "A Neuroscientist's Quest to Reverse Engineer the Human Brain." *Scientific American*, March 20.

Cooter, Robert, and Thomas Ulen. 2011. *Law and Economics*, 6th ed. Pearson Hall, February.

Corrado, Carol, Charles Hulten, and Daniel Sichel. 2009. "Intangible Capital and U.S. Economic Growth." *Review of Income and Wealth* 55(3): 661–685.

Costa Jr., Paul, Antonio Terracciano, and Robert R. McCrae. 2001. "Gender Differences in Personality Traits Across Cultures: Robust and Surprising Findings." *Journal of Personality and Social Psychology* 81(2): 322–331.

Costinot, Arnaud, and Dave Donaldson. 2016. "How Large Are the Gains from Economic Integration? Theory and Evidence from U.S. Agriculture, 1880–1997." NBER Working Paper No. 22946, December.

Cover, Thomas, and Joy Thomas. 2006. *Elements of Information Theory*, 2nd Edition. Wiley-Interscience, July 18.

Cramton, Peter, Yoav Shoham, and Richard Steinberg. 2005. *Combinatorial Auctions*. MIT Press, December 9.

Credé, Marcus, Michael Tynan, and Peter Harms. 2017. "Much Ado About Grit: A Meta-Analytic Synthesis of the Grit Literature." *Journal of Personality and Social Psychology* 113(3): 492–511.

Croson, Rachel, and Uri Gneezy. 2009. "Gender Differences in Preferences." *Journal of Economic Literature* 47(2): 1–27.

Cummins, Neil. 2013. "Marital Fertility and Wealth During the Fertility Transition: Rural France, 1750–1850." *Economic History Review* 66(2): 449–476.

Currey, Mason. 2013. *Daily Rituals: How Artists Work*. Knopf, April 23.

Curry, Andrew. 2013. "Archaeology: The Milk Revolution." *Nature* 500(August 1): 20–22.

Cutler, Ben, Spencer Fowers, Jeffrey Kramer, and Eric Peterson "Dunking the Data Center" March 2017. *IEEE Spectrum*, pp.27–31.

Dababneh, Awwad, Naomi Swanson, and Richard Shell. 2001. "Impact of Added Rest Breaks on the Productivity and Well Being of Workers." *Ergonomics* 44(2): 164–174.

Dacey, Mike. 2017. "Anthropomorphism as Cognitive Bias." *Philosophy of Science*, March 22.

Dafoe, Allan, John Oneal, and Bruce Russett. 2013. "The Democratic Peace: Weighing the Evidence and Cautious Inference." *International Studies Quarterly* 57(1): 201–214.

Dalgaard, Carl-Johan, and Holger Strulik. 2014. "Physiological Constraints and Comparative Economic Development." University of Copenhagen Department of Economics Working Paper, October. http://www.econ.ku.dk/dalgaard/Work/WPs/geo_reversal_oct2014.pdf.

Dalvit, Dean. 2011. "Price Per Square Foot Construction Cost for Multi Story Office Buildings." EV Studio website, July 14. http://evstudio.com/price-per-square-foot-construction-cost-for-multi-story-office-buildings/.

Damian, Rodica, Rong Su, Michael Shanahan, Ulrich Trautwein, and Brent Roberts. 2015. "Can personality traits and intelligence compensate for background disadvantage? Predicting status attainment in adulthood." *Journal of Personality and Social Psychology* 109(3): 473–489.

Dari-Mattiacci, Giuseppe. 2009. "Negative Liability." *Journal of Legal Studies* 38(1): 21–59.

Dave. 2015. "Why is computer RAM disappearing?" *Nerd Fever*, June 18. http://nerdfever.com/?p=2885.

Davies, James, Susanna Sandström, Anthony Shorrocks, and Edward Wolff. 2011. "The Level and Distribution of Global Household Wealth." *Economic Journal* 121(551): 223–254.

Dawson, John, and John Seater. 2013. "Federal Regulation and Aggregate Economic Growth." *Journal of Economic Growth* 18(2): 137–177.

De Witt, John, W. Brent Edwards, Melissa Scott-Pandorf, Jason Norcross, and Michael Gernhardt. 2014. "The Preferred Walk to Run Transition Speed in Actual Lunar Gravity." *Journal of Experimental Biology* 217(September 15): 3200–3203.

Deal, W.R., V. Radisic, D. Scott, and X.B. Mei. 2010. "Solid-State Amplifiers for Terahertz Electronics." Northrop Grumman Technical Report. http://www.as.northropgrumman.com/products/mps_mimic/assets/SState_Amp_Terahertz_Elec.pdf.

Debey, Evelyne, Maarten De Schryver, Gordon Logan, Kristina Suchotzki, and Bruno Verschuere. 2015. "From junior to senior Pinocchio: A cross-sectional lifespan investigation of deception." *Acta Psychologica* 160 (September): 58–68.

DeBrohun, Jeri. 2001. "Power Dressing in Ancient Greece and Rome." *History Today*, 51(2): 18–25.

Desmet, Klaus, and Esteban Rossi-Hansberg. 2009. "Spatial Growth and Industry Age." *Journal of Economic Theory* 144(6): 2477–2502.

Dhand, Rajiva, and Harjyot Sohal. 2006. "Good Sleep, Bad Sleep! The Role of Daytime Naps in Healthy Adults." *Current Opinion in Pulmonary Medicine* 12(6): 379–382.

Dhyne, Emmanuel, Amil Petrin, Valerie Smeets, and Frederic Warzynski. 2017. "Multi Product Firms, Import Competition, and the Evolution of Firm-product Technical Efficiencies." NBER Working Paper No. 23637, July.

Diaz, Jesus. 2015. "Wow, China Builds Complete 57-story Skyscraper in Record 19 Days." *Sploid.* March 9. http://sploid.gizmodo.com/china-builds-complete-57-story-lego-like-skyscraper-in-1690315984.

Diener, Ed. 2013. "The Remarkable Changes in the Science of Subjective Well-Being." *Perspectives on Psychological Science* 8(6): 663–666.

Doeswijk, Ronald, Trevin Lam, and Laurens Swinkels. 2017. "Historical Returns of the Market Portfolio." Working Paper, June 2. https://papers.ssrn.com/sol3/papers.cfm?abstract_id=2978509

Dolan, Kerry, and Luisa Kroll. 2014. "The World's Billionaires." *Forbes*, March 3. http://www.forbes.com/billionaires/.

Domar, Evsey D. 1970. "The Causes of Slavery or Serfdom: A Hypothesis." *Journal of Economic History* 30(1): 18–32.

Douglass, Frederick. 1845. *Narrative of the Life of Frederick Douglass: An American Slave*. Anti-Slavery Office.

Drechsler, Rolf, and Robert Wille. 2012. "Reversible Circuits: Recent Accomplishments and Future Challenges for an Emerging Technology." *Progress in VLSI Design and Test, Proceedings* 7373: 383–392.

Drexler, K. Eric. 1992. *Nanosystems: Molecular Machinery, Manufacturing, and Computation*. Wiley. October.

Drexler, K. Eric. 2013. *Radical Abundance: How a Revolution in Nanotechnology Will Change Civilization*. Public Affairs. May 7.

Drouvelis, Michalis, and Julian Jamison. 2015. "Selecting Public Goods Institutions: Who Likes to Punish and Reward?" *Southern Economic Journal* 82(2): 501–534.

Drust, Barry, Jim Waterhouse, Greg Atkinson, Ben Edwards, and Tom Reilly. 2005. "Circadian Rhythms in Sports Performance—an Update." *Chronobiology International* 22(1): 21–44.

Dubois, David, Derek Rucker, and Adam Galinsky. 2015. "Social class, power, and selfishness: When and why upper and lower class individuals behave unethically." *Journal of Personality and Social Psychology* 108(3): 436–449.

Duckworth, Angela, and Patrick Quinn. 2009. "Development and Validation of the Short Grit Scale (Grit-S)." *Journal of Personality Assessment* 91(2): 166–174.

Duhigg, Charles. 2016. "What Google Learned From Its Quest to Build the Perfect Team." *New York Times Magazine*, MM20, February 28.

Dunbar, Robin. 1992. "Neocortex Size as a Constraint on Group Size in Primates." *Journal of Human Evolution* 22(6): 469–984.

Dunbar, Robin, Jacques Launay, Rafael Wlodarski, Cole Robertson, Eiluned Pearce, and James Carney. 2017. "Functional Benefits of (Modest) Alcohol Consumption." *Adaptive Human Behavior and Physiology* 3(2): 118–133.

Dunne, Timothy, and Mark Roberts. 1993. "The Long-Run Demand for Labor: Estimates From Census Establishment Data," Center for Economic Studies, U.S. Census Bureau, Working Paper 93–13. http://ideas.repec.org/p/cen/wpaper/93–13.html.

Duranton, Gilles, and Hubert Jayet. 2011. "Is the Division of Labour Limited by the Extent of the Market? Evidence from French Cities." *Journal of Urban Economics* 69(1): 56–71.

Dutta, Rohan, David Levine, Nicholas Papageorge, and Lemin Wu. 2017. "Entertaining Malthus: Bread, Circuses, and Economic Growth." *Economic Inquiry*, July 25.

Eckersley, Peter, and Anders Sandberg. 2014. "Is Brain Emulation Dangerous?" *Journal of Artificial General Intelligence* 4(3): 170–194.

Edmans, Alex, and Xavier Gabaix. 2016. "Executive Compensation: A Modern Primer" *Journal of Economic Literature* 54(4): 1232–1287.

Edmans, Alex, Xavier Gabaix, and Dirk Jenter. 2017. "Executive Compensation: A Survey of Theory and Evidence." NBER Working Paper No. 23596, July.

Edmond, Mark. 2015. "Democratic vs. Republican occupations." Verdant Labs Blog, June 2. http://verdantlabs.com/blog/2015/06/02/politics-of-professions/.

Edmondson, Amy. 1999. "Psychological Safety and Learning Behavior in Work Teams," *Administrative Science Quarterly* 44(2): 350–383, June.

Eeckhout, Jan. 2004. "Gibrat's Law for (All) Cities." *American Economic Review* 94(5): 1429–1451.

Egan, Greg. 1994. *Permutation City*. Millennium Orion Publishing Group.

Enke, Benjamin. 2017. "Kinship Systems, Cooperation and the Evolution of Culture." NBER Working Paper No. 23499, June.

Environmental Process Systems Limited. 2014. "Slurry-Ice Based Cooling Systems Application Guide." http://www.epsltd.co.uk/files/slurryice_manual.pdf.

Enz, Karalyn, David Pillemer, and Kenneth Johnson. 2016. "The relocation bump: Memories of middle adulthood are organized around residential moves." Journal of Experimental Psychology: General 145(8): 935–940.

Erdkamp, Paul. 2016. "Economic growth in the Roman Mediterranean world: An early good-bye to Malthus?" *Explorations in Economic History* 60: 1–20.

Erdogan, Berrin, Talya Bauer, Donald Truxillo, and Layla Mansfield. 2012. "Whistle While You Work: A Review of the Life Satisfaction Literature." *Journal of Management* 38(4): 1038–1083.

Esmaeilzadeh, Hadi, Emily Blem, Renee Amant, and Karthikeyan Sankaralingam. 2012. "Power Limitations and Dark Silicon Challenge the Future of Multicore." *Transactions on Computer Systems* 30(3): 11.

Eth, Daniel, Juan-Carlos Foust, and Brandon Whale. 2013. "The Prospects of Whole Brain Emulation within the next Half-Century." *Journal of Artificial General Intelligence* 4(3): 130–152.

Evstigneev, Igor, Thorsten Hens, and Klaus Schenk-Hoppé. 2009. "Evolutionary Finance." In *Handbook of Financial Markets: Dynamics and Evolution* 9: 507–566, edited by Thorsten Hens and Klaus Schenk-Hoppé. North-Holland.

Fagerberg, Jan, and Martin Srholec. 2013. "Knowledge, Capabilities, and the Poverty Trap: The Complex Interplay between Technological, Social, and Geographical Factors." In *Knowledge and Space* 5(March 6), edited by Peter Meusburger, Johannes Glückler, and Martina el Meskioui. New York: Springer, 113–137.

Faghri, Amir. 2012. "Review and Advances in Heat Pipe Science and Technology." *Journal of Heat Transfer* 134(12): 123001.

Farr, Robert. 2007a. "Fractal Design for Efficient Brittle Plates under Gentle Pressure Loading." *Physics Review E* 76(4): 046601.

Farr, Robert. 2007b. "Fractal Design for an Efficient Shell Strut under Gentle Compressive Loading." *Physics Review E* 76(5): 056608.

Farr, Robert, and Yong Mao. 2008. "Fractal Space Frames and Metamaterials for High Mechanical Efficiency." *Europhysics Letters* 84(1): 14001.

Feathers, Michael. 2004. *Working Effectively with Legacy Code*. Prentice Hall, October 2.

Feldman, Gilad, Huiwen Lian, Michal Kosinski, and David Stillwell. 2017. "Frankly, we do give a damn: The relationship between profanity and honesty" *Social Psychological and Personality Science*, January 15. 10.1177/1948550616681055

Fernald, John, and Charles Jones. 2014. "The Future of US Economic Growth." *American Economic Review* 104(5): 44–49.

Feron, James. 1995. "Rationalist Explanations for War." *International Organization* 49(3): 379–414.

Fincher, Corey, Randy Thornhill, Damian Murray, and Mark Schaller. 2008. "Pathogen Prevalence Predicts Human Cross-cultural Variability in Individualism/collectivism." *Proceedings Royal Society B* 275(1640): 1279–1285.

Fletcher, Jason. 2013. "The Effects of Personality Traits on Adult Labor Market Outcomes: Evidence from Siblings." *Journal of Economic Behavior & Organization* 89(May): 122–135.

Flynn, James. 2007. *What Is Intelligence?: Beyond the Flynn Effect*. Cambridge University Press. August 27.

Flynn, Kathleen, and Josh Katz. 2016. "Style and Substance." *New York Times*, p.BR13. July 16.

Flyvbjerg, Bent. 2015. "What You Should Know About Megaprojects and Why: An Overview." *Project Management Journal* 45(2).

Forbes Israel. "Forbes Ranking of Billionaires: The World's Richest Jews." 2013. *Forbes Israel*, April 17. http://www.forbes.co.il/news/new.aspx?pn6Vq=J&0r9VQ=IEII.

Fogel, Robert, Stanley Engerman. 1974. *Time on the Cross: The Economics of American Negro Slavery*. W. W. Norton & Company.

Foote, Brian, and Joseph Yoder. 2000. "Big Ball of Mud." Chapter 29, in *Pattern Languages of Program Design 4*, ed. Neil Harrison, Brian Foote, and Hans Rohnert, Addison-Wesley.

Foster, Lucia, John Haltiwanger, and C. J. Krizan. 2006. "Market Selection, Reallocation, and Restructuring in the U.S. Retail Trade Sector in the 1990s." *Review of Economics and Statistics* 88(4): 748–758.

Foster, Richard. 2012. "Creative Destruction Whips through Corporate America: An Innosight Executive Briefing on Corporate Strategy." *Strategy & Innovation* 10(1).

Fox, J.G., and E.D. Embrey. 1972. "Music—an aid to productivity." *Applied Ergonomics* 3(4): 202–205.

Frattaroli, J. 2006. "Experimental Disclosure and its Moderators: A Meta-analysis." *Psychological Bulletin* 132(6): 823–865.

Freitas, Robert. 1999. *Nanomedicine, Volume I: Basic Capabilities*. Landes Bioscience.

Freitas, Robert, and Ralph Merkle. 2004. *Kinematic Self-Replicating Machines*. Landes Bioscience. October 30.

Fridley, Jason, and Dov Sax. 2014. "The Imbalance of Nature: Revisiting a Darwinian Framework for Invasion Biology." *Global Ecology and Biogeography* 23(11): 1157–1166.

Friedman, David. 1973. *The Machinery of Freedom: Guide to a Radical Capitalism*. New York: Harper and Row.

Friedman, David. 2000. *Law's Order: What Economics Has to Do with Law and Why It Matters*. Princeton University Press.

Friedman, Daniel, and Ryan Oprea. 2012. "A Continuous Dilemma." *American Economic Review* 102(1): 337–363.

Fyfe, W.D. 2011. "8 Simple Rules for Ghosts" March 28. http://wdfyfe.net/2011/03/28/8-simple-rules-for-ghosts/.

Gal, Eyal, Michael London, Amir Globerson, Srikanth Ramaswamy, Michael Reimann, Eilif Muller, Henry Markram, and Idan Segev. 2017. "Rich cell-type-specific network topology in neocortical microcircuitry." *Nature Neuroscience* 20: 1004–1013.

Galenson, David. 2006. *Old Masters and Young Geniuses*. Princeton University Press.

Galor, Oded, Omer Ozak, and Assaf Sarid. 2017. "Geographical Origins and Economic Consequences of Language Structures." February 4. http://papers.ssrn.com/sol3/papers.cfm?abstract_id=2820889

Garcia-Macia, Daniel, Chang-Tai Hsieh, and Peter Klenow. 2016. "How Destructive is Innovation?" NBER Working Paper No. 22953, December.

Garvin, David, and Joshua Margolis. 2015. "The Art of Giving and Receiving Advice." *Harvard Business Review* 93(1/2): 60–71.

Gavrilov, Leonid, and Natalia Gavrilova. 2006. "Models of systems failure in aging." *Handbook of Models for Human Aging*. pp.45–68.

Gayle, Philip. 2003. "Market Concentration and Innovation: New Empirical Evidence on the Schumpeterian Hypothesis." April. http://www-personal.ksu.edu/~gaylep/jpe.pdf.

Gensowski, Miriam. 2014. "Personality, IQ, and Lifetime Earnings." IZA Discussion Paper No. 8235, June. http://ftp.iza.org/dp8235.pdf.

Gervais, Will. 2017. "Global evidence of extreme intuitive moral prejudice against atheists." June 12. https://osf.io/preprints/psyarxiv/csnp2

Gibson, Matthew, and Jeffrey Shrader. 2014. "Time Use and Productivity: The Wage Returns to Sleep." Working Paper, Department of Economics, U.C. San Diego. July 10.

Giesen, Kristian, Arndt Zimmermann, and Jens Suedekum. 2010. "The Size Distribution Across all Cities—Double Pareto Lognormal Strikes." *Journal of Urban Economics* 68(2): 129–137.

Giuliano, Paola, and Nathan Nunn. 2017. "Understanding Cultural Persistence and Change." NBER Working Paper No. 23617, July.

Glaeser, Edward, Joseph Gyourko, and Raven Saks. 2005. "Why Have Housing Prices Gone Up?" *American Economic Review*, 95(2): 329–333.

Glasser, Matthew, Timothy Coalson, Emma Robinson, Carl Hacker, John Harwell, Essa Yacoub, Kamil Ugurbil, Jesper Andersson, Christian Beckmann, Mark Jenkinson, Stephen Smith, and David Van Essen. 2016. "A multi-modal parcellation of human cerebral cortex." *Nature* 536: 171–178.

Glück, Judith, and Susan Bluck. 2007. "Looking Back across the Life Span: A Life Story Account of the Reminiscence Bump." *Memory and Cognition* 35(8): 1928–1939.

Göbel, Christian, and Thomas Zwick. 2012. "Age and Productivity: Sector Differences." *De Economist* 160: 35–57.

Goldstein, Evan. 2012. "The Strange Neuroscience of Immortality." *The Chronicle Review*, July 16.

Goldstone, Jack, Robert Bates, David Epstein, Ted Robert Gurr, Michael Lustik, Monty Marshall, Jay Ulfelder, and Mark Woodward. 2010. "A Global Model for Forecasting Political Instability." *American Journal of Political Science* 54(1): 190–208.

Good, Arla, and Frank Russo. 2016. "Singing promotes cooperation in a diverse group of children." Social Psychology, Vol 47(6): 340–344.

Gorodnichenko, Yuriy, and Gerard Roland. 2011. "Which Dimensions of Culture Matter for Long-Run Growth?" *American Economic Review* 101(3): 492–498.

Gorodnichenko, Yuriy, and Gerard Roland. 2017. Culture, Institutions, and the Wealth of Nations." *Review of Economics and Statistics* 99(3): 402–416.

Gorton, Gary, and Frank Schmid. 2004. "Capital, Labor, and the Firm: A Study of German Codetermination." *Journal of the European Economic Association* 2(5): 863–905, September.

Grace, Katja. 2013. "Algorithmic Progress in Six Domains." Technical report 2013–2013. Berkeley, CA: Machine Intelligence Research Institute. October 5. http://intelligence.org/files/AlgorithmicProgress.pdf.

Grace, Katja. 2014. "MIRI AI Predictions Dataset." *AI Impacts*. May 20. http://aiimpacts.org/miri-ai-predictions-dataset/.

Grace, Katja. 2015. "Costs of human-level hardware." *AI Impacts*. July 26. http://aiimpacts.org/costs-of-human-level-hardware/.

Grace, Katja, John Salvatier, Allan Dafoe, Baobao Zhang, and Owain Evans. 2017. "When Will AI Exceed Human Performance? Evidence from AI Experts." May 30. https://arxiv.org/abs/1705.08807

Grant, Adam. 2013. *Give and Take: Why Helping Others Drives Our Success*. Viking, April 9.

Gray, Heather, Kurt Gray, and Daniel Wegner. 2007. "Dimensions of mind perception." *Science* 315: 619.

Gully, Philippe. 2014. "Long and High Conductance Helium Heat Pipe." *Cryogenics* 64(November-December): 255–259.

Herbert Gutman. 1975. *Slavery and the Numbers Game: A Critique of Time on the Cross. University of* Illinois Press.

Haldane, John. 1926. "On Being the Right Size." *Harper's Magazine*, March.

Haltiwanger, John. 2012. "Job Creation and Firm Dynamics in the United States." In *Innovation Policy and the Economy*, edited by Josh Lerner, and Scott Stern. v. 12, 17–38. University of Chicago.

Haltiwanger, John, Ron Jarmin, and Javier Miranda. 2013. "Who Creates Jobs? Small versus Large versus Young." *Review of Economics and Statistics* 95(2): 347–361.

Hampshire, Adam, Roger Highfield, Beth Parkin, and Adrian Owen. 2012. "Fractionating Human Intelligence." *Neuron* 76(December 20): 1225–1237.

Hanna, Awad, Craig Taylor, and Kenneth Sullivan. 2005. "Impact of Extended Overtime on Construction Labor Productivity." *Journal of Construction Engineering and Management* 131(6): 734–739.

Hanson, Robin. 1992. "Reversible Agents: Need Robots Waste Bits to See, Talk, and Achieve?" Workshop on Physics and Computation (October): 284–288. doi: 10.1109/PHYCMP.1992.615558.

Hanson, Robin. 1994a. "Buy Health, Not Health Care." *Cato Journal* 14(1): 135–141, Summer.

Hanson, Robin. 1994b. "If Uploads Come First." *Extropy* 6(2): 10–15.

Hanson, Robin. 1995. "Lilliputian Uploads." *Extropy* 7(1): 30–31.

Hanson, Robin. 1998. "Economic Growth Given Machine Intelligence." October. http://hanson.gmu.edu/aigrow.pdf.

Hanson, Robin. 2000. "Long-Term Growth as a Sequence of Exponential Modes." October. http://hanson.gmu.edu/longgrow.pdf.

Hanson, Robin. 2001a. "How to Live in a Simulation." *Journal of Evolution and Technology* 7(September).

Hanson, Robin. 2001b. "World Peace, Thanks To Old Men?" January 11. http://hanson.gmu.edu/Worldpeace.html

Hanson, Robin. 2003. "Combinatorial Information Market Design." *Information Systems Frontiers* 5(1): 105–119.

Hanson, Robin. 2005. "He Who Pays The Piper Must Know The Tune." April. http://hanson.gmu.edu/expert.pdf.

Hanson, Robin. 2006a. "Decision Markets for Policy Advice." In *Promoting the General Welfare: American Democracy and the Political Economy of Government Performance*, edited by Eric Patashnik and Alan Gerber, 151–173. Washington D.C.: Brookings Institution Press, November.

Hanson, Robin. 2006b. "Five Nanotech Social Scenarios." In *Nanotechnology: Societal Implications II, Individual Perspectives*, edited by Mihail Roco and William Bainbridge, 109–113. Springer, November.

Hanson, Robin. 2007. "Double Or Nothing Lawsuits, Ten Years On." Overcoming Bias blog, October 30. http://www.overcomingbias.com/2007/10/double-or-nothi.html.

Hanson, Robin. 2008a. "The Rapacious Hardscrapple Frontier." In *Year Million: Science at the Far Edge of Knowledge*, edited by Damien Broderick, 168–192. New York: Atlas Books, May 19.

Hanson, Robin. 2008b. "Economics of the Singularity." *IEEE Spectrum*, 45(6): 37–42.

Hanson, Robin. 2009. "A Tale Of Two Tradeoffs." Overcoming Bias blog. January 16. http://www.overcomingbias.com/2009/01/a-tale-of-two-tradeoffs.html.

Hanson, Robin. 2010a. "Two Types of People." Overcoming Bias blog. October 4. http://www.overcomingbias.com/2010/10/two-types-of-people.html.

Hanson, Robin. 2010b. "Compare Refuge, Resort." Overcoming Bias blog. December 10. http://www.overcomingbias.com/2010/12/compare-refuges-resorts.html.

Hanson, Robin. 2010c. "Am I A Sim?" Overcoming Bias blog. August 3. http://www.overcomingbias.com/2010/08/am-i-a-sim.html.

Hanson, Robin. 2010d. "Bill & My Excellent Hypothesis." Overcoming Bias blog. August 16. https://www.overcomingbias.com/2010/08/billandme.html.

Hanson, Robin. 2011. "Space vs. Time Genocide." June 16. https://www.overcomingbias.com/2011/06/space-v-time-genocide.html

Hanson, Robin. 2012a. "AI Progress Estimate." Overcoming Bias blog. August 27. http://www.overcomingbias.com/2012/08/ai-progress-estimate.html.

Hanson, Robin. 2012b. "Meet The New Conflict, Same As The Old Conflict." *Journal of Consciousness Studies* 19(1–2): 119–125.

Hanson, Robin. 2013. "Shall We Vote on Values, But Bet on Beliefs?" *Journal of Political Philosophy* 21(2): 151–178.

Hanson, Robin. 2014. "Conservative vs. Liberal Jobs." Overcoming Bias blog. November 18. http://www.overcomingbias.com/2014/11/conservative-vs-liberal-jobs.html.

Hanson, Robin. 2017a. "A Post-Em-Era Hint." Overcoming Bias blog. July 4. https://www.overcomingbias.com/2017/07/a-post-em-era-hint.html.

Hanson, Robin. 2017b. "'Human' Seems Low Dimensional." Overcoming Bias blog. July 15. http://www.overcomingbias.com/2017/07/human-seems-low-dimensional.html

Hanson, Robin, and Tyler Cowen. 2004. "Are Disagreements Honest?" August 18. http://hanson.gmu.edu/deceive.pdf

Hanson, Robin, and Eliezer Yudkowsky. 2013. *The Hanson-Yudkowsky AI-Foom Debate*. Berkeley, CA: Machine Intelligence Research Institute.

Harris, Sam. 2017. "Former Air Force data scientist explains why the US won't see a violent political revolution anytime soon." *Business Insider*, April 22. http://www.businessinsider.com/the-us-isnt-on-the-brink-of-a-violent-political-revolution-because-it-doesnt-have-enough-teenagers-2017-4

Hart, Kevin. 2017. "In Wondering Admiration Before the World." *Los Angeles Review of Books*, January 24. https://lareviewofbooks.org/article/wondering-admiration-world/

Hartshorne, Joshua, and Laura Germine. 2015. "When Does Cognitive Functioning Peak? The Asynchronous Rise and Fall of Different Cognitive Abilities Across the Life Span." *Psychological Science* 26(4): 433–443.

Haub, Carl. 2011. "How Many People Have Ever Lived on Earth?" Population Reference Bureau, October. http://www.prb.org/Publications/Articles/2002/HowManyPeopleHaveEverLivedonEarth.aspx.

Hausmann, Ricardo, César Hidalgo, Sebastián Bustos, Michele Coscia, Alexander Simoes, and Muhammed Yildirim. 2014. *The Atlas of Economic Complexity: Mapping Paths to Prosperity*. MIT Press.

Hawkins, Jeff. 2008. "Tech Luminaries Address Singularity." *IEEE Spectrum*, June 1.

Hawks, John. 2011. "Selection for Smaller Brains in Holocene Human Evolution." arXiv: 1102.5604, February 28.

Hayworth, Kenneth. 2012. "Electron Imaging Technology For Whole Brain Neural Circuit Mapping." *International Journal of Machine Consciousness* 4(1): 87–108.

Healy, Kevin, Luke McNally, Graeme Ruxton, Natalie Cooper, and Andrew Jackson. 2013. "Metabolic Rate and Body Size are Linked with Perception of Temporal Information." *Animal Behaviour* 86: 685–696.

Heintzelman, Samantha, and Laura King. 2016. "Meaning in life and intuition." *Journal of Personality and Social Psychology* 110(3): 477–492.

Hektner, Joel, Jennifer Schmidt, and Mihaly Csikszentmihalyi. 2007. *Experience Sampling Method: Measuring the Quality of Everyday Life*. Thousand Oaks, CA: SAGE.

Helliwell, John, Richard Layard, and Jeffrey Sachs. 2013. *World Happiness Report 2013*. United Nations Sustainable Development Solutions Network, September 9.

Helliwell, John, and Shun Wang. 2015. "How was the Weekend? How the Social Context Underlies Weekend Effects in Happiness and other Emotions for US Workers." NBER Working Paper No. 21374, July.

Henig, Robin. 2008. "Taking Play Seriously." *New York Times Magazine*, February 17.

Henrich, Joseph. 2015. *The Secret of Our Success: How Culture Is Driving Human Evolution, Domesticating Our Species, and Making Us Smarter*. Princeton University Press, October 27.

Herodotus. 440BC. *The Histories*. Translated by A.D. Godley, 1920.

Herzer, Dierk, and Holger Strulik. 2017. "Religiosity and income: a panel cointegration and causality analysis." *Applied Economics* 49(30): 2922–2938.

Hill, Patrick, and Nicholas Turiano. 2014. "Purpose in Life as a Predictor of Mortality Across Adulthood." *Psychological Science* 25(7): 1482–1486.

Hill, Patrick, Nicholas Turiano, Daniel Mroczek, and Anthony Burrow. 2016. "The value of a purposeful life: Sense of purpose predicts greater income and net worth." *Journal of Research in Personality* 65: 38–42, December.

Hofstede, Geert, Gert Hofstede, and Michael Minkov. 2010. *Cultures and Organizations: Software of the Mind*. 3rd ed. McGraw-Hill. May 24.

Hölzle, Patricia, Joachim Hermsdörfer, and Céline Vetter. 2014. "The Effects of Shift Work and Time of Day on Fine Motor Control During Handwriting." *Ergonomics* 57(10): 1488–1498.

Horn, John, and Raymond Cattell. 1967. "Age Differences in Fluid and Crystallized Intelligence." *Acta Psychologica* 26: 107–129.

Hotz, V. Joseph. 2015. "Strategic parenting, birth order, and school performance." *Journal of Population Economics* 28(4): 911–936.

Howe, Neil, and William Strauss. 1992. *Generations: The History of America's Future, 1584 to 2069*. Quill. September 30.

Huang, Fali, Ginger Zhe Jin, and Lixin Colin Xu. 2016. "Love, Money, and Parental Goods: Does Parental Matchmaking Matter?" NBER Working Paper No. 22586, September.

Huber, Evelyne, and John Stephens. 2014. "Income inequality and redistribution in post-industrial democracies: demographic, economic and political determinants." *Socio-Economic Review* 12(2): 245–267.

Hummels, David, and Georg Schaur. 2013. "Time as a Trade Barrier." *American Economic Review* 103(7): 2935–2959.

Hunter, Emily M., and Cindy Wu. 2015. "Give Me a Better Break: Choosing Workday Break Activities to Maximize Resource Recovery." *Journal of Applied Psychology* 2016 101(2): 302-11.

Iannaccone, Laurence. 1994. "Why Strict Churches Are Strong." *American Journal of Sociology* 99(5): 1180–1211.

Ichniowski, Casey, and Anne Preston. 2014. "Do Star Performers Produce More Stars? Peer Effects and Learning in Elite Teams." NBER Working Paper No. 20478, September.

Idson, Todd. 1990. "Establishment Size, Job Satisfaction and the Structure of Work." *Applied Economics* 22(8): 1007–1018.

Iliev, Rumen, Joe Hoover, Morteza Dehghani, and Robert Axelrod. 2016. "Linguistic positivity in historical texts reflects dynamic environmental and psychological factors." *Proceedings of the National Academy of Sciences of the United States of America* 113(49): E7871–E7879.

Inglehart, Ronald, and Christian Welzel. 2010. "Changing Mass Priorities: The Link Between Modernization and Democracy." *Perspectives on Politics* 8(2): 554.

International Labour Organization 2012. "International Labour Organization Global Estimate of Forced Labour 2012: Results and Methodology." June 1. http://www.ilo.org/washington/areas/elimination-of-forced-labor/WCMS_182004/lang–en/index.htm.

Jacobs, Emma. 2015. "The Strange World of the Humans Who Loaned Their Voices to Siri." *Financial Times*, February 12.

Jahncke, Helena, Staffan Hygge, Niklas Halin, Anne Green, and Kenth Dimberg. 2011. "Open-plan Office Noise: Cognitive Performance and Restoration." *Journal of Environmental Psychology* 31(4): 373–382.

Jaspers, Esther, and Rik Pieters. 2016. "Materialism across the life span: An age-period-cohort analysis." *Journal of Personality and Social Psychology* 111(3): 451–473.

Jay, Timothy, and Kristin Janschewitz. 2012. "The Science of Swearing." *Observer* 25(5).

Jensen, Robert, and Emily Oster. 2009. "The Power of TV: Cable Television and Women's Status in India." *Quarterly Journal of Economics* 124(3): 1057–1094.

Johnson, Justin, and David Myatt. 2006. "On the Simple Economics of Advertising, Marketing, and Product Design." *American Economic Review* 96(3): 756–784.

Johnson, Steven. 2016. *Wonderland: How Play Made the Modern World*. Riverhead Books, November 15.

Jones, Benjamin, E.J. Reedy, and Bruce Weinberg. 2014. "Age and Scientific Genius." *Wiley Handbook of Genius*, edited by Dean Simonton, 422–450. Wiley-Blackwell, June.

Jones, Dan. 2017. "Your true self: Why it's morals that make the human." *New Scientist* 3122, April 22.

Jones, Garett. 2011. "IQ and National Productivity." In *New Palgrave Dictionary of Economics*, Online Edition, edited by Steven Durlauf and Lawrence Blume. London, New York: Palgrave-Macmillan.

Jones, Garett, and Niklas Potrafke. 2014. "Human Capital and National Institutional Quality: Are TIMSS, PISA, and National Average IQ Robust Predictors?" *Intelligence* 46: 148–155.

Jones, Rhys, Patrick Haufe, Edward Sells, Pejman Iravani, Vik Olliver, Chris Palmer, and Adrian Bowyer. 2011. "RepRap—The Replicating Rapid Prototyper." *Robotica* 29(January): 177–191.

Jones, Richard. 2016. *Against Transhumanism: The Delusion of Technological Transcendence*. Self-published, January 15, http://www.softmachines.org/wordpress/wp-content/uploads/2016/01/Against_Transhumanism_1.0.pdf.

Jordan, Gabriele, Samir Deeb, Jenny Bosten, and J. D. Mollon. 2010. "The Dimensionality of Color Vision in Carriers of Anomalous Trichromacy." *Journal of Vision* 10(8): 12.

Jordani, Joseph. 2011. *Why Do People Sing? Music in Human Evolution*. Logos, March 25.

Josef, Anika, David Richter, Gregory Samanez-Larkin, Gert Wagner, Ralph Hertwig, and Rui Mata. 2016. "Stability and change in risk-taking propensity across the adult life span." *Journal of Personality and Social Psychology* 111(3): 430–450.

Joshel, Sandra. 2010. *Slavery in the Roman World*. Cambridge University Press, August 16.

Judge, Timothy, and Robert Bretz. 1994. "Political Influence Behavior and Career Success." *Journal of Management* 20(1): 43.

Juliana, María, Leone, Diego Slezak, Diego Golombek, and Mariano Sigman. 2017. "Time to decide: Diurnal variations on the speed and quality of human decisions." *Cognition* 158: 44–55, January.

Kaestle, Carl, and Helen Damon-Moore. 1991. *Literacy in the United States: Readers and Reading Since 1880*. Yale University Press. April 24.

Kahn, Herman, and Anthony Wiener. 1967. *The Year 2000: A Framework for Speculation on the Next Thirty-Three Years*. Collier Macmillan. February.

Kahneman, Daniel, and Alan Krueger. 2006. "Developments in the Measurement of Subjective Well-being." *Journal of Economic Perspectives* 20(1): 3–24.

Kahneman, Daniel, and Dan Lovallo. 1993. "Timid Choices and Bold Forecasts: A Cognitive Perspective on Risk Taking." *Management Science* 39(1): 17–31.

Kamilar, Jason, Richard Bribiescas, and Brenda Bradley. 2010. "Is Group Size Related to Longevity in Mammals?" *Biology Letters* 6(6): 736–739.

Kandler, Christian, Anna Kornadt, Birk Hagemeyer, and Franz Neyer. 2015. "Patterns and Sources of Personality Development in Old Age." *Journal of Personality and Social Psychology* 109(1): 175–191.

Kang, Joonkyu. 2010. "A Study of the DRAM Industry." Masters Thesis, Sloan School of Management, MIT. http://hdl.handle.net/1721.1/59138.

Kantner, John, and Nancy Mahoney, 2000. *Great House Communities Across the Chacoan Landscape*. University of Arizona Press.

Kaplan, Steven, and Joshua Rauh. 2010. "Wall Street and Main Street: What Contributes to the Rise in the Highest Incomes?" *Review of Financial Studies*. 23(3): 1004–1050.

Karabarbounis, Loukas, and Brent Neiman. 2014. "The Global Decline of the Labor Share." *Quarterly Journal of Economics* 129(1): 61–103.

Katz, Leo. 1996. *Ill-Gotten Gains: Evasion, Blackmail, Fraud, and Kindred Puzzles of the Law*. University of Chicago Press, May 8.

Kauffeld, M., M.J. Wang, V. Goldstein, and K.E. Kasza. 2010. "Ice Slurry Applications." *International Journal of Refrigeration* 33(8): 1491–1505.

Kell, Harrison, David Lubinski, and Camilla Benbow. 2013. "Who Rises to the Top? Early Indicators." *Psychological Science* 24(5): 648–659.

Kelly, Raymond. 2000. *Warless Societies and the Origin of War*. University of Michigan Press, November 7.

Kemeny, Anna. 2002. "Driven to Excel: A Portrait of Canada's Workaholics." *Canadian Social Trends* 64, March 11.

Kessler, Donald, and Burton Cour-Palais. 1978. "Collision Frequency of Artificial Satellites: The Creation of a Debris Belt." *Journal of Geophysical Research* 83(June 1): 2637–2646.

Khazan, Olga. 2016. "The Best Music for Productivity? Silence." *Atlantic*, December 8.

Kiger, Derrick. 1989. "Effects of Music Information Load on a Reading Comprehension Task." *Perceptual and Motor Skills* 69: 531–534.

Killingsworth, Matthew, and Daniel Gilbert. 2010. "A Wandering Mind Is an Unhappy Mind." *Science* 330(6006): 932.

Kim, Jungsoo, and Richard de Dear. 2013. "Workspace Satisfaction: The Privacy-communication Trade-off in Open-plan Offices." *Journal of Environmental Psychology* 36(December): 18–26.

Klein, Gerwin, June Andronick, Kevin Elphinstone, Toby Murray, Thomas Sewell, Rafal Kolanski, and Gernot Heiser. 2014. "Comprehensive Formal Verification of an OS Microkernel." *ACM Transactions on Computer Systems* 1(32): article 2.

Klein, Mark, and Ana Garcia. 2014. "High-Speed Idea Filtering with the Bag of Lemons." September 27. http://papers.ssrn.com/sol3/papers.cfm?abstract_id=2501787.

Koch, Christof, Giulio Tononi. 2008. "Can machines be conscious?" *IEEE Spectrum* 45(6): 55.

Koene, Randal. 2012. "Experimental Research in Whole Brain Emulation: The Need for Innovative In Vivo Measurement Techniques." International Journal of Machine Consciousness 4(1): 35–65.

Kohli, Rajeev, and Raaj Sah. 2006. "Some Empirical Regularities in Market Shares." *Management Science* 52(11): 1792–1798.

Kok, Suzanne, and Baster Weel. 2014. "Cities, Tasks, and Skills." *Journal of Regional Science* 54(5): 856–892.

Koomey, Jonathan, and Samuel Naffziger. 2015. "Moore's Law Might Be Slowing Down, But Not Energy Efficiency." *IEEE Spectrum* 52(4): 35.

Korotayev, Andrey, and Sergey Tsirel. 2010. "A Spectral Analysis of World GDP Dynamics: Kondratieff Waves, Kuznets Swings, Juglar and Kitchin Cycles in Global Economic Development, and the 2008–2009 Economic Crisis." *Structure and Dynamics* 4(1): 3–57.

Kruse, Kevin. 2016. "15 Surprising Things Productive People Do Differently." *Forbes*, January 20.

Kubanek, Jan, Lawrence Snyder, and Richard Abrams. 2015. "Reward and Punishment Act as Distinct Factors in Guiding Behavior." *Cognition* 139(June): 154–167.

Kurzweil, Ray. 2005. *The Singularity Is Near: When Humans Transcend Biology*. Viking Press, September 22.

Kuster, Dennis, and Aleksandra Swioderska. 2016. "Moral Patients: What Drives the Perceptions of Moral Actions Toward Humans and Robots?" 340–343, in *What Social Robots can and Should Do*. Ed. Johanna Seibet, Marco Norskov, Soren Andersen. IOS Press, October 14.

Kyaga, Simon, Paul Lichtenstein, Marcus Boman, Christina Hultman, Niklas Langstrom, and Mikael Landen. 2011. "Creativity and Mental Disorder: Family Study of 300,000 People with Severe Mental Disorder." *British Journal of Psychiatry* 199: 373–379.

Kydland, Finn, and Edward Prescott. 1982. "Time to Build and Aggregate Fluctuations." *Econometrica* 50(6): 1345–1370.

L'Her, Jean-François, Rossitsa Stoyanova, Kathryn Shaw, William Scott, and Charissa Lai. 2016. "A Bottom-Up Approach to the Risk-Adjusted Performance of the Buyout Fund Market." *Financial Analysts Journal* 72(4): 36–48.

La Ferrara, Eliana, Alberto Chong, and Suzanne Duryea. 2012. "Soap Operas and Fertility: Evidence from Brazil." *American Economic Journal: Applied Economics* 4(4): 1–31.

Laland, Kevin. 2017. *Darwin's Unfinished Symphony: How Culture Made the Human Mind*. Princeton University Press, March 7.

Lalley, Steven, and E. Glen Weyl. 2014. "Quadratic Voting." December. http://papers.ssrn.com/sol3/papers.cfm?abstract_id=2003531.

Landes, David. 1969. *The Unbound Prometheus: Technological Change and Industrial Development in Western Europe from 1750 to the Present*. New York: University of Cambridge Press.

Lawrence, Robert. 2015. "Recent Declines in Labor's Share in US Income: A Preliminary Neoclassical Account." NBER Working Paper No. 21296, June.

Lawson, David, and Ruth Mace. 2011. "Parental Investment and the Optimization of Human Family Size." *Philosophical Transactions of the Royal Society B* 366(1563): 333–343.

Lawson, R., R. Ogden, and R. Bergin. 2012. "Application of Modular Construction in High-Rise Buildings." *Journal of Architectural Engineering* 18(2): 148–154.

Laxman, Kiran, Kate Lovibond, and Miriam Hassan. 2008. "Impact of Bipolar Disorder in Employed Populations." *American Journal of Managed Care* 14(11): 757–764.

Lee, Anthony, Courtney Hibbs, Margaret Wright, Nicholas Marting, Matthew Keller, and Brendan Zietsch. 2017. "Assessing the accuracy of perceptions of intelligence based on heritable facial features." *Intelligence* 64: 1–8.

Lee, Kenneth. 2011. "Essays in Health Economics: Empirical Studies on Determinants of Health." Doctoral dissertation, Economics, George Mason University.

Lehman, M., and L. Belady. 1985. *Program Evolution: Processes of Software Change*, San Diego, CA: Academic Press Professional, Inc., December.

Lentz, Rasmus, and Dale Mortensen. 2008. "An Empirical Model of Growth Through Product Innovation." *Econometrica* 76(6): 1317–1373.

Levitin. Daniel. 2016. "Your Em Goes to Bermuda." *Wall Street Journal*, June 10.

Levy, David. 1989. "The Statistical Basis of Athenian-American Constitutional Theory." *Journal of Legal Studies* 18(1): 79–103.

Levy, David. 2008. *Love and Sex with Robots: The Evolution of Human-Robot Relationships*. Harper Perennial.

Liberman, Nira, and Yaacov Trope. 2008. "The Psychology of Transcending the Here and Now." *Science* 322(5905): 1201–1205.

Lindberg, Henrik. 2017. "The people who keep us company" June 7. https://twitter.com/hnrklndbrg/status/872555621807267840

Lindenberger, Ulman. 2014. "Human Cognitive Aging: Corriger la Fortune?" *Science* 346(6209): 572–578.

Llinas, Rodolfo. 2001. *I of the Vortex: From Neurons to Self.* MIT Press, April 2.

Longman, Phillip. 2006. "The Return of Patriarchy." *Foreign Policy* 153: 56–60, 62–65.

López, Héctor, Jérémie Gachelin, Carine Douarche, Harold Auradou, and Eric Clément. 2015. "Turning Bacteria Suspensions into Superfluids." *Physical Review Letters* 115(2): 028301, July 7.

Lu, Jackson, Jordi Quoidbach, Francesca Gino, Alek Chakroff, William Maddux, and Adam Galinsky. 2017. "The dark side of going abroad: How broad foreign experiences increase immoral behavior." *Journal of Personality and Social Psychology*, 112(1): 1–16.

Luo, Jinfeng, and Yi Wen. 2015. "Institutions Do Not Rule: Reassessing the Driving Forces of Economic Development." Federal Reserve Bank of St. Louis, Working Paper 2015–2001A. January.

Lupien, S.J., F. Maheu, M. Tu, A. Fiocco, and T.E. Schramek. 2007. "The Effects of Stress and Stress Hormones on Human Cognition: Implications for the Field of Brain and Cognition." *Brain and Cognition* 65(December): 209–237.

Lykken, David, and Auke Tellegen. 1996. "Happiness Is a Stochastic Phenomenon." *Psychological Science* 7(3): 186–189.

MacCormack, Alan, John Rusnak, and Carliss Baldwin. 2012. "Exploring the Duality between Product and Organizational Architectures: A Test of the 'Mirroring' Hypothesis." *Research Policy* 41(8): 1309–1324.

Macey, Jonathan. 2008. "Market for Corporate Control." In *The Concise Encyclopedia of Economics*, edited by David Henderson. http://www.econlib.org/library/CEE.html.

Madrigal, Alexis. 2015. "The Case Against Killer Robots, from a Guy Actually Working on Artificial Intelligence." *Fusion*, February 27. http://fusion.net/story/54583/the-case-against-killer-robots-from-a-guy-actually-building-ai/.

Magalhaes, Joao, and Anders Sandberg. 2005. "Cognitive Aging as an Extension of Brain Development: A Model Linking Learning, Brain Plasticity, and Neurodegeneration." *Mechanisms of Ageing and Development* 126: 1026–1033.

Magee, Christopher, and Tansa Massoud. 2011. "Openness and Internal Conflict." *Journal of Peace Research* 48(January): 59–72.

Mandel, Michael. 2014. "Connections as a Tool for Growth: Evidence from the LinkedIn Economic Graph." November. http://www.slideshare.net/linkedin/mandel-linked-in-connections-reportnov-2014.

Mankiw, N. Gregory, and Matthew Weinzierl. 2010. "The Optimal Taxation of Height: A Case Study of Utilitarian Income Redistribution." *American Economic Journal: Economic Policy* 2(1): 155–176.

Mannix, Elizabeth, and Margaret Neale. 2005. "What Differences Make a Difference? The Promise and Reality of Diverse Teams in Organizations." *Psychological Science in the Public Interest* 6(2): 31–55.

Marcinkowska, Urszula, Mikhail Kozlov, Huajian Cai, Jorge Contreras-Garduño, Barnaby Dixson, Gavita Oana, Gwenaël Kaminski, Norman Li, Minna Lyons, Ike Onyishi, Keshav Prasai, Farid Pazhoohi, Pavol Prokop, Sandra L. Rosales Cardozo, Nicolle Sydney, Jose Yong, and Markus Rantala. 2014. "Cross-cultural variation in men's preference for sexual dimorphism in women's faces." *Biology Letters* 10(4): 20130850.

Marett, Kent, Joey George, Carmen Lewis, Manjul Gupta, and Gabriel Giordano. 2017. "Beware the dark side: Cultural preferences for lying online." *Computers in Human Behavior* 75: 834–884.

Markoff, John. 2016. "Microsoft Unit Dives Deep for a Data Center Solution." *New York Times*, B1, February 1.

Martin, G.M. 1971. "Brief Proposal on Immortality: An Interim Solution." *Perspectives in Biology and Medicine* 14(2): 339.

Martin, Leonard, and Kees van den Bos. 2014. "Beyond Terror: Towards a Paradigm Shift in the Study of Threat and Culture." *European Review of Social Psychology* 25(1): 32–70.

Martin, Rod, and Nicholas Kuiper. 1999. "Daily occurrence of laughter: Relationships with age, gender, and Type A personality." *Humor* 12(4): 355–384.

Marusek, David. 2012. *The Wedding Album*. General Genius Digital, January 30.

McAndrew, Francis, and Sara Koehnke. 2016. "On the nature of creepiness." *New Ideas in Psychology* 43: 10–15, December.

McCarty, Christopher, Peter Killworth, H. Russell Bernard, Eugene Johnsen, and Gene Shelley. 2000. "Comparing Two Methods for Estimating Network Size." *Human Organization* 60(1): 28–39.

Mednick, Sara, Ken Nakayama, Jose Cantero, Mercedes Atienza, Alicia Levin, Neha Pathak, and Robert Stickgold. 2002. "The restorative effect of naps on perceptual deterioration." *Nature Neuroscience* 5, 677–681.

Melnick, Michael, Bryan Harrison, Sohee Park, Loisa Bennetto, and Duje Tadin. 2013. "A Strong Interactive Link between Sensory Discriminations and Intelligence." *Current Biology* 23(11): 1013–1017.

Melzer, Arthur. 2007. "On the Pedagogical Motive for Esoteric Writing." *Journal of Politics* 69(4): 1015–1031.

Mercier, Hugo, and Dan Sperber. 2011. "Why do Humans Reason? Arguments for an Argumentative Theory." *Behavioral and Brain Sciences* 34(2): 57–74.

Merkle, Ralph. 1989. "Large Scale Analysis of Neural Structures." CSL-89-10, November. http://www.merkle.com/merkleDir/brainAnalysis.html

Merkle, Ralph, Robert Freitas Jr., Tad Hogg, Thomas Moore, Matthew Moses, James Ryley, "Molecular Mechanical Computing Systems," IMM Report No. 46, April 2016; http://www.imm.org/Reports/rep046.pdf

Merolla, Paul, John Arthur, Rodrigo Alvarez-Icaza, Andrew Cassidy, Jun Sawada, Filipp Akopyan, Bryan Jackson, Nabil Imam, Chen Guo, Yutaka Nakamura, Bernard Brezzo, Ivan Vo, Steven Esser, Rathinakumar Appuswamy, Brian Taba, Arnon Amir, Myron Flickner, William Risk, Rajit Manohar, and Dharmendra Modha. 2014. "A Million Spiking-neuron Integrated Circuit with a Scalable Communication Network and Interface." *Science* 345(6197): 668–673.

Miceli, Thomas, and Kathleen Segerson. 2007. "Punishing the Innocent along with the Guilty: The Economics of Individual versus Group Punishment." *Journal of Legal Studies* 36(1): 81–106.

Mikula, Shawn, and Winfried Denk. 2015. "High-resolution Whole-brain Staining for Electron Microscopic Circuit Reconstruction." *Nature Methods* 12(6): 541–546.

Millar, Jonathan, Stephen Oliner, and Daniel Sichel. 2013. "Time-To-Plan Lags for Commercial Construction Projects." NBER Working Paper No. 19408, September.

Miller, Kenneth. 2015. "Will You Ever Be Able to Upload Your Brain?" *New York Times*, October 10.

Miller, Mark, Ka-Ping Yee, and Jonathan Shapiro. 2003. "Capability Myths Demolished." Systems Research Laboratory, Johns Hopkins University, Technical Report SRL2003–2002. http://srl.cs.jhu.edu/pubs/SRL2003-02.pdf.

Miller, Shawn. 2009. "Is There a Relationship between Industry Concentration and Patent Activity?" December 17. http://ssrn.com/abstract=1531761.

Miner, Andrew, Theresa Glom, and Charles Hulin. 2005. "Experience Sampling Mood and its Correlates at Work." *Journal of Occupational and Organizational Psychology* 78(2): 171–193.

Minetti, Alberto, Yuri Ivanenko, Germana Cappellini, Nadia Dominici, and Francesco Lacquaniti. 2012. "Humans Running in Place on Water at Simulated Reduced Gravity." *PLoS ONE* 7(7): e37300.

Minkov, Michael. 2013. *Cross-Cultural Analysis: The Science and Art of Comparing the World's Modern Societies and Their Cultures*. Thousand Oaks, CA: Sage. June 6.

Minsky, Marvin. 1991. "Conscious Machines." in *Machinery of Consciousness*, Proceedings, National Research Council of Canada, 75th Anniversary Symposium on Science in Society, June.

Mlodinow, Leonard. 2012. *Subliminal: How Your Unconscious Mind Rules Your Behavior*. Pantheon. April 24.

Mogilner, Cassie, Sepandar Kamvar, and Jennifer Aaker. 2011. "The Shifting Meaning of Happiness." *Social Psychological and Personality Science* 2(4): 395–402.

Mokyr, Joel, Chris Vickers, and Nicolas Ziebarth. 2015. "The History of Technological Anxiety and the Future of Economic Growth: Is This Time Different?" *Journal of Economic Perspectives* 29(3): 31–50.

Montemurro, Marcelo, and Damián Zanette. 2016. "Coherent oscillations in word-use data from 1700 to 2008." *Palgrave Communications* 2: 16084.

Montgomery, Douglas. 2008. *Design and Analysis of Experiments*. John Wiley and Sons. July 28.

Moravec, Hans. 1988. *Mind Children: The Future of Robot and Human Intelligence*. Harvard University Press, October.

Morgan, Timothy. 2014. "A Rare Peek Into The Massive Scale of AWS." *Enterprise Tech Systems Edition*, November 14. http://www.enterprisetech.com/2014/11/14/rare-peek-massive-scale-aws/.

Morris, Ian. 2015. *Foragers, Farmers, and Fossil Fuels: How Human Values Evolve*. Princeton University Press. March 22.

Mrazek, Michael, Michael Franklin, Dawa Phillips, Benjamin Baird, and Jonathan Schooler. 2013. "Mindfulness Training Improves Working Memory Capacity and GRE Performance While Reducing Mind Wandering." *Psychological Science* 24(5): 776–781.

Mueller, Dennis. 1982. "Redistribution, Growth, and Political Stability." *American Economic Review* 72(2): 155–159.

Mulder, Monique. 1998. "The Demographic Transition: Are we any Closer to an Evolutionary Explanation?" *Trends in Ecology & Evolution* 13(7): 266–270.

Mullainathan, Sendhil, and Eldar Shafir. 2013. *Scarcity: Why Having Too Little Means So Much*. Times Books, September 3.

Müller, Vincent, and Nick Bostrom. 2014. "Future Progress in Artificial Intelligence: A Survey of Expert Opinion." In *Fundamental Issues of Artificial Intelligence*, edited by Vincent Müller. Berlin: Springer.

Mulligan, Casey, Richard Gil, and Xavier Sala-i-Martin. 2004. "Do Democracies Have Different Public Policies than Nondemocracies?" *Journal of Economic Perspectives* 18(1): 51–74.

Myers, David. 2017. "Religious Engagement and the Good Life." January 1. http://www.sydneysymposium.unsw.edu.au/2017/chapters/MyersSSSP2017.pdf

Myers, David, and Ed Diener. 1995. "Who Is Happy?" *Psychological Science* 6(1): 10–19.

Nagy, Bela, J. Doyne Farmer, Quan Bui, and Jessika Trancik. 2013. "Statistical Basis for Predicting Technological Progress." *PLoS ONE* 8(2): e52669.

Nakamoto, Satoshi. 2008. "Bitcoin: A Peer-to-Peer Electronic Cash System." November. https://bitcoin.org/bitcoin.pdf.

National Bureau of Economic Research. 2017. "US Business Cycle Expansions and Contractions." Downloaded February 13, 2017. http://www.nber.org/cycles.html

Navarrete, C. David, Robert Kurzban, Daniel Fessler, and Lee Kirkpatrick 2004. "Anxiety and Intergroup Bias: Terror Management or Coalitional Psychology?" *Group Processes & Intergroup Relations* 7(4): 370–397.

Nesse, Randolph, Caleb Finch, and Charles Nunn. 2017. "Does selection for short sleep duration explain human vulnerability to Alzheimer's disease?" *Evolution, Medicine, and Public Health* 2017(1): 39–46.

Nguyen, Anh Ngoc, Jim Taylor, and Steve Bradley. 2003. "Job Autonomy and Job Satisfaction: New Evidence." Doctoral dissertation, University of Lancaster, Lancaster.

Niederle, Muriel. 2014. "Gender." NBER Working Paper No. 20788, December.

Nikolaev, Boris, and Raufhon Salahodjaev. 2017. "Historical Prevalence of Infectious Diseases, Cultural Values, and the Origins of Economic Institutions." *Kyklos* 70(1): 97–128.

Nishijima, Sadao. 1986. "The Economic and Social History of Former Han." in *Cambridge History of China: Volume I: the Ch'in and Han Empires, 221 B.C.–A.D. 220*. Ed. Denis Twitchett and Michael Loewe. Cambridge University Press.

Nitsch, Volker. 2005. "Zipf Zipped." *Journal of Urban Economics* 57(1): 86–100.

Niven, David. 2006. *The 100 Simple Secrets of Successful People: What Scientists Have Learned and How You Can Use It*, Harper One, November 7.

Nordhaus, William. 2015. "Are We Approaching an Economic Singularity? Information Technology and the Future of Economic Growth." NBER Working Paper No. 21547, September.

Oi, Walter, and Todd Idson. 1999. "Firm Size and Wages." In *Handbook of Labor Economics* 3(3), edited by Orley Ashenfelter and David Card. Elsevier.

Oishi, Shigehiro, and Ed Diener. 2014. "Residents of Poor Nations Have a Greater Sense of Meaning in Life Than Residents of Wealthy Nations." *Psychological Science* 25(2): 422–430.

Oishi, Shigehiro, Thomas Talhelm, and Minha Lee. 2015. "Personality and geography: Introverts prefer mountains." *Journal of Research in Personality* 58: 55–68.

Olson, Mancur. 1974. *The Logic of Collective Action: Public Goods and the Theory of Groups*. Harvard University Press; Revised edition, July 1.

Olsson, Ola, and Christopher Paik. 2015. "Long-Run Cultural Divergence: Evidence From the Neolithic Revolution." University of Gothenburg Working Papers in Economics No. 620. May. http://hdl.handle.net/2077/38815.

Organski, A. F. K. 1958. *World Politics*. Knopf.

Ostry, Jonathan, Andrew Berg, and Charalambos Tsangarides. 2014. "Redistribution, Inequality, and Growth." IMF Staff Discussion Note, February.

Otterbein, Keith. 1985. *The evolution of war: a cross-cultural study*. Human Relations Area File: New Haven, CT.

Pagel, Mark. 2009. "Human language as a culturally transmitted replicator." *Nature Reviews Genetics* 10: 405–415, June.

Paine, Sarah-Jane, Philippa Gander, and Noemie Travier. 2006. "The Epidemiology of Morningness/Eveningness: Influence of Age, Gender, Ethnicity, and Socioeconomic Factors in Adults (30–49 Years)." *Journal of Biological Rhythms* 21(1): 68–76.

Pang, Alex. 2017. "Darwin Was a Slacker and You Should Be Too." *Nautilus* 46, March 30.

Papaioannou, Sotiris. 2017. "Regulations and productivity: Long run effects and nonlinear influences." *Economic Modelling* 60: 244–252.

Parker, Alice. Saeid Barzegarjalali, Kun Yue, Rebecca Lee, and Sukanya Patil. 2016. "Modeling Brain Disorders in Silicon Nanotechnologies." in *Wireless Computing in Medicine: From Nano to Cloud with Ethical and Legal Implications*, ed. Mary Eshaghian-Wilner, John Wiley & Sons.

Parker, Gordon, Amelia Paterson, Kathryn Fletcher, Bianca Blanch, and Rebecca Graham. 2012. "The 'Magic Button Question' for Those with a Mood Disorder—Would They Wish to Re-live Their Condition?" *Journal of Affective Disorders* 136(3): 419–424.

Partridge, Bradley, Stephanie Bell, Jayne Lucke, Sarah Yeates, and Wayne Hall. 2011. "Smart Drugs 'As Common As Coffee': Media Hype about Neuroenhancement." *PLOS One* 6(11): e28416.

Paulhus, Delroy, Paul Trapnell, and David Chen. 1999. "Birth Order Effects on Personality and Achievement Within Families." *Psychological Science* 10(6): 482–488.

Pavan, Ronni. 2016. "On The Production of Skills and the Birth Order Effect." *Journal of Human Resources*, 51: 699–726.

Pellegrino, Renata, Ibrahim Halil Kavakli, Namni Goel, Christopher Cardinale, David Dinges, Samuel Kuna, Greg Maislin, Hans Van Dongen, Sergio Tufik, John Hogenesch, Hakon Hakonarson, and Allan Pack. 2014. "A Novel BHLHE41 Variant is Associated with Short Sleep and Resistance to Sleep Deprivation in Humans." *Sleep* 37(8): 1327–1336.

Penrose. Roger. 1989. *The Emperor's New Mind: Concerning Computers, Minds and The Laws of Physics*. Oxford University Press, November 9.

Pepinsky, Tom. 2017. "Everyday Authoritarianism is Boring and Tolerable." January 6. https://tompepinsky.com/2017/01/06/everyday-authoritarianism-is-boring-and-tolerable/

Perkins, Adam, and Philip Corr. 2005. "Can Worriers be Winners? The Association between Worrying and Job Performance." *Personality and Individual Differences* 38(1): 25–31.

Pfeffer, Jeffrey. 2010. *Power: Why Some People Have It—and Others Don't*. HarperCollins. September 14.

Philippon, Thomas. 2015. "Has the US Finance Industry Become Less Efficient? On the Theory and Measurement of Financial Intermediation." *American Economic Review* 105(4): 1408–1438.

Pickena, David, and Ben Ilozora. 2003. "Height and Construction Costs of Buildings in Hong Kong." *Construction Management and Economics* 21(2): 107–111.

Piff, Paul, Pia Dietze, Matthew Feinberg, Daniel Stancato, and Dacher Keltner. 2015. "Awe, the small self, and prosocial behavior." *Journal of Personality and Social Psychology* 108(6): 883–899.

Piller, Frank. 2008. "Mass Customization." In *The Handbook of 21st Century Management*, edited by Charles Wankel, 420–430. Thousand Oaks, CA: Sage Publications.

Pindyck, Robert. 2013. "Climate Change Policy: What Do the Models Tell Us?" *Journal of Economic Literature* 51(3): 860–872.

Pinker, Steven. 2007. *The Stuff of Thought: Language as a Window into Human Nature*. Viking Adult, September.

Pinker, Steven. 2011. *The Better Angels of our Nature*. New York: Viking, October.

Piore, Adam. 2014. "The Neuroscientist Who Wants To Upload Humanity To A Computer." *Popular Science*, May 16.

Pizzola, Brandon. 2015. "The Impact of Business Regulation on Business Investment: Evidence from the Recent Experience of the United States." Working Paper, May 11.

van der Ploeg, Hidde, Tien Chey, Rosemary Korda, Emily Banks, and Adrian Bauman. 2012. "Sitting Time and All-Cause Mortality Risk in 222,497 Australian Adults." *Archives of Internal Medicine* 172(6): 494–500.

Porat, Ariel. 2009. "Private Production of Public Goods: Liability for Unrequested Benefits." *Michigan Law Review* 108: 189–227.

Porter, David, Stephen Rassenti, Anil Roopnarine, and Vernon Smith. 2003. "Combinatorial Auction Design." *Proceedings of the National Academy of Sciences* 100(19): 11153–11157.

Poschke, Markus. 2014. "The Firm Size Distribution Across Countries and Skill-Biased Change in Entrepreneurial Technology." IZA Discussion Paper No. 7991, March 1. https://papers.ssrn.com/sol3/papers.cfm?abstract_id=2403128

Posner, Richard. 2014. *Economic Analysis of Law*, 9th ed. Wolters Kluwer, January.

Post, Felix. 1994. "Creativity and psychopathology: A study of 291 world-famous men." *British Journal of Psychiatry* 165(1): 22–34, July.

Potter, Andrew. 2010. *The Authenticity Hoax: Why the "Real" Things We Seek Don't Make Us Happy*. Harper, April 13.

Pozen, Robert. 2012. *Extreme Productivity: Boost Your Results, Reduce Your Hours*. Harper Business. October 2.

Preckel, Franzis, Anastasiya Lipnevich, Sandra Schneider, and Richard Roberts. 2011. "Chronotype, Cognitive Abilities, and Academic Achievement: A Meta-Analytic Investigation." *Learning and Individual Differences* 21: 483–492.

Prelec, Dražen. 2004. "A Bayesian Truth Serum for Subjective Data." *Science* 306(5695): 462–466.

Prelec, Dražen, H. Sebastian Seung, and John McCoy. 2017. "A solution to the single-question crowd wisdom problem." *Nature* 541(7638): 532–535.

Provenzano, Davide. 2015. "On the World Distribution of Income." *Review of Income and Wealth* 63(1): 189-196.

Raa, Thijs Ten. 2003. "A Simple Version of the Henry George Theorem." *Finance India* 17(2): 561–564.

Rammstedt, Beatrice, Daniel Danner, and Silke Martin. 2016. "The association between personality and cognitive ability: Going beyond simple effects." *Journal of Research in Personality* 62: 39–44, June.

Ramscar, Michael, Peter Hendrix, Cyrus Shaoul, Petar Milin, and Harald Baayen. 2014. "The Myth of Cognitive Decline: Non-Linear Dynamics of Lifelong Learning." *Topics in Cognitive Science* 6(1): 5–42.

Randall, Jason, Frederick Oswald, and Margaret Beier. 2014. "Mind-Wandering, Cognition, and Performance: A Theory-Driven Meta-Analysis of Attention Regulation." *Psychological Bulletin* 140(6): 1411–1431.

Rao, Venkatesh. 2012. "Welcome to the Future Nauseous." Ribbon Farm blog, May 9, http://www.ribbonfarm.com/2012/05/09/welcome-to-the-future-nauseous/.

Rayneau-Kirkhope, Daniel, Yong Mao, and Robert Farr. 2012. "Ultralight Fractal Structures from Hollow Tubes." *Physics Review Letters* 109(20): 204301.

Reed, William. 2003. "Information, Power, and War." *American Political Science Review* 97(4): 633–641.

Reed, William, and Murray Jorgensen. 2004. "The Double Pareto-Lognormal Distribution: A New Parametric Model for Size Distributions." *Communications in Statistics, Theory and Methods* 33(8): 1733–1753.

Regalado, Antonio. 2013. "The Brain Is Not Computable." MIT Technology Review, February 18.

Regan, Pamela, Saloni Lakhanpal, and Carlos Anguiano. 2012. "Relationship outcomes in Indian-American love-based and arranged marriages." *Psychological Reports* 110(3): 915–924.

Richter, Eugene. 1893. *Pictures of the Socialistic Future*. Translated by Henry Wright. London: Swan Sonnenschhein.

Rimfeld, Kaili, Yulia Kovas, Philip Dale, and Robert Plomin. 2016. "True grit and genetics: Predicting academic achievement from personality." *Journal of Personality and Social Psychology* 111(5): 780–789.

Roberts, Brent, Nathan Kuncel, Rebecca Shiner, Avshalom Caspi, and Lewis Goldberg. 2007. "The Power of Personality: The Comparative Validity of Personality Traits, Socioeconomic Status, and Cognitive Ability for Predicting Important Life Outcomes." *Perspectives on Psychological Science* 2(4): 313–345.

Robinson, Robert, and Elton Jackson. 2001. "Is Trust in Others Declining in America? An Age–Period–Cohort Analysis." *Social Science Research* 30(1): 117–145.

Rockenbach, Bettina, Abdolkarim Sadrieh, and Barbara Mathauschek. 2007. "Teams Take the Better Risks." *Journal of Economic Behavior & Organization* 63(3): 412–422.

Rohrer, Julia, Boris Egloff, and Stefan Schmukle. 2017. "Probing Birth-Order Effects on Narrow Traits Using Specification Curve Analysis." *Psychological Science* in press.

Root-Bernstein, Robert, Lindsay Allen, Leighanna Beach, Ragini Bhadula, Justin Fast, Chelsea Hosey, Benjamin Kremkow, Jacqueline Lapp, Kaitlin Lonc, Kendell Pawelec, Abigail Podufaly, and Caitlin Russ. 2008. "Arts Foster Scientific Success: Avocations of Nobel, National Academy, Royal Society, and Sigma Xi Members." *Journal of Psychological Science and Technology* 1(2): 51–63.

Rosso, Brent, Kathryn Dekas, and Amy Wrzesniewski. 2010. "On the meaning of work: A theoretical integration and review." *Research in Organizational Behavior* 30: 91–127.

Rothman, Wilson. 2016. "The Camera That Doesn't Let You Lie." *Wall Street Journal*, October 24.

Sabelman, Eric, and Roger Lam. 2015. "The Real-Life Dangers of Augmented Reality." *IEEE Spectrum* (July): 51–53.

Sahal, Devendra. 1981. *Patterns of Technological Innovation*. Addison-Wesley.

Sailer, Steve. 2003. "Cousin Marriage Conundrum: The ancient practice discourages Democratic Nation-building." *The American Conservative*, January 13, 20–22.

Salvador, Fabrizio, Martin de Holan, and Frank Piller. 2009. "Cracking the Code of Mass Customization." *MIT Sloan Management Review* 50(3): 70–79.

Samson, David, Alyssa Crittenden, Ibrahim Mabulla, Audax Mabulla, and Charles Nunn. 2017. "Hadza sleep biology: Evidence for flexible sleep-wake patterns in hunter-gatherers." *American Journal of Physical Anthropology* 162(3): 573–582, March.

Sandberg, Anders. 2013. "Feasibility of Whole Brain Emulation." pp. 251–264, *In Theory and Philosophy of Artificial Intelligence*, ed. Vincent Muller, Springer.

Sandberg, Anders. 2014. "Monte Carlo model of brain emulation development." Working Paper 2014–1 (version 1.2), Future of Humanity Institute. http://www.aleph.se/papers/Monte%20Carlo%20model%20of%20brain%20emulation%20development.pdf.

Sandberg, Anders, and Nick Bostrom. 2008. "Whole Brain Emulation: A Roadmap." Technical Report #2008–2003, Future of Humanity Institute, Oxford University. http://www.fhi.ox.ac.uk/__data/assets/pdf_file/0019/3853/brain-emulation-roadmap-report.pdf.

Sandstrom, Gillian, and Elizabeth Dunn. 2014. "Social Interactions and Well-Being: The Surprising Power of Weak Ties." *Personality and Social Psychology Bulletin* 40(7): 910–922.

Savage, Van, Eric Deeds, and Walter Fontana. 2008. "Sizing Up Allometric Scaling Theory." *PLoS Computational Biology* 4(9): e1000171.

Scafetta, Nicola. 2010. "Empirical evidence for a celestial origin of the climate oscillations and its implications." *Journal of Atmospheric and Solar-Terrestrial Physics* 72: 951–970.

Schacht, Ryan, Douglas Tharp, and Ken Smith. 2016. "Marriage Markets and Male Mating Effort: Violence and Crime Are Elevated Where Men Are Rare." *Human Nature* 27(4): 489–500, December.

Schafer, Markus, and Laura Upenieks. 2016. "The Age-Graded Nature of Advice: Distributional Patterns and Implications for Life Meaning." *Social Psychology Quarterly* 79: 22–43.

Scheidel, Walter. 2017. *The Great Leveler: Violence and the History of Inequality from the Stone Age to the Twenty-First Century*. Princeton University Press, January 24.

Scheve, Kenneth, and David Stasavage. 2009. "Institutions, Partisanship, and inequality in the long run." *World Politics* 61: 215–253.

Schmitt, David. 2012. "When the Difference is in the Details: A Critique of Zentner and Mitura (2012)—Stepping out of the Caveman's Shadow: Nations' Gender Gap Predicts Degree of Sex Differentiation in Mate Preferences." *Evolutionary Psychology* 10(4): 720–726.

Schoemaker, Paul. 1995. "Scenario Planning: A Tool for Strategic Thinking." *Sloan Management Review* 36(2): 25–40.

Schrank, David, Tim Lomax, and Bill Eisele. 2011. "2011 Urban Mobility Report." Texas Transportation Institute, September.

Schwartz, Shalom, Jan Cieciuch, Michele Vecchione, Eldad Davidov, Ronald Fischer, Constanze Beierlein, Alice Ramos, Markku Verkasalo, Jan-Erik Lönnqvist, Kursad Demirutku, Ozlem Dirilen-Gumus, and Mark Konty. 2012. "Refining the Theory of Basic Individual Values." *Journal of Personality and Social Psychology* 103(4): 663–688.

Schwartz, Shalom, and Tammy Rubel. 2005. "Sex Differences in Value Priorities: Cross-cultural and Multimethod Studies." *Journal of Personality and Social Psychology* 89(6): 1010–1028.

Scott, James. 1998. *Seeing Like a State: How Certain Schemes to Improve the Human Condition Have Failed.* Yale University Press, March 30.

Scott, James. 2017. *Against the Grain: A Deep History of the Earliest States*. Yale University Press, August 22.

Sedikides, Constantine, Tim Wildschut, Wing-Yee Cheung, Clay Routledge, Erica Hepper, Jamie Arndt, Kenneth Vail, Xinyue Zhou, Kenny Brackstone, and Ad Vingerhoets. 2016. "Nostalgia Fosters Self-Continuity: Uncovering the Mechanism (Social Connectedness) and Consequence (Eudaimonic Well-Being)." *Emotion* 16(4): 524-539.

Sedivy, Julie. 2017. "Why Doesn't Ancient Fiction Talk About Feelings?" *Nautilus* 47, April 27.

Seung, Sebastian. 2012. *Connectome: How the Brain's Wiring Makes Us Who We Are.* Houghton Mifflin Harcourt, February 7.

Shapiro, Carl. 2016. "Patent Remedies." *American Economic Review* 106(5): 198–202.

Shapiro, Carl, and Hal Varian. 1999. *Information Rules: A Strategic Guide to the Network Economy.* Boston: Harvard Business School Press.

Shavell, Steven. 2004. *Foundations of Economic Analysis of Law.* Harvard University Press.

Shea, John. 1993. "Do Supply Curves Slope Up?" *Quarterly Journal of Economics* 108(1): 1–32.

Shiota, Michelle, Dacher Keltner, and Amanda Mossman. 2007. "The nature of awe: Elicitors, appraisals, and effects on self-concept." *Cognition and Emotion* 21(5): 944–963.

Shleifer, Andrei. 2000. *Inefficient Markets: An Introduction to Behavioural Finance.* Oxford University Press, March 9.

Shulman, Carl. 2010. "Whole Brain Emulation and the Evolution of Superorganisms." Machine Intelligence Research Institute working paper. http://intelligence.org/files/WBE-Superorgs.pdf.

Shulman, Carl, and Nick Bostrom. 2013. "Embryo Selection for Cognitive Enhancement: Curiosity or Game-Changer?" *Global Policy* 5(1): 85–92.

Shumpeter, Joseph. 1942. *Capitalism, Socialism, and Democracy.* New York: Harper.

Shy, Oz. 1996. *Industrial Organization, Theory and Applications.* MIT Press.

Simler, Kevin, and Robin Hanson. 2018. *The Elephant in the Brain: Hidden Motives in Everyday Life.* Oxford University Press. January 2.

Smith, Rosanna, and George Newman. 2014. "When Multiple Creators Are Worse Than One: The Bias Toward Single Authors in the Evaluation of Art." *Psychology of Aesthetics, Creativity, and the Arts* 8(3): 303–310.

Snir, Raphael, and Itzhak Harpaz. 2002. "Work-leisure Relations: Leisure Orientation and the Meaning of Work." *Journal of Leisure Research* 34(2): 178–203.

Society for Human Resource Management. 2012. "2012 Employee Job Satisfaction and Engagement." Society for Human Resource Management. October 3. http://www.shrm.org/Research/SurveyFindings/Documents/12–0537%20 2012_jobsatisfaction_fnl_online.pdf.

Solomon, Sheldon, Jeff Greenberg, and Tom Pyszczynski. 2015. *The Worm at the Core: On the Role of Death in Life.* Random House, May 12.

Song, Jae, David Price, Fatih Guvenen, and Nicholas Bloom. 2015. "Firming Up Inequality." NBER Working Paper No. 21199, May.

Sorensen, Morten, Neng Wang, and Jinqiang Yang. 2014. "Valuing Private Equity." *Review of Financial Studies* 27(7): 1977–2021.

Soto, Christopher, Oliver John, Samuel Gosling, and Jeff Potter. 2011. "Age Differences in Personality Traits from 10 to 65: Big Five Domains and Facets in a Large Cross-Sectional Sample." *Journal of Personality and Social Psychology* 100(2): 330–348.

Sousa-Poza, Alfonso, and Alexandre Ziegler. 2003. "Asymmetric Information about Workers' Productivity as a Cause for Inefficient Long Working Hours." *Labour Economics* 10: 727–747.

Spengler, Marion, Martin Brunner, Rodica Damian, Oliver Lüdtke, Romain Martin, and Brent Roberts. 2015. "Student characteristics and behaviors at age 12 predict occupational success 40 years later over and above childhood IQ and parental socioeconomic status." *Developmental Psychology* 51(9): 1329–1340.

Spolaore, Enrico, and Romain Wacziarg. 2016. "War and Relatedness." *Review of Economics and Statistics* 98(5): 925–939, December.

Staats, Bradley, and Francesca Gino. 2012. "Specialization and Variety in Repetitive Tasks: Evidence from a Japanese Bank." *Management Science* 58(6): 1141–1159.

Stanovich, Keith. 2004. *The Robot's Rebellion: Finding Meaning in the Age of Darwin*. University of Chicago Press. May 15.

Stanovich, Keith, Richard West, and Maggie Toplak. 2013. "Myside Bias, Rational Thinking, and Intelligence." *Current Directions in Psychological Science* 22(4): 259–264.

Stapleton, Karyn. 2010. "Swearing." In *Interpersonal Pragmatics*, edited by Miriam Locher and Sage Graham. 289–305. De Gruyter Mouton. October 15.

Stebila, Douglas, Michele Mosca, and Norbert Lütkenhaus. 2010. "The Case for Quantum Key Distribution." *Quantum Communication and Quantum Networking* 36: 283–296.

Steen, Todd. 1996. "Religion and Earnings: Evidence from the NLS Youth Cohort." *International Journal of Social Economics* 23(1): 47–58.

Stephens. Mitchell. 2007. *A History of the News*, 3rd ed. New York: Oxford University Press.

Stern, Chadly, Tessa West, and Peter Schmitt. 2014. "The Liberal Illusion of Uniqueness." *Psychological Science* 25(1): 137–144.

Stojmenovska, Dragana, Thijs Bol, and Thomas Leopold. 2017. "Does Diversity Pay? A Replication of Herring (2009)." *American Sociological Review*, July 7.

Stoll, Gundula, Sven Rieger, Oliver Lüdtke, Benjamin Nagengast, Ulrich Trautwein, and Brent Roberts. 2017. "Vocational Interests Assessed at the End of High School Predict Life Outcomes Assessed 10 Years Later Over and Above IQ and Big Five Personality Traits." *Journal of Personality and Social Psychology*, 113(1): 167–184.

Strand, Clark. 2015. *Waking Up to the Dark: Ancient Wisdom for a Sleepless Age*. Spiegel & Grau, April.

Stratmann, Thomas. 1996. "Instability of Collective Decisions? Testing for Cyclical Majorities." *Public Choice* 88(1–2): 15–28.

Stross, Charles. 2006. *Accelerando*. Ace. June 27.

Stutzer, Alois, and Bruno Frey. 2013. "Recent Developments in the Economics of Happiness: A Selective Overview." In *Recent Developments in the Economics of Happiness*, edited by Bruno S. Frey and Alois Stutzer. Cheltenham, UK: Edward Elgar.

Sun, Wei, Robin Hanson, Kathryn Laskey, and Charles Twardy. 2012. "Probability and Asset Updating using Bayesian Networks for Combinatorial Prediction Markets." *Proceedings of the Twenty-Eighth Conference on Uncertainty in Artificial Intelligence*, Catalina Island, August 15–17, ed. Nando de Freitas and Kevin Murphy, 815–824.

Sutin, Angelina, Paul Costa Jr., Richard Miech, and William Eaton. 2009. "Personality and Career Success: Concurrent and Longitudinal Relations." *European Journal of Personality* 23(2): 71–84.

Sutter, Matthias. 2005. "Are Four Heads Better than Two? An Experimental Beauty-contest Game with Teams of Different Size." *Economics Letters* 88(1): 41–46.

Swami, Viren, and Rebecca Coles. 2010. "The Truth is Out There." *The Psychologist* 23(7): 560–563.

Sylos-Labini, Francesca, Francesco Lacquaniti, and Yuri Ivanenko. 2014. "Human Locomotion under Reduced Gravity Conditions: Biomechanical and Neurophysiological Considerations." *BioMed Research International*: 547242.

Syverson, Chad. 2004. "Product Substitutability and Productivity Dispersion." *Review of Economics and Statistics* 86(2): 534–550.

Syverson, Chad. 2011. "What Determines Productivity?" *Journal of Economic Literature* 49(2): 326–365.

T.A.W. 2017. "Want to be a sport star? Don't specialise as a youngster." *Economist, Game Theory*, January 19. https://www.economist.com/blogs/gametheory/2017/01/tiger-parents-beware

Tabarrok, Alexander. 1998. "The Private Provision of Public Goods Via Dominant Assurance Contracts." *Public Choice* 96(3–4): 345–362.

Talhelm, T., X. Zhang, S. Oishi, C. Shimin, D. Duan, X. Lan, and S. Kitayama. 2014. "Large-Scale Psychological Differences Within China Explained by Rice Versus Wheat Agriculture." *Science* 344(6184): 603–608.

Tammen, Ronald, Jacek Kugler, and Douglas Lemke. 2011. "Power Transition Theory." Transresearch Consortium, Working paper 1, December. http://transresearchconsortium.com/s/Power-Transition-Theory.pdf

Tay, Louis, Vincent Ng, Lauren Kuykendall, and Ed Diener. 2014. "Demographic Factors and Worker Well-being: An Empirical Review Using Representative

Data from the United States and across the World." In *The Role of Demographics in Occupational Stress and Well Being (Research in Occupational Stress and Well-being, Volume 12)*, 235–283, edited by Pamela Perrewé, Christopher Rosen, and Jonathon Halbesleben. Emerald Group Publishing Limited.

Thomas, Frank, and Ollie Johnston. 1981. *The Illusion of Life: Disney Animation*. Abbeville Press.

Thompson, Ben. 2013. "What Clayton Christensen Got Wrong." Stratechery blog, September 22. http://stratechery.com/2013/clayton-christensen-got-wrong/.

Torelli, Carlos, and Andrew Kaikati. 2009. "Values as Predictors of Judgments and Behaviors: The Role of Abstract and Concrete Mindsets." *Journal of Personality and Social Psychology* 96(1): 231–247.

Tormala, Zakary, Jayson Jia, and Michael Norton. 2012. "The Preference for Potential." *Journal of Personality and Social Psychology* 103(4): 567–583.

Tovee, Martin. 1994. "How Fast is the Speed of Thought?" *Current Biology* 4(12): 1125–1127.

Towers, Grady. 1987. "The Outsiders." *Gift of Fire* 22(April).

Treleaven, Michelle, Robyn Jackowich, Lesley Roberts, Richard Wassersug, and Thomas Johnson. 2013. "Castration and Personality: Correlation of Androgen Deprivation and Estrogen Supplementation with the Big Five Factor Personality Traits of Adult Males." *Journal of Research in Personality* 47(4): 376–379.

Trougakos, John, and Ivona Hideg. 2009. "Momentary Work Recovery: The Role of Within-Day Work Breaks." In *Current Perspectives on Job-Stress Recovery*, vol. 7, edited by Sabine Sonnentag, Pamela Perrewe, and Daniel Ganster, 37–84. Bradford, U.K.: Emerald Group.

Tschacher, Wolfgang, Fabian Ramseyer, and Sander Koole. 2017. "Sharing the Now in the Social Present: Duration of Nonverbal Synchrony Is Linked With Personality." *Journal of Personality*, February 17.

Tsiolkovsky, Konstantin. 1903. "The Exploration of Cosmic Space by Means of Reaction Devices." *The Science Review* 5.

Turchin, Peter. 2003. *Historical Dynamics: Why States Rise and Fall*. Princeton University Press.

Turchin, Peter, and Sergey Nefedov. 2009. *Secular Cycles*. Princeton University Press. August 9.

Ulku, Hulya. 2004. "R&D, Innovation, and Economic Growth: An Empirical Analysis." International Monetary Fund Working Paper, September.

United Nations. 2013. *World Population Prospects: The 2012 Revision*. United Nations, Department of Economic and Social Affairs, Population Division. DVD Edition.

Vakarelski, Ivan, Derek Chan, and Sigurdur Thoroddsen. 2015. "Drag Moderation by the Melting of an Ice Surface in Contact with Water." *Physics Review Letters* 115(July 24): 044501.

van de Ven, Niels, Marcel Zeelenberg, and Rik Pieters. 2011. "Why Envy Outperforms Admiration." Personality and Social Psychology Bulletin 37(6): 784–795.

Varnum, Michael, and Igor Grossmann. 2016. "Pathogen prevalence is associated with cultural changes in gender equality." *Nature Human Behaviour* 1: 0003.

Vélez, Juliana. 2014. "War and Progressive Income Taxation in the 20th Century." BEHL Working Paper WP2014-03, September. http://behl.berkeley.edu/files/2014/10/WP2014-03_londono_10-3-14.pdf.

Ventura, Jaume, and Hans-Joachim Voth. 2015. "Debt into Growth: How Sovereign Debt Accelerated the First Industrial Revolution." NBER Working Paper No. 21280, June.

Vermont, Samson. 2006. "Independent Invention as a Defense to Patent Infringement." *Michigan Law Review* 105(3): 475–504.

Vestling, Monika, Fertil Tufvesson, and Susanne Iwarsson. 2003. "Indicators for Return to Work after Stroke and the Importance of Work for Subjective Well-being and Life Satisfaction." *Journal of Rehabilitation Medicine* 35(3): 127–131.

Viamontes, George, Igor Markov, and John Hayes. 2005. "Is Quantum Search Practical?" *Computing in Science and Engineering* 7(3): 62–70.

Vinge, Vernor. 2003. "The Cookie Monster." *Analog* 123(10): 10–40.

Vohs, Kathleen, Joseph Redden, and Ryan Rahinel. 2013. "Physical Order Produces Healthy Choices, Generosity, and Conventionality, Whereas Disorder Produces Creativity." *Psychological Science* 24(9): 1860–1867.

von Soest, Tilmann, Jenny Wagner, Thomas Hansen, and Denis Gerstorf. 2017. "Self-Esteem Across the Second Half of Life: The Role of Socioeconomic Status, Physical Health, Social Relationships, and Personality Factors." *Journal of Personality and Social Psychology*, February 2.

Voth, Hans-Joachim. 2003. "Living Standards During the Industrial Revolution: An Economist's Guide." *American Economic Review* 93(2): 221–226.

Vrecko, Scott. 2013. "Just How Cognitive Is 'Cognitive Enhancement'? On the Significance of Emotions in University Students' Experiences with Study Drugs." *AJOB Neuroscience* 4(1): 4–12.

Walker, Mark. 2016. Comment on Facebook post, October 20. https://www.facebook.com/robin.hanson.754/posts/10103087761308537?comment_id=10103088991747727

Walker, Mirella, and Thomas Vetter. 2016. "Changing the Personality of a Face: Perceived Big Two and Big Five Personality Factors Modeled in Real Photographs." *Journal of Personality and Social Psychology* 110(4): 609-624

Wang, Jing, Vladimir Cherkassky, and Marcel Just. 2017. "Predicting the Brain Activation Pattern Associated With the Propositional Content of a Sentence: Modeling Neural Representations of Events and States." *Human Brain Mapping*, June 27.

Wassersug, Richard. 2009. "Mastering Emasculation." *Journal of Clinical Oncology* 27(4): 634–636.

Watkins Jr., John. 1900. "What May Happen In The Next Hundred Years." *Ladies' Home Journal* 18(1): 8.

Watts, Steve, Neal Kalita, and Michael Maclean. 2007. "The Economics of Super-Tall Towers." *The Structural Design of Tall and Special Buildings* 16(November 5): 457–470.

Waytz, Adam, Nicholas Eply, and John Capioppo. 2010. "Social cognition unbound: Insights into anthropomorphism and dehumanization." *Current Directions in Psychological Science* 19: 58–62.

Wei, Shang-Jin, and Xiaobo Zhang. 2011. "The Competitive Saving Motive: Evidence from Rising Sex Ratios and Savings Rates in China." *Journal of Political Economy*, 119(3): 511–564.

Weil, David. 2012. *Economic Growth*, 3rd ed. Prentice Hall, July 9.

Weiner, Mark. 2013. *The Rule of the Clan: What an Ancient Form of Social Organization Reveals about the Future of Individual Freedom*. Farrar, Straus and Giroux.

Weingast, Barry, and Donald Wittman. 2008. *The Oxford Handbook of Political Economy*. Oxford University Press. August.

Weinstein, Netta, Andrew Przybylski, and Richard M. Ryan. 2009. "Can Nature Make Us More Caring? Effects of Immersion in Nature on Intrinsic Aspirations and Generosity." *Personality and Social Psychology Bulletin* 35(10): 1315–1329.

Weiss, Alexander, and James King. 2015. "Great Ape Origins of Personality Maturation and Sex Differences: A Study of Orangutans and Chimpanzees." *Journal of Personality and Social Psychology* 108(4): 648–664.

Wiley, Keith. 2014. *A Taxonomy and Metaphysics of Mind-Uploading*. Alautun Press. September 13.

Williams, Alex. 2012. "Friends of a Certain Age: Why Is It Hard to Make Friends Over 30?" *New York Times*, July 13.

Wimsatt, William. 1986. "Developmental Constraints, Generative Entrenchment, and the Innate-Acquired Distinction." *Integrating Scientific Disciplines*, vol. 2, edited by William Bechtel. 185–208. Dordrecht: Martinus Nijhoff.

Woolley, Anita, Christopher Chabris, Alex Pentland, Nada Hashmi, and Thomas Malone. 2010. "Evidence for a Collective Intelligence Factor in the Performance of Human Groups." *Science* 330(6004): 686–688.

Woolley, Kaitlin, and Ayelet Fishbach. 2015. "The experience matters more than you think: People value intrinsic incentives more inside than outside an activity." *Journal of Personality and Social Psychology* 109(6): 968–982.

Wout, Félice van't, Aureliu Lavric, and Stephen Monsell. 2015. "Is It Harder to Switch Among a Larger Set of Tasks?" *Journal of Experimental Psychology: Learning, Memory, and Cognition* 41(2): 363–376.

Wu, Lynn, Ben Waber, Sinan Aral, Erik Brynjolfsson, and Alex Pentland. 2008. "Mining Face-to-Face Interaction Networks Using Sociometric Badges: Predicting Productivity in an IT Configuration Task." *International Conference on Information Systems 2008 Proceedings*. 127.

Yang, Mu-Jeung, Lorenz Kueng, and Bryan Hong. 2015. "Business Strategy and the Management of Firms." NBER Working Paper 20846, January.

Yao, Shuyang, Niklas Långström, Hans Temrin, and Hasse Walum. 2014. "Criminal Offending as Part of an Alternative Reproductive Strategy: Investigating Evolutionary Hypotheses using Swedish Total Population Data." *Evolution and Human Behavior* 35(6): 481–488.

Yetish, Gandhi, Hillard Kaplan, Michael Gurven, Brian Wood, Herman Pontzer, Paul Manger, Charles Wilson, Ronald McGregor, and Jerome Siegel. 2015. "Natural Sleep and Its Seasonal Variations in Three Pre-industrial Societies." *Current Biology* 25(October 15): 1–7.

Yetman, Norman. 1999. *Voices from Slavery: 100 Authentic Slave Narratives*. Dover, May 27.

Youngberg, David, and Robin Hanson. 2010. "Forager Facts." May. http://hanson.gmu.edu/forager.pdf.

Younis, Saed. 1994. "Asymptotically Zero Energy Computing Using Split-Level Charge Recovery Logic." Doctoral Thesis, Electrical Engineering, Massachusetts Institute of Technology.

Yudkowsky, Eliezer. 2008. "Cognitive Biases Potentially Affecting Judgment of Global Risks." In *Global Catastrophic Risks*, edited by Nick Bostrom and Milan Ćirković. 91–119. Oxford University Press.

Yudkowsky, Eliezer. 2013. "Intelligence Explosion Microeconomics." Technical report 2013-1, Machine Intelligence Research Institute. September 13.

Yule, Morag, and Lori Brotto. 2017. "Sexual Fantasy and Masturbation Among Asexual Individuals: An In-Depth Exploration." *Archives of Sexual Behavior* 46(1): 311–328, January.

Zaman, Tauhid. 2016. "Does the Amount You Sweat Predict Your Job Performance?" Wall Street Journal, October 27.

Zamyatin, Yevgeny. 1924. *We*. Translated by Gregory Zilboorg. New York: Dutton.

Zerzan, John. 2005. *Against Civilization: Readings and Reflections*. Feral House, May 10.

Zhai, Yao, Yaoguang Ma, Sabrina David, Dongliang Zhao, Runnan Lou, Gang Tan, Ronggui Yang, and Xiaobo Yin. 2017. "Scalable-manufactured randomized glass-polymer hybrid metamaterial for daytime radiative cooling." *Science* 355(6329): 1062–1066, February 17.

Zimek, Arthur, Erich Schubert, and Hans-Peter Kriegel. 2012. "A survey on unsupervised outlier detection in high-dimensional numerical data.:" *Statistical Analysis and Data Mining* 5(5): 363–387.

Zimmermann, Harm-Peer, and Heinrich Grebe. 2014. "'Senior Coolness': Living Well as an Attitude in Later Life." *Journal of Aging Studies* 28(January): 22–34.

INDEX

A

abstraction 115, 323, 327, 396
adaptations 144, 204, 206, 261, 364, 391
  behavior 30–31
  to new situations 2
adiabatic gates 91
advice 205, 214, 238–239, 423
  on call 367–370
  legal 315
  prediction markets 296
  relationship 198
  safe-based 200
age 5, 10, 184, 229, 338, 379
  peak productivity 11, 230–232, 423
agglomeration 247
aggression 201
aging 143, 144, 153, 195, 238, 425
air 86, 101–104, 107, 380, 428
  pressure 107, 250
aliens 173, 432–433
alms 349
ancestors 1, 2, 34, 147, 358, 384, 424, 452
  see also farming era; foragers
animals 5, 18, 26, 28, 33, 83, 85, 98, 143, 166, 349
  emulations of 119, 182
anti-messages 93
appearances 111–121
  comfortable 114–116
  merging real and virtual 119–121
  of shared spaces 116–119
  of virtual reality 111–114
application teams 239
archives 82, 92, 263, 315
  frequency made 81
  memory costs 80
  message 92
art 231
artificial intelligence 6, 421, 437, 450
  intelligence explosion 407–412
  research 59–63, 69
artificial light 21
asexuality 11
assets 131, 207, 209, 224, 302, 318, 319, 431, 446, 447
  assumptions 50–63
  alternative 421–426
  artificial intelligence 59–63
  of brains 50–52
  complexity of emulations 57–59
  of emulations 52–55
attacks 120, 389, 421
auctions 252–254 *see also* combinatorial auctions
audits 148, 198
authenticity 127, 352
autonomy 372, 375

B

bacteria 72, 104
baseline scenarios 8, 40–41, 42, 49, 421, 426
base speed 80–81, 147, 255, 308
beauty 185
behavior, energy-efficient hardware and 92
beliefs, false/biased 302
bets 131, 199, 210, 214, 427
biases 45–49, 200
bipolar disorder 188
birth cohort 230, 379
bits 89, 92
blackmail 319

bodies 83–84, 116, 120, 203
quality of 84
bosses 198, 202, 228
bots 127–128
brain cells 51
brain emulations *see* emulations
brain scanners 51
brain, the 6, 50–52, 398, 399, 403, 411
aging of 143
cell models 51
complexity of 57
emulating brain processes 68
function of 50
modeling 431
reaction time 83
size changes 423
synapses 90
brand loyalty 352
breach of contract 318
buildings 104–107, 219
bulk buying 265
Burj Khalifa, Dubai 105
business 204–215
combinatorial auctions 210–212
cycle fluctuations 226
institutions 204–206
new institutions 206–210
organizations 229
prediction markets 212–215

C

capacities 397, 398, 400, 401, 403, 404
capital 217, 218, 221, 428
careers 227–230
castration 331
celebrities 243, 345, 346
charity 349–350, 445–446
childhood 12, 54, 238, 240–244
children 240–243, 350, 451 *see also* youth
choices, regarding em world 434–448
charity 445–447
evaluation of 434–438
policies 441–445
quality of life 438–441
success 447–448
cities 20–21, 96–97, 247–249, 280, 350, 443
air-cooled 101–104
auctions 252–254
centers 97, 101, 102, 105–107, 154, 250–252, 267, 274, 289, 297, 337, 377
first em 427–428, 429
optimal size 253
peripheries 101, 250–252, 256, 377
structure of 249–252
transport of items 260
water cooled 101–104
civilization 147, 148, 149, 151
clans 10, 160, 261–263, 338, 345
clan-specific computer hardware 422
concentration 174–176, 181, 273, 279–280
and finance 223
firm-clan relations 270–272
governance 299, 301–306
identity 351–355, 369
inequality between 284
managing 263–266
nostalgia 356
one-name em 175
sexuality 332
signals 347, 348, 349
stories 388–389
voting via mindreading 308
classes 10, 13, 19, 298, 312, 358, 380
lower 364, 365
upper 364, 365
Cleisthenes 312
climate 96–110
clumping 247–260
clutter 116
CMOS (complementary metal–oxide–semiconductor) materials 89
coalitions 309–312
cold war 290
collaboration 357–373
combinatorial auctions 105, 210–212, 252, 302–303
communication 33, 67, 75, 81, 86, 100, 140, 209
hardware 96, 97, 166
networks 75, 93, 140
commuting 258

competition 160, 169, 171, 193, 216
  clan 174
  efficiency 175–179
complexity 57–59, 396
computer capital 221
computer chips 89
computer gates *see* logic gates
computers 51
computer security 71
conceptual art 231
conflict 278–296
congestion 208, 248, 249
conscientiousness 185, 188
consciousness 54, 55, 400
consensus theories 41–44
conservatives 381
consortiums 431
construal level theory 28, 43, 47, 370
contract law 319
conversations 365–367
cooling 97–101, 140
  fluids 101–104
  systems 99
  towers 102
coordination 228, 266, 268
copies 59, 81, 126, 127, 263
copy identity 353–356
copying 133–135, 160, 170, 376
cosmic rays 68
costs 69–70, 147, 268, 269, 271, 273, 276
  and bulk buying 265
  business cycle 226
  communication 419
  of cooling 423
  and speed 80
critics 449–451
cultures 30, 46, 374–377
  attitudes toward death 154
  fragmentation 21, 298, 380
  future 33, 34
  global 34
  identity 350, 353, 355
  proto-industry 20

D

data centers 103
data redundancy 82
death 126, 150–151, 152–155, 361
  accidental 82
decentralization 209, 211
decision markets 213–215, 301–303
decisions 305
defense 421
democracy 306–309
demographic transitions 29
descendants 1–2, 34, 433, 450, 452
development
  cost of 422
  research and 427
disasters 126, 436–437
discrimination *see* inequality
diversity 436
divisions 377–380
doubling time, of economy 217, 218, 219, 220–221, 229–230, 254
drama 387
dreamtime 28–31, 34, 212
Drexler, K. Eric 38
dust 115

E

early scans 167, 169
earthquakes 105
eating 344
economic analysis v
economic growth 32
economics 42–43, 451
economy 145, 204, 217–218, 320, 323–324, 443
  doubling time of 217–221, 229–230, 254
  early em 427
  growth of 11, 104
  size of 222
efficiency 174–191, 323
  clan concentration 174–176
  competition 176–179
  eliteness 182–184
  implications 179–182
  qualities 184–189
elections 208, 209, 308
eliteness 182–184
ems *see* emulations
emotion words 363

emulations 2, 6, 8, 145, 394
assumptions 52–53
brain 2
compared with ordinary humans 12–13
enough 171–173
envisioning a world of 39–41
inequality 279–282
introduction to 1–2
many 137–139
mass 356
models 54
niche 356
one-name 175–176
opaque 70
open source 70
overview of 5–8
precedents 14–17
slow 297
start of 5–13
summary of conclusions 8–13
technologies 51
time-sharing 75, 254
energy 80, 81, 84, 85, 94 *see also* entropy
control of 140
influence on behavior 94
entrenchment 401
entropy 88–92 *see also* energy
eras 14–15, 16 *see also* farming era; foraging era; industrial era
present 21–25
prior 17–21
values 25–28
erasures of bits 92, 93, 94
logical 89
rate of 91
reversible 90
eunuchs 331, 400
evaluations 434–438
evolution 26, 28, 30, 31, 151, 173
animal 28
em 172, 173
foragers 28, 29, 273
human 151, 173, 261
systems 400
existence 133–141
copying 133–135
many ems 137–139
rights 135–137
surveillance 139–141
existential risk 436
expenses 423
experimental art 231
experts, fake 295–296
exports 98, 108, 258

F

faces 115, 344
factions 312–314
factories 108–109, 218, 219, 220, 221
failures 238
fake experts 295–296
fakery 126–128
farmers 1, 5, 8, 14, 19–20
communities 248
culture 380–383
farming era 5, 14, 16, 217, 293
firms 294
inequality 278
marriages 335
stories 385
wars 288
fashions 297, 311, 345, 358, 378, 379
clothes 21
intellectual 348
local 343
music 33
fast ems 297
fears 400
fertility 30, 31
fiction 1, 2, 46, 389 *see also* science fiction
finance 223–226
financial inequality 282
fines 319
firms 266–269, 281
cost-focused 268
family-based 267
firm-clan relations 270–272
managers 269
mass versus niche teams 274–277
novelty-focused 268
private-equity owned 267

quality-focused 268
teams 272–274
first ems 166–169
flexibility 211, 231, 236, 258, 335, 448
flow projects 219
foragers 1, 5, 6, 8, 28–29, 34, 175, 217, 273
communities 14
pair bonds 335
foraging era 15, 18
inequality 278
stories 385
forecasting 37–38
fractal reversing 90, 92
fractional factorial experiment design 130
fragility 142–145
friendship 372, 438
future vi, 1, 31, 33, 35–37, 449
abstract construal of 46
analysis of 450, 451
em 452
eras 31, 34
evaluation of 434
technology 2, 7
futurists 39

G

gates, computer 89
gender 337–338, 379
imbalance 338–340
geographical divisions 380
ghosts 148–150
global laws 139
God 367
governance 226, 299–304
clan 304–306
global 425
governments 431
gravity 84, 114
grit 190, 448
groups 261–277
clans 261–263
firm-clan relations 270–272
firms 266–269
managing clans 263–266
mass versus niche teams 274–277
signals 346–349
teams 272–274
growth 15, 17, 32, 33, 34, 216–226
estimate 220–221
faster 216–219
financial 223–226
modes 15
myths 222–223

H

happiness 47, 188, 233, 267, 274, 282, 293, 350, 360, 372, 395, 438–439
hardware 63, 66–70, 73, 75, 323
clan-specific 422
communication 97
computer 97
deterministic 67, 97, 110, 201
digital 67
fault-tolerant 67
parallel 73–76
reversible 93
signal-processing 51, 67, 68
variable speed 93, 94
heat transport 103–104
historians vi, 39
history 35, 36, 46, 283, 348
leisure 232, 236
personal 124
homosexual ems 339
homosexuality 11
hospitals 349
humans 1, 5, 7, 8, 15
introduction of 14

I

identical twins 261
identity 55, 350–353, 369
ideologies 380
illness 352
implementation of emulations 64–76
hardware 66–70
mindreading 64–65
parallelism 73–76
security 70–73
impressions 341, 347
incentives 205, 206, 208, 209, 318

inclinations 399
income tax 208
individualism 23
industrial era 21–25
  firms 294
  stories 358
industrial organization 179
industrial revolution 266, 431
industry 5, 6, 14, 15
inequality 278–279
information 122–132
  fake 126–128
  records 124–126
  simulations 129–132
  views 122–124
infrastructure 96–110
  air and water 101–104
  buildings 104–107
  climate controlled 96
  cooling 97–101
  manufacturing 107–110
innovation 216, 221, 320–322
institutions 204–206
  new 206–210
intellectual property 139, 140, 165–166, 321, 378, 429, 447
intelligence 185, 222, 341, 344, 346, 403–405
intelligence explosion 407–412
interactions 94, 122–123
interest rates 146, 225–226, 258

J

job(s)
  categories 171
  evaluations 181, 268
  performance 187
  tasks 423
  see also careers; work
judges 150, 199, 200, 302, 304, 310, 313, 316, 322, 333

K

Kahn, Herman 37
kilo-ems 257
Kingdom Tower, Jeddah 105

L

labor 63, 159–173, 217, 428
  enough ems 171–173
  first ems 166–169
  Malthusian wages 162–166
  markets 272
  selection 169–171
  supply and demand 159–162
languages 18, 143, 198, 323, 402
law 263, 315–317
  efficient 317–320
lawsuits 318
leisure 112, 115, 144, 193, 236, 444
  activities 384
  fast 298
  speeds 256
liability 263, 316, 318, 321
liberals 381
lifecycle 227–244
  careers 227–230
  childhood 240–244
  maturity 233–234
  peak age 230–232
  preparation for tasks 235–237
  training 237–240
lifespan 12, 281, 282
limits 31–34
logic gates 89, 91
loyalty 129, 131, 343, 346
lying 234

M

machine reproduction estimates 220
machine shops 220
maladaptive behaviors 30
maladaptive cultures 30
Malthusian wages 162–166
management 228
  of physical systems 122
  practices 267–268
manic-depressive disorder 188
marketing 386
mass-labor markets 275, 378
mass-market teams 275–277
mass production 108

mating 331–340, 372, 399
gender 337–338
gender imbalance 338–340
open-source lovers 333–334
pair bonds 334–337
sexuality 331–333
maturity 233–234
meetings 86–88, 359
memories 54, 126, 153, 161, 237, 252, 351, 355
memory 74–76, 80–81, 90, 161, 252
mental fatigue 195
mental flexibility 231
mental speeds *see* minds, speeds
messages 92–93, 118
delays 87
methods 37, 39, 41, 45, 46, 47
Microsoft 427
military 427
mindfulness 188
minds 11, 390–415
features 401–402
humans 390–395
intelligence 403–405
intelligence explosion 407–411
merging 425
partial 397–400
psychology 400–403
quality 84
reading 64–65, 308, 315, 359, 365
speeds 75, 222, 227, 254–257
see also speed(s)
theft 11, 70, 72, 87, 139, 349
unhumans 395–397
modeling, brain cell 431
modes of civilization 14–34
dreamtime 28–31
era values 25–28
limits 31–34
our era 21–25
precedents 14–17
prior eras 17–21
modular
buildings 106
functional units 58
Moore's law 63, 68, 91
moral choices 351
morality 2, 436
motivation, for studying future emulations 35–37
multitasking 197
music 359, 362, 382
myths 222–223

N

nanotech manufacturing 109
nations 43, 98, 179, 186, 211, 223, 248, 278, 279, 280, 293
democratic 307
poor 26
rich 26, 43, 83, 106, 248, 269
war between 299
nature 93, 350
Neanderthals 25
nepotism 293–295
networks, talk 272
neurons 79
niche ems 356
niche-labor markets 275, 378
niche-market teams 274–277
normative considerations 49
nostalgia 356
nuclear weapons 288

O

office politics 271
offices 112, 116, 117
older people 233–234
see also aging; retirement
open-source lovers 333–334
outcome measures 301
ownership 134

P

pair bonds 332, 334–337, 339–340
parallel computing 73–76, 323, 324, 325, 419
parents 451
partial sims 129
past, the *see* history
patents 322
pay-for-performance 206–207

peak age 230–232
period 74–75, 80, 83, 87, 123
  reversing 90, 94
perseverance 190
personality, gender differences 337
personal signals 343–346
phase 75, 87, 93, 95, 123, 255
physical bodies 83–84, 86
physical jobs 84
physical violence 117
physical worlds 92
pipes 98, 99
plants 18, 98, 217, 350
police spurs 425
policy analysis 441–445
political power 420
politics 297–314, 375, 387
  clan governance 304–306
  coalitions 309–312
  democracy 306–309
  factions 312–314
  governance 299–304
population 140
portable brain hardware 289
portfolios 224, 307, 447
positive considerations 49
poverty 281, 283, 285, 288
  em 166, 173, 379
  human 394
power 201–203
power laws 278
prediction markets 210, 212–215, 289, 296, 319, 369
  city auctions 253
  estimates 265
  use of 321
pre-human primates 17–18
pre-skills 159–160, 171–172, 178, 423
preparation for tasks 235–237
prices 207–210, 214
  of manufactured goods 161
  for resources 204
printers, 3D 220
prison 318
privacy 198
productivity 13, 184, 196, 239–240, 241, 439
progress 2, 51–52, 57, 60, 62, 63
psychology 400–403
punishments 263, 318
purchasing 110, 208, 323, 352

Q

qualities 184–189
quality of life 438–441
quantum computing 424

R

random access memory (RAM) 80
rare products 346
reaction time 83–84, 86–88, 94, 250
  body size and 83
  physical em body 257
real world, merging virtual and 119–121
records 124–126
redistribution 282–286
regulations 33, 42–43, 120, 123, 138, 171, 180, 249, 254, 307, 422, 425, 426
religion 321, 360–362, 380
research 222–223, 445
retirement 123, 142, 146–148, 151, 195, 201, 254–255, 391–395
  human 8
reversibility 88–92, 93, 94, 107
rewards 180–181
rights 135–137
rituals 357–359
rulers 299
rules 187, 315–327

S

safes 198–199
salt water 103
scales 79–95
  bodies 83–84
  Lilliputian 84–86
  speeds 79–82
scanning 167, 170, 431
scans 167–169
scenarios 39–41, 421–426, 430, 432

schools v, 24, 190, 193, 207, 268, 341–342, 349, 357, 388, 450
science fiction v, 2, 7, 361
scope 44–45
search teams 239
security 70–73, 82, 113, 117, 123, 131, 265, 354, 421, 424
  breaches 96, 131
  computer 117, 289, 424
  costs 87
selection 6, 28, 31, 126, 154, 169–171, 173, 179, 183, 201, 305, 339, 396, 403
self-deception 200, 302, 342
self-governance 264
serial computing 419
sexuality 331–333, 382
shared spaces 116–119
showing off 341–342
sight perception 398
signals 341–356
  copy identity 352–356
  groups 346–349
  identity 350–353
  personal 343–346
  processing 51
sim administrators 130
simulations 129–132
singing 359
sins 361
size 79, 83, 84, 85, 86, 123
slaves 19, 70, 135, 137–138, 166, 168, 281, 349, 381, 399
sleep 21, 70, 95, 149, 188
sleeping beauty strategy 147
social bonds 274
social gatherings 310
social interactions 274
social power 201–203
social reasoning 398
social relations 377
social science 451
social status 298
society 13, 374–389
software 63, 140, 321–325, 421
software developers 325–327
software engineers 228, 323, 325
souls 120
sound perception 398
spaces 123–128
space travel 259
speculation 44
speed(s) 79, 123, 155, 281, 387
  alternative scenario 421, 425
  divisions 378, 380
  em 8, 10, 419–420
  em era 419
  ghosts 148, 150
  human-speed emulation 53
  redistribution based on 283
  retirement 146, 147
  talking 344
  time-shared em 75
  top cheap 79, 80, 94, 101, 150, 255, 325, 327
  travel 383, 384
  variable speed hardware 93
  walking 85
spurs 10, 123, 153, 194–197, 316, 339
  social interactions 197
  uses of 197–201
stability 147, 148
status 297–299, 348
stories 36, 40, 115, 379, 384–388
    see also fiction
  clan 388–389
stress 24, 116, 151, 154, 187, 364
structure, city 249–252
subclans 261, 263
  conflicting 423
  inequality between 283
subordinates 228
subsistence levels 285
success 447–448
suicide 156
supply and demand 159–162
surveillance 139–141, 316
swearing 364–365
synchronization 357, 370–373

T

takeovers 224
talk networks 272
taxes 286, 393

teams 272–274, 342, 346, 349, 354, 355
  application 239
  intelligence 403
  mass versus niche teams 274–277
  training 232
technologies 430–432
temperature 96, 99–102
territories 444
tests 128–131
theory 42, 43, 159
tools, non-computer-based 324
top cheap speed 79, 80, 94, 101, 150, 255, 325, 327
track records 207, 295
training 166, 170, 238–239, 243
transexuality 11
transgender conversions 339
transition, from our world to the em world 426–430
transport 257–260
travel 21, 25, 34, 48, 86, 115, 247, 250–252, 350, 383–384
travel times 115
trends 419–420
trust 237, 271
  clans 261, 262, 269, 270
  maturity and 233, 234
Tsiolkovsky, Konstantin 38
tweaking 169, 170

U

undo action 118
unhumans, minds of 395–398
unions 271
United States of America 27
uploads *see* emulations
utilitarianism 438

V

vacations 236
values 25–27, 273–274, 375, 451, 452
variety 23, 27, 108, 177, 181, 216, 227, 269, 345, 444
views 122–124, 449, 450, 451
virtual meetings 250
virtual reality 9, 115, 116–117, 125, 334, 338, 429
  appearances 111–114
  authentication 126
  cultures 377
  design of 118
  leisure environments 115
  meetings 87
  merging real and 119–121
  nature 93
  travel 257
voices, pitch of 343
voting 209, 308–309

W

wages 10, 13, 138, 160–161, 280, 391, 425
  inequality 269, 284
  Malthusian wages 162–166
  rules 136, 137
  subsistence 420
war 18–20, 40, 147, 286–289, 381, 421, 428
water 98, 101–104
Watkins, John 37
wealth 27, 30, 281, 375–376, 379, 392–393
weapons 288
Whole Brain Emulation Roadmap (Sandberg and Bostrom) 53
Wiener, Anthony 37
wind pressures 104, 105
work 192–203, 381, 382, 386
  conditions 194
  culture 374, 376, 377
  hours 192–194, 346, 440
  methods 231
  social power 201–203
  speeds 254
  spurs 194–197
  teams 272–274
workers, time spent "loafing" 195
workaholics 188, 192
World Wide Web 38

Y

Year 2000, The (Kahn and Wiener) 37
youth 11, 445 *see also* children

Z

zoning 211, 212